SIX TUDOR QUEENS

KATHERINE OF ARAGON
The True Queen

Quick Reads
Traitors of the Tower

Non-fiction
Britain's Royal Families: The Complete Genealogy
The Six Wives of Henry VIII
The Princes in the Tower
Lancaster and York: The Wars of the Roses
Children of England: The Heirs of King Henry VIII 1547–1558
Elizabeth the Queen
Eleanor of Aquitaine
Henry VIII: King and Court
Mary Queen of Scots and the Murder of Lord Darnley
Isabella: She-Wolf of France, Queen of England
Katherine Swynford: The Story of John of Gaunt and
His Scandalous Duchess
The Lady in the Tower: The Fall of Anne Boleyn
Mary Boleyn: 'The Great and Infamous Whore'
Elizabeth of York: The First Tudor Queen
The Lost Tudor Princess

As co-author
The Ring and the Crown: A History of Royal Weddings, 1066–2011

ALISON WEIR

SIX TUDOR QUEENS

KATHERINE of ARAGON
THE TRUE QUEEN

headline
review

First published in Great Britain in 2016 by
HEADLINE REVIEW
An imprint of HEADLINE PUBLISHING GROUP

1

Cataloguing in Publication Data is available from the British Library

ISBN 978 1 4722 2747 8 (Hardback)
ISBN 978 1 4722 2748 5 (Trade paperback)

Typeset in Garamond MT by Avon DataSet Ltd, Bidford-on-Avon, Warwickshire

Printed and bound in Great Britain by Clays Ltd, St Ives plc

HEADLINE PUBLISHING GROUP
An Hachette UK Company
Carmelite House
50 Victoria Embankment
London EC4Y 0DZ

www.headline.co.uk
www.hachette.co.uk

SIX TUDOR QUEENS

KATHERINE OF ARAGON
THE TRUE QUEEN

1501

SPAIN
(House of Trastámara)

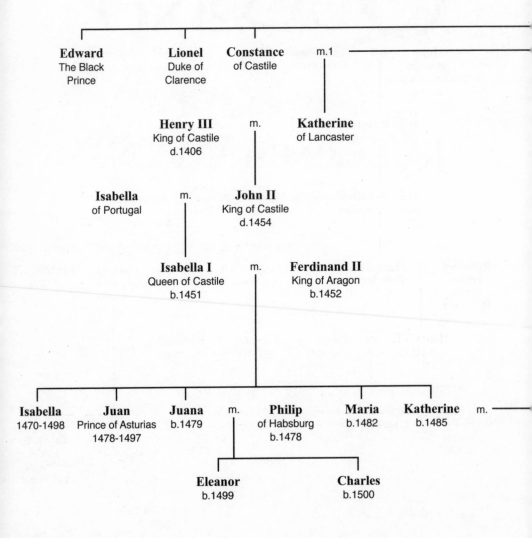

Edward
The Black
Prince

Lionel
Duke of
Clarence

Constance
of Castile

m.1

Henry III
King of Castile
d.1406

m.

Katherine
of Lancaster

Isabella
of Portugal

m.

John II
King of Castile
d.1454

Isabella I
Queen of Castile
b.1451

m.

Ferdinand II
King of Aragon
b.1452

Isabella
1470-1498

Juan
Prince of Asturias
1478-1497

Juana
b.1479

m.

Philip
of Habsburg
b.1478

Maria
b.1482

Katherine
b.1485

m.

Eleanor
b.1499

Charles
b.1500

ENGLAND

(House of Tudor)

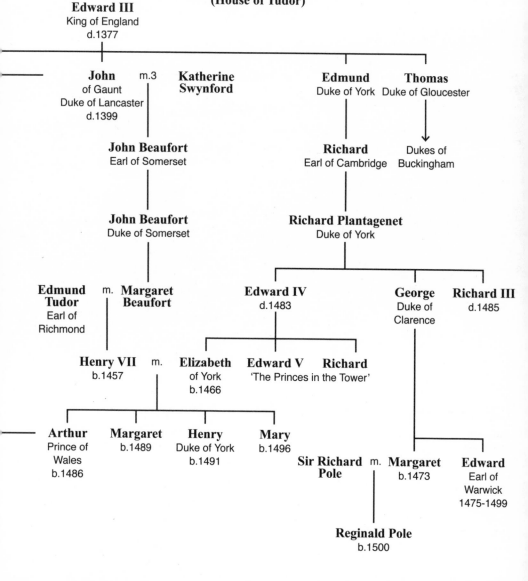

Edward III
King of England
d.1377

John   m.3   **Katherine**
of Gaunt   **Swynford**
Duke of Lancaster
d.1399

Edmund   **Thomas**
Duke of York   Duke of Gloucester

John Beaufort
Earl of Somerset

Richard   Dukes of
Earl of Cambridge   Buckingham

John Beaufort
Duke of Somerset

Richard Plantagenet
Duke of York

Edmund   m.   **Margaret**
Tudor   **Beaufort**
Earl of
Richmond

Edward IV
d.1483

George   **Richard III**
Duke of   d.1485
Clarence

Henry VII   m.   **Elizabeth**   **Edward V**   **Richard**
b.1457   of York   'The Princes in the Tower'
                    b.1466

Arthur   **Margaret**   **Henry**   **Mary**
Prince of   b.1489   Duke of York   b.1496
Wales   b.1491
b.1486

Sir Richard   m.   **Margaret**   **Edward**
Pole   b.1473   Earl of
                                   Warwick
                                   1475-1499

Reginald Pole
b.1500

With all my love to the best and dearest of mothers.
The wheel comes full circle: this is where it all began.
A thousand thanks for your belief in me
and for your unconditional love and support.
May God bless you.

I named my daughter for Katherine,
because Katherine was a woman of integrity and principle, as you are.

'. . . her
That, like a jewel, has hung twenty years
About his neck, yet never lost her lustre;
Of her that loves him with that excellence
That angels love good men with; even of her
That, when the greatest stroke of fortune falls,
Will bless the King.'

(William Shakespeare, *King Henry VIII*, Act 2, Scene 2)

As the holly grow'th green
And never changeth hue,
So I am, e're hath been,
Unto my lady true.

(King Henry VIII)

Part One

The Princess from Spain

Chapter 1

The coast of England was closer now. Standing at the balustrade of the deck, high above the stern of the ship, with tendrils of red-gold hair whipping about her face, Catalina could see green and brown hills and the spires of churches, with houses huddled together beside them; and, at a dizzying distance below, between the land and the rolling vessel, the grey churning sea. How different it all looked from La Coruña, with its warm blue waters and its mighty Tower of Hercules, or the dramatic wide sweep of the bay of Laredo! Everything was going to be different from now on.

Her maid-of-honour and dear friend, Maria de Salinas, was standing beside her.

'It cannot be long now till we come into port,' Catalina said. 'When I think how many years I have dreamed of coming to England, I cannot quite believe I am nearly there. I thank God that you are with me, Maria. I would not want to face this alone.' There was no one else to whom she would have admitted that.

'And I am glad of Your Highness being with me,' Maria replied. She was two years older than Catalina, and they had been friends all their lives. It was typical of Maria to have pulled off her cap and let her rippling long night-black hair blow free in the wind. She was almost dancing with anticipation, her large eyes luminous as she gazed at the land ahead. Catalina reminded herself that Maria was also going into the unknown. It was expected that she and the other young ladies in attendance on their infanta would be found well-born husbands in England. But where Catalina was facing the future with a certain trepidation, Maria could barely contain her excitement.

'Soon I will come face to face with Prince Arthur,' Catalina said. She had been told countless times that her betrothed was a golden prince, beautiful and graceful, with many excellent qualities, and that the English people hailed him as their great hope for the future. 'I pray that I may please him.' And that all will be well.

'Judging by his letters, he is as eager to meet your Highness as you are to see him. You are lucky to have a husband who loves you.' Maria smiled encouragingly – and not a little enviously.

'But how can he love me when he has never met me?' Catalina asked, voicing a concern she had kept to herself for a long time. 'Was he that much taken by my portrait?' Master Miguel, her mother's court painter, had taken an excellent likeness.

'He could hardly have failed!' Maria said. 'You are so pretty.'

'He is just fifteen!' Catalina retorted. 'He is nearly a year younger than I am. I think he has been told what to write, just as I was. And—' she bit her lip, 'I fear he is young for his years. Remember how my coming was postponed for a year until he was ready to be married, and then it was postponed again?' That had been a strange business, veiled in secrecy. Not even to Maria would Catalina confide her secret suspicions that all might not be quite well with Arthur – and that some dreadful deed had finally made possible her coming to England. It was as if saying them out loud would confirm them. 'At least it gave me time to learn French!' she said brightly. King Henry's Queen and his mother, the Lady Margaret, had specially requested it, as they spoke no Spanish or Latin. And they had urged that Catalina cultivate a taste for wine, as the water in England was undrinkable. She had duly complied. She had expected many such requests and instructions to prepare her for her life in England, but there had been just one more, one that had immeasurably troubled her.

'King Henry wants me to forget Spain,' Catalina revealed. 'He thinks I will be happier not remembering it. Dr de Puebla wrote that to the King my father.' Dr de Puebla was Spain's resident ambassador in England, and it was he who had negotiated her marriage.

'King Henry means well, I am sure, Highness,' Maria soothed.

'I can *never* forget my homeland,' Catalina declared, tears welling as

4

visions of the land of her birth came to mind, 'but I am determined to be a good Englishwoman.' She blinked the tears away.

'We must make ready,' she said. And then, mimicking her duenna, 'I must always remember that, as soon as I set foot on English soil, I am longer the Infanta Catalina but the Lady Katherine, Princess of Wales!' Catalina had been told that her name must be anglicised to please her husband's future subjects, for one day, when King Henry died and Prince Arthur succeeded to the throne, she would be Queen of England.

Maria laughed – Catalina had Doña Elvira to the life! Catalina smiled, but as she went ahead of Maria down the steep stairs to the sterncastle, where she and the ladies of her suite had been allocated cabins, she was dutifully resolving to think of herself as Katherine from now on.

The cabins were cramped and creaking, with barely room for a feather bed, and they were unpleasantly stuffy after four days at sea. Mercifully it had been a smooth crossing, unlike the earlier one from La Coruña. It was hard to believe that she had set out on her wedding journey more than five weeks ago, excited at the thought that the long-awaited new life was about to begin, yet grief-stricken at leaving her own country and the mother she loved and revered.

Four days on raging, storm-tossed seas had made homesickness pale into insignificance beside the fear of drowning and the constant irregular buffeting of the waves. Katherine and her ladies had been horribly, disgustingly sick. All those hours she had intended to devote to improving her English had been spent lying prone, clinging to her wooden cot as the ship bucked and dipped, and praying in terror for the tempest to stop. Her greatest fear had been that the storm had been sent by God as punishment for the great sin that had made her marriage possible, and that they would all be drowned. But God, it had seemed, was reserving His vengeance for another day. Never would Katherine forget the relief she had felt when the ship's master had managed by a miracle to dock at Laredo; and she had been full of devout thanks for the four weeks' respite there while they were forced to wait for the seas to calm. She had hated boarding the ship again, dreaded entrusting herself once more to the unpredictable temper of the waters of the Bay of Biscay and the English Channel. Mercifully they had been calm, but she had still been horribly seasick.

Katherine and Maria found Doña Elvira in the largest cabin, which Katherine herself occupied. Her duenna came from an old and respected Castilian family, and was devoted to Queen Isabella and determined to do her duty by Isabella's daughter. In the absence of Katherine's mother, Doña Elvira's word was now law in the Infanta's household. She was a stern, proud woman in her late fifties, with a disdainful eye and a sharp tongue, too vigilant for comfort – and too old to remember what it was to be young and bursting with life! And yet, for all her strictness and rigid outlook on life, the Queen trusted her implicitly, and had told Katherine that she must do so too.

Katherine watched as Doña Elvira heaved her bulk around the narrow spaces of the cabin and cast a critical eye over the four gowns laid across the bed and the travelling chest, gowns of red and gold damask, woven silk, velvet of the costliest black, cloth of gold. Queen Isabella had commanded that her daughter go to England dressed as befitted a future queen, and had paid for a sumptuous trousseau that reflected the glory and majesty of Spain. The chests that lay in the ship's hold were packed with more magnificent gowns, undergarments edged with fine blackwork lace, hoods of velvet with biliments of gold, silver or pearls. There were night robes bordered with lace for summer and fur for winter, cloth stockings and lined kirtles, as well as the stiff, decorous Spanish farthingales that belled out the skirts of Katherine's gowns. Also packed in locked and weighty coffers was the gold and silver plate that was to form part of her dowry, and her jewellery. She had exclaimed in amazement when her mother had shown her the intricate bejewelled necklaces, the ornate collars, the gold chains, the crucifixes and the brooches that had been provided for her.

Then Queen Isabella had laid across her daughter's outstretched hands a beautifully embroidered christening robe. 'For your children,' she had said. 'I pray that God blesses you with many fine sons. I hope you will be the source of all kinds of happiness in England.'

Katherine felt like weeping at the memory.

'This one,' the duenna said, pointing to the damask, 'if your Highness approves?'

'Of course,' Katherine agreed. Her mother had instructed that she must trust Doña Elvira's judgement in all things.

She stood patiently while three of her maids – Maria de Salazar and twin sisters called Isabel and Blanche de Vargas – stripped her to her farthingale and chemise, dressed her in a kirtle and the rich gown, laced up the back and tied on the wide, hanging sleeves. Doña Elvira herself placed around Katherine's neck the heavy gold collar adorned with gem-encrusted 'K's and pomegranates, the Princess's personal badge.

'The pomegranate stands for fertility,' Queen Isabella had said. 'Your first duty to Prince Arthur will be to bear him sons.'

Katherine was ten when the collar was made, and ensuring the royal succession had been far in the future. But now she wished she knew more about the process of getting sons. Her mother and her duenna had told her that it was a wife's duty to submit to the will of her husband in all things, and that children were born at his pleasure. Her mother, with many references to Scripture, had told her a little about how children were begotten, but there was still much mystery surrounding the whole business. Isabella's obvious embarrassment and the euphemisms she had used had left Katherine confused, and showed that decent people did not like to talk about such things. And yet, in a few weeks, she would be married, and know the whole truth.

Doña Elvira lifted up a length of the finest white lawn, exquisitely hemmed. 'Her Majesty's command was that your Highness be veiled in public until you are married,' she reminded her charge, as she combed Katherine's long hair and arranged the veil over her golden head. And so it was that, when the Princess emerged on the main deck to see sailors leaping across to the busy quayside to fling stout ropes around the bollards there and secure the ship in dock, her view of Plymouth, the crowds gathered to welcome her, and the banners gaily flapping in the breeze, was a misty one, glimpsed through the folds of her veil.

Once the gangplank was in place, her train began disembarking, led in stately fashion by the hero of Granada, the Count de Cabra, who commanded her escort. There followed Katherine's first chamberlain,

Don Pedro Manrique, who was Doña Elvira's husband, the second chamberlain, Juan de Diero, Katherine's chaplain, Alessandro Geraldini, three bishops and a bevy of ladies, maids, gentlemen and servants, all tricked out in their finest clothes and liveries. Never let it be said that the Spanish sovereigns, their Most Catholic Majesties King Ferdinand and Queen Isabella, had sent their daughter lacking in any way into England!

Katherine came last, escorted by Doña Elvira, whose bulk was resplendent in yards of green damask and black velvet, her grey hair covered by a voluminous hood. After waiting all her life – or so it seemed – for this moment, Katherine could hardly believe that it had arrived. She carried herself with conscious dignity and pride, aware that she was representing her parents and Spain, the greatest power in Christendom. Ahead of her swelled the sound of cheering voices, and when she stepped on land, even though she felt a little giddy after four days in motion on the sea, she knew a sense of triumph tempered with awe. This was the kingdom of which she would one day be queen. God send that she would be worthy of it, and of the unknown Prince, her husband.

The Mayor of Plymouth and his brethren, splendid in their furred scarlet robes, were waiting to receive her, bowing low.

'Welcome, your Highness!' the Mayor boomed. 'Welcome to England!'

'I thank you, good sirs,' Katherine replied, inclining her head. She had practised the words on board ship. Her English was not very good, and it was heavily accented, but she was determined to master it.

The people were roaring their approval. Some were gaping and pointing at the dark-skinned Moorish servants in her Spanish retinue, but most were jostling each other to gain a better sight of their new Princess. Katherine felt humbled to be the focus of such wild excitement, even though she knew that her father considered the King of England lucky to have a Spanish bride for his son.

'They could not have received your Highness with greater joy had you been the Saviour of the world!' exclaimed one of Katherine's gentlemen. Doña Elvira frowned. Men were not supposed to address the Princess familiarly. But even the stern duenna was gratified by her charge's reception.

'His Grace the King sends his greetings, my lady,' the Mayor said. 'He looks forward to welcoming you himself in London, with Prince Arthur. But for now, at your pleasure, a great feast awaits your Highness.'

Katherine was feeling a little disorientated; the ground was still tilting disconcertingly. But she must not let that detract from the good impression she meant to make. 'Please thank the Mayor for me,' she said to Don Pedro Manrique, who spoke some English. 'I will be honoured to be his guest.'

Behind her there were shouts as the crew unloaded her possessions from the ship. The Count de Cabra was watching anxiously as the coffers containing the hundred thousand crowns that were the first instalment of Katherine's dowry were brought ashore. It was his responsibility to guard them at all times.

The Mayor, beaming and puffed up with pride, took an obvious pleasure in escorting Katherine on foot through the celebrating, cheering crowds to the feast. Her first impressions of Plymouth and its inhabitants were startling. In Spain she had been used to seeing stone facades on houses built around patios, but here there were streets crammed with stout, half-timbered houses, some – the more prosperous – with glittering diamond-shaped panes in the windows, and most with roofs of thatch above upper storeys that overhung the narrow, crowded thoroughfares. The smell of fish pervaded everywhere in this bustling port. She stared as women openly greeted the homecoming sailors with kisses on the mouth – and in public too! That would never be tolerated in Spain, where ladies led almost cloistered lives and thought themselves fortunate to be allowed glimpses of the world from their balconies.

In a fine mansion called Palace House, the nobles and worthies of Devon were assembled, standing respectfully behind long tables laden with a hearty display of food. Everyone bowed low as Katherine and her entourage entered the hall, then a trumpet sounded and grace was said.

She could barely eat. She was still feeling a little nauseated, the food looked and tasted strange, and it was difficult trying gracefully to convey it from the plate to her mouth when the constricting veil kept getting in the way. She felt uncomfortable partaking of a meal with strange gentlemen watching her, for the privacy of young girls of high birth was closely guarded in Spain. But clearly this was how they did things in England, and she must accustom herself to it. So she responded to everyone's compliments through her chamberlain, and did her very best to be courteous and friendly, remembering how her mother exerted herself to set people of all ranks at their ease. And when the time came for Katherine to bid the good folk of Plymouth farewell, she knew that they had warmed to her for her own sake, and not just because of who she was.

Her most pressing need now was to give thanks for her safe arrival in England. As she left Palace House, she asked if she might go to some holy place. The Mayor willingly led her to a church dedicated to St Andrew, where the rotund and rather excited little priest celebrated Mass for her. She knelt, filled with exultation, thanking God for His goodness to her, and praying that His wrath might not be visited upon her for the secret sin committed by others to her advantage, and that she might do as well in the rest of England as she had done in Plymouth.

Outside the horse litter was waiting, with the lords of Devon mounted beside it, ready to accompany Katherine's train to Exeter, where they were to lay that night. Katherine would have liked to stay in Plymouth and rest, but the Mayor had given Doña Elvira a letter from Dr de Puebla, saying that the King of England was eager to see her, and that he had been kept waiting long enough, so she must press eastwards to London with all speed. As she climbed into the litter and seated herself comfortably on its embroidered silk cushions, Doña Elvira, whose English was good, commanded that the curtains be closed, for Spanish etiquette demanded that none should look on the face of the royal bride until she was wed.

Katherine could not sleep. The weather vane on the spire of St Mary Magnus next door to Exeter's deanery kept creaking, and she had sent a servant to complain. But that was not the only thing keeping her awake. After two days in this alien land, she had found herself crying into her

10

pillow, filled with an overwhelming longing to be at home in Spain, and to see her mother. And when she thought of how Queen Isabella must herself be feeling, now that the last of her children had gone from her, she wept even more. '*Madre, madre!*' she sobbed.

For as long as she could remember, her mother had been the guiding presence in her life, even though Isabella had often been busy with state affairs and with war. For many centuries Spain had been occupied by the Moors, who were cruel and savage infidels and in league with the Devil. They had haunted Katherine's childhood nightmares, terrifying her as much as El Roba-Chicos, the man who was said to carry children off in his sack.

Katherine had imbibed with her nurse's milk the story of how, for hundreds of years, the rulers of the Christian kingdoms of the Spanish peninsula had fought bravely against the Moors, gradually reconquering their land, inch by inch. She had been told of the great rejoicing when her father, the King of Aragon, and her mother, the Queen of Castile, had married and united Spain under their joint rule. Both had been zealous in ridding the land of the Moors, and in 1492 the last infidel kingdom, Granada, had fallen to the victorious sovereigns.

Katherine had been six then, but she remembered as clear as day riding across the River Vega with her parents, her brother Juan and her sisters, and looking ahead in awe to see King Ferdinand's great silver cross set up on the watch tower of the Alhambra Palace, and the royal standard being hoisted beside it. That was the signal for the royal procession to enter the city. She would never forget the shouts of 'For King Ferdinand and Queen Isabella!' resounding from hundreds of triumphant onlookers, or her father and mother falling to their knees to thank God for vouchsafing this magnificent victory.

They had all been together then, the royal siblings. Sad Isabella, in her widow's black, mourning Alfonso of Portugal, her husband of just seven months, cruelly dead after a fall from his horse; Juan, Prince of Asturias, the cherished heir to the throne – 'my angel', as their mother called him; tempestuous Juana, the beauty of the family, passionate and longing to be a bride; placid Maria; and Katherine, the youngest of them all. Those had been the happy years. After the conquest of Granada, Katherine and her sisters had lived in the Alhambra. For the children, the old fortress had been a magical place, and they had loved exploring the old palaces with their colourful tiles and strange Moorish decorations, the pavilions, the arched patios, and the water gardens with their pools and cool, splashing fountains, where once the caliphs had kept their harems. The views of the Sierra Nevada mountains from the Generalife Palace, where the sultans had once retreated in summer, were breathtaking.

The Christian princesses had rarely left their sunny home, except for the great occasions of state at which their presence was required, nor had Katherine wanted to. She wept afresh when she remembered those long, spacious days in the Alhambra when the future seemed so far ahead and she had been content to play in its courtyards or apply herself to her studies. How sad it was not to know how happy you were until it was too late.

Her mother, believing that princesses benefited from a good education, had appointed the pious Alessandro Geraldini as Katherine's tutor. He had taught her to read and write, instructed her in Latin and the ancient classics, and given her devotional books to improve her mind and teach her virtue. Now he had come to England as her chaplain. From her duenna she had learned needlework and dancing, lacemaking and the intricacies of Spanish blackwork embroidery. It would be committing the sin of pride to say that she was good at the embroidery, but it could not be denied that she had mastered the skill well.

The year when she turned seven had been an exciting one. Not long after the fall of Granada, Cristóbal Colón had returned to Spain to report that he had discovered a new world across the Atlantic Ocean. Queen Isabella had financed his voyage, and it was to the Spanish court that he brought the gold and the natives he had captured on his voyage. The dark-skinned savages were outlandishly dressed, but they looked terrified and ill, poor heathen creatures. Katherine had preferred the beautiful birds and plants that Colón showed her, his eyes afire at the prospect of many more voyages to come. Her tutor impressed on her how important Cristóbal Colón's discovery was, for now that the

Turks controlled the eastern Mediterranean, it was vital to find new trade routes to the East. One day, Father Alessandro told her, with a faraway look in his eyes, he hoped to visit this wonderful new world and see it for himself.

It had been inevitable that Katherine's older sisters would marry and go away before she did. She was ten when Juana had eagerly left for Flanders to marry the Archduke Philip the Handsome, Duke of Burgundy, and life had been very quiet after that. The Infanta Isabella had wanted to enter a nunnery and drown her grief in prayer, but King Ferdinand was having none of it, and she was packed off back to Portugal to marry the new King, Manuel, her late husband's cousin. Three years later young Isabella was dead, Maria was married to her widower, and Katherine was all alone.

That was after the great tragedy that had befallen her family. She still grieved for her beautiful, chivalrous brother Juan, who had died four years ago in the flower of his youth and promise, at just nineteen. Her parents had been inconsolable at the loss of their angel. The delicate Juan had not long been married to the lively young Margaret of Austria, the Archduke Philip's sister, and Katherine had heard gossip that he had died as a result of overexerting himself in the marriage bed. She had not quite understood what that meant, but she was painfully aware – as was everyone else – that Spain had been left without a male heir, and that Juana was now next in line to the throne. Unstable, unhappy Juana, whose temperament had been volatile from childhood, and whose husband was making her life a torment with his infidelities.

Queen Isabella had aged in these years, worn down by worry and grief. Her once-fair skin became puffy and lined, her green-blue eyes dulled by care. Yet to Katherine, her pious mother remained the perfect example of a Christian queen. There were people who said that women should not rule and should not wield dominion over men, but Isabella had proved them wrong. She had governed her kingdom and even led armies; not even female frailties had stalled her. Katherine had heard that, when campaigning against the Moors, her mother had given birth to Maria and been back in the saddle within days.

It was true that Isabella had had little time to devote to her family, yet she had always loved her children. She had constantly looked to their welfare, and personally supervised their education whenever she could. She was their champion, whereas their wily, self-seeking father, Ferdinand, was more interested in what advantages his children could bring him. Katherine had been brought up to respect and obey her father, but she did not love him in the way she loved her mother. Isabella was everything that Katherine wanted to be, and she had resolved always to emulate her example.

She had been thrilled when, shortly before they bade each other farewell (God, let it not be for ever, Katherine now prayed), Isabella had said, 'You, Catalina, are the most like me of all my children. I pray that your life will be happier.' Katherine had felt sure in that instant that it would be, especially with her mother's prayers behind her.

She did not want to think of the moment she had had to say goodbye. It had been postponed so often she had begun to think it might never come. But, inexorably, the day had arrived when she had knelt for the last time for her mother's blessing, been raised by loving arms and folded into one last embrace. And at that memory she wept afresh into her pillow, racked with longing.

The maid-of-honour on duty that night was Francesca de Cáceres. She had been asleep on the pallet at the foot of Katherine's bed, her dark locks spread out on the pillow, but now she sat up, rubbing her almond-shaped eyes.

'Highness? What is amiss? Why do you cry?'

Katherine did not like Francesca as much as she did Maria, but she needed to talk to someone.

'I think I am a little homesick,' she sniffed, trying to compose herself. 'Francesca, are you missing your mother?'

'Of course, Highness,' Francesca said. 'I think we would be unnatural if we did not.'

'Do you think we will ever see our mothers again?' Katherine asked.

'Maybe not for a while, Highness. But Prince Arthur might one day wish to visit Spain, or Queen Isabella may come to England.'

Katherine thought mournfully that neither eventuality was very likely. She could not remember her mother ever leaving Spain. Again, the need to be with Isabella swamped her. If I go on like this I shall go mad, she told herself. Her grandmother had been mad – she could remember visiting the older Queen Isabella at the grim castle of Arévalo, and hearing the old lady say she was being pursued by ghosts. It had been a frightening experience for the young Catalina, one she had never forgotten. And now there were rumours that Juana had become more unbalanced, throwing tantrums and attacking ladies at the Flemish court because Philip's eye had lighted upon them. Dear God, let me not end up that way, Katherine prayed silently.

She made herself dwell on Prince Arthur. All her life she had thought of him as her husband, yet they had not been married by proxy until two years ago, and then again last year, just to make sure that the alliance was watertight. Now King Henry was planning a state reception and wedding of such magnificence as had never been seen in England, even though her parents had urged that he outlay only moderate expense, for they did not want their daughter to be the cause of any loss to her adoptive realm. But the King had insisted, and Katherine guessed why. He had pursued this marriage to seal his sovereignty, for he was king by right of conquest only, and needed the reflected glory of mighty Spain to legitimise his title. Spending a fortune on celebrations was a small price to pay for recognition by Ferdinand and Isabella.

She knew that her father had worried that the English King was insecure on his throne. Henry had vanquished King Richard at the Battle of Bosworth, yet reports had reached Spain that there remained many kinsfolk of the late monarch to claim or contest the crown, and there had also been pretenders who had tried to unseat Henry. Yet Ferdinand had told Katherine last year that there now remained no doubtful drop of royal blood in England to threaten his throne. She did not like to dwell on what that had meant, and kept trying to put it from her mind. But she could not forget the whispers of what King Henry had done to ensure it . . .

Again she wondered what Arthur would be like. His portrait showed a youth with pink cheeks, narrow eyes with heavy lower lids, and a pursed rosebud mouth. He seemed so young, so girlish, and so unlike the princely hero people had described. But then portraits often lied. As did people, whispered her inner voice.

She would not listen or pay heed. These were night thoughts, and things would look different in the morning. The vane had now mercifully stilled. Francesca was lightly snoring, and Katherine resolved to do the same. She turned over and shut her eyes tightly, trying to think only of pleasant things.

At Dogmersfield Katherine was so cold she could not stop shivering. The upstairs chamber of the Bishop's Palace had a large fire roaring up the chimney, and she had had the table pulled over in front of it so that she could copy out her English sentences, but while the side of her nearest to the fire was warm, the rest of her was chilled to the bone, and when she had to force herself to get up and use the close stool in the privy at the far corner of the room, her teeth started chattering. The warmth from the hearth did not penetrate the stone walls. Winter was setting in with a purpose now, and she was trying harder than ever not to wish herself back in the warmer climes of Spain. How was she going to endure months of this freezing, bitter weather?

The bedchamber, with its fire stoked high, was only marginally warmer. Maria was preparing her for bed, and had just unlaced her gown when they heard the loud clatter of many hooves on the cobbles below. There was a stir and some commotion, then a man's voice raised in anger echoing from beneath them.

Minutes later Doña Elvira burst into the bedchamber, her normally severe features flushed, her erect figure bristling with rage. She was panting heavily.

'The King is here with Prince Arthur,' she announced, in a hoarse voice. Katherine began to tremble with anticipation, but Doña Elvira did not notice. 'His Majesty is acting outrageously!' she fumed. 'We told him that your Highness had retired for the night, but he said he wished to see you. I said you could see no one, it was not fitting, and he gave me a very evil look, as if I had spirited you away somewhere.'

It was bad enough hearing that the King had been angered, but almost worse to realise that Doña Elvira's judgement was not as rock-sound as Katherine had always believed. It was as if the foundations of her world were suddenly shifting beneath her feet. But it just would not do to offend the King at this first, crucial meeting. Her whole future lay in his hands, and he was all-powerful here, as she of all people had cause to know. What was Doña Elvira thinking of?

'I must go to His Majesty, if he commands it,' she said. 'Maria, please lace up my gown.'

Maria moved to obey, but Doña Elvira stopped her with a furious gesture.

'Your Highness will stay here!' she insisted, plainly shocked at this unaccustomed defiance. 'This English King is a rude, uncouth fellow. Despite what the Queen your mother told me to expect, he has no respect for Spanish customs! He demanded to know why I would not let him see you, and when I told him, he asked, "What is wrong with the Princess? Is she ugly or deformed?" Highness, I would not have repeated this, but you should know.'

This was getting worse by the minute. Doña Elvira had to grasp that they were in England now, and she could not always stand fast on Spanish ideas of ceremony. It seemed that the duenna's insufferable pride was about to wreck years of careful and courteous diplomatic negotiations.

'I said to him,' Doña Elvira was saying, 'that in Spain a young lady must be veiled when presented to a gentleman. I repeated that you had retired for the night. And do you know what he said?'

Katherine's heart sank further.

'He said that this is England, and that he would see you even though you were in your bed. The very shame of it! We are come among savages!'

This had to stop. 'Doña Elvira,' Katherine said firmly, 'the King is my father-in-law and this *is* his kingdom. We are bound to obey his orders and observe English customs. I pray you, do not think ill of me, but I must do as he commands.'

Doña Elvira looked at her as if a lamb had just roared. There was a short, charged silence, then she said, 'I am not a fool, Highness. I had not the courage to argue further, even to preserve propriety, so

I told him that he might see your Highness. I had no choice, as you say! Maria – lace up that gown and bring me the veil.' Having reasserted her authority, she picked up a comb and began raking it none-too-gently through Katherine's hip-length, wavy red-gold hair.

Katherine stood there bearing it patiently, looking at herself in the mirror. Duenna or no duenna, if the King asked her to lift her veil, she would. Her mother would surely hear about it – Doña Elvira was assiduous in sending reports – but Katherine trusted her to understand. Isabella would want her to comply with King Henry's wishes. She stared at her reflection, her heart pounding; she was still shivering, although not just from the chill in her room. She could only hope that the King and Prince Arthur liked what they saw. A pretty, round face, a determined little chin, gentle grey eyes, soft lips and a clear brow.

'If he insists that you remove the veil, Highness, remember what I taught you about custody of the eyes,' Doña Elvira said, her voice cold. 'Keep them demurely downcast, as befits a virtuous maiden! Do not stare.'

In a trice Katherine was ready, the veil in place, and Maria gave her a mischievous smile and sped down the stairs to make her curtsey and invite the King to come up to her mistress's chamber.

In a moment, just a heartbeat, Katherine would come face to face with her destiny. And here, entering her chamber, was the debonair Count de Cabra, bowing and obsequious, and with him a tall, middle-aged man in riding clothes, booted and cloaked against the cold. His face was angular, his nose a prominent beak, his greying sandy-brown hair sparse on his fur collar, and he was regarding her almost greedily with shrewd eyes. His rich furs and velvet bonnet with its jewelled ornament left her in no doubt that this was His Grace King Henry VII of England, first sovereign of the House of Tudor. She sank to her knees, her attendants following her example.

'Welcome to my kingdom, Princess Katherine,' the King said. As the Count translated, Henry stepped forward, took her hands and raised her to her feet. His voice was high but manly, almost musical. She had been told that he had Welsh blood from his father's ancestors, and the Welsh were renowned as a musical race.

Before Katherine could reply, the King let go of her hands and raised her veil – and smiled.

'The ambassadors of the sovereigns have not lied,' he said delightedly. 'I had heard of the wealth of Spain, but here is her most priceless treasure. Your Highness is doubly welcome for your beauty and your pretty face.' He lifted her hands and kissed them, as Don Pedro Manrique translated his words.

'I thank your Grace,' Katherine said, reciting the sentence she had practised earlier. Ignoring the stony-faced Doña Elvira, she ventured a smile.

'They told me you did not look like a true Spaniard,' Henry told her. 'By your red hair, you are a Lancastrian, like me and Arthur. By God, you look as English as we do! The kinship is plain, for we all descend from old John of Gaunt and King Edward the Third! I could not have found a more fitting match for my son.'

'I am very proud of my English royal blood,' Katherine said in Spanish. 'I am named for my great-grandmother, Catalina of Lancaster.'

'Gaunt's own daughter! Well, well. But you must not let an old man keep you from your husband!' the King declared jovially, stepping aside to reveal a youth standing in the doorway, flanked by several lords.

Katherine's first reaction was dismay, although she took care to keep smiling. It was the boy in the picture, grown slightly older, yet different. Prince Arthur was tall and auburn-haired, like his father, and had the air of confidence that was customary in those born of princely rank, but the thinness of his limbs was not concealed by his heavy travelling clothes. They hung on him. Even in the candlelight she could see that his cheeks were not rosy at all, but white with a ruddy flush.

Again she knelt. Arthur gave her an uncertain smile, bowed courteously and raised her to her feet. His hands were colder than hers. Then he bent to brush her lips briefly with his, just as she had seen people doing in Plymouth. She had been told since that it was the custom in England. She dared not look at Doña Elvira.

Speaking in Latin, Arthur asked her if she had had a pleasant journey. His voice was light and melodious. She assured him, in the same language, that she had.

'I have been received warmly and made welcome everywhere in England,' she said.

'I heard that your Highness had nearly been shipwrecked,' Arthur said. 'We were all much alarmed, and relieved when we had news that you had made land safely.'

'It was a frightening experience,' Katherine told him, searching his face for some spark of warmth, some indication that he found her appealing.

'Well, you are here now,' Arthur replied. They smiled awkwardly at each other, for want of anything else to say, until the King rescued them, calling for wine to celebrate this happy meeting and talking about the lavish wedding celebrations he had planned.

Arthur said little. Although he politely asked if she had been comfortably accommodated, and what she thought of the food in England, and other such pleasantries, Katherine was unnerved by his reserve. Compared to King Henry's hearty welcome, her husband's had been lukewarm. She thought of the letters he had sent, so full of longing for her coming. It was hard to believe now that he had written them. Her heart plummeted. Was he disappointed in her? She could detect no ardour in him, none of the passion her brother Juan had shown from the first towards his bride. But she could see something in Arthur that she had seen, belatedly, in Juan – the signs of ill-health. Indeed Arthur looked so poorly that she feared he was ailing from some dread disease. Yet this was the young man it was her duty to love, as her husband. Her mother had said that it was up to her to win his love.

'You must be tired after your journey here, sir,' she said, thinking the Latin sounded very stilted and resolving again to learn English as quickly as she could. 'It's cold, and the ground must be hard for riding.'

'I am freezing to my bones, your Highness,' Arthur admitted. 'I expect you find England very cold after Spain.'

'I do, but already I have grown to love England,' Katherine replied. It was not wholly truthful, for she had seen little of the country on her long journey, enclosed in her litter, with only occasional peeps when the curtains gaped – but it was politic, and one day, God willing, it would be true. 'Come to the fire, my lord,' she invited, noticing the

King watching them approvingly as they walked together across the room. Arthur accepted a glass of wine, sipped it and coughed.

'Is your Highness quite well?' Katherine asked.

'A winter rheum, nothing more,' he replied, coughing again.

'Then I hope you will soon be better!' she said brightly.

'Your Highness is most kind,' Arthur said. 'Forgive me if I did not welcome you as warmly as I should have done. I was tired by the ride to and from Easthampstead, where I met up with the King my father. I will be more myself soon, and better company, I hope. I *am* pleased that you are here.' He flushed, and Katherine warmed to him. She had mistaken weariness and perhaps shyness for indifference. Suddenly the world had shifted again. Everything was going to be all right.

It was midnight before everyone retired. Katherine had enjoyed herself immensely. At the King's request, she had summoned her musicians to entertain him and Arthur, and to the melodic sound of hautboys and sackbuts, she and her ladies had danced the slow, stately *pavaniglia* with its two beats to a step. Arthur, somewhat restored after the wine and sweetmeats, wanted to join in, so she and her ladies taught him a dignified *baja*. Afterwards, as everyone clapped, he raised her hand to his lips and kissed it.

When he took his leave the next morning, he looked a little better.

'Farewell, my lady,' he said, still speaking Latin. 'I look forward to seeing you in London.' He bent to kiss her hand, bowed to her curtsey, and walked off to join his father and their retinue. Her heart went out to him, poor, thin, sickly boy. She sent up a prayer that God would soon restore him to health.

Chapter 2

1501

Soon they would be nearing London. That night they would lodge in Kingston, and tomorrow they would lie at the Archbishop of Canterbury's palace at Lambeth, just south of the great River Thames. They were following its course, riding across the gently undulating hills of Surrey. The winter landscape was bleak and overcast, with a hint of snow in the air. Katherine huddled in her litter, her furs muffling her up to her chin, longing for nothing more than to be warm.

In the distance she could hear the sound of a great body of horsemen approaching. They came closer and closer, and peering through a chink in the leather curtains, Katherine saw that all the riders – a veritable army – were dressed in a livery of red and black, and that at their head rode two finely dressed people: a young man and a boy, both sitting proud and erect in their saddles. As they drew near, the young man, a florid and rather portly gentleman in a velvet cloak edged and lined with sable, signalled to the rest to halt.

'Masters, we seek the Princess of Wales,' he cried. 'The King's Grace has sent us to escort her party to Lambeth.'

'I am here, sir,' Katherine said, drawing aside the curtains of her litter, as the Count de Cabra came alongside to act as her interpreter.

The man and the boy immediately dismounted, swept off their plumed hats and knelt in the road.

'Edward Stafford, Duke of Buckingham, at your service, my lady,' the florid man said with a flourish. 'And I have the honour of presenting Prince Henry, Duke of York, second son of the King.'

Katherine's eyes swivelled to the boy kneeling beside him. He was a well-grown lad with plump, rosy cheeks. He had narrow eyes and rosebud lips like Arthur's, but that was where the likeness ended. Where Arthur was pale and thin, his brother was stocky and blooming with health; even kneeling he exuded vitality and self-assurance. There was no doubting that this was a prince.

She asked them to rise, noticing that Prince Henry's gown was a splendid scarlet furred with ermine, and that he was grinning broadly at her, the bold imp!

'Welcome to England, your Highness,' he said. His voice had not yet broken, yet it carried authority. 'The Prince my brother sends greetings, and bids me say that he is counting the days until the wedding with impatience.' Prince Henry's bold gaze suggested that he would be counting them even more fervently were he in Arthur's place. How old was the boy? Surely he could not be five years younger than Arthur, as she was certain she had heard? He was acting as if he were sixteen, not ten!

'If your Highness will make yourself comfortable in the litter, we will lead you into Kingston,' the Duke of Buckingham said. 'The nights are drawing in and you will be glad of shelter. If there is anything you need, you have only to call.'

Katherine thanked him, drew the curtains and huddled back into her furs. She had found Prince Henry a little disturbing. He was a handsome boy with undeniable charm, and even in those brief moments he had dominated the courtesies. Arthur had been reserved and diffident, and she could not stop herself from wondering how different things would have been had she been betrothed to his brother. Would she have felt more excited? More in awe? She felt disloyal even thinking about it. How could she be entertaining such thoughts of a child of ten? Yet it was so easy to see the future man in the boy. And it was worrying to realise how effortlessly Arthur could be overshadowed by his younger brother. Pray God Prince Henry was not overambitious!

Katherine stood as still as her inner excitement permitted, while Doña Elvira and the maids-of-honour made her ready for her state entry into the City of London. Already dressed in rich Spanish gowns ornamented with goldsmiths' work and embroidery, they helped her step into the wide-hooped farthingale, laced her kirtle as tight as she could bear it, then drew on the heavy velvet gown with bell-shaped sleeves and a full, gathered skirt.

Katherine surveyed herself critically in the mirror, catching Maria's eye as her friend hid a smile.

'It makes me look as broad as I am tall. I am too short to wear this attire. Why can I not wear an English gown?'

Doña Elvira was shocked. 'Because they are unseemly, Highness!' she snapped. She had made no secret of her horror at seeing English-women wearing low-cut, figure-revealing gowns without hoops. 'And your lady mother the Queen chose this gown for you. It was most costly!' Doña Elvira was in a bad mood. The rolls of fat under her chin were quivering. She had already lost the battle over the litter. Katherine had been determined to ride on horseback through London, so that the people could see her. She had insisted, and got her way – but Doña Elvira was set on reasserting her authority.

'You must wear this too!' she commanded. 'This' was a little hat with a flat crown and wide brim, like a cardinal's hat. The duenna placed it on Katherine's head, over the bejewelled Venetian coif, and tied the gold lace under her chin. No one, thankfully, had mentioned a veil. Fortunately the November sky was bright and it was not too cold; she was gradually getting used to the English climate, and thought she could bear to go out without a cloak. She wanted to look her best for the citizens. This was to be her day. The King, the Queen and Prince Arthur would play no formal part in it.

Outside the great doors of Lambeth Palace Katherine's Spanish retinue – prelates, dignitaries, nobles and knights, all richly dressed in her honour – had formed a procession. A gaily caparisoned palfrey was waiting, a sumptuous padded seat affixed to its saddle. With careful dignity she stopped beside it, as an ugly, crookbacked little man with a sparse beard, a hooked nose and a cloak of yellow damask stepped forward. Doña Elvira, her manner stiff and disdainful, introduced him as Dr de Puebla. The doctor bowed low, with great courtesy, and Katherine gave him her hand to kiss. As her father's ambassador to King Henry's court, he had done much to bring her to this day – more, perhaps, than she would ever know. She wondered how far Puebla had been complicit in the dark deed that had led to her marriage. He must have his secrets. Yet there was no doubt that he had skilfully driven and concluded the negotiations, and so she supposed she should be filled with gratitude. More than that, she felt sorry for him, being so crippled and unprepossessing, and she hoped that the duenna had not taken against him on that account.

'I will be your Highness's escort,' he told her. He had earned the honour.

Once Katherine had mounted, and the bent little Dr de Puebla had climbed on his own steed with some difficulty, the procession set off at a stately pace along the river to Southwark, Puebla pointing out the sights of London on the way. On the opposite bank Katherine saw the great abbey of Westminster rising above the lofty pinnacled roofs of Westminster Palace.

'That is where the English kings are crowned, Highness,' Dr de Puebla said. 'And ahead on that side, see the town houses of the nobility along the riverbank and the Strand, the road that leads to the City.' There were many of them, all with fine gardens sloping down to the river. Beyond, she was told, lay the Inns of Temple and the magnificent monastery of the Black Friars.

Dominating the City's skyline was St Paul's Cathedral, a vast edifice with a mighty spire, and clearly the largest church by far in a sea of spires. And on her right there was another great monastery, the Priory of St Mary Overy. Just past that was London Bridge – a bridge with shops and houses crammed in on both sides, and even a chapel!

Katherine felt herself beginning to warm to Dr de Puebla, who was proving such a knowledgeable and entertaining escort, and whose unfortunate appearance belied his friendliness.

'The bridge links the City to the Surrey shore of the Thames,' he explained as they crossed it through packed crowds. At the end was a great gatehouse, and it was through this that Katherine entered the City of London itself.

She was immediately surrounded by hordes of eager, expectant citizens, all jostling for a good view of her. Everywhere she looked, colourful banners and tapestries were hanging from the windows of tall, prosperous-looking houses, and her ears were assailed by the endless joyous pealing of bells from what seemed like a hundred churches. The tremendous ovation was deafening, though she was offended to see some of the common people laughing at her attendants' clothes, and pointing at the Christianised Moors among them, crying out, 'There go the Ethiopians, like devils out of Hell!'

Her progress was slowed by the press of citizens, and six times along the route she paused to admire elaborate pageants that had been mounted in her honour. This city must be rich indeed to be able to afford such outlay on pretty tableaux adorned with gaudy heraldic shields, and people dressed as saints and mythical heroes loudly lauding their future Queen with music and verse. The sight of a fierce Welsh dragon perched atop a mock castle made her gasp, and she was relieved to hear that it was meant to be the red dragon of Cadwaladr, a near-legendary Welsh ancestor of the King.

The procession wound its way along Fenchurch Street to Cornhill, and then to Cheapside. Here Katherine glimpsed King Henry and Prince Arthur watching her from the windows of a fine house. The King raised his hand in greeting, the Prince bowed. With them was a plump lady with a kind face, wearing a velvet gable hood with long lappets, and smiling down at Katherine. She must be Queen Elizabeth, Katherine concluded. The Queen had corresponded with her own mother, saying how thrilled she was at the prospect of having Katherine for a daughter, and how lovingly she would look after her. Katherine looked forward to meeting her. She seemed charming, and certainly the people thought so too, for many were cheering her.

When her cavalcade came to a halt beside an elaborate stone cross Katherine was formally welcomed to London by the Lord Mayor, who stood at the head of a large deputation of men in furred robes with heavy gold chains. These were the aldermen and sheriffs of the City, and the representatives of the wealthy craft guilds and livery companies.

The Lord Mayor spoke, with Dr de Puebla translating. 'Your Highness may be interested to know that this cross was erected by the first King Edward in honour of his much-loved Queen, Eleanor of

Castile, your Highness's own forebear. After she died, the King had thirteen of these crosses built at every place where her body had rested overnight on its way to Westminster Abbey. It is our prayer that your Highness's own marriage to our Prince may be as happy.'

When the Mayor and civic dignitaries had finished their loyal address, Katherine and her train passed on to St Paul's Cathedral, where she was to be married in two days' time. Here, in the cool of the vast nave, she knelt for a magnificent service of thanksgiving, the climax to the day's celebrations.

Back at Lambeth that evening, she gratefully accepted a goblet of wine and bade her maids join her by the fireside. They were all full of the excitements and spectacles of the day.

'Those pageants!' Isabel de Vargas cried. 'They must have cost this King a fortune.'

'They were splendid,' Katherine agreed, then saw Maria's raised eyebrows and started giggling. 'You noticed too! Ladies, in one of the pageants, the "Archangel Gabriel" reminded me that my chief duty was to bear children, because it was for this that God gave mankind the capacity for sensual lust. And in another, a man dressed as Our Lord appeared to me and said, "Blessed be the fruit of your belly; your fruits I shall increase and multiply." If I had not known before, I was left in no doubt as to what is expected of me here. But, oh, I did blush! It would never have been said so publicly in Spain!'

At Baynard's Castle by the Thames, in a great chamber hung with tapestries, and filled with curtseying ladies-in-waiting clutching their embroidery, Katherine was received by her mother-in-law, Queen Elizabeth.

'I cannot welcome your Highness warmly enough,' the Queen said in French, raising Katherine from her own curtsey and kissing her on both cheeks. She smelt of rose water and ambergris.

'I have longed to see your Grace,' Katherine told her, trying out the English she had practised so often during the past days. She could understand a good deal of what people said now, but speaking the language herself was more challenging.

'And I have longed to see your Highness. Come, let us sit and get to know each other,' the Queen said, leading Katherine to a cushioned window seat. It was easy to see that Elizabeth of York, with her burnished red hair and fair skin, had once been a woman of great beauty. She was beautiful still, but her face was pale and she looked tired.

'I trust you are comfortably lodged?' she enquired.

'Yes, your Grace, thank you,' Katherine said.

Elizabeth smiled at her. 'From now on you must regard me as your mother, my child. If there is anything you need, or that you are worried about, come to me, and I will do my best to help. I have some influence with the King. Soon you will meet his mother, the Lady Margaret. She too has been longing for your coming. Her chief wish is to see all our children happily settled and provided for.'

Katherine had heard of the Lady Margaret by repute. She was renowned even in Spain as a learned and holy lady.

'Your Highness has already met my son Henry,' the Queen smiled. 'He is a rogue! Arthur was sent away when he was small, to Ludlow Castle on the Welsh border, to be taught how to rule his principality of Wales. It is a sound preparation for kingship – yet it was a wrench to part with him, of course. But Henry grew up under my care, with his sisters. You will like Margaret and Mary. Margaret is not much younger than your Highness, and is to be the Queen of Scots.'

'And the Princess Mary?' Katherine asked.

'She is but five,' the Queen said. 'We must wait to see what God will provide. I had two other children, but alas, God saw fit to take them to Himself. Edmund died only last year. He was fifteen months old.' Her voice faltered.

Had that been a judgement of God? Katherine wondered. The sins of the fathers being visited upon the young? Forgetting etiquette, she reached across and laid her hand on the Queen's.

'My mother also lost two children – two babies. And when my brother Juan died, she was very sad.'

'That must have been the hardest cross to bear,' the Queen said. 'We were grief-stricken ourselves to hear the news.' She squeezed Katherine's hand. 'But today let us speak of happier things, for you are to be

28

married tomorrow, and there are going to be great celebrations and disports! Lady Guildford tells me that you like to dance. She was with the King's party at Dogmersfield and saw how accomplished you are.'

'I love to dance!' Katherine cried.

'Do you know any English dances?' the Queen asked, rising to her feet.

'No, your Grace.'

'Then I will teach you some!' Clapping her hands, Elizabeth bade her ladies leave their embroidery and summon the musicians. Katherine was enchanted by her spontaneity and warmth. Her own mother had never been so informal, even with her children. Soon the Queen and her ladies had Katherine gliding across the tiled floor in a *branle* or skipping in a lively *saltarello*. It was a wonderful evening; she had not enjoyed herself so much in a long while.

When it grew late and the time came for her to bid the Queen farewell, Elizabeth took her hand.

'I know you will be a good wife to Arthur,' she said. 'Be patient and kind with him. He has not been well, and he is not himself. He thinks I fuss too much, but we all pray he will amend soon.' She spoke lightly but Katherine detected the concern in her voice.

'I know he will,' she said, wishing to comfort the Queen. 'At Dogmersfield he said he was getting better.'

Elizabeth kissed her. 'God bless you for your sweet heart,' she said.

It was near midnight when Katherine returned to Lambeth Palace to make her final preparations for her wedding day. Everything *was* going to be all right. She knelt and said her prayers, thanking God and His Holy Mother for all their blessings, and hugging to herself the comforting knowledge that Queen Elizabeth would be there to help her prepare for the role she would one day occupy, and initiate her into the realities and mysteries of life at the English court.

Sleep came fitfully. Katherine was too tense to relax. Tomorrow she was to be married, and initiated into another mystery. The prospect of the high ceremonies and what was to follow overwhelmed her. In the end, she could lie there tossing and turning no more, and got up and knelt again at her prie-dieu, praying earnestly that she might be blessed with the strength to do well all that was expected of her.

On her wedding morn, the fourteenth of November in the year of Our Lord 1501, Katherine rose very early to be dressed in her bridal robes. Her wedding gown was of heavy white and gold satin, pleated and wide-skirted. Her glorious golden hair was to be worn loose in token of her virginity, and on her head Doña Elvira placed a jewelled coronet, and over it a voluminous veil of silk, edged with a sparkling border of gold, pearls and precious stones. When Katherine looked in her mirror, she saw there a reflection of a glittering, gorgeously robed icon, and there were gasps of admiration from her assembled household when she emerged from Lambeth Palace.

'Prince Arthur is indeed fortunate to have such a bride!' Dr de Puebla observed, bowing low. 'Your Highness does us all proud.'

Behind her, Doña Elvira sniffed, and Katherine turned, to catch only fleetingly the contemptuous glance that the duenna was casting upon the ambassador. But there was no time to wonder why the duenna seemed so disapproving, as a flotilla of barges was waiting at the jetty to convey Katherine and her train to the Tower, where the royal entourages were to assemble.

Already there were people lining the banks of the Thames, waving and cheering, but as the grey riverside fortress loomed ahead out of the morning mist, Katherine suppressed a shiver. On this day, of all days, she did not want to think about what she had heard about the Tower. Instead, as the barge drew up by the Queen's Stairs and she entered the Tower through a small postern, she focused her mind on the Constable's enthusiastic greeting. He conducted her to the broad tournament ground below the giant white keep, which was called Caesar's Tower, because, the Constable said, it had been built by Julius Caesar. Here the King and Queen and their retinues were waiting to depart for St Paul's. Katherine sank into a deep curtsey, and was embraced by both Henry and Elizabeth.

'Your Highness makes a beautiful bride!' the Queen exclaimed.

The King was eyeing Katherine appreciatively. 'We could not have asked for better,' he said. 'Very becoming!'

Katherine blushed. Henry himself was resplendent in red velvet robes, with a breastplate studded with diamonds, rubies and pearls, and a belt of rubies at his waist.

Katherine travelled with Queen Elizabeth in an open chariot to St Paul's Cathedral, with the King riding ahead, magnificent on a white horse. The cheering crowds were back in force, and the streets still decorated from her reception two days before. She saw wine flowing from the conduits, and was amazed when the Queen said that it was provided free for the people, so that they too could celebrate.

'There will be much merrymaking today, and many sore heads tomorrow,' Elizabeth said wryly.

The press of people by St Paul's was great, the clanging of the bells deafening. They alighted at the adjacent Bishop's Palace, where the Lady Margaret was waiting for them. Wearing the dark robes and white wimple and barbe of a widow, she cut a sombre figure and her long, thin face looked stern, but when she broke into a delighted smile at the sight of Katherine, it was transformed. And when Katherine refused to allow this venerable lady to kneel to her, the Lady Margaret's eyes were bright with tears of emotion.

'Sweet Princess, we are blessed to have you,' she said, and kissed Katherine. The King was nodding enthusiastically in agreement.

'Come, my lady mother,' he said. 'We must go and take our places.' He accompanied the Queen and the Lady Margaret through a door that led directly to the cathedral, leaving Katherine alone with her ladies for a few moments. As Maria briefly grasped her hand, Katherine breathed deeply and lifted her chin. Then the door opened and Prince Henry walked in, looking splendid in a gown of silver tissue embroidered with gold roses. Again he had about him that air of assurance that had impressed her before.

'I am come to escort your Highness into the cathedral,' he said, kneeling and kissing her hand before swiftly rising and offering her his arm. As she was not tall, they were much of a height, and she was very conscious of her closeness to him and the strength of his arm. He really was an extraordinary boy.

They emerged from the Bishop's Palace to the sound of trumpets, shawms and sackbuts. The people went wild when they saw Katherine, calling down blessings on her and roaring their approval. At the west door the Queen's sister, Cecily of York, was waiting to carry the bride's train, and behind her, in a line that stretched along the west front of the church, a bevy of English ladies – there must have been a hundred of them, all expensively gowned.

Inside the cathedral the guests were already gathered. A high walkway, covered with a red worsted carpet, had been raised along the nave, from the west door to the crossing, so that all might witness this marriage that would bring glory to the Tudor dynasty and ensure its continuance. When the trumpets sounded, Prince Henry again offered Katherine his arm, and they mounted the steps to the walkway and advanced slowly. To one side she could see the King and Queen watching from the privacy of their latticed pew, again to ensure that everyone's attention was on the bridal pair; and on the other she saw the Lord Mayor and the City fathers.

Ahead, under the crossing, steps led on all four sides up to a higher platform, where the Archbishop of Canterbury, magnificent in his ceremonial cope and jewelled mitre, was waiting to conduct the service. Ranged behind him was a score of bishops and abbots, the princes of the Church come in state to see the Spanish alliance properly concluded, and to sanctify it. And there was Arthur, waiting at the foot of the platform, tall, dignified, but looking shrunken inside his padded white satin robes. His pale face impassive, he bowed as Katherine approached, and at his nod she left Prince Henry behind and ascended the stairs on one side to the platform, as Arthur went up the other. And there, in the sight of God and – it seemed – of all the world, they were made man and wife.

After the wedding ceremony the Archbishop and the clergy formed a procession and led Arthur and Katherine to the high altar, where the nuptial High Mass was celebrated. Then, hand in hand, the newly married couple walked back along the platform and knelt to crave the blessing of the King and Queen, who gave it jubilantly. Katherine noticed that, behind them, the Lady Margaret was dabbing her eyes, overcome once more with emotion.

It felt strange to be married at last. Everything seemed unreal. She stole a glance at Arthur as they descended into the nave. There was a quiet grace about him, an impassive, regal quality, as he nodded to left and right, but when he caught her eye he did smile, and that smile broadened as they emerged through the cathedral doors to greet crowds erupting in a joyous ovation. They stood for several moments, acknowledging the acclaim, until the King and Queen joined them. Then, at a signal from his father, Arthur raised his hand.

'Good people,' he cried, 'be it known that this day I give to my wife, the Lady Katherine, her dower of one-third of my revenues as Prince of Wales.'

There were hearty shouts of approval. 'King Henry! Prince Arthur!' the people cried, and the trumpets, shawms and sackbuts blared out once more in celebration. It was then that Katherine happened to glance at Prince Henry watching his brother, and caught the fleeting, hostile glimmer of naked envy in his eyes. Then it was gone and he was beaming again, waving and bowing to the crowds as if their applause were all for him. She supposed it was natural for him to be jealous of the brother who would outrank him at every turn, but nonetheless it was disconcerting to see such hostility in a young boy's eyes.

But she forgot about it when Arthur took her hand in his clammy one and she noticed the sheen of sweat on his forehead. He did not look well, and she was concerned about him having to endure all these high ceremonies and celebrations. It troubled her that he was still suffering from the malady he had dismissed as a mere rheum ten days before. Yet there was no time to worry, as he was steering her in the wake of Prince Henry, who had been chosen to lead the grand procession back to the Bishop's Palace, where a great feast was waiting.

As Katherine entered the hall she almost collided with the Lord Mayor and aldermen, all craning their necks to get a good view of her, and there was much laughter. She was impressed to see that not only the royal family but the whole company was dining off solid-gold plate ornamented with pearls and precious stones. In the candlelight the myriad jewels and heavy gold chains of the noble guests winked and glittered. The feast went on for what seemed like hours, as course after course was brought in to the sound of fanfares, and the wine flowed endlessly. At the high table she was seated in the place of honour at the King's right hand, and next to her was the witty Don Pedro de Ayala. He was supposed to be her parents' ambassador in Scotland, but he had come to London on diplomatic business some years ago and stayed there.

'I like it here, Highness,' he told her. 'It suits my health, for Scotland is too cold by far for a Spaniard. And, of course, it proved useful to King Ferdinand and Queen Isabella to have me in London in the time leading up to your marriage.' Katherine gained the impression that Don Pedro had no intention of resuming his duties in Scotland. In fact, he told her, now that she was married, he was expecting to go home. He seemed popular with the English courtiers and the King, and she rather liked him too, but she noticed that Dr de Puebla was glowering at him from his lowlier position further down the table. It did not take much imagination to deduce that Puebla, their Most Catholic Majesties' resident ambassador, felt his position had been usurped by Don Pedro.

The King chatted amiably, speculating keenly on the value of the plate on display, and wondering aloud how this or that lord had been able to deck himself out so finely when he was late with his taxes. The Queen steered the talk around to how moving the ceremony had been, and how delicious the food was. Katherine politely agreed, although privately she thought English food bland and nowhere near as varied as the rich diet she had enjoyed in Spain. It was all roasted meats and hard-crusted pies!

Prince Henry could talk of little but the tournaments and pageants that were to be held over the coming days, in honour of the marriage. He was desperate to take part, and in the end the King had to say no, quite firmly. He was too young. Henry sulked for a bit, until his sister Margaret told a joke, then he was all smiles again. Katherine liked Margaret, a russet-haired, lively, headstrong girl of twelve, and hoped that it would be some time before she was sent north to wed the King of Scots. She guessed that Queen Elizabeth would miss her daughter sorely, for it was plain that they were close.

Arthur said little, and picked at his food. Katherine wondered if he was as nervous as she was at the prospect of the wedding night to come. She knew her duty, and so must he, but it was daunting, and she was embarrassed to think that every person in this crowded hall was aware of what she and Arthur would be doing later.

'It is a good dinner,' she said in her halting English, trying yet again to draw him into a conversation and find out what was wrong with him. Again, she saw that he was perspiring. The smoke from the central hearth was making her cough, so Heaven knew how he was feeling.

'Do you find it hot in here?' she asked.

'It is indeed, my lady,' Arthur agreed. 'I'd give much to be in bed.' There was a pause as he realised what he had said, then – at last – he smiled. In that moment the tension was broken, and Katherine giggled nervously. The King and Queen leaned forward to see what was going on.

'Time for some merriment, I think!' King Henry said, signalling for the tables to be cleared. 'It would please us greatly if the Princess and her ladies treated us to a display of Spanish dancing.'

'It would please me too, sire,' Arthur concurred.

When the cloths had been lifted and the trestles carried out, the musicians assembled in the gallery above. Katherine stepped down to the floor of the hall and beckoned to her ladies to join her. Holding up their trains, they performed a *pavaniglia* for the company to the accompaniment of shawms and a slow, rhythmic drumbeat. Katherine was conscious of everyone's eyes on her as she dipped and stepped in dignified style. She was aware of Arthur watching her, and of the intent gaze of King Henry, and of Prince Henry casting bold eyes upon her, hardly able to sit still.

There were cries of 'Bravo!' when the dance came to an end, and then, as a compliment to the Queen, Katherine glided into the *branle* that Elizabeth had taught her the day before. Elizabeth clapped in delight, and kissed and embraced Katherine when she returned to the royal dais.

'That was very well done, my lady,' Arthur complimented her.

'Now it is your turn, Arthur,' the King said.

Arthur seemed about to refuse, but he dutifully rose. Katherine was expecting him to lead her down to the floor, but he turned away and bowed before one of his mother's ladies before taking her by the hand. Katherine's cheeks burned. It was embarrassing to be ignored and spurned. She would not have expected to dance with Arthur while they were merely betrothed, for that would have been unseemly, but they were married now, and this was their wedding day! *She* was the bride, not Lady Whatever-Her-Name-Was. But no one seemed to think anything strange of Arthur's choice of partner, so Katherine was forced to conclude that this was yet another outlandish English custom. And her humiliation – for so it felt – did not last long, for Arthur returned to her side after just the one dance.

'Will you dance again, my lord?' she asked hopefully.

'I am a little weary,' he said, to her disappointment. 'I do not dance often.'

'Well, I do!' cried Prince Henry, jumping up and pulling his sister down to the floor, where he whirled her about in a lively *dompe*. Everyone clapped in time, and when the dance was over, the Prince cried, 'Another!' Throwing off his gown, he proceeded to jump about with Margaret in the *saltarello*, showing off outrageously, to the applause of his parents and his doting grandmother. Katherine thought it strange that none of them had suggested that Arthur should dance with his bride on his wedding day, of all days.

She had known before leaving Spain that in England there was such a thing as a bedding ceremony, when a bride and bridegroom were put to bed together by their guests, and the bed was blessed by a priest before everyone left the couple alone in their bedchamber. She had known it, but had been dreading it, and hoping that Doña Elvira, usually so outspoken about anything she deemed unseemly, would protest against it. But the duenna had remained silent. When Katherine had voiced her reluctance to be on public show in so immodest a manner, Doña Elvira had surprised her.

'The Queen your mother approved, and you should not question her wisdom. She wanted this public ceremony, so that all the world should see you bedded as man and wife together, for the avoidance of any doubt.'

Katherine had said no more, realising that, if her mother had wanted this, her duenna would be immovable. But she cringed at the very thought of it, and when the King called for hippocras and wafers to be served, signalling the end of the evening's festivities, she knew that the moment was at hand. Normally abstemious, she accepted a large goblet of the sweet spiced wine, hoping that it would calm her nerves. Maria, speaking in a whisper, and giggling, had confided that her married sister had said that the first time could be painful . . .

Arthur's pallid face looked tired and drawn as the King summoned him to attend him. They left the hall followed by a host of lords and gentlemen, amid gusts of hearty laughter. The Queen rose and beckoned Katherine to go with her, and Doña Elvira and the ladies crowded behind them. Upstairs in the vast nuptial chamber the great tester bed had been made up with plump pillows and fine sheets, then spread with an ermine-trimmed counterpane and strewn with dried petals and herbs. The headpiece was adorned with the royal arms of England, newly painted and gilded.

Katherine stood trembling while the Queen herself assisted Doña Elvira with the disrobing.

'There is nothing to fear,' her mother-in-law said, with a reassuring smile.

Doña Elvira frowned. 'The Princess has been taught her duty, your Highness.'

Elizabeth raised an eyebrow. 'There should be more to it than duty, I hope,' she observed. 'Well, daughter, that is a strange garment you are wearing!'

'It is my farthingale,' Katherine explained. 'We wear them under our gowns in Spain.'

'Now that you are married you will wear English dress,' the Queen said.

'I will be pleased to do so,' Katherine told her, glad to obey.

Doña Elvira's eyes flashed fire as she undid the ribbons holding the farthingale in place, tugging them viciously. 'Hand me the night-rail,' she barked at Maria.

Maria exchanged glances with Katherine and reverently picked up a long night-rail of the finest lawn, embroidered with blackwork at the low neck and the wide cuffs. Doña Elvira divested her charge of her chemise and for a moment Katherine stood there, naked and blushing, before the duenna lifted the night-rail over her head. Then she combed her hair while the maids sprinkled Katherine with Hungary water scented with rosemary and thyme.

The Queen took Katherine's hand and assisted her into bed.

'Prop yourself up on the pillows,' she instructed. Katherine did as she was told, pulling up the covers over her breasts as Doña Elvira thrust forward and briskly arranged her hair like a fan over her shoulders. Katherine could tell that the duenna resented the Queen being there and was making it clear that she was the proper person to prepare her charge for her bridegroom.

Katherine sighed inwardly. Queen Isabella had insisted that Doña Elvira remain with her after marriage, to be a friend and mentor to her in a strange land, but Katherine was beginning to see that things would not be as simple as that. She had found it impossible to warm to her duenna, who – for all her rectitude and vigilance – was not the most lovable of mortals, and she feared there would be struggles ahead. But there was no time to fret because moments later the sound of approaching voices and guffaws announced Arthur's coming.

Chapter 3

1501

Katherine could have died of shame. She felt the hot blush rising from her chest to her face, for the Prince's voice could be heard, boasting that he felt lusty and amorous, which met with a burst of earthy male laughter.

'To it, lad, to it!'

'For England and St George!'

Led by his father, Arthur entered the bedchamber, wearing a voluminous nightshirt embroidered along the gathered yoke with red and white roses. The men crammed in behind him, their leering eyes seeking the bride as she lay in her bed. Katherine's cheeks were crimson as Arthur lifted the covers and climbed in beside her. They lay there stiffly together, two feet apart, as goblets were raised and bawdy jests made. Prince Henry was the most incoherent of all; there was no doubt he had had too much wine. The Queen saw Katherine's embarrassment and caught the King's eye. He nodded.

'Make way for His Grace of Canterbury!' he cried. Reluctantly the men stood aside to allow the Archbishop through, and there was a semblance of hush as he raised a hand in blessing and prayed that God would make the union of the Prince and Princess fruitful.

'Amen!' said the King. 'And now, my lords and ladies, we must leave these young people alone together. A hearty good night to you both!' Taking the Queen's hand he escorted her out, dragging Prince Henry with the other hand, and the company straggled off unwillingly behind him. Doña Elvira, last of all, blew out all the candles but one, hauled herself out of the room and closed the door.

*

Katherine lay there, her heart thumping. She heard Arthur swallow. He sounded as nervous as she was. The silence between them deepened.

'Are you tired, Katherine?' he asked suddenly.

'A little, sir,' she said, knowing she must not appear to be evading his attentions.

'I am exhausted,' he said. 'I could sleep for a week.' He coughed.

'Are you ill, my lord?' Katherine asked in concern.

'It is nothing. This rheum lingers.' He turned to face her and sighed deeply. 'Do not look so frightened,' he said, reaching across and laying a hand on her shoulder. 'It is my first time too.'

She did not know what to do. Isabella's euphemisms had not covered the practical aspects of the business.

Arthur drew her towards him. She could feel his damp breath on her cheek. Now he was pulling up her night-rail. He was breathing heavily. Then he turned his face away and coughed.

She could feel his hand gently probing her breasts before moving down to the secret places between her legs. Her cheeks burning, she lay there unmoving, bearing it, not understanding if she needed to do anything in return. Suddenly Arthur clambered on top of her, and she braced herself for the pain she feared was coming.

Arthur moved his body against hers, getting more and more agitated, but nothing else was happening. This wasn't how the act had been described to her. There was supposed to be some sort of joining of flesh, she was sure. But after several minutes of grappling and ineffectual thrusting, in which their bodies kept sticking together sweatily, although not in the right way, Arthur fell back on the bed, coughing violently, and in the moonlight Katherine glimpsed his poor little member resting limply against his thigh before he pulled down his nightshirt and lay there panting.

'I am sorry,' Arthur said. 'I am not well.'

'It does not matter,' Katherine whispered.

'I think not.' He was really out of breath. 'Whatever he says in public, my father does not want us to have children yet.'

Katherine turned towards him, astonished. This went against everything she had been told.

40

'He said we might consummate our marriage, but not cohabit afterwards for a few years,' Arthur explained, his breathing slowing now. 'He fears that I am too young to lie with you, and that it will ruin my health, especially with this cough.'

Katherine felt a pang. 'The King is right. My brother died at nineteen from too much indulgence in the marriage bed.'

'That is one of the reasons my father gave me when he commanded me to wait. He is overanxious because I've been unwell. I keep telling him he should not worry, but he does, and he is adamant. We cannot disobey him. He is the King.'

Katherine, watching Arthur as he lay silhouetted against the firelight, his face in shadow, could not tell whether he was grieved or not at his father's decision. In fact, she had the slight impression that he had been glad of an excuse not to do his husbandly duty. But King Henry was right. Arthur was unwell, worryingly so. He was clearly unfit for the duties of marriage. And it was obvious now that he must have been ailing for some time. Why, oh why, had they not informed her?

'Have my parents been told?' she asked.

'Certainly, and they are content.' They, of all people, had good reason to be, after what had happened to Juan.

'Then *I* am content to abide by what the King has decreed,' Katherine said. 'We are to make a pretence of . . . of marriage?'

'That is what he has commanded. We are to spend some nights together, to avoid talk. And I think we must let the world believe that we are man and wife in every way.' He paused. 'In truth, I am glad that I did not give an account of myself this night, for I fear that, even if I had not been interrupted by this foul cough, I would have failed you miserably, I am so very weary.' It was a face-saving lie, of course, for he had given up before the cough had attacked. Now he was seized by another paroxysm, harsher and more prolonged this time.

'It does not matter,' Katherine said, when the fit had subsided. 'I'm weary too. It's been a long day, and I shall be glad to get some sleep. Do you know when the King means us to – to—'

'When I am recovered, and maybe some time after that. He thinks that we should wait. He says we have our whole lives ahead of us.'

Arthur rose early the next morning and disappeared into his privy chamber next door, where his gentlemen were waiting to assist with his robing.

Reluctant to leave the warmth of the comfortable bed – and who could blame a bride for lying late on the morning after her wedding? – Katherine could hear them talking, although she could not understand every word they said.

'Willoughby, give me a cup of ale.' That was Arthur. 'My throat is so dry today, for I have been this night in the midst of Spain. It's good pastime to have a wife!' He repeated this several times, until Katherine – who had grasped the gist of it – began to fear that his bluff would be detected.

There was some chuckling, and some bawdy talk to which she closed her ears, then the conversation turned to the coming tournaments and the wagers that were to be laid. Presently the outer door closed and all was silent. Katherine turned over and dozed. There were to be no entertainments today; she and Arthur were to be allowed some privacy before they appeared in public again. She lay there remembering what Arthur had said, and trying to analyse her reaction. Yes, she was relieved. Despite the intimacy they had briefly shared, there was still a distance between them. Maybe he was holding aloof because he was unwell; or he was keeping that distance deliberately because he knew he was unable to make her his properly.

Yet she could not help feeling a little cheated. How different her wedding night might have been – and how different her future would be – with a proper man in her bed. How would it look when the months passed and there was no sign of an heir? It would reflect badly on her, as if she had failed in her duty. But the King would understand, she was sure, because he was concerned about his son's health, which was, of course, the greater issue. Did Henry know something that Katherine didn't? Or was he just being cautious? He was a prudent, calculating man, her father had once said – like recognising like. She comforted herself with that thought. If Arthur was that ill, he would surely not have been allowed to consummate the marriage at all.

A little later Doña Elvira entered with Francesca de Cáceres.

'Good morning, Highness,' Doña Elvira said. 'I trust you slept well. Francesca, make up the fire and help your mistress to dress when she is ready. I will return presently.'

Katherine sat up, rubbing her eyes. Now she must begin the great pretence.

'Good morning, Francesca,' she greeted the slender, raven-haired girl bending at the hearth. 'It's time I arose.' She flung back the covers and lowered her bare feet to the rush-matted floor.

'My nightgown, please,' she commanded, reaching for her velvet slippers. Then she saw that Francesca was staring at the bed.

'What is it?' she asked.

'Nothing, Highness.' Francesca hastily collected herself.

'No, there was something. You were looking at the sheets.'

Francesca looked embarrassed. 'Highness, I could not but notice that they are clean.'

'Of course they are clean.' Katherine was puzzled.

'But they should not be. My mother told me that a girl always bleeds the first time.'

Francesca's cheeks were pink.

'Bleeds? Why?'

'Highness, it is the breaking of the maidenhead.'

That made some sense, and it explained why the process would be painful, but Katherine realised that, in their ignorance, she and Arthur had not considered this bar to their pretence.

She thought rapidly. He had said they were to act as if they were one flesh, but he had not specifically forbidden her to tell the truth to those who would be in a position to help her. And Doña Elvira was coming back soon. She was a married lady herself, and little escaped her eagle eye.

Katherine was desperate to unburden herself. 'Francesca,' she said, her voice catching in her throat, 'nothing passed between Prince Arthur and me.'

Francesca looked shocked. 'Highness, I – I am sorry to hear that.'

Katherine felt tears threatening. This was not how things should be!

'I fear the Prince may never be able to have relations with me,' she said bleakly. 'He is too ill, and too weak.'

Francesca stared at her.

'I see, Highness.' She paused uncertainly. 'Doña Elvira should be told.'

'And *I* will tell her, but I must rely on your discretion.'

'Yes, Highness.'

Katherine said no more. She was dreading discussing the problem with her duenna. Doña Elvira had an adult son, but it was impossible to imagine her in the act of conceiving him!

Presently the duenna bustled in and dismissed Francesca. She stood there, her eyes boring into Katherine.

'Highness, I must ask, as the Queen your mother will wish to know. Is all well between you and the Prince of Wales?'

'Perfectly well,' Katherine said.

'I mean – I should make myself plain – is your marriage consummated?'

Katherine could feel herself flushing. 'No. The Prince was not well enough.' She explained what the King had ordered.

Doña Elvira frowned. 'One can only applaud His Highness's love and care for his son.'

The last thing Katherine wanted to hear, from an indignant Maria, was that Francesca de Cáceres had wasted no time in telling her fellow maids-of-honour how sad it was that the Princess was a virgin still.

'Tell her, and the others, from me,' she said, with the new-found authority that came from being married, even if it was in name only, 'that if I hear of any of them repeating what was told to Francesca in confidence, I will report them to the King.'

Then she prayed that no one would dare, because she too should have held her tongue.

Fourteen days of jousts, feasts, plays and dancing had passed, days filled with pageantry, colour, laughter and excitement.

The court had come to the brand-new palace at Richmond the day before. To Katherine, approaching on the River Thames at the head of a flotilla of barges, it had seemed like a place out of legend, rising above the River Thames like a vision. The King had smiled to see her marvelling at the fantastic pinnacles, the turrets surmounted by onion domes, the forest of gilded weather vanes, and the vast windows with their tiny diamond panes reflecting the winter sun. Proudly he told her that he had built the palace to his own specifications after the previous one had been badly damaged in a fire. He himself escorted her, the rest of the royal family following behind, along wide paths leading through courtyards with spouting fountains, fair gardens and fragrant orchards, and along galleried cloisters. Everywhere there were brightly painted badges – roses, portcullises, coats of arms – and gilded statues of fantastic beasts.

'Of course, it is meant to impress,' Henry said. 'People expect magnificence of a king. Magnificence betokens power. If I have great palaces, I must be rich enough to fund great armies!' Katherine noticed Prince Henry avidly hanging on his father's every word.

'But riches,' Arthur observed, 'can also exist in the mind. There is no greater wealth than in learning.'

'Which is why I welcome so many scholars to my court,' the King said. 'Then people are doubly impressed!'

When they entered the palace Katherine gasped to see azure ceilings, like the heavens, studded with more Tudor emblems, brilliant tapestries, murals in deep reds and golds, in which the figure of the King loomed large, and the wealth of portraits that adorned the walls. No one, seeing Richmond, could have failed to be awed by it.

It was here, the next day, that she bade a sad farewell to the Count de Cabra and the other lords of Spain who had escorted her to England.

'We will go home, Highness, and tell the King and Queen how magnificently your nuptials have been celebrated,' they told her, kissing her hand one by one. Then they were gone and another link with Spain was broken.

Afterwards, feeling somewhat dejected, and not a little homesick, she had sought out Arthur in the hope that he would play music or walk with her in the gardens, but he said he was tired and wanted to rest. So, thrusting down her ever-present anxiety about him, and dismissing her maids, she wandered into the royal library, which the King had said she might use whenever she pleased. Everything was so quiet today, after the excitements of the past fortnight. They had been sufficient to ward off melancholy humours, but today everything seemed flat and sad, and Katherine found herself once more longing for her homeland and her mother.

She chose a book on astrology, written in Latin, and sat down at a desk to read it, but it was dull, dull, dull. She could not help thinking about Arthur, and fretting because he seemed no better. She had seen the King, the Queen and the Lady Margaret looking anxiously at him, and was sure that they were concerned too. It worried her that he did not seem to want her company. She wondered if she might join her ladies and do some blackwork embroidery, to take her mind off things, but lacked the will to make a move. Suddenly, a wave of misery overcame her. She was condemned to spend her life in this kingdom as an exile, a wife but not a wife, a daughter without a mother. Engulfed by sadness, she buried her head in her arms and sobbed.

There was a hand on her shoulder. She looked up, startled. It was the King, gazing down at her with concern.

'What is it, child?'

She made to get up but he would not allow it.

'Tell me what is wrong,' he said. 'Have we not made you welcome?'

'You have,' she wept. 'Sire, you have made me very welcome. It is that – I miss my mother and my home!'

To her amazement, King Henry put an arm around her shoulders.

'Ah, poor Katherine! I, of all people, understand that. I was a fugitive and an exile from the time I was five, and separated from my mother for many years. Think you I do not know what it is to live among strangers? Of course I do! But we cannot change our destiny. You would not want to go home to your mother and father leaving all their hopes unfulfilled, would you? You are of sterner stuff than that, am I right?'

Katherine nodded through her tears, understanding what he was telling her.

'I have been impressed by your beauty, your bearing and your dignified manners,' he went on. 'I know you will try to do your duty with a happy heart, however hard it is. And remember, Katherine, in me you may be sure that you have found a second father who will ever watch over your happiness.'

'Thank you, sire,' she faltered, thinking how much easier it was to talk to the King than to Arthur. 'Forgive me. I worry about Prince Arthur. He is ill.'

The King's arm tightened about her shoulder. 'Fear not. The doctors now say it is no rheum but a quartan fever, which can last for weeks and recur. You must not worry. All will be well. Now dry your eyes and send for your ladies, for I have a surprise in store for you!'

Katherine allowed herself to be reassured, and while they were waiting for her maids to arrive, Henry showed her some of the books in his library: exquisitely illuminated manuscripts, new printed books with marvellous woodcuts, and tiny devotional volumes with embroidered covers and chased-gold clasps. Thus diverted, she calmed down, and she was even more cheered when the King's goldsmith was ushered in and commanded to spread his glittering wares on the table.

'You may choose as many pieces as you like!' Henry told her. Now her eyes were brimming with gratitude for his kindness. Taking care not to appear greedy, she selected from the treasures before her a necklace of pearls and sapphires, a ruby and gold cross and a rich collar of goldsmith's work. The King nodded his approval at her taste, and then informed her delighted ladies that they might have their choice of the other pieces. Katherine wondered how people could think that he was miserly; she had heard it repeatedly from her father, during his frequent haggling over her dowry. Look what Henry had outlaid on her reception and her wedding! Look at his munificence today!

Two days later she began to wonder if Ferdinand had been right. Don Pedro de Ayala came to her, craving a few moments of her time. They walked in the knot garden, well wrapped against the December chill.

'Your Highness will be aware that the first instalment of your dowry has been delivered to King Henry,' Don Pedro said. 'The trouble is he wants the rest of it. On the advice of Dr de Puebla, he asked your chamberlain to deliver the gold and silver plate and the chest of jewels, but, as you know, that portion of your dowry is not due for a year.' Katherine had been instructed not to touch or use any of the treasure she had brought from Spain, but to hand everything over to the King when her father commanded it.

'Dr de Puebla knows of this, none better,' Katherine said. 'He negotiated the marriage treaty! I have received no orders from King Ferdinand about it.'

'Nor I,' Don Pedro told her. 'And your Highness's chamberlain told the King that he was obliged to retain the jewels and plate. The fact is that His Grace of England would rather have their equivalent in coin. What I have to tell you is distasteful to me in the extreme. I fear that Dr de Puebla has connived with him to persuade your Highness to use the plate and jewels yourself, so that, when the time comes, the King will refuse to accept them, being used and second-hand, and perhaps dulled and tarnished, and your father would be shamed into sending him their value in money instead.'

'But then my father would be paying twice,' Katherine protested.

'Assuredly,' Don Pedro said. 'And Dr de Puebla has told the King that you approve of his little scheme.'

'I? That is a lie!' she cried.

It sounded all wrong to Katherine. She could not believe that her father's ambassador would even think up such a duplicitous plot, let alone involve her in it.

'But why? He acts for my parents. Why would he suggest something that is so patently against their interests and mine?'

'Because he desires to please the English King. He has been manipulated, and has forgotten where his loyalties should lie! That is why I felt it my duty to inform your Highness of this. Doña Elvira is aware of the matter. She agreed that you should know.'

'Doña Elvira does not like Dr de Puebla,' Katherine told him.

'Doña Elvira is a wise woman. She distrusts him, and rightly so.'

'I am glad you have told me,' Katherine said.

'His Grace wants to see you,' Don Pedro said. 'He asked me to tell you to go to him immediately.'

Trembling with anger and trepidation, she went straight to the King, and was ushered into his study, where she found Henry trying to prevent his pet monkey from ripping up his account book.

'Desist, Peterkin!' he commanded, setting the animal on the floor. 'He ruined my ledger once, you know, Katherine. The whole court was laughing about it. I know what they say of me – and no doubt it serves me right!' His smile faded. 'I wish to make you an apology,' he said. 'I am exceedingly sorry that I have asked for the plate and jewels. I should not like to be thought of as a person who asks for what is due before the specified time. I beg that you will write to King Ferdinand and Queen Isabella and explain that I was deceived by Dr de Puebla.'

Katherine gathered her courage. She had to be careful not to accuse the King of conniving at treachery. 'Sir, Don Pedro told me that Dr de Puebla suggested I use the plate and jewels myself, so that they be made unacceptable to you. I must stress that I knew nothing of this plan, nor gave my consent.'

Henry frowned. 'Nor I, Katherine.' He got up and began pacing. 'It is a monstrous idea.' He paused. 'Of course such an arrangement would be greatly to my advantage, but it would be fraudulent, and I would never consent to it. I am content with what the marriage treaty stipulates.' He sat down on the edge of his desk, drawing his furred robe around his spare frame. 'I am very angry with Dr de Puebla for advising me to ask for them now, and King Ferdinand should be aware of how his ambassador is conducting himself. But he has never suggested to me that you use the plate and jewels. You may have noticed, Katherine, that there is much hatred between Dr de Puebla and Don Pedro, and that, whatever one says, the other will try to discredit. If you take my advice, you will make little account of this, for I fear it proceeds from jealousy. Remember that Don Pedro would like to be ambassador here.'

Katherine went away, promising to think no more of it, but she could not help but worry lest the deadly enmity between Dr de Puebla and Don Pedro lead to further trouble. It was clear that she could not trust Dr de Puebla – but could she trust Don Pedro? And was even King Henry telling the truth?

That evening she dismissed her maids and bade Doña Elvira join her by the fire, then she related all that had happened that day.

The duenna's moon-shaped face creased into a frown.

'Highness, I will not say anything against the King. But Dr de Puebla is an evil man who owns no loyalty to the sovereigns, your parents.'

'But is there proof of his treachery?'

'Don Pedro was present when Dr de Puebla and the King discussed it; he can vouch for it.'

'The King denies it.'

'They are liars both – he and Dr de Puebla!' Doña Elvira flared.

Katherine turned on her. 'You must not say such things of the King! And I must not hear them!'

Doña Elvira's face flushed darkly. 'I beg your Highness's forgiveness,' she muttered, in a voice that sounded anything but humble.

Katherine decided not to repeat what the King had said about the jealousy between the two ambassadors. She said, 'You have never liked Dr de Puebla, I think – right from the start, and certainly before this happened. Why is that?'

'He is a Jew!' Doña Elvira's proud Castilian blood was up. 'A lying *converso*! He should have been expelled from Spain like the rest after Granada fell.'

Katherine remembered the edict being passed, and the great exodus of Jews that had followed. Ferdinand and Isabella had been determined to purge their realms of heresy.

'But many of my father's officers chose to be baptised as Christians, rather than go into exile. Dr de Puebla was one such.'

'Hypocrites, all of them! Once a Jew, always a Jew! They always relapse. And this Dr de Puebla is of low birth too.'

Katherine said no more. She was sure that Doña Elvira's deeply ingrained prejudices were colouring her judgement. No doubt some Jews had made a pragmatic decision to convert, but Katherine had known several who had embraced their new faith with sincerity.

And she had seen no sign of Dr de Puebla scanting his religious observances.

She sighed. Adjusting to a new life was difficult enough without having to take into account all the nasty petty rivalries and intrigues that surrounded her. And it was impossible to decide who was telling the truth and who was lying. On the whole, she was rather inclined to believe Don Pedro.

The court moved on to the castle of Windsor, a mighty fortress many centuries old that commanded breathtaking views across the surrounding countryside. Katherine and Arthur were allocated lodgings in the medieval royal apartments in the upper ward, with windows overlooking a rather sad vineyard. But the bed, which was eleven feet square, was sumptuous, with its gold and silver canopy and silken hangings. One could get lost in such a bed, and she did feel lost, sleeping there alone.

Arthur was no better. Katherine thought he had lost weight. He was coughing more, and complained of suffering terrible sweats at night. Yet still he made light of his illness, refusing to give in to it. At a feast in the magnificent St George's Hall, Katherine saw the Queen watching her son intently, and heard Arthur, who had eaten little, reassuring her that he was better, his appetite was improving, and his cough was on the mend. Whether the Queen heard only what she wanted to hear, Katherine did not know.

'Ought you not to see a doctor?' she ventured one day.

'I have seen too many doctors!' Arthur retorted. 'There is nothing wrong with me! Stop fretting!'

But she could not. She had seen people suffering from a quartan fever, and none of them had coughed. True, Arthur sweated and had headaches, but his fever was constant, not intermittent.

She confided her fears to her own physician, Dr Alcaraz.

'This must go no further,' she told him as she described Arthur's symptoms. The doctor listened gravely.

'His Highness does seem to me to be over-thin, and what you tell me is worrying, but I can make no diagnosis without examining him,

51

and I cannot be seen to be questioning the expertise of the English physicians. But I will discreetly observe His Highness as much as I can.' He paused. 'Forgive me, my lady, but it would be wise not to tax his strength by lying together.'

'The King agrees with you,' Katherine revealed, feeling her cheeks growing hot. 'We do as he commands. Our marriage is in name only.'

'Very wise, Highness,' Dr Alcaraz said.

One evening, after dinner, the King summoned Katherine to his study. As Dr de Puebla was present, she knew that she was there to discuss a matter of importance.

'Be seated, child,' Henry bade her, swooping up Peterkin from the floor and settling him on his lap, caressing his ears. 'As you will be aware, it is necessary for Prince Arthur to go back to Ludlow to continue learning how to rule his principality of Wales. It is an excellent apprenticeship for kingship.'

Katherine was shocked. Ludlow, Arthur had informed her, was a hundred and fifty miles from London – and he ought to know, having lived there since he was seven. She was on the point of protesting that he was not well enough to travel so far, especially in the middle of winter, but in truth she was too in awe of the King, and feared to be seen to be questioning his judgement. Arthur was his son, after all; he must know all about his state of health, and he had surely considered the risks and the dangers.

As if he had read her mind, Henry said, 'I have had a long talk with Arthur. It had been agreed that he should return to Ludlow after the wedding festivities, yet I did say to him that, if he did not feel well enough, he could wait until the spring. But he is adamant that he should be at Ludlow.'

Arthur would say that, Katherine thought. She knew enough of her young husband to appreciate that he wanted no one to think him not meet for the duties required of him.

'The question is,' the King said, 'whether you should go with Arthur, or stay with the Queen and Princess Margaret, at least for the winter. For myself, I do not wish you to go. I feel, as I know he has told you, that Arthur is not old enough to give free rein to the duties of a husband, and that you should wait a while before you live together. My councillors agree, on account of the tender age of my son. And we are all worried that, coming from Spain, you would find it hard wintering on the Welsh border. We would not want the King and Queen your parents to think that we had made you do it, especially if it affects your health.'

Katherine said nothing. This was a matter for the King to decide, and it sounded as if he had already made up his mind that she should stay.

'However,' he was saying, 'I do not wish to risk offending King Ferdinand and Queen Isabella by keeping you and Arthur apart, so I have consulted Don Pedro de Ayala and Doña Elvira. They have both urged that you remain behind. I honestly do not know what to think. Tell me, Katherine, what is your opinion?'

She noticed Dr de Puebla shaking his head at the mention of Don Pedro and Doña Elvira.

'Your Grace, my advice is that the Princess should go,' he said. She was not surprised – he would disagree with them on principle.

She had the impression that she was being embroiled in an elaborate game of strategy, and that the real issues were beyond her comprehension. Would her parents be content for her to make the decision herself? It might be that the King's care for her really was the chief issue, although she knew he feared for his son, and guessed that he was worrying that, once alone together in their remote castle, she and Arthur might be tempted to forget his command to wait. Yet she could not help wondering if this had something to do with the matter of her dowry. If the King sent her to Ludlow and she found that she needed to use the plate, her parents might say that he had forced her to it. Yet if she went to Ludlow of her own volition and did so, knowing what the repercussions would be, that would be her fault – wouldn't it?

'I will be content with what your Grace decides,' she said.

Henry left it at that. 'Think on it,' he said. 'We will talk another time.'

She went to her chaplain, Father Alessandro, and asked for his advice. 'As Dr de Puebla can confirm,' he said, 'it is the wish of the King and Queen your parents that you and Prince Arthur should not be separated; if you are, they will be displeased.'

Greatly torn, Katherine thought hard about his words, praying for guidance. She wanted to do the right thing – but what *was* the right thing?

For four days she fretted, not knowing what to say to the King. Then Prince Arthur came to her.

'My father wishes to know what you have decided,' he said. 'You know it would please me very much if you came to Ludlow with me.' He has been told to say that, Katherine thought.

'It is for His Grace to decide,' she insisted.

'But what do you want to do, Katherine?'

'I wish to do his pleasure and yours in all things.'

Arthur sighed and went away. At dinner that evening the King, looking sorrowful, bent his head to her ear.

'It pains me to say this, Katherine, but I have decided that you should go to Ludlow, although there is nothing in the world I regret more.' He shook his head mournfully. 'We will miss you, but I must defer to the wishes of the King and Queen your parents, even though allowing you to go might be to the danger of my son.'

Why should that be? She almost uttered the question. But, of course, the King's words had been for the benefit of others seated nearby. The pretence had to be kept up.

'As your Grace pleases,' she said, smiling despite her misgivings. Not only was there Arthur's health to consider, but also she realised that she felt daunted at the prospect of being alone with him on that distant, freezing border.

Of course, Doña Elvira made a fuss.

'Nothing is ready for your Highness's departure, and I suspect that no provision has been made for you at Ludlow. I suppose we must be grateful that the King is permitting your Spanish servants to accompany you.'

'That is one blessing,' Katherine said.

'It is the only one!' fumed the duenna. 'Do you know what Don

Pedro told me? His Highness has given nothing to Prince Arthur for the furnishing of his house.'

That seemed odd. If it had been known that Arthur was returning to Ludlow, why had his apartments there been stripped? He had not needed his furniture and other household stuff at court, and yet it sounded as if they had been returned to the King.

Doña Elvira was beside herself. 'And, would you believe, there isn't even any table service. Your Highness will have *no choice* but to use your plate! Don Pedro says you should give it all, and the jewels, to the King now, to avoid further trouble.'

'But my parents told me that I must wait until they instruct me to do so,' Katherine protested. 'Have they so instructed Don Pedro?'

Doña Elvira looked evasive. 'No, Highness,' she admitted.

'Then the plate and jewels must be packed,' Katherine ordered.

Chapter 4

1501–1502

Katherine could not remember ever having felt so cold. Privately she had thought all along that it was madness to embark on such a long journey in the middle of a harsh winter, and that the King had taken leave of his senses to send Arthur to Ludlow at this time, but she had ventured no protest, and when the time came to make their farewells, she had warmly embraced the King, the Queen, Prince Henry, Princess Margaret and the Lady Margaret. Queen Elizabeth had clung to Arthur as she kissed him goodbye.

'God protect you, fair, sweet son!' she had prayed, as he knelt for her blessing. Then he had mounted his horse – insisting on riding in the proper place at the head of his entourage – as Katherine climbed into the waiting litter, shivering inside her furs. And there was Doña Elvira, firmly closing the curtains.

The December landscape was bare and unforgiving, with fields silvered with frost and skeletal trees bending in the bitter winds. The ground was iron-hard and rutted in places, so the going was uncomfortable, and slow, for a train of baggage wagons and pack horses followed behind, and they were lucky if they covered more than ten miles in a day. The feast of Christmas was celebrated in dismal, disjointed fashion in inns and monastic guesthouses along the route.

Even Maria could find little to cheer her, and Katherine felt wretched. She was cold, cold, cold, to her very bones. She yearned for the interminable journey to be over, and she trembled for Arthur, exposed to that whip-sharp wind on his horse. When she had suggested he join her in the litter he had answered her abruptly, so she had kept her peace since.

Maidenhead, Oxford, Gloucester, Hereford . . . Pulling aside the curtains when Doña Elvira was looking the other way, or had fallen asleep, she saw that the scenery had changed, and that they were passing through a wild, hilly region. In summer it might be green and beautiful, but it was now bleak and inhospitable, and the little towns and villages seemed largely deserted. Several times she heard the passing bell tolling in churches and chapels along the way.

They were travelling north now, parallel with the Welsh border. There was great sickness in the area, she was told. Best to make haste! They spent the last night of the journey in a cheerless castle, and by then Katherine was utterly miserable. One look at Arthur's fleetingly unguarded face told her that he was feeling infinitely worse. Not long now, she told herself. Only a few more miles and then this nightmare would be over.

The next day, to her inexpressible relief, they entered Shropshire, and not long afterwards she saw Ludlow Castle looming grimly ahead in the morning mist. The massive grey fortress stood sentinel high above the pretty town, and looked dauntingly impregnable, although Arthur, riding beside Katherine, assured her that the Welsh no longer came raiding over the border. Doña Elvira sniffed loudly, conveying to Katherine just what she thought of this place they had been sent to.

They rode across the drawbridge and through the gatehouse below the keep into the inner bailey, where a gentleman was waiting to receive them. Behind him were drawn up ranks of officers in furred gowns and liveried servants.

'May I present my chamberlain, Sir Richard Pole,' Arthur said. Sir Richard bowed low as his young master dismounted and offered his hand to be kissed; he made a courteous obeisance to Katherine too, as she alighted stiffly from her litter. His eyes were twinkling and appreciative.

'Welcome, your Highness! This is a great day for Ludlow.'

Katherine warmed to him. He was handsome in that blond, English way, and his strong, angular features seemed to exude kindliness and humour. She was soon to learn that her first impression had been correct, and that Sir Richard Pole was unfailingly amiable, supportive without being obtrusive, and helpful, anticipating his young master's every need.

She followed the chamberlain as he led the way across the bailey towards a high and imposing range of apartments. Behind them, the business of unloading the baggage had begun.

'This is where we will hold our court,' Arthur said, indicating the broad sweep of lordly buildings. 'The great hall and the great chamber are there, in the centre, and our lodgings are in that building on the left. My rooms are on the upper floor, yours are below it.'

'What of the tower on the right?' Katherine asked.

'The Pendover Tower?' Arthur's drawn face clouded over. 'That was occupied by the last Prince of Wales. He was my uncle. I will tell you about him later.'

Inside, the castle was palatial. Katherine was pleased to find that her rooms had been made welcoming with tapestries, cushions and fine oak furniture. What she appreciated most was the roaring fire that was already ablaze on the great hearth. At last she could get really warm.

Waiting in the great chamber to receive her was a tall, fair woman, rather plain with a narrow, flat face and gentle eyes, who sank into a graceful curtsey.

'I am Lady Pole, your Highness, Sir Richard's wife,' she introduced herself. 'I trust that everything is to your liking.'

Understanding the gist of her words, Katherine raised her with a smile. 'Thank you, Lady Pole. I know I will be comfortable here.' The woman – she must have been nearing thirty – looked pleased. Katherine liked her immediately, feeling that Lady Pole might prove to be the friend of whom she had great need.

Doña Elvira bustled in, carrying Katherine's jewel casket.

'Who is this, Highness?' she bristled.

The chamberlain's wife smiled. 'I am Lady Pole, madam, and I am here to see that everything is to Her Highness's satisfaction. If there is anything that either of you need, just send for me.'

'Hmm,' sniffed the duenna. 'I will see to Her Highness's needs, thank you, my lady.'

'Of course,' Margaret Pole said. 'I just wanted to make sure that you are all comfortable.'

Doña Elvira looked about her with an expression that said she would never be comfortable in such a place.

'We are most grateful for your kindness, Lady Pole,' Katherine said. 'Doña Elvira looks after me, but as strangers in England we will both be glad of your guidance and help.' She beamed at the chamberlain's wife, hoping she was not offended by Doña Elvira's antipathy. 'Won't we, Doña Elvira?' she said to the duenna.

Doña Elvira's face creaked into what passed for a smile. 'Yes, Highness,' she said.

'I will leave your Grace to settle in,' Margaret Pole said warmly.

That evening Katherine descended to the hall and took her place at the high table next to Arthur, gratified to see that the service was of heavy English silver-gilt, and that her plate had not been plundered.

Over the roast meats Arthur, speaking in a mix of English and Latin, and unusually talkative at the head of his own table, told her something of the castle's past.

'It was the seat of my ancestors, the Mortimers, and then of my mother's family, the House of York. Thirty years ago my grandfather, King Edward the Fourth, sent her brother Prince Edward to be educated here. It was he who stayed in the Pendover Tower, and it was there that he learned of his father's death. He was only twelve, yet he was now king, and he had to leave Ludlow for London to be crowned. But he was captured on the way by his uncle Richard of Gloucester, who imprisoned him in the Tower with his little brother Richard, and made himself king in his stead. Poor Edward was never seen again. King Richard had the boys murdered.'

Katherine shivered. 'How terrible – and how awful for your mother, to lose her brothers in that way.'

Arthur laid down his knife. Most of his meal lay untouched on his plate. 'It was. Some years ago my father was plagued by a pretender who claimed to be Prince Richard, and my mother went through agony wondering if this imposter really was him. Of course he wasn't, but it was a long time before his claim was proved false.'

'You are talking about Perkin Warbeck,' Katherine said.

'Yes. My father was very lenient, and after Warbeck confessed he allowed him to live at court under house arrest. But he tried to run away, so he was sent to the Tower. And there he plotted against the King. He brought his fate upon himself.'

Katherine couldn't bear to think about the pretender's end. What she had learned of it, piecing together her father's censored version of events and the bits of gossip she had overheard, had haunted her for two years now. Because Warbeck had not been the only one to suffer. There had been, in the Tower, another prisoner. The Earl of Warwick had been a cousin of Queen Elizabeth. He was a simple-minded young man, but dangerous on account of his having a strong claim to the throne. According to King Ferdinand, as soon as King Henry had won the crown at Bosworth, he had immured Warwick in the Tower and left him without any books or creature comforts. It must have been a living death for a hapless youth who had not the wits to understand how he had offended. But what happened to him in the end had been far worse . . .

'Katherine?' It was Arthur, drawing her back to reality. 'You were miles away. I asked if you wanted to hear about our castle ghost.'

'I'm sorry, I was thinking of how your poor mother must have suffered,' Katherine lied. To speak of Warwick's fate might be seen as accusing King Henry of the worst kind of crime. Not that her own father's hands were clean of blood . . .

'I've seen the ghost myself,' Arthur was saying. 'It was last autumn, at dusk. I was walking across the bailey when I saw a strange woman standing on the battlements of Mortimer's Tower. I asked the guards who she was, and they told me it was the ghost of Marion la Bruyère, a maiden who lived here hundreds of years ago. The story goes that she fell in love with the enemy of the castle's lord, and one night she lowered down a rope from the tower so that he could climb up to meet her. But he betrayed her, and left the rope dangling, enabling his men to get into the castle and capture it. Marion's love turned to shame and hatred. She grabbed her lover's sword and stabbed him, then threw herself to her death from the tower. They say that her appearance portends some tragedy, but I'm not sure that I believe it.'

Sir Richard Pole, sitting at Katherine's right hand, chuckled. 'Forgive me, your Highnesses, but I think that tale is the result of too much ale in the guardroom!'

'But I did see her,' Arthur said.

'Many have,' said Sir Richard, 'but tragedy hasn't always followed. It's an old wives' – or should I say soldiers' – tale, your Highness, and I would take no notice of it!'

Arthur translated and Katherine smiled.

Lady Pole leaned forward. 'My cousin Edward saw the ghost,' she said.

'Edward?' Katherine asked.

'The last Prince of Wales, later King Edward the Fifth,' Arthur explained. 'Lady Pole is our kinswoman, Katherine; she is the niece of King Edward and King Richard, and the daughter of my great-uncle the Duke of Clarence, and sister to the late Earl of Warwick.'

Katherine sat there shocked, appalled at her own ignorance, although how could she have known that Warwick had a sister? She was horribly embarrassed. It was a miracle that Lady Pole had been civil to her. For it was because of Katherine that Warwick had died.

But Margaret Pole was behaving as if nothing were amiss.

'You see this bracelet I wear,' she said, showing Katherine a tiny barrel on a chain. 'It is in memory of my father, who was executed by drowning in a butt of Malmsey wine. My mother had died in child-bed and he blamed the then Queen for practising witchcraft on her. My uncle King Edward was furious, and himself condemned his brother to death. I was but four at the time, so I remember nothing of the scandal.'

But you, Katherine thought, have had three tragedies in your life. Mother, father, brother – all dead, two by violence. Do you know your brother died because of me?

Maria burst into the great chamber, her face glowing, then stopped abruptly as she caught Doña Elvira's frown. Katherine beckoned her

61

over, eager to hear the latest gossip that her friend always managed to extract from cooks or courtiers. Life at Ludlow had settled down quickly into a routine, and any news brightened their conversation.

Katherine's days were spent with Doña Elvira, Maria, her other ladies and Lady Pole, and they would have been pleasant but for the strangeness of life in England and her persistent homesickness for Spain. It did not help that the duenna was still hostile towards Margaret Pole, and clearly jealous of Katherine's friendship with her. She would seize every opportunity to belittle Margaret or ignore her. Katherine sometimes resented having been forced into a wearisome role as mediator, almost – she felt – a placater, but she liked Margaret Pole immensely and wanted to make up for the terrible tragedy that had overshadowed her life, for which she felt in some way responsible; and she sensed that Margaret understood how hard Katherine was trying to keep the peace. Doña Elvira, on the other hand, seemed concerned only to prevent Margaret from enjoying any influence with Katherine.

Maria sat down beside Katherine and took up her embroidery, briefly mimicking the duenna's severe gaze before grinning widely. Katherine struggled to contain her laughter. Maria's cheerful company was a blessing. She shared Katherine's sense of the strangeness of living in Ludlow, and was forever complaining of the cold, but for her life was an adventure, and she relished each new day. When Katherine grew tired of Doña Elvira being difficult, Maria was there to offer a sympathetic ear and a rallying jest.

For the past few weeks they had embroidered endlessly, sung, played music, danced and chatted as much as they could, given the language barrier. But Katherine was working hard at learning English, urging her women to do so too, and she was becoming more fluent daily. With prayers in the chapel of St Mary Magdalene in the inner bailey, and happy hours of play with Margaret Pole's young children, Henry, Ursula and Reginald, a solemn infant who had just learned to walk, the winter was slowly passing.

Katherine had seen little of Arthur. He had returned to his studies with his tutor, the amiable and learned Dr Linacre, and on some days presided over the Council of the Marches, which met in the lodge by the castle gate. Katherine occasionally stayed there with him, or at Tickenhill, Arthur's beautiful palace at nearby Bewdley, but he was kept busy for most of the time. She suspected that he drove himself in order to live up to his father's high expectations, but he was still unwell – and still making light of it. Sometimes Katherine noticed Dr Alcaraz watching the Prince, but he never said anything, and she dared not ask what he was thinking, in case he said something she did not want to hear. Five times she and Arthur had bedded together, for the sake of appearances, but all they did was talk for a while before drifting into sleep. Deep in the night Katherine was invariably awakened by Arthur's coughing.

They had few visitors, due to the great sickness that was carrying off so many in these parts. The heir to the throne could not risk contagion. Occasionally a local lord or a member of the Prince's council had been their guest at dinner, but Katherine would have preferred it if they had stayed at home. She was terrified that Arthur would catch whatever plague it was, for she feared he would have no resistance to it. He was looking almost skeletal these days. His arms and legs were like sticks.

At Shrovetide Arthur bade her accompany him to bed once more. After a restless night, when he tossed and turned, sweating despite the February chill, they lay there waiting for dawn to break, not touching, as usual, but talking about the possibility of a visit to court in the summer.

'It has to be the summer,' Katherine said. 'I could not face that journey again in the winter.' Arthur did not answer, and when she turned to look at him she saw that he was clutching his chest and gasping for air.

'The pain, the pain!' he groaned. Then he was racked with a horrible paroxysm of coughing, and when he lay back, spent, his hand still pressed to his chest, there were spots of bright blood on the pillow.

Katherine stared at it for a few heartbreaking moments, then leapt out of bed, pulling on her nightgown and calling for Dr Alcaraz and Sir Richard Pole. When they came she sat in the antechamber, where Margaret Pole joined her, holding her hand and looking concerned as Katherine recounted, in her halting English, what had happened. Doña

Elvira arrived, froze at the sight of someone else comforting her Princess, then thawed when they explained what had occurred. Even her stern eyes filled with tears. She took Katherine's other hand and squeezed it.

They waited, none of them saying much. Father Alessandro came to them and said prayers for Arthur.

Presently Dr Alcaraz emerged, his face grave. 'Highness, you must be brave. It is as I have suspected for a while. The Prince is very ill. In my humble opinion, he is in the final stages of consumption.'

'Oh, merciful God,' Katherine whispered, crossing herself, shocked, but not entirely surprised. 'Poor, *poor* Arthur. He is so young . . .' Her eyes brimmed.

'God calls to Himself those whom He loves best,' Father Alessandro murmured, laying a hand on her shoulder.

Grief had evidently banished all differences, for Doña Elvira and Margaret Pole were crying in each other's arms. At the chaplain's behest, they all knelt and prayed that Arthur's sufferings might be mitigated, or brief. And as the implications of Dr Alcaraz's diagnosis began to sink in, Katherine found that her sorrow was more for Arthur's family than for herself.

'This will come as a dreadful shock to King Henry and the Queen. All their hopes were in Arthur!' she said, and then the tears did fall as she thought of what this news would do to them. 'How long?' she asked the doctor.

'Not long,' he told her. 'I am so sorry for your Highnesses.'

'Does he know?'

'I have prepared him.'

'I must go to him,' Katherine said.

Arthur looked as bleached as the pillow when she returned to the bedchamber. He was no longer gasping for air, although his breathing was laboured. He turned to her, and she was reminded once more of Juan, for his skin also had that translucency that was so beautiful, yet so deadly. But Juan had sickened and died suddenly, and nothing in Katherine's sixteen years had equipped her to deal with someone who had just been told that death was facing them.

Yet Arthur made it clear at once that the subject was not to be mentioned.

'Do not worry, Katherine,' he said, attempting a smile, 'I am feeling somewhat restored now. Would you kindly ask Willoughby and Gruffydd to attend me? I think I shall get up and go to the Council.'

'Would it not be better to rest?' she asked.

'There will be plenty of time for rest,' he said, the fierce expression on his face warning her to say no more.

'I will summon your gentlemen.' She tried not to notice that he was blinking back tears.

She hastened through the antechamber and began descending the stairs. As she neared the bottom she heard voices below, which made her pause. One belonged to Maurice St John, Arthur's groom. 'He is ill because he lay with the Lady Katherine,' he was saying.

'Aye, but can you blame him? If she were my wife, I'd bed her every night.' That was Anthony Willoughby. Katherine grew hot. It was shaming to hear herself discussed in such terms.

'From what I hear, it's a good thing the lad took his pleasure when he could,' Gruffydd ap Rhys said mournfully. 'I cannot believe it. All that promise . . . I never had a better master.'

Katherine tiptoed back up the stairs and sent a page to summon the men. Then she went to her chamber, threw herself on the bed and sobbed her heart out.

Arthur rallied a little. He went about his daily round as usual, and was well enough to wash the feet of fifteen poor men – one for every year of his age – on Maundy Thursday, but after that it was clear to everyone that time was running out for him. At the end of March, so weak that he was forced to take to his bed, he called for pen and parchment, and his lawyer, and announced that he was making his will.

By then Katherine herself was unwell, confined to bed in her chamber below, suffering a purgatory of chills, pains in her joints and all-encompassing fatigue. Soon her head was swimming, her body shuddering, and she could hardly stand. Between them Doña Elvira and Maria helped her to bed. She stayed there, too ill to rise, too weak even to lift her hand above the counterpane. Margaret Pole sent up choice delicacies to tempt her appetite, but she could not eat, and could take only sips of wine from a goblet held to her lips. Most of the time she slept fitfully. When she woke, it was to ask after Arthur, only to be told that he was comfortable. She felt terrible about not being with him, but Dr Alcaraz, supported by her other Spanish physicians, Dr de la Saa and Dr Guersye, had warned that, if he caught her malady, it would finish him. They told her, though, that Arthur was in good spirits and talking of getting up again. She hoped it was true.

One afternoon, to allow Doña Elvira to rest, Margaret Pole came to sit with Katherine, filling the room with her serene, reassuring presence. It was clear that she bore no rancour towards Katherine, or to Doña Elvira, with whom she was now quite companionable, both of them united in their concern for their Princess. She stitched while Katherine dozed, plumped the pillows when she awoke, and stoked up the fire when it threatened to die on them.

'You are so kind to me,' Katherine said.

'Nonsense, madam! It's my pleasure to look after you. Would you like something to eat?'

'I couldn't face anything, but thank you. You are a true friend.'

Katherine felt ill and homesick, and miserable about not being with Arthur when he might die at any moment. She kept crying when she thought of his young life being cut short, and how cruelly Margaret Pole had suffered because of her, yet was ready to comfort her nonetheless.

She could not help herself. She had to say something.

'Lady Pole, forgive me, but I must say how deeply sorry I am about your brother of Warwick.'

Margaret lowered her eyes, but not before Katherine had glimpsed the pain that name had evoked. 'That is kind of you, madam,' she said. 'My poor brother was too trusting, too gullible by far. He was a simple soul; he could not have told a goose from a capon. Alas, he was led astray by that fool Warbeck luring him into his mad plot.'

'I fear there was more to it than that.' Katherine swallowed.

'More? How so?'

'Both of them were lured into treason – I am convinced of it. My father said that I would never go to England while any lived who could challenge the crown. Some weeks later we heard that your brother and Warbeck had been executed. Then my father summoned me and told me that his ambassador had assured him that not a doubtful drop of royal blood remained in England, and therefore it was safe for me to depart. I drew my own conclusions from that. I was – I still am – horrified to think that I was the cause of two men's deaths.'

Margaret was shaking her head. 'Not you, madam, never you. It was nothing to do with you, and I will not speak ill of the King your father, or King Henry. No doubt they did what they thought they had to do. I did wonder at the time if all was as it seemed. It was such a silly plot: as if those two young fools could have hoped to take the Tower and the throne!'

'I can never make it up to you,' Katherine said, 'and God is punishing me. My marriage was made in blood, and so it will end soon in tragedy.'

'Do not say such things!' Margaret reproved. 'God is our loving father, and everything happens by His providence. He knows you are innocent of this deed.'

'I wish I could believe it,' Katherine sighed.

'Pray to Him; ask Him to reassure you. If I do not hold this against you, He certainly does not.'

'Thank you, my dear friend,' Katherine sobbed. 'Thank you! You cannot know how relieved I am to hear you say that.'

Later that evening Maria came in with a ewer of wine and a goblet.

'Please try to drink something, Highness.' She placed both by the bed and poured the wine, then held the goblet to Katherine's lips.

'There is a strange woman up on Mortimer's Tower,' she said. 'I called up to her as I passed from the ewery, but I don't think she heard me. She was just standing there.'

'I've told the servants before that the roof of that tower is out of bounds,' Margaret fumed. 'It's unsafe up there. I'll go and summon her down.'

She was soon back. 'There's no one there,' she said.

Katherine felt a twinge of fear. She could not look at Margaret, in case Margaret knew what she was thinking.

On the second day of April, Katherine woke to find Margaret Pole sitting beside her bed, telling the beads on her rosary.

'How is your Highness?' she enquired.

'I won't know until I try to sit up,' Katherine told her.

'Then lie there for a while,' Margaret advised. Katherine noticed that she looked drawn.

'You are tired, my friend,' she said.

'I am well, your Highness, but I have been up all night and now am come to perform a sad duty.' She laid her hand on Katherine's. 'I am deeply sorry to tell you that Prince Arthur died this morning, between six and seven o'clock.'

Katherine had been expecting it, but still the news came as a shock. He had died and she had not been there. She wondered what she should feel for the loss of this boy who had been her husband, yet had always seemed a stranger.

'God rest his soul,' she said at last, crossing herself, and trying not to cry. 'Was it – was it peaceful?'

'Mercifully, yes. He died in his sleep, with Richard and me watching over him. It was an easy passage. If only the Fates had granted him a longer stay in this world.'

If only. The great marriage alliance, sealed in the interests of peace, had in the end lasted less than five months. Four little months in which she had been neither wife nor lover. She wished she could have loved Arthur more, or that it had hurt, rather than worried her, that he had not loved her. She thought of those closest to Arthur who would be affected most deeply by his death, and her heart bled for them.

'The King should be informed,' she said.

'A messenger is already on his way.' Pray God he would break the news kindly. And yet such news would always be a brutal blow, however gently broken.

As Katherine lay there, feeling weak and waiting for Margaret Pole to summon Doña Elvira to attend her, she wondered what would happen to her now. At just sixteen, she was a widow, and a virgin. There was no reason for her to stay in England. The new heir to the throne was Prince Henry, a child, even if he seemed old for his years. Maybe she could go home to Spain. At this moment she wanted nothing more than to be with the mother she had not seen in months, to be in a warm climate, away from this cold, damp, grey land, and to know what the future held for her. It cheered her to think that, within weeks, she might be back in Spain, with England a sad memory that would fade as the years passed.

She missed the funeral. Although her health was slowly mending, she was still too weak even to go down to the great hall, where Arthur's body lay in state. Sir Richard Pole had made all the arrangements. Katherine had no energy to do anything but lie abed, as the cortège battled its way through gales and mud to Worcester Abbey, where the Prince was to be buried. Afterwards Margaret Pole told her how the mourners had wept and made great lamentation as the coffin was lowered into the new vault at the side of the altar. The hope of England had gone, and the dreams of a dynasty were dust. It was fitting that people should weep. He had been so young, so full of promise.

Katherine felt no pang when she learned that Arthur had left all his robes and household stuff to his sister Margaret. She herself had merited no mention in his will. It was no surprise to her. He had not loved her, nor she him. They had done their best with each other, as she supposed many married couples did, but it had availed them little. There had never been any spark of passion between them.

The coming of May blossom brought with it a summons from the Queen. Katherine was touched that Elizabeth, grief-stricken as she must be, had thought of her.

'Her Grace fears that you are in an unhealthy place because of all this sickness,' said Doña Elvira, looking up from the Queen's letter. 'She wants you moved as soon as possible, and is sending an escort to take you to London.'

Katherine heard the news with relief. She had come to hate Ludlow and its grim associations with death and illness. She was better now and chafing at being confined to her black-draped rooms, wearing mourning weeds and a nun-like veil over a wimple with an irritating chin barbe, as became a widow. When the litter sent by the Queen arrived, Katherine was dismayed to find it covered with black velvet and black cloth, and fringed with black valances and black ribbon. She stood regarding this doleful equipage dubiously, then turned to Margaret Pole and embraced her warmly, as Sir Richard bowed.

'I shall miss you, dear Lady Pole, and you, Sir Richard. You have been true friends to me, and I hope that one day we shall meet again,' she said. Margaret hugged her.

'We will miss you too, dear Princess. I will write to you. God keep you. Have a safe journey.'

The ever-ready tears were in Katherine's eyes as she climbed into the litter and settled back into its gloomy depths. Soon Ludlow was left far behind and she was travelling back across England, an England awakening to the promise of spring. When Doña Elvira's face was turned away, she peered through the curtains to see lush green fields, woodlands, copses and small villages with timbered houses clustered around stone churches. People ran to see her, and called down blessings on the tragic Princess who had been widowed so young. And so she came to Richmond.

Chapter 5

1502–1503

Katherine gazed out of the window on the gardens of Croydon Palace. When she had first arrived in Richmond, Queen Elizabeth, her face ravaged with grief, had offered her a choice of houses to reside in while she awaited the decision on her future. Here, in the Archbishop of Canterbury's red-brick palace, she was comfortable enough, but she longed to go home. Her parents had written to say that they could not endure that a daughter whom they loved should be so far away from them in her trouble, and Queen Elizabeth had assured her the King would do all for the best, but no plans had yet been made.

'Why can we not go home to Spain?' Francesca de Cáceres had asked only that morning. Of all Katherine's maids, she was the one who missed their homeland the most.

'In truth, I do not know,' she had told the girl.

What is to happen to me? she kept asking herself.

Doña Elvira swept into the room, interrupting her thoughts, and Katherine could tell from her face that she had something important to impart.

'Their Majesties have sent a new ambassador, Highness. His name is Don Hernán Duque de Estrada and he is a knight of the Order of Santiago; you may remember him, as he served in your brother's household. He comes with instructions to preserve the alliance with England, and to ask for the immediate return of your Highness and all your dowry.'

Katherine's face lit up and she caught her breath to speak.

'But heed me!' Her duenna held up a hand. 'They are only throwing out a cheap fish to bait a larger one! Dr de Puebla has instructions too, so Don Hernán tells me; if possible he is to secure your betrothal to Prince Henry.'

'But he is a child!'

'He is nearly eleven, and at fourteen will be ready for marriage, by the look of him.'

Katherine could not help thinking of young Henry's vitality and forwardness. Somehow she did not think there would be any question that he would be potent at fourteen. He was bursting with health, and there was something very engaging and – yes – attractive about him. But—

'I am more than five years older,' she protested. 'I would then be nearly twenty.'

'It matters not,' dismissed the duenna. 'The alliance must be preserved. The sovereigns and King Henry are both anxious for that. But there is a delicate matter I am to discuss with you. King Henry still hopes that you will bear Prince Arthur a child.'

'You know that is not the case.'

'I do, but I must know what you wish me to say. You see, Highness, if your marriage to Prince Arthur was consummated, a union with his brother would be incestuous. But King Ferdinand is certain that the Pope will provide a dispensation if it can be shown that there was no consummation. Your mother has asked Don Hernán to get at the truth.' Doña Elvira's stern face betrayed a hint of a smile. 'Of course, decorum prevents him from asking your Highness outright, so he has been making discreet inquiries of your ladies – and even of your laundresses. And then that fool, Father Alessandro, told him that the marriage had been consummated. So, with your Highness's permission, I will write to Queen Isabella and inform her that you remain a virgin.'

'Very well,' Katherine said, her heart sinking. So she was not to go home after all. She must hide her longing for the hot sunshine on her face, the taste of oranges and the embrace of her beloved mother. What she wanted did not matter. When her parents commanded, she must obey.

Soon afterwards Father Alessandro was summoned home to Spain, under a cloud. Doña Elvira explained, in an offended tone, that his insistence that Katherine was no virgin had not gone down well in Madrid. Katherine's farewell was cool, because she knew that he had incurred her parents' displeasure, but she was sorry to see him go, for he had been her tutor for years before he had become her chaplain, and she was fond of him.

'And now I lack a spiritual director,' she complained, when he had gone.

'The Queen your mother has directed that you be confessed by my private chaplain,' Doña Elvira said. 'You know Father Duarte; he is a good man, and most holy in his living.' Katherine did know him; he was a rotund, grizzly tonsured cleric with an avuncular manner. He would do very well.

During the months of court mourning Katherine stayed mainly at Croydon, impatient to hear if her betrothal to Henry would be permitted. Gossip had it that the King of France had offered a French princess for Prince Henry. It was unthinkable that she should be jilted for a marriage with France, Spain's great enemy. Despite her hope that she would one day see her homeland again, she had come to regard marriage to the Prince as her true calling.

She made only a few visits to court, and when she did go there it was almost as a private person, because a pall of grief still hung over the royal palaces, and the usual entertainments had been curtailed. In the summer Queen Elizabeth confided to her that she was expecting her seventh child, which must have been conceived soon after Arthur's death.

'I said to the King, on that dreadful night they brought us the news, "God is where He was, and we are still young enough,"' the Queen said, her eyes misty. 'I pray that He will send us another prince.'

Katherine hoped it would be so, though she was concerned to see that her kindly mother-in-law was not in the best of health, no doubt because of her grief at losing Arthur. But then Elizabeth departed on a long progress through the kingdom, and Katherine had to return to Croydon. It was only at Christmas, when the King ordered that the usual festivities go ahead, that she was struck – and alarmed – by the change in the Queen, who looked drained and ill, and seemed to have little energy for anything.

Katherine wondered if she should voice her fears to the King when he summoned her to his study one day. He too looked drawn, and grief had etched harsh lines on his brow, but he was very much in command of himself.

'Sit down, Katherine,' he said, leaning back in his chair and facing her across a desk laden with documents and ledgers. There was no sign of his monkey today.

Katherine sat, smoothing her black velvet skirts.

'I wanted to talk to you about your marriage to Prince Henry,' the King said. 'There are those who are against it. The fiercest is William Warham, the Bishop of London. He insists that, if a man takes his brother's wife in marriage, it is an unclean thing and unlawful. There has been a lot of heated debate.' He grimaced. 'But fear not! Whatever you may have heard in regard to your betrothal, I am assured by many learned divines that the Pope will almost certainly grant a dispensation, since your marriage to Arthur was, shall we say, no true marriage. And even if it had been, the Pope still has the power to dispense with such an impediment. There are precedents. I will confound the critics!'

Katherine had listened to this with mounting concern, so her relief was profound.

'I am so grateful to your Grace,' she said, the words heartfelt. The King gave her a long look and nodded.

'My son will be a lucky man,' he observed.

'Sir,' she ventured, 'is the Queen's Grace in health?'

King Henry frowned. 'She is tired, but the doctors say that all will be well. Do not worry.' He rose to indicate that the conversation was at an end, extending his hand to be kissed. She knelt and pressed her lips to it, wondering why, if all that ailed the Queen was tiredness, he looked so heavy-hearted.

Queen Elizabeth was dead. Katherine wept bitterly when Doña Elvira broke the news on a dark February morning.

'She died in the night. The child came too early,' the duenna said, peering at a letter bearing the royal seal, then handing it to Katherine. Through her tears Katherine read what the King had written. His entirely beloved wife had planned to be confined at Richmond, but the baby had come when they were visiting the Tower. 'She was recovering from her travail, but then, all of a sudden, she lost a lot of blood, and we sent for the physician, who had gone home. He came as fast as he could, but he could not save her. She died on her thirty-seventh birthday.'

To die like that! It was horrifying, and it brought home to Katherine the reality of what every woman risked merely by conceiving a child – and that she herself, when the time came, would be no exception. That was a chilling thought. How the Queen must have suffered. To have come through her ordeal only to die days later – when she was getting well. How did such things happen?

Katherine would dearly have liked to ask the duenna that, but Doña Elvira was not one for confidences, especially those of an intimate nature. She was shaking her head sadly. 'She called the babe after you, Highness.'

'Poor little thing,' Katherine mourned.

As ever, Doña Elvira was thinking of the practicalities of etiquette. 'The court will be back in mourning,' she said. 'We must look out your black gown – or the blue one, if your Highness prefers.' Katherine had been surprised to learn that blue was the colour of royal mourning in England.

But although she put on her weeds, she did not go to court immediately, for word came that King Henry had shut himself away to mourn his wife's death, and – hard on its heels – that of the infant she had borne. Poor man, he must be utterly bereft. There was no doubt that he had loved her dearly: it had been plain for all to see. Who could not have loved Elizabeth? And those poor motherless children, especially Margaret, who was soon to go north to marry the King of Scots, and little Mary, not quite seven years old. Katherine's tender heart bled for them.

She herself felt deep sadness. Queen Elizabeth had been a true and loving friend to her ever since she had come to England. And this was not her only grief, for word had come from Spain that Maria's beloved mother had died. Seeing her friend so stricken with sorrow, Katherine could empathise even more with the bereaved royal family. It was a terrible thing to lose a mother, especially when you were young. She prayed – how she prayed – that her own mother would be spared to her for many long years.

The Queen's death had come at a critical moment, for Don Hernán had just drawn up the contract for Katherine's marriage to Prince Henry, and the sovereigns were eager for it to be concluded. All the conditions had been agreed, which was nothing short of miraculous, given that it had taken fourteen years to negotiate her marriage to Arthur. King Henry was to keep the first instalment of Katherine's dowry, and the second would be handed over when her marriage to Prince Henry was consummated. In the meantime, Queen Isabella had insisted, the King was to maintain Katherine out of his own pocket. That would give him the right to order her household, although her mother was adamant that Doña Elvira remain as duenna. Katherine had sighed when she heard that. Was she ever to know just a modicum of freedom? The duenna still treated her as if she were a child! It was so hard having to observe strict Spanish etiquette in a land where manners were much freer, but Doña Elvira did not seem to understand that.

On her visits to court Katherine had seen nothing of Prince Henry. While she was willing to do her duty, she sometimes doubted the wisdom of this marriage. Certainly years would have to pass before she could be a proper wife. She had hoped to be a mother long ere then. Yet she had to admit that the prospect of becoming Queen of England was as attractive as it had ever been, and now she had seen for herself how magnificently queens were treated in this kingdom. Above all, she had envied the late Queen the degree of freedom she had enjoyed. At present Katherine's life was a cloistered round of prayers, needlework, practising English, reading and gossiping with her attendants. Doña Elvira had decreed that, as a widow, it was not fitting for her to dance in public or take part in court entertainments. But a betrothal to Prince Henry would hopefully put an end to all that, and Katherine was coming to depend on it as her escape from all the constraints that chafed her.

After the Queen's funeral she was summoned to Greenwich, another great Thames-side palace much favoured by the King. Like Richmond, it was surrounded by beautiful gardens, little versions of Paradise with railed flower beds in neat rows, gilded statues of royal heraldic beasts on green-and-white striped poles, pretty fountains and lush orchards.

She was escorted through spacious courtyards to the massive red-brick tower that housed the royal apartments, and shown into King Henry's closet, an exquisite little room with vivid murals depicting the life of St John. She sat when invited, as the King faced her across his ledger-laden desk. Swathed in deep blue velvet, he looked ravaged, his drawn face a death mask, but he managed a smile.

'I asked you here, Katherine, to find out for myself if you are content to be betrothed to Prince Henry.'

'So long as you are content, sire, and my parents, I am happy.' She spoke English passably well now, and did not need a translator.

The King leaned forward, coughing. She had heard such a cough before, and the sound of it chilled her.

'But the Prince is a boy. Would you not prefer a man in your bed?'

Katherine was shocked to her core. No man had ever spoken of such intimate matters to her. She felt herself blushing furiously. 'I do not think about it,' she stammered.

'Be assured I do,' said Henry. 'It is something to consider. Were a husband of mature years to be found, your father and mother agreeing, you would also be content?'

'I am theirs to command,' she replied, worrying where this was leading. Pray God the French match had not been agreed. She would never outlive the shame.

The King was staring at her. His eyes flickered momentarily to her breasts, then back to her face, so fast she wondered if she had imagined it. But it made her feel distinctly uncomfortable.

'You are a good girl,' Henry said, smiling bleakly, and coughed again. 'Now, leave an old widower to his grief and go and enjoy the gardens. They are lovely at this time of year.'

Katherine left, wondering what all that had been about. Summoning the Vargas sisters to attend her, she wandered along a tree-lined alley that led to what looked like a church in the distance. And there, coming in the opposite direction, was Prince Henry, tutor in tow.

She could not believe the difference in him. He looked older, of course, and his face was leaner, hinting at the man he would become; but he was so sad, all his joyful ebullience having fled. Yet he seemed delighted to see her, and she found herself thinking once more what a charming and attractive boy he was.

'Lady Katherine,' he cried, bowing deeply. Katherine curtseyed.

'Your Highness. I was so very sorry to hear of your loss.'

Tears filled the blue eyes. 'Thank you. I know not how to bear my grief for my dearest mother. Never did I receive such hateful news. I wait only for time to bring me insensibility.' A tear escaped down Henry's cheek. He brushed it away, plainly making an effort to control himself.

'Time is a great healer,' Katherine said, thinking this sounded feeble in the face of so much sorrow. 'I lost my brother and my sister. I know something of what your Highness is suffering. I loved your mother too.' She held out her hand and he took it. Her response startled her. It was like a warmth flooding through her.

'Sweet Princess, your kindness is balm to me,' Henry said, appearing not to have noticed. 'Alas, I must learn to live with the pain of my loss. Those things that are decreed by Heaven must be accepted by mortal men. I have been at the Observant Friars' convent, trying to resign myself to God's will.' In later years Katherine would learn that God's will and Henry Tudor's were much the same thing in Henry's mind, but there was now no doubting that his mother's loss had been a heavy blow.

'I have also lost two brothers and two sisters,' he said. 'I cannot bear to think of illness and death, especially not in relation to her . . .' He broke off and bent his head, trying – and almost failing – to master himself. 'She was so beautiful, such a kind and loving mother. There could not have been a more perfect queen – faithful, dignified, pious, virtuous and fruitful. She was all those things. Dear Katherine, I know you admired her too, although you had the misfortune not to know her for as long as I did.'

'My heart grieves for your Highness. It is a great loss, for you, for the King and for England.'

'Thank you, my lady,' Henry said. 'Now I must leave you. Master Giles here has come to fetch me for my French lesson.' He bowed and walked away, and Katherine and her two maids continued on to the convent. There the grey-habited friars showed her into their chapel, pointing out the new stained-glass window that the King had donated. She knelt there for a while, ostensibly in prayer, trying to make sense of all the confusions of the day. The King's strange demeanour, and that odd conversation they had had. Her response to Prince Henry. It was only now that she realised that, on this, the first occasion they had met since a marriage between them had been mooted, he had not said a thing about it.

Dr de Puebla came banging on the door. It was Maria who admitted him.

'I must see Doña Elvira at once!' Katherine heard him say, and then she heard Doña Elvira inviting him to speak in private. Her heart was pounding. This must be about her marriage. Why else would the doctor be so insistent? Something of moment must have happened. Katherine nodded at Maria to leave the door open so that she would know when the duenna reappeared, and the two girls clasped hands in silent concern.

Katherine did not have long to wait. Soon she saw the ambassador slinking off, sketching a hasty bow when he saw her watching him, and avoiding her gaze. Then Doña Elvira came bursting into Katherine's chamber, outrage personified.

'Words fail me, Highness,' she railed. 'That King is a devil. His Queen is not cold in her grave, yet he must needs go lusting after another. He needs to remarry and get more heirs, or so he told Dr de Puebla. And what does that villain of a doctor suggest? I am amazed that the Almighty has not struck him dead—'

'*What* has he suggested?' Katherine interrupted.

'Dr de Puebla, traitor that he is, has suggested that the King marry *you*. And he but a weak man and sickly!'

Katherine was appalled. King Henry was an old man – if not in years, then certainly in every other respect. And he was not a well man; that cough he had reminded her of Arthur's. The very idea of marrying him, of bedding with him, was utterly distasteful, especially after she had seen Prince Henry and understood for the first time something of the attraction between a man and a woman.

'No,' she said, abandoning the obedience drummed into her over a lifetime. 'I will be torn in pieces first, whatever my parents say.'

'Be assured I will support your Highness,' Doña Elvira declared, like a general amassing his forces for battle. 'I will write to Queen Isabella.'

Katherine did not know how she endured the three weeks of waiting for her mother to reply – three weeks in which she managed to avoid seeing the King and refused to have anything to do with Dr de Puebla. By the time she received the letter she was in an agony of trepidation. But as she read it, she exhaled with relief.

'Doña Elvira!' she called. The duenna came running; she knew the letter had come.

'I will not be marrying the King!' Katherine informed her. 'The Queen my mother is furious. She says it would be an evil thing, one never before seen, and that the mere mention of it offends her ears.'

'I knew Her Majesty would never countenance it!'

'There is more. You will be gratified to hear that she has severely censured Dr de Puebla for his meddling.'

'Ha! Serves him right,' Doña Elvira exulted.

'My mother says that King Henry is known to be ailing, and that the best I could hope for is a short marriage followed by a long widowhood, with no influence. She is sure that marrying Prince Henry would assure me of a far more stable and glorious future. So if the King pursues the matter, I am to speak of it as a thing not to be endured. In the meantime my mother is proposing another bride for him.'

She wondered what King Henry would say when he received this snub, but her fear that he might react angrily was unfounded. In no time Don Hernán came to say that His Grace had no wish to offend

Spain, and was ready to conclude the treaty of betrothal between the Princess and his son.

'But, Highness,' the ambassador added, 'the King of England is still haggling over the dowry, so we have agreed that the remaining hundred thousand crowns will be made up of sixty-five thousand crowns in gold, and thirty-five thousand in the plate and jewellery in your possession.' The plate and jewellery were still safely packed in chests in a locked attic at Croydon.

'You will be married to Prince Henry two years hence, when he reaches his fourteenth birthday,' Don Hernán continued. 'In the meantime, the sovereigns and King Henry will approach the Pope for a dispensation that resolves all the canonical difficulties. His Grace will sign the treaty this week.'

Her future was almost settled. If the Pope granted the desired dispensation, she would be the Princess of Wales, and in God's good time, Queen of England.

Katherine walked gracefully into the chapel, barely able to contain her joy. This June day was glorious not only on account of the dazzling sunshine but because it was her betrothal day. After weeks of prevaricating, Pope Julius had finally issued a dispensation permitting Henry and Katherine to marry, even if she had perhaps been Arthur's wife in every sense.

It felt good to be out of mourning weeds, and free of the constricting Spanish fashions and the cumbersome farthingale. Katherine wore a gown in the English style in virginal white silk, her hair flowing loose in token of her purity. The gown had hanging sleeves, heavy skirts that flared out from the waist, and a long train that was looped up at the back to show the rich damask kirtle beneath. The neckline was low and square, edged with tiny pearls, and around her neck she wore the heavy collar of Ks and pomegranates that she had brought from Spain.

Prince Henry, watching her approach with a confident smile, was no less splendidly dressed, in cloth of silver and crimson velvet. He had grown in height since she had last seen him, and his red hair was nearly shoulder-length. Again she was struck by what she could only describe as something of royalty in his demeanour, his innate dignity, his courtesy as he greeted her. They stood together in the chapel of the Bishop of Salisbury's house in Fleet Street, her small hand in his firm one, and made their formal promises to each other, the King looking on, a satisfied expression on his face. Katherine was relieved that there was nothing in his manner towards her that was not in keeping with his proper role as her father-in-law.

Afterwards they all moved into the low-ceilinged parlour, where wine, fruit and wafers had been laid out on the polished oak table. A toast was drunk to the Prince and Princess of Wales, and young Henry gallantly raised Katherine's hand and kissed it exuberantly.

'This is like something out of legend,' he said to her later, as they stood in a latticed window looking down on the busy thoroughfare below.

'Highness?' Katherine asked, not understanding his meaning.

'It is the proper reward of a true knight to win his lady,' Henry said. 'Usually he has to perform great deeds before she will consent to be his, but all I had to do was possess my soul in patience. I have dreamed of this day, Katherine. Never did I think that you would be mine.'

Katherine had to remind herself that he was but twelve. She supposed he had been raised on tales of love and chivalry – and she remembered that cold, envious glance at Arthur on her wedding day. What Arthur had had, Henry must have. That was how it seemed to her. The title, the succession, and now the Princess.

She smiled at him. He thought he was grown up, but he seemed so young in that moment, with his fresh, eager face and his high ideals. She remembered that he had not long lost his mother, and surprised herself by feeling very protective towards him. As his betrothed, and later his wife, it would be her duty to comfort and console him, perhaps even guide him. She sensed it would be not just a duty, but a pleasure.

'I am overjoyed to be betrothed to your Highness,' she said, and meant it.

'Do you know what my first tutor, that rogue Skelton, told me?' Henry said. 'Choose a wife for yourself. Prize her always, and uniquely. I assure you I mean to take his advice.' They smiled at each other.

The warm feeling coursed through Katherine's veins.

Later they talked of books they had enjoyed. Henry had read most of the great classical authors – Homer, Virgil, Plautus, Ovid, Thucydides, Livy, Julius Caesar and Pliny, or so he boasted. What was so striking was his evident love of learning, something she could share with him, although her education had been more traditional and less comprehensive. He said that he could speak both French and Latin, and promised to learn Spanish, just for her.

'I hear that your Highness is a musician,' she said.

'It's in my Welsh blood,' he told her, 'and my mother loved music.' A shadow crossed his face, but it was quickly gone. 'I play and I write songs. I will compose one for you, Katherine!' His enthusiasm was infectious.

'Do you enjoy sports?' he asked.

'I like riding and hunting,' Katherine said, 'although I have had little chance to do either since I have been in England.'

'I *love* sports,' Henry enthused. 'Daily I practise horsemanship, archery, fencing, jousting, wrestling, swordsmanship and tennis.' No wonder he looked so fit and strong.

'That's an impressive list,' she said. 'And you still have time for all that study!'

'I want to excel at everything!' Henry cried. 'There is not enough time in one life to do all the things I want to do.'

'You will be king. You will have all at your command. You will be able to do all those things.'

'I dream of it!' Henry sighed. 'Alas, I do not enjoy the freedoms I once had.' His glance flickered to his father, who was standing at the other end of the room, deep in conversation, yet watching his son.

'I sympathise with that,' Katherine replied. 'But you are the Prince of Wales!'

'It's true,' Henry said, seeing her surprise. 'Since my brother died, everything has changed. Yes, I am now my father's heir. Yes, I am the second person in the kingdom. But I enjoy far less freedom. I am stifled, Katherine. My father never ceases reminding me that he has lost two sons; he says that my life is all that stands between peace and civil war, so I must be kept safe. That means holding me apart from the world. I might as well be in a cloister. I see barely anyone but my tutors, and I am kept out of the public eye. Do you know, my bedchamber can be accessed only from a door in my father's room? I cannot go anywhere, even riding in the park, without his permission.'

'You have my sympathy,' Katherine said. 'I thought *my* life was ordered by rules and etiquette. Sometimes I could scream at my duenna, she makes such a fuss about little things.' She would have liked to say more, but she could not be seen to be criticising the King. No doubt he had good reasons for being overprotective towards his only heir.

'I knew you would understand, Katherine!' Henry said, taking her hands and squeezing them. She realised she was enjoying his company. He was like a breath of fresh air after the dull routine of her life. And they had more in common than she could ever have suspected. She felt sorry for Henry too, but she was deeply gratified that he had confided in her. All in all, she thought, they had made a good beginning. She looked forward to many such meetings over the next two years. And then they would be married.

It had never been like this with poor Arthur.

Chapter 6

1504–1505

Katherine lay on her bed at Durham House, wondering if she could feel more wretched. This ague and derangement of her stomach just would not go away. It had ruined her stay at Richmond with Prince Henry and the King, and in the end, as autumn came, she had been sent to Durham House, where she was feeling worse than ever. Every day she shivered, first with cold, then with heat. She had to force food down, and her face had developed an unnatural pallor. Her doctors kept reassuring her that she would soon recover, but she had lost faith in their prognoses.

The worst thing about this illness was that it was keeping her away from Prince Henry. They had had such a merry time at Windsor and Richmond. Every day they had gone out hunting, accompanied by a train of courtiers. There had been picnics under the trees, and long talks with her betrothed on every subject from mathematics and astrology to siege engines and guns – in fact, she had thought he would never cease talking of war!

Maria came in, her pretty face concerned. 'The King has sent again to ask after your health, Highness.'

'He has sent every day,' Katherine said. 'It is thoughtful of him. He treats me as though I were his own daughter.'

'Once more he offers to visit you.' Maria bent down and gently wiped Katherine's brow with a damp cloth.

Katherine groaned. She did not want King Henry seeing her in her bed, or looking so poorly. 'No, Maria, please tell the messenger that I thank His Grace, but I am too ill to receive him.'

She lay back on her pillows, giving in to lethargy, rousing herself only to read a letter that arrived from Margaret Pole. True to her word, Margaret had kept in touch for more than two years now. Her letters had always been cheerful and full of news of her growing family and life on the Welsh Marches. But this one was brief and despairing.

Sir Richard Pole had died. He had been well, to all appearances, until he'd started getting pains in his stomach, where an ominous swelling could be felt. The doctors had been unable to do anything for him. The genial blond man had died in agony, and Margaret had been plunged into grief and financial embarrassment, for there was no money and only a small pension to live on. She was thinking of seeking refuge at Syon Abbey, and of dedicating little Reginald to the Church. Offering a son to God would be a way of laying up treasure in Heaven, she explained. It would also, Katherine knew, relieve Margaret of some of the expense of keeping her children. Katherine wept for her, and wished she had money to give her so that poor Reginald could stay with his mother. How desperately sad that they had to be parted.

The December sky was lowering and the rooms dark, even at noontide. Doña Elvira insisted on having all the candles lit; her eyesight was not good these days, she said. She needed light so that she could see to embroider. More likely to see if I am transgressing, Katherine thought. On the day the sun broke through the clouds, she thought she might suffocate within the four walls of her overheated, overcrowded, dazzlingly lit chamber. At least Christmas would soon be here. Her recovery from illness had been slow and tedious, yet as her spirits returned she had felt ever more constrained by her duenna's strict rules. So she had worn English dress, danced and sung at court, conversed with courtiers, ridden out and tasted a little freedom – why did that scandalise Doña Elvira so much that she must write to King Henry and her father, Ferdinand, insisting that Katherine was disgracing herself?

'I might as well live in a nunnery!' she complained to Maria and Francesca.

'Amen to that,' Maria pouted. 'We are all constrained to poverty, obedience and chastity!'

'I shall cut off my hair and wear a veil!' Francesca threatened.

Katherine smiled, despite herself. 'We would make awful nuns!'

But Doña Elvira's letters to Their Highnesses had made things worse. When the King had invited Katherine to the Palace of Westminster for the feast of All Souls, he had instructed her to keep the same rules as in her house. To her frustration, she had to stay mostly in her own apartments, wear her old, outdated Spanish gowns, and, worst of all, she had little chance of seeing Prince Henry. And her appeals to her father had no effect. He had not replied to Doña Elvira's complaints, or to her own, increasingly desperate, letters.

She called for her cloak and emerged into the courtyard of Durham House. The wind was brisk and invigorating, the shadows of the turrets sharp on the sunlit cobbles. Pulling Maria after her – for, of course, it was unthinkable that she be left unattended; heavens, she might speak to a gardener, or hum a tune in a groom's hearing – she made her way through the archway on the river front to the lawns leading down to the Thames. As they stood on the jetty above the swirling grey water, Katherine could see the broad sweep of the river, with the hospital of the Savoy and the City of London to the north, Westminster to the south, and all along the shore in between the houses and gardens of the nobility. The river was crowded with boats of all kinds; with the streets being so narrow and congested, it was London's main highway.

'It is good to feel the breeze,' Katherine said. 'I could not have stayed in there a moment longer.'

'How long do we have to endure this existence?' Maria asked.

'I wish I knew!' Katherine replied, watching the gulls swooping over the water. The stink of the Thames assailed her nose, but it was preferable to the stuffiness of her apartments.

She was still standing there, drinking in the view, when Doña Elvira appeared.

'Your Highness, I beg you to come indoors,' she said.

Katherine turned, in no mood to have the duenna interrupt her snatched moments of solitude. But then she saw Doña Elvira's face.

*

She lay on her bed, sobbing into the velvet counterpane. She wanted only Maria with her, for Maria knew what it was to lose the person she loved most. Katherine made her lock the door against everyone else. She had suffered her fair share of blows in her short life, but this was the worst, and she did not know how she could bear it.

Her mother was dead. Isabella had been ailing for some time, but Katherine had not known. She suspected that her parents had kept it from her so as not to alarm her, because, after all, what could she have done to help, being so far away in England, save offer up prayers? And this, unknowing, she had done, for she always prayed daily for the good health and happiness of her parents.

Spain was in mourning for the greatest of its queens. Isabella's fame was legendary; there would never be another like her. Katherine did not need to be told that. This was the mother she had adored and would always try to emulate. But Isabella's conquests, her achievements, her brilliance, were as nothing compared with the love she had inspired in her youngest child.

Her head cradled in Maria's lap, Katherine lay utterly bereft, beyond speech. She had always envisaged herself visiting Spain one day and being reunited with Isabella. She had dreamed of being swept into her mother's embrace, of hearing her dear voice – now stilled for ever. It was hard to accept that she would never see that beloved face again on this earth.

For two days she kept to her room, refusing food, spending hours on her knees praying for Isabella's soul, which must surely be in Heaven, and weeping uncontrollably. Maria, for all her kindness and under-standing, was unable to do anything with her. She offered sympathy, she cajoled, she bullied – but to no avail.

At length a calm descended on Katherine, and the first sad glimmer of acceptance. The door was unlocked. On the third day she emerged, pale, red-eyed, shrouded in the mourning weeds she had worn for Arthur. She resisted Doña Elvira's attempts to comfort her, wanting only Maria. No one else would do.

Dr de Puebla came to see Katherine. She received him warily in her black-draped chamber, the duenna standing guard, Katherine glowering at the little man, unable to forget how he had tried to wed her to the ageing King. She stood stiffly as he explained he had come to offer his condolences and to discuss the implications of Isabella's death.

'Spain is once more divided,' he said, looking unusually perplexed. 'Castile is now ruled by your Highness's sister Queen Juana, the next heir to your mother, and your father, King Ferdinand, is again King of Aragon.'

The significance of that did not escape Katherine. Ferdinand was no longer King of Spain, but the ruler of a much smaller kingdom. How hard it must be for her father, having for thirty years governed Castile too! He had lost not only a wife but a crown.

And Juana – beautiful, passionate, unstable Juana. How would she fill Isabella's shoes?

'The question is,' Puebla was saying, 'will Philip of Burgundy – or King Philip, as we must now call him – leave the rule of Castile to King Ferdinand?'

Katherine saw Doña Elvira purse her lips.

'My sister is queen,' Katherine said. 'It is she who will rule there, as our mother did.'

'She has the right,' declared Doña Elvira, glaring at Puebla.

'There are those who would prefer Philip.' He glared back.

Katherine did not go to court at Christmas; it would not have been fitting for one in mourning. But soon afterwards the King summoned her to Richmond, and she arrived hoping that she would soon see Prince Henry again. She longed to talk to him, knowing that he too understood what losing a mother meant. But when the King received her, the Prince was nowhere to be seen.

'I hope you will stay with us for some time,' King Henry said as Katherine knelt before him. She rose from the floor, aware that his words were a mere courtesy, for his eyes were unaccustomedly cold. She took her leave feeling puzzled, hoping that she had not offended him in some way.

As she entered her lodging she found Dr de Puebla sparring with Doña Elvira. The duenna, usually adept at controlling her emotions, looked distressed.

'What is the matter?' Katherine asked.

'Highness, I must be honest with you. My husband tells me that we are running out of money. King Henry has not paid your allowance.'

Katherine looked at Dr de Puebla for help.

'The King says that your Highness lacks for nothing,' he told her. 'He says you have the means to support your household.'

Katherine was dumbstruck. 'But, lacking money, how am I to pay my servants? Are they expected to work for me for love alone? This will put me in a very embarrassing situation. What of my maids? They have come to England hoping to make good marriages, but without an income I can give them no dowries. Doña Elvira, will you ask Don Pedro if there is enough to pay this quarter's wages?'

There was not.

It occurred to Katherine that the King meant her to use the plate and jewels he had long coveted, and thus devalue them, so that he must ask her father for their value in cash. Heaven forbid that she should be driven to that! Probably that was why the perfidious Puebla had not made a fuss on her behalf.

'I will see the King myself!' she declared.

'No!' protested Doña Elvira, rubbing her eyes, a habit she had developed lately. 'It is not fitting. You cannot go begging to him.'

'Would you rather we starved?' Katherine snapped, and asked Dr de Puebla to request an audience; and asked again. The King was busy, she was told. It seemed a most discourteous way to treat her, a princess of Spain and the future Queen of England. Clearly she *had* offended Henry, although she was bewildered as to how.

She wished she could see the Prince and enlist his help, but she was kept cloistered in her apartments and he in his; they would be unlikely to meet by chance, and Doña Elvira's rules precluded Katherine seeking a meeting. In fact, to her dismay, she did not see Prince Henry at all.

It was now April, now May. Katherine was in no doubt that something was very wrong. There had been no word from the King, nor any sight of her betrothed. Dr de Puebla had done nothing but write to her father, and she could only hope that King Ferdinand would remind Henry of his obligations.

She sat by the open window of her chamber with Maria, unable to enjoy the spring sunshine. She knew her face was etched with worry over the expenses that she could not meet. Her servants at least understood her plight. They loved her, and were willing to serve her without pay. Where, after all, could they go in this strange land? Here at court they had bed and board, and the company of their own kind. She could not speak her gratitude, her heart was so overwhelmed.

Nor could she bear to think what this was doing to her dear friend. Maria was longing to be married, but no man of status would look at her without a dowry. Katherine must not let Maria down, or deprive her of the chance to escape from this miserable existence. She had even written to her father, begging King Ferdinand to provide what was needful, but after weeks of waiting there had still been no reply.

'You have served me well, Maria,' Katherine said now, dreadfully embarrassed. 'You do not deserve this. I am so shamed.'

'Highness, I would rather be with you than marry anyone,' Maria said bravely, not quite concealing her disappointment. 'Maybe God does not wish me to wed.'

Katherine hugged her, her heart heavy with guilt.

She felt sad for Maria, and wearied by Francesca de Cáceres's constant pleas to return to Spain. She had written to the girl's parents in Extremadura, but they wanted Francesca to remain with her. At that, Francesca had wept, and sulked for three days.

These were not the only crosses Katherine had to bear. The gowns she had brought from Spain four years ago were now becoming shabby, and she could not afford to replace them. At court, even if you were confined mostly to your chambers, there was a certain standard of dress to be maintained. She could not shame herself and Spain by appearing in public in rubbed velvet and splitting seams. Already she was turning her gowns, or cutting up one to refurbish another. And there was Doña Elvira, whose eyesight had deteriorated to the point where she could not see the flaws in the gowns properly, clucking about decorum and propriety and the correct behaviour to be observed by a Spanish princess! It was intolerable. Did she not realise that Katherine had far more pressing matters on her mind?

It was early June, and the roses were in full bloom, before her father wrote to say, quite correctly, that it was King Henry's responsibility to provide for Katherine and her household.

'But that is of no help to me!' she cried, throwing the letter down. 'I *must* go to the King.'

'No!' snapped Doña Elvira. 'You cannot ask him outright for money. The very idea!'

'Then Dr de Puebla will have to do it for me!' Katherine flung back.

'Much joy you will have of him!' Doña Elvira retorted.

And Puebla did refuse to help. Of course, he did not want to compromise his rapport with King Henry.

'So we are to tighten our belts!' Katherine challenged him. 'What I cannot understand is why! What have I done to deserve such treatment?'

Dr de Puebla looked uncomfortable.

'If you know, you must tell me!' Katherine commanded.

'I am as perplexed as your Highness,' he said. 'My advice is to be content with what the King has decreed. At the end of this month Prince Henry will be fourteen, and you will soon be married. Then all will be remedied.'

That was true. Once they were wed, Prince Henry would be responsible for her maintenance, which he would provide out of his revenues as Prince of Wales, as Arthur had. King Henry would be aware of that. He was not, after all, pushing her into a situation where she had to use the plate – he would get it soon enough. Suddenly she knew all would be well. She must just be patient. It was time to go back to Durham House to make ready for her wedding.

The Prince's birthday came and went. No one mentioned it. No one said anything about the marriage. There was no invitation to court. Soon it became glaringly obvious that no preparations were being made for a wedding. Why? she asked herself, again and again. Why?

By the autumn her financial situation was desperate.

'The time has come for your Highness to resort to the plate and jewels you have in keeping,' Doña Elvira said.

Katherine stared at her. 'But we have always agreed that I should never touch them. They are part of my dowry.'

'Who would know if a few pieces go missing? And if anyone complained, your Highness could say that necessity drove you to it. It is the truth! Your creditors are clamouring for payment.'

Katherine thought about this. The idea was tempting – and if she did not do something soon, she would be horribly embarrassed financially.

'All right,' she capitulated. 'But we must take the minimum of pieces to satisfy the creditors.'

Doña Elvira agreed. That night, when everyone else had gone to bed, they unlocked the chests. Katherine gasped at the riches that lay within them – gold, silver and a multitude of precious stones, winking in the candlelight. Feeling like a thief she took out a collar of goldsmith's work and four pieces of gold plate.

'Will those suffice?'

'They will, Highness.' Doña Elvira appeared very satisfied with their night's work.

Two days later she informed Katherine that the creditors had been paid. But that was only one problem solved. There was still no money to pay the servants, and even though Doña Elvira urged her to do so, Katherine dared not purloin more of her plate.

She could not look her people in the face, lest she see reproach there. Her nights were spent wakeful, as she went over in her mind what she could possibly have done to cause the King to treat her like this. What of her marriage? Why had nothing been said? And why would the King not see her?

Again she entreated her father to pay her servants' wages, but in vain. King Henry had sent her a small sum, but it was only for food. And all the while Dr de Puebla did nothing, and Doña Elvira spent her days castigating him for it.

Katherine had stopped listening to her complaints, but one day her duenna's words caught her attention.

'It is his fault that you are kept from the court!' Doña Elvira insisted. 'He feeds King Ferdinand with lies, so that he has no idea of what you suffer. No doubt he has poisoned King Henry's mind against you, and that is the cause of the King's coldness.'

'But why is the doctor doing this?' Katherine asked in bewilderment.

'Because he is a traitor who has abandoned his true master for the King of England's bribes!'

'Then truly I am alone!' Katherine cried. 'What can I do?'

Doña Elvira put her head on one side and considered. 'Your Highness could write to Queen Juana and explain to her how ill you are served. Once she learns how you are forced to live, she and King Philip will force King Henry to treat you properly, and you will be restored to your former happiness!'

It was not often that Katherine felt warmly towards her duenna, but at that moment she could have kissed her. This might be the perfect solution to her problems.

'How shall I approach Queen Juana?' she asked.

'This is in confidence, Highness, but my brother, Juan Manuel, who is at the court of King Philip and Queen Juana, has told me that they have an envoy at court here just now, come to negotiate a marriage between the King and your sister-in-law the Archduchess Margaret. I myself will approach him on your behalf.'

Katherine seized her hands. 'You are a true friend to me, Doña Elvira!'

It was the happiest day she had had in a long while. Not only might there be an end in sight to her misery, but also the heartening prospect of her warm and lively sister-in-law becoming the Queen of England!

The very next day Doña Elvira ushered Herman Rimbre, King Philip's envoy, into Katherine's chamber. Rimbre was a suave, elegantly dressed Fleming with long flaxen hair and warm blue eyes, and Katherine liked him immediately.

'Doña Elvira has acquainted me with your Highness's plight,' he told her. 'I am sorry to hear it, and I am confident that I can help. Queen Juana has often said of late that she is eager to see your Highness.'

'She cannot long to see me as much as I long to see her!' Katherine exclaimed.

'Then why not write to her and suggest that you both meet?' Doña Elvira suggested.

'King Henry can hardly refuse you leave to visit your sister,' Herman Rimbre said, 'and it so happens that I have a courier waiting to depart with my dispatches. He could take a letter from your Highness to the Queen. I am happy to wait while you write it.'

'That would be so kind!' Katherine replied. 'Doña Elvira, please fetch my writing chest.'

Within the week she had a reply. Queen Juana would be delighted to meet with her as soon as possible. King Henry was invited too, and if he was pleased to cross the sea to Saint-Omer, Philip and Juana would be waiting there to greet him and Katherine. 'We will have celebrations and fireworks to mark this special occasion,' Juana promised, 'and King Philip and I will speak to King Henry on your behalf and make all right. I long to see you, dearest sister.'

Katherine could not wait. King Henry must agree to the visit, he *must*!

'Doña Elvira! My sister has written a very kind letter! Listen to what she says . . .' She read it aloud to the duenna, who beamed happily.

'We must look out your best gowns, and see how we can make them as new,' she said. 'But first, your Highness should write to the King. My brother has heard that King Henry is eager for an alliance with King Philip. I think you will find His Grace amenable to your request.'

When she had written her letter, Katherine left it unsealed so that she could read it to Doña Elvira for her approval. Nothing must be left to chance in this important matter.

Walking along the passage in search of the duenna, she came face to face with Dr de Puebla. He eyed the letter, a frown on his brow. She could not help herself: she had to let him know that there were some intrigues that he could not manipulate.

'Ambassador!' she said. 'I hope to see my sister soon. She has written to me about it, and I am writing to the King, begging him to grant our request. Maybe you would like to see my letter.' She handed it to him. Let him wonder what was afoot! Let him know that, although he had failed her, others were ready to help!

Dr de Puebla's eyes scanned the paper. His ugly face creased into a grimace. He swallowed. 'Very commendable, Highness.' His voice came out as a croak. She had bested him! Now she knew why they said revenge was sweet!

In a firmer tone, Puebla said, 'It would be more regular for a request for such a meeting to come direct from the King, through me, as Queen Juana's ambassador. Let me take your letter to him.'

Interfering again! 'No!' Katherine snatched back the letter. 'There is no reason why I should not write to the King myself, and I will send this by one of my own servants!' And she swept on past him.

She found Doña Elvira in the great chamber and handed her the letter. The duenna nodded approvingly.

'Seal it,' she said. 'The chamberlain is waiting below, ready to take it to the King at Richmond.'

Katherine had just sat down to dinner in her chamber when she heard a commotion outside and voices raised in anger. One of them was Dr de Puebla's.

'I must see the Princess!' he was shouting. 'This is a matter of the highest import!'

'I said, Her Highness is at table and must not be disturbed.' That was Doña Elvira.

'Madam, the fates of Spain and England are at stake! Dinner can wait!'

Katherine laid down her knife, gripped with a sense of foreboding. 'Come in, Dr de Puebla,' she called.

The door opened and Doña Elvira charged in. 'Highness, do not listen to him! He is a traitor!'

'That is rich coming from you, madam!' Puebla retorted, hard on her heels. 'Highness, may I speak with you alone?'

'No, you may not!' cried the duenna. 'He has come here full of lies!' she told Katherine.

It was at that moment that Katherine saw the doctor's face. It was a mask of fury and fear, stained with tears and streaked with sweat. Obviously he was deeply troubled about something. It occurred to her that, whatever he had to say, he was agonising over it, and that was so unlike him, who was renowned as a subtle and wily intriguer.

'Doña Elvira, please leave us,' she said.

'Highness, I beg of you—'

'Please leave us!'

Red-faced and outraged, the duenna heaved herself out of the room. Katherine waited until her footsteps had died away, then turned to Dr de Puebla, who was mopping his brow.

'Please be seated,' she said, trying to stay calm and cool. 'Now, Ambassador, tell me about this matter that can so affect England and Spain.'

Dr de Puebla sank gratefully down on a bench. Katherine poured him some wine, which he downed quickly.

'Highness, I hardly know where to begin.' His voice was choked with emotion. 'Please be calm and hear me out.'

'Speak freely,' Katherine said.

'Your Highness may not be aware that the court of Burgundy is riven by two parties, both eager to settle the future of Castile. Juana is queen, but how shall she rule? Certainly not alone! The Aragonese faction is led by King Ferdinand's ambassador, Fuensalida; they want King Philip to entrust the government of Castile to your father. They say that Philip is slow and lazy and not very interested in Spanish affairs, whereas King Ferdinand is vastly experienced, having ruled Castile with Queen Isabella for many years. It makes sense, and it is by far the most advantageous solution for your Highness, for with your father back in power in Castile, your former status as a princess of Aragon and Castile will be restored. I believe it is the devaluation of that status, Highness, and nothing I have said or done, that has caused King Henry to become cold towards you, you understand.'

Katherine nodded, but she was not convinced, and not sure where this was going.

'But there is another party at King Philip's court, a party led by a

97

skilful and dangerous man, a true Castilian who hates King Ferdinand. This man is Juan Manuel – ah, yes, I see you are understanding a little now – and he is, as you know, Doña Elvira's brother. He is hated and feared, but he is powerful and commands a strong following. His party wishes to oust King Ferdinand from Castile and set up Juana and Philip as joint sovereigns. To this end, Juan Manuel wants an alliance between King Philip and King Henry, who will unite to expel the Aragonese. And like many alliances, it is to be sealed with a marriage – or two, in this case. For the plan is that the Archduchess Margaret will marry King Henry – and Eleanor, the daughter of King Philip and Queen Juana, will marry Prince Henry.'

Katherine could not stop herself. 'No!' she cried. '*I* am to marry Prince Henry!'

'Not if Juan Manuel has his way, Highness – or King Henry. For while Philip is irresolute, the King is ready to proceed, and therefore Juan Manuel wants this meeting you have so willingly arranged.'

Katherine was speechless. 'You are lying!' she challenged.

'Do I look like a man who is lying?' Puebla countered. 'Highness, I know that Doña Elvira has turned you against me. She hates all Jews, and for years she has done her best to undermine me. I did not want to come here; I know where I am not welcome. But earlier today, when you showed me your letter and I realised what was brewing, I confronted Doña Elvira. I was tactful: I suggested that she did not appreciate what this meeting at Saint-Omer was about, or know of the grave issues involved. I assured her that nothing could be more harmful to Spain, to King Ferdinand and to your Highness. She did not like that, but she agreed that writing to King Henry was a mistake. So the chamberlain was sent away and I went home. Fortunately I left one of my fellows on watch near your gates, and as I was myself sitting down to dinner, he came racing to tell me that the chamberlain had just ridden off to Richmond.'

Katherine felt stunned. She had been manipulated and deceived by the people she had trusted most, to her own detriment! She could not doubt that Puebla was telling the truth – she had never seen him so distressed and agitated – or that Doña Elvira and Juan Manuel had used her most treacherously. The realisation hit her like a blow. That Doña Elvira could have actively pursued a marriage for Prince Henry that would leave her, Katherine, publicly abandoned, humiliated and heartbroken was dreadful, beyond belief. It was the worst act of betrayal.

Dr de Puebla was regarding her with sympathy. 'Highness, you alone can frustrate this conspiracy,' he said. 'Write again to the King. Persuade him against the meeting. Your duty to your father demands no less.'

'I will do it,' she said. 'But I feel such a fool. I have been incredibly naive.'

'Your Highness is but nineteen years old, too young to have learned how perilous life in courts can be. But I am an old man, and I have seen it all – the plotting, the lies, the crooked schemes, the enemies who turn a friendly face, the deceivers . . .'

'But to find such things in my own household is terrible,' Katherine said.

'There is something else,' Puebla told her. 'Your second chaplain tells me that some of your plate and jewels are missing, and I fear that Doña Elvira may have stolen them to compromise the terms of your marriage contract.'

Katherine felt the hot tide of shame rising from her chest. 'I agreed to it, God forgive me! It was to pay my creditors. The need was pressing.'

The doctor regarded her with sympathy. 'But she suggested it?'

'Yes.'

'Her motive was the same. Highness, you should be grateful that she has been exposed. You have been nurturing a viper in your bosom.'

Katherine got up, her knees almost giving way under her, went to the buffet and poured some wine, which she drank to steady herself. Then she walked shakily into the inner chamber, fetched her writing chest, and returned to her place. Taking out a sheet of paper, inkpot and quill, she turned to Dr de Puebla.

'Tell me what I must write.'

*

When Puebla had left for Richmond, Katherine braced herself and summoned Doña Elvira. She did not relish the prospect of a confrontation, but anger and honour demanded one, and righteous indignation would bolster her.

The duenna came in looking truculent, defiant even. Katherine did not bid her to be seated. She let her stand there, while she herself recited what Dr de Puebla had told her.

'What do you have to say to this?' she asked.

'It is all lies!' Doña Elvira spat. 'You should know better than to believe that lying, crippled Jew.'

'But I do believe him,' Katherine said. 'He was most agitated, and deeply worried. No, Doña Elvira, it is you I do not believe. You and your brother intrigued to overthrow my marriage and bring about an alliance detrimental to King Ferdinand, to whom you owe unquestioning loyalty.'

'I owe Aragon nothing!' screeched the duenna. 'I am a Castilian, and a proud one too. While your sainted mother lived, I was pleased to bow the knee to your father, but it is her daughter who rules Castile now, and he has no right to its governance!'

Katherine stared at her, shocked. She had had no idea that Doña Elvira held such strong opinions. She swallowed. 'Out of your own mouth you have condemned yourself,' she said, anger taking over. 'You have betrayed my father's trust, and you have betrayed me! What was I supposed to do once Prince Henry was married to Princess Eleanor? Go back to Spain in disgrace, rejected and scorned? That was the fate you had in mind for me! You, whom my mother entrusted with my safekeeping!'

Doña Elvira bridled. 'I have done my duty by you, God knows, but my first duty is to Castile and its Queen.'

'You are a traitor!' Katherine shouted, losing her temper completely. 'A traitor to my mother, to my father, and to me! If I had my way, you would be locked away somewhere, but I have not that power. What I can and will do is send you away. You will have to go to the court of Burgundy – for be assured you will not be welcome in Spain, where the long arm of my father reaches far. And then you and your unspeakable brother can meddle in things that don't concern you to your hearts' content!'

Doña Elvira's plump face sagged and turned a nasty pasty colour.

'Highness, maybe we should not be so hasty . . .'

'We? My mind is made up. Do not try to change it. Think yourself fortunate that you have got away with this without worse punishment.'

'But what will your Highness do for a duenna? No one knows how to manage your household like I do.'

'I will manage it myself!' Katherine cried. 'At my age, I do not need a duenna. Now go, and make ready to leave. I will order the chamberlain to arrange your passage to Flanders.'

'Forgive me, Highness! I have been most remiss.' The old woman sounded desperate.

'Doña Elvira, my mind is made up!'

The duenna opened her mouth to protest, then thought better of it. 'What will you say about my departure?' she asked meekly.

'In justice, everyone should be told the reason for it!' Katherine said. 'You deserve nothing less. But I do not care to look a fool in the eyes of the world.' She thought for a few moments. 'It is known that you have had trouble with your eyes. I will say that you have gone blind in one eye, and are losing the sight in the other, and that I have sent you to Flanders to be treated by the physician who healed the eye trouble of my late sister, the Queen of Portugal. In the circumstances, I think that is a very generous explanation. You will not, of course, return.'

'But, Highness, I do not wish to end my days in Flanders!'

Katherine erupted. 'Do you wish to end them on a gallows in Spain? You do not seem sensible of how lucky you are. If I sent you back to my father, he would deal with you as a traitor!'

'I beg your pardon, Highness!'

'Just go!' Katherine commanded.

Much on her dignity, Doña Elvira curtseyed and left the room without another word. Katherine slumped in her chair, her heart pounding, tears streaming down her cheeks. She had hated having to confront and dismiss the duenna, but she had had no choice but to assert her authority. Still, the interview had left her feeling drained and with a horrid sense of guilt. Yet what else could I have done? she asked herself.

There was a tap on the door. Maria came in, a look of grave concern on her face as she saw Katherine's distress.

'Highness?'

'What a terrible hour this has been,' Katherine said, wiping away her tears.

'We all heard you,' Maria said. 'You were shouting. I could not believe it was your Highness. Whatever did she do to deserve it?'

'I cannot tell you – even you,' Katherine said. 'But I have dismissed her. She has gone for good.'

'God be praised!' Maria exclaimed. 'I never could stand her.'

'If only you knew,' Katherine said, rising and embracing her friend.

'Highness, you are shaking,' Maria said.

'I know.' Katherine sighed with relief. And then came the realisation. She was her own woman, at last.

Chapter 7

1505–1507

While Katherine had believed Dr de Puebla when he revealed how the Manuels had used her, she could not accept that it was purely her reduced status that accounted for King Henry's treatment of her. She suspected that some of what Doña Elvira had said had been the truth, and that the doctor was susceptible to bribes and wanted an easy life at the English court. It took a lot to stir him to a remembrance of his proper role, as she had seen. And while Herman Rimbre had gone home to Flanders – on the same ship as Doña Elvira and her husband and their servants, she had heard – and there had been no more talk of the meeting at Saint-Omer, she herself had received no word from King Henry, and her situation was no better. In December, the December in which she was twenty – and still unwed – she wrote again to her father, leaving him in no doubt as to her plight. It was Dr de Puebla's fault, she told him; the doctor had transacted a thousand falsities against Ferdinand, and done her a great disservice. She stressed how troubled she was at seeing her servants so at a loss, and unable to buy the new clothes they so badly needed.

Two other matters were bothering her. Before she left, Doña Elvira had pleaded with her to find a new duenna. Katherine had ignored her advice, but she feared that some of her people, and Dr de Puebla, who were all Spaniards, would find it scandalous that she should take control of her household herself. They would assuredly feel that she should have an older woman to chaperone her, at the very least. And King Henry might be of the same opinion. She realised that she could not take it upon herself to assert her authority.

Then there was the problem of finding a new chaplain. Doña Elvira

103

had taken Father Duarte with her, and Katherine had no priest to hear her confessions. She had invited the local parish priests from St Martin's and St Mary le Strand to Durham House, but her English was not good enough, she believed, to make herself properly understood, and it was impossible trying to confess in stilted Latin, so she gave up, feeling bereft without a chaplain to guide her and give the spiritual consolation she so badly needed.

To add to her troubles, the tertian fever had returned, and never a day went by when she was not shivering with ague or feeling like death. Constant worry only made her worse. She had to do something, so she gathered her strength and consulted Dr de Puebla. There was no one else to ask.

'My advice is that your Highness go to court to see the King yourself,' he said. It was clear that he was not interested in speaking on her behalf.

Reluctantly she summoned her maids and an escort and, ill as she felt, took a barge to the court. She felt desperately self-conscious as the Lord Chamberlain, despite her sorry state, led her through the palace to a guest chamber. She would have preferred to go by a more discreet route, but clearly he thought that her rank entitled her to go by the public halls and galleries, which were crowded with people, many of them staring at her. There she goes, the poor, slighted Princess from Spain. How they have made a fool of her!

Katherine was aware that her finest gown, in brown velvet with bands of goldsmiths' work, was well past its best. She knew that she looked haggard and ill. So she was horrified when, as she was coming from the Chapel Royal one morning, having gone to be confessed by one of the royal chaplains, she met the Prince coming the other way. Flustered, she sank into a deep curtsey, waiting for him to raise her, but all he did was bow, then walk on, averting his eyes from her. How she got to her feet she did not know, and when she gained the privacy of her chamber, she lay on her bed and wept. She felt so weak and ill and wretched that she thought she would never get up.

That evening Dr de Puebla asked to see her. She splashed water on her face, smoothed her hair and forced herself to receive him.

'I have talked to the King and negotiated a solution to your Highness's problems,' he announced.

Immediately Katherine was suspicious. 'But *I* was to speak to the King!' she said angrily. 'That is why I am here.' And I wish to God I had never come.

'Will your Highness let me finish? The King says there is no need to replace Doña Elvira. He will dismiss most of your servants and disband your household. That way, money can be saved. Henceforth you will live at court.'

That was exactly what she had hoped to avoid. 'And this serves my interests best?'

'I believe it will.'

'Then you are a traitor!' she cried. 'Can't you see that the King does not wish to pay for the upkeep of a separate household, and that you have played right into his hands by agreeing to this? Negotiating indeed!'

'Under the terms of the betrothal treaty the King is entitled to order your household as he sees fit,' Dr de Puebla said, unruffled.

'Not to my dishonour!' Katherine stormed. 'I will write to the King my father and tell him everything!'

Her quill flew across the parchment. Even though she was wilting with fatigue, she must send this letter.

I entreat your Highness to consider that I am your daughter! Dr de Puebla has caused so much pain and annoyance that I have lost my health in a great measure. For two months I have had severe tertian fevers, and because of this I shall soon die.

She almost believed it. Surely her father would not ignore so desperate an appeal?

She urged him to send gold in lieu of the plate and jewels; she did not dare mention that she had been forced to take more pieces from her store, which she had pawned and never redeemed. With gold coin in his coffers the King of England would be content, and all would be well again. 'I will be lost if I am not assisted from Spain,' she wrote.

105

There was no reply. It seemed that her father had abandoned her. Feeling alone and desperate, she had no choice but to tell most of her servants that their sacrifices had been in vain and that they must now go home to Spain. She hated doing it, hated to see the disappointment in their faces, hated to say goodbye. She had failed them – but it had been none of her doing. She was at pains to make that clear.

Francesca de Cáceres was among those who were to remain. As Katherine had anticipated, the girl protested. 'Your Highness knew I wanted to go home!' Her sallow, olive-skinned face was mutinous.

'Francesca, I have to bear in mind your parents' wishes, and I still have need of young ladies of good family such as yourself to serve me,' Katherine explained.

'Highness, why do you stay?' Francesca burst out. 'There is nothing for any of us here but want and humiliation!'

'Go to your chamber,' Katherine said coldly. 'It is not for you to dictate royal policy. When you are ready to show a proper humility, you may return.'

Francesca fell to her knees and apologised, with tears in her eyes. Of course, she did genuinely long to go home, and who could blame her? But if Katherine herself could endure suffering and privation, and others did without complaint, then Francesca must do so too.

With her much-diminished train, she obeyed the King's command and went to court, where she was assigned a small suite of rooms at some distance from the royal lodgings. There were just four chambers, including her privy chamber and bedchamber, into which she and her remaining servants would somehow have to squeeze themselves. The diamond-paned windows looked out over a narrow courtyard, and the wall hangings were so old and faded it was hard to tell what they were meant to depict. The rush matting on the floors was grubby and needed replacing, and the furnishings looked like cast-offs from the last century. Mortified, Katherine asked to see the King. It took some negotiating and pleading, but finally she was admitted to the royal presence.

Henry looked up as she entered his study. His face had aged and was scored with deep lines. The once-red hair was grey and hung in lank strands over his fur collar. He sat hunched in his heavy robes, regarding her warily. It was hard to believe that he had once treated her with kindness.

'Your Highness asked to see me,' he said. His voice was brisk, business-like.

Katherine looked at him pleadingly. 'Your Grace, I have no money. I am destitute. I have closed up my household, but I cannot pay the servants who remain with me. I have no money to buy the clothes I need . . .'

'Stop there!' the King commanded. 'I am credibly informed that you do have the wherewithal to support yourself.'

'Sire, I do not. And, if I may remind your Grace, under the terms of my betrothal—'

'I know the terms of your betrothal. I have provided for you. You live at my court. I pay for your food. *I* have kept faith with the treaty.'

'Sire, it is not enough. I implore you to help me! I am all but naked, my gowns are so worn. My servants have been reduced to begging for alms. And the rooms I have been assigned here are not fit for scullions! It has all made me ill. I have been at death's door for months!' She was weeping uncontrollably now, past caring if she angered the King.

'I am not responsible for your plight,' Henry barked, then began coughing, clutching a kerchief to his face as the spasm passed. When he spoke again his voice was harsh. 'Be grateful for what I have done for you. I am under no obligation. I have been cheated out of your dowry.'

'How so?'

'Dr de Puebla informed me that the King your father promised to pay it all in cash. So far I have not seen a penny. Now go. Be grateful that I give you bed and board.' The heavy-lidded eyes were cold, the mouth a tight-lipped slash.

Anguished, Katherine dipped the briefest of curtseys and fled to her dismal chamber, feeling as if she were about to collapse. How could everything have gone so wrong?

*

Katherine smoothed her new gown, and straightened her spine, ignoring the dizziness that kept threatening to overwhelm her. She could not wait to greet her older sister after so many long years. Juana and Philip had been shipwrecked off the English coast while sailing from Flanders to Spain, and had battled their way through the January winds to Windsor Castle. Even now they would be in the great hall, ready to celebrate their deliverance at a feast hosted by King Henry. How much they would have to talk about! And, as Queen of Castile, Juana would surely understand Katherine's plight, and take steps to put things right.

Earlier that evening two new Spanish gowns had been delivered to her apartment – gifts from the King. Katherine was astonished at this unlooked-for munificence, but then understanding dawned. The gowns had been sent to give the lie to any complaints of ill-treatment that she might make to Philip and Juana. Still, they were beautiful, one in black velvet and one in yellow damask with crimson sleeves. She had chosen the black, even though it emphasised her pallor. If only she felt better. She had needed Maria to help her out of bed to dress, and her friend was a step behind her now, one hand ready to steady her.

As they entered the great hall, Katherine searched for the beautiful face of her sister. There was the King; there, to her delight, her own Prince Henry. Seated with them at the high table was a strikingly attractive man, who turned to watch as she walked slowly past the crowded tables. She could feel him examining her with almost indecent interest and knew this must be Philip.

Katherine could see why they called him 'the Handsome'. Tall, with long dark locks, his full, sensual lips and narrow-lidded eyes hinted at a powerful, barely concealed sexuality. No wonder Juana was possessive! Yet there was a coldness too, which left Katherine in little doubt that ruthless self-interest was what drove her brother-in-law. As she reached the table, he addressed her as his dear sister, but his eyes had already moved on to other ladies.

Juana was nowhere to be seen.

Katherine was surprised to find herself seated in the place of honour beside King Henry. It only confirmed her suspicion that Henry meant Philip to return to Spain with glowing reports of how honourably she was being treated; she could hardly believe that it marked her return to favour. As she sat down, she looked again for Juana, but she was not there.

'I hope my sister is joining us?' she asked the King.

Overhearing, Philip flicked a wrist as if in dismissal. 'She is still recovering from the journey. No doubt she will be in better spirits tomorrow.'

Katherine tried not to show her dismay. She had placed such hope in this meeting. Suppressing her desire to demand that she be taken straight to her sister, Katherine turned to Prince Henry, who was seated at the King's other hand. At least she would be able to speak with him. At fourteen, he had already shot up in height, and was taking on the image of manhood. As he greeted her he was as courteous as ever, but she saw in him something of the reserve she had found daunting in his brother Arthur. Was it because Henry was older now – or did it mean he no longer wanted her? She prayed that was not true. As the first course arrived – all twenty dishes of it – she tried to engage him, but his answers were short, with little of the passion she remembered in their previous conversations.

When the feasting was done, the King asked her to dance with her ladies for Philip's entertainment. She could feel the fever rising, making her light-headed, but she stepped forward for Prince Henry's benefit, and was gratified when he clapped her loudly. At his father's bidding she invited Philip to join the dancers, but he refused, and remained deep in conversation with his royal host, talking politics.

And that was the way it remained – the weeks that followed were dominated by interminable parleys and meetings, in which she had no part, nor would have expected to. But something secret was definitely being discussed, and she suspected that it concerned herself. When she was invited to join the two monarchs and their parties, she was dismayed by the disrespectful way Philip spoke of her father, making no attempt to hide his dislike for King Ferdinand.

Her wariness of her handsome brother-in-law only increased when she was finally able to see Juana. They met in the bustling great hall, surrounded by whispering courtiers and watching eyes. Katherine longed to embrace her and confide her deepest worries, but from their first meeting her sister was distracted and tearful because Philip was ignoring her. Juana's famous beauty was furrowed by misery, and her heart-shaped face was set into a permanent tight-lipped mask. Beneath the sumptuous gown, the richly trimmed velvet hood, the cloth-of-gold sleeves and the armorial cloak of silk, there stood a deeply unhappy woman.

In the whole three months of the visit Katherine managed to contrive just half an hour alone with Juana, but it was not long enough to divert her sister's attention from her own problems. Katherine guessed that their separation was by the King's design, but Juana was not interested in Katherine anyway; that much was clear. She had eyes for no one but Philip. Katherine tried to get her to talk about her children, especially the heir, the six-year-old Archduke Charles, but that was another conversation which foundered as soon as Philip hove into view. Juana watched him constantly, her eyes hopeful, beseeching, full of devotion, like a lapdog. Katherine cringed to see it. Where was Juana's Spanish pride, her queenly dignity?

It was plain that Juana was no queen such as their mother, Isabella, had been. She was too self-absorbed, too emotional, and it was soon obvious that the real power lay in the hands of her husband. Juana wasn't interested in the talks between the two kings, and certainly didn't want to discuss them with Katherine. She wanted only to talk about Philip. In April, when Katherine bade farewell to her sister, she felt not so much disappointment at the failure of her hopes, but a deep sadness for Juana.

'Dead?' Katherine echoed, horrified. 'It isn't possible. He is only twenty-eight.' And handsome and vital and compellingly attractive, or so he had been that spring. But she, of all people, had reason to know that Death is no respecter of age.

'Highness, my information is that the Archduke Philip succumbed to a brief enteric fever,' Dr de Puebla said. 'Please accept my condolences.'

'I did not know him well,' Katherine said. 'While I grieve for him, I am thinking of Queen Juana, and the suffering this loss will cause her.' Her heart went out to her difficult, envied sister, now to be envied no more. For the adored Philip was dead, and Juana would no doubt be going mad with grief.

'How I sorrow for Her Highness,' Katherine said to Dr de Puebla. 'And she with child too. How will she rule Castile?'

'King Ferdinand will be there to assist her,' the doctor reminded her.

'Of course. There is none more experienced in Castilian affairs.' Katherine could easily imagine how eager her father would be to restore his authority in Castile. 'Her Highness will be able to rely on him.'

Now that Ferdinand's standing in the world had improved, Katherine's did too. She was made very welcome at Richmond. King Henry was all benevolence and warmth once more, and the Prince's reserve seemed to vanish overnight. Young Henry took to seeking her out for dances and walks in the gardens, all in the glow of paternal approval. When they conversed with others, he took evident pleasure in deferring to Katherine. It was now, 'What does the Princess my wife think of that?' or, 'My most dear consort would agree with you, I'm sure . . .' She thrilled to hear him speak of her like that, revelling in being at the heart of the court once more. She sold two of her bracelets and used the money to buy a fine new gown of crimson velvet. Now she could appear in public looking as a princess should; she had recovered from the tertian fever at last, and her mirror told her that the gown certainly became her, setting off her long golden locks and fair complexion, or matched with a beguine hood of the same material. She could not believe that Fortune's wheel had turned again. It seemed, once more, that everything was going to be all right.

Katherine was not used to the King opening his mind to her.

'It is a delicate matter,' he said, leaning back in his chair in his study one dull January day, and looking gauntly at her down his proud, high nose, 'one that involves a lady, so I thought it fitting to ask for your advice. The truth is, I want to marry Queen Juana.'

Katherine stared, almost forgetting that she was in the King's presence.

Henry scooped up his monkey from the floor and plumped it in his lap, popping a nut into its mouth. 'I was struck by the Queen's beauty when she came to England, but then of course she was married, and naturally I did not think of her in any special way. But now she is alone, and clearly in need of a husband who can rule Castile for her.'

Katherine's heart was leaping at the prospect of Juana becoming Queen of England. In her joy it was easy to dismiss how reluctant she herself had been to wed King Henry; she had been much younger than Juana was now, and had been dismayed to envisage a short time as queen, then years of dreary dowagerhood. But Juana was a queen in her own right; she already had six children. Marriage to King Henry would solve all Juana's problems, and Katherine's too, for it would certainly ensure that hers to Prince Henry would follow, doubly cementing the alliance between England and Spain; and it would be so wonderful to have her sister here in England.

'Naturally I hope you approve of the idea, Katherine,' Henry said, eyeing her shrewdly.

'Wholeheartedly, sire,' she said.

'And I hope the King your father will too. You see, I need his permission – and his goodwill.'

'I do not think my father will demur, sire,' she said. 'His friendship with England is very important to him.'

'Yes, but he is at present ruling Castile himself, and may wish to continue to do so.'

Of course, Henry wanted Castile as much as he wanted Juana.

'He can have no formal role in Castile,' Katherine said. 'He cannot marry his own daughter!'

'Very true,' Henry agreed, grinning. 'Now, Katherine, I would like you to write to your father and lay my proposal before him.'

*

Katherine wrote, and was pleased to receive word that her father was himself amenable to the marriage going ahead. It was too soon, of course, to know whether Juana was inclined to marry again, yet if she was, Ferdinand was certain that it would be with no other person than the King of England.

She hurried off to beg an audience with King Henry, and when she told him the good news his craggy face was transformed.

'Katherine, I am deeply grateful. This gives me the greatest joy.'

His mother, the Lady Margaret, was with him, looking frailer than ever but beaming broadly.

'You have done His Grace a signal service,' she told Katherine, 'one that will bring much happiness. Bless you, child.'

Katherine returned to her apartments light of step and heart, anticipating a glorious future, with England and Spain more closely bound by ties of love than ever.

But there was Dr de Puebla waiting to see her, his brow furrowed, his expression grim. He seemed to have some difficulty in speaking. Then it all poured out. There were fears for her sister's sanity.

'She has been much stricken by grief, of course, but it is more than that. Highness, she will not give up King Philip's body for burial.'

Katherine's hand flew to her mouth in horror. In her mind there loomed the distant memory of that mad, terrifying old lady at Arévalo, her grandmother and Juana's.

'The Queen takes the coffin with her everywhere she travels in Spain,' Dr de Puebla said. 'The body is embalmed, but one report I have received informs me that Her Highness had the coffin opened, and embraced and kissed it. She will not consent to its being laid to rest.'

Of course. She had Philip all to herself at last.

Katherine crossed herself. She felt sick. Her mind strove to reject the terrible images that Dr de Puebla had conjured up.

'I can hardly believe this,' she whispered. 'It is too dreadful for words. I will pray for her.' Juana must be deranged by grief. Thank God and His Saints that their father was there to rule Castile for her.

When Katherine sat down to dinner in her chamber that evening, her heart was heavy. Should she say anything to King Henry? Morally, perhaps, yes, but she so wanted this marriage with Juana to go ahead. All evening she agonised, proving such a bad opponent at chess that Maria got cross with her for not concentrating. And when a groom arrived with a summons from the King, her spirits plummeted still further. But she could tell from Henry's face that he knew the worst.

'I have had this letter from your father.' He handed it to Katherine to read, and she saw that Ferdinand had told him everything. Now Henry would tell her that the marriage negotiations were at an end.

But no.

'When we are married, the Queen your sister will soon recover her reason,' Henry said. Then he saw Katherine's face. 'I do not much mind her infirmity, if that is what is worrying you. It does not prevent her from bearing children.'

Katherine was shocked. The King's words brought home to her how little he cared about Juana or her mental state. He was only interested in her beauty, her fecundity and the kingdom she would bring him. Katherine supposed that was how most men thought of marriage. How fortunate she was to have as her future husband young Henry, who loved her for herself.

'I will tell your father that I am happy to proceed,' the King said, oblivious to her disapproval.

As the spring approached Katherine again became a martyr to tertian fevers, and even the King expressed concern more than once. But what grieved her more than being unwell was a new suspicion: that he was keeping her and Prince Henry apart. For weeks had gone by since she had set eyes on her betrothed.

'Seeing His Highness so seldom is the most difficult thing for me to bear,' she confided to Dr de Puebla. 'As we all live in the same house, it seems to me a great cruelty.'

'I will speak to the King,' the ambassador promised.

The response was not what Katherine wanted to hear. 'His Grace tells me that he keeps you both apart for your Highness's good.'

'What good could it possibly do me?' she cried.

'He did not say, but assuredly he meant that, if you accustom yourself not to be with the Prince, it will hurt less if the betrothal is broken off.'

'Broken off?' Katherine echoed, appalled. 'Who said anything of that?'

'Forgive me, Highness, I was merely trying to foresee all possibilities. He has been offered many other princesses for the Prince of Wales, all with greater marriage portions.'

It may have been a bluff, but it put the fear of God into Katherine, and she begged her father to comply with Henry's wishes. 'Please do so, to prevent these people from telling me that they have reduced me to nothingness.'

There was still little money, for all that she was supposed to be in favour. Her servants were walking about in rags, and she felt deeply ashamed that they lived in such misery. She again beseeched her father to help them. She was aware that their patience, like their clothes, was becoming frayed at the edges. But King Henry would not act unless he received her dowry, while all Ferdinand seemed to care about was that she preserved intact her plate and jewels. In this, her time of need, she still very much felt the lack of a Spanish confessor. One advantage of living at court was the availability of several royal chaplains, but they served the King, and their loyalty was primarily to him. King Ferdinand had remained deaf to her pleas to send a friar of the Order of St Francis, for which she had a special affection and reverence, so she determined to shift for herself and wrote to the head of the Franciscan order in Spain, asking for help in finding a new confessor.

And that was how, in April 1507, Fray Diego Hernandez came into her life.

He was announced as she was seated at the rickety table in her chamber with her illuminated psalter open in front of her. She looked up to see a tall young man with swarthy good looks and intense black eyes, dressed in the grey habit of the Franciscans. Even as he stood unmoving before her, she could sense a physical dynamism more natural to a man of action than one of the cloth. There was a suppressed energy about him, and an air of authority that commanded instant respect.

She extended her hand and he knelt to kiss it. The touch of his lips startled her. Many men had done a similar duty, but none, apart from Prince Henry, had aroused such a response in her. She found herself inexplicably drawn towards Fray Diego, and as she spoke the formal words of welcome she felt herself blushing. God forbid that he had noticed!

'You are welcome, Father,' she said, as she bade him be seated. She told him of the months of spiritual deprivation. 'It has been a great grief to me. I long only to be properly confessed and absolved of my sins.'

'I will hear your confession this evening,' the friar said, his dark eyes boring into hers. 'It seems my coming is long overdue. Well, I will remedy all, and make sure that none of your people has fallen into error. Be of cheer: the dark days are over.'

He whirled into her household and charmed nearly everyone with the sheer force of his personality. Her maids instantly fell in love with him.

Katherine's first confession was a revelation. She knelt, admitting her few sins – Heaven knew, she had no opportunity to commit many, but the tensions in her household bred venial sins, and she had been guilty of anger and envy and pride. Yet where Father Alessandro would have dismissed her with a few Hail Marys, the new friar was unexpectedly strict.

'Your Highness must set an example! All sins offend God, and venial sins can lead to mortal ones. Omit nothing!'

So she racked her brains and remembered that she had accepted a second helping of lamb at dinner, which of course she should not have done when money for food was in short supply.

'I accuse myself of the sin of gluttony,' she whispered.

'Very reprehensible!' Fray Diego barked. 'As penance you will fast tomorrow. Fasting – and any form of self-denial – purges the soul.'

He absolved her and blessed her, and she suffered her penance, but his strictures were not confined to the confessional, for he was not reticent in reminding Katherine and her household where they had sinned. If they showed anger or impatience, it was a sin; drinking what the friar considered to be too much wine was a sin; even laughing immoderately, as he put it, earned censure.

Katherine did not mind, for from the first Fray Diego had set out to be her champion. He understood how valuable Katherine's role in England could be to her father. He was as eager as she to see her marriage concluded. One evening, as they sat at supper, she found herself confiding to him her fears about her betrothal, her father's failure to pay her dowry, and being kept apart from the Prince.

'I am sorry to hear it.' Fray Diego leaned forward and laid a sympathetic hand on her shoulder. 'It is Dr de Puebla's fault, I have no doubt. He has been dilatory in his duties.'

'Duplicitous, as ever,' she said, very much aware of the friar's touch and his brilliant eyes, like dark pools. 'If he had been any kind of man, he would not have consented to my being treated so shabbily. And now he is ill, and has to be carried from his house to the palace.'

'Your Highness should urge the King your father to send a new ambassador, someone who will dare to speak an honest word at the opportune time.' The friar's eyes were boring into her; they seemed to be saying something else entirely.

She felt her voice falter. 'I have asked him several times already, but I will write again.'

'Tell him that any new ambassador coming to England would be appalled at what you have suffered, and worried about your future.'

Katherine stood up, at once glad and sorry to see the friar's hand drop. Had it been presumptuous of him to touch her? Or had it been purely a kindly gesture, intended to comfort her? Of course it had been! He was a man of God, and had seen the troubled soul, not the Princess of Wales.

She wrote to her father that very evening. Then she and Fray Diego spent a very pleasant hour in which he gave her news of Spain and they discussed St Thomas Aquinas's views on Aristotle. She had been pleased to find the friar well read and very learned, and to discover that she could easily confide in him. It was thanks to Fray Diego that her situation was improving, and that she no longer felt so alone in her troubles.

She looked at the letter from her father in disbelief, then read it again. Never in all the histories she'd read had a woman been so honoured!

She summoned her household, bubbling with jubilation.

'I have very important news,' she announced. 'King Ferdinand has appointed me to act as his ambassador in England.'

'It is a great honour,' said Fray Diego approvingly, his dark eyes warm.

'It is not usual,' Katherine said, 'but the King my father believes it a necessity. He says there is no one else who knows the situation in England as well as I do. Of course, it is only until a proper replacement can be found.'

For now, though, she could work for a closer bond between England and Spain, and perhaps move her father and King Henry to understand how difficult it had been for her to be caught in the middle of their squabbles.

'Be wary of the sin of pride!' Fray Diego warned, but she could not help being gratified to see people regarding her with a new respect when she passed through the palace on her way to see the King. No longer did he receive her in his study, but enthroned in his presence chamber, with courtiers standing around at a respectful distance.

'Come, you must meet my council,' the King said, and led her into an adjacent room, where there was much scraping of benches as the men seated along an oak table rose to their feet and bowed.

Henry took his place at the head of the table and bade Katherine be seated next to him. The talk was all of pleasantries and court entertainments. She tried to steer it round to the subject of her marriage, but soon realised that she was being deftly thwarted at every turn. She left it there, not wishing to provoke any unpleasantness during this first meeting.

Back in her chamber she flung off her hood in disgust.

'They fancy that I have no more in me than appears outwardly!' she fumed.

'It is because your Highness is a woman,' Francesca observed.

'Well, they will find out that I am not a woman to be trifled with!'

Katherine was determined to take her new responsibilities seriously. She made herself go out into the court and talk to influential people. She organised couriers to take her dispatches to Spain. She made her father agree to use a special cipher for sensitive information, and spent time carefully coding and decoding their messages. It was good to be busy and to have a say in affairs. Above all, she knew that her marriage depended on the preservation of strong relations between England and Spain, and she worked hard to maintain them. But it required the patience of a saint.

The more she saw of the King and his councillors, the more confident, and exasperated, she became. Tiring of evasive tactics, she soon resolved on open confrontation.

'Your Grace, we *must* discuss my marriage,' she said one morning, as soon as the courtesies had been dispensed with. 'My father is not bound to pay the second instalment of my dowry until my marriage to the Prince is consummated.'

King Henry raised his thin brows at her boldness. 'That was not my understanding,' he said. 'King Ferdinand has promised to pay the dowry several times, so he clearly thinks it is due.'

'He has done that to please your Grace, but he was not obliged to.'

'Indeed he is.'

'May we look together at the betrothal treaty?'

'Your Highness does not believe me?'

'I would never question your Grace's honesty or wisdom, but I need to quote it to my father.'

'It will be sent for. But I assure you, the dowry is due, and until it is here, the marriage cannot proceed.'

When she saw the King a few days later there was no sign of the treaty.

'An oversight on my part, your Highness. I am sorry,' he said. Somehow, though, she knew that the treaty would not be there on the next occasion, or the next – and so it would go on. In the end she urged her father to send the new ambassador to take her place.

'I am getting nowhere,' she told Fray Diego. 'They have no scruples, these people. I have tried to play the game their way, but I am no good at it.'

It was galling to think that she had failed, but she took comfort in the knowledge that even the wily Dr de Puebla had been no match for King Henry. Puebla was still in England, and at court when his gout permitted; it irritated her to hear that he remained friendly with the King, and active on Spain's behalf. It saddened her that her days as ambassador were numbered, for she had enjoyed her role. Having that interest in her life, the status it gave her, and the support of Fray Diego, had done marvels for her health. The fevers had gone, and there was a healthy glow to her cheeks.

Despite the time Katherine spent at court attending to Spain's business, she rarely encountered Prince Henry. But in June she was delighted to be invited to a tournament to celebrate his sixteenth birthday.

'Maybe he will ask you to wear his favour!' Maria speculated, excited for her mistress. She and the other maids were chattering about the gallant knights who would be taking part.

'At least I will see him!' Katherine breathed, not daring to hope for too much.

When the day of the tournament came, she put on the crimson velvet gown, wore her hair loose, and took her place in the royal box with the King, the Lady Margaret and the Princess Mary, a sweet, pretty, red-haired child of eleven, who could barely sit still until the jousts began.

'I saw our dear boy just now; he is so eager to enter the fray!' the Lady Margaret said, her pride in her grandson obvious. 'You have an heir to be proud of, my son. There is no finer youth in the world.'

'Aye,' the King agreed. 'And here he is now!'

Katherine leaned forward to see the Prince, mounted on a horse caparisoned in the Tudor colours of green and white, advancing into the tiltyard at the head of a colourful procession of knights. He was wearing chased silver armour and was bareheaded, his helm being borne by the squire who was leading his mount. Henry's long red-gold hair fanned out in the breeze as he drew up before the royal stand and bowed from the saddle to his father. Then he turned his face to Katherine.

She stared, entranced. Her betrothed was no longer a boy, but almost a man, with all the beauty a man could command. His eyes flashed blue fire, his lips were full and red, his cheeks flushed pink with youth. His skin glowed. And he had grown so tall! His limbs were gigantic, his shoulders broad. He was Mars's lusty knight!

He was bowing now to her, dipping his lance as a token of respect. There was that in his face that made her feel weak.

'My lady!' he cried, his voice strange and broken, high-pitched still yet manly.

'My lord!' Katherine said, smiling, her heart full. 'I wish you good luck!'

He trotted away to prepare for the contest, not having asked to wear her favour. It did not matter; she had not expected it, and his eyes had told her all she needed to know. She was unable to settle or calm her raging thoughts. She feasted her gaze on him, watching him showing off his prowess in the lists, carrying off his fair share of the prizes. He was a keen and skilful horseman and jouster, but even so, every time his opponent was charging towards him, her heart leapt in fear. And every time he parried the onslaught expertly. The people roared their approval, and Katherine watched the Prince bend down to receive the acclaim of first one, then another, regardless of rank. It was plain that he had the common touch, something he had from his mother. But he seemed to take the most pleasure in her own applause, bowing again and again in her direction, and smiling broadly, delighting in her joy at his triumphs. His father looked on benignly. Surely he could see that the pair of them were made by God for each other?

Afterwards refreshments were served in a silken pavilion, and once again Katherine came face to face with Prince Henry.

'Sir, you were magnificent!' she said, and blushed hotly.

He looked down tenderly on her from his great height.

'I feel exhilarated, Katherine! You know, I dream of war and deeds of chivalry. I want to earn glory in the field, and a tournament is the next best thing!'

'Your Highness dreams of war?'

'Of victories, Katherine, over the French, our mutual enemy. I would win another Agincourt, be a second Henry the Fifth!'

'All in good time, all in good time,' said the King, coming upon them. 'I'm not dead yet!' He smiled thinly. 'If your Highness will excuse us, I wish to present a Venetian envoy to the Prince.' He bowed, and led his son away; Henry looked back once and smiled reassuringly.

Katherine did not see him again, but returned to her apartments nursing a new emotion in her heart.

She knew, beyond a doubt, that she had fallen in love.

Chapter 8

1507–1509

Katherine had been increasingly disturbed by reports that Castile had fallen into disorder for lack of firm rule, so she was much relieved when she heard that King Ferdinand had seized his chance. Despite Juana's protests, he had forced her to surrender sovereign power in Castile to him. She was not fit to rule, he had declared. It was the best solution for everyone.

Katherine rejoiced. Now, with Ferdinand's standing in the world as high as it had ever been since her mother was alive, she was sure that he would be better able to remedy all her troubles. Seizing the moment, she wrote, asking him to redress the wrongs done to her servants, who were still in utter misery for lack of wages.

She was delighted when, that autumn, her father finally sent her some money – not a large sum but enough to clear some of her debts.

'I hardly know which wants to satisfy!' she told Juan de Diero, who had replaced Don Pedro Manrique as first chamberlain. 'Do I pay off my creditors, recompense my servants or buy new clothes?'

Plainly her status had gone up in the world with Ferdinand's. When she next saw King Henry – for there was still no word of a new ambassador – she gave him a gentle dig about his neglect. 'My father sent me some money,' she told him pointedly. 'I was in such need.'

But the King had had yet another change of heart.

'Katherine,' he said, 'I love you so much that I cannot bear the idea of your being in poverty. I will give you as much money as you want for your person and servants.'

She thought she had misheard him, but no, he repeated himself, and understanding dawned, along with relief.

'I thank your Grace,' she said. She was not going to effuse. It was his responsibility to maintain her, and until now he had failed woefully.

He told her that the money would be paid immediately, then paused. 'This business of the marriage with Queen Juana has occasioned me great perplexity,' he said at length. 'I may look elsewhere for a wife, in view of what has happened.' You mean because you are unlikely to wrest Castile from my father, she thought. 'I must ask you to bring some pressure to bear on King Ferdinand,' the King concluded.

'I will do my best,' Katherine told him. If she could get her father to agree to the marriage, her credit with King Henry would soar still higher.

She appealed to Juana, telling her of his great love for her. She appealed to Ferdinand, who promised to persuade Juana by degrees to agree to the marriage. But from Juana there was no reply.

Nevertheless, King Henry was treating her with far more affection and respect, and she was hopeful that her marriage to Prince Henry might now go ahead, if only her father would send her dowry. She took care to do as Ferdinand had commanded her, and always spoke of her marriage as a thing beyond all doubt.

But that autumn the six months of grace that King Henry had given Ferdinand expired with no payment of the dowry in sight. He excused himself, saying he had been away fighting in Naples. Katherine could have cried, but King Henry was magnanimous.

'I will extend the term until March,' he said.

'He does not lose anything by that,' she told Fray Diego, who by degrees had become her mentor in all matters, especially her marriage. 'On the contrary, he gains. For, as he has told me, so long as he is not paid, he regards me as bound and his son as free.' It pained her to say it, for her yearning for Prince Henry was with her always.

'Your Highness must always act as if this marriage is a certainty,' Fray Diego commanded.

'But it isn't!' she cried.

She even confided her fears to Dr de Puebla. He was at court less frequently now, on account, he said, of his gout, but it was plain that he was ailing from something more serious.

'Your Highness must face reality,' he told her. 'King Henry does not believe that your marriage will be concluded.'

'That cannot be true!' Katherine said angrily, wishing she hadn't broached the matter with him. He always took a pessimistic view, but she feared he could be right.

Puebla spoke no more; with tears in his eyes he merely bowed and backed away.

After ten months as Spain's ambassador, Katherine received her replacement with mixed feelings. Don Guitier Gómez de Fuensalida, the Knight Commander of Membrilla, was a florid, corpulent man, very much on his dignity. As he entered her chamber, his greeting was everything she could have asked for, even if his manner was pompous and a little brusque.

'King Ferdinand is in Castile as we speak, raising money to pay your Highness's dowry,' he told her. 'I am to tell the King that it will be delivered before March, in the care of Signor Francesco de Grimaldi, of the banking house of Genoa.'

Katherine's heart leapt. At last! At last!

'Your Highness will be aware that it is an enormous sum to raise,' Fuensalida went on. 'I hope His Majesty has not been over-optimistic.'

She bridled at that. It was not an ambassador's role to criticise his betters.

'I am sure His Majesty will keep his word,' she said firmly. She dared not think of what would happen if he did not.

Fuensalida's expression showed what he thought of Ferdinand's promises.

'What of the marriage with Queen Juana?' Katherine asked, reining in her temper. She needed this man's support, and could not afford to offend him, but she did not like his manner.

'Out of the question, Highness. Her Majesty is completely deranged. And so I will tell King Henry.'

It was not a good beginning. And things did not improve.

She fretted all the while that Fuensalida was with the King. She was waiting for him in the hall when he emerged from the audience. He

125

looked at her as if she had no business to be there; his face warned her that he was the ambassador now.

'What did His Grace say?' she asked, determined not to be intimidated.

'About Queen Juana? Highness, the King did not believe it! He said he had heard that King Ferdinand keeps her shut up and spreads this rumour about her being insane. I had to make it very clear that it is no rumour, and that there will be no marriage.'

Katherine wondered how forcefully Fuensalida had made it clear. Tact did not seem to be among his virtues.

'And what did the King say about my dowry being paid soon?'

'His Grace was not in the most receptive of moods . . . He is angered by King Ferdinand's failure to pay the dowry.'

You angered him, Katherine thought. 'But he knows it will be coming soon?'

'I intimated as much, Highness.'

'You left him room for doubt?'

'Rest assured, Highness, I told him to expect it. But he did not seem convinced.'

Of course, he would not. There had been too many broken promises before.

King Henry was in the process of affiancing his daughter, the Princess Mary, to Juana's son, the young Archduke Charles. The powerful Holy Roman Emperor Maximilian was Charles's grandfather, and this new alliance would assuredly bring great prosperity, as King Henry pointedly told Katherine the next time they met. Maximilian's dominions included the Low Countries, with which England had long enjoyed a lively and lucrative trade. It seemed that the King thought he no longer had any need of Ferdinand's unreliable friendship.

She was dwelling mournfully on this late one night, when, just before retiring, she slipped back to her chamber to retrieve her book and found Fray Diego there, looking for her. His finger to his lips, he drew her into her closet. No one was watching. The maids were in the bedchamber.

'I cannot stay long!' Katherine whispered.

'Your Highness can be at prayer whenever you wish!' the friar muttered. 'This is important. Today I overheard a conversation between two of the King's councillors. I was in the chapel closet, fetching some books, and they obviously thought that the chapel was deserted. They spoke of the King negotiating for a French marriage for himself.'

'No!' Katherine was appalled to think that the Spanish alliance might be under threat.

'That was not all, Highness. They were also talking about some secret negotiations with the Emperor Maximilian for a marriage for Prince Henry—'

'Oh dear God!' Katherine interrupted.

'Your Highness!' The friar's face was stern. 'That is the sin of blasphemy, and you know better than to commit it. Pray let me finish. The King is thinking of betrothing the Prince to the Archduke Charles's sister Eleanor.'

'But he is betrothed to me!'

Fray Diego frowned. 'Your Highness knows as well as anyone else that betrothals can be broken. Moreover, these men were saying the King had told them that the Prince himself is now hardly inclined towards marrying you.'

That hit her like a poisoned dart. It could not be! Not after the way that great golden youth, her Henry, had looked at her. She struggled to find an explanation.

'Probably he says what the King expects of him!' She felt the tears welling.

Fray Diego saw. He took her hands in his. It made her aware that she was alone with him. If he were not her confessor, it would not have been appropriate.

'Highness, I also heard that King Henry has expressed concern that a marriage between you would be of questionable validity anyway.'

'But the Pope has granted a dispensation!'

The friar sighed. He was still holding her hands. 'This English King is slippery as an eel, Highness. He would sell his mother to achieve an advantage. Prince Henry must obey his father, although from what I

127

hear he chafes at the bit. You need to know what is going on. Forewarned is forearmed.'

'The King of England must keep faith. He must!' Katherine was beside herself. 'Maybe I should speak to Fuensalida.'

'That posturer! It is well known in the court that the King does not like him.'

'That is because he is too rigorous in his approach.'

'He will wreck all, if he continues unchecked. It is a thousand pities that he was sent to replace you.' It was true. Things had only got worse. And Katherine was painfully aware that the respect accorded to her as her father's official ambassador had diminished since Fuensalida's coming.

'I do not trust him,' she said. 'He professes to have my interests at heart, but does he know what they really are?'

'Do not talk to him!' the friar insisted.

It was all too much. Katherine could not stem the tears, and suddenly Fray Diego's strong arm was around her shoulders and she could smell the wine on his breath as he bent his head to her ear.

'Do not weep, Highness. All will be well. I will make it well for you, if I have to strangle Fuensalida with my bare hands!'

She had never heard such passion in the friar's voice. It unsettled her. Surely a priest should be detached? And then she felt him press closer to her, and for a moment, the briefest of moments, before she drew away, she felt a curious sensation, like a beautiful warmth flooding through her body. She knew it had come from feeling Fray Diego's body against hers.

As he bade her good night and closed the door softly behind him, Katherine sank to her knees. This was terrible! That she should feel a shameful attraction to a man other than her betrothed – and a priest at that! She loved Henry – she had eyes for no other. It was impossible that she could be drawn to anyone else! And yet – and she had always striven to be honest with herself – she had always been aware of the friar's physicality and his good looks; they were as much a part of him as the authority and power he exuded. And – being honest again – she had warmed to that as much as to his spirituality. As the friar had said

128

many times, sinning in the imagination was as bad as sinning in fact. And for that one moment, that treacherous moment, she must do penance – but she could never confess her sin to Fray Diego.

The next morning she was able to forgive herself a little. It had been an involuntary sin, and in future she would have more control of herself. She had been upset and she was lonely: those had been the causes of her lapse from grace. All the same, she put on her cloak, pulling the hood down to shadow her face, made her way to the Chapel Royal, slipped into the confessional, admitted to impure thoughts, and received absolution from one of the King's chaplains. And when she encountered Fray Diego later, she was mightily relieved to detect no sense of his having noticed anything amiss.

Katherine was desperate to find out how seriously she should regard what she had heard about those secret marriage negotiations. If anyone was in a position to know, it would be Fuensalida. In the end, after several sleepless nights, and days of anguish, she sent for him.

'Where did your Highness hear of such things?' he asked, looking at her as if she were making it up.

'A well-wisher told me.'

'Could it be a certain friar? Madam, I am bound to say that he is a bad influence.'

She felt her cheeks grow warm and her heart begin to race. 'How may that be?'

'I am informed by persons in your household that you spend much time alone with him, and that he rules all here.'

'*What* precisely have they been saying?' she asked.

'They have voiced the same concerns as I have.'

'No one has said anything to me! I can only assume that jealousy is at the root of it. Fray Diego is a good man. He has my interests close to his heart. And I am entitled to be alone with my confessor!' She was allowing anger to mask her own shame. 'Might I be correct in saying that my servants have in fact said very little at all, and that you are inventing things against Fray Diego because you know what he thinks of you?'

'Highness, how can you say that? I did not make any of it up. There is talk about you in the court. Some say you are too close to this friar, that he has too much sway over you. Highness, it is causing scandal!'

'That is untrue and wicked! No one who knows me could doubt it. You will refute such talk whenever you hear it. That is an order! And you will be answerable to my father if you disobey. Now, we will speak no more of this. Pray tell me what you have heard of these marriage negotiations with the Emperor.'

'Nothing,' muttered Fuensalida, his face red with fury.

She had expected him to deny all knowledge. They would not have made him privy to their secrets. But any ambassador worth his salt kept his ear to the ground. Dr de Puebla would have known, that was for certain. She almost felt affection for the old rogue.

Again, she did not sleep. Fuensalida's words haunted her. It was not Fray Diego who deserved his censure; Fray Diego, who had always behaved with the utmost decorum. Fuensalida must be jealous of his influence, for in giving her good counsel the friar was only doing what the ambassador should have been doing. All the same, she could not bear to think that she, who had lived in the most circumscribed manner and had had only one impure thought in her entire life, should be the subject of court gossip. She would have to warn the friar to be vigilant – and spend less time alone with him.

By the summer the gossips had something of far more import to occupy them.

'Highness, I must tell you,' Maria said, bustling into Katherine's chamber and shutting the door firmly behind her. 'They are saying that the King is dying.'

'I think it is true,' Katherine said, and tried to summon some sympathy for the man who had rarely shown much to her. 'He has been looking very ill lately, and his cough is worse.' It sounded like Arthur's had, six long years ago.

Maria's eyes met hers. They held an unspoken question. What would this mean for both of them?

Far away in Spain her father had heard the rumours too. He wrote that, since the King was in the last stages of consumption, it would not be worthwhile to press for Katherine's marriage to take place before his death.

Fuensalida informed her loftily that he was courting the favour of the Prince. 'I tell him of the great love that King Ferdinand bears him. I assure him that he may command His Majesty in anything. Highness, I am doing everything in my power to bring about your marriage.'

Katherine was grateful, but still she could not bring herself to like Fuensalida. And soon she was to despise him even more.

She was seated at her embroidery frame, sewing tiny stitches in black silk thread and chatting with her maids, when she heard footsteps approaching, angry voices and violent coughing. Then the door was flung open and there was the King, his cadaverous face red and furious, his hand gripping Fuensalida's arm, pushing him into the room. Immediately she rose and dropped a curtsey, her ladies making themselves scarce at the King's abrupt signal.

'The Princess shall see how you handle her affairs!' Henry barked, letting go of the ambassador.

Fuensalida was the image of bruised dignity. Ostentatiously he began smoothing his sleeve, but the King, coughing again, spluttered that he must now make account of himself to Katherine.

'This fellow here has jeopardised your Highness's marriage because he has failed to press the King your father for your dowry. He thinks to ingratiate himself with the Prince instead, but I still rule here!'

'His Grace is determined on having the dowry before committing to the marriage,' Fuensalida explained, in an injured tone.

Henry's eyes blazed. 'It is my right, and I want no more empty promises. Your King wears many crowns, but lacks the coin to pay his daughter's dowry!'

Fuensalida bridled. '*My* master does not lock away his gold in chests, but pays it to the brave soldiers at whose head he has always been victorious!'

Katherine drew in her breath, horrified that Fuensalida had dared to insult King Henry to his face. The whole world knew that the King was miserly with money, but he too had won great victories.

'The dowry is here in England, in the keeping of Signor Grimaldi, and will be delivered at the appropriate time,' Fuensalida went on, unheeding. Katherine was praying that he would not mention the plate and the jewels.

'Remember that, in the circumstances, I am not obliged to honour my part of the treaty,' the King said, his voice menacingly quiet. 'Princess Katherine, I bid you good day.' Then he left.

'Now see what you have done!' Katherine burst out, as Fuensalida stared at her. 'You are a fool, just as Fray Diego said. How dare you insult the King! My father would never countenance that.'

'Everything I have said or done has been in your Highness's interests,' the ambassador protested.

'And look where it has led! You saw the King just now; you heard him. My marriage is now in greater jeopardy than ever! You made him angry, and he took it out on me. Because of you he thinks he can break my spirit.'

'Believe me, Highness . . .'

'I believe what I choose. I am not as simple as I seem. Now go!'

In the midst of all this unpleasantness Katherine decided that it was at least gratifying to know that her dowry was in England. Surely it would tempt the King to forget his anger and honour his part of the marriage contract. At the thought of that her pulse quickened. Soon she might be married!

But for now, what was she to do for money? She dared not pawn any more plate, but with the news about her dowry was born a possible solution.

She called for writing materials and wrote a letter to Signor Grimaldi. She explained that she hoped to be married to Prince Henry soon – and of course he would understand about that, because he knew about the dowry – and asked if he might see his way to giving her a small loan, which she would repay as soon as her circumstances changed.

She did not have to wait long for a reply. Signor Grimaldi would be honoured to arrange a loan. In return, he would ask for her bond for the principal sum and the interest, which were to be repaid within a month of her marriage. The interest rate he quoted – fifty per cent – seemed high, but she reasoned that she had no choice, and hoped that Prince Henry would understand. She had to eat, after all!

It was a bitter January day, and the pitifully few logs on the fire were losing their battle with the freezing draughts that rattled the windows. Katherine laid down her embroidery and shivered. Her fingers were too numb to continue.

Nothing had changed, and all her hopes were as dust.

'I cannot bear any more,' she wept to Maria. 'Things get worse every day.'

'Do not cry, Highness,' Maria begged. 'You know I hate to see you distressed.' They were alone in Katherine's bedchamber, the other maids having gone to bed. Maria rose, poured some wine and handed it to her mistress.

'But I have every reason to cry!' Katherine sobbed. 'Here I am, twenty-three years old, still unwed, and with no hope of anything changing. The King is angry because my father will still not authorise the handing over of my dowry. He has lost patience with Fuensalida. He is cold towards me. And I cannot help you, or Francesca, or any of my people. It is impossible for me to endure any longer.' Now she was sobbing in earnest, her face buried in her hands.

'Hush, now. This is doing you no good,' Maria murmured, putting an arm around Katherine's heaving shoulders.

'Nothing ever does me any good! Oh, Maria, I am so unhappy I fear I might do something that no one would be able to prevent.'

'No!' Maria cried. 'Don't say such things! It is a mortal sin even to think it.'

'I appealed to my father,' Katherine said brokenly. 'I told him I might be driven to it, unless he sends for me and lets me pass the few remaining days of my life in God's service, as a nun, for sometimes I think that I can have no other future. But he has not replied.' She burst into a fresh flurry of weeping.

Suddenly Fray Diego was in the room. 'What is going on?' he asked. 'I could not help but overhear. Is Her Highness in distress?'

'Her Highness is upset.' Maria sounded deeply concerned. 'She is talking of ending her life.'

'Never let me hear your Highness speak of that again!' the friar commanded, at which Katherine sobbed all the more, unable to stop herself. He laid his hand on her arm. Even in her extremity, she turned away, hoping he would remove it.

'No, my daughter,' he said, with great authority. 'You will not do it. To contemplate such a thing is a heavy sin against God. It is for Him to call us out of this world. We do not go to Him when we please.'

'But I do not know where to turn!' Katherine cried, shaking his hand off. 'There is no money. I do not know how to maintain myself, or all of you. You know I have sold all my household goods and stuff from my wardrobe. Now even that money has gone. When I begged King Henry for help, he said he was not bound to give me money, even for food.'

'But he gave you something,' Maria said.

'Just enough to defray the expenses of my table! I felt so humiliated. To be reduced to such a state! Not to be able to pay your wages. And to be reminded that even my food is given me as alms!'

'Despair, as I have told you, is also a sin against God,' the friar said sternly, his black eyes flashing. 'Tribulations are sent to test us. Remember, we never come to the kingdom of Heaven but by troubles.'

'God would surely understand if I find my troubles too burden-some,' Katherine protested. 'Our situation is desperate. All of us face destitution. When I think of how faithfully you good people have served me, and how you have had nothing but want for your reward, I am shamed. It hurts me. It weighs on my conscience.'

She cried afresh when she thought of what had happened that very morning. Of all her household, her chamberlain had been the least forbearing. She had been complaining to him, for the hundredth time, about the lack of money; but he had rounded on her accusingly.

'Highness, you have failed to order this household properly!'

She had smarted at the unfairness of it, but she knew that he too was reaching the end of his endurance. And she had said nothing; she could not pay him, so she could neither reprimand nor dismiss him.

Then Fuensalida had brought her the most unwelcome news from Spain. King Ferdinand had publicly declared Juana mad and unfit to reign, and had shut her up in a convent at Tordesillas.

'Officially she is sharing the government with her son, the Archduke Charles, who is to be King of Castile.'

It was an unbearable thought. And that poor little boy – not only deprived of his mother, but also burdened with a crown at just nine years old. But, as Fuensalida explained, his grandfather Ferdinand was to govern both Castile and Aragon until Charles reached his majority.

When Katherine calmed down, she took heed of Fray Diego's words, remembering that those desperate enough to take their own lives would never see God. But that morning she had felt as if her life were un-ravelling uncontrollably, and that she could fight no more. It was thanks to the friar that she had pulled herself back from the brink. She was truly blessed in her confessor, and could not believe that she had ever responded to him as a mere man. But that was all behind her. She had fought her battle and won. Now she would pray for the strength to cope with her many troubles, and for serenity, as he had often urged her to do, and for patience to endure until things got better.

Katherine was uncomfortably aware of petty jealousies and disputes developing among her much-tried servants. She could not find it in her heart to blame them, for they had suffered so much, but she had noticed too a scanting of respect towards her. Some had not served her as well as they should, yet she dared not call them to account lest they abandon her.

She was determined to ignore all that – and what Fuensalida had said about Fray Diego. He had accused her of causing scandal, yet where was the evidence? No one in the court had looked disapprovingly at her; none of her maids had come running with tales of scurrilous gossip, and they would certainly have told her if they had heard anything. She could only conclude that the ambassador was jealous of the friar's influence.

'Do people say anything of me and Fray Diego?' she asked Maria.

'The chamberlain thinks he has too much influence over your Highness. He says you will do nothing without the friar's advice and blessing.'

'Is that all? No scandal to report?'

Maria's eyes widened. 'Never, Highness! Why would anyone think that of you, of all people?'

'There is no reason why they should. It was something Fuensalida said. But he has it all wrong. Fray Diego is the best confessor any woman in my position ever had. I cannot fault his devout way of life or his learning – or his kindness. It grieves me that I am too poor to maintain him in the way his office demands, for he has served me untiringly.'

But here was Fuensalida again, relentless as the plague, demanding to see Katherine. One look at his pompous, disdainful face set her hackles a-quiver.

'Highness, I have been most concerned about the disorders in your household, and I have promised the King your father to see that they are remedied.'

Katherine rose to her feet. 'You exceed your instructions, Ambassador. This is my household, and I will run it as I think fit.'

'As Fray Diego thinks fit, I suspect!'

'Ah, there we have it,' she snapped. 'Some of my people have poisoned your mind against him.'

'Madam, they had no need. I can see for myself that there is much need of a person who can rule this household, and so I have informed King Ferdinand, for it is clearly governed by that young friar, and in my view he is unworthy, for he has caused your Highness to commit many errors.'

Guilt flared again for a moment, but fury took over. 'What errors?'

'Dismissing Doña Elvira, for one.'

Katherine bristled. The *ignorant* fool! 'That had nothing to do with Fray Diego. What else?'

'I am told that the friar makes a sin of all acts.'

'Some would say that he keeps us on the path of virtue.'

Fuensalida glared at her. 'Highness, do not quibble with me. It is well known that the beginning, middle and end of these disorders in your household are the friar.'

'That is a lie!' Katherine cried. 'How dare you complain to King Ferdinand of matters of which you plainly know nothing!'

'It is my duty,' Fuensalida said. 'I am sorry that it grieves your Highness, but my allegiance is to a higher power.'

He bowed and left her standing there, trembling with anger.

Francesca de Cáceres came to her. Alone of her household, Francesca had never stopped urging Katherine to return to Spain. She hated England and the privations she was forced to suffer, and made no secret of her yearning for her homeland.

Fray Diego had told Katherine to pay no heed to her. 'Your Highness's place is here. You are the future Queen of England. Do not let a foolish girl persuade you otherwise.'

Katherine suspected that Francesca had overheard him, because since then her manner towards the friar had been cool, and she had put even more pressure on Katherine to leave England for good.

'Would your Highness not like to go home? Think of how good it would be to be back in Spain. To bask in the sunshine and eat oranges whenever we want to . . .'

'My place is here,' Katherine would reply. 'I am the Princess of Wales. I cannot leave.'

But of late, unlike the other hard-pressed servants, Francesca had been in a buoyant mood, laughing readily and humming as she performed her tasks. Now the reason became clear.

Francesca was looking nervous yet determined. Katherine put down her embroidery, expecting to hear more complaints, but her maid surprised her.

'Highness, there is a banker of Genoa, in whose house the ambassador lodges. His name is Francisco de Grimaldi, and with your permission we wish to marry.'

Katherine winced inwardly at the mention of Signor Grimaldi. She had taken his loan and given him her bond, but there was now no hope of her being able to repay him, with her marriage seeming as remote a prospect as ever. She was in a difficult position, but duty had to come first.

'Francesca, the answer must be no. Your family is an ancient one; they would never forgive me for allowing you to marry a mere banker.'

'But, Highness, he is very rich. It is a good match.'

'I am sorry, Francesca, but it is out of the question.'

'Highness, we love each other!' Francesca pleaded. She did not notice that Fray Diego had come in and was standing behind her.

'You heard your mistress,' he said. 'You are bound to obey her.'

'You!' she rounded on him. 'Are you interfering again?'

'You will not speak to Fray Diego like that,' Katherine said. 'Remember the respect due to his office.'

Francesca was seething. 'I would that he deserved it, Highness!'

Fray Diego's temper flared. 'Francesca, if you have any complaint to make of me, you may say it now in front of Her Highness.'

His steely eyes were fixed on the girl's face.

'For shame, I would not speak of it,' she muttered.

'This is monstrous,' said the friar.

'All I will say is that a man such as you should not be allowed in a household of women!'

'You will kindly explain what you mean,' Katherine erupted, shocked.

'Ask him!' Francesca flung back.

'I have no idea what the woman is talking about,' Fray Diego said.

'Ask Fuensalida!' Francesca challenged.

'There we have it!' he retorted. 'That man will say anything against me.'

'He knows what he has heard.'

'Then your complaint is third-hand,' Katherine said, 'and it is prejudiced. Francesca, I cannot have anyone making unfounded allegations against my confessor, whom I would trust with my life. I understand that you are disappointed about being forbidden to marry Signor Grimaldi, but there is no need to take it out on Fray Diego.'

'That man is poison!' Francesca cried, pointing at the friar. 'Your Highness is too full of goodness to see it.'

'I think I am in a good position to judge his character. He has served me unfailingly well for two years.'

'You are a fool!' Francesca said, then realised to whom she was speaking, and clapped her hand to her mouth. 'Highness, I beg your pardon. That was unforgivable.'

'I fear it was,' Katherine said, perilously close to tears. She hated confrontations like this, but she could not allow a maid-of-honour to speak to her so disrespectfully. 'I will not have anyone causing trouble in my household. You must consider yourself dismissed.'

'Highness! I beg of you . . .'

'No, Francesca.' Katherine's heart was pounding. 'My mind is made up.'

Francesca flounced out of the door. As soon as she was out of earshot, Katherine sank down on a stool and gave way to weeping.

'Highness,' Fray Diego said, laying a hand on her shoulder, 'I assure you, her complaint was without foundation. I have no idea what she meant.'

'Fuensalida has got to her,' Katherine sighed, moving away. 'He is determined to have you dismissed. But I will never allow it.'

Francesca had gone.

'She told me that Fuensalida placed his lodgings at her disposal. She and Signor Grimaldi are to be married,' Maria told Katherine.

'That does not look well, considering the ambassador's official position as my father's representative,' Katherine fumed.

Things looked even worse when Fuensalida appeared with Signor Grimaldi in tow. The banker was an elderly man, and Katherine guessed that, for Francesca, the lure had been his wealth.

'I ask your Highness to pay something of what you have promised me,' Grimaldi said, regarding her implacably. She suspected that this was in revenge for her dismissal of Francesca.

'If you will give me two days' grace, I will do so,' she said, resolving desperately to pawn some more of her diminished store of plate.

'If your Highness does not pay,' Fuensalida said nastily, 'you must surrender your jewels and plate to me for safekeeping, as surety for Signor Grimaldi.'

'But they are part of my dowry,' she protested, fearful of Fuensalida finding out that her store was alarmingly depleted. 'I cannot give them to you.'

'Then we look forward to your settlement, Highness,' he said.

When they had gone, Katherine saw that she was in an impossible position. She had planned, should her father order the handing over of the plate and jewels, to appeal to Signor Grimaldi to lend her the money to redeem the pieces she had pawned. But now – what in Heaven was she to do?

Later that day she received a summons from the King. She had not set eyes on him for weeks and was shocked to find him skeletally thin and much wasted. Seeing his eyes burning with anger in his skull-like face, she shrank back.

'Why is your Highness obstructing payment of your dowry?' he demanded to know.

'Your Grace, I promise I am not. I but wait for my father's command to hand it over.'

'His ambassador tells me you refused to do so.'

So Fuensalida was lying about her now. 'No, sire,' she replied. 'I said I could not repay a loan. That was nothing to do with the payment of the dowry.'

'That's not what he told me. And he said also that your household is under the sway of an insolent friar who is young, light-minded, haughty and causing scandal.'

'Sire, that is not true. Whatever you have heard—'

'The Knight Commander is most concerned. He urged me to speak to you . . .' The King broke off, attacked by a bout of coughing so violent that he could not speak for several minutes, but sat barking into his handkerchief. Katherine did not know whether she should go and comfort him, or stay where she was. At length, the King lay back wearily against his chair, clutching the bloodstained cloth. She stared at it, appalled.

'Katherine, I urge you to dismiss this friar. Remember that his conduct is damaging your reputation. Remember to whom you are betrothed. If I hear one more complaint, out that man goes. Do I make myself plain?'

'Yes, sire,' she murmured.

'And if the Knight Commander asks again for the plate and jewels, give them to him!'

'Sire, if I may—'

'No, you may not. Now go.' The King's voice cracked and he began coughing again. Katherine fled from the room, trembling with the injustice of it all.

With Fray Diego's connivance she sold some of her jewels. The price he obtained was not a fair one, but it was enough to repay Signor Grimaldi. Katherine entrusted the bag of gold to her chamberlain and told him to go to the banker's house and deliver it into his hands, and to wait for a receipt. She did not stop shaking until he returned with it.

When next Fuensalida came asking to see her, Katherine refused to receive him, and Maria, who had now taken upon herself some of the authority that Doña Elvira had once exercised, sent him away.

'He was furious!' she reported. 'He said that Fray Diego has put him out of favour with your Highness, and if he had committed some treason you could not have treated him worse. He bade me tell you he is asking King Ferdinand to recall Fray Diego and replace him with an old and honest confessor.'

The friar was listening. 'I do not wish to cause grief to your Highness. It might be better if I leave your service.'

'No!' Katherine cried. 'What would I do without you? You have been a true friend. And who would I rely on for spiritual advice?'

'Highness, I cannot feel comfortable knowing that I am the cause of such dissension. Give me leave to go back to Spain.'

Katherine felt tears brimming. 'No, I will not hear of it! The greatest comfort in my troubles is the consolation and support you give me. I will write myself to my father and warn him that Fuensalida is a liar.'

In desperation, she scribbled the letter, complaining of how badly the ambassador had behaved. 'Things here become daily worse, and my life more and more insupportable. I can no longer bear this. Your ambassador here is a traitor. Recall him, and punish him as he deserves. He has crippled your service.'

That night Katherine felt really ill. Her stomach was heaving and she vomited three times.

'It is all the worry you suffer,' Maria said, shaking her head and covering the bowl with a cloth.

The next morning, when Katherine had made herself rise from her bed and was trying to force down some breakfast, a royal messenger arrived, commanding her to make ready to move with the court to Richmond.

'You cannot go,' Fray Diego said, regarding her with concern. 'You are unwell.'

'I am better,' Katherine lied, knowing that it would be foolhardy to risk offending the King further. 'I want to go.'

'Listen to me!' he said, stern. 'I tell you that, upon pain of mortal sin, you will not go today.' He turned to the messenger. 'And so you may tell the King.'

Katherine raised a small protest.

'I *am* well enough to travel. I do not see why going is a mortal sin.'

'Disobeying your confessor is,' Fray Diego said. 'Look at you. You are ill. You have not slept. I am making you stay for your own good. If you are better tomorrow, we will leave.'

When Katherine did arrive at Richmond the next day, Fuensalida was waiting for her.

'The King was very much vexed that you did not come yesterday,' he told her. 'He knows that his order was countermanded.'

'Then I must go to him and apologise,' she said.

'He will not see you.'

In fact the King did not speak to her for three weeks, nor did he send to enquire after her health. Her only consolation was that he had again quarrelled with Fuensalida and was refusing to see him too, or to transact any business with him.

*

142

Katherine was overjoyed to hear from her father that he was recalling his ambassador, and sending another, Luis Caroz, in his place. She began reading Ferdinand's letter out loud to Maria, as they sat together in her shabby chamber, knowing her friend would share her sense of victory. But her voice faltered as she took in the next words. Her father was sending Caroz to England to escort her home to Spain, so that he himself could arrange a new marriage for her.

She looked at Maria, unable to speak. She was to go home, after more than seven years in England? For a moment she could not take it in. She did not know what to feel. She would be returning to a Spain that had changed greatly since she had left it. There would be no beloved mother there to welcome her, no sisters, for all had married or died – only the father who she could not help but feel had betrayed her. It would be good to see her homeland again; it would be wonderful not to live at the English court on sufferance, not to live in poverty, not to feel guilty about the privations of her people, and not to endure the interminable squabbles in her distressed household.

But leaving England would mean giving up all hope of marrying Prince Henry. She had not seen him for so long, yet she had never forgotten that day of the tournament, and how he had looked at her. Did he think of her now as she thought, so often, of him? All her life she had envisaged herself as the future Queen of England; she wanted to be Prince Henry's Queen, not to marry someone else, go to another foreign land and learn another set of customs, another language. She was quite proficient in English now.

King Henry was dying, that much was clear. She could never wish for anyone's death, and prayed daily for his recovery, but she had dared to speculate that, once he had departed this life, Prince Henry would come like a knight errant to claim her, and they would live happily ever after, as in all the old romances. But evidently her father knew that would not happen; otherwise, why summon her home?

The unpalatable truth was that what she wanted was immaterial. She knew she was powerless to affect her future. It would be decided to the advantage of others. That was the way it had always been if you were a princess.

Katherine sat at table, her household about her. No one commented on the bad smell emanating from the fish before them; they were too used to eating fish a day old from the market. It was Lent, and they were fasting, and with Fray Diego in charge no laxity was permitted, so there was very little else on the table. We could not have afforded much anyway, Katherine reflected.

She felt nauseous and shivery.

'I cannot eat any more,' she said. 'I must go and rest.'

Maria rose. 'Go to bed, Highness. I will help you.'

In the bedchamber Katherine lay down, fully dressed, on her bed.

'Leave me; just let me sleep,' she murmured, when Maria protested. Sleep would not solve her problems, but it would give her some respite from worrying about them.

She lay ill for two days, kept to her chamber over Easter, and rested for another week or so. She was still convalescing, but dressed and seated in her chair with her maids and ladies around her, when Luis Caroz, the new ambassador, arrived.

'Do bring him to me, Maria,' Katherine commanded.

Caroz was a neat, dark-bearded man in his thirties, his oval face just shy of handsome, but pleasing. Maria was looking at him most appreciatively.

'You are very welcome, Señor Caroz,' Katherine said.

'Highness, the pleasure is mine. I have heard so much about your unfortunate situation, and it is my fervent hope that I can serve you usefully. You will be glad to know that King Ferdinand is well, and sends his dearest love.'

'And Queen Juana?'

Caroz looked pained. 'I have not heard, Highness. I believe she is well looked after, poor lady.'

'Have you seen King Henry yet?'

'Highness, that is what I came to tell you. The King is too ill to see me. My instructions are to wait on events.'

'Then I am not to go home immediately?' Katherine could feel the women around her draw breath, anxious to hear of their future.

'No, Highness. Let us see what transpires.'

Katherine saw the King only once after that. She was walking in the palace gardens, enjoying the April sun and the spring breeze, when she happened to look up and saw him watching her from his window. He looked grey and spectral, and it seemed to her that he had aged a hundred years. But to her astonishment he smiled at her and raised his hand in greeting. She swept a hasty curtsey and waved back. She saw that he was nodding at her, nodding as if in approval.

Three days later she heard that he had died.

Chapter 9

1509

'They are saying that His late Majesty was a great king,' Luis Caroz reported.

That may be so, Katherine thought, but he was not a great man. She sat there in her faded mourning garments, the same ones she had worn for Arthur and her mother. She was thankful that they mostly still fitted, even though they hung on her with room to spare, for she had lost weight in the years of her privations.

'My sources tell me that he has left over a million pounds in his treasury.' That did not surprise her. The King had not spent a penny unless it had brought some advantage to himself. She had not sensed much grief in the court at his passing. The poor, frail, ageing Lady Margaret was devastated, of course, as was the Princess Mary, who had loved – and been loved by – her father, and Katherine's thoughts were also with the young Queen Margaret, who had yet to hear the dread news in faraway Scotland; but generally there was rather an atmosphere of anticipation, of suppressed excitement. She had heard the late King called miserly, grasping, even harsh. She thought that these unpleasant aspects of his character had been more manifest since Queen Elizabeth's death.

Now Prince Henry was king – King Henry VIII. She still had not seen him. He would be mourning his father, and busy with the affairs of his kingdom. But there had undoubtedly been a change. It was like being her father's ambassador all over again, for when she emerged from her lodging to go to chapel or walk in the gardens, people were quick to make obeisance and be noticed by her. She did not dare to hope what this might betoken.

*

The King was buried beside his Queen in the magnificent Lady Chapel he had built in Westminster Abbey. Katherine did not attend. In charity, she spent the day praying for the old miser's soul.

Then came the order to move from Richmond to Greenwich, the great red-brick palace by the Thames, the beautiful Placentia that the new King was known to favour, for he had been born there. Here Katherine found herself lodged in a finely furnished apartment with large diamond-paned windows that glittered in the sunshine and afforded prospects of dancing fountains, immaculate lawns and beds of flowers, and beyond them magnificent views of London and the Thames. It was all a far cry from the dismal, overcrowded rooms at Richmond and other palaces. But still there was no summons from the young King.

Soon there came a letter from King Ferdinand, who explained that he had not paid her dowry because he had not trusted the late King, whom he believed had no intention of marrying her to Prince Henry. He had been beset by the fear that his son might obtain too much power by his connection with Spain. Now Katherine must rest assured that things would change. 'I love you the most of my children,' Ferdinand wrote, 'and I look on the King of England as a son. I will give him advice about everything, like a true father. Your duty will be to bring about an understanding between us, and ensure that the King heeds my guidance in matters of state.'

That was all very well, she thought – but where *was* the King?

It was now June, and the roses were opening their delicate petals in full bloom. The old King had been dead for six weeks, and the court was still abuzz with excitement at the prospect of change and preparing eagerly for the coming coronation. Luis Caroz was cautiously optimistic – Katherine suspected he was cautious in all things, even love – and her ladies were predicting that she would be queen ere long. She wished she could believe it. Fray Diego counselled her to have patience, and to leave her future in the hands of God. But it was hard to remain positive. She could not help reading something ominous into this long silence.

Everyone was praising the new King – how wisely he behaved, how he loved goodness and justice. It was universally agreed that he was the most gentle and affable prince in the world; quick to laugh, and intelligent, with a jolly look; he would always talk to people in a friendly way, with exquisite courtesy. He had made no secret of his determination to distance himself from the parsimonious reign of his father, and to be rid of unpopular advisers. His was to be a new golden age, an age of open-handedness, magnificence and glory. Katherine stored up every bit of gossip and praise she heard, and was thrilled to learn that this eighth Henry was still filled with dreams of conquering France. 'What a hero he now shows himself!' his courtiers applauded. 'Our King does not desire gold or gems, but virtue, glory, immortality!'

'He seems, by all accounts, to be prudent, sage and free from every vice,' Fray Diego said. 'England is blessed in having such a king!' Of course it was! She knew that better than most; she could have said much about Henry's high ideals and chivalrous nature, his learning and his zest for life. If only she could see him, she thought, and know his intentions towards her.

The hours dragged. She filled them with prayer, endless embroidery, reading and walks in the gardens. Maria insisted that she dress becomingly every day – 'just in case the King comes courting'. Ignoring Fray Diego's oft-repeated warnings of the sins of pride and vanity – although surely even he must see that it was all in a good cause – she dressed hopefully, donning yellow damask or the good black velvet. Her hair she wore loose, betokening her maidenhood. She kept looking into her mirror. Did her five years' seniority show? If he came, would Henry still find her attractive?

One morning, towards the dinner hour, Katherine was playing tables with Maria when there was a small commotion outside and the door opened to reveal a tall, dazzlingly handsome, elegant young man in a suit of black silk, who swept her a most gracious bow. She caught her breath, for by the glorious grace of God, it was the King himself – Prince Henry, grown older, the planes of his face chiselled in the lines of manhood, his mass of shining red hair framing his beautiful face, his eyes ardent, hopeful. There was eagerness in every pore of him.

She saw all this before, almost belatedly, she sank to the floor in a deep curtsey; she saw too, to her astonishment, that he had come alone. In that musical voice – deeper now than she remembered – he smilingly dismissed her attendants, then raised her with his own hands, held hers and lifted them to his lips, not letting them go, all the while gazing down into her face. There was, in his grasp and his expression, an authoritative possessiveness that was irresistible. She looked into his piercing blue eyes and was lost.

'Katherine, my lady,' he said. 'We must talk.' He made no move to be seated, but just stood there holding her hands. 'I am sorry I could not come before. There was so much to do, and my councillors go into every why and wherefore. But I made plain to them one thing: that I have waited too long to make you my wife, and I will not wait any longer. My heart is yours, and always has been.' Suddenly, he dropped to one knee and gazed up at her. 'I long to be your servant, and it would complete my happiness if you would consent to be my wife and my Queen.'

Katherine could not speak. This was the moment of which she had dreamed through all those long, penurious, barren years, the moment she had imagined so many times.

'You are my true love, Katherine!' Henry said, with that irresistible boyish enthusiasm. 'I want no other. Say yes! Say you will be mine.'

Could it be true? This glorious, fresh-faced young man, this Adonis – for Nature surely could not have done more for him – still wanted to marry her!

'Yes!' she said through joyful tears. 'Yes! Oh, yes!'

For answer he leapt up, swept her into his arms and kissed her, a kiss so sweet, so tender and so loving that she thought she would swoon from the pleasure of it.

The King stayed to dinner; he did not want to break the moment. They had been kept apart too long, he declared. They had years of catching up to do.

Katherine could not quite believe that it was all happening. There was Fray Diego, blessing them both before saying grace, with Katherine momentarily wondering how she could ever have felt attracted to him; and Maria and the other maids blushing as the King paid them compliments; and even the dour chamberlain – now become instantly obsequious – unbending sufficiently to join in a toast to their happiness.

This was the culmination of all her hopes. God had seen fit to answer her prayers, and she was filled to the brim with thankfulness. She was to be Queen of England, raised by this magnificent young man to be the bride of his heart and the mother of his heirs. Those who had scorned her and tried to humiliate her would now have to defer to her – she tried not to relish the prospect, but she was only human. The days of want were gone for good; very shortly she would be the wife of the richest king ever to reign in England.

She apologised for the poor fare on the table – pottage, of which she was heartily sick, coarse bread, a cheese and a dish of cherries.

'No matter, no matter,' Henry said, waving away her concerns. 'I love cherries. And after today, you shall never be in want again.' He raised her hand to his lips.

With his great, silk-clad frame seated at table, he made the room feel small; he filled it with his presence; he put everyone at ease. He was quick to laugh and talked to her people in a friendly, knowledgeable way. In no time at all Katherine was laughing out loud at his jests.

'Here's another!' he said, grinning. 'A knight returned from the northern shires, bringing his King many prisoners and much gold. The King asked him what he had been doing. He said he had been plundering and pillaging, burning all the villages of the King's enemies in the north. The King was appalled. "But I have no enemies in the north," he said. "You do now," said the knight.' Henry roared with laughter.

Katherine laughed too, unable to tear her gaze from him as he sat there at his ease, his quick and penetrating eyes repeatedly straying in her direction, making her blush all the way down to her pearl-edged neckline. Her people were relaxed now in his company; she had noticed this before, his common touch. No one within its compass could fail to love him. He was more like a good fellow than a king.

She could not quite believe that he was hers. She had been told often enough while she was growing up that she was a great prize for any man, but the long years of struggle had eroded her confidence. She was twenty-three; Henry was almost eighteen. Not so many years' difference, and clearly it did not matter to him. He could have had his pick of every princess in Christendom, but he had chosen her, loved her, and waited for her, just as she had done for him. And now he had rescued her from poverty, ignominy and humiliation. She was ready to give her passionate, loving heart unreservedly to this glorious young man – her King, her knight errant, her lover.

In the afternoon they sat together in a tree-shaded arbour in the gardens, for they had much to talk about and plan.

'We must be married immediately!' Henry said. 'The coronation is planned for midsummer, and I want you to share it with me as my Queen, sweet Katherine.'

He broke off a pink rosebud and gave it to her. Raising it to her lips, she smiled at him. She wanted him to go on talking. She loved listening to him. Every word from his lips was as a pearl of wisdom to her.

'You know my father wanted me to marry you,' Henry said. 'On his deathbed, he gave me his express command that I should do so. Not that I needed any, for my mind had long been made up.' He gazed at Katherine, his eyes warm. 'My Council are also in favour. They extolled your virtues; they said you are the image of your mother, and have the wisdom and greatness of mind that win the respect of nations. They told me that in every way you would be the perfect Queen. But Katherine, know this: that whatever anyone else has said, and whatever good reasons there are for our marriage, *I* desire you above all women; I love you, and I have longed to wed you for yourself.'

His arm had crept along the back of the stone seat; his hand was resting lightly on her shoulder. She had never dreamed that a man's touch could have such a powerful effect. Nothing in her life had ever truly awakened her to the realities of physical love. Now she understood why the poets and minstrels made so much of it, why people were ready to languish, die or kill for it. And a light touch was as nothing to what was to come when they were married . . . Her heart began racing at the thought.

'I am sorry for the way my father treated you,' Henry said, his face becoming more sober. 'I protested about it many times, but he would not listen. Nothing I said carried any weight with him. I looked out for you, although I knew he was keeping us apart. I heard from others how bravely you coped with a difficult situation. Believe me, Katherine, if I could have rescued you, I would. I hated my father for what he was doing to you.' From the passion in his voice, she guessed he had hated the late King for many other things besides.

'But that is all in the past,' Henry said firmly. 'I am not my father! We are in a new age. There is money aplenty in the treasury, and that gives me the power to make changes. My father dreamed of a new Arthurian age, and it was my poor brother who was to usher it in, but I will do it in his place. It will be a new age of chivalry! I mean to revive England's ancient claim to the throne of France. I will make such a war on the French that Agincourt will seem like a skirmish, and I swear to you, Katherine, that one day I will have you crowned at Rheims.' His eyes were alight at the prospect of such a glorious future.

'My father will support you,' she assured him, thrilling at his words. 'France is no friend to Spain.'

'Together England and Spain will be invincible!' Henry said, his eyes dancing with fervour. 'King Ferdinand has already written to me, urging me to marry you without delay. He has promised that your dowry will be punctually paid. His banker, Signor Grimaldi, has put the arrangements in hand.'

His news burst the bubble of Katherine's happiness. Her plate and jewels! Dare she tell Henry how depleted they were? She began trembling, fearing that, with her confession, he might well change his mind about marrying her.

'Sir,' she faltered, 'part of it was to be paid in jewels and plate. I had to sell some, to buy food and other necessities.'

Henry leaned forward and kissed her. 'We will not waste time over trifles,' he reassured her. 'The plate and jewels are of no importance.'

And with those few words he banished the anxiety that had been consuming her for years. Never had woman felt so loved!

'I cannot thank you enough for your understanding,' Katherine said, kissing him back, 'and I am deeply thankful that the alliance between our countries is to be preserved.'

'And I am thankful that you are to be my wife and Queen!' Henry said, bending forward and kissing her soundly on the lips. 'I love that pretty Spanish accent of yours. You are the most beautiful creature in the world.' He pulled off her velvet hood and she shivered in pleasure as he ran his hand down the length of her hair, which was now so long that she could sit on it. Then he took her in his arms and held her close. Willingly she surrendered to his kisses, thankful that the trees gave them privacy and that the King's Yeomen of the Guard were standing watch at the entrance to the privy garden. A lifetime would not be long enough to express the love and gratitude she felt.

There was much to be done, and all in haste. An army of craftsmen and labourers were set to work refurbishing the long-empty queen's apartments for Katherine. Furniture and tapestries were delivered from the Royal Wardrobe, painters were refreshing the decorations, and linens and napery were purchased, all of the finest quality. Henry was busy appointing a great household for Katherine, numbering one hundred and sixty persons, and many of those who had faithfully served his mother had been recalled to serve her. It was to be headed by a new chamberlain, William Blount, Lord Mountjoy, a personable man in his early thirties who had studied under Erasmus in Paris and was now renowned as a friend of the great scholar and a learned humanist in his own right.

Mountjoy's assured manner inspired confidence. Katherine had no doubt that this urbane, cultivated man would run her household with effortless ease. And she was delighted to learn that Mountjoy had fallen in love with one of her maids, Agnes de Vanagas, and proposed marriage.

She was so grateful to Henry for allowing her to retain most of the Spanish officials who had been in her train since she came to England.

He liked Fray Diego and approved of him staying on as her chaplain. Another Observant Friar, the devout and gentle Jorge de Atheca, who had served as her clerk since her coming to England, was now promoted to the post of household chaplain. Dr Alcaraz was going back to Spain, for family reasons, but her other physicians, the patrician Dr de la Saa and the avuncular Dr Guersye, would remain to look after her.

In her happiness Katherine could find it in her heart to forgive those servants who had been disrespectful and insubordinate when her fortunes had been at a low ebb. Henry had readily paid the arrears of salary due to them, and she had asked her father to chastise them for their boldness and then pardon them.

'If it pleases you, I wish to keep Maria, and she desires more than anything to remain with me,' she had entreated Henry.

'You may keep whoever you wish, sweetheart, as long as you have some English ladies waiting on you.'

'I should like that very much,' she said, kissing him in gratitude.

She was pleased with the ladies-in-waiting he chose for her, and delighted that Margaret Pole was among them.

'I know you have an affection for her,' Henry said, 'and she is of royal blood and highly suitable.'

'You could not have chosen better!' she cried, kissing him again.

Margaret Pole had changed. Widowhood had taken flesh from her already slender frame and etched lines on her face, and she was paler than Katherine remembered, but every bit as warm and kind-hearted as when they had been together at Ludlow, and Katherine quickly found that they were as comfortable with each other as if they had last met only a week ago, rather than seven years.

Three other ladies-in-waiting were descended from the Plantagenet royal house. Elizabeth, Lady FitzWalter, and Anne, Lady Hastings, were the sisters of Henry's distant cousin, the mighty, over-proud and bombastic Duke of Buckingham. The Countess of Surrey was Buckingham's feisty daughter, Elizabeth Stafford, whom Katherine liked enormously. They were all to serve as great ladies of her household, alongside the countesses of Suffolk, Oxford, Shrewsbury, Essex and Derby.

'I would also recommend the wife of my comptroller, Sir Thomas Parr,' Henry said. 'He and his family have given excellent service to the Crown, and my grandmother, the Lady Margaret, thought highly of them. Thomas's mother and grandmother were ladies-in-waiting, and while I know it is not usual to appoint one who is not a noblewoman, I think you will like her.'

Katherine did. Maud Parr was a warm and delightful lady, unusually literate and learned. The two women took to each other on sight and found they had much in common. Like Katherine, Maud was fortunate enough to love the husband chosen for her. She was seventeen years old, curly-haired, pretty and elegant. Margaret Pole got on very well with her, despite the twenty-year age gap between them, as did Maria, who preferred the approachable Maud to most of the other great ladies of the household, since they tended to be much on their dignity.

Once the word was out that the Queen was to have thirty maids-of-honour, there arose a great clamour for places in her household, with the highest families in the land vying like hucksters to secure appointments for their daughters. To Katherine's relief, Henry did not object when she asked if she might also retain her Spanish maids; all he wanted to do was please her, he declared. He approved several names himself, and appointed some who had done good service to his mother. One was French: Jane Popincourt, a petite, glossy-haired lady in her late twenties with a neat, precise manner and an elegant taste in dress. Katherine would have preferred not to have a Frenchwoman in her household, but Henry thought highly of Jane, who had served both his mother and his sister Mary, and Katherine made no protest but welcomed the woman for his sake.

The rest he allowed her to choose herself – with his advice – and when she interviewed the likeliest candidates, she looked above all for virtue and beauty, so that her maids would be ornaments to their mistress whenever she appeared in public, and their exemplary conduct would be a credit to her. She ordered that the lucky selected few wear only black and white, in contrast to the deep shades of purple, crimson and tawny that she favoured herself.

'Your virtuous conduct is crucial,' she told them, when they were all assembled before her. 'Your families expect me to find you good husbands, so no breath of scandal must touch you. Remember that it would reflect very badly on me too.'

They nodded earnestly, plainly proud to have been chosen among so much competition, and aware of their good luck.

'You must choose a badge as queen,' Henry told Katherine.

'It will be the pomegranate, which is *granada* in Spanish and was adopted by my mother after the fall of Granada as a symbol of the reconquest.'

'And it is a symbol of fertility,' Henry said, smiling. 'Very apt, for I hope we will have many sons!'

'I have longed for children,' Katherine admitted, thrilling at his words.

'God willing, your prayers will be answered soon!' Henry drew her to him and kissed her. 'The sooner we make an heir to England, the better!'

She blushed at that.

She chose for her motto the device 'Humble and Loyal', and soon it was blazoned, with an array of pomegranates, and castles for Castile, everywhere in the King's palaces, where carpenters, stonemasons and embroiderers were also busy chiselling, carving and stitching her initials and Henry's, 'H' and 'K', on every available surface.

Another army of tailors, seamstresses, silkwomen and goldsmiths had been set to work on a sumptuous new wardrobe for Katherine, most of it in the English fashion. Only rarely now did she wear a farthingale or put on Spanish dress. Her days were a busy round of choosing fabrics and having fittings. Every day new gowns arrived, to be hung on pegs or laid out on the bed for her inspection. After years of wearing an increasingly shabby and sparse wardrobe, she took a near-sensual pleasure in adorning herself once more in rich materials – glossy silk, heavy damask, thick-piled velvet, stiff with raised gold embroidery, and royal cloth of gold.

Henry lavished jewels upon her. Already he had given her the crown jewels of the queens of England, pieces that had been worn by former consorts, which were not her own but royal property, and would one day be passed down to her son's wife. They included the ancient crown of the Saxon Queen Edith, wife of St Edward the Confessor, a pretty diadem fashioned of silver-gilt and enriched with garnets, pearls and sapphires. There were diamonds, necklaces, rings, earrings and many fine pieces. Most were old-fashioned, of course, but Katherine appreciated them not just for their great value and their historical worth, but because many had been the gifts of devoted kings to their beloved wives. There were elaborate collars here that she had last seen around the neck of her beloved mother-in-law, Queen Elizabeth. There was a garnet cross that had been the gift of Edward III to his adored Queen Philippa. And there was a gold reliquary that had once belonged to Eleanor of Castile, whose grief-stricken husband had set up the memorial crosses she had seen on her arrival in London so many years ago. Yes, these jewels were very precious indeed. She tried on Queen Edith's crown with great reverence.

She cherished too the jewels that Henry had given her as personal gifts: ropes of pearls; an array of rings; diamond pendants; crucifixes studded with gemstones; brooches fashioned to depict St George, England's patron saint, or the letters 'IHS', representing Christ, which she proudly wore pinned to the centre of her bodice. The gift she loved best, because Henry had suggested its exquisite design, was a large cross set with sapphires and three pendant pearls. He also gave her some of his mother's personal jewels, and her missal too, and in it he wrote, 'I am yours for ever, Henry R.' Her joy was overflowing.

This time there would be no cathedral bells pealing, no crowds and no feasting. It was to be a private wedding, for Henry and Katherine were still officially in mourning for the late King. They had decided that it would take place, auspiciously, on the feast day of St Barnabas, the patron saint of peacemakers, for certainly their marriage would bring peace.

Early that morning, Katherine entered her closet at Greenwich, attended by a beaming Maria and some of the new English ladies, all in white. She had donned the new wedding gown, a ceremonious affair of silver tissue that belled out over her farthingale, and her long hair flowed free under a circlet of gold, a wedding gift from her future husband.

Henry came clad in a suit of white Florentine velvet with raised embroidery in gold thread, in company with a few of his lords and gentlemen. At the small altar Archbishop Warham was waiting to perform the ceremony. The little oratory was filled with the scent of June roses – a scent that Katherine was forever after to associate with this wondrous time in her life.

Henry bowed to her, his eyes telling her that she looked beautiful, and she curtseyed. They knelt on rich cushions, and as the Archbishop pronounced them man and wife and blessed them, Katherine was filled with a strong sense of destiny, and overwhelmed with love and gratitude for the young man kneeling next to her. When she stood up, she was Queen of England, and Henry was looking down on her with adoration in his eyes.

Laughing joyously they led their small wedding party out of the palace, through the gardens and along the lime walk to the chapel of the Observant Friars for the nuptial Mass. Then it was back to the palace for a quiet dinner in Henry's privy chamber, where Katherine sat beside him under the cloth of estate and their food was served on gold plates with great ceremony by impassive pages on bended knee, with lords and ladies standing in attendance around them.

No one had said anything about her being publicly put to bed with Henry, and she had not liked to ask him about it. In fact, she was praying that they would be allowed some privacy.

She need not have worried. As the cloth was lifted and they stood up to have the crumbs brushed off their clothes, Henry smiled down at her. As soon as the servitors were out of earshot, he bent forward and murmured in her ear, 'I will come to your chamber tonight, by the secret stair. It leads up from my rooms to yours. Until then, my Queen!'

Katherine had not even known that there was such a stair.

'It's behind the arras, in the corner,' Henry told her. 'Our marriage is not proclaimed yet. I thought it meet to allow us a few days of privacy to get to know each other.' His intent expression set her cheeks aflame; there was no mistaking his meaning.

*

He came before darkness had fallen, when the late-evening air smelt cool and sweet, and the trees silhouetted against the dying light lent the gardens below her window an air of enchantment. He came full of youth and vigour, wearing a trailing damask robe embroidered in gold over his fine lawn nightshirt. He came like a lover, gathering Katherine in his arms and tumbling her on the bed.

'The candles,' she murmured through his kisses.

'Let's leave them,' he said, laying her back against the pillows. 'I want to see you.'

Katherine had expected to feel embarrassed, but she was carried away by Henry's insistent eagerness, and began kissing him back with fervour, surprising herself by her body's response to his caresses, which grew ever more bold. Soon they were lying naked together on the velvet counterpane, lost in the joy of discovering each other fully.

'I've said it before, but it's true – you are the most beautiful creature in the world,' Henry breathed.

Katherine took delight in exploring a man's body for the first time, and in his burgeoning desire, hard and insistent against her. Then Henry reared up and positioned himself on top of her, parting her thighs and thrusting between them. But he was not yet inside her, just pushing to one side, then the other, which awoke in her the memory of Arthur moving uselessly against her all those years ago. But Henry was no Arthur – he was hard and ready, and all that was needed was for her to reach down her hand and guide him to where he should be. As he thrust again and slid inside her, she felt a hot, stinging pain, and gasped, but he seemed oblivious. Immediately he tensed, and suddenly there was a throbbing sensation and a warm, sticky wetness flooding her.

When he had withdrawn from her and lay back panting, he flung out an arm and drew her towards him.

'How I do love you, Katherine!' he whispered. 'My Katherine!'

'And I love you, my Henry,' she answered. She lay blissful in the crook of his arm, a true wife at last. The soreness he had left behind mattered little. What had surprised her was how quickly their coupling had taken place. But soon she was to be surprised afresh, because as the night passed Henry wanted to do it again – and again. And suddenly, the third time, she felt desire awakening in her, like a flower opening out, and then – oh, the wonder of it! – an explosion of the purest pleasure she could ever have imagined, followed by a great calm and a deep sense of well-being. Now she understood what being one flesh meant. If she had loved Henry before, she loved him a thousand times more now for giving her the gift of such joy. And what was so wonderful was that they had all their lives ahead of them to share this rapture . . .

Part Two

The Queen of England

Chapter 10

1509

When she rose from her marriage bed in the morning Katherine was surprised to find that, although the sheets were stained, there was no blood. But Henry, lying there watching her appreciatively, did not mention it, or even seem to notice, so she decided that she had been lucky. Obviously not every woman bled the first time.

Covering her nakedness with her nightgown, she sat down beside her new husband on the bed and put on her gable hood.

'Now that I am wed I must cover my hair,' she said.

'You do not have to,' Henry said. 'It is the privilege of a queen to let her hair flow free like a virgin. Your virginity is symbolic, of course.' He grinned. 'And I love to see your hair.' He drew her back into his arms.

'Marriage is merry sport!' he whispered in her ear, nuzzling her. And then, of course, all was to do again . . .

'Did you like that, Katherine?' Henry asked, some time later.

'How could I not?' she giggled.

'You are the first woman I have ever known,' he said, gazing at her.

That was unexpected. 'I am glad,' she told him. 'I imagined that ladies had been throwing themselves at your feet! You are the King, after all.'

'You know there were few ladies at my father's court after my mother died,' he said. 'And he made me lead a cloistered life. There was never an opportunity for dalliance. But it was you I wanted all along, Katherine. Beside you, all other ladies were wanting. And now I have you; by God's good grace, I am blessed indeed!' He looked at her intently. 'I must know. Did Arthur ever . . . ?'

'No, Henry. He was too ill, the poor boy.'

'Then all their carping was for nothing,' Henry muttered.

'What carping?'

'Oh, Warham and a few councillors, bleating on about our marriage being forbidden by Scripture.'

'But we have the Pope's dispensation!' she cried. Nothing must mar this new-found bliss.

'So I told them. Do not worry, my sweet. All is well. Think you I would have married you if there had been the slightest doubt? I would not have risked your future, or mine. But the Pope has given us his blessing, and now you are my wife in the eyes of God.' And he began kissing her fears away.

Over the next three days they enjoyed a precious period of privacy. Katherine was utterly swept away by the new joy in her life, and forgot about that brief conversation. Her head was too full of Henry, her body surprised by the unsuspected pleasure he had awoken in her. They spent most of the time in bed, even taking their meals there. When they were not loving each other they played cards, dice or backgammon, or made music. Henry was an excellent musician, she discovered. He could play on almost every instrument, and was especially accomplished on the lute, the recorder and the virginals. Lying back on the pillows, Katherine watched him singing from the book, reading the music effortlessly. He could compose too, as she well knew.

'Do you remember, Katherine, the day we were betrothed, and I promised to make a song for you?' he asked.

'How could I forget?' she answered.

'Well, how like you this?' And he sang in his high, perfect tenor:

'Without discord
And both accord
Now let us be;
Both hearts alone
To set in one
Best seemeth me.

164

For when one soul
Is in the dole
Of love's pain,
Then help must have
Himself to save
And love to obtain.

Wherefore now we
That lovers be,
Let us now pray,
Once love sure
For to procure
Without denay.
Where love so sues
There no heart rues,
But condescend;
If contrary,
What remedy?
God it amend.'

Her eyes filled with tears when he sang of their being lovers, for no word could have described it better. She loved the way he thought about things, the sensitivity he showed in both his lovemaking and his verses. She loved the fresh, clean smell of him, his innate fastidiousness, the newly washed linen he put on every day. It was scented with the herbs in which his laundress laid it away, a scent she would always associate with her husband. She truly was the luckiest woman alive!

When it was proclaimed that they were man and wife, she made her first appearance at court as Henry's Queen, wearing a blue mourning gown with a low-slung golden girdle, and a rich mantle lined with ermine.

'From now on, my Queen, you will be at my side at all state and court ceremonies,' Henry told her, his eyes alight with pride.

That night he told her to be ready for him, so she dismissed her ladies and sat down on the great tester bed to await his arrival, expecting him to emerge from behind the arras at any moment. But then she heard the tramp of several feet approaching, and suddenly the door to her bedchamber was flung open and he came in, wearing his damask robe. Behind him, she heard the outer door to her apartments shut.

'Why did you not come up the secret stair?' she asked.

'I was escorted by my guards and two of my gentlemen,' he answered. 'People know we are married now, and it is customary in England for kings to be seen to visit their wives. It is a matter of public interest, you understand. The succession must be seen to be assured. Don't worry, my guards will remain outside until I am ready to leave.' He grinned. 'They might have a long wait!'

They made love; at first Katherine found it a little hard to relax, but she told herself she would get used to this new arrangement. It was not for her to question English customs. Then the familiar joy overwhelmed her, and she forgot all else except Henry's touch and his melodious voice murmuring love talk in her ear.

Henry looked magnificent. His robe was crimson velvet trimmed with ermine, and beneath it he wore a coat of raised gold embroidered with diamonds, rubies, emeralds, great pearls and other previous stones. Katherine was wearing her wedding gown. It was midsummer, and they were seated on cushions in the royal barge, which was gliding majestically along the Thames surrounded by a flotilla of gaily decorated boats. Behind them was Greenwich, ahead London and the Tower, where they would lie that night; Henry had explained that it was customary for English monarchs to lodge in the Tower before they were crowned.

Crowds lined the riverbanks, waving and cheering as they passed. Henry acknowledged them with smiles, nods and a raised hand, and Katherine bowed her head to left and right, touched by the people's acclaim. It was the same all along the river.

'They love you!' Henry turned to her. 'They love you not only because this marriage has strengthened our trade, but for yourself too!'

'I am humbled that they have so taken me to their hearts,' she said.

They alighted at the Court Gate and entered the Tower by the Byward postern, where they were received by the Constable and his Yeomen Warders, and thence conducted in procession along Water Lane to the royal apartments. The court crowded into the ancient rooms in the Lanthorn and Wardrobe towers, where, in the afternoon, the King created twenty-four Knights of the Bath, with Katherine seated beside him.

She did not like the Tower. It was not just the knowledge that the hapless Earl of Warwick had been imprisoned there a decade ago; there was something sinister about the place, and she was glad that they were spending only one night there – and that Henry had spent a fortune in refurbishing the gloomy old chambers. Even so, she disliked the Queen's lodging; the June sunlight did not penetrate far beyond the narrow windows, and there was a miasma of sadness in the very air. Of course, Queen Elizabeth had died here. No wonder the apartments felt dismal, despite the rich new furnishings.

That evening, as Henry and Katherine took the air along the high walkway that led from the Wakefield Tower to the Lanthorn Tower, and looked out over the inner and inmost wards, Henry was in such a buoyant mood that Katherine forbore to speak of her aversion to the Tower. But then he turned to her.

'Tonight, my love, I will not be coming to you. I wish to keep vigil before my crowning, in the Chapel of St John.' He had taken her up to the top floor of the massive keep, Caesar's Tower, and shown her the exquisite little chapel earlier.

Her heart sank, but she smiled and said, of course, that was only fitting. One of the things she loved most about Henry was his piety. Like her, he heard five Masses every day, and he had instituted the habit of coming every evening to her chamber so that they could hear Vespers together. Theology was a passion with him, and he basked in the reputation of being an acknowledged authority on religious doctrine. His faith was pure and fervent, and she understood his need to keep this vigil.

That night she chose Mary Roos, one of her maids, to sleep on a pallet bed in her chamber, instructing her to leave it discreetly, if by any chance the King came. Then she tried to sleep, but the fate of young Warwick was preying on her mind. She wondered where he had been held, and if he had understood the consequences of his plotting and what awaited him. She shuddered, imagining his terror on the day they had come for him. Then her mind turned to the fate of those two little princes, done to death in the Tower by the wicked King Richard a quarter of a century ago. No one spoke of it even now, save in whispers. She shivered, although the bed was warm. The bones of those children were here somewhere, and yet to be discovered . . .

It was a long time before she drifted off.

She awakened to the sound of sobbing. It was still dark.

'Mary?' she said softly. There was no reply, yet the sobbing did not cease.

Katherine sat up. There was a woman seated in a chair in the corner, her face in her hands, her shoulders shaking. She was not Mary. Her dress looked black, and her hood was a strange shape.

'Who's there?' Katherine asked, wide awake now and wondering which one of her women would have needed to take refuge in her room to have a good cry – and why.

The woman ignored her and went on weeping, obviously in great torment. Katherine leaned over the side of her bed, wondering if Mary had been woken too, but she saw that her maid was still soundly asleep.

'Whoever you are, please let me help you!' Katherine said. Again the woman took no notice. Katherine's eyes were becoming accustomed to the darkness, and she could see that although her visitor was wearing a hood in the familiar gable shape, its lappets were very short – a fashion she had never seen.

She still could not get a glimpse of the woman's face, for it remained buried in her hands. Clearly she was in the most terrible distress.

Katherine slid out of bed, intending to touch the woman gently on the shoulder and rouse her, but then a strange thing happened. The figure was just not there any more. There was no chair where she had been sitting, and the only sound in the room was Mary Roos's even breathing. Katherine stared at the place for a few moments, then climbed back into bed, puzzled, and not a little shaken. Had she been dreaming?

The next morning she was glad to hear the door close behind her on the Queen's lodging. And there, banishing the last vestiges of shadows, was Henry, ebullient as ever, glittering in gold and gemstones, eager to make his state entry into London.

'I cannot wait to show you off to my subjects!' he said, planting a hearty kiss on her cheek. The tournament ground at the Tower was packed with lords, ladies, officers of state, royal servants in the green and white Tudor colours, and a host of clergy, all scrambling to get into their places in the grand procession. Henry mounted his horse, then Katherine climbed into a litter dressed with cloth of gold, to which were harnessed two white palfreys, and thus they rode forth, through the roaring crowds who lined their route, which wound from Tower Hill to Cheapside, Temple Bar and the Strand, and finally to the Palace of Westminster. The streets were hung with fine tapestries, the conduits flowed with wine, and on every corner there stood priests swinging censers. For Katherine, the day held vivid echoes of her state entry into London, nearly eight years before.

That night, exalted at the prospect of their coronation on the morrow, Midsummer Day, she and Henry retired to the vast Painted Chamber, which was decorated with ancient murals of the coronation of St Edward the Confessor and biblical battles. A fine oak bed, carved with symbols of royalty and fertility, stood beneath them.

'My parents' marriage bed,' Henry said. 'It is called the Paradise Bed.'

The bed was adorned with rich damask curtains and had been sumptuously made up, but the chamber felt dank even on this warm June night. There were ominous patches of green mould discolouring the reds, blues, silvers and golds of the murals, and a damp miasma arose from the Thames.

Henry turned to Katherine.

'Hallowing sets a king apart from the ordinary species of men,' he said. 'Tomorrow I will be different – anointed, crowned, invested

169

with divine authority. It is a strange and daunting thought. My father always said that kings are given wisdom and insights denied to mere mortals.'

'What is even more important, my Henry, is that you rule with the love of your people,' Katherine replied, taking his hand. 'And you have that in abundance already. The whole world is rejoicing; they are glad to have such a king.'

Henry leaned forward and kissed her. 'You would say that, sweetheart!'

'It's true, and I am not the only one. I watch and I see. The people love you for your youth, your beauty, your courage, and most of all for your common touch. It is not something one learns, but a gift. They know you understand the things that touch their lives. If you go on as you have begun, you will hold their love and loyalty all your life.'

'I mean to do it, Katherine! And you must help and support me.'

'I will always be there for you, Henry,' she vowed.

He smiled at her. 'Will you come with me to St Stephen's Chapel and keep vigil?'

'Are you not tired? You kept vigil last night.'

'I feel it is a sacred duty.'

'Then I will come.'

They made their way hand in hand to the chapel and knelt together before the altar, which was lit only by the lamp glowing in the sanctuary. Above them tall Gothic windows soared to the vaulted roof, but all was in shadow, and the night was still. Katherine's senses were assailed by the lingering smell of incense and the sound of Henry's low voice intoning prayers. She tried to pray herself, but for once the words would not come. She was too conscious of Henry kneeling devoutly beside her, golden head bowed, hands clasped together – the epitome of a Christian king.

They went to bed at four, but Katherine felt little the worse for the lack of sleep, even when she was woken early. She rose feeling refreshed, to hear Mass with Henry. As she again knelt beside him at the altar rail, she glimpsed his face, exalted, rapt, gazing up at the painted statue of the Virgin and Child, and knew that he was ready for his great task, for the years of kingship that lay ahead.

When Henry had left for his own lodging to be made ready by his lords and gentlemen, Katherine's ladies attired her in an exquisite gown of white satin embroidered in gold. They left her hair falling loose down her back, and on her head they placed a coronet set with Orient pearls and precious stones. Then they lifted on her shoulders the crimson mantle lined with ermine.

Henry was waiting for her.

'You are beautiful,' he breathed. 'I'm so very proud of you.' Then he handed her into her litter, and took his place under a canopy of estate borne by the five barons of the Cinque Ports. The long procession moved forward, with Katherine's officers and ladies following her in chariots and on palfreys, and the King coming last. They advanced slowly along a bright scarlet runner that had been laid from the palace to the great west door of Westminster Abbey, and on either side there were dense crowds, rejoicing loudly.

For Katherine, the day of her coronation passed in a haze. There were so many moments to savour and treasure, so many images that she would cherish in memory. Henry seated in majesty in the venerable coronation chair; the sparkle of the jewels in St Edward the Confessor's crown as it was placed on his anointed head; the shouts of acclaim from the assembled lords spiritual and temporal, and head after head bending in homage. She would never forget the sacred moment of her own anointing, or the moment when the Archbishop of Canterbury reverently placed the heavy gold diadem glittering with sapphires, rubies and pearls on her head. Her heart was full; with all her being she was ready to dedicate her life to God and to the service of her husband's realm.

When they at last emerged from the abbey, undoubted and sanctified king and queen, their crowns on their heads, their hands joined, the people went wild. The red runner had gone, ripped to shreds, they were told later, by those greedy for mementos. They walked through the throng of well-wishers to Westminster Hall, where, beneath the lofty hammerbeam roof, they mounted the steps to the high table and sat down to their coronation feast.

Katherine thrilled to see Sir Robert Dymoke, the King's champion, ride on horseback into the hall, daring anyone to challenge his master's right to the throne. It was an awe-inspiring moment, and Dymoke – whose family, Henry explained, had been champions of England for over a century – performed his office with a flourish, casting down his gauntlet on the floor and glaring around him, daring anyone to pick it up. No one came forward, of course, and Henry merrily presented Sir Robert with a golden cup. Then the feasting began.

There followed days of celebrations. Henry loved nothing more than a tournament, and had arranged for a series of them to be held in the gardens of the Palace of Westminster. Katherine sat beside him in a wooden pavilion hung with tapestries and decorated with crowns, roses and pomegranates. With her ladies clustering behind her, she presided over the jousts in true courtly fashion, while beside her Henry roared his approbation of the victors, impatient to be among them. So far he had heeded his councillors' pleas not to put his royal person at risk until the succession was assured. Katherine hoped fervently that before long it would be.

She felt for Henry, forced to watch impatiently and cheer on his friends, the privileged young men whom he had appointed gentlemen of his privy chamber. Heading his chamber was his fair-haired Groom of the Stool, William Compton, who had been Henry's page since infancy and was now closer to him than most. Then there was Charles Brandon, one of the comeliest men at court, and who, even at close range, could have been taken for the King, he was so like him. Brandon owed his position at court to the fact that his father had died fighting for the late King at Bosworth. He was so charming that Katherine could not but warm to him. Compton, she felt, was over-amorous with her ladies, and a dubious influence on the King, yet his courtesy towards her was unfailing.

Feast followed feast, and the days were a bright whirl of pageantry, dancing, hunting and hawking, and at every event she and Henry donned new clothes. It seemed that the treasury was as bottomless as Henry's love for her.

He could not stop telling people of the joy he had found with her.

'It is clear that His Grace adores you,' Fray Diego observed.

'And I adore him,' Katherine smiled. 'I never dreamed there could be such happiness in this world.' She had been schooled to gravity and decorousness, and had had little cause for rejoicing in the past seven years, but now, freed at last from care and constraints, she gave herself up to love and to life's pleasures.

'Your Highness looks in high health,' the friar said, gazing at her approvingly.

'I am in the greatest gladness and contentment there ever was,' Katherine told him. She felt better than she ever had. Gone were her ailments, gone her depression.

One afternoon she bent down and watched over Henry's shoulder as he wrote to her father: 'My wife and I are as much in love as any two creatures can be. Her virtues daily more and more shine forth and increase so much, that if we were still free, I would choose her for my wife before all others.' She kissed him for that.

'I have never met your father, but I desire to serve him as if he were my own,' Henry said. It touched her to hear him. Since her marriage, she had felt as if the kingdom of England had become a part of her father's dominions, and it was her sincere wish that Henry would be guided by Ferdinand.

Her heart full of gratitude, she herself sent a letter to her father. 'I want to thank you for seeing me so well married, and to a man I love so much more than myself,' she wrote, 'not only because he is my husband, but also because he is the true son of your Highness, and desires to show greater obedience and love to serve you than ever son had to his father.'

'I rejoice to find that you love each other so supremely,' Ferdinand replied, 'and hope you may be happy to the end of your life. A good marriage is not only for the blessing of the man and woman who take each other, but also to the world outside.' And this *was* a good marriage, she knew it. It could not fail to be, for it was built upon a sure foundation of love, respect and sound political sense.

Her father had made it quite clear that, now she was married, her chief role in England was to represent his interests. She was to be an unofficial ambassador.

'My father is a great king,' she said to Henry one night, as they lay entangled in the sheets, relaxing after making love. 'He will always give you wise advice.'

Henry gazed into her eyes. His were of a piercing, intense blue. 'I intend to place myself entirely in his hands,' he murmured. 'I am very hearty for his service!'

It delighted Katherine to see how deeply Henry loved and respected her. He did nothing without her approval. He often brought his councillors and foreign ambassadors to see her, saying, 'The Queen must hear this.' 'This will please the Queen,' he would enthuse, hastening to show her some letter or book he had received. Soon he would do nothing without first discussing it with her and asking for her father's opinion.

Katherine herself met frequently with Luis Caroz. She thought he would be pleased to see her enjoying such influence, but as they walked together in the rose-scented gardens, he uttered a word of warning.

'These English are insular,' he said. 'They dislike strangers from other lands interfering in their affairs. The King's councillors fear your power over him. I have heard it said that England will shortly be ruled at one remove by Spain.'

'But I would do nothing against England's interests,' Katherine protested, a little shocked.

'Of course not,' Caroz soothed. 'Your Grace is much loved here, that is plain, but if you are thought to be putting Spain's interests before those of England, you would incur much hatred.'

'I would never do that,' she assured him. 'And surely they are one and the same. King Ferdinand and King Henry are eager to see France conquered. My lord hates the French as much as my father does.' She did not tell Caroz that she had persuaded Henry to enter into a secret agreement with Ferdinand to undermine King Louis's power in Italy, which she had to admit would not benefit Henry much, but would be greatly to Ferdinand's advantage. After all, it could not hurt England.

And she said nothing of Ferdinand's instruction that she herself was to communicate all Henry's plans to him. Henry trusted her to do the right thing, and as she returned to his side, to watch England's finest young knights vie for honour, she knew for a certainty that through her the interests of both kingdoms would be well served.

And so that brilliant, golden summer passed, an endless round of pleasure, entertainment and hospitality. Henry revelled in displaying the riches at his disposal. He kept a splendid court; it literally glittered with jewels and gold and silver. Hundreds of people flocked to it – gold-chained nobles, lavishly dressed, ambitious young men, officers of the King's and Queen's households, Privy councillors puffed up with their own importance, lawyers, churchmen, ambassadors from many lands – and most of them did nothing but jostle for preferment, eager to take advantage of their new King's open-handedness.

Henry was full of his plans to build new palaces or renovate his existing ones. He did not know exactly how many he owned.

'Dozens!' he said. 'And I will make them all fitting places to receive my lovely Queen!' She was forever to associate the smell of sawdust and fresh paint with the early years of her marriage.

Katherine remembered the Spanish court as being very formal, yet here the high ceremonial was unprecedented, for Henry was determined to be an even more magnificent sovereign than his father. But he knew – to a fine art – when not to stand on ceremony. It was what drew people to him. Katherine had been amazed to see him playing at dice with the master of his wine cellar, which her father would never have condescended to do. And she would not forget the astonishment on the faces of some Venetian envoys when, while walking with her in the gardens one day, Henry saw them watching him from a window and went over and joked and laughed with them, even speaking a little Italian.

'This is a great honour,' they told him, clearly unable to believe that a king could be so free and easy, so companionable. He really was the most gentle and affable prince in the world.

Henry was at his ease too with the numerous scholars he welcomed to his court, many of them from Italy. Often, when he and Katherine dined, doctors, philosophers and divines surrounded their table, and the conversation was brilliant.

'The wealth and civilisation of the world are here,' one awed Venetian visitor observed to Katherine, his gaze taking in the King engrossed in discussion with a host of soberly clad men and the contrasting magnificence of the presence chamber, its tapestries, its gilded ceiling and the carved frieze of gambolling cherubs on its walls.

'I wish to surround myself with learned men,' Henry told Katherine as they sat together in the palace library one afternoon. 'I would rather be with them than with anyone else, saving yourself.' He could have been a scholar himself, she realised. He loved to debate, and was preparing himself for this evening's battle of wits by reading the works of Thomas Aquinas and Gabriel Biel the philosopher. Katherine was to test his logic and his rhetoric. He was a good sparring partner because whatever arguments he put forth – and he could be quite incisive – he always did so with remarkable courtesy and an unruffled temper.

'Biel is right when he says that all ecclesiastical jurisdiction is derived from the Pope,' he declared, putting down the scholar's book.

'I am surprised that anyone would question that,' she said.

'Some have held that authority within the Church should rest in an ecumenical council. Francis Bryan is taking that stance tonight, and I intend to oppose it.'

'Too many people want change,' Katherine reflected. 'They question the things they should not question. They complain of abuses within the Church.'

'Oh, there are abuses, Kate, to be certain. But that is not the fault of the Church; it lies with the individuals who perpetrate them, and they can and should be dealt with. And that's another debate entirely!'

Everyone commented on the affection Henry bore to the learned. It was well known that the great humanist scholar Erasmus had called him a universal genius, and that, she was sure, was not mere flattery. Surely no monarch before him had possessed greater erudition and judgement. He was gifted with acute powers of reasoning and observation, and could sum up a person or situation immediately. She never ceased being astonished at his vast store of general knowledge – he seemed to know something about everything. He spoke French and Latin fluently, and with her help was now learning Spanish. He spent a lot of his leisure time reading, a pleasure she shared. They often exchanged, or recommended, books, and enjoyed discussing them.

It was obvious, she thought indulgently, that he had a good opinion of himself – but he had good reason, for there were few to equal him! She knew that, because she was becoming used to welcoming scholarly guests and assessing their talents. She even held her own in the stimulating discussions that took place in her chamber.

'This does not seem like a court,' one foreign cleric said to her, 'but a temple of the Muses.'

'I have loved learning for as long as I can remember,' Henry told her one evening, when she had engaged her wits in a particularly lively debate. 'That was thanks to my parents and my grandmother. I have never neglected my studies, and do not intend to do so. And now I have a wife who is a miracle of learning. Even Erasmus sings your praises, Kate!' That was now his private name for her.

'I was lucky to have enlightened parents who believed that their daughters should receive an education. Few women do.'

'That will change,' Henry declared. 'We will have our daughters taught as well as our sons.'

Katherine looked at her husband, his eyes alight with passion for a bold and bright future, and knew it was time to tell him the secret she was cherishing.

Henry whooped with glee and gathered her into his arms.

'Think of it, Kate,' he exulted, 'a son, to crown our happiness and safeguard my royal line! Now we will be free from the threat of civil war – and I can go jousting!'

Henry came into her chamber a few days later, wearing an anxious expression, and waved her ladies away.

'Kate, Dr de la Saa approached me this morning. He'd heard that I

177

have been visiting your bed, and urged me not to do so while you are with child. He said it was not fitting, and it might be dangerous.'

Her first reaction was to rail against her physician for interfering. What did the celibate doctor know of love? How dare he try to come between her and Henry?

But then she saw the conflict in Henry's face.

'Kate, it grieves me to say it, but we cannot take any chances at this time,' he said, putting his arms around her. 'In truth, I do not know how I will bear to sleep alone, but I know how strongly I desire you, and I dare not risk losing control and harming our son.'

She clung to him. This was terrible. She had come to need him in her bed at night as much as she needed light and air and food. It was not just their lovemaking that was so precious: it was the privacy, the being together alone – all too rare in their very public lives. She did not know how she would do without all that.

But she concurred, as was ever her way. He was looking into her face, his eyes beseeching her to understand.

'Of course,' she said, forcing a smile. 'We must put the child first.'

How she missed him, oh, how she missed his solid form beside her in bed, his arms around her in the dark, his tender murmuring in her ear, their physical completeness. However attentive and loving he was by day – and he was, give him his due – it was not the same. But her married ladies assured her that it was perfectly normal for husbands to absent themselves from their wives' beds during pregnancy. Some of the women even welcomed it . . . So she was persuaded to see it as proof of Henry's care for her and their child.

At Henry's behest, Katherine had reluctantly agreed to receive Fuensalida one last time. He offered her a thousand profuse apologies for having failed her, and formally took his leave before departing for Spain. With him went Dr de Puebla, old and frail, with Death's mark on him. Some months later, when she heard that Puebla had died, she felt unaccountably sad. Perhaps she had misjudged him all along, believing him to have behaved treacherously towards her. It had been Doña Elvira who had fuelled her mistrust and enmity, and look how false she had proved! Henry insisted that the doctor had always done his best for her, for his father had said so – and maybe he was right. She just wished she had known it at the time. But already the desperation that had then blighted her life felt like a distant nightmare. The people who had endured it with her had been well rewarded, and those few who had deserted her were almost forgotten. Katherine had heard that Francesca de Cáceres was bitter about missing out on the benefits of serving in the Queen's household, though she now felt only pity for the girl.

Henry approved of Fray Diego remaining in Katherine's service. 'I hope to keep him for as long as I am able,' she told him. 'I rely on him for spiritual counsel.' Naturally she told the friar of her frequent talks with Caroz – there was little she did not tell him – but he seemed uneasy, and a little resentful, to hear of their increasing friendship. Finally, Katherine asked him why he was so concerned.

'The ambassador wishes to get rid of me,' he said. 'You are not to heed him. He has given you bad advice. You must be guided by King Ferdinand in all things.'

'Why would he wish to be rid of you?' Katherine asked.

'Because he knows I tell you the truth! And he wants you to bend to his will, not your father's.'

She sighed. 'Fray Diego, how am I to fare well if the two people best placed to advise me are at odds with each other?'

The friar frowned. 'You must decide where your loyalty lies.'

'But I do not believe that Don Luis wishes to be rid of you. You are imagining it. He is a good and conscientious man. Please show him every courtesy, as you love me.'

'Very well, Highness. I am happy to be proved wrong. But I will be watchful.'

When Fray Diego had gone, Katherine went to her closet and knelt at her prie-dieu. But she had too much on her mind to pray. Once again Fray Diego appeared to be the object of hatred and criticism. Why was it that people disliked him so much? Were they jealous of his influence over her? She thought carefully about his actions and behaviour since she had become queen, but she could not see anything that had not been beneficial. So what cause had Luis Caroz to resent him?

No, she must trust her own judgement now. She got up and smoothed her skirts. Henry approved of the friar; he liked him too. And if Henry had no complaints about him, neither did she.

Chapter 11

1510–1511

Katherine was resting contentedly in her chamber at Greenwich, one hand on the mound of her stomach, watching her ladies sorting through fabrics, ribbons and trimmings for the costumes they planned to wear for the Twelfth Night feast.

She smiled, remembering how, when the babe had quickened in October, Henry had almost burst with pride, and had written to tell her father the wonderful news. Hearing her husband, you might have thought that no child had ever been born before; certainly not one as special as this babe.

Beside her on a table lay the beautiful illuminated missal that Henry had given her this morning for her New Year's gift. She picked it up and leafed through its pages, tracing her finger gently over the exquisite miniatures and delicate floral borders. She was enjoying a peaceful respite from all the revelry, and taking the opportunity to rest before the evening's feasting, when there came the sound of approaching music and laughter, and suddenly the door burst open and a dozen masked men came leaping and crashing into the room. Katherine rose in startled amazement as the babe, surprised by her thumping heart, wriggled inside her, and her women dropped their fripperies, gaping; but then she saw that her boisterous visitors were all dressed alike in green velvet and feathered caps, and carried bows and arrows.

'May it please your Grace, Robin Hood and his merry men are at your service!' cried their leader in the unmistakable voice of her husband. 'We outlaws crave the pleasure of dancing with the ladies!'

On cue, the musicians who had crowded in behind the players struck up a tune and amid much laughter the women entered into the spirit of the occasion, allowing themselves to be partnered with the outlaws and joining in a lively dance.

Then Robin Hood bowed low before the Queen.

'One stately measure, madam!' he cried. 'I would not tire you in your condition.' He led her into a slow pavane, keeping time to a beating drum as the shawms sounded and the pipes trilled. Dance followed dance, until Robin Hood held up his hand.

'My lords of the greenwood, you have put up a brave showing tonight, but it is now the time to unmask,' he said, and bowed before Katherine. 'Madam, will you do me the honour?'

Katherine rose and pulled down his visor, revealing Henry's handsome, gleeful face and tousled hair. She pretended to be delightfully surprised and kissed him, and there were squeals and giggles as the ladies discovered the identity of their dancing partners. Then wine was served and there was much laughter and flirtation among the ladies and gentlemen. Katherine ended the afternoon in Henry's arms, thanking him warmly for the entertainment.

How good life was! And soon – for she was near her time now – they would be moving to Westminster, where they wanted their son to be born.

Katherine had never known such pain, and what was worse, when the contractions weren't torturing her, was the awareness that it was all for nothing. It was too soon, too soon!

There had never been any doubt in Henry's mind that the baby would be a boy. He had spent months happily planning the Prince's household, his christening, the tournaments that would follow, what he would wear . . .

But today, this last day of January – oh, the pity of it! – all those plans had come to naught. Katherine had woken with a dull cramp low in her belly, spreading up to her back. When she arose, she had seen, to her horror, bright wet blood on the sheet. It was then that she'd screamed for help.

Her women had come running, and a midwife was sent for. By the time she arrived Katherine was in the grip of powerful pains, and they lifted her on to the pallet bed so that she could be delivered. Her agony lasted for several hours until she felt an overwhelming need to push. Then it was over. Exhausted, she averted her eyes as the midwife, busy at her end of the bed, handed a tiny cloth-wrapped bundle to one of the chamberers, who scurried out of the door with it, tears streaming down her cheeks.

Katherine was too weary to cry. She must bear the trial that God had sent her, bear it with courage and patience.

'What was it?' she asked weakly.

'A girl, your Grace,' the midwife said. 'Never you mind. Them as has a stillborn the first time often has a healthy babe the second.'

And all to do again! Katherine thought.

Henry came to her, loving and reassuring, but she could tell he had been weeping. It seemed all wrong that a young, strong man like Henry should weep.

'It is a great calamity!' she cried. 'I am so sorry!'

'You must not worry, Kate,' he soothed, stroking her damp hair back from her forehead.

'I have failed you,' she sobbed. 'I had so desired to gladden you and the people with a prince.' She was shaking with the awfulness of her loss – Henry's loss, England's loss.

'And you will, my love,' he said, grasping her hand and squeezing it. 'There will be other babes, you'll see. As soon as you are well, we will make another.'

Katherine turned her head away, mourning for the child she had lost, and for her shattered hopes.

She recovered quickly, and was allowed to sit up only a week after the delivery. The child had been small, so she had suffered no tearing, the midwife told her. All would be well next time. Soon she was allowed to get up and rest in a chair, and then it was time for her churching. That was a quiet ceremony, for there was no child for which to thank God; she could only offer up gratitude for her safe delivery from the pains and perils of childbirth.

Blessed and purified, she returned to everyday life, uncomfortably aware of the sympathetic looks of concern people were giving her. And no wonder, for when she glanced in her mirror she saw that her face was white and tragic; in fact she looked ill.

Her ladies did their best to comfort her. There would be other children, they said. It was common to lose the first.

'I lost my son at two months,' Maud Parr said, her eyes misting over. 'I know how devastating it is. But you learn to live again.'

Henry did all he could to cheer her, from bringing her books he thought she would like, to sending to Spain for the oranges and salad stuffs she loved. He sat with her for hours, forgetting affairs of state and offering her every word of comfort in his vocabulary. He brought his portable organ and played for her a beautiful anthem he had recently composed, 'O Lord, the maker of all things', which was now being sung regularly in the royal chapels. He was working on two Masses, he told her, each in five parts. She tried, how she tried, to respond, to be interested, to smile, to be her old self, but she knew she was not giving a convincing performance.

She felt overwhelmed by guilt. The loss of her baby must have been her fault. She tried endlessly to think back to what she had done or not done in the days leading up to it. There were no answers. Maybe she had displeased God in some way. On her knees, she sought His forgiveness, and fasted to absolve her guilt.

'Have you written to your father?' Henry asked, his face overcast with concern.

'What, to tell him how I failed you?' she answered. 'I do not have the heart.'

'You have not failed me, sweetheart,' Henry said, for the hundredth time. 'Let me write to King Ferdinand.'

'No!' she cried.

'Very well. But, Kate, he would welcome a letter from you, I am sure.'

She thought about it for a few days, then forced herself to put pen to parchment. She begged her father, 'Pray, your Highness, do not storm against me. It is not my fault, it is the will of God. The King my lord took it cheerfully, and I thank God that you have given me such a husband.' She repeated, for emphasis, 'It is the will of God.'

It was May, and Katherine had quickened again.

'That is the most welcome news!' Henry cried, and folded her in his arms. 'I never expected it so soon.'

'You did not waste time,' she reminded him, smiling, remembering his urgent embraces as he'd claimed her again.

'You needed comforting,' he said, 'and England needs an heir. This time, God willing, we will have our son!'

'I thought, after what happened, that I had offended God in some way, and that He might not vouchsafe me another child,' Katherine admitted, 'but now it has pleased Him to be my physician. We must thank Him for His infinite mercy.'

'I will render thanks a thousand-fold,' Henry vowed fervently. 'And look, even now you have a high belly.' He patted her below her girdle. It was true: she had only missed two courses, yet here she was, already unlacing her gown.

'I hope this is the beginning of a hundred grandsons for my father!' she said, her eyes shining.

'Your Grace, may I speak to you in private?'

Katherine looked up from her embroidery frame, where an intricate blackwork design of flowers and fruit was taking shape. It was her lady-in-waiting Elizabeth FitzWalter who had spoken. Of Buckingham's two sisters, Lady FitzWalter, plump, sensible and motherly, was Katherine's favourite. Looking around the room at the bent heads of her ladies, busy with their stitching, she noticed that the other sister, Anne Hastings, was not among them.

'Of course,' she said, rising. 'Come into my closet.' She led the way into the linenfold-panelled room that served as her oratory at Greenwich. 'Now, what can I do for you?'

Elizabeth FitzWalter looked uncomfortable. 'Madam, I would not for the world say what I have to say to you, but you will find out anyway, and better from me than from anyone else.'

'What is it?' Katherine asked, alarmed.

'I have been concerned about my sister's reputation. I wanted to spare my family any scandal, so I confided in her husband and my brother, the Duke.'

But what had this to do with her? Katherine wondered, puzzled. Was Lady FitzWalter worried about her sister's poor reputation reflecting on the Queen? Well, she would speak to her.

'What has happened?' she asked.

'Your Grace, forgive me – there has been much talk in the court of late, of her becoming too close to Sir William Compton.'

Ah, that was it. The rakish but amusing Compton, the King's lifelong friend. Of course, Lady FitzWalter would want her to speak to Henry.

But that lady had not finished. 'Some say that these love intrigues involve the King, and that Sir William is providing a diversion to stop tongues wagging.'

Katherine was outraged. 'Who says this?'

'The Spanish ambassador, madam. He had heard gossip, and was worried that you would hear it too.'

'I will speak to the King!' Katherine said, unable to credit what she was hearing. She could not believe that Henry would even look at another lady. He had been so loving lately, so attentive, although since she had told him of her condition he had of course abstained from her bed.

'He already knows it is discovered, madam!' Lady FitzWalter cried, her face working in distress. 'My brother, the Duke, went to Anne's lodging and asked for an explanation, but while he was there Sir William Compton arrived, and there was a fearful quarrel, with the Duke severely reproaching him and using many hard words. Sir William complained to the King, who was so offended that he reprimanded the Duke personally, after which my brother left court.'

'But that is not proof that the King was involved in this intrigue,' Katherine protested.

'Alas, madam, when her husband confronted Anne, she confessed it.'

Katherine stood there like stone. This could not be happening. Not Henry – not her beloved Henry.

'Send your sister to me,' she commanded.

'Madam, she is gone. Lord Hastings carried her off to a nunnery sixty miles away. And now I fear that the King will blame me.'

'Let me think on this,' Katherine said. 'Now go.'

Left alone, she sank to her knees at the prie-dieu, her legs having dissolved into water. What was she to believe? What should she do?

After hours of lying sleepless and sobbing into her pillow, she dragged herself out of bed, trying to compose her features as her women entered the chamber to make her ready to face the court. There was to be a reception for some Milanese envoys.

Lady FitzWalter was not there.

'Where is she?' Katherine asked.

'Your Grace, she is just coming,' Jane Popincourt said. Like the rest, she seemed unusually subdued. Katherine was aware they were all giving her furtive looks.

She was dressed and feeling for the first time the nausea of early pregnancy when Elizabeth FitzWalter arrived, in outdoor attire. Like Katherine, she looked as if she had been crying.

'Your Grace, I am come to bid you farewell,' she said. 'The King has banished me and Lord FitzWalter from the court.'

'But why?' Katherine was horrified.

'His Grace is in great displeasure. He summoned me this morning and said he knew that I was telling tales to your Grace. He accused me of employing women to spy on his every unwatched movement, in order to tell you what he is doing. He said he would like to turn them all out of the court, but for his fear that it would cause too great a scandal.'

'But it isn't true . . .'

'No, it is not, madam. I do not employ spies, as the King thinks, and I was only trying to do you a kindness by telling you what I knew. Now I must go, as I fear to incur His Grace's anger by lingering.'

'You may leave this with me,' Katherine said.

Never had she criticised or opposed Henry in any way. She had been raised to be aware that it was up to her to preserve the love and harmony between her and her lord, and until now she had had no cause for the slightest complaint. But in return she expected fidelity. The suggestion that Henry had strayed cut her deeply, and she needed to know the truth. She must remember that *she* had done nothing wrong.

She sent a page to the King's privy chamber, requesting an audience with His Grace. The next thing she knew, Henry was bursting through her door, waving away her ladies. His expression was steely, his handsome face flushed.

'Sir, why has Lady FitzWalter been banished?' Katherine asked, shrinking inside, but determined to stand her ground.

'Because she has been telling lies,' Henry said, glowering over her. She gathered her courage.

'She told me that you and Lady Hastings have become too close, and that Sir William Compton was pretending to court the lady to divert suspicion from you. She wanted to avoid my hearing of it from others. Henry, I must know: is it true?'

'Of course not!' he shouted. 'She had no business to be saying such things to you. It was a mere flirtation on William's part.'

'Then why did Lady Hastings say it was you?'

'Because she is a foolish woman who likes to think I fancy her! Kate, I will not have you question me like this.'

'You are my husband, Henry, and owe me fidelity.'

'I *have* been faithful! But even if I had not, it is a wife's duty to be silent.'

'I have no intention of being silent!' Katherine declared. 'You should have taken greater care not to get into a situation that was open to more than one interpretation.'

Henry's face was puce. 'I should – *I should* . . . Who are you to tell me what I should and should not do? I have honoured you with my marriage, and my body, and I expect unquestioning obedience. You have no right to criticise me – I am the King, the Lord's anointed!'

'And that is why you should ensure you are above suspicion! And don't shout – my ladies will hear you.'

'Let them! Let them hear how you forget your duty to me!'

'Henry—' Katherine grasped his arm, but he pushed her away. This was terrible. They could not be quarrelling like this. 'Henry, please – I must know. Has there been anything between you and Lady Hastings?'

'No! I've already told you. Do you doubt the word of a prince?'

'No,' she said, her anger subsiding, leaving her uncertain and near to tears.

'Good! Then I'll leave you to reflect on a wife's proper duty to her lord!'

The whole court knew of their quarrel. Henry was avoiding her company, and when they did meet his manner was frosty. Katherine wanted to believe his denials, but if she was honest she had not been convinced, so she was frosty too. And to Sir William Compton she would not speak, but let her displeasure be evident.

Luis Caroz came to see her, with Fray Diego in his wake. For once they were in agreement.

'Highness, I am concerned about this situation,' Caroz said. 'It seems to me that the King has been at pains not to humiliate you publicly, and you are only making matters worse by your ill will towards his friend. I do fear that, if you continue in this behaviour, you might compromise your great influence with the King.'

'Much is at stake,' Fray Diego chimed in. 'We have the fortunes of Spain to consider. King Ferdinand relies on your Grace. It would be a sin to neglect your duty towards him.'

Katherine was still deeply hurt. Did no one understand that *she* was the one who had been wronged, not Henry? But she was with child, nauseous and fatigued – she did not need all this. She realised that she could choose to fight a battle she would not win, or swallow her pain with dignity and regain her position.

'Very well,' she said. 'I will make my peace with His Grace.'

She asked to see Henry in private, and when he came, so promptly that she suspected that he too was anxious to put an end to this horrible rift, she sank into a deep curtsey and remained there.

'I fear I have displeased you,' she said in a low voice, 'and I am truly sorry for it. I would not hurt the one I love more than anything in this world.'

Strong arms were suddenly raising her, then she was looking up into her husband's handsome face, and he was smiling at her. It was as if the sun had burst forth.

'No matter, sweetheart,' Henry said. 'Let us be friends again.'

As he moved to kiss her, smelling familiarly of the fragrant herbs stored with his body linen, she felt the gentle kick of the child she carried, the heir that would ensure England's future and seal Henry's love for her. This was what mattered, and she knew now that she had the strength to trust the bonds of their marriage and disregard what would only wound her.

On 8 November the court moved to Richmond. Big with child now, Katherine sat in a cushioned chair while Henry fought mock battles and put on private disguisings, all for her diversion. He was now leaving a lot of state business to his almoner, Thomas Wolsey. Henry constantly praised Wolsey to Katherine as a capable, loyal servant, but there was something about the man's heavy-set, fleshy face and unctuous manner that repelled her. He never failed in his courtesy to her, and he took many burdens from the King's shoulders – burdens that Henry was all too willing to slough off – but she found herself resenting his influence, and avoiding his company if she could.

'He is the son of a butcher!' Maria snorted with all the disdain of the long line of noble ancestors behind her. 'It is not fitting that he should advise the King.'

Katherine agreed – as, she was aware, did most of the great lords at court. They hated Wolsey for being a low-born upstart who was usurping their time-honoured role of chief advisers to the King, and they made no secret of their enmity – unless, of course, the King was within earshot. But Katherine did not want to be seen to be criticising Henry – or Wolsey – in any way.

'Wolsey went to Oxford,' she pointed out to Maria. 'He is clever, and you cannot doubt that he is able and hard-working. The late King promoted him to chaplain.'

'He is too worldly for a churchman! He loves luxury for its own sake.'

'The King has seen fit to reward and promote him, and he would not do so without cause,' Katherine said, wondering why she was standing up for Wolsey. In truth, she was concerned that the almoner was making himself indispensable to Henry by relieving him of the many duties of state that bored him. She had noticed that, on days when her husband was supposed to be in the Council chamber, he was often out hunting or playing tennis, or on wet days gambling and making music in his privy chamber.

'My councillors – and Bishop Foxe in particular – are so slow in getting anything done,' he complained in disgust that very day.

'Then tell them what you want done, and make them do it,' she counselled, weary of hearing it.

'There's always a reason why I can't do this or that,' he grumbled. She suspected it was an excuse, for she knew he preferred to be enjoying himself in the company of the young gallants of his chamber, many of whom had grown up alongside him at court.

'My councillors make me feel like a schoolboy,' Henry complained, a peevish frown on his face. 'They moan about me spending my father's wealth. Squandering, they call it, reminding me that he spent years carefully saving it. They accuse me of neglecting state affairs for *frivolous pastimes*' – he was Bishop Foxe to the life – 'and they nag me to sit in on their interminable meetings, with which I cannot endure to be troubled.'

'But should you not be keeping an eye on those who are governing your kingdom?' she asked gently.

'They know my will in most matters. If they need any advice they can come and ask me, or Wolsey. Wolsey knows everything.'

She sighed inwardly. That was what she was worried about. Wolsey had not troubled him, or complained. He had got on with things, quietly gained influence and taken control of many state duties before anyone realised it, leaving Henry free to hunt, plan glorious campaigns, lavish his inheritance on revelry and write love songs. None of this Katherine could say out loud, even to Maria. Nor could she confide her

191

fears that Henry was coming to rely too much on his new friend. If this continued, the day would come when Wolsey would be the power behind the throne.

Later, she watched Henry as they sat at table with Wolsey and Brandon. The men were laughing and joking, and she noticed that Henry continually deferred to Wolsey, seeking his opinion, which Wolsey was clearly only too happy to give. To be fair, Henry was also making efforts to draw Katherine into the conversation, as was the amiable Brandon, but she thought that Wolsey would have been happy to exclude her.

Henry was saying that he wanted to invade France as soon as possible.

'Bravo!' cried Brandon, smiling at Katherine.

'Greater victories are made in diplomacy than on the battlefield,' Wolsey observed.

'There speaks a churchman!' Henry said. 'Thomas, I want to win glory for England! By right, I am King of France, and I mean to conquer it.'

'Then I will assist your Grace in every way I can,' Wolsey said.

Along the table the Duke of Buckingham leaned forward. 'Your Grace may rely on your *nobility* to support you,' he said. There was no love lost between him and Wolsey. But Henry ignored the barb and raised his goblet to Buckingham.

'We'll have some fun in France, eh, Ned!'

'It will be a wonderful day when your Grace is crowned at Rheims,' Katherine said, hoping to avert harder words.

'And with you beside me, my darling,' Henry smiled, raising her hand to his lips. 'How delighted your father will be!'

Wolsey said nothing. Already Katherine suspected that he had no love for Spain. She could not have said why, and maybe she was mistaken and it was her own influence he resented – and, by implication, Spain's, of course. Always she was aware of his eyes on her, and they were calculating, assessing . . . It occurred to her that he could prove a formidable enemy.

While they were talking the babe had fidgeted and kicked lustily.

When Katherine placed Henry's hand on her belly, he grinned.

'A fine commander we have in there, my love! He will be Prince of Wales and, God willing, Dauphin of France!' Of late he had been ordering luxuries for his son's nursery and drawing up instructions for his daily care. Again, he was utterly convinced that the infant would be a boy, and Katherine had given up reminding him that there was an equal chance that it could be a girl. And she had forced herself not to think of the tiny, still body carried from her chamber not a year ago.

She would be retiring from public life some weeks before her confinement. 'My father laid down ordinances for the confinement of a queen,' Henry had told her, 'and I would like you to follow the precedent set by my mother. No man will be admitted to your presence during the last weeks of your pregnancy, save I myself and Fray Diego. You will need to arrange for your ladies to take over the duties of all your male officers; they must serve as butlers and servers and pages, and they can receive all the things you need at the door to your chamber.'

Katherine had done as she was bidden, and now all was in readiness. Her chamber was prepared. There was gold plate in the court cupboard, kindling for the fire, and a portable altar. In the great chest at the foot of her state bed were swaddling bands, tiny bonnets, binders and bearing cloths, as well as all the linen and holland cloth thought requisite for the birth. She wondered if Wolsey had had a hand even in this.

Shortly before Christmas she went into seclusion. First she attended Mass and prayed that she might be vouchsafed a safe delivery and a healthy child. Then she went, her belly high before her, in procession from the chapel to her presence chamber, where she gratefully sank into her chair of estate. Wine and wafers were served, after which her chamberlain, Lord Mountjoy, came forward and bowed low to her.

'My lord, I bid you and all present farewell,' Katherine said. 'Now I must take to my chamber.'

Mountjoy turned to her assembled household. 'I desire you all, in the Queen's name, to pray that God will send her a good hour!' he cried.

There was applause and blessings as, accompanied by her ladies, Katherine departed to her privy chamber, and thence to her bedchamber. Behind her the heavy traverse of arras was drawn across the door. A good fire was burning on the hearth, and the room was very warm, for tapestries had been hung not only on every wall, but also across all the windows but one. They depicted the 'Roman de la Rose', amid a thousand colourful flowers. Henry had assured her that there would be no gloomy or staring figures to frighten the babe. His father had been particular about that.

For the next three weeks Katherine kept to her bedchamber, resting on the rich tester bed, on silver damask cushions, sheets of fine lawn, and a counterpane of bright scarlet velvet bordered with ermine and cloth of gold. The curtains and hangings were of crimson satin embroidered with crowns and her coat of arms. It was a peaceful and pleasant time. Her ladies played music or sang with her, read aloud and entertained her with the latest gossip. She and Maria spent hours lovingly stitching a layette of tiny garments for the baby. Fray Diego attended diligently to her spiritual needs, and Henry came every day to sit with her and tell her what was going on in the world beyond her chamber. He fussed over her, begged her to tell him if there was anything she needed, and exhorted her repeatedly to take care of herself.

'Whom shall we have for sponsors?' he asked one evening after they had dined together with her ladies waiting on them.

Katherine was touched that he had asked her. 'The Archbishop of Canterbury?' she suggested, dabbing her napkin to her lips.

'An excellent idea!' Henry approved. 'I think we should also have the Earl of Surrey and my aunt, the Countess of Devon.' Katherine had grown to like the Countess, who was sister to Henry's late mother, and a princess of the House of York; and Thomas Howard, the Earl of Surrey, was a nobleman of the old school, a man of great integrity and courtesy. 'I suppose I'll have to ask King Louis,' Henry added.

Katherine stiffened. She could not bear to have her father's enemy sponsoring her precious child, but she held her peace.

'Maybe we could have the Duchess of Savoy too,' she countered. The Duchess was that same Margaret of Austria who had married her poor brother Juan, and had once, briefly, been Katherine's rival for Henry's hand.

'It shall be as you wish,' Henry had agreed, beaming. 'You know I can deny nothing to the mother of my son.'

Christmas came and went. Festive fare was served to her, boar's head and roast peacock, pies and brawn, and Henry came as often as he could, although he was keeping open court and was busy hosting the feasting and disports.

One morning he brought her a gift, a great diamond set in a pendant.

'I wanted you to have this before New Year, in case you have no leisure to enjoy it then,' he said, kissing her. In return Katherine presented him with an illuminated book for his library, which she had commissioned months before. He thanked her warmly, and described for her the gorgeous mummeries, the pageants, the disguisings and feasts, the carols danced and sung in the great hall while the Yule log crackled on the hearth.

'Next year you will share them with me,' he told her. 'You and our son. That fighting boy in your belly will be old enough to take notice of it all by then.'

Katherine smiled at him, her heart full. She could see Henry with their son; he would make a good father.

'I've composed a new song,' he told her. 'I will play it for you.' He had brought his lute, on which he played most skilfully, and when he sang his voice was rich and true.

'Pastime with good company
I love and shall until I die;
Grudge who lust, but none deny,
So God be pleased, thus live will I!
For my pastance,

195

Hunt, sing and dance,
My heart is set:
All goodly sport,
For my comfort,
Who shall me let?'

There were three verses, in which he sang of putting to flight Idleness, the chief mistress of all vices, and how he himself meant to follow the path of Virtue through enjoying mirth and play in honest company.

'Bravo!' Katherine smiled, clapping. She loved the intimacy of making music together in private.

A few days after Christmas, Henry arrived bearing something very special. 'This was brought for you today by the Abbot of Westminster.' Reverently he laid a bundle of damask on the chest and unwrapped it to reveal a fragile, cracked blue silk cincture. 'It is Our Lady's girdle, one of the abbey's most precious relics. The Abbot said they had lent it to my mother, and now he wishes you to borrow it. It offers special protection in childbed.'

Katherine gazed at the girdle in awe. To think that it had once been worn by the Mother of Christ, and now she herself was vouchsafed the special privilege of wearing it in her hour of need.

'Bring it to me,' she said. She took it with reverence and kissed it. It was feather-light and smelt of age and incense. 'I will guard it with my life,' she promised. Now she was sure she had nothing to fear. All would be well.

On the last day of the old year Katherine's pains began, gently at first, then strongly gathering momentum. Her women helped her on to the pallet bed, and when they carefully looped the sacred girdle around her swollen body, she felt safe, and thanked God that He had permitted her pregnancy to run its full span this time.

For hours she laboured, until, hearing the bells chiming midnight, heralding the new year of 1511, she felt so exhausted that she thought she could bear no more.

'Not long now, your Grace,' the midwife said. 'Soon the head will be crowning!'

'Please, Holy Mother of God, let it be over soon!' Katherine prayed. She was pushing now, mustering all her remaining strength to deliver her child into the world.

'Just one more push!' the midwife instructed.

Katherine pushed again, with all her might.

'God be praised! A fair prince!' the midwife cried.

Chapter 12

1511

Henry was beside himself. He stood there, cradling his son, tears streaming down his cheeks.

'I can never thank you enough, Kate!' he kept saying. 'You have given me an heir to England! He looks like me, don't you think?'

Lying in the tester bed, washed, clad in a clean night-rail and supremely happy, Katherine smiled up at him. 'He does indeed. He has your red hair and mine.'

Henry laid the swaddled babe in her arms. It was true, he was Henry to the life. She gazed in adoration at his little yawning mouth, his tiny, star-like hands, the milky blue eyes that regarded her gravely, the sweet rosebud mouth. He was perfect in every way. She put him down in his cradle of estate, a vast bed upholstered in crimson and gold fringe. He looked so tiny lying there beneath the painted arms of England.

'He shall be called after me,' her husband declared. 'Henry the Ninth!' He bent and kissed Katherine. 'You have brought great gladness to me and my realm. Can you hear the church bells ringing? They'll be singing the *Te Deum* throughout the land. They tell me the citizens have lit bonfires all over London, and I've arranged for free wine to flow in the conduits.'

'I wish I could see it all!' Katherine said.

'You lie there and get better!' Henry commanded.

Five days after his birth the little Prince was borne off to his christening, wearing the robe Katherine had brought with her from Spain and a purple velvet bearing cloth with a long train. Well on the way to recovery, Katherine lay against her pillows. Maria had helped her dress in a sumptuous mantle of crimson velvet trimmed with ermine, fitting attire in which to receive the guests after the ceremony. Henry sat beside her, resplendent in green and gold, colours that set off his red hair to advantage.

'It is not the custom in England for the King and Queen to attend their child's christening,' Henry had informed her. 'It is the godparents' day.'

They could hear the procession returning from the chapel, and the sounds of excited chatter and happy rejoicing. Soon the Queen's chamber was full of richly dressed guests, and ambassadors from the Pope, France, Spain and Venice were bowing low, congratulating Katherine on her noble offspring. When the Countess of Devon, smiling, lay the little Prince Henry in her arms to be named for the first time and to receive his mother's blessing, Katherine's happiness was complete.

Luis Caroz came to pay his respects. 'Highness, I was in London on the night of the christening, and the people were thronging the streets, celebrating. I wish you had heard them! They were crying, "Long live Katherine and the noble Henry! Long live the Prince!"'

'The people of England have always made me feel welcome,' Katherine reflected, 'which is something to marvel at, for the King tells me that, as a rule, the English hate foreigners!'

Henry announced that he was going on a pilgrimage to Norfolk to give thanks for his son at the shrine of Our Lady of Walsingham.

'She is the special patron of mothers and babies,' he explained. 'I will thank Her on your behalf too, my love. While I am gone, rest and concentrate on recovering for your churching, for I have great celebrations planned! Everyone must share in our joy at the birth of our son!'

He left her serene and full of gratitude for God's great blessings, and when he returned a week later she was up and bustling around her apartments, impatient to be back in the world again.

'I rejoice to see you so well, Kate!' Henry cried, embracing her lustily, regardless of the stares of her women, who clearly thought that such conduct was unbecoming for a woman not yet churched. 'How I have missed you, my love. It would have been wonderful to have you kneeling beside me at the Holy House – did you know it was built by angels, in the shape of Mary's house at Nazareth? And you have to walk the last mile of the pilgrimage barefoot, and leave your shoes in the Slipper Chapel. I did it gladly, with everyone else, but you should see the state of my feet! And I saw the holy relic, the precious milk of the Virgin, and paid it great reverence. Oh, Kate, my heart was bursting with thanks!'

She drank in his every word. 'I will go to see Her one day,' she vowed. 'I will thank Her in person.'

Henry began telling her what he had planned for the celebrations.

'You must be churched as soon as possible, so that we can leave for Westminster and the rejoicings can begin.'

'And the Prince – he will come with us?'

Henry shook his head. 'I would not risk our precious jewel, even for your sake. Here at Richmond the air is purer and there is less risk of infection.'

'But I cannot bear to leave him! He is so tiny! He needs his mother.' Katherine felt as if her very lifeblood were being leached; no one, she was certain, could care for her baby as well as she. 'Let me stay here, Henry, I beg of you!'

'Sweetheart, your place is at my side. People will expect you to be there. Little Harry is in good hands – never had a child better or more loving nurses. You have done your duty – now enjoy the applause. And after we have celebrated, you can come back to Richmond and see him. It is not so far away.'

She allowed herself to be persuaded, hardly able to bear the prospect of the inevitable moment of parting. And when it came, and she had hugged and kissed her tiny baby as if she would never let him go, she gathered her courage, laid him in the arms of his lady mistress and let herself be carried away to Westminster, knowing that she had left her heart at Richmond.

'Oh, Henry!' Katherine breathed as the magnificent mounted knight paused before the royal stand in which she and her ladies were seated.

The splendid hangings were of cloth of gold and purple velvet, which the King had ordered to be embroidered with the letters 'H' and 'K' in fine gold, in honour of his love for her. And now here he was, entering the lists as her champion, Sir Loyal Heart.

He was in his element. Tournaments were in his blood, and he was exultant at the prospect of participating himself, which he could safely do now that he had an heir.

'From now on I will be holding tournaments twice a week!' he had informed Katherine, his eyes shining in anticipation. 'We'll have them every May Day too!'

His armour gleaming, his surcoat and the trappings of his horse emblazoned with the words 'Coeur Loyal' and embroidered 'H's and 'K's, Henry bowed low in the saddle, dipped his lance and extended it for Katherine's favour. She stood up, wrapped in furs against the February chill, and herself tied on her yellow silk kerchief, her ladies doing likewise for their chosen knights. Then Henry blew her a kiss and cantered away, to the cheers of the spectators and the admiring gaze of the ladies.

Katherine held her breath each time he thundered down the lists to meet his opponent. She need not have worried. There were many young men who excelled in this dangerous sport, as she well knew, but today the most conspicuous among them all, the most vigorous in the combats, both on horseback and on foot, and the most dedicated, was her husband. He jousted expertly, and broke more staves than any other contestant, easily surpassing everyone else. He ran several courses against his favourite jousting partners, William Compton and Charles Brandon – and won them all. Those eagerly watching were enthralled, and there were cheers of acclaim from Henry's friends and the crowds in the stands as Katherine stood to present Henry with the prize as he drew up on his horse before her.

'My lady!' he cried, flashing her that devastating smile. 'The mother of my son!'

Henry and Katherine made love that night for the first time since the Prince's birth. Katherine had been worried that all would not be as it had been before, and that Henry would find her body too much altered, for she had still not lost the weight she had gained in her pregnancy, and her breasts had lost a little of their firmness. But she need not have concerned herself. He was so thrilled to be reclaiming her that she was sure he had noticed nothing amiss, and if his ardour was anything to go by, he loved her so much that it would not have mattered anyway. Again, she thanked God for such a husband.

Cherishing the secret knowledge that they were lovers again, and firmly suppressing her nagging need to be with her son, Katherine found herself enjoying the elaborate pageants that Henry had devised with his master of the revels. She caught her breath with everyone else as a band of wild men clad in animal skins and leafy garlands came leaping into the hall, growling and snarling, as behind them rumbled a pageant car pulled in by a golden lion and a silver antelope. On the wooden stage a forest had been created, with rocks, hills, dales, trees, flowers, hawthorns and grass, all fashioned from velvet, silk and damask; and from it emerged dancers dressed as foresters in green velvet. Rising in the middle of the forest was a golden castle, in front of which sat a gentleman making a garland of roses for the Prince. As the pageant drew to a halt before Katherine, armed knights burst from the castle and summoned the whole court to the tiltyard for yet another tournament.

There were several other pageants, along with feasts, banquets and of course dancing, in which Henry acquitted himself marvellously, leaping and jumping and proving himself indefatigable. He was in such an expansive mood that he commanded that the doors to the White Hall be left open to allow the common people to come in and watch the festivities. Katherine could not take her eyes off him, he looked so debonair. The gold 'H's and 'K's from his tilting costume had now been sewn on to his purple satin doublet and bases, so that he could continue to proclaim his love for her to the world.

Luis Caroz admired these ornamental initials. 'They are surely not real gold, your Grace?'

'I don't think so,' the Earl of Surrey chimed in.

'Oh, but they are, I assure you both,' Henry said, 'but if you don't believe me, I will prove it!' He jumped in one lithe leap on to his chair of estate, and a hundred pairs of eyes turned to him.

'My lords and ladies!' he cried. 'There are some here that doubt that these ornaments are gold, so now we will dance, and I invite all of you, if you can, to divest me of them for largesse, so that you can see for yourself that they are! Let the music begin!'

The consort of musicians in the gallery broke into a lively brawl, and Henry took Katherine's hand and led her to the floor, where he twirled her around, bowed, skipped and whirled her by the waist, as his courtiers tried to snatch the golden initials from his clothes. But now the common people, thinking that the King's largesse was for them too, surged forward and began grabbing and pulling, and before long Henry's doublet had been ripped apart, his bases were torn, and he was standing there in his shirt and breeches, laughing helplessly, for his good commons were now setting about his lords and divesting them too of their finery.

Katherine had taken refuge with her ladies on the dais, where Henry hastened to join her.

'Don't you think they should be stopped?' she asked nervously, but Henry just chuckled.

'Let them have their largesse in honour of the Prince!' he said. 'I will cry it! Largesse! Largesse! Mother of God, look!'

Katherine looked up to where he was pointing, and there was Sir Thomas Knyvet, the Chancellor of the Exchequer, shinning up a pillar to escape the rapacious hands of the mob. He was stark naked, and affording the ladies a comprehensive view of his manly parts. Henry was vastly amused.

'They have gone too far, for shame!' Katherine protested, rising to her feet as the milling crowd began edging towards the dais. She was horrified to see two homespun-clad fellows reach out for her ladies and tug at the green and white silk gowns they had worn for the pageant. Henry had seen too.

'Enough!' he said in a voice like a trumpet, signalling to his guard, and suddenly armed pikemen were in the midst of the throng, pushing the people back towards the doors and ejecting them from the hall, leaving the King and his tattered courtiers staring at each other.

Someone threw poor Knyvet a torn gown. Then again Henry laughed. There was a pause, and others followed suit, until the rafters were echoing with the sounds of mirth.

'Let us to the banquet!' the King cried. 'As you are!' And he took Katherine's hand and led his merry, bedraggled throng into the presence chamber.

As the trumpets sounded, Henry and Katherine headed the procession into the great hall, followed by the Queen's ladies, the foreign ambassadors and all the nobility. Henry himself showed the ambassadors to their seats, then sat down beside Katherine at the high table on the dais, beneath the canopy of estate bearing the royal arms of England.

Katherine was wondering if she could face another feast. It seemed to her that she had done nothing but eat and drink for the past weeks, and she felt that she was putting on more weight daily. She had heard that at the French court a tiny waist and a full bosom were the ideal; well, she had the bosom, but she doubted that her waist would ever be tiny again. Yet Henry, unbothered about his trim figure, which stayed trim thanks to all the exercise he got, was hungrily eyeing the huge platters of food that were being borne towards him with great ceremony. There were meats garnished with costly spices and sauces, raised pies with rich crusts, and – most magnificent of all – a peacock roasted and re-dressed in its plumage.

A nobleman placed before the King a gold platter of meats.

'Let me serve you, Kate,' Henry said, all courtesy, and speared with his knife the choicest portions, placing them on the silver-gilt plate in front of her. 'Wine for the Queen!' he commanded. A page was instantly at the table with his ewer.

Katherine raised her goblet.

'To your Grace, my beloved lord!'

Henry's eyes drank her in. 'And ever shall be!' he declared. 'I have written a new song for you, Kate, a winter ballad. After dinner you shall hear it!'

'I will look forward to that,' she said.

Henry could not remain seated for long. He was soon walking

around the tables, chatting to his guests. He then disappeared for a time. When he came back he was wearing Turkish robes and was accompanied by a troupe of players, with whom he proceeded to dance for the delight of the assembled company. Then, flushed with his exertions, and basking in the ovation, he rejoined Katherine at table, just as the subtlety was carried in, a monumental sculpture of sugar in the form of a great castle, which drew many an admiring gasp.

'That's something for valiant teeth to assault,' Henry muttered in Katherine's ear, and politely waved it away as it was presented at the high table. Then he tried unsuccessfully to conceal his mirth as he watched others trying to eat the rock-hard confection.

'At least it looks impressive,' Katherine smiled.

When the cloth had been lifted and the trestles taken away, hippocras was served, and Henry called for his lute. A hush descended as his clear, true voice sang out.

'As the holly grow'th green
And never changeth hue,
So I am, e'er hath been
Unto my lady true!

As the holly grow'th green
With ivy all alone,
When flowers cannot be seen
And greenwood leaves be gone.

Now unto my lady
Promise to her I make:
From all other only
To her I me betake.

Adieu, mine own lady,
Adieu, my special,
Who hath my heart truly,
Be sure, and ever shall!'

As he sang the final lines his eyes met those of Katherine, who thought she would swoon with the joy of it.

'Bravo!' she cried, clapping her hands and leading the applause. 'That is a beautiful song.'

'Thank you, sweetheart,' Henry said, bowing and acknowledging the applause. 'I think I might add a chorus, something like, "Green grow'th the holly, so doth the ivy . . ." I haven't got the last lines yet.'

'Another, sire!' cried a voice from the near end of a lower table. It belonged to Sir Thomas Boleyn, one of Henry's tilting partners.

'Yea! Yea!' others called.

'Please, sir!' Katherine echoed. Then she became aware that the Earl of Surrey had appeared and was murmuring something in the King's ear. Henry turned to her.

'Urgent business calls me, Kate. I'll return as soon as I may.' He got up, bowed to her and preceded Surrey through the door at the side of the dais.

'Maybe our minstrels will play us a tune!' Katherine cried. 'Let the dancing begin!'

She had sat there for five, maybe ten, minutes, enjoying the music and the sight of the couples treading a stately measure down the hall, when Surrey returned, without the King.

'Madam.' His long, wall-like face was grave. 'His Grace requests your presence in his closet.'

Katherine rose, wondering what this could be about, and hastened with Surrey to the King's lodgings, her ladies following. As they passed through the deserted presence and privy chambers, the guards sprang to attention, then in the antechamber beyond Surrey turned to Katherine.

'His Grace would see you alone, madam.'

'You may go,' she said to her women, then pushed open the door, her heart full of foreboding.

Henry had lit two candles. Their dancing light illuminated his tear-stained, tragic face in the dark room. She knew then what it was he had to say to her, but her whole being was gathering its resources to deny the truth of it. If the words were not said, they could not be true. But then Henry reached out his hands to her and spoke. Suddenly she was screaming and screaming, and then strong arms were around her as she sank down and down into the terrible darkness . . .

She lay on her sodden pillow, unable to stem the tears that had been flowing for hours now.

'After such great joy . . . to be cursed with such sorrow,' she sobbed.

'Kate, I know not what to say to you.' Henry's voice was choked. He had been with her all the while, lying at her side, trying in vain to comfort her. His arms were again tight around her.

'He did not suffer,' he had said.

'His soul is now among the innocents of God,' he had said, his own eyes now brimming.

'We are young; we can have other children,' he had said.

'I want my baby!' Katherine wept. 'I want my little son! I should never have left him. I am his mother, but I was not there when he needed me.'

'We must not question the wisdom of God,' Henry said. 'If you had been there, you could not have saved him. A sudden chance like that, a chill – he was so young.' His voice threatened to break again.

'I wish God had taken me!' Katherine wailed. 'I cannot face life without him. I cannot bear the pain. My little babe . . .' And she would not be comforted.

Fray Diego came and spoke sternly to her. 'God understands your loss, my daughter, but this excessive grief is a sin against His will. Did not St Paul speak of the dead as them that are asleep, not them that have died? Your son sleeps in the Lord, and assuredly knows the joy of eternal life.'

Dutifully she tried to be positive, but her arms ached with emptiness, and her longing to see and touch her child was agony.

Henry was her only comfort. Hiding his own sorrow, he stayed with her during the darkest days of her grief, holding her through every storm of weeping, and trying to divert her with music and pastimes.

'There will be no court mourning,' he decreed. All the same he wore black on the day the little Prince was buried in Westminster Abbey, and spent a fortune on the funeral. All that pomp – vigils, candles and torchlight – for one tiny babe, but it was fitting that the King's son be laid magnificently to rest among his forefathers, as his mother grieved and keened for him in the seclusion of her chamber and brokenly laid away the layette that was no longer needed.

Chapter 13

1513

Katherine frowned as she read the letter. It was from Francesca de Cáceres, who was begging to be taken back into her service. Her husband had died, and she desired nothing more than to serve the Queen.

Katherine showed it to Fray Diego.

'Under no circumstances should your Grace agree,' he commanded. 'She is a troublemaker and I will not have her entering the palace!'

Katherine thought his reaction excessive. He seemed almost to fear Francesca, and she wondered fleetingly if he had cause to, and if she had misjudged her maid four years ago. But those accusations of immorality could not have been true – she could not imagine the friar ever behaving that way. Nothing in all his long years in her service had given her cause to doubt his virtue.

Then another letter from Francesca came, and another. Clearly the woman was not going to give up. She might make trouble, which could reflect badly on Katherine.

There came an evening when Katherine was dining with Henry in her privy chamber with just Wolsey and Maria present. The subject of dishonest servants was raised – Wolsey had had to dismiss one for thieving – and Katherine mentioned Francesca's importunings, relating what had happened years before.

'I know Fray Diego to be a man of integrity. What she said was just not true. But she is prejudiced against him, and he fears she may make more false accusations.'

'We cannot have that,' Henry said. 'What touches him touches you. Thomas, can you advise in this?'

Wolsey steepled his hands under his chin.

'Why not send her abroad and get rid of her?' he suggested. 'If you write a letter of recommendation, she will be assured of a place in some foreign court. Might I suggest approaching the Regent of the Netherlands?'

Katherine shook her head. 'I fear it would be dangerous to take that course. Francesca was a party to Fuensalida's blackmail, and claimed he had told her secrets about Fray Diego. Dare we risk her making mischief abroad, or spreading unfounded gossip that might reflect adversely on me? The Regent Margaret was my sister-in-law. I would not inflict such a person on her.'

'Then, madam, we will pack her off back to Spain,' Wolsey said. Suddenly she could see why Henry relied on Wolsey. Finding solutions and relieving others of their worries came effortlessly to him. But although she was profoundly grateful, still she could not warm to him.

When she told Fray Diego that Francesca was to be sent home, his eyes filled with tears of gratitude and relief. 'That woman is poisonous!' he fumed. 'Your Grace is well rid of her, as am I.'

Again she thought his reaction disproportionate. *Had* he had something to hide?

'You must forget what happened, Henry,' Katherine said, keeping her voice low. She was standing beside him as he let loose his arrow at the butts in Greenwich Park, her own bow on the grass beside her. The mild spring weather had prompted a mass exodus from the stuffy confines of the palace, and a large crowd of avid courtiers stood respectfully at a distance, watching the sport.

'The shame of it!' her husband fumed. 'If only your father had been there when he should have been. Damn!' His arrow had gone wide of the mark.

'It was a misunderstanding,' Katherine insisted, watching him take aim again. 'My father could not help the fact that your army was poorly provisioned.' She wasn't having the failure of their joint offensive against France blamed on Ferdinand, when it was Wolsey who had been remiss. His lauded efficiency had failed him on this occasion.

Henry frowned as his second arrow missed the centre of the target. He practised daily and was a superb shot; Brandon said he drew a bow with greater strength than any man in England, but today he was too upset to concentrate properly. He took another arrow from the chest beside him.

'It wasn't all Wolsey's fault,' he muttered. 'My lord of Dorset told me that he waited in vain in the north for your father to attack from the south.' They had had this conversation several times now, and still the ignominy of his army's withdrawal rankled. 'He complained that King Ferdinand wasted valuable time in trying to enlist his aid in attacking Navarre.'

Katherine was aware that that would have been much to Ferdinand's advantage, but did not say so. She could not bear to have Henry doubt her father's wisdom or think ill of him.

'My father was not responsible for the dysentery that laid your army low,' she said. 'Had there not been great sickness, he would have come, I am sure of it. But it was clear that nothing could be gained after that.'

'It was an inglorious retreat,' Henry sniffed.

'It is best not to dwell on it. Gather another army; invade again this year! My father is planning to do the same. Together you can win this time!'

Henry took her at her word; he was easily influenced because he loved her, and he longed to make her smile. She knew he sometimes caught the sadness in her eyes when some small memory brought back the pain of losing her tiny son. And it did warm her heart to see him throwing himself eagerly into preparations for a second campaign.

'I myself will lead my men to victory!' he announced. His talk was all of the Black Prince and Henry V, and England's past triumphs in France. He could think of nothing else but the glory of the battlefield.

Luis Caroz requested an audience with the Queen. She saw that he looked worried.

'Highness, as you know, Spain is as eager as King Henry to invade France, but here, it seems, the people are not so keen. Master Almoner loves the French, and he and other councillors are trying to talk the King out of it.'

'They will not succeed. He is bent on war.'

'And your Highness?'

'I am for it too, and I think he will listen to me.'

'Good.' Caroz looked relieved. 'I have heard it said that even the wisest councillors in England cannot stand against the Queen.'

She waited for an opportunity, and seized it when, walking in the palace grounds one day, she came across Henry and a group of courtiers playing bowls, with Wolsey standing by, watching them. She joined him, and they stood together, applauding every time someone scored.

'Master Almoner, I understand that you are trying to dissuade the King from invading France,' Katherine murmured.

Wolsey gave her a quizzical look. 'I am for peace, madam, not war.'

'My father's ambassador believes that you favour the French.' She was watching him closely, but he was inscrutable.

'Then he is mistaken, madam. I would not wish you to think that I was in any way hostile to Spain. My aim is to protect English interests. This is a small kingdom, and Christendom is dominated by two great powers, Spain and France.' He was explaining this patiently to her, as if a woman would find it hard to understand. 'England's friendship tips the balance of power and preserves peace, and so if the King favours Spain or France, he does so for a good reason.'

'I can hardly think that he will ever favour France when he is married to Spain,' Katherine said.

'Naturally your Grace thinks that, but history shows us that alliances can founder and shift.'

'Rest assured that I am doing everything in my power to preserve this one,' she said firmly.

Wolsey merely inclined his head, as if deferring to her. 'I see that Brandon is set to win,' he said, turning back to the game.

She walked back with Henry, leaning on his arm.

'You will not let them talk you out of this war with France,' she said.

'You've been talking to Wolsey,' he said.

'He has been explaining how alliances work,' Katherine told him, making a face.

Henry laughed. 'As if you did not know, my love! Wolsey hates the idea of war. He would dissuade me if he could. But do not worry, Kate, I am for France, whatever he says!'

Katherine felt a sense of triumph at having for once outmanoeuvred Wolsey.

Late that spring, Henry signed a treaty with Ferdinand and their ally, the Emperor Maximilian, pledging himself to invade France that year.

'It will be a marvellous adventure!' he cried, fired up with martial fervour. Katherine knew he was seeing himself returning victorious, adorned with laurel wreaths and the crown of France. 'More than that,' he added, 'it will be a holy war, nay, a crusade.'

'Louis has ever been an enemy of the Church,' Katherine said. She could feel nothing but contempt for the French King. 'What kind of man would dare invade the Pope's own territory?'

'Fear not,' Henry assured her. 'I am determined never to rest or desist until he is utterly destroyed. I thank God for my dear father of Spain. I know I have his support and that he will never desert me.'

'You have my support too, my Henry,' Katherine told him.

'Aye, I know I can count on you,' Henry said, kissing her. Then he straightened and regarded her gravely. 'Kate, I have decided to name you Regent of England, to rule while I am in France.'

Her heart swelled. 'It is a great honour,' she whispered.

'I'll swear you'll be as good a ruler as your mother, Isabella,' Henry declared.

'I will do all that is needful,' she promised. 'I will not fail you.'

'Wolsey is coming with me, but I am leaving behind Archbishop Warham and the Earl of Surrey to act as your advisers, and every precaution has been taken to safeguard the border in case the Scots decide to take advantage of my absence.'

'They will not do that, surely? Your sister is married to King James.'

'And Scotland is France's friend! I do not trust James. He supported the pretender Warbeck against my father. Just be on your guard. You can rely on Surrey to keep an eye on things. He has vast experience.' Henry paused. 'I am glad you are with child, Kate. I would not have gone otherwise.'

Katherine patted the slight mound beneath her unlaced stomacher. 'I am in high hopes that this will be another son,' she said, knowing it was what Henry wanted to hear. In truth, she was frightened to hope that this third pregnancy would be successful. They had waited long enough, for it had been more than two years since the birth of poor little Henry. She still mourned for him; she would always hold his memory in the secret places of her heart.

'You must take great care of yourself,' Henry said. He had never reproached her for her long failure to conceive.

'I will do everything the midwife tells me to do,' she promised him, 'and I will pray every day that God will send us a healthy boy.'

'And I will pray that you are safely delivered,' Henry said, his lips seeking hers. 'You are very precious to me.'

'I do not know how I will bear your absence,' Katherine murmured. 'Keep safe, my lord! Do not take any unnecessary risks!'

'Never fear,' he soothed, stroking her hair.

Katherine's litter jolted as it was borne up the steep hill to Dover Castle. Ahead of her rode the King, and behind came his lords, his officers, and – marching in unison – eleven thousand men. Crowds had lined the route as the great procession wended its way through Kent, crying out blessings on their King and cheering him and his brave soldiers. Now it had reached the edge of the kingdom and the great fortress that stood sentinel on the white cliffs, overlooking the sea. Above, seagulls wheeled and squawked in the clear June sky, and far below the grey waves churned in the harbour where the mighty fleet lay at anchor.

In the Great Tower of the ancient castle Katherine stood before the whole court as Henry invested her with the regency, and assured him that she would do her utmost for him and for England.

That night, despite her pregnancy, he came to her bed and she lay within the circle of his strong arms, aware that he was dreading the moment of parting as much as she was. In the morning, when she heard him singing marching songs in his bath next door, she knew he had gone from her already. It was always easier for those going away than for those left behind, and Henry was going to war, which he had always wanted to do. He would have much to occupy him. Fortunately there would be many things to fill her empty days too.

They said farewell at the quayside, as the great warships bobbed and creaked on the roiling waves, gulls screamed and the sky was a canopy of blue.

'Thanks be to God for a magnificent fighting force!' Henry said, waving an expansive hand at the ranks of well-equipped men boarding the ships. 'Have you ever seen anything so gorgeous as this fleet?' He turned away from her, his mind busy with campaign plans and the glory to come.

She had resolved to be brave, but when Henry broke away from her embrace she could not stem the tears, and suddenly the gallant Surrey was beside her, his arm protectively around her while they watched the King board his flagship, turning to wave at the assembled throng as he did so. He had never looked more handsome, tall and debonair with his red-gold hair blown by the wind. She felt sick as she saw the anchors pulled up and the vessel move away in stately fashion out of the harbour, and she would have stood there until it had disappeared from sight, but for Surrey insisting that it was time to depart.

'It only prolongs the unhappiness to watch a loved one leaving,' he said.

I must be strong, she told herself. She was the custodian of her husband's kingdom, and she must guard it well for him. Nodding to Surrey, she turned and walked away, her head held high.

As he escorted her back towards Richmond, the elderly Earl regaled her with tales of his youth.

'I am seventy now, and I have seen much,' he told her. He made no secret of the fact that he had once served King Richard. 'And why should I not have done?' he asked. 'Of course, I was sent to the Tower for it after Bosworth. The late King asked me why I had fought for the tyrant, and I replied that he had been my crowned King, and if Parliament had set the crown upon a stock, I would have fought for that stock. I think the King liked my words, for I was soon pardoned and allowed to serve him. But I was not allowed to succeed to my father's dukedom of Norfolk.'

'That is very sad,' Katherine commiserated, deciding to speak to Henry. Such a great and noble lord should have his reward.

'I do not blame His Grace,' Surrey said. 'He has always been good to me. But there is another who does not like me. The antagonism is mutual, I must admit.'

Wolsey, of course. She had known that Surrey hated him as much as Buckingham and many lords did. Here was this butcher's son rising higher and higher, usurping their place. But she said nothing, lest Surrey think she was criticising the King. At least Master Almoner's influence did not extend into the bedchamber! She knew – for had she not had proof? – that Henry would heed her rather than Wolsey.

Katherine soon came to realise that Henry, busy with the campaign, was no great letter writer. She had arranged for relays of messengers to be posted between London and France to bring her word of his progress, but after several days of silence she desired nothing more than to hear of his health, especially when it was made clear to her that the French were drawing ever closer. Daily she was on her knees in her closet, beseeching God to have her husband in his keeping. She could not rest until she had news.

Wolsey was with the army in France and would surely know everything that was happening, so she wrote to him too, asking for word of the King. 'I trust in God that he shall come home soon with as great a victory as any prince in the world,' she ended. It was a fortnight before she heard back, by which time she was about to go mad, worrying that something had happened to Henry. Great was her relief, therefore, when Wolsey reported that all was well.

She replied that she had been filled with alarm at reports of the risks the King was taking. Wolsey wrote to reassure her that he was watching over him, and, full of gratitude, she thanked him. 'I pray you, good

Master Almoner, remind the King always to continue thus, so that nothing in the world shall come to him amiss, by the grace of God. If you remember in what condition I am, without any comfort or pleasure unless I have news, you will not blame me for troubling you.'

In the August heat, she and her ladies were busy sewing standards, banners and badges destined for the army in France. She also made new body linen to send to Henry, for she knew how fastidious he was about having clean undergarments, and it would not be easy to get laundry done regularly while on campaign. As she sewed and sewed, her heavy sleeves rolled back and her hood discarded in the heat, she could feel the child stir under her girdle.

For four years she had watched and counselled Henry as he governed England, absorbing the intricate and unspoken rules of the English court. Now she felt ready to act as his regent, attending council meetings, listening to the views of the lords and considering their advice. Much of the business they dealt with was mundane in the extreme. She was in the process of discussing the sending of hay, oats and beans for the King's horses when Surrey came bursting into the council chamber and, without ceremony, threw a letter on the table.

'The Scots are preparing to invade, madam!' he cried.

There was a moment's stunned silence as the lords looked at each other, nonplussed, before Katherine stood up. This was her proving time, she knew. As her mother's daughter, she must be bold and decisive.

'Then we must face them,' she said. 'Gird yourselves, my lords, for we too must go into battle.'

'Your Grace, you cannot possibly . . .' Surrey's voice tailed off. He was looking at her high belly.

'Good Surrey, I do not mean to lead you myself, of course, but I can rally troops and support you in every other way I may.' She added mischievously, 'I might remind you that my mother, Queen Isabella, rode with her armies right up till the time she was confined, and was back in the saddle soon afterwards. But I mean to be guided by you, my lords.'

They cheered her for that and settled down to the serious business of defending the realm. They seemed glad, she thanked God, to be busy with the Scots. Of course, England and Scotland were ancient enemies; the English would be glad of a chance to best the treacherous King James. What an underhanded thing to do, invading England while its King was away fighting in a holy cause!

When all was finally in readiness, and the men were mustered, the veteran Surrey rode out at the head of his army.

'I am glad, despite my grey hairs, to be useful again,' he told Katherine as he bade her a courteous farewell. 'I am hot to go north to trounce the Scots. May God give us the victory!'

She watched him go, the brave old man, and prayed fervently that he would win the day.

Soon there arrived news that King James had invaded Northumberland.

'His army is eighty thousand strong!' Katherine told Archbishop Warham, in some alarm. 'I hope we can prevail against it.'

'Never fear, madam,' he replied. 'In my lord of Surrey we have a commander without parallel.' All the same, Katherine wished that Henry, young, strong and vigorous, was here to deal with this menace.

Three days later there arrived the most wonderful news from France. Henry and Maximilian had taken the town of Thérouanne. Then, hard on the heels of that, came brave tidings from Henry himself of another great victory, in which he and his allies had routed the French. 'Their army took one look at our superior forces and fled,' he had written, 'so we are calling it the Battle of the Spurs.'

She wondered how significant these victories were. Would they pave the way to Rheims? Surely Henry would have said. Maybe they were but a preliminary to greater conquests to come. Pray God there would be a decisive triumph, like Agincourt!

But she would not belittle her lord's achievement. She hastened to write to Wolsey. 'The King's victory has been so great that I think none such has been seen before. All England has cause to thank God for it, and I especially.'

Soon afterwards she had a letter from Henry himself. He had heard that the Scots had invaded, and commanded her in all haste to prepare to defend his kingdom.

'We have done that and more, with great diligence,' she informed him. 'Your realm is in safe hands.'

Her pregnancy was advancing now, the child becoming ever more active. It must be a boy, she thought; it has to be a boy, by God's grace. Heavy and encumbered as she was, she journeyed north to Buckingham, where she would await news from Surrey. He had left his reserve forces – all thirty thousand of them – camped outside the town, and to a man they greeted Katherine joyfully when she came to see them. Alighting from her litter, she stood on a mounting block, helped up by a sturdy captain, and spoke to the men massed before her, taking care to project her voice into the distance, as she remembered her mother doing all those years ago in Spain.

'I urge you to victory!' she cried. 'The Lord God smiles on those who stand in defence of their own – and remember, English courage excels that of all other nations!' How they cheered her!

She stayed as the guest of Edward Fowler, a wealthy merchant, at Castle House, his well-appointed brick and timber home in the town. It was here, one afternoon in the middle of September, that a letter from Surrey was brought to her. Trembling, she broke the seal.

'Your Grace, I write to inform you that God has vouchsafed us a great victory,' she read. 'The King of Scots and the flower of his nobility lie dead on the field of Flodden.'

'Thanks be to God!' Katherine exclaimed, crossing herself, her heart pounding and the babe leaping within her. This was more than she could ever have hoped for.

She read on. 'Our Englishmen fought like heroes. There was great slaughter, and ten thousand Scots were slain.'

Katherine spared a thought for her sister-in-law Queen Margaret, widowed at a stroke, and of her infant son, another James, who would now be king in his father's place, which would mean a long regency. The teeth of Scotland had been drawn; with so many of her lords dead, it would be years before she recovered. England was safe. Truly this was a great victory.

Katherine went to the parish church of Buckingham and gave thanks, the townsfolk cramming in behind her. She prayed especially for Surrey. That brave old man – how well he had acquitted himself! She would see that the King gave him his just reward.

Another letter from Surrey arrived the next day, informing her that King James's body had been found among the dead. The messenger had also brought her a parcel. When she unwrapped it, she found the King's banner bearing the royal arms of Scotland, and his torn and bloody coat. That gave her a jolt, but she did not flinch from it. Instead she ordered the herald to take the banner and the coat to the King in France.

'Tell His Grace that I am now returning to Richmond,' she instructed him. And there, God willing, his son will be born. By her reckoning the child would arrive in a few short weeks. She had prayed constantly, and fasted, for a safe delivery. What more could she do to ensure it?

Katherine paused, her quill poised above the parchment. It was early evening, and all was quiet in the guesthouse of Woburn Abbey, where she had broken her journey. The nights were drawing in now, and she had ordered candles to be lit, so that she could see to write to Henry.

'Sir,' her letter read, 'by now you will have heard of the great victory that Our Lord has sent to your subjects in your absence. To my thinking, this battle has been to your Grace and all your realm the greatest honour that could be, even more than if you should win the crown of France.' She read over it again. Would Henry think that she was belittling his gains across the Channel by extolling the triumph over the Scots? Surely not! He would realise how important it was in the grand scale of things. Yes, she would leave it as it was.

She began writing again. 'Your Grace shall see how I keep my promise, sending you for your banners a king's coat. I thought to send his body to you, but our Englishmen's hearts would not suffer it.' Instead, the embalmed corpse was being stored in a lumber room in Richmond Palace. 'My lord of Surrey, my Henry, would know your pleasure in burying the King of Scots. I pray that God will send you home shortly, for without you no joy can here be accomplished.'

She wondered if she ought to tell Henry what she was about to do. Would he chide her for making such a journey so late in her pregnancy? Or would he feel it was a risk worth taking? She thought, on balance, that he would approve. So much was at stake that she felt compelled to go, even though she was weary after so many weeks of being busily occupied and travelling. So she told him: 'And now I go to Our Lady of Walsingham, that I promised so long ago to see.' She was sure that Our Lady, herself the mother of a king, would understand the need for a healthy heir to England. How that would crown these victories!

Katherine approached the shrine barefoot, standing in line with the other pilgrims. Here, in the sight of God, all were equal. After the blinding sunshine outside, the chapel entrance was dark. But ahead, to the right of the altar, was a vision of lights, a small statue of Our Lady of Walsingham enthroned, shining with precious stones, gold and silver, and illuminated by numerous candles.

In awe, she knelt to pray and receive the Blessed Sacrament. Having accepted her offering, a monk brought to her a crystal and gold phial containing a creamy liquid.

'The sacred milk of Our Lady,' he said low, offering it to her to kiss. She did so fervently, her heart beseeching Mary to bless her with a son. And suddenly she knew that it was a son, and she was filled with thanks.

Afterwards, when she emerged into the sunlight, the people crowded around her, calling down their blessings and wishing her a happy hour.

'That's a boy you've got there, my lady,' a woman called. 'I can tell by the way you're carrying it.' As she said it, the babe shifted. Not long to go now, Katherine thought, heartened as much by the woman's words as by the certainty she had felt at the shrine. Nearly there. Just let me get through the birth, then all will be well.

Henry had won another town, Tournai. Surrey and Warham brought her the news as she was taking the air in the privy garden at Richmond.

'It's a French town, but it lies isolated in Burgundy,' Surrey explained.

'His Grace has done marvels,' Katherine said. 'To have won so many victories! And to come through it all unscathed. God has indeed been watching over him.'

'The messenger said that the King was fresher after his exertions than before.'

'I do not know how he can stand it,' Warham observed.

'You know the King – he is never still or quiet,' Katherine said, smiling. It was strange, but she had the impression that neither Surrey nor Warham were rejoicing as much as they should have been. 'From here he will go on to great things,' she said. 'I am beginning to believe that he really will conquer France.'

'It is the hope of us all, madam,' Surrey answered, 'but it is now autumn and the end of the campaigning season. The King is in Lille with his allies. They are pledging themselves to launch a combined invasion of France before next June.'

'The King is also arranging for the marriage of the Princess Mary to the Archduke Charles to take place,' Warham told her.

'That is good news,' Katherine said. 'An alliance with Queen Juana's son can only strengthen the ties of friendship between our two nations.' She thought sadly of her sister, still shut up at Tordesillas with no word of her; often she prayed that Juana was too far gone in madness to understand what had happened to her. She wondered too what young Charles thought of his mother, and if her loss, and the macabre end of his father, had badly affected him. Poor child – to be virtually orphaned, so cruelly, and he just thirteen. Her maternal heart ached for him. God grant that the lively and beautiful Princess Mary brought joy into his life.

'It will be a popular union,' Katherine said. 'I thank God that all is going well for us after so many weeks of worry.'

'This has all been a great strain on your Grace,' Warham said. 'You are with child, and for that we owe very much to God.'

'You forget, Archbishop, who my mother was!' Katherine laughed. 'And I have felt very well and equal to the tasks set me.'

*

'The King is here!' Maria cried, breathless. 'I saw him just now from the gallery, riding through the gatehouse with a small company.'

Katherine stood up, smoothing down her skirts and straightening her hood. There would be no time to change. She picked up her mirror and pinched her pale cheeks. How she had longed for this moment in the four months since he had left. And how, latterly, she had dreaded it.

She wished now that she had written to him, but there would have been no guarantee that a letter would have reached him while he was journeying home, and anyway, she had not wanted to write. And now it was too late, and he would see at once . . .

'Kate! Kate!' She could hear him calling her name, hear eager footsteps approaching, and by the sound of it he was not alone. And here he was, every inch the returning hero, looking so virile and handsome in his riding clothes, taller than she remembered him, and mantled with a new and attractive confidence.

'I came with all speed!' he said, and drew her close to him, covering her lips with his, heedless of their avidly watching attendants, or the grins of Brandon, Compton and Boleyn.

'My lord, I am so proud!' Katherine told him, when she could speak. 'And my eyes have longed to behold you. It has been so long. I can hardly believe that you are here at last.'

'I have missed you, my darling,' Henry said, kissing her again, then murmured in her ear, 'Shall we get rid of all these people so that we can be private together?'

'I would like that more than anything,' she whispered. So far there had been nothing in his manner to indicate that he was aware that she was not as he had expected to find her. But he was a good dissembler. She prayed he would not reproach her when they were alone.

He did not. Instead he took her chair by the fireside and drew her down on to his lap, folded her into his arms and kissed her, long and hard this time.

'I fear I have overburdened you with duties, Kate,' he said gently. 'They told me what happened. I am very, very sorry.' He pulled her closer.

She was determined not to cry. Nothing must mar their reunion.

'I too am sorry, Henry. I am deeply sorry to have let you down. I should have had more care for myself, but there was so much to do – and I was happy to do it.' Never let him think that she had grudged doing the task he had entrusted to her.

'It is the will of God,' Henry said, his face tautening, 'and we should not question it. He has blessed us in so many other ways. All I care about is that you are all right.'

She thought of the long hours of labour, the pain, the blood, that tiny, fragile babe being coaxed by the frantic midwife to breathe, mewling weakly, then lying waxen and limp in his nurse's arms as she herself opened her mouth in a soundless scream . . .

'I am much restored,' she lied. 'The sight of you, my Henry, is all I needed to return to perfect health.'

'God be thanked! Kate, we must not mourn, for this is a time to be joyful. Come, let me greet the ladies!'

He lay with her that night, even though she was still bleeding slightly. She knew she had flesh to lose, and that her breasts had been left slacker than before, after the milk dried up. Three pregnancies had taken their toll on her body – and what had she to show for them?

But Henry took his pleasure as passionately as usual, though gently, mindful of her comfort. Afterwards he kissed her and lay beside her, his arms curled around her.

Long after he had drifted into sleep she lay wakeful. It troubled her beyond measure that God had seen fit to take all three of her children. How joyful life would be if He had permitted her to keep them. Young Henry would have been nearly three now, his sister a year older, and this last babe thriving in his cradle. There would have been two male heirs to England – and she a happy mother, not empty-armed and tormented by failure and fear for the future.

She envied Maud Parr, who now had a healthy son, William, and a daughter, sweet little auburn-haired Kate, to whom she herself was godmother, and who had been named in her honour. Maud's grief for her own lost son had been tempered by these blessings;

Katherine could only mourn for the children she had lost.

She knew that Henry must feel the same. She wanted above all things to present him with that thing he needed most, a living son, and God knew that she had done her very best. Three pregnancies in four years of marriage – yet still she was barren.

How have I offended You? she kept asking God. Surely a sin that merited such punishment would be obvious to her. She had searched her conscience again and again, and found it quiet, but her mind would not be stilled.

She rested her hands on the soft mound of her recently pregnant belly and wept for all the hopes that had been dashed. She could not stop thinking of that tiny dead baby – she had never even held him – and a great sob escaped from her.

It woke Henry up.

'Darling,' he said, instantly alert. 'Oh, darling.' He turned and took her in his embrace, holding her tightly. 'Put it behind you, Kate. These things happen. My mother lost three young children, and yet she had me and Arthur and Margaret and Mary.'

'What have I done that God should take my babies?' Katherine wept.

'You have done nothing. *We* have done nothing.' He stroked her hair, soothing her.

'It is a judgement of God!' she cried out.

'For what?' he asked, drawing back and looking at her directly.

'I do not know! I wish I did.'

Henry closed his eyes. He looked pained.

It was then that a terrible thought occurred to her.

'Is it our marriage?' she faltered. 'There were some – Warham, I think – who thought it against Scripture. But the Pope sanctioned it. We have his dispensation.'

'It is not our marriage,' Henry said firmly. 'Would you have every couple who lost three children in the church courts? The queue would be endless. What of my sister Margaret? God saw fit to take five of her children. Sweetheart, you should not take this so seriously. There is no cause for concern. We are young yet – you are not twenty-eight. We will get other children, I promise you. Now try to sleep and forget your fears.'

They kissed good night, and Katherine sought – in vain – for oblivion. But she was still awake when the dawn broke, and when she looked across at Henry, who had his back to her, she could see, in the dim light from the mullioned window, that his shoulders were quietly heaving.

Chapter 14

1514

The new horses were superb. Henry and Katherine watched in admiration as the two mares, gifts from the Marquis of Mantua, were put through their paces by their master in the stables courtyard at Greenwich.

'Bravo!' Henry called, shielding his eyes against the harsh June sunlight.

'And now, your Graces, they will give a display of horsemanship in the Spanish manner, as a compliment to Her Grace,' the Italian envoy announced. Katherine watched, captivated, memories of her father and brother flooding back. They had been expert horsemen.

The display ended with the horses making obeisances to her and Henry.

'I send a thousand thanks to His Grace of Mantua for his kind gift,' Henry said, and he and his sister Mary went over to pat the horses and give them titbits.

'What think you, my Lord Duke?' Henry asked, turning to one of the lords in attendance. It was the French Duc de Longueville, who had been taken prisoner at the Battle of the Spurs and been held hostage ever since. He was a handsome man in his mid-thirties, with a dark spade beard and high cheekbones, dressed in an ash-coloured short gown with great puffed sleeves. He had spent the first months of his captivity comfortably lodged in the Tower of London, on Katherine's orders, but when Henry had returned in the autumn, he had summoned Longueville to court, liked him and kept him there. The Duc was treated with great honour and enjoyed everything the court had to offer, but it was a gilded cage nonetheless, and he would be confined within it until the exorbitant ransom demanded by Henry was paid.

But it seemed he was in no hurry to go home, for it was apparent to all that he had found consolation with Jane Popincourt. Katherine frowned to see Jane standing near him, when she should be attending her mistress. But it was the woman herself who was the mistress now, by all accounts. She made a mental note to warn Jane that her behaviour was causing scandal. Already there had been gossip, and that reflected on her, the Queen!

'They are the finest steeds I have ever seen, your Grace,' Longueville said, in his perfect English, which – God knew – he had had enough leisure to perfect. But his eyes were lingering on Jane rather than on the horses.

'Your Grace did say that I might attend you to discuss the affairs of Mantua,' the envoy said.

'Not now,' Henry told him. 'Let us speak another time. We are late for dinner already, and there is to be dancing afterwards.'

The Italian looked put out. Katherine hid her disquiet at yet another example of Henry's lack of diligence in attending to state business. And after the envoy had travelled all this way with such handsome presents! No doubt Wolsey would end up doing the honours, as usual.

They walked back to the palace together. Katherine held her peace. At the moment she had other priorities. She was fretting about the coming confrontation with Jane Popincourt, and wondering if now was the time to tell Henry her own wonderful news, then thought better of it. Brandon, Compton and those rakes Nicholas Carew and Francis Bryan were not far behind. As usual, Brandon was with the Princess Mary, hanging on her every word. It was another thing weighing on Katherine's mind. Brandon was old enough to know better, yet he was making no secret of his amorous interest, and Mary was encouraging him, for all that she was to be the bride of the Archduke Charles.

Katherine wanted to make Henry understand how worried she was about Mary. She had voiced her concerns to him twice now, but he had made light of them.

'It's a harmless flirtation,' he had said. 'Mary knows her duty. By all accounts the Archduke is a serious boy. Let her have her fun while she may.'

'But, Henry, she loves Brandon – it is as plain as day.'

'She knows he is not for her.'

'Ask him to stay away, please.'

Henry had got impatient with her then. He could refuse Brandon nothing, it seemed. 'All they do is laugh and jest. Brandon has never touched her. He would not dare.' His voice had grown testy. 'You are worrying about nothing, Kate.'

After five years of wedlock she knew when to hold her peace, and she would hold it now, despite her fears for that headstrong girl, because she knew that Henry would not welcome her advice. Then the thought came unbidden: what if Wolsey had said it?

The ever-increasing influence of Wolsey continued to disturb her. She did not like or trust him. The former almoner was now Bishop of Lincoln, now Archbishop of York. The rich revenues from his sees enabled him to support a lavish household that rivalled that of his royal master, and he was forever engaged on building projects. York Place, his episcopal residence, was well on the way to becoming the greatest house in London after Lambeth Palace; even the royal residences looked diminished beside it. And now he had started building himself a palace, Hampton Court, by the Thames in Surrey.

It was not right, Katherine thought, for a humble butcher's son – and a man in holy orders – to have so much, nor was it right for him to exploit his high rank in the Church to enrich himself. He was insincere, too complacent, too smoothly spoken, and singularly lacking in the humility desirable in a prince of the Church. Worse than that, she remained convinced that Wolsey had too great a love for the French, if only to counterbalance her own influence, for certainly he resented that. She could not understand why Henry, who considered himself to be the rightful King of France, should allow himself to be persuaded to formulate foreign policies that favoured England's ancient enemy, and – never forget it – Spain's too!

She should have continued to hold her tongue, but there was too much at stake. That night, after Henry had made love to her, she judged that he would be in a receptive mood and ready to heed her, just as he had always done. She was certain that, after she had told him her news, he would be prepared to agree with everything she said.

'Maybe we should not have loved tonight, my Henry,' she murmured against the rough skin of his cheek.

'Mmm? Darling, are you not well?' he asked, smiling down at her and kissing her temple.

'I am perfectly well,' she said, gazing up at him, 'as well as befits a woman in my condition!'

Henry's blue eyes widened. 'God be praised, Kate! Are you certain?'

'It's three months now. I did not like to tell you before. I wanted to be sure. But I am now, and I am so happy!'

Henry's arms tightened around her and he kissed her joyously. 'That's the best news I've had since the Spurs! Darling, I am so pleased. I told you that God had not forsaken us. This time, all will be well – I know it! When will it be?'

'At Christmas, I think.'

They lay there, talking of the prince he was sure she had in her belly, the household he would have, the jousts that would celebrate his birth.

'Wolsey must be godfather,' Henry said.

'I should prefer not,' Katherine ventured, knowing that she must speak now.

'Why ever not?'

'I fear that Wolsey loves our enemies the French too much. I think he resents my influence and he seems to work constantly against the interests of Spain.'

She felt Henry stiffen in her arms.

'I do not think so,' he said at length. 'He is completely loyal, and a pragmatist when it comes to foreign policy. I would trust him with my life and my kingdom.'

'That is what he wants! To rule here, while you play at being king.' Immediately she wished the words unsaid.

'Is that what you think, Kate?'

'Henry, while you spend your time in sport and revelry, Wolsey is making himself indispensable, and usurping the power that is rightfully yours as an anointed king. It is not just what I think – Wolsey is resented by many of your nobles.'

Henry lay back on the pillow. 'They are just jealous. None of them can hold a candle to him.'

'Henry, your lords should be your natural counsellors. They are born to it, of ancient families with long records of service to the Crown.'

Henry rounded on her. 'Kate, from time immemorial church-men have wielded influence in this realm, much as they do in Spain. Did not your mother rely on the monk Torquemada, who made her found the Inquisition? You have no right to criticise me. And before you say more, remember that in my court it is ability that now counts, not lineage. The days of over-mighty subjects are gone. I prefer new men to the older nobility – men like Brandon, Boleyn, Compton and Wolsey – and I am ready to reward good service above long pedigrees.'

'But Wolsey serves you ill! How can a man who favours your enemy be relied upon? And what devout churchman amasses such wealth?'

'You sound like Warham, forever bleating on about Wolsey's riches. If only *he* served me so well! As for Wolsey influencing my foreign policy – and, believe me, he does not favour the French – you must allow me to be the judge of that. These are matters for men.'

It was as if he had slapped her. Never had he spoken so dismissively; until now he had heeded her advice, spoken as if he valued it, yet in an instant he had made her feel as if her opinions counted for nothing. And it was all Wolsey's fault. Wolsey, that clever, subtle, unscrupulous fellow, was ousting her from her rightful place in the King's counsels, and Henry would not, or could not, see it. How could she protect Spain's interests if her husband would not listen to her? What of the trust that had built up between them?

'I am sorry if I have offended you, my lord,' she said, turning her back on Henry and pulling the covers over herself.

'You are forgiven, Kate,' Henry said kindly, as if it were she who was at fault. 'I understand that you have fancies at this time. Forget about Wolsey and state matters – you have more important things to think about now, like preparing for the birth of our son.' He patted her shoulder, rose from the bed, put on his nightgown, cap and slippers and padded to the door.

'Good night, Kate,' he said softly, and departed.

The next she heard was that he was ill. With long faces his physicians came to her with the dread news that it was smallpox, and she swayed as if she would faint. They sat her down, opened the window, brought wine and assured her there was nothing to worry about.

'His Grace has a strong constitution,' they told her. 'He will recover soon.' Yes, she wondered, but would all that red-gold manly beauty be marked for life? She begged to see him.

'It is out of the question, madam, especially in your condition. The risk of infection is too great.'

So she had perforce to wait in agony for news, wondering what was going on behind the closed doors of Henry's privy chamber, and hoping that bad news was not being kept from her. She could not bear to think of what might happen if he died. She would lose her King, her lover and her protector, and England would be without an heir until the child beneath her girdle was born. There might even be a civil war, for Heaven knew there remained enough descendants of the old royal line who might decide to press their debatable claims to the throne. So she prayed, and prayed again, for Henry's recovery. And God answered her prayers. Within a week he was up again, full of his usual boundless energy, and happily planning his next campaign against France.

Katherine had put off speaking to Jane Popincourt because of Henry's illness, but now she summoned her, and kept her standing.

'There is talk of your having become too close to the Duc de Longueville,' she said. 'Do you know that he is a married man?'

Jane coloured. 'Yes, madam, but unhappy in his marriage.'

Katherine sighed. 'That is no excuse. My maids must be above reproach. And rumour has it that you are his mistress, and not just in the courtly sense.'

Suddenly Jane's customary control broke and she threw herself on her knees before Katherine. 'I love him, madam! I live for him. And I know he feels the same about me.'

Katherine pitied her. She knew what it was to love someone while thinking that any chance of happiness with them was as far away as the moon.

'It is not just a matter of love,' she said gently. 'It is a matter of what is acceptable behaviour, which you should know, having lived at court for sixteen years.'

Jane was weeping, her shoulders heaving. 'What shall I do?' she sobbed. 'I cannot give him up!'

Katherine laid a hand on her head. 'The game and play of love is one thing, and I have no objection at all to that. But anything more is a sin in the eyes of God. Flirt with your lover, enjoy his company, keep things light-hearted and honest – but do not put your reputation, and mine, at risk.'

Jane seized Katherine's hands and kissed them. 'Oh, thank you, madam – I will, I will, I promise!'

The Princess Mary was glowing, all brilliant red hair and sparkling green eyes, as she seated herself next to Katherine in the gallery at the side of the tennis court. Henry and Brandon were stripped to their shirts and drawers, ready to play, and Mary could not take her eyes off the amiable Brandon. Listening to the men discussing strategies, while Mary, with the bloom of youth on her, chimed in admiringly, Katherine, still upset about Henry's rejection of her advice, felt as if she were on the outside looking in. Her preoccupations were so far removed from theirs, and beside them she felt old and staid – a sad reflection upon one who was not yet twenty-nine! Yet she knew she had gained flesh in the five years since her marriage, and that next to Mary she paled by comparison. God be thanked that Henry did not seem to see her any differently.

When the men had taken up their positions on the court, Katherine took the opportunity of speaking to Mary as they watched the game, which was fast and furious. She loved to see Henry play, his fair skin glowing through his fine-textured shirt. But today she was preoccupied.

'Good sister,' she said, laying her hand on Mary's, 'I have noticed that you and Brandon are good friends.'

Mary flushed. 'I love him,' she whispered. 'And he loves me.'

'You must not say that!' Katherine chided her softly, sorry that her concern over the girl had been so accurate. 'You are betrothed to the Archduke. Princesses like ourselves have no choice in these matters.'

'It's all very well for your Grace,' Mary retorted. 'You married my brother, and you love each other. But by all reports the Archduke is a cold fish. They say his jaw is so misshapen that he cannot even close his mouth properly.'

'That's mere gossip,' Katherine reproved. 'I have not heard anything like it, and he is my nephew. And if he *is* reserved, he is deserving of your sympathy, for his father died when he was six, and his mother is mad and shut up in a convent. It will be your duty to love him and heal those hurts.'

'Yes, madam,' Mary said, looking doubtful. She was not an ill-natured girl, just one whose heart had succumbed to the wrong man. Katherine's own heart bled for her.

'I do understand how you feel,' she assured Mary. 'But for your own sake, try to distance yourself from Brandon and spend less time in his company. Otherwise it will be harder for you when the time comes for you to go to Brussels.'

'I may never go!' Mary burst out. 'No date has been set.'

'It cannot be long, I'm sure. Under the terms of the treaty made by your father, you will be married this year. The King your brother has written to ask the Council of Flanders if they are ready to receive you as the Archduke's bride. We await their reply.'

Mary swallowed. 'Pray for me!' she whispered.

'You may depend on it,' Katherine promised, then rose smiling to clap Henry, who had bested his friend and was standing there flushed with victory, pulling on his black velvet tennis coat.

Henry's face was red with rage.

'Your father has deceived me!' he roared, erupting into Katherine's chamber and scattering her women with one fierce glare.

'I will not believe it!' she cried. 'My father loves you.'

'Hah! You are an innocent, Kate – or so you pretend! I have been duped, and made a fool of in the eyes of Christendom. Hear this: Ferdinand and Maximilian, who are supposed to be my allies, have signed secret treaties with King Louis, leaving me to fight France alone. No, hold your peace, you will hear me out before you spring to your father's defence, for it is clear now that neither of them ever had any intention of helping me to win the French crown. Those victories I had at Thérouanne and Tournai benefited only Maximilian, and the worst of it is that Louis had agreed with him and your father beforehand that I should be allowed to win them, so that I would go home satisfied and leave them all to pursue their devilish ends.'

'But why would they do that?' But she knew, she knew . . . She had indeed been an innocent, had allowed hope to cloud judgement, for it was now as clear as day that neither of those seasoned princes would ever seriously have agreed to help Henry become King of France. Why would they do that when they might carve it up for themselves? But if Henry had been duped, so had she, for her father had cozened her too with fair words and promises . . .

She could not speak for shame, but it made no difference, for Henry was not interested in hearing what she had to say. He was beside himself with righteous anger.

'Now the Council of Flanders has refused to accept Mary as a bride for the Archduke Charles! Maximilian has broken the treaty, and you may depend on it that your father had a hand in it. How those two could prate about the perfect love we had as allies, when they were deceiving me all the time, is beyond belief! It is an appalling betrayal, and it exposes me as a fool for having trusted them. I do not see any faith in the world save in me only, and God knows that!'

Katherine began to cry. This was a side of Henry she had never seen, and it shocked her.

He was brutal. 'This is your fault!' he shouted. 'For years you've been urging me to heed your father's advice. Well, see where it has led me! And you had the nerve to criticise me for listening to Wolsey – and you accused him of having too much love for the French! Well, madam, I will listen to you no more. You must bear the responsibility for your father's desertion!'

'I did nothing,' Katherine cried out at last. 'I swear that I knew no more than you did.'

Henry was implacable. 'You did your best to make me sacrifice England's interests to those of Spain. You tried to make me a vassal of your father. May I remind you that the kings of England have never ceded place to anyone but God!'

'You told me you valued my father's advice!'

'I listened to *you*, Katherine, fool that I was. I heeded you rather than Wolsey. Now I find myself wedded to the daughter of a man who was my enemy all along.'

'It does not matter who my father is,' she wept, deeply distressed now. 'What matters is the love and trust we have between us—'

'Don't talk to me of love and trust!' Henry spat. 'That has been betrayed, and in future, madam, I will not be listening to you!'

Without another word he stamped out of the door and slammed it.

Katherine broke down when she told Fray Diego what had happened.

'Highness, your duty is clear,' he said. 'You must forget Spain and everything Spanish in order to keep the love of the King and the English.'

'But what of my loyalty to my father?' she asked in dismay. 'And what of the alliance between England and Spain, which it is my duty to preserve?'

'Your first duty is to your husband!' he insisted.

Bewildered, she sent for Luis Caroz. It was essential that she explain to him what had happened and how angry Henry had been with her.

'I should not be here, Highness,' he said. 'The King has made it clear to me too that my master is his enemy, and it would not do for me to be seen to be counselling you.'

'I beg of you, listen and help me,' Katherine urged, near to tears again. 'It is essential that I regain the King's confidence.'

'Highness, my advice is to do as King Henry wishes for now. Refrain from involving yourself in politics. Perform your ceremonial duties, order your household. Give him no cause for complaint. There has always been great love between you, and when the King's anger dies, he will remember that.'

'But what of Spain's interests? Fray Diego says I must forget Spain.'

'Highness, at this time the best way you can serve Spain is in obeying your husband the King. In pleasing him, you may yet recover your influence. That is what we must hope for.'

It was going to be hard, she thought, after Caroz had gone. For five years she had been at the centre of events, and Henry had confided in her and consulted her. He had respected her views, so it was dreadful to think that he now held them in contempt. Worse still, the door was now open for Wolsey to usurp her place fully in the King's counsels, and that she could not endure. But she knew that Caroz had given her wise advice. She must be patient, and trust in God to heal this terrible breach between her and Henry. And if she bore him an heir, she might yet win back her influence. That was something Wolsey could not do!

But Wolsey could demonstrate his predominance in other ways. Katherine was appalled when she learned that he had brokered a new French alliance. Of course, it was what he had wanted all along, and once she was out of favour he had seized his chance.

Throughout these long, terrible weeks Henry had treated her with cold courtesy. He listened to Wolsey these days, and no longer heeded her opinions. The whole court seemed to know of his displeasure with her, and she burned with the injustice of it, yet she held her peace and showed herself cheerful and gracious when she and Henry were together in public. In private it was a different matter, for he had ceased visiting her apartments and she could not but mourn his absence. Many were the days when Maria had to offer her a shoulder on which to weep, many the nights when she cried into her pillow. And there was another thing, a new and uncomfortable awareness that she was a Spaniard in a court in which all things French were now the fashion. She did not think she could bear to lose the love of the English people as well as that of their King.

At last – just when she thought her breaking heart could take no

237

more – Henry came to her, rosy from his exertions at tennis. She got to her feet in hope, full of love and forgiveness, and sank into the deepest of curtseys; but his manner was cool and distant.

'Katherine, I have come to tell you that the Princess Mary is to marry King Louis,' he announced.

Wolsey had done his work well! To have convinced Henry to make friends with the enemy he had not long since sworn to overthrow must have taken a special kind of cunning – although Henry, furious at Maximilian and Ferdinand's betrayal, would have been glad to acquire a powerful ally against them, even if it *was* Louis.

How she kept the smile on her face she never knew. Poor, poor Mary . . . To be wasted on that horrible man, that French monster! At least the Archduke had had youth on his side, but Louis of France was old before his time, decrepit and in bad health. He had divorced his saintly first wife for her barrenness, and his second had only just died, worn out by many pregnancies, which had resulted in just two daughters, which meant – because women were barred from ruling in France – that Louis would be after making sons. Would a crown be compensation for all that in the eyes of a beautiful eighteen-year-old girl who was in love with someone else?

Henry was watching Katherine closely. 'It is a great alliance,' he said. 'Never before has an English princess become Queen of France. And it is because I alone have acted with the purest faith that God favours my designs.' He gave her a hard look.

'Sir, I rejoice with you and Mary,' Katherine said, trying to sound as if she meant it. 'When is the wedding to be?'

'In October,' Henry told her. 'Longueville is acting for Louis in finalising the arrangements. We will hold the proxy ceremony here at Greenwich, next week. I trust you are in good health and able to be present.'

'I am well,' she said. 'The child has quickened.'

'God be praised.'

There was a flicker of warmth in his eyes, and for a moment she thought he would unbend and show her some gesture of affection, but he merely bowed and walked away. At least he had come. The ice had been broken, and now it was up to her to win back his love and respect. She must suppress her hatred of the French, put on a brave face and endure these ceremonies. And when Mary came weeping to her, as she had known she would, Katherine urged her to obey the King and be content with the great marriage he had made for her.

Well pleased with Jane Popincourt, who had made an honest show of heeding her advice, she lent her maid to Mary to help her perfect her French. Soon it became clear that the Duc de Longueville was also assisting. Katherine hoped that the lovers were being discreet. She reminded Jane of her promise.

'I assure you, madam, I have done nothing for which you could reproach me,' Jane assured her. Katherine trusted that she was telling the truth. Nothing at this late stage must be allowed to tarnish Mary's reputation.

Shimmering in ash-coloured satin with gold chains slung across her bodice, and a cap and caul of cloth of gold, Katherine sat in state next to Henry on a sweltering August day and watched Archbishop Warham join the Princess and the King of France – represented by the magnificently attired Longueville – in holy matrimony; and afterwards she was present with the King and the whole court in the ceremonial bedchamber to see Mary lie down fully dressed on the state bed, and Longueville lie down beside her, each with one leg bared to the knee. Then, as everyone watched avidly, Longueville pressed his naked calf against the Princess's. Jane Popincourt was going pink at the sight.

'Now we may deem the marriage consummated,' Henry said, with an air of satisfaction. Katherine saw him smile at Archbishop Wolsey, whose face bore a triumphant beam. She realised then that it would be impossible at this time to challenge his influence, and that any attempt on her part to do so could only be detrimental to her own interests, and Spain's. So she sat there, in her chair of estate, smiling and nodding and exchanging pleasantries as if nothing were amiss in her world.

Katherine helped Mary to draw up for King Louis's approval a list of those she wanted to attend upon her and accompany her to France.

'Would your Grace object if I took Jane Popincourt with me?' Mary asked. 'I like her well, and she would be glad of the opportunity to return to France. Besides, there is a certain lord who is accompanying me, with whom she is much enamoured.'

'A married lord,' Katherine said. 'Well, I will not stop her. Take her with my blessing.'

Wolsey looked over the list and nodded, and then Henry approved it. But, two weeks later, back it came with Jane Popincourt's name struck out in the French King's own hand. Mary was very upset. She had come to value Jane's friendship and had been relying on her to help negotiate the etiquette and customs of the French court.

'Wolsey's information is that our ambassador in Paris warned him that she was leading an evil life as Longueville's mistress,' Henry told his wife and his sister. 'Moreover, Madame de Longueville will be attending the King's wedding.'

'Is there nothing to be done?' Mary pleaded.

'No,' Henry said. 'Louis has written to me in adamant terms. He insists that his only concern is for the moral welfare of his new Queen. And to compensate you, dear sister, he has sent you this.' He handed Mary a small silver-gilt casket. Inside, nestling on a bed of the finest Florentine velvet, was the largest diamond Katherine had ever seen, with a shimmering pendant pearl attached.

Mary gasped.

Henry was eyeing the jewel covetously. 'It is the famous Mirror of Naples, and it is worth at least sixty thousand crowns!' he told her. 'You are the most fortunate of women!' Katherine could hear the envy in his voice.

Mary was delighted with her gift, and declared that she would wear it at her wedding, but then her voice broke as she remembered that she would shortly be going to a foreign land to marry a stranger, and leaving not only Brandon but her dear friend behind. Katherine watched her turn away so that Henry should not see. And she could only imagine how poor Jane Popincourt would feel at losing her lover when he returned to France with the bridal train.

*

At least this time Henry would not be sailing away and leaving her behind, Katherine told herself as she stood beside him on the windswept quayside at Dover to bid Mary Godspeed. Countless chests of baggage had been loaded on to the ships that were to escort the Princess to France, her officers and servants had boarded, and her ladies were standing shivering in the wind as they waited to attend her on deck. The October weather had been appalling, and the court had been holed up here in Dover Castle for two weeks, waiting for the gales to subside. Katherine prayed that this calm would hold until her sister-in-law reached France. She had never forgotten how seasick and terrified she herself had been on her voyage to England.

Mary, composed and white-faced, said her farewells to the lords and ladies of the court. When it came to Brandon bowing and kissing her hand, no one would have guessed that this was a desperately sad moment for both of them, for Mary's poise was admirable. Katherine reflected that life had not been kind to Henry's sisters: here was Mary, forced to renounce the man she loved, and in Scotland there was Margaret, who had lost her cherished King James to a bloody death at Flodden, and then, as they had heard only last month, impulsively taken a second husband, the Earl of Angus, and lost custody of her sons to the outraged Scots nobles, who hated Angus and were determined not to allow him any influence over the young King.

And there was Jane Popincourt, barely concealing her misery as the Duc de Longueville made her a courtly bow and formally kissed her hand in farewell. How she must be longing to give him one last embrace, one final kiss on the lips . . . Katherine pulled herself up. It was for the best, she told herself.

All the while Henry was growing fidgety, and she guessed that, for all his fine words about the French alliance, he was dreading the parting from his sister, and sure enough, when the time came for Mary to kiss him and crave his blessing, there were tears in his eyes.

'Be of good cheer, brother,' Mary said. 'I pray God we will meet again soon.'

'And I pray that Louis proves a kind husband to you,' Henry replied, sounding very emotional.

'A kind husband is a blessing from God,' Katherine observed, looking pointedly at Henry and being startled by the misery in his face as he returned her glance.

'There is one thing I would ask, brother,' asked Mary. 'I beg this favour of you. King Louis is a sickly old man, by all reports. If he dies, will you give your promise that I may choose my next husband?'

'It's a fine thing to be going to your wedding and thinking of widowhood,' Henry said, forcing a laugh. 'Very well, I promise. Now I commit you to the sea and to the King your husband, and may God go with you.'

As Mary was assisted up the gangplank, Katherine noticed a dark-haired young girl hanging back at the end of the train of ladies who followed her, and looking nervously at the churning sea below.

'It looks as if that little maid doesn't want to board,' Katherine said.

'That's Boleyn's daughter Mary,' Henry told her. 'She's new to court.'

'He has two daughters, doesn't he?' It felt so good to be talking normally to Henry again.

'Yes. The younger one is at the court of the Archduchess Margaret in Brussels. He tells me she is very accomplished.'

Katherine gave no thought to the little Boleyn. She was remembering the Archduchess, Maximilian's daughter, in those far-off days when young Margaret had been married to the Infante Juan. Her memories of Margaret were of a boisterous, laughing, vital girl. By all accounts that girl had matured into the gracious and capable woman who was now acting as regent for her father in the Low Countries, and bringing up her nephew, the Archduke Charles. Katherine wished she could see her again.

Mary Boleyn was now in tears. Her father had stepped forward and was haranguing her to hurry up and get on the ship, shooing her up the gangplank. Katherine shook her head, pitying the child. She knew Thomas Boleyn to be an ambitious man set on his own advancement. Henry liked him enormously. He was learned and capable, useful as a diplomat, thanks to his gift for foreign tongues, and an expert jouster, a talent guaranteed to win his master's favour.

'She's gone,' Henry remarked, grinning. 'You can rely on Tom

Boleyn to prevail. There's no skilled negotiator to equal him. Bravo, Tom!' he called, as Sir Thomas walked towards him, shaking his head.

'Little minx,' he muttered. 'What use are daughters if they don't do as they're told? Good riddance, I say, eh, Harry?'

The King laughed, but Katherine thought Boleyn's manner over-familiar. She did not like or trust the man. Even Henry had said Boleyn would sooner act from interest than from any other motive.

She watched as Boleyn joined his wife, Elizabeth Howard, Surrey's daughter. It was easy to see that she had once been a great beauty, with her oval face, delicate features and dark eyes. Years ago the poet laureate John Skelton had written verses about her that were still in circulation at court. Katherine had read them, and had been shocked at the implication that Lady Boleyn was no better than she should be. Small wonder that she rarely visited the court, if that was what people were saying about her. Today, naturally, she looked unhappy, for she was here to see her daughter off; yet Katherine sensed that there was a distance between husband and wife.

There was no time to ponder on that now. The ship was moving away from the quayside, the Princess and her ladies were waving and blowing kisses as they were borne away, and Jane Popincourt was crying on Isabel de Vargas's shoulder. Henry raised his hand in farewell, tears streaming down his cheeks. When Katherine discreetly laid her hand on his, he did not draw it away.

Soon after the court returned to Greenwich, Luis Caroz came craving an audience of the Queen.

'He would like to speak to you in private, madam,' Lord Mountjoy informed her.

'Very well, have him announced,' Katherine directed.

Caroz, that consummate diplomat, seemed uncomfortable. He stood before her tense and frowning. 'Highness, there are delicate matters that I have to discuss. May I speak freely?'

'By all means,' Katherine said, wondering what was coming.

'It concerns your confessor, Fray Diego. He is very suspicious of me.'

'Alas, he has always believed that you would like to have him dismissed.'

There was a pause. 'Actually I would, Highness,' Caroz said. 'I fear his mind is not quite right.'

'You had better explain what you mean.'

'Naturally Fray Diego has considerable influence with your Highness, but he does his best to prevent me and others from obtaining audiences with you. It is becoming increasingly difficult to see you; nearly every time he puts me off, saying that you are at prayer or indisposed. Your servants go in fear of him. They dare not cross him, as they know he can have them dismissed if he so pleases.'

Katherine had listened in mounting disbelief.

'Excellency, I fear that you are as crazed in your mind about Fray Diego as he apparently is about you. I wish you would both make an effort to be friends with each other. It has got to the point where I feel guilty if I show favour to either one of you.'

'Highness,' Caroz said, 'there are things you do not know about Fray Diego, things I would blush to tell you. I have never seen a more wicked person in my life.'

This was insupportable! 'You have been listening to gossip!' Katherine reproved him. 'I know that is what ambassadors do, but I pray you, use your judgement. I know what people say about Fray Diego, but it is all lies and jealousy. I assure you he is not wicked, but a good man.'

Caroz looked as if he badly wanted to say more, but Katherine did not want to listen to any further complaints. The friar had served her exceptionally well and deserved her loyalty.

'You said there was another matter,' she said firmly.

'Yes, Highness.' There was a long pause.

'Well?'

'I have received a report from the Venetian ambassador in Rome. It may well be unfounded – you know how things get garbled in the telling – but there was a rumour in August in the Papal Curia. I thought you should see this.'

He drew out of his bosom a letter and handed it to her, then stepped back.

Katherine saw the seal bearing the lion of Venice. She scanned the letter quickly, then read it again, out loud, in disbelief.

'"The King of England means to repudiate his present wife because he is unable to have children by her, and intends to marry a daughter of the French Duc de Bourbon. It is said he means to annul his marriage and will obtain what he wants from the Pope."'

She realised she was trembling. Her thoughts returned to that conversation she had had with Henry last year, when she had voiced her fears about the validity of their marriage. He had reassured her that there was nothing to worry about – but a chill went through her when it occurred to her that she might have awoken his own doubts.

She made a tremendous effort to calm herself.

'This cannot be true,' she declared. 'It is certainly unfounded. Well before August His Grace knew that I was to bear him a child. He loves me. He would never think of divorcing me, especially when we are both praying for a son to be born to us.'

'Of course not, Highness. It is unthinkable that the King would make suit to the Pope at such a time. We are all praying for a prince.'

She was glad to dismiss Caroz. Her thoughts were in turmoil. Was it possible that, back in June, when Henry was furious with her, he had said something in anger that gave the impression he wished to be rid of her? Wolsey would have leapt on it, of course. He had always seen her as a rival, and might well have placed a more serious interpretation on his master's remarks than they merited. She would not have put it past Wolsey to make preliminary inquiries about the possibility of an annulment. He would be delighted to be rid of her, on many counts, not least because he knew she disapproved of him and saw through the bonhomie to the corruption beneath.

She wished she could confide her worries to Henry, but they had only just established a fragile accord and she feared to upset it. He was now showing himself solicitous about her comfort. He visited her daily to ask after her health, often placing his hand on her stomach to feel the child leap. He was once more according her every respect and courtesy as his Queen. But she sensed that he was still resentful of her for her father's sake. He was out hunting for much of the time, spending the short November days in the saddle, and in the evenings he would be gambling or dancing or flirting, often with her ladies. He had always done that, considering such courtesy an obligation of his chivalry, and she had never thought amiss of it, but now she felt threatened. Seven months pregnant as she was, she could not compete with the young women who clustered around her husband, all graceful flowers newly in bud. He was only a man, after all, and young men were always hot in pursuit of sensual love; it would be hard to resist such charms, especially as he had abstained from her bed these many months. Yet their long-ago quarrel over Lady Hastings had taught her that it was best not to cast any doubt on his faithfulness; and her married ladies were mostly of the opinion that wives should turn a blind eye to their husbands' infidelities. Far better to hold her peace and preserve her dignity.

The birth of this child could not come quickly enough, and several times a day she was down on her knees, beseeching God for a son. Once she had a male heir in her arms, she would be forgiven, and all would be well again. But as to what might happen if the child was lost, she dared not think.

Chapter 15

1514–1515

Katherine began to hear the name of Bessie Blount on people's lips. Bessie, a distant relative of Lord Mountjoy, was one of her maids-of-honour, an enchanting girl of sixteen, so it was not surprising that people remarked upon her beauty. Unlike her learned kinsman, she was not blessed with brains, but you could not help but like Bessie – she was gentle and kind, and willing.

Too willing, as it turned out. Katherine could not avoid overhearing her women gossiping and linking Bessie's name with the King's. She was so shocked that she had had to slip away to her bedchamber, where she'd dismissed her chamberers and sat down on the bed, waiting for her churning heart to return to normal. She picked up her glass and stared at her reflection. A plump, tired woman with sad eyes stared back at her. Small wonder that Henry had looked elsewhere.

She was too appalled even to cry. How could she lure him back, eight months pregnant and worn down by misery as she was? Did he not cherish the memory of the five wonderful years in which they had been all in all to each other? Surely he could not have forgotten how much he loved her? This flirtation with Bessie Blount – it could be nothing more – was doubtless a fleeting fancy to divert him while his wife's bed was forbidden him.

How long she sat there she did not know, but the evening shadows were lengthening when she finally got up, smoothed down the covers and drew the curtains, not even registering that she was performing tasks normally done by servants. Then, stiffened in her resolve not to be defeated by this latest trial, she summoned her women and bade them dress her in her finery, for she had a mind to grace the court with her presence this night. There was to be a supper in the presence chamber, followed by music and dancing. She would wear a brave shade of red for that.

She called for her bath to be prepared, stepped into the tub lined with holland cloth, sat down on soft sponges and luxuriated in the herb-scented water as the Vargas sisters sponged her with Castile soap.

'I'll wear the scarlet velvet with the slashed sleeves. Maria, please fetch my cross with the pearl and the quatrefoil necklace.'

Maria regarded her warily. 'Would your Grace like a brooch for your corsage?'

'Yes, the IHS. And I should like my hair loose over my ears and gathered into a plait at the back. Fetch my Venetian cap, please.' She knew she was being too much on her dignity, but she could not face unburdening herself, even to Maria. If she did, she would start crying and never stop.

When she was ready she was gratified with the transformation. The dress was becomingly low-cut, displaying to advantage the fullness of her pregnant bosom. She bit her lips to redden them, splashed on some damask rose perfume, then smiled approvingly at the ladies who were to attend her, all of them sumptuously dressed in their black and white gowns.

She could tell that Henry was impressed when he raised her from her curtsey and kissed her.

'You look very fine, Kate,' he said. It was the first time he had called her Kate in months, and she dared to hope that he had at last forgiven her.

They sat together at table and chatted quite happily. There was no sign of Bessie Blount at supper, but she appeared afterwards when the courtiers assembled in the presence chamber for the dancing. Katherine saw her across the room, in a group with Compton, Elizabeth Carew and Brandon, now newly created Duke of Suffolk. They were all laughing and Katherine saw that Suffolk was gaily consoling himself in Mary's absence; no doubt a dukedom and two pretty maidens were sufficient to distract him.

Seeing Bessie flirting with him and Compton, she was now convinced that Henry's interest in the girl had been a passing one – if that. Once she saw Suffolk beckon Henry over, but Henry shook his head and turned back to Katherine. He had sat out every other dance with her, and dutifully taken to the floor in between with every married lady present, as was courteous. Never once did Katherine see his eyes stray in Bessie's direction. It was over, she told herself. It must be. Maybe it had never happened.

Two days later Henry came to see Katherine.

'I have a serious matter to discuss, Kate. Some of your household came to me this morning and complained that your confessor is fornicating with women of the court. Has anyone said aught of this to you?'

'Fray Diego fornicating?' Katherine echoed, setting aside the rich hood she had been lining. 'I would not believe it of him. But I do know that several of my servants are jealous of the influence he enjoys, and I would not put it past them to make it up.' Or Caroz, she thought, but she did not mention him, lest she give Henry cause for further complaint against Spain.

'You will not object if I question him?' Henry said. 'Nothing must be allowed to touch the honour of my Queen.'

'Not at all,' Katherine agreed, her eyes drawn to Bessie Blount bending her blonde head over the altar cloth she was sewing. 'By all means question him.' She beckoned a page and sent him to fetch the friar.

Fray Diego stood before the King, his swarthy face reddening angrily when he heard what had been said against him.

'I deny it, sire!' he growled.

'Then you are saying you have been badly used?' Henry replied.

'I certainly am. And if I am badly used, the Queen is still more badly used!'

Katherine saw Henry's face tauten. He frowned. Did he fear that the friar was about to throw discretion to the wind and accuse his sovereign of fornication with Bessie Blount?

'You had better explain yourself,' he said, 'and be careful what you say. I would not have you impugning anyone without good cause.'

Fray Diego almost glared at him. 'I meant, your Grace, that you had best take a look at my accusers before paying heed to them. I know who they are, and that they resent me for refusing them absolution. They should be dismissed from Her Grace's service. One is a perjurer and traitor, one has a bastard son, and one leads an unclean life.'

'Then you have never had any connection with Thomasine Haverford or Cecily Swan?' Katherine started in surprise at his naming of her laundresses.

Fray Diego had started in surprise too. His hot denial came after too long a pause, and Henry pounced.

'Ah, but you did meddle with them, you cur, didn't you?'

'No, sire, I did not!' barked the friar.

'I don't believe you,' Henry said, 'and I cannot allow any taint of scandal to stain the honour of my Queen. You are forthwith dismissed from her service and will return to Spain.'

Katherine was about to protest, but Fray Diego forestalled her.

'Your Grace, that is unjust. For nine years I have served the Queen faithfully. I have endured many evils for her sake. Now your Grace has called me a fornicator. By the Holy Gospel, I swear this charge is false. Never in your kingdom have I had to do with women. I have been condemned unheard! Those who complained of me are my enemies and disreputable rogues. Yet I am willing to forget all this unpleasantness, and I am prepared to remain in Her Grace's service if you desire it – but only on condition that I be heard by honest judges.'

No one, Katherine was sure, had ever spoken to Henry in such a condescending manner, and it was small wonder that he had gone red with fury.

'*You* are prepared? *You* are willing to forget . . . ? Do you question my justice? Am I a dishonest judge?' He was almost spluttering in rage. 'Get out. Go!'

Fray Diego bowed. 'As your Grace pleases.' His voice shook. 'Wherever I go I shall pray that you have sons.' He stood up and bowed to Katherine. 'God go with you, my daughter.'

Then he was gone.

Henry was still seething. 'The man is a liar as well as a womaniser.'

'You had no choice but to dismiss him, if it was true,' Katherine answered, trying to come to terms with the shattering of her illusions about the friar.

'It *was* true,' Henry insisted. 'The women concerned made a complaint about him pestering them. He was overfamiliar with them in the confessional; he tried to seduce them. I will not go into details.' Outside their bedchamber he was prudish about discussing such matters.

Katherine thought back to before her marriage and the times when Fray Diego had touched her, and she had thought it merely a gesture of comfort. Had there been more in it than that? She could hardly bring herself to believe it, but . . .

'Have I been a fool?' she whispered at length. 'Was Francesca right all along, and Don Luis? But I refused to heed them. Did I treat Francesca unjustly?'

'You are too full of goodness to see evil even when it is under your nose,' Henry said, then fell silent. Was he thinking of another evil she could have seen, in the person of a fair-haired wench with a winning manner? But maybe – hopefully – she was mistaken. Henry cleared his throat. 'Do not reproach yourself, Kate. I'd rather you had a pure mind than a prurient one.'

When he had gone, promising to find her a new confessor, she was troubled in her mind. After all Fray Diego's years of service to her, she felt she had let him down. She had not even questioned him herself, or insisted he be given a chance to explain. No doubt Henry was right, and the friar had behaved immorally, but she felt that she too had come out of the affair badly.

Had Fray Diego confessed his vile sins? If he had not, or he had backslid, there was little hope of Heaven for him. Because a priest occupied a position of the greatest trust, and to take advantage of it was the worst kind of betrayal. Yet how could she have been blind to his wickedness all these years? There was still in her mind some worm of doubt, some guilty sense that Henry – and she herself – had not dealt fairly with the friar. But all she could do now was recommend Fray Diego to King Ferdinand and appoint Jorge de Atheca her personal chaplain in his stead. Hopefully his dismissal would have taught him a lesson.

'He has served me very faithfully all the time he has been in England, and much better than certain persons pretend,' she wrote to her father, lest Francesca de Cáceres tried to spread her calumnies in Spain. Katherine did not want Ferdinand thinking that she herself had been so unwise as to retain in her service a man of bad character. And she did understand why Henry had summarily dismissed him. Even the slightest breath of scandal could rebound on her.

All told, it had been a miserable year. There was still some awkwardness between her and Henry, and she was beginning to doubt that they would ever recapture the joy they had once shared. The child she carried should bring them together, but too often Katherine could think only of the babes she had lost, and the pain she had yet to endure before this one was safely in the world. Wolsey had undermined her influence over her husband. England was shackled to France, although at least Mary's letters were cheerful, and it sounded as if she were leading her feeble husband a merry dance. And now Katherine had been deprived of the confessor upon whom she had always relied. Justified or not, that was a cruelty at such a time.

When Henry spoke of her father, Ferdinand, he still did so with contempt. And when Ferdinand wrote of Henry, he was scathing. 'If someone does not put a bridle on this colt, it will be impossible to control him,' he raged. Katherine found her loyalties brutally torn. When Henry got into a fury about Ferdinand, he spared her nothing, and after he had ranted and roared she would seek refuge in her bedchamber to cry. Once that November she cried so much that her nose bled all evening.

The next morning, her pains started.

'Mother of God, it is too soon!' she sobbed. She had not even taken to her chamber.

The midwife, summoned in haste, spoke sternly to her Queen. 'If you carry on like that, your Grace, you won't do yourself or the child any good. Now stop fretting. I've delivered many an eight-months child that's thrived.'

For hours Katherine laboured, hoping and praying it would all be worth it, and that this prolonged travail meant that the babe was healthy. And then she could reason no more, for it seemed she had entered a long dark tunnel of agony and that her only aim was to rid herself of the relentless pains. They were all shouting at her to push, but they did not seem to understand that she needed *them* to do something to ease her suffering. It was only when she felt a great wrench, as if her body were being torn in two, that she remembered she was birthing a child, and then she did push, with all her remaining strength, and soon there was a violent, wet, slithering feeling between her legs as the babe was drawn out of her.

All she heard was silence. Maria, sitting by the bed with her hood abandoned and her sleeves rolled up, was holding her hand tightly and shaking her head.

'What is it?' Katherine croaked.

'A boy, your Grace,' the midwife said, gathering up a bundle in her arms and laying it on the chest at the foot of the bed.

'A prince!' Katherine said weakly. 'I have borne a prince!' Then she realised that she had heard no cry from the infant. She struggled to raise herself and saw a tiny bloodied form lying on a towel. The midwife was frantically massaging its breast.

'Get me water,' she was panting. 'That might revive him.'

Water was brought, and splashed liberally over the child's crumpled blue face. It gave a slight cough, then did not stir again.

'No!' Katherine screamed, the sound a long howl of misery.

This time Henry was devastated and could not hide it.

'What have I done to deserve this?' he stormed. 'How have I offended God?'

Katherine had no words that could soothe or comfort him. The only one in whom she could confide was Maria, who sat up with her every night of her lying-in, talking her through what happened.

'I was already out of favour,' Katherine cried, 'and now I know that the King's love for me has died. He still holds me responsible for what he is pleased to call my father's treachery, and I fear he thinks that the loss of our son is down to some fault in me. But I was desperate for that child. I longed for him. I wanted him to live so much.'

'I am sure His Grace understands. You have both suffered a bitter blow,' Maria commiserated, looking distraught herself.

'God must love me to confer upon me the privilege of such suffering,' Katherine wept.

One night, as Maria sat late beside Katherine's bed, she confided to her that she had fallen in love with the most wonderful man, who wanted to marry her.

'I cannot believe it is happening at last!' she told Katherine, her eyes shining.

'And who is the lucky gentleman?'

'It is my Lord Willoughby. He wants to speak to your Grace.'

Katherine knew him slightly, a great blond giant with a winning manner and thousands of acres. It would be a fitting match.

'I will look forward to receiving him,' she said, forcing herself to look cheerful. 'I am so happy for you, my dear friend. You deserve to be happy.' It barely touched her, Maria's joy, so great was her own misery.

When she had been churched and was ready to return to the life of the court, she looked in her mirror and saw a tragic wraith. With this last pregnancy she had begun to lose her figure; the stiffened bodice of her English kirtle no longer provided effective underpinning, and her ladies had to make her a Spanish *vasquina* to wear under her gown, and lace it up tightly. She was painfully aware that she looked faded next to Henry's maturing golden beauty and vitality. She found herself wishing that she had not chosen her ladies for their looks as well as their gentle birth, because they no longer complemented her – they exposed all that was lacking in her and made her look old.

She knew she must continue to put a brave face on things, however. She and Henry were both making an effort to put their grief behind them and make a display of happiness. At Christmas, when he staged a disguising at Greenwich, she showed herself especially delighted; and when he brought masked lords and ladies into her chamber for dancing, it felt like old times, and she thanked him heartily for such an enjoyable evening and kissed him, surprising herself at her boldness.

Immediately he kissed her back, a proper, lingering kiss, and everyone present clapped and whooped. That night, for the first time in months, he came to her bed and was gentle with her, even affectionate. He did not stay the whole night, but when he had gone she lay there thinking that this augured well for the future. It was a new beginning.

Hard on the heels of the new year came the news that King Louis was dead. Katherine's thoughts were with Mary, a widow after less than three months of marriage. Judging by her letters, Louis had been a loving and indulgent husband, so Katherine did not know whether to feel relieved or sad for her. She wondered if Mary had got over her infatuation with Suffolk.

'It sounds like she wore him out,' Henry said. They were at dinner with Wolsey in his privy chamber, all suitably attired in black.

'By all accounts he was not a well man,' Wolsey said. 'God rest him.' He crossed himself.

Aye, you were his creature, Katherine thought, and probably in his pay.

'This new King, Louis's cousin, Francis of Angoulême,' Henry said. 'What do we know of him?'

Katherine could sense a tension in him. Already he was jealous of this unknown young rival – for what else could he be, given England's long history of enmity with France?

'He is not king yet, sire,' Wolsey said. 'It is not yet known whether the Queen your sister is with child.'

A gleam came into Henry's eye. 'An English king on the French throne! That would suit me very well! She wrote that she had gone into seclusion.'

'Her Grace must keep to her chamber for forty days, by which time it will be known whether she is *enceinte* or not.'

'God send that she is!' Henry cried.

'Amen to that,' Katherine said. 'But I pity her. I have heard that in

France the chamber of a widowed queen is hung with black, with even the windows covered, and that the only light permitted is from candles. And there must she lie, in her white mourning, with only her ladies for company.'

'I'll wager that Francis's mother is keeping an eagle eye on her,' Henry speculated.

'The ambitions of Madame Louise are well known,' Wolsey observed.

It transpired that it was not only Madame Louise who was taking an interest in Mary. Soon Henry was getting increasingly hysterical letters from his sister, complaining that Francis himself was becoming an all-too-frequent visitor, and that she had no idea what his intentions were, and that they might not be honourable, and if they weren't, God only knew what he had in mind for her, and if her dearest brother did not send envoys to bring her home, she did not know what she might do, for he had no idea how difficult her position was, and she dared not offend King Francis, for God knew she was not with child, and so he was the rightful King after all, but she feared that what he was scheming would be detrimental to Henry and England, and even more so to her, for he saw her as nothing more than a pawn on a political chessboard, and could Henry see his way urgently to bringing her home before something awful happened, and if he did not . . .

Henry crumpled the latest letter and put his head in his hands.

'Was ever man so beset? But for all her ranting, she is shrewd, my beloved sister.' And he showed Katherine what Mary had written.

'I would not trust Francis, or any Frenchman,' Katherine said at length. 'I would hate to be in her position. It must be intolerable.'

'She will not be in it for much longer,' Henry declared, standing up. 'It's clear that Francis means to marry her off to his own advantage. Well, I'm having none of that. If anyone is finding a husband for her, it's me!'

This, of course, was not the right time to remind him of his promise made to Mary, as she boarded her ship to France, that she could choose her next husband herself. But then, of all the people he could have chosen, Henry sent Suffolk to Paris to escort Mary home.

Katherine thought she would never forget Henry's anger when he found out that Suffolk had secretly married Mary, with the connivance of the French King. She was only glad that his sister had not witnessed that explosion.

'But, Henry, you did promise that she could choose her next husband,' Katherine remonstrated, taken aback at such an unprecedented display of the royal Tudor temper. 'I heard you myself.'

There was no reasoning with him. His anger against Katherine had been a cold fury; this time he was at white heat.

'Are you stupid, Kate?' he bellowed. 'Mary's marriage would have been a valuable political asset to me. Her marriage could have secured an important foreign alliance for England, and brought great advantages.'

'They love each other,' Katherine said.

Henry snorted. 'Much joy they will have of each other when I've finished with them! I have loved Suffolk, he has been my boon companion and friend, and I have advanced him and showered favours on him. And he repays me with this! Of all the cursed ingratitude!' He was stamping up and down now. 'The son of a knight, however puffed up he is with a dukedom, is no fitting match for my sister.'

If he said it once, he said it countless times, or rather shouted it, to anyone within range. There was no limit to the punishments he intended to mete out to the hapless Suffolk once he returned to England. He would have his head for this, he threatened, at the very least . . . He even threatened to send Mary to the Tower. By now he was kicking the furniture.

Katherine knew better than to argue with him. He was like the enraged bulls she had seen as a child in the arena in Spain, and there was no reasoning with him. Even Wolsey was keeping his distance. But behind the scenes he had been working to bring about a reconciliation. It was Wolsey who finally calmed Henry down and stilled the troubled waters. Give him his due, he managed it all most diplomatically. In the end, the Suffolks agreed to pay a crippling fine and gave Henry the Mirror of Naples – and Henry, miraculously restored to a good humour, graciously consented to take them back into favour. And so they were summoned home.

What made that sweet spring special for Katherine was the May Day pageant that Henry staged for the ambassadors of Venice. Wearing a gorgeous Spanish gown of crimson velvet, she rode on horseback at his side, followed by a vast train of courtiers, into the woods of Greenwich Park, bound for a secret destination. Henry was waxing very mysterious, and indeed could hardly contain himself, until suddenly the track opened out and they found themselves in a glade where there were tables beneath the trees, set with a lavish feast.

'Welcome to Robin Hood's hideout, masters all!' Henry cried excitedly. 'We are now in the heart of Sherwood Forest, and will make merry!' It was a favourite theme of his, one he returned to again and again.

As if on cue birds began carolling sweetly – Katherine glimpsed cages almost hidden in the branches of the trees. The melodious sounds of shawms, crumhorns, lutes, sackbuts, regals, pipes and tabors echoed from a leafy bower where musicians played unseen. Then, dressed in the familiar Lincoln green and carrying bows, Robin and his merry men emerged from the woodland.

'Your Graces, we invite you heartily, and all your company, to come into the greenwood to see how we outlaws live!' Robin Hood cried. Katherine recognised William Cornish, Henry's talented musician and deviser of revelry, behind the disguise.

Chattering delightedly, everyone sat down to dinner, at which the King and Queen were served succulent venison.

'Poached from my own royal forests, no doubt!' Henry jested, raising his wine goblet to their hosts.

Afterwards an archery contest was held for the entertainment of the foreign visitors, and of course Henry had to have a go, and of course he won.

The afternoon's entertainments culminated with the crowning of the May Queen – Margaret Pole's pretty, giggly daughter, Ursula, who blushed furiously when Henry placed the garland on her head. Then the magical day was over and it was time to return to the palace. A fleet of gilded triumphal cars adorned with figures of giants was waiting to convey everyone back, and as these were borne on their way, escorted by the King's guard, music played and everyone sang. Word of the revels in the woods had spread, and people came running to see the spectacle. Behind the last car, in which Henry and Katherine sat, smiling and waving, thousands followed as they made their way home.

And then Mary Tudor returned, luminously beautiful and basking in the love of her husband. The two of them knelt abjectly before Henry, and he forgave them with expansive magnanimity and warm embraces.

'The irony was,' Mary confided to Katherine later, 'Henry thinks that Charles had his wicked way with me – but it was me who forced *him* into marriage. I warned him that if he refused, I'd go into a nunnery. I cried a lot . . .' She smiled mischievously at the memory.

A week later there was another wedding, this time with the proper royal trappings, at Greenwich. Henry could not bear the thought of his sister being wed in that furtive, secret ceremony in Paris; no, she must have all the magnificence that was due to a Tudor princess! And he himself must have a new suit of clothes in cloth of gold to set off the Mirror of Naples.

From her place of honour by the chancel of the chapel of the Observant Friars, where her own nuptial Mass had been celebrated, Katherine watched the couple taking their vows, and marvelled that, only the summer before, Mary had been distraught at the prospect of a loveless marriage. How the wheel of Fortune had spun! Now that Louis was dead, Mary had been able to arrange for Jane Popincourt to return to France, and she had gone, rejoicing, to be reunited with her lover. Katherine was so glad that both Mary and Jane had found happiness, and that all was rosy once more between Henry and his sister.

Chapter 16

1516–1517

'A beautiful healthy daughter, your Grace!' beamed the midwife, reverently laying the cloth-wrapped bundle in Katherine's outstretched arms. Katherine looked down into the tiny face and gazed in wonder at a miniature image of herself – the same uptilted nose, firm chin, rosebud lips and wide eyes. But the colouring, the red hair – that was also Henry's. This child was a true Tudor – and a true Trastamara.

She could not feel disappointed that the baby was a girl and not the longed-for son. This little one was bawling forcefully and likely to thrive, and after losing four babies Katherine found it miraculous to have a healthy child in her arms at last. She could not stop thanking God for this precious gift, could not take her eyes from the beautiful little face.

It was soon after four o'clock, still dark outside on this February morning, and the palace of Greenwich was cloaked in the hush of night. But as soon as Katherine had been washed, clad in a clean night-rail and lifted into her bed of estate, someone had been sent to wake the King and inform him that he had a daughter. It was only minutes before he arrived, and when he entered the room, the skewed clasps of his furred nightgown bearing witness to his haste, he stopped and stared in wonder at Katherine with the babe in her arms.

'God be praised!' he exclaimed, hastening over to kiss her and taking the child, as the ladies looked on beaming or wiping away a tear.

'A right lusty princess!' he declared, his voice filled with emotion. 'May God bless and preserve you all the days of your life – my little daughter!' He looked at Katherine. 'You have done well, Kate, very well,' he said. 'She is a beauteous babe. I do trust that all is well with you?'

Katherine smiled up at him, enraptured at the sight of him cuddling their child. 'I am tired,' she said, 'but so thankful that all went well. I would have been yet more pleased had I borne you a son.'

Henry shook his head. 'What matters is that you have come through your ordeal safely and that we have a healthy child. We are both young; even if it was a daughter this time, by the grace of God sons will follow. We will name her Mary, in honour of the Blessed Virgin. Does that please you?'

'I could not think of a better name,' Katherine said contentedly. 'And it is in honour of your sister.'

'We will have a splendid christening in the Observant Friars' chapel,' Henry said. 'Margaret Pole must be one of the godmothers. But we can talk about that later. For now, you must get some rest. Where is the nurse?' A woman stepped forward and he laid the baby in her arms. 'Put her in her cradle and see she is rocked to sleep gently.'

He stood up. 'Bless you, Kate,' he said, stooping to kiss Katherine tenderly. 'I will visit you when you are rested.'

The Princess Mary, now Duchess of Suffolk but known to all as the French Queen, was one of the first to visit Katherine after her upsitting. Katherine was relieved to be upright after days of being made to lie flat, and she was even gladder to see Mary's lovely face smiling down at her. During the past months they had become close.

'What a beautiful babe!' the French Queen exclaimed, peering into the great cradle and pulling back the cloth-of-gold coverlet so that she could see little Mary, who lay there swaddled and bonneted, sweetly slumbering. 'I hope God vouchsafes me such a pretty child!' She was nearing the time when she would have to take to her own chamber, and Katherine hastily bade her sit down.

'The whole court is celebrating,' the French Queen told her. 'There is so much joy in England at the birth of the Princess.'

'There is much joy here too,' Katherine said. 'Henry and I are now in as perfect love as ever we were.'

'I know that the last two years have not been easy,' her sister-in-law said. 'Even Louis said he felt sorry for you. He knew that the alliance with France would be hateful to you.'

'It was not just the alliance, but the fact that Henry blamed me for what he saw as my father's treachery.'

'That was unjust of him. I'm sorry I could not help. I knew that things were going hard for you, but it was not my place to criticise my brother, and I had troubles of my own. I was dreading leaving England and all I held dear to marry Louis.'

Katherine squeezed her sister-in-law's hand. 'But he was not such a bad husband.'

The French Queen sighed. 'He was very kind. He had laid on so many celebrations in my honour, and was so generous and loving to me. He told me I was his Paradise, would you believe? And he kept apologising because his health did not permit him to join in all the festivities. It was easy to feel affection for him. I had not expected that. And the other . . .' She flushed slightly. 'It was not so bad, except that Louis went around boasting to the court that he had thrice crossed the river on our wedding night! He hadn't, but I wasn't going to deny it. It was embarrassing, though, but as nothing to what poor Charlotte d'Albret suffered when she wed Cesare Borgia. People were spying on them through the keyhole. That marriage was consummated six times! They say I wore Louis out in bed, but it's a long way from the truth. He was ill for most of those few weeks we were married.'

'Poor man. I am glad he was good to you,' Katherine said, though she felt uncomfortable discussing such intimacies. They were best kept private between the two persons concerned. 'But you are happy now,' she said, changing the subject.

'Never happier,' the French Queen declared, her eyes brilliant pools of sapphire blue. 'Especially now that Henry has truly forgiven us. I wish I could come to court and see you more often. You do understand that we can't afford to?'

Katherine knew that it would take the Suffolks years to pay their debt to Henry. 'You are here now,' she said, stretching out her hand again, 'and I am so glad. I have been feeling weepy these past few days. It's silly, when I am so happy, but the midwife says it is normal at this time. Henry has been marvellous. He's been coming twice a day to see me and he adores Mary. You should see him with her!' She smiled to think of it.

Yet she had sensed that Henry was holding something back. There was no doubting his delight in his daughter, but she suspected that he was nursing disappointment about not having a son. She could not blame him, for it was only natural that he was concerned about the succession, and every man wanted a boy to carry on his line, be he king or yeoman. But Katherine, the daughter of Isabella of Castile, did sometimes wonder why it was seen as essential for a man to rule. Her mother had been a great queen, and pray God that Mary would take after her; and thus she herself could see no good reason why Mary should not rule. Yet now was not the time to say that to Henry. That conversation would have to wait on an opportune moment.

Henry came to see her that evening after Vespers. The baby was sleeping – she was such a good little mite – and Katherine was propped up on her pillows, trying to read her missal but spending most of the time gazing adoringly into the cradle. When she saw Henry in the doorway she laid her book aside, for it was as if the room had lit up with his presence.

He sat down on the bed beside her and took her hand. 'I trust you are feeling stronger today, darling,' he said.

'I am,' she told him. 'I'm not bursting into tears at everything, thank goodness. Hopefully I'll be allowed to get up soon. I am longing to be back to normal.'

Henry's smile did not reach his eyes. He seemed distracted. 'Kate,' he said, 'there is some news that I felt I should keep from you until you were strong enough to bear it, but I feel I should keep it no longer. Your father has died, God rest him.'

She wept then, real tears born of grief, not of female vagaries. It was so terribly sad to lose the man who had been a guiding presence all her life, to see such greatness brought to dust; sad too that Ferdinand had been taken just when he and Henry had become friends again. It had taken a long time, but by last autumn Henry's anger had burned itself out, and a new accord had been established between them.

Henry had still made it clear that he would never again be in tutelage to Ferdinand. 'I will not allow anyone to have it in his power to govern me,' he had said. But by then Katherine was happy enough knowing that the two men who meant most to her were no longer enemies.

The accession of the new King of France had had much to do with that. King Francis was three years younger than Henry, elegant, accomplished, notoriously lecherous and extremely rich. Already his court was the most brilliant in Christendom, a magnet for artists and men of letters and beautiful women, and already he had shown himself to be as devious as any of his wily predecessors when it came to politics.

Henry was not a little jealous. No longer was he the youngest, most handsome, most sought-after sovereign in Europe. Right from the beginning, especially after he had been told that the new French King had tried to seduce his sister while she was secluded in mourning, he had distrusted and resented Francis; the jealousy was mutual, and there had developed a strong sense of rivalry between the two monarchs.

Henry was determined to prove himself the better king, in every respect. Katherine had been present when he'd asked the Venetian ambassador if the King of France was as tall as he.

'Is he as stout? What sort of legs has he?'

'Spare, your Grace,' the ambassador told him.

'Look here!' crowed Henry. 'I also have a good calf to show!' And he opened his doublet to display a shapely and well-muscled leg, much to the ambassador's discomfiture.

Happily anticipating a new war with France, he had ordered the construction of several great ships to join the navy he was proudly building. Katherine had gone down to Southampton with him to review the fleet, and they had clambered all over the *Henry Grace à Dieu* and the *Mary Rose*. He had been in his element that day, dressed up in a sailor's coat and breeches of cloth of gold. He'd been as delighted as a schoolboy to act as pilot, blowing the large whistle of his office as loud as a trumpet, deafening everyone nearby. That had been a happy day.

Inevitably he had turned away from France and looked to Spain for friendship. Katherine had been overjoyed to find Henry his old loving self, and to be once more at his side at pageants and revels, with him paying her every attention and courtiers competing for her favour – and Bessie Blount standing meekly with her other ladies. But what would happen now?

Henry was holding her, gentling her as she poured out her grief. She was devastated that she could not tell her father that she had at last borne a healthy child. She had been about to write to him with the news. Now the Lord who had given had taken away, with perfect timing. He had sent her child to comfort her. The thought calmed her.

'What will happen now?' she asked, disentangling herself and lying back on the pillows.

'Your nephew Charles has succeeded as King of all Spain and Naples,' Henry said. 'At sixteen he can take over himself. Nominally he is joint King of Castile with your sister Juana, but effectively he will rule alone.'

'He will have a great inheritance,' Katherine observed.

'He will one day be the most powerful ruler in Christendom. When Maximilian dies he will have the Low Countries and Austria, and may one day be emperor. Thank God you are his aunt, and we have strong trade links with the Low Countries, for we will need his friendship.'

'I think of him as a mother does, since Juana cannot be a mother to him. And though I would give anything to have my father alive again, it is good to see Spain reunited.'

'It is a very good thing,' Henry said. 'I never told you that when your mother died and your father ceased being King of Spain but was merely King of Aragon, my father made me secretly repudiate my betrothal to you because he thought he could wed me to a greater princess. But I held steadfast to you all those years, and now you are a princess of Spain once more.'

'I never knew that!' Katherine said. 'I remember my grief at his coldness, and that he would forever keep us apart. It all makes sense now, the change in your father's attitude towards me, and his demands to my father. I could never understand why he was so unkind to me when he had been so eager for me to marry Arthur.'

'My father was a changed man after my mother died. He ceased being human.' Henry's mouth set grimly. 'I hope I have made it up to you, Kate. And Kate . . .' He paused, then squeezed her hand. 'I know I said some harsh things about your father, and about you. I regret them now, very much.'

'They are forgotten,' Katherine said, thinking that out of sadness something good and precious had been born.

That spring Katherine was overjoyed to be standing beside Henry when he welcomed King Charles's ambassadors to England. Her husband looked exceptionally magnificent leaning against his gilded throne, wearing a cap of crimson velvet, a doublet of striped white and crimson satin, scarlet hose, slashed from the knee upwards, and a mantle of purple velvet falling in heavy folds at his feet. From his gold collar there hung a diamond the size of a large walnut.

It delighted her to preside with him over the feast given in the envoys' honour, even if it did drag on for seven hours, and she felt she would burst after eating so much rich food. She loved sitting in the royal stand at the jousts given in honour of her countrymen, marvelling with them and the French Queen as Henry showed off his horsemanship in a breathtaking display. They all gasped in wonder as Governatore, his noble charger, performed almost supernatural feats, making what seemed like a thousand jumps in the air. Then, changing mounts, the King made his fresh steed fly rather than leap, to the delight of everybody.

From feasts to jousts to private dinners in Katherine's chamber, Henry offered her countrymen every honour. There was a lavish reception in the great hall, at which Katherine looked on proudly as Henry showed off Mary to the envoys, his delight in his daughter lighting up his face.

The only cloud in her sky was the relentless presence of Wolsey.

Last year the Pope had made him a cardinal, which was far more than he deserved, the worldly, arrogant knave. Then Henry had appointed him Lord Chancellor, immeasurably increasing his power. She watched Wolsey making his stately way about the court in his red silk robes, the great chain of office weighted about his neck, and her resentment festered. She knew that he would never again let her enjoy the influence that had once been hers. Henry was so busy disporting himself and spending his father's riches that, more than ever, he was willing to leave affairs of state in Wolsey's capable hands. The Cardinal was now virtually running the country, and her heart sank to think that Henry was happy to let him do it.

Luis Caroz had been quick to raise his concerns. 'It is impossible to speak to His Grace these days,' he said, drawing Katherine aside after attempting to meet with Henry. 'It is essential to speak first of any serious matter to the Cardinal, and not to the King. Highness, whatever you do, do not cross this man.'

'I have no intention of doing so,' Katherine declared. There were subtle ways in which she too could make herself indispensable to Henry, and if God sent them a son next year, she would be in a very strong position. So when Wolsey invited her and Henry to see his new palace of Hampton Court, she resolved to put on a smiling face. Yet when His Eminence, bustling about in his gaudy finery, proudly showed her his massive red-brick residence, his private apartments lined with gilded linenfold panelling, the vast wall paintings by Italian masters, the ceilings delicately carved and painted in gold leaf, the accommodation for thousands of retainers, and a host of other wonders, she burned with anger, for this house of the Cardinal's far excelled any of the King's palaces in its luxury and its grandeur. And well could Wolsey afford such extravagance, for the King had been fabulously generous to him. But it was not right for a servant to appear richer than his master!

She saw Henry looking enviously at the riches unfolding before him, and thought he was thinking the same things as she was. Yet when they were seated in their barge, being rowed back to Greenwich, he was in a buoyant mood and seemed in no way jealous of Wolsey.

'Seeing Hampton Court has made me realise that many of my houses still need refurbishment,' he said. 'I'm going to enlarge and beautify Greenwich and Richmond and Eltham, and one day soon they will excel Hampton Court in magnificence.'

It was dusk when they alighted and made their way through the gardens by the light of torches, their retinue trailing behind them. Then, out of the evening darkness, a man's voice sang out above the chatter:

'Why come ye not to court?
To the King's court or to Hampton Court?
The King's court hath the precedence,
But Hampton Court hath the pre-eminence!'

There was a burst of jeering laughter, but Henry was frowning. Surely he must have heard what people were saying about Wolsey, Katherine thought. He said nothing, though. It was clear from his shut-off expression that he did not want to know.

Katherine thought that Henry would have been pleased to receive his sister the Queen of Scots, but she could tell that he wasn't. He made a good show of it, of course, riding out himself to welcome Margaret Tudor at Tottenham, taking with him the white palfrey that Katherine had sent for her; and he had escorted her in procession through his capital, both of them acknowledging the cheers of the people who had flocked to see them: the golden young King and the poor, much-wronged Scottish Queen, forced to flee from her adopted country after its lords had seized the regency from her. Back at Greenwich, Henry and his two sisters were reunited, and to see them feasting joyously and catching up on the last dozen years you would never have guessed that Henry was feeling disgruntled with Margaret.

'Her proper place is with her husband,' he said later, when he and Katherine were lying in bed. 'Yes, I know she's been badly treated in Scotland, and that she's been wrongly deprived of her office and her son the King – my God, she hasn't stopped complaining about it – but she insisted on that rash marriage with the Earl of Angus. She knew the lords hated him. Heaven knows, it was the worst thing she could have done.'

'They did imprison her,' Katherine pointed out. 'She was forced to flee to England when she was near her time. It's a wonder she did not lose her baby.'

'Yes, and because of that I have to spring to her aid, for I cannot have them treating my sister like that. But I've suffered years of her complaints – you have no idea, Kate, for I would not weary you with them all. And now I have all to do to make peace between her and the lords of Scotland. As if I haven't enough on my hands!'

Katherine felt sorry for Margaret. She knew that the Earl of Angus had stayed with his wife only to see her safely delivered of his child, then raced back to Scotland, hoping to secure the regency for himself. She admired Margaret's tiny daughter and namesake, who was being cared for with the Princess Mary in the royal nursery at Greenwich. Henry was much taken with his niece – little Marget, as he called her – who was just five months older than his own adored child; the cousins looked very alike, and Katherine liked to think that already they were friends.

She spent many long, happy hours with her sisters-in-law, the Scots Queen and the French Queen. Three queens together, they had much in common. Margaret had lost five of her children in infancy, and understood exactly how Katherine had suffered; all had known a great love, and all had recently been made mothers. Katherine, holding Mary on her lap, looked on enviously as the French Queen proudly showed off her newborn son, named Henry for the King.

The sisterly idyll lasted only a short time. The French Queen could not afford to stay at court for long, and had to go home; and Henry made available to his sister Margaret Scotland Yard, the London palace of the kings of Scots.

'I'm not having her at court nagging me any more!' he declared.

Maria was leaving court too. Having just become a naturalised subject of the King of England, she was to marry Lord Willoughby. Radiance shone from her; she was headily in love, and Katherine was glad that her friend had finally made a good match.

'Oh, I shall miss you, my dear,' she said, hugging Maria tightly as they bade farewell. 'You have been with me through so much these past fifteen years.'

'I shall miss you too, Highness,' Maria declared, with tears in her eyes, 'but we can visit each other. I will come to court as often as I can, and I hope your Grace will visit us in Lincolnshire in our new house.' The King had bestowed Grimsthorpe Castle on the couple as a wedding gift.

'Willingly!' Katherine agreed. 'My Lord Willoughby.'

The personable big man with the kind eyes stepped forward and bowed.

'I know I do not need to tell you to take good care of my Maria, for I know that you will,' Katherine said, 'but I beg you to spare her to me sometimes. She has been a true friend to me.'

'Madam, it will be my pleasure to bring Maria to court whenever you wish it,' the kind man said. Then, after many embraces and kisses, they were gone, and Katherine felt bereft. At least Maria was happy, with her William.

Fortunately there was the baby Mary to distract her, and Margaret Pole and Maud Parr were at hand to fill the gap left by Maria. Maud now had permanent lodgings at court, and she divided her time between there and her husband's house in the Strand, so that she could supervise her children's upbringing. Henry had restored to Margaret Pole the earldom of Salisbury, which had been borne by her noble forebears, and with the upturn in his mother's fortunes, and to her evident relief, her clever and gifted son Reginald had been rescued from his miserable existence at Syon Abbey. He had become Henry's special protégé, and was now at Oxford at the King's expense. Katherine suspected that, like her, Henry felt the need to make up to the Pole family for the injustices and tragedies they had suffered in the past, although he would never say so. That would be to admit that his father had connived in judicial murder.

He was forever praising Margaret Pole.

'She is the saintliest woman in England!' he declared. 'I know few ladies as devout and learned – and you are one of the others, Kate!' It did not trouble him that the new Lady Salisbury was of the old royal blood, for her loyalty shone forth.

Katherine loved the happy hours she spent with Margaret, talking about their children. The older, more experienced woman was ready with advice when Katherine needed it, and even Henry listened avidly to her.

'I always thought that two was rather late for weaning,' Margaret said one crisp morning when the rusty red of autumn was tinting the leaves outside, and they were all three together in the royal nursery, and Katherine was holding Mary and kissing her downy red head. 'Not that your Grace has to worry about that yet! But what a dear, sweet child my goddaughter is, and so good.'

'We are truly blessed,' Katherine said, hugging her baby tightly.

Lady Bryan, Mary's motherly lady governess, caught her eye and nodded, smiling. 'Indeed you are, your Graces,' she said. 'She is no trouble at all – a princess to be proud of.'

Henry lifted Mary from her mother's arms and swung her high in the air as she squealed with delight. 'This little one acquitted herself well yesterday,' he said. 'When I showed her to the Venetian ambassador and he kissed her hand, she behaved most regally. I told him that she never cries.'

'That is true, sir,' Lady Bryan said. 'She is the most contented child I ever saw.'

'She looked at the organist and said, "Priest! Priest!"' Henry told them. 'Didn't you, my little lady?'

Mary laughed at him, showing three pearly new teeth.

'Lady Bryan, you have schooled her well,' Katherine said approvingly.

'Her natural grace is inherent, having such parents. It's a joy to see how well she loves her father,' the governess said. 'Every time she sees His Grace, she leaps up in my lap.'

'God could not have sent us a sweeter child,' Henry declared, handing Mary to Margaret Pole, to whom the little girl had taken an immediate fancy.

Later, when Henry had gone and Katherine walked with Margaret in the autumnal gardens, and Margaret spoke of her plans for her castle of Warblington, she was wistful, thinking of those other children who had not lived. What would they have been like? She could not but imagine them romping around in the alleys and bowers, healthy, happy heirs to England, delighting their mother's heart.

'If God would send us a son, I would count myself perfectly happy,' she said.

'Your Grace is young. There is plenty of time yet.'

'You are lucky, Margaret. You had five sons and a daughter before you were thirty. I am thirty and have just the one daughter.'

'Just have patience, and pray, madam. I'm sure your prayers will be answered.'

A germ of an idea was born in Katherine's mind at that moment. Henry, she knew, did not trust most of his other Plantagenet relations. Like his father before him, he regarded them as threats to his security as king, fearing that they would plot to take his throne.

'Some of them would like nothing better than to see the House of York restored,' he had confided. 'They think we Tudors are usurpers. They forget that my father married the rightful heiress of the House of York. I tell you, Kate, I will brook no challenges to my crown!' Three years ago he had executed his cousin Edmund de la Pole, the previous Duke of Suffolk, for that very crime. Yet abroad there lurked de la Pole's exiled brother, Richard, who liked to call himself 'the White Rose'. The year before last, Henry was certain, he had tried to invade England from Brittany, although it had been given out that his purpose there was to look to the duchy's defences.

'I'm having him watched,' Henry had growled. 'I wouldn't put it past that fox, King Francis, to offer him support just to discountenance me, as Louis did.'

The teeth of several of the King's other dynastic rivals had been drawn over the years, and their children were too young to pose any threat. But when they grew up, they too might take up the old cause . . .

Katherine pondered. It seemed to her that there was a way to bring to an end this rivalry and insecurity – a better way than anyone had yet thought of.

'Margaret,' she said one day, pausing from her blackwork, 'has it ever occurred to you that a marriage between your Reginald and the Princess would bind the old royal line with the new one in amity? It would be like the union between the King's parents, the uniting of Lancaster and York that brought the late civil wars to an end. It would seal a bond between the houses of Tudor and Plantagenet, and it would unite our families in perpetual love.'

Margaret stared at her, her long, pale face working with emotion.

'You know, madam,' she said, breaking into a smile, 'sometimes I think they should leave the politics to us women!'

The May Day of 1517 dawned golden-pink, heralding glorious weather. The palace servants had been up for hours, preparing for the day's celebrations. Henry had chosen a place in Eltham park that afforded a spectacular vista of London, and it was here that a royal picnic had been set out on tables beneath the trees. On the nearby heath, deer and their young were grazing peacefully; the hunters would not trouble them today.

Katherine sat on her cushioned chair, Lord Willoughby's letter crushed in her hand. She was delighted for Maria, thrilled to hear her news – but desperately envious, and hating herself for it. For Maria had borne her first child, a healthy son whom, naturally, she and William had named for the King. Lord Willoughby asked if Their Graces would do them the honour of being godparents. Of course, *of course*, they would, and Katherine was going to send her chaplain, Jorge de Atheca, now made Bishop of Llandaff by Henry, to officiate at the baptism. Yet she could not help comparing herself with the fortunate Maria. It seemed so unfair that her friend had borne a son with satisfying speed, but that all her own sons had died. What was God thinking of?

Henry turned to her. 'Wake up, Kate! Have some of this pie. It's wonderful.' He munched contentedly, serving her himself, unaware of her conflicting emotions. She wondered if she should tell him Maria's news. She did not want to depress his buoyant mood.

They had just finished the second course and their goblets were being refilled when Katherine caught sight of Cardinal Wolsey approaching at speed like a vast scarlet galleon, with several Privy councillors in his wake.

'Your Grace,' he called breathlessly, as soon as he came within earshot, 'there are riots in the City. The apprentices have risen against all foreigners.'

Henry jumped to his feet. He had been laughing moments earlier, but his face was now like thunder. 'By God, how dare they? For years I've been encouraging foreign merchants to set up trade in London, yea, and seen they were made welcome.'

'Aye, sir, and they have prospered. Many of them are Her Grace's countrymen.' Wolsey bowed his head briefly in Katherine's direction.

'England has prospered because of it,' Henry said, still flushed with anger. 'How dare these knaves attack those under my special protection!'

'Sir, there is much resentment. The people do not like foreigners stealing their business, as they see it. But whatever the rights and wrongs, we have to act. Mobs of apprentices are fighting in the streets, and I fear for the safety of our foreign guests.'

'I will leave for the City at once,' Henry said. 'Send my guards ahead, and tell them to bring the rioters under control as quickly as possible.'

Wolsey sped away and Henry hastened back to the palace with Katherine and his courtiers. Then he was gone, riding like fury to London.

The next day, word came to Katherine that the riots had been suppressed and that hordes of apprentices had been herded into Westminster Hall to await the King's justice. She was to take her barge and go there immediately.

On arrival she was escorted to the high dais in the vast, crowded hall, where once she had sat for her coronation feast. Henry was already enthroned there, with Wolsey seated magisterially at his side. His face stern, her husband kissed her hand and bade her be seated next to him. She looked down the steps before her at a multitude of young men, all with halters about their necks. Their terrified faces were upturned as one, beseechingly, to the King's implacable visage.

Henry leaned over to Katherine. 'The world must see that I am determined to avenge these outrages that have been committed against our foreign guests, so I intend to be terrible in my judgement. I wanted you present, Kate, so that you can see justice done, for some of the victims are your countrymen. But you may feel that a degree of mercy is in order.' He raised an eyebrow at her. 'I leave that to you.'

She understood immediately what she was required to do. She was really here to allow the King to temper justice with mercy. He would not lose face if she begged it of him.

Henry addressed the prisoners from the throne in a voice of steel. 'You are all guilty of a most heinous and grievous crime against innocent persons who are under my royal protection, as guests in my kingdom. After this evil May Day, what foreign merchant would risk his business by coming to London? It must be made plain to them that London is a safe place, and that they are welcomed by all. Those who have risen against them, and made a mockery of my protection, must be made an example of. I sentence every one of you to be hanged.'

The faces of the apprentices – most of them youths and young boys – registered shock, as from the back of the vast hall came an outburst of the most pitiful weeping and wailing.

'We made sure that their mothers and sisters were present to hear my judgement,' Henry murmured. Some of the apprentices themselves were crying now.

'Oh, the poor souls,' Katherine breathed. As a mother herself, she could imagine how those women were feeling. How terrible to lose their sons so young and so shamefully! Some of the condemned looked as if they were not even old enough to shave.

She knew what Henry expected of her, but she would have done it anyway. She rose from her seat, knelt before him and raised her joined hands in supplication, her tears falling unprompted.

'Sir,' she pleaded, 'for my sake, and the sakes of those poor ladies who are about to lose their sons, I beg of you, spare the apprentices.'

To her surprise, Wolsey was also sinking stiffly to his knees. 'May I add my plea to Her Grace's?' he beseeched the King. Katherine could not help thinking that this was a gesture calculated to enhance his own popularity with the people – and Henry's too.

It was as if the collective breath and tears of the wretches in the hall had been stilled in expectancy, as Henry looked down thoughtfully on the two supplicants kneeling at his feet. Katherine prayed that he would show his humanity; surely he would not turn down such an opportunity of winning the love of his subjects.

His eyes were tender now as he rested them on Katherine. 'I can refuse you nothing,' he said. Then he turned to Wolsey. 'Your prayers are heard, my faithful minister.'

He stood up. His voice rang out. 'All are pardoned and restored to liberty. You young fellows may thank the Queen and the Cardinal for your lives.'

There were shouts and whoops as the apprentices threw their halters into the air and fought their way through the throng to be reunited with their families. Peals of laughter and joy echoed through the cavernous hall, and everywhere there was praise for the good Queen, whose gentle plea had prevailed. Katherine heard it and was deeply touched.

Henry was beaming broadly, standing with arms akimbo, as he watched the joyful scene below him.

'You have done a good day's work, Kate,' he said. 'And you too, Thomas.' He raised a hand, acknowledging the cheers for himself. There was little he loved more than the acclaim of his people. 'Now everyone is pleased, and no harm is done.'

Katherine had to agree that it had been a masterful piece of statecraft. She wondered if it had been Wolsey's idea.

Soon afterwards Katherine bade a somewhat relieved farewell to Margaret Tudor and her little girl. They had been living at Scotland Yard for nearly a year now, on Henry's charity. Margaret's husband, the Earl of Angus, had refused to join them, much to her distress, and had revealed his mercenary motives in marrying her by appropriating her rents in Scotland. Since then, she had done nothing but lament and complain, and even Katherine, sorry for Margaret as she was, had grown weary of it.

Henry had concluded a new truce between England and Scotland, which gave her hope of recovering the regency and custody of the young King James and allowed him, at last, to send her home. With unflattering alacrity Henry appointed the Earl of Shrewsbury to escort Queen Margaret north. The farewells between brother and sister were strained, and when Margaret's cavalcade had disappeared up the Great North Road, Henry turned to Katherine and let out a long sigh.

'Thank God!' he murmured. 'If there's any talk of her coming here again, I might just need to plan a campaign in France!'

Chapter 17

1517–1518

'We must leave London right away, Kate,' Henry said, his eyes wild.
'I've just had a report that there is a case of the sweating sickness in the
City.'

Katherine's first thought was of Mary, secluded in her nursery at
Richmond. She had heard of the dreadful epidemic of the sweating
sickness, which had visited England in the year in which Henry's father
had won the crown, but that had been long ago. The late King's enemies
had deemed it a judgement of God, for thousands had died of the
disease.

For a man of such great courage in nearly every other respect, Henry
had an inordinate fear of illness and death. They disgusted and terrified
him. Katherine had lost count of the times he had shown her a blemish
or rash and asked if she thought it was a symptom of some dread
malady. If he caught a cold he treated it like a serious illness. He could
not bear to be in the company of anyone afflicted by sores or disease.

She wondered if the loss of his brother Arthur, closely followed by
that of his mother, had instilled this fear in him. She guessed that it was
made worse by the heavy awareness that, if he died, there was as yet no
son to succeed him. But she was sure that it was not just the threat of
civil war that panicked him. This was something far more personal.

She had seen him flee from the plague that visited London nearly
every summer and flourished in the filthy, narrow streets. She had seen
him hide himself away in some remote house, with only a few attendants,
to escape it. Plague, he often said, was no respecter of persons, and
he had to keep himself safe. Yet she had never seen him as terrified as he
was now.

He drew her to him distractedly. He was trembling.

'The sweat is deadly,' he muttered, 'far worse than the plague. Kate, we've been fortunate never to have experienced an outbreak of the sweating sickness, but I've heard awful things about it.' He turned to his hovering physician. 'Dr Chambers knows how virulent it is.'

'Indeed, your Grace. It is a loathsome disease, and frightening, because a man can be well at dinner and dead by supper time.'

'Most of those struck down with it die,' Henry said gloomily.

'It is highly infectious too,' the doctor added. 'It spreads with terrifying speed. Your Grace is wise to get away from London.'

'But what happens to those who catch it?' Katherine wanted to know, still thinking of Mary.

'Madam, it begins with stiffness, shaking, a headache, sometimes giddiness. The victim suffers severe prostration. Between one and three hours later, they develop a violent, drenching sweat and a rapid pulse, which worsens until the crisis is reached.'

Katherine shuddered. 'Will the Princess be safe?' she asked.

'I have sent orders that, at the first report of any cases within five miles, she is to be removed,' Henry replied. He relinquished Katherine and began shouting for her women. 'Make ready! Make ready! We're leaving for the country!' he cried, greatly agitated.

Katherine hastened to scribble a note to be sent to Margaret, Lady Bryan, who was in charge of Mary's nursery household, urging her to take the strictest precautions. 'See that this goes to Richmond now!' she commanded one of her grooms, thrusting the letter into his hand as she hurried out of her lodgings.

Wolsey was waiting in the porch to say farewell. He had had the sweat in childhood and recovered, so was immune and able to stay in the capital, looking after affairs.

'Make it clear to everyone, without fail, that under no circumstances is anyone who has been in contact with the sweat to approach us,' Henry said. Then he mounted his waiting steed and was away. It seemed to Katherine that they had packed up and taken to the road within ten minutes.

Several hours later, after pushing the horses to the limit of their strength, they arrived at Woking Palace, which had been hardly used since the days when Henry's grandmother, the Lady Margaret, had owned it. As soon as they had clattered over the drawbridge, Henry shut himself up in his hurriedly prepared lodgings, devising preventatives for the sweat. He had a wide knowledge of physic and enjoyed mixing his own medicines.

Katherine left him to it, not supposing for a moment that any remedy he made would be efficacious against this dreadful disease. A headache had been threatening all day, giving her no small cause for concern, and she retired to her bedchamber to lie down for the rest of the afternoon. Yet she could not sleep; she kept worrying about young Mary and wishing she was with her. She was also praying that her headache would subside, but it did not, and when Henry came to her apartments for a private supper, she was too unwell to join him – and becoming increasingly worried. She was not surprised to hear that he had left in rather a hurry.

The next day she was decidedly unwell and stayed in bed, coughing until her chest ached, terrified that she was going to die and leave Mary motherless. Dr Chambers reassured her that it was most certainly not the sweating sickness, and prescribed an infusion of butcher's broom leaves, berries, iris petals and comfrey roots mixed with honey. It tasted vile, but she dutifully drank it. The arrival of a letter from Lady Bryan reassured her that Mary was well, and that there were no cases of sweat reported in the area, but it had been written two days ago and anything might have happened since. Worry about what might be happening at Richmond kept Katherine from the healing rest she needed.

It was on the sixth day of her illness, when she was beginning to feel a little better, that she realised she had missed her courses for the second time. *Oh, please, Almighty Father, let me be pregnant*, she prayed. She arose from her sickbed; she spent hours on her knees in chapel; she made bargains with God; she fasted.

'Madam, you are doing yourself no good,' Margaret Pole admonished. 'If you are with child, you must look after yourself.'

'But I need to show God that I am worthy of this child,' Katherine protested.

'He knows that, you may be sure,' Margaret said. 'Please go back to bed. You do not look well. Let *me* pray that you may have the blessing of a son.'

Katherine gratefully sank into the pillows. Presently she slept, and when she awoke there was Henry's anxious face peering down at her.

'How are you, Kate?' he asked, taking her hand and squeezing it. 'I have been worried about you. Chambers said I was not to see you, for fear of infection, but I have been asking after you continually.'

'I am on the mend,' Katherine assured him, squeezing his hand in turn. 'And, Henry, I think I am with child!'

She was up and about again, and Henry was treating her as if she were made of fragile glass like his Venetian goblets. But she felt much restored, and the news from Richmond was still reassuring. She was suffering only a little nausea in the mornings, and had a good presentiment about this pregnancy, although she dared not voice it.

Maud Parr was newly pregnant too, and it was pleasant to sit and talk about their coming babies, while stitching tiny layettes in the finest lawn and soft woollen cloth. And – joy of joys – there was a letter from Maria, full of news of her darling baby Henry and her wonderful William. Her lively, witty style evoked memories of the years when she and Katherine had been girls together, and then queen and confidante. Always they cheered Katherine.

But the reports about the sweat were nerve-racking. It was raging in London and had spread well beyond its suburbs. The death toll was rising, with a resurgence of Katherine's anxieties about Mary.

In September, Lord Willoughby wrote to inform her that his and Maria's baby son had succumbed to the sweat. Maria had taken it heavily, and Katherine, her heart aching for her beloved friend, understood only too well what that meant. It was not two weeks since she had been reading of little Henry's pretty ways, his silky dark curls and first tooth. She knew what it was to look upon an adored child's face and see Death claim it. She longed to go to Maria, to comfort her, as

281

Maria had comforted her in the losses of her own children, and she was desperate to see her own child and know that she was well. But it was impossible. Only a crazed person would travel across country with the sweat raging. It could be lurking around any corner. So she lit candles for the soul of little Henry Willoughby, which must surely be with God, and for his grieving parents. She sent them a beautifully illuminated copy of the Lady Julian of Norwich's book, *The Revelations of Divine Love*, and herself wept over the words of comfort it contained: 'God did not say, You will not be troubled, you will not be belaboured, you will not be afflicted; but He said, You will not be overcome.' It was a favourite of Katherine's, and had brought her consolation in her own dark hours.

Henry held her when she told him the news. He closed his eyes, his face pained. He too understood what the Willoughbys were going through. But he was distracted.

'There are cases in Surrey now,' he said nervously. 'We must leave Woking.'

'At Richmond?' she cried.

'No, Kate. Mary is safe there for now. Surrey is a big shire.'

They travelled west into Hampshire. This time Henry rode ahead, and Katherine followed in a litter. Whether it was the jolting on rutted roads, or the effects of her recent illness, she could never tell, but when they arrived at the small, remote, private house that Henry had commandeered from its owner, there was blood dripping down her legs to the floor . . .

Katherine watched Mary lift up her skirts and try to copy Lady Bryan in a curtsey.

'Now try it again for your lady mother,' the governess instructed.

Mary wobbled before Katherine then toppled into a heap of skirts, giggling. She really was the most enchanting child, so blithe, so willing and so sweet-natured.

Sir Thomas More, standing by, laughed merrily. This new Privy councillor of the King's was a renowned scholar and a delightful man. In the short time he had been at court, both Katherine and Henry had come to love him. Today she had invited him to meet Mary, knowing that he advocated the education of women and that in time to come she might want to seek his advice.

'Do it again!' More said to Mary. The two-year-old scrambled to her feet, eager to please the kindly man with the gentle eyes.

'Watch me,' she commanded, and curtseyed beautifully. Everyone clapped and smiled, even Maud, who had had little to smile about since the death of her husband from the sweating sickness last November, and the stillbirth that had followed, brought on by shock and grief. She and Katherine had clung together in sorrow as both mourned their losses. Katherine had found some solace in her daughter, and then in the new child now stirring in her belly, and it was good to see Maud taking an interest in life again.

Margaret Pole led Mary away, as it was time for her walk. Katherine liked her daughter to get some fresh air every day.

'The Princess is enchanting,' More said to Katherine as they strolled along the gallery that overlooked the gardens of Greenwich.

'I hear that your own daughters are very learned, Sir Thomas.' As she spoke the child under her girdle shifted and kicked.

'I have been criticised for giving them the same education as my son, but I see no reason why they should not have it. They are every bit as able – as we see in your Grace too. England is lucky to have as its Queen such a virtuous and learned lady.'

'You flatter me, Sir Thomas!' Katherine smiled. 'Tell me, how is Lady Alice?'

'My wife is in perfect health, madam, and her usual forthright self!' More chuckled. 'I jest, of course, madam! I am singularly blessed in my family. And Alice, while she prefers to ignore St Paul's injunction to learn of her husband in all submissiveness at home, is yet a valiant and redoubtable lady!'

Katherine smiled. 'I look forward to meeting her.' As she paused by a window to watch Mary skipping about in the privy garden below, her cloak discarded on the ground for all it was November and cold, More stopped in front of a portrait hanging on the wall. 'Well, if it isn't my friend Erasmus!'

'He is a great scholar. The King and I think very highly of him.'

'And a great humanist. I count myself proud to know Erasmus. As he says, life without a friend is no life, but death, and ours has been a very special and long friendship. I always keep a room in my house ready for him, should he honour me with a visit.'

'He is always welcome at court too,' Katherine said. 'The King loves little more than entertaining learned men. Sir Thomas, he has asked me to invite you to sup with us tonight. Will you come?'

'I shall be most honoured, madam,' More told her, bowing and kissing her extended hand.

Henry had planned an intimate supper in Katherine's chamber, with just the three of them present. He wanted the chance to talk in depth about the subjects that interested both him and his new friend.

Sir Thomas arrived promptly and confessed to feeling some-what relieved at being accorded such an honour. 'I was so pleased when I was summoned to your Grace's chamber,' he told Katherine. 'It is hard to carry on a conversation amid the clamour of a dinner at court.'

'Welcome, Thomas,' Henry said heartily, clapping More on the back. 'Be seated. We'll have no ceremony tonight. I've been reading your *Utopia* again, and there are many points I would like to put to you. It's incredible, your vision of an ideal state. I would that we could have such in England!'

'I too have read and enjoyed *Utopia*,' Katherine said.

'Then I am doubly honoured!' More beamed.

Henry himself poured the wine, and after the first course had been served he laid More's book on the table. There were several markers in it.

'This part struck me as very wise,' he said. 'If a ruler suffers subjects to be ill-educated, and then punishes them for crimes they commit in their ignorance, what else can we conclude but that he first makes thieves and then punishes them!' He helped himself to roast capon.

'Which leads us to another argument,' More said, looking a little more relaxed. 'Instead of inflicting horrible punishments on those who offend, it would be far more effective to provide everyone with some means of livelihood.'

'Some are incorrigible villains,' Henry observed.

'That is true, sire, but there is much injustice in this world. Poverty and ignorance are at the root of many crimes – and envy. For what justice is there in this: that a rich man who does nothing at all should live in great luxury and splendour; while a mean man – say, a carter, a smith, or a ploughman – who works harder even than the beasts themselves, can only earn a poor livelihood and must lead so miserable a life that the condition of the beasts is much better than his?'

Henry grimaced. 'Thomas, you are a heretic! Who has the right to question the station to which God called him in life?'

More smiled. 'I am the last man you could call a heretic. But I am not making a case for material wealth. It is through learning that ignorance and want are banished. Your Grace knows this better than anyone, for you have cultivated all the liberal arts and possess greater erudition and judgement than any previous monarch. In Utopia nobody owns anything, but everyone is rich.'

'But someone has to push the plough,' Katherine said.

'Very true,' Henry said. 'And some are called to be kings. Thomas would have us all equal!'

'We are all equal in the sight of God, sire – and a happy ploughman will be a better ploughman. But remember that Utopia is a state in which everything is perfect.'

'And therefore it can never exist. But something like it *could* work – perhaps one day. These are powerful ideas, Thomas, ideas that all kings should read. I will give it to my son when he is old enough to read it.' He smiled at Katherine, looking proudly at her high stomach.

Katherine smiled back, sipping her wine. 'Sir Thomas, I did think it a little indecent that Utopians have the bride and bridegroom presented naked to each other before marriage.'

Henry laughed and More grinned.

'Ah, but, madam, they would wonder at our folly! If we buy a horse, we want to see every part of him, so that there may be no secret hid under any trappings; and yet, in the choice of a wife, on which depends a man's happiness for the rest of his life, he ventures into marriage on trust. Not every man is so wise as to choose a wife only for her good qualities. A pretty face may be enough to catch a husband.'

'Bring in that custom and you'll have all the women in Christendom running for cover into nunneries!' Henry observed, grinning. 'Many a man may marry on the strength of a pretty face, so I suppose it's a fair point. Yet it can only be true of poor men, for princes have no choice; they must take the wives others have chosen for them. I was lucky.' He raised Katherine's hand to his lips.

'Beauty may attract a man, but it also takes character and good nature to hold him,' More observed. 'No woman could compete with Her Grace in those qualities. I rejoice to see your Graces so happy together.'

Spiced wine, wafers and candied plums were brought.

'It took a lot of persuading to get this fellow to come to court,' Henry told Katherine. 'He accepted only with great reluctance, when everyone else is baying at me for preferment and offices.' He pretended to be put out.

More looked pained. 'Do not think me ungrateful, sire. I was unhappy about leaving the peace of my home for public life.'

'And are you enjoying being at court?' Katherine asked him.

'Madam, I must be honest. As I feared, I hate it. I am as uncomfortable here as a bad rider is in the saddle. But His Grace is so courteous and kindly to all, and you have both done all in your power to make me welcome. I feel honoured to be singled out for special friendship.'

'I know what a sacrifice you made to humour me,' Henry said, serious again. 'I should not like to think that my presence had in any way interfered with your domestic pleasures. I am just intrigued by a rare man who has no ambition and is content with his family and his books and his animals.'

'In my view, sire, anyone who actively campaigns for public office disqualifies himself for holding any office at all!' More quipped, and they all laughed. What stimulating company the man was.

'Well, Thomas, there is one thing you will enjoy while you are at court. I hear you like astronomy. I have a great love for it myself, and tonight we will go up on the roof and look at the stars together!'

'That will be both an honour and a pleasure, sire!' But as the two men rose, and Henry put his arm around More's shoulders and led him away, Katherine thought she had detected a note of falsity in More's response. He had been hoping, she was sure, to get home and spend the rest of the evening with his family.

'It is hateful – horrible – to think that the Princess is to be the bride of the Dauphin!' Katherine blurted out to Thomas More. They were wrapped in fur-lined cloaks and striding briskly through the wintry landscape of Greenwich Park, far out of earshot of Katherine's ladies and the few others who had ventured forth on this cold day.

She had not been able to contain herself. Fortunately she knew she could rely on More's discretion, even though she felt slightly disloyal to Henry for voicing her complaint. And yet it was not so much Henry as Wolsey with whom she was angry. She would never say anything against the King. She knew that More, no friend to Wolsey, would understand that and respect her confidence.

He shook his head sadly, regarding her sympathetically with his kind, intelligent eyes. 'Treaties between princes are never set in stone,' he murmured.

'Pray God you are right! I had so hoped that Mary might be married to Reginald Pole or to King Charles of Castile himself – but to be wasted on France! And she so precious to me. The prospect is unbearable, dear friend.'

'I may not criticise the King's policy, your Grace,' More said, 'but I understand your feelings.'

Katherine shrank from the implied criticism. 'I myself do not venture to criticise His Grace's decisions, so I have never mentioned the idea of a marriage with King Charles to Henry; and when I brought up the subject of Reginald Pole, he was dismissive. He said that he was no match for the Princess, and that she was destined for greater things. But, Sir Thomas, Reginald is of the old royal blood and surely a fit husband for her!'

'I imagine that marriage with one of Plantagenet blood is a touchy subject with the King,' More observed, his smile wry.

'It is.' She remembered the shuttered look on Henry's face that had told her the matter was closed.

She sighed and sank down on a low stone wall. The unborn infant was busy beneath her girdle. Not long to wait now . . . She invited More to sit beside her.

'My only comfort lies in the fact that the Dauphin is just a babe in arms,' she told him. 'It will be years before he and Mary are of an age to wed, and much can happen in those years. Betrothals can be broken . . . Do you know, it galled me to be present at the celebrations marking the signing of the treaty, but I forced myself to smile and be gracious to the French ambassadors.' She grimaced, remembering how, at the centre of it all, there had been Wolsey, now Papal legate in England.

'I have the Cardinal to thank for this alliance,' she fumed. 'It seems that he now rules both the King and the kingdom. I can recall a time, years ago, when he would say, "His Grace will do this or that." Then it was, "We shall do it." Now – and I have heard him say it several times – it is, "*I* will do it." The Cardinal is king. Everyone says it, even Luis Caroz.'

She got up, feeling the chill through her cloak, and began walking back in the direction of the palace. More kept pace with her.

'Even the King hardly knows in what state matters are,' he said in a low voice. 'The Cardinal rules all. He is a clever man. I have noticed that he always tells the King what he ought to do; he never tells him what he is able to do. In that he is shrewd, for if the lion knew his strength, it would be hard to rule him.'

Katherine stared at him, but the genuine concern in his face convinced her that he meant no disrespect to Henry. She knew better than to press the matter, but More's words troubled her. Was he implying that Wolsey was preventing Henry from realising his full potential as a king? Or – but surely not! – that it would be better for everyone if Henry did not reach that potential?

'I hope, if this child is a boy, to enjoy sufficient influence to counteract that of the Cardinal,' Katherine told him. Henry, she knew, would refuse the mother of his son nothing.

'I pray God heartily that this child of your Grace's may be a prince,' More responded. 'Nothing would be more welcome, for the surety and comfort of the realm.'

'I am praying hard too, as you may imagine,' Katherine replied.

He smiled at her. 'God will surely listen to the prayers of so devout a lady.'

If only I could believe that, she thought.

'How is Lady Alice?' she asked, determinedly changing the subject.

'It is kind of your Grace to ask. She is well, and merry. I hear that you had a triumphant visit to Oxford; I was told that the students welcomed you with as many demonstrations of joy and love as if you had been Juno or Minerva.'

Katherine smiled at the memory. 'I was deeply touched. They made me most welcome. There was talk that the Cardinal plans to found a new college at Oxford.'

'The Cardinal again!' More mused. They walked in silence for a while, then he asked, 'Did His Grace tell you that he has asked me to join him on the leads again tonight to look at the stars? I do hope that you will be coming too.'

'If I can get up the stairs!' Katherine laughed, looking down at her great belly.

She was aware that Henry was becoming more and more frustrated by his lack of an heir.

'The Turks are encroaching on Europe in the east,' he told Katherine. 'They will be at the gates of Vienna before we know it. How I long to lead a crusade against them. Alas, it cannot be!' And he sighed and thumped his fist hopelessly on the arm of his chair. He could not risk himself while the succession was still not settled.

Fearful of it ending in another disaster, they had kept this pregnancy secret until Katherine could conceal it no more. As the months had gone by with no mishap, they had allowed themselves to hope; Henry had even given a feast to celebrate her quickening. Now she was near her time and about to take to her chamber, and he was refusing to leave her lest anything went wrong. He would hardly let her move, he was so afraid of her losing the child. So she had rested and rested, and her ankles were now badly swollen. And here was Henry, hovering around her, to the ill-concealed exasperation of her women, who regarded birthing children as a strictly female occupation.

'I'm loath to leave you, sweetheart,' he said. 'I'm not going to London until you are safely delivered.'

'I am in perfect health,' Katherine protested. It was true.

'You know very well that a happy outcome is not an ensured thing,' Henry said sternly. 'Remember, I have great hopes of it.'

It was because she did remember that she did everything he asked, to please him. All she wanted now was for the birth to be over – and her son safely in her arms.

She took to her chamber, grateful to have got this far, and while she was warmly ensconced there, the King, the court – and indeed, the whole realm – waited anxiously for news. And then, to Katherine's great comfort, Maria arrived to be her gossip at her lying-in: an older Maria, honed by love and loss, and plumper than she had been, but still the same, beloved friend. When she removed her riding cloak, it seemed strange to see her in a rich gown of crimson damask, instead of the black and white she had always worn as Katherine's maid-of-honour. But then she turned, and Katherine saw that her stomacher was unlaced.

'My dear! You are expecting too!' she cried.

'Next spring, Highness. This little one is very active.' Her face clouded. It was clear she was thinking of that other little one who was irrevocably lost to her.

'Then she will surely take after her mother,' Katherine declared.

'Poor little thing!' Maria smiled. 'How is your Highness keeping?'

'I am much better, thank you, and just longing to hold my child in my arms.'

'Looking at you, it will not be long!'

Maria was right. The baby was born in the night – a girl, a tiny, mewling creature with a fluff of gold hair. Although Katherine's heart plummeted when they told her the child's sex, she took one look at her new daughter and fell in love. Isabella, she thought. I will call her for my mother, if Henry agrees.

Henry. She could not bear the thought of his disappointment. She feared to face him with the news of her failure. Would he love this child as he loved Mary, for all that she was a girl?

He came to her bedside, crestfallen. He took the child in his arms and gave it his blessing, but there was no mistaking the chagrin in his eyes, and he did not stay long, much to Maria's ill-concealed disgust. Katherine wept for hours that night, fearing she had lost his love for good. But it was her hopes that had been dashed too. What have I done to deserve this ill fortune? she asked herself.

'What are they saying in the court?' she demanded of Margaret Pole and Maria the next day.

Margaret regarded her with sad eyes. 'There is much disappointment. They are saying that, had this child been born before the betrothal, the Princess would not have been promised, for people now think she will succeed here. The sole fear is that England might be lost to France through her marriage.'

'They are speaking as if my childbearing days are done! But, Margaret, I will have other children, surely. I am but thirty-three.'

'I have known women much older than that bear sons.' Margaret's tone was robust and encouraging.

'I'm older than your Highness, and look at me,' Maria said, patting her belly. 'Thirty-three is not old!'

Katherine smiled weakly. 'You are both very kind.'

Margaret sighed. 'Take some rest, please, dear madam. You need to make a good recovery so that you can get those sons!'

Henry and Katherine bent over the cradle, their faces fraught with anxiety. Katherine felt as if her heart would break. The new Princess, just two days old, was weak and failing, and the King had been summoned. As they watched and prayed, the little hands fluttered and fell. Katherine gasped, disbelieving, and scooped up the limp body.

'Isabella, my little Isabella,' she keened desperately, as if rocking the child violently might bring her back to life.

'Kate, please,' Henry remonstrated, more affected than she would have believed. 'It is God's will.'

'How many times have you said that to me?' she cried.

'Who are we to question it?' he asked helplessly, tears streaming down his cheeks. 'She is my child too! Let me hold her.'

He prised the tiny bundle out of Katherine's arms and sat down with it, emitting great shuddering sobs.

'I cannot bear another loss,' Katherine wept. 'Why is God punishing us?'

'In faith, I do not know,' Henry said, staring into the waxen little face.

'She did not even live to be christened,' she mourned. 'Now her soul is in limbo and she will never know God.'

'Never believe that!' Henry flared. 'I have read that the souls of the unbaptised enjoy every kind of natural felicity. You must hold to that, Kate. And we must let her go.' His voice broke. 'I will arrange for her to be buried by the wall of the friars' burial ground.'

This seventh pregnancy had finally ruined her figure.

'Lace me tighter,' she instructed her maids on the day of her churching, but it made little difference. Her body was like a stout column, her great breasts strained at the low square bodice of her gown, and her face was puffy with grief. How would Henry ever desire her now? And how could she herself, weighted as she was with the burdens of loss and failure, ever surrender joyfully to his embrace again?

But Henry gave no sign that he had noticed a change in her. He came to her chamber an hour after she'd left the chapel and kissed her as heartily as usual.

'It is good to have you back with us, Kate,' he said. 'We must try to put this sadness behind us.'

'Yes,' she said, thinking that she would never be happy again, and worrying about her misery affecting Mary, who she had with her at court as often as possible. God forbid that Mary would ever think that her parents did not love her as much as they would have loved a son. But that was not her only worry.

'Henry, can we talk?' she asked.

'Of course.' He settled himself down by the fire opposite her, his hound at his feet.

'Something is tormenting me,' Katherine said, pouring him some wine. 'I fear that there must be some reason for the loss of our children, and I have been wondering – Henry, I must say this: is it a judgement of God because my marriage to Arthur was made in blood?'

'Made in blood?'

'Surely you must know of the fate of the Earl of Warwick, Lady Salisbury's brother?'

Henry frowned. 'What of it?'

'My coming to England was conditional upon Warwick being removed. I know it; I heard my father say so.'

The frown deepened. 'Mine never mentioned it. Not that he would have. He was as crooked as a rotten bough, and secretive. Aye, I can believe it. My father was ever one for expediency.'

'Think of it, Henry. Seven children we have made together, and of them just Mary lives, and with one daughter you are as good as childless in the eyes of men. Is God saying something to us?'

Henry got up, came to her, crouched on his haunches and took her hands. 'Kate, you are overwrought. This is nonsense. It was not your fault.'

'You know what they say about the sins of the fathers!'

'But, Kate, whatever *your* father or mine may have said or done, Warwick was plotting with the pretender Warbeck. He committed treason.'

'He was a simpleton, easily led, Margaret says. And it would have been easy to lead him into wrongdoing.'

'Has Lady Salisbury been putting these fancies in your head?'

'No, certainly not. The matter has troubled me for years. Henry, there has to be a reason for our children dying – or it is my fault! I have borne my losses with resignation, but the burden of failure is heavy, and it falls on me. People will say that I am deficient as a wife. They will say you should not have married me, that I am too old for you. God knows, I feel it! Do you know what the King of France said of me? I heard it from Luis Caroz. Francis said that you have no son because, though young and handsome, you keep an old and deformed wife.'

'Hush, Kate. I will not listen to such calumnies. You have nothing to reproach yourself for. We are all in God's hands.'

'But it is true!' she burst out. 'I am not pretty any more. My figure is ruined.'

'Nonsense!' Henry was quick to deny it, much to her relief. 'To me, you are beautiful, and it is what I think that matters. By all accounts Francis has deplorable taste in women!'

'I am so blessed in having you for my husband,' Katherine said, grasping Henry's hand and pressing it to her cheek. 'But tell me truthfully, do you never wonder why God should deny us this one crucial gift of a son?'

'I do wonder, all the time, but I live in hope. I am a good son of the Church, I live a virtuous life. I won't pretend I don't worry about the succession. My throne is based on firmer foundations than my father's was, but there are still those who might challenge it, and I fear what they would do if I died tomorrow. There could well be civil war. Mary's very life would be in danger and my dynasty might topple. It gives me nightmares. We must hope that you will conceive again soon.'

'I pray God you will be spared to reign over us for many years to come, my Henry, yet Mary has great qualities; she could be another queen such as my mother.'

'Kate, we've spoken of this. We do not have queens ruling over us in England. Your mother was exceptional, but it is against Nature for a woman to hold dominion over men. Hundreds of years ago there was a king's daughter, Matilda, who claimed the throne and fought a civil war against her cousin, King Stephen. She was victorious, but after just two weeks the people of London threw her out before she could be crowned. They could not stand her arrogance. It was unnatural in a woman. Since then no one has wanted a queen in England.'

Katherine knew it was useless to argue. On this point, Henry's views were entrenched.

Chapter 18

1519–1520

The masquers were disguised in the Italian fashion in visors and caps of gold, yet there was no mistaking the identity of the tall, broad-shouldered man in their midst. Henry never seemed to tire of disguising himself, or of being unmasked. He delighted in performing incognito, even though he must know that any element of surprise had long since disappeared. Yet tonight he was Troilus to his sister Mary's Criseyde – both of them being fond of the works of old Geoffrey Chaucer – and he was in his element, bowing to the ladies and cajoling them into the dance, not that they needed any persuasion.

The court was at Penshurst Place, being lavishly entertained by the Duke of Buckingham. Katherine loved the beautiful, rambling old building, which lay amid enchanting gardens in the lush green countryside of Kent, at their best in this lovely month of June. She was impressed by the magnificent hall in which the masque was taking place, and by the hospitality of her host. Yet there was something about Buckingham that disquieted her. He was the perfect courtier, noble of bearing and deferential to his sovereign, but proud and outspoken, and he cared not whom he offended, even if it be the great Cardinal himself. He made no secret of his enmity for Wolsey, who for the main part ignored it – look at the Cardinal now, engrossed in the masque and talking animatedly to his neighbour, the Countess of Surrey. Katherine had long had the feeling that Buckingham did not like Henry either – it was as if he were always trying to out-king him! And Henry, she noticed, was often watching Buckingham.

But that was the least of her worries, because she had sensed that her women were keeping something from her. She had not missed the covert glances they kept giving her – and each other – and she was aware of an undercurrent of whispers. She was sure she hadn't imagined it all. In the last few days she had noticed a palpable tension in her chamber, and conversations being suddenly hushed when she approached. She feared it might concern Maria, who had just written with the happy news that she had borne a daughter – her own god-daughter, named Katherine after herself – but, reading between the lines, it was clear that she had suffered a hazardous confinement. Katherine prayed that nothing had happened to Maria or the child. Surely they would not keep it from her?

'Margaret,' she asked Lady Salisbury as they walked in the gardens the next morning, 'has something happened? Please don't pretend there isn't anything. I'm aware that people are giving me odd looks.'

Margaret looked as if she would rather be anywhere else. 'Your Grace is right, there is something, and I would give much not to be the one to have to tell you.'

'What is it?' Katherine sat down on a stone bench, bracing herself.

'The talk is that Bessie Blount has borne the King a son.' Margaret's cheeks were pink with embarrassment.

Katherine gasped. Suddenly she could not breathe. She felt dizzy and thought she might die. People had dropped dead after receiving bad news, hadn't they?

She made herself stay calm and take deep breaths.

'Is it true?' she whispered, forcing the words out, and knowing the answer. For Bessie, all honey-blonde, meek and demure, had come to her in February begging leave to go home to be with her mother, who was sick. Taking pity on the girl, but relieved to see her depart, Katherine had agreed, and she had not given much thought since to her maid-of-honour's continued absence.

'If you listen to the gossip it is,' Margaret said, sitting down beside her and taking her hand. 'I try not to, but it seems to be the sole topic of conversation.'

It would be, Katherine thought: how the King's mistress can give him a son, and his wife cannot.

'And I am the last to know!' she said, her breathing coming more evenly now. But the pain of betrayal, the immensity of Henry's betrayal, was intensifying, swelling into something horrible and obscene. Worse still was the terrible realisation that it must be her fault that they did not have sons. Either there was some bodily deficiency in her, or she had offended God. Yet surely Bessie Blount's offence was greater? So why had *she* been vouchsafed a son?

Katherine could no longer blame Henry for straying. The fair Bessie – her allure could not be denied – was a merry girl with a love of singing, dancing and revelry. She had youth and vitality on her side, and could offer light-hearted companionship and more – and more . . . Whereas Katherine knew that her looks had faded and that the loss of six children had aged her and made her more serious and devout and introspective. She was no longer the golden princess whom Henry had married.

And yet, give him his due, he was still loving towards her, still kind, still caring. He came to her bed regularly, and their loving was everything she could have wished for. It would have been better, she thought, for her not to have known about Bessie Blount, otherwise there would have been no clue that anything was amiss. But now she had to deal with this dreadful pain, and face public humiliation.

'What are people saying?' she asked. 'Tell me the truth.'

Margaret sighed. 'Apparently His Grace sent her to a house in Essex. It had an unusual name – Jericho.'

'I know the house. The King leases it from a priory. He keeps apartments and uses it as a hunting box.' And as a secret trysting place, obviously.

Margaret seemed reluctant to go on. 'You may be aware that there is a lot of gossip about the house,' she said, and swallowed. 'They say that no one is allowed to approach His Grace when he stays there, and that his servants are warned not to ask where he is or talk about his pastimes or the hour he goes to bed.'

It was horrible, hateful.

'And this is where the child was born?'

'Indeed. Madam, I am so sorry. This must be very difficult for you.'

'Thank you, Margaret. But I wanted to know the truth. What is the child called?'

'Henry – Henry Fitzroy.'

Fitzroy – son of the King. Henry, who was usually so discreet, could not have been more obvious in proclaiming to the world that he had a son at last. And who could blame him? All men wanted sons, especially kings, and Henry was a magnificent, virile man of twenty-eight; the lack of a male heir diminished him and reflected on his manhood. But not any more. The whole world would soon know that Henry Tudor was capable of siring boys.

She imagined Henry's joy when they brought him the news, the moment when the child was presented to him, his gratitude to the woman who had made it possible. It pained her that someone else should have given him this gift – it should have been her, his wife, who gave him this one thing his heart desired.

'There is more, madam,' Margaret said, as they got up and walked back towards the house. 'Cardinal Wolsey is appointed the child's godfather, and he is arranging for Bessie to marry Lord Tailboys. An honourable marriage for a dishonourable woman!' Margaret was uncharacteristically savage.

Katherine was shocked. 'Has the Cardinal forgotten his calling, that he must descend to this?'

'Fear not, madam – there is much outrage about it. People openly criticise. They say he is encouraging young women to indulge in fornication in order to find husbands above their station.'

'And so he is.'

She felt a burning anger towards both Henry and Wolsey. Henry was still devoting himself to amusements day and night, intent on nothing else, and leaving all business to the Cardinal. The man ruled everything! And now he had shown himself little better than a procurer.

She wondered what her nephew would make of this – not that she would ever be so disloyal as to complain to him, or that it would do any good if she did, for all Charles's power. For Maximilian had just died, and at only nineteen Charles was now Holy Roman Emperor and the master of half of Christendom. Overnight, Katherine's status had soared. She might be barren, but in England she represented the combined might and glory of Spain and the Empire.

But what was it all worth? she wondered, as she lay wakeful that night, watching the dying embers of the fire. Henry was friends with King Francis now, and absorbed in plans for a meeting between them this summer, which precluded any close alliance with Charles. She herself enjoyed little influence in affairs of state these days, and her role as Henry's Queen had been whittled down to a merely ceremonial one. She stood by his side on state occasions; she received foreign ambassadors; she presided with him at feasts, banquets and masques. For the rest of the time she stayed mainly in her apartments. Her days were governed by the offices of the Church, and she spent hours on her knees in her private chapel, praying for a son. She had been several times to see Our Lady of Walsingham too, but it had done her no good. She passed as much time as she could with Mary, or embroidering endless church vestments and altar cloths, or stitching clothing for the poor. She made music with her ladies, played cards or dice, or read devotional books. She felt she had outlived her usefulness. She had failed in every way that mattered.

Katherine was dizzy with exhaustion through torment and lack of sleep, and was looking wrecked the next morning when Henry came to see her. He stared at her for a long moment, then that shuttered look came down. He did not ask how she was, for surely he did not want to hear her answer.

He kissed her cheek and sat down, resplendent in cloth of gold; they were to dine with some French envoys later.

'God, I have a foul headache,' he grumbled.

'Another one?' she asked, concerned despite herself. Henry had complained several times lately of headaches and megrims.

He rubbed his forehead. 'It makes reading and writing somewhat tedious and painful.'

She wondered if this was a bid for sympathy, intended to deflect her suspicions or her anger.

Henry was looking at his feet. He would not meet her eyes. 'Kate,

299

I came to tell you that Francis and I have agreed to postpone our summit until next year. We both feel that it would not be appropriate to hold it in the wake of the Emperor's death.'

She nodded, cheered to hear that. If the meeting was delayed for a year, it might never happen. 'I think that is fitting,' she said, trying not to think about Henry Fitzroy and how he had changed everything between her and the man seated opposite her – the man she loved, but who now seemed like a stranger.

'As a token of good faith, Francis and I have agreed not to shave until we see each other, so I am growing a beard, Kate.' Already there was golden stubble on his chin.

Katherine was dismayed. She hated to see a man unshaven, and to her Henry's new beard, its appearance coinciding with what she now knew of him, seemed to symbolise all that was wrong in their marriage.

'Oh, please, Henry,' she protested, before she could stop herself. 'Don't grow a beard! I love you as you are.'

'But I've given my word,' Henry said. 'I think a beard will suit me.'

Did he think a beard an outward symbol of the virility he had proved in another way?

'You know I dislike beards,' Katherine persisted, knowing herself defeated.

'You will get used to it, Kate, I'm sure. I rather like it.' He stroked his chin. 'However, I didn't come to talk about that. I've been disturbed by reports from Germany about that pestilential monk Martin Luther. You remember, he nailed his protests against what he called abuses in the Church to a church door in Wittenberg a couple of years ago? I assumed he was just a little crazed, but his ideas are gaining ground over there, and he must be stopped. I don't want this canker in England. We can't have every Tom, Dick or Harry spouting forth against the Church. So I'm going to write a book, Kate, demolishing the arguments of this Luther.'

'He sounds a highly dangerous man. This is a worthy cause to take up. I applaud you for doing it.'

'It needs someone like me, someone who has influence in the world and is a good son of the Church. Luther does have a point about indulgences, though. Why should people have to pay for a pardon for their sins and have to buy themselves out of purgatory?'

'It is wrong,' Katherine agreed. 'Greed is a sin. It does not become the priests who sell these indulgences.'

'Alas, the practice is widespread. The fellow is right to protest against it, but I would that he had left it at that. The rest of what he says is dangerous. Do you know that he denies all but two of the seven sacraments? Well, I intend to defend them vigorously! The Christian unity of Europe must be maintained in the face of this threat.'

Seeing Henry so zealous to champion the Church, Katherine found it hard to reconcile him, this man of conviction and principle, with the man who must have been secretly making adulterous love to Bessie Blount for God knew how many years, and who had sired a bastard with her. How could she be sitting here with him calmly discussing the heresies of that fool Luther? Why was she not raking her fingernails down his face, or beating her fists against his chest? How was it possible both to love and hate someone at the same time?

To Katherine's dismay, the French summit was to go ahead. In May the entire court was to be shipped across the English Channel to the Pale of Calais, where it would lodge for a short time in Henry's castle at Guisnes. The Pale of Calais was part of England, the last remaining outpost of the empire that Henry's ancestors had carved out for themselves in France. Mary would be left at Richmond in the care of Margaret Pole, who had replaced Margaret Bryan as her lady mistress – an appointment Katherine had urged, since there was no one she trusted more to look after her child.

Wolsey was in his element. This meeting was his idea, and he was in charge of all the arrangements, from the vexing questions of precedence and courtesy to the design of the silken pavilions that were to be set up in the field chosen for the meeting, which lay between the towns of Guisnes and Ardres.

Katherine made no secret of the fact that she was against the visit. She summoned her council, which had been appointed by the King to advise her and help administer her estates.

'The Cardinal is arranging what I am sure will be one of the most expensive charades ever staged,' she told them. 'No expense is being spared on either side, and for what? So that our court and the French court can vie with each other to prove which is the superior in wealth and magnificence. And what good will that do anyone? England and France are ancient enemies; they can never be true friends. England should look to where its trade is, to the lands of the Empire.'

They had regarded her dubiously at first, and she guessed that they were thinking it was wrong of her to criticise the King's policy. But now, with her mention of the trade with Flanders that was at the root of England's prosperity, there was respect in their eyes, and heads were nodding, and she knew she had touched a chord.

Then the door opened and Henry walked in. There was a scraping of benches as the men rose and bowed, and Katherine sank into a curtsey. The King signalled to them all to be seated, and took the empty chair at the end of the board opposite his wife.

'You are all looking very serious, my lords,' he said. 'May I know what you are discussing?'

'Sir, we were speaking of the French visit,' Katherine said.

'Ah.' There was a pause. 'I see why there are so many long faces.'

'You may tell His Grace what I said,' Katherine said.

'Sir,' said Lord Mountjoy, 'Her Grace has made more representations against the voyage than we would have dared to do.' He repeated her arguments, looking uncharacteristically nervous. But Henry was himself nodding now, and there was approval in his eyes.

'I am impressed by your grasp of affairs, madam,' he said. 'You are right to speak out, and I hold you in greater esteem for it – and I am sure my councillors will agree. You have given me something to think about.'

Katherine felt herself flushing pink with pleasure. It was a long time since Henry had heeded her political opinions.

'The truth is,' he said in bed that night, after yet another attempt to sire an heir for England, 'I am having second thoughts about this French alliance. I don't trust Francis, and I must confess that I find the prospect of friendship with the Emperor more appealing.'

His words brought joy to Katherine's heart. She hoped that her own arguments had helped to sway him. He was too much under the thumb of Wolsey, who had overmuch love for the French and allowed it to override all other considerations when making policy.

Henry raised himself on one elbow and began twisting a strand of Katherine's hair through his fingers.

'Charles is coming to England,' he said, grinning. 'I heard today.'

Katherine sat up and flung her arms around him.

'That is wonderful news!' she cried.

'I thought you would be pleased, my love,' Henry murmured, kissing her tenderly. 'He will arrive before we leave for Calais. He says he is eager to bind himself in friendship with England.'

'Even better news!' Katherine exclaimed, jubilant at this wonderful turn of events. 'My Henry, you should cancel this meeting in France. There is no point to it.'

'My love, I would if I could, but it's too late. Wolsey's plans are far advanced, and I've outlaid too much money. Besides, it would be an unforgivable insult to Francis to cancel at this late stage; he would have every right to be offended, and where would that leave us? Wars have been fought for less! Anyway, I want to meet him, to discover what I'm up against.'

Katherine gave up the fight. She knew Henry too well to think she could dissuade him. For all his adverse comments, he was excited about the visit, and had been for weeks. He never could resist an opportunity to show off, especially when it was to his French rival. She had no choice but to prepare to go to France with as much grace as she could muster, while praying that something would happen to prevent the visit.

Katherine could hardly contain her joy as, on a pleasant afternoon in May 1520, she stood waiting at Christ Church Gate, before Canterbury Cathedral, to meet her nephew the Emperor. Her great train of fair ladies ranged about her, and excited crowds thronged the streets; no one was more impatient than she to see the King's party approaching. This meeting between Henry and Charles was all-important to her; it

303

might tip the balance against the French alliance, the prospect of which she could not bear.

She and Henry had outlaid a king's ransom on new clothes for themselves and their attendants in honour of the Emperor's visit. For Henry, it was crucial that he appear to be a wealthy and magnificent monarch, a fitting equal to this young man who held dominion over half of Christendom. Katherine, all too aware that her youth was behind her, nevertheless felt that she looked regal in her gown of cloth of gold and violet velvet embroidered with Tudor roses, its skirt parted in the front to show off her kirtle of silver taffeta; on her head she wore a black velvet hood in the Flemish style, ornamented with gold, jewels and pearls, and her neck was encircled by a carcanet of fine pearls from which hung a costly diamond cross.

She turned to the French Queen, who was almost as splendidly attired as she was herself. It was a joy to have her sister-in-law with her, and a shame that they saw each other too seldom, for the Suffolks were still burdened with debt, and now the French Queen had three young children to occupy her.

'I have long dreamed of meeting my sister's son,' Katherine said, elated at the thought. 'I thank God I shall see his face. It will be the greatest good I can have on earth.'

The French Queen gave her a searching look. She knew what Katherine wanted but dared not voice. Katherine was counting on Charles to dissuade Henry from meeting Francis.

The Emperor's procession was approaching now; Katherine could see the banners bearing the two-headed sable Imperial eagle and the arms of Castile and Aragon, and was thrilled to her soul. There was Henry – who was styling himself 'His Majesty' now, since Charles had adopted the title, and Henry felt it lent to his own magnificence as king. He rode next to his guest at the head of the long column of lords and dignitaries, raising a hand to point out the soaring cathedral ahead. The two sovereigns dismounted, and Henry embraced Charles warmly, then led him over to where Katherine was waiting. She sank into her curtsey, and when the Emperor raised her, greeting her in Spanish and doffing his wide-brimmed hat as he bowed, she saw that he was not the comely young man she had expected the son of Philip the Handsome and Juana to be. He had Juana's dark hair, cut short and straight at the chin and across his forehead, but also the heavy Habsburg jaw, so pronounced in his case that he could not close his mouth, as the French Queen had long ago asserted. Katherine had thought Mary was exaggerating, and was saddened to find that she was right.

Charles's manner was correct rather than warm, but she could not fault his courtesy to herself. In the ordinary exchange of pleasantries she would have asked about his mother, but did not like to. As far as she knew, Queen Juana was still shut up at Tordesillas. She had been there for eleven years now – goodness knew in what state of mind and health. She hoped that Charles was a dutiful son and visited her.

Like the Emperor, Henry was clean-shaven. He had held out against Katherine's complaints until November. Sir Thomas Boleyn, his ambassador in Paris, had placated King Francis by explaining that it was all the Queen's fault.

'Far from being offended,' Henry had told her, 'Francis was amused, and thanks to you, Kate, I am now known throughout Europe as a Samson to your Delilah!'

'At least peace has been preserved!' she had laughed. 'I am happy to take the blame.'

It was painful to watch Charles eating during the feast given in his honour. Because he could not close his mouth he could not chew his food properly, and between this and his innate reticence, conversation at the high table was a challenge. But afterwards, when they had all three retired to Katherine's privy chamber and hippocras was served, Charles came quickly to the point.

'I would prefer it, brother, if you would cancel this proposed summit with King Francis,' he said. 'We both know where your true interests lie. Why go ahead with this great farce when you know it will lead nowhere?'

Henry explained why the meeting had to go ahead. 'The Queen agrees with you, nephew,' he said, 'yet my hands are tied. But when I am done in France, let us meet up again in Flanders and seal our pact.'

'We will do that, you have my word on it,' Charles promised. It was not quite what Katherine had hoped for, but it was enough to sustain her during the coming ordeal.

The great retinue – more than five thousand persons in all – wound its lengthy way into Guisnes on a beautiful warm day in early June. Katherine gazed up in awe, despite herself, at the new palace that Wolsey had had built there – a miracle of illusion, for it was in reality a temporary structure in wood and canvas. Yet she thought it extraordinary, the most noble and royal lodging she had ever seen. She almost gasped when she beheld the unsurpassed magnificence of her apartments. Her closet was hung with cloth of gold and jewels; in the chapel the altar was adorned with pearls and precious stones, and on it stood twelve great images of gold; even the ceiling was lined with cloth of gold and precious stones.

The French Queen stared in awe. 'It's superb!' she declared. 'Tragic to think they'll take it all down afterwards.'

'I shudder to think of how much money has been lavished on this,' Katherine said. Now that she had had time to acclimatise herself to the splendour of her surroundings, she was beginning to find them slightly on the vulgar side – just what one might expect from a butcher's son!

'You know my brother!' the French Queen said, laughing. 'He never does anything by halves.'

'I rather think this is Wolsey's doing.' Katherine could not hide her chagrin.

The French Queen took her hand. 'I understand how you feel, Kate, but I owe much to Wolsey. If it hadn't been for his intercession, my husband might not have a head on his shoulders. So I have an affection for the man; he does have a heart, you know. There was nothing in it for him, but he helped us all the same.'

Katherine forbore to say that Wolsey, in negotiating that steep fine, had made his master the richer and therefore all the more grateful, and had thereby further entrenched himself in Henry's good opinions. 'Yes, but he loves the French too much!'

'You should learn to hide your distaste for him, Kate. And you make it too clear that this visit is against your will. Just smile and bear it. In two weeks all the mummery will be over.'

'I long for the day!' Katherine sighed. Her baggage was being carried in now. Two new and very willing chamberers, Margery and Elizabeth Otwell, sisters in their early twenties, had started unpacking the chests. Margery was handling the Queen's gowns as reverently as if they were altar frontals. She had come to Katherine on a recommendation from Sir John Peche, whose wife she had served, and Katherine was pleased with her. Margery, with her russet curls and open, heart-shaped face, was honest and diligent. Elizabeth was a paler copy of her sister, but as good at her duties.

Katherine smiled at them both, then beckoned to Mistress Carey, one of the ladies who had been accorded the honour of waiting on the Queen during this visit, by virtue of being married to gentlemen of the King's Privy Chamber.

'Be so good as to fetch us some wine,' she said. 'It is a hot day.'

Mistress Carey smiled and hastened away. The smile had lit up her docile face, and Katherine suddenly remembered her as a weeping young girl who was frightened to board a ship.

'I see you have Mary Boleyn in your household,' the French Queen said, her voice a trifle tart.

'She served you in France,' Katherine recalled.

'She did, and nearly got herself a reputation. There were whispers that she was bedded by King Francis himself. Her father carted her off to the country before her good name was irrevocably damaged.'

'I can see what Francis saw in her. She is very pretty.'

'She is, and I suppose – if I am to be fair – that she had no choice. I should know – Francis laid siege to *my* virtue, the devil! He can be very persuasive, and he *is* the King. Little mouse Boleyn would not have stood a chance against him.'

'Well, she is safely married now,' Katherine said, glad that Mistress Carey was not one of her permanent ladies, for she could not have in her service any whose virtue was in question.

'That's no proof against anything!' the French Queen said, laughing once more.

*

Even the ground had been levelled, so that neither king should be higher than the other. To this field between Guisnes and Ardres, Henry and Francis came in peace, swearing undying love for each other, but each had an army at his back. They met against a backdrop of silken pavilions the colours of jewels, and it was hard to say what was the most brilliant – the magnificently clad monarchs, their resplendent courts or the fantastic landscape of gaudy tents. There was so much peacock finery on display, in rich apparel and marvellous treasure; the courtiers glittered in cloth of gold, and countless gold chains and collars, way beyond estimable price, winked and shone in the sunlight.

Katherine watched as Henry and Francis saluted and embraced each other. She made herself smile as they exchanged gifts, and tried not to show her distaste when they signed a new treaty of friendship. She prayed that Charles would not take it amiss when he heard, and was relieved to hear Henry tell Francis of his hopes for a reconciliation between France and the Empire.

Outwardly Henry and Francis were brimming with goodwill. They behaved like brothers and best friends. But Katherine knew Henry, and her intuition told her that Francis was playing a part too. They were not just rival kings but rival males, and they were not at peace. It was clear to her – and Henry had as good as told her – that they hated each other cordially. If anything, Katherine thought, this empty charade that had cost such a fortune had actually served to seal the rivalry between them. It was obvious that Henry's jealousy of Francis was driving him directly into the arms of the Emperor.

For all that, Henry and Francis made a brave show of amity, revelling in the endless round of festivities, jousts and feasts laid on to celebrate their meeting. As the days passed, one extravagant entertainment succeeded another for the delectation of the two courts. Every one saw Henry and Francis posturing in new outfits of increasing splendour, barely concealing their jealousy of each other.

Against all expectations Katherine found herself liking Francis's Queen, the pious, plump, ungainly, cross-eyed Claude. Katherine felt sorry for her, for Claude limped badly and did not look well at all. Next to Francis's sister, the Queen of Navarre, a kindly, brilliantly learned woman with violet-blue eyes, Claude was a sorry thing. And Francis had called her, Katherine, old and deformed! At least she stood straight and was in health, even if she was thirty-four and too stout. But Claude was to be admired and envied in one vital respect, for she had borne sons.

'She has been continually pregnant since Francis married her,' the French Queen murmured, 'and she has to suffer his constant infidelities. Small wonder she is strict with her maids!'

Katherine's heart went out to Claude. They had taken to each other immediately.

When first they had attended Mass, each kept insisting that the other kiss the Bible first – until they solved the problem by kissing each other instead. In that moment a friendship had been born.

Then came the day when Henry challenged Francis to a wrestling match and Katherine's heart sank. Henry, who loved his food, had begun to put on weight – she had even heard one Frenchman calling him fat, which was untrue and unfair; but Francis was definitely slimmer, and younger. There was a dreadful moment when he threw Henry to the floor, at which the two queens and the spectators had held their collective breath in horror. Henry, red with fury, got up and would have hit Francis, had not Katherine and Claude been there to pull them apart and make light of things.

Thankfully Henry did better in the jousts, and honour was vindicated. Katherine took great pleasure in appearing in the stands wearing a Spanish headdress. Let these French remember who she was!

On the evening she saw Henry off to Ardres, where he was to be the guest of Queen Claude, she herself entertained King Francis at Guisnes with a sumptuous banquet. Exchanging pleasantries with him in her limited French as they helped themselves to elaborate fruit pies with decorated crusts, marchpane comfits garnished with gold leaf, and sugared fruits, she was aware of the wit and charm that had women falling into bed with him, yet he was not the type of man she would fancy. He was too saturnine in appearance, with his long Valois nose and his sardonic eyes – a very devil of a Frenchman. He was a cultivated man and engaging, but seemed to think it perfectly acceptable to be talking to his royal hostess and ogling her maids-of-honour at the same time. And afterwards, when her ladies danced for him, he did not ask if she would do the honours with him, but kept leering at poor Mistress Carey, who coloured and looked away.

By the time Henry returned, Katherine was furious. 'Words fail me!' she huffed. 'That man is the greatest Turk there ever was! No woman is safe with him.'

Henry frowned. 'I trust he did not behave dishonourably to you, Kate?'

'Only in that he ignored me when his eye lighted on one who pleased him better. Poor Mistress Carey was quite embarrassed. He kept staring at her.'

'Will Carey won't be pleased to hear that. Francis is a lecher, and doesn't care who knows it. They say that in Paris his chief mistress, Madame de Châteaubriant, queens it over the court – and no one even thinks it scandalous.'

Katherine shuddered. Poor Claude. Thank goodness Henry had never humiliated her publicly like that. He had been unfaithful, but he had also been discreet.

It galled her that she had to be polite to Francis in the days that followed, as the extravagant festivities continued. She grew weary of sitting for endless hours in the tiltyard watching the interminable sporting contests that Henry loved; of eating too much rich food at feast after feast; and of reining in her impatience as her ladies dressed her in new finery for each different event. She would much rather have been at home in England with Mary, whom she was missing sorely. She dared not think what this was all costing. And there was Wolsey, revelling in it all, enjoying the reflected glory that should have belonged wholly to his King, and crawling to the French.

At last, at long last, the great pantomime came to an end. Wolsey celebrated Mass before the assembled courts. After a farewell feast, everyone went outside into the velvety June night to watch a firework display, and there were gasps of delight as a fiery salamander, King Francis's emblem, burst into the sky, fizzled there for a few moments, then scattered in myriad sparks. As the crowds began to disperse, Katherine saw Mistress Carey with a dark-haired girl wearing a halo-shaped French hood, a fashion that was apparently all the rage in Paris. Katherine had never adopted it. She found it a little too daring for a married woman, for it exposed hair that should be kept covered. But her sister-in-law, the French Queen, wore one, and very becoming she looked in it.

The dark-haired girl was laughing, a little too loudly, which belied the air of elegance she carried so gracefully. The two young women embraced, then the dark girl turned away with a swish of her train, and Mary Carey hastened to join her mistress.

'I beg your pardon, your Grace, but I had to say farewell to my sister. I have not seen her for five years. She has been at the French court. She served Queen Claude, and is now with King Francis's sister.'

'She has done well,' Katherine observed, watching the retreating figure disappearing into the crowds, and thinking that, while no beauty, she had a certain grace about her.

'Our father has been hoping she will find a husband at the French court, but Anne knows her own mind. She will have none but the best!'

'Then I hope she will find her heart's desire – and please your father. Now we must to bed. I am to host a farewell dinner for King Francis tomorrow, and wish to be up early, as we depart the next day and there is much to be done.'

As Katherine walked back to the gaudy, transient palace, there was a spring in her step. Only thirty-six hours, and they would be on their way to rendezvous with the Emperor!

And now there was another round of revelry, almost as lavish as the one that had just flagged wearily to an end, but this time Katherine threw herself into the festivities with zest because Henry and Charles were in perfect amity, and there was no hint of rivalry between them.

They had met the Emperor at Gravelines and escorted him back to Henry's town of Calais to lodge in the Exchequer Palace. Now Katherine could take delight in hosting suppers, revels, masques and banquets, because they were in Charles's honour. Unresponsive as he was by nature, he represented Spain and all that she held dear.

'I hear that Francis is spitting mad to learn of our friendship,' Henry crowed. He had still not forgiven Francis for throwing him, and was delighted to be able to trump his rival. Willingly he signed a new treaty of friendship with Charles, each agreeing not to make any new alliance with France in the next two years. When Charles departed, Katherine was sorry to see him go, and parted with many good wishes for his health and happiness, consoling herself with the happy knowledge that England and Spain were once again allies.

And now it was time to board their flagship for England – and home!

Chapter 19

It was one of the proudest days of Katherine's life when Henry told her that Charles had asked for Mary's hand in marriage. She looked at her five-year-old daughter playing gravely and quite competently on the virginals, and her heart swelled almost unbearably at the realisation that this little one would not only be Queen of Spain but also Empress of half of Europe. It was a breathtaking destiny, one for which it was patently clear that Mary was admirably fitted. Already she had taken part most prettily in court pageants; even at four years old, she had received foreign envoys all by herself, and played for them. She loved to dance, and could twirl as beautifully as any lady of honour. In every respect she was a princess to be proud of, and as far as Katherine was concerned, Charles could have chosen no better wife. Henry had been right. This was a far better match than any Mary might have made with Reginald Pole.

There was, of course, the age gap of sixteen years. It was a lot to ask a young man in his prime to wait for at least seven years until Mary was mature enough to be married, yet Katherine hoped – for the thought of parting with her child was unbearable – that the waiting time might be longer, as Mary was small for her age.

'I am more thrilled than I can say,' she told Henry.

'I thought you would be,' he replied, hugging her.

'I have always hoped for a Spanish marriage for Mary,' she told him. 'I was not happy when she was betrothed to the Dauphin, but it was not my place to question your wisdom.'

'Wolsey has dealt with that,' Henry said. 'The betrothal is broken.'

'That is such a relief!' She bent down and stroked her daughter's silky red hair.

'The Emperor is the greatest match in Christendom,' Henry said proudly, scooping a delighted Mary up in his arms and kissing her. 'Who's going to be empress?' he chuckled.

'Me!' cried the child.

And so the marriage treaty was signed, and the Imperial ambassadors were now at Greenwich to make arrangements for Charles to come to England later in the spring for the betrothal. Katherine went about with a smile on her face and a spring in her step, feeling benevolent towards all humanity, even to Wolsey, who had negotiated the new treaty.

She knew that Wolsey had had an ulterior motive for favouring the Emperor. He had made no secret of the fact that he wanted to be pope one day, and of course the Emperor had great influence in the Vatican. When Pope Leo had died in December, the Cardinal's hopes had leapt high.

But Wolsey had been overlooked. Charles had chosen to support the rival candidate, who happened to be his old tutor and his regent in Spain, and it was no surprise to many that the Emperor's choice was duly elected. The smile had frozen on Wolsey's face.

'I had so hoped that His Imperial Majesty would favour me,' he told Henry at supper, on the day news of the election had come speeding into London. 'There would have been so much I could have done, as pope, for your Majesty.'

Henry toyed with his wine goblet and frowned. 'It wasn't for lack of pressure,' he said. 'I sent a hundred thousand ducats to buy you votes. I asked the Emperor to support you and to send an army to Rome to show that we meant business. Thomas, I am sorry that it was all for nothing. Still, the King of France is hopping with rage because the Emperor's subject has been elected.' He smiled wickedly. 'Maybe it wasn't all a wasted effort!'

Katherine said nothing but she was uneasy. If Wolsey took against the Emperor, he might try to undermine the new alliance. Wolsey was all-powerful. Think of what had happened to the Duke of Buckingham last year.

Buckingham had been accused of treason – not, she believed, because he had a claim to the throne and had conspired to seize it, but because of his hatred of Wolsey. A rumour had conveniently reached the King's ear that Buckingham had designs on his crown: the Duke had been rash enough to express the opinion, not considering that there were informers among his hearers, that God had punished Henry for the Earl of Warwick's death by smiting down his sons. Buckingham himself, the Duke had then implied, was more fitted to rule.

It was no secret that Buckingham, the descendant of a long line of kings, had despised Wolsey. Katherine had been present on the day when the Cardinal had been about to wash his hands in the same bowl as the Duke, and Buckingham had deliberately tipped the water over Wolsey's shoes. He had paid dearly for that, and other slights. He had died on the block, and at that bloody stroke, his vast lands had come into the King's hands and Henry had been rid of a rival for his throne, which gave him more good reasons to be grateful and beholden to Wolsey.

Katherine had not liked Buckingham, but she did not believe that he had been guilty of treason. If guilt were to be apportioned in the whole grim, appalling affair, it belonged to Wolsey. In future, she was going to be very, very careful of antagonising Wolsey. Already she feared he had enough grudges against Spain.

These days, whenever Henry dined in private with Katherine, he invariably sent for Thomas More to be merry with them, as Henry put it. Frequently he summoned More to his study, and kept him there for hours discussing astronomy, theology and geometry, a subject that fascinated Henry but left Katherine bored beyond endurance.

She worried that Henry was monopolising More. The King still teased him about his lack of enthusiasm for the court, but More had recently let drop in conversation that he had not had leave for a month to go home to his wife and children. Yet Henry was impervious. He loved More's company, and for months he had sought his advice in regard to his Latin treatise against Martin Luther. Henry had spent more than a year working on it, and Katherine had been present at many a late-evening discussion with him and More, who shared his master's concerns about heresy.

More's devout Catholicism, no less than his integrity, appealed to Katherine. She was gratified that such a man so stoutly supported the King's desire to stamp out this new heresy.

'I see nothing wrong in disputing points of doctrine,' Henry had said one night as the three of them were sharing a late supper, 'but heresy is another matter entirely, and I am appalled that any credence should be given to the teachings of this weed.'

'I am in absolute agreement with your Majesty,' More declared. Normally a gentle man, his eyes were blazing with fervour. 'Heresy is a canker in the body politic of the Church. It must be rooted out and eradicated.'

'Amen to that,' Katherine said. 'I fear for those poor ignorant souls who are taken in by these dangerous teachings.'

'I'm a reasonable man,' Henry said. 'I know there are abuses within the Church, but I will not countenance heresy as a means of correcting them. It undermines the divinely appointed order of our society, and it encourages disaffection among the lower classes.'

'It means eternal damnation,' More added. 'That is why burning heretics is an act of mercy, for it gives them a foretaste of the fires of Hell, and thereby may spur them to repent at the last. And if they do not, then they cannot hope for the resurrection of the body, and the world has been purged of its canker.'

Henry nodded enthusiastically. 'I will not tolerate heresy in my realm, or allow Luther's ideas to gain hold. He even rejects the sacrament of marriage. Well, I am determined to defend that sacrament, which turns the water of desire into wine of the finest flavour. Whom God hath joined together, let no man put asunder!' He smiled at Katherine. 'Luther also rejects the authority of the Pope, but I have written that all true believers in Christ honour and acknowledge Rome for their mother. In truth, I am so bound to the See of Rome that I cannot do enough to honour it. I am determined to set forth the Pope's authority to the uttermost.'

Katherine smiled back, proud to see him with the crusading light in his eyes, and so zealous in the Church's defence.

*

The Pope had received Henry's treatise with rapturous praise, and gratefully rewarded him with the title 'Defender of the Faith'. The King's book was printed, critically acclaimed and tremendously popular. Henry had basked in the adulation.

Then had come a letter from Martin Luther himself.

'He dares to accuse me of raving like a strumpet in a tantrum!' Henry roared. 'He says he will stuff my impudent falsehoods – if you please – down my throat. He even suggests that someone else wrote the book for me. Well, he will be made to eat his words, for I will write and tell this dilapidated, sick and evil-minded sheep that it is well known for mine, and I vow that it *is* mine!' He had fumed and glowered all through the feast given that evening as part of the celebrations at court to mark his new title.

Katherine tried to cheer him.

'It matters not what that misbegotten monk says,' she soothed. 'Why fret about his opinion when the Pope so honours you?'

'I had hoped to silence him for good with my arguments!' Henry said.

The King's fool, seeing his master's woebegone expression, leapt up and jingled his stick of bells, pulling a wry face.

'What ails you, good Harry?' he cried. 'Come now! Let you and I defend and comfort one another, and let the Faith alone to defend itself!'

Ill-tempered though he was, even Henry had to laugh at that.

At the lavish tournament that was laid on that March in honour of Charles's ambassadors, Katherine took her place in the royal stand above the tiltyard, her ladies seating themselves about her, all avid to watch the jousts, for today the King himself was to take part.

And there he was, riding into the lists on a magnificently caparisoned horse, wheeling his steed around before them, bowing in his saddle to his Queen and acknowledging the admiring applause of the ladies. Then he reined in his mount and turned, and Katherine saw what was embroidered on the cloth-of-silver caparisons: 'She has wounded my heart.'

It threw her for a moment. She wondered what she had done to upset him, then reasoned that he had not acted in any way like a man she had wounded. Then it dawned on her that the words were not intended for her, and suddenly she felt faint. The tiltyard, the stands, the sea of faces all seemed to blur.

It was not unusual for knights to have such mottos embroidered on their horses' caparisons. It was all part of the elaborate game of love that had been played in royal courts for centuries. A gentleman – usually a single gentleman, of whom there were many at court, often with no prospects – dedicated himself to a lady whom he longed to serve, a lady who would enjoy mastery over him, even if she were married or far above him in rank. He might languish for years for love of her, for she was, in theory, unattainable. But secrecy was all-important: her identity must never be revealed. Hence the tantalising mottos.

As a princess, and then a queen, Katherine had never played the game. She could have encouraged admirers aplenty, but her virtuous Spanish upbringing had ensured that she could never bring herself to do it. Yet she had not discouraged her ladies from these seemingly harmless flirtations, and enjoyed hearing about them.

But Henry had always been discreet. He had never openly practised the art of courtly love – at least, not since his brief courtship of Katherine. She thanked God that he had never flaunted any mistress at court, but had kept his indiscretions private. It was so out of character, and unconventional, for him, a married man, to proclaim to the world – for that was surely what he was doing – that he was pursuing a lady.

She so wanted not to believe it. Henry had discarded Bessie Blount long ago. Bessie was now married, and Katherine had heard that she had borne a daughter. At any rate, she had never returned to court, so it could not be her.

Who, then?

She sat there, trying to focus her tear-filled eyes on the contest. When the crowd cheered, she did too. When the victors came to receive their prizes, she presented them graciously. She smiled, she applauded loudly when Henry unseated his opponent. And all the while she was dying inside.

She tried to tell herself that it probably meant nothing, that the game of courtly love was harmless fun. It was just that, of course – a game. But Katherine knew, as well as any, that such games were often a cover for something less chivalrous. Henry was the King, handsome, athletic and powerful – irresistible, as she well knew – and there were probably numerous women ready to give themselves to him without hesitation.

She looked around at her ladies, all of them most becoming in their striking black and white, and wondered if it was one of them. None seemed to be acting suspiciously. And that evening, at the dinner given for the ambassadors, Henry was his usual genial self, full of the jousts and the Imperial alliance, which he spoke of as if it were all his own achievement. There was nothing in his manner towards Katherine to indicate that anything had changed. But then, she reminded herself, he was a good dissembler.

That night he came to her. He still visited her bed often, hoping to get her pregnant again. It was three and a half years since her little Isabella had been born, and both of them were beginning to feel desperate.

Katherine had not had the heart or the courage to tell Henry that there had been three occasions in the past year when her courses had not flowed. Three times her hopes had been raised, then dashed a month later. She, who had been as regular as the phases of the moon, was regular no longer. She fretted about what that portended, and prayed constantly that, while there was still time, God would make her fruitful. A son, she pleaded, an heir to gladden England and her husband; grant, O Lord, the boon of a son. Please, please . . . Was it so much to ask? Everywhere she looked she seemed to see women with strapping sons of all ages. Why was she denied even one boy?

Henry never reproached her. He understood that she was as devastated as he was at her failure to bear him an heir. It was not her fault, he assured her, time after time. He'd tried to cheer her by saying that getting a boy was as good an excuse as any to bed with her. But the constant pressure to conceive had robbed the act of love of its former joy. It was more a means to an end these days. Henry was loving, yes, but she wondered whether, if they had a palace full of sons, he would come to her as often.

Tonight was no exception. As usual he knelt to say his prayers, climbed into bed, kissed her, murmured a few endearments, then took his vigorous pleasure. It never lasted long, but that did not matter. Then they would lie and talk for a while until he left and went back to his own apartments. In many of his residences he had built secret stairs connecting his bedchamber with hers, so that they could enjoy more privacy. He liked the traditional public nature of his conjugal visits no more than she did. But the best nights were the ones when he fell asleep and remained with her until morning, because then he would make love to her again.

She could not believe that a man who was hers on an almost nightly basis was pursuing another woman. But then, as Henry began snoring gently beside her, she thought about what that motto had actually said. *She has wounded my heart.* Of course! The lady had rejected him, unbelievable as it seemed. Katherine wondered who would have dared, who would have had the confidence to do it.

She was still wondering two days later, when she and Henry attended a feast for the ambassadors hosted by Wolsey at York Place, the London house of the archbishops of York, which the Cardinal had transformed into yet another great palace. She found herself watching Henry for signs that his attention was focused on a particular lady.

After dinner the great hall was cleared and there were shouts of appreciation as a pageant car was wheeled into the hall.

'*Le Château Vert*,' announced the Cardinal, rising from his seat beside the King to acknowledge the acclaim. The pageant setting had three towers, from which hung three banners: one with three broken hearts; one with a lady's hand holding a man's heart; and the other a lady's hand turning a man's heart. Katherine wondered, with a pang, if they were in any way connected with the King's wounded heart of two days before. Hopefully – she brightened at the thought – they were all part of some elaborate conceit. She was almost convinced of it when Henry got up and left the hall.

Suddenly eight ladies sprang from the castle, all clad in gowns of white satin embroidered with Milan-point lace and gold thread, and wearing on their heads silk cauls in different colours and Milanese bonnets of gold encrusted with jewels. Each had the name of her character embroidered in gold on her bonnet. Leading the troupe was the French Queen, still as lovely as ever at twenty-six, in the apt role of Beauty. One of Katherine's most cherished ladies, Gertrude Blount, played Honour; the half-Spanish Gertrude, with her olive skin and striking black hair, was the daughter of Lord Mountjoy and Agnes de Vanagas, and had recently married the King's cousin Henry Courtenay. Constancy was personified by a newcomer to court, Lord Morley's daughter Jane Parker, who was affianced to Sir Thomas Boleyn's heir, George, a handsome, unruly young page about the court. There too was Boleyn's daughter Mistress Carey, as Kindness, and her sister, the girl Katherine had first seen in France, as Perseverance.

Anne Boleyn was now in her own household as a maid-of-honour. Sir Thomas had approached Katherine only last month and explained that his daughter was no longer welcome at the French court now that King Henry had negotiated a rapprochement with the Emperor, especially as war between England and France seemed a certainty. Taking pity on the girl, Katherine had agreed, and been rewarded, for although Anne Boleyn was not as beautiful as she liked her ladies to be, she was elegant, accomplished, musical and witty, and she had livened up Katherine's rather staid household already with her vivacious charm. She danced superbly too, Katherine thought, watching her. Her prettier sister paled beside her.

Eight splendidly dressed lords entered the hall, their hats of cloth of gold, their voluminous cloaks of blue satin. They were named Love, Nobleness, Youth, Devotion, Loyalty, Pleasure, Gentleness and Liberty, and despite the disguise it was obvious that the imposing figure of Love was the King himself, something else that made Katherine uneasy. The lords were led into the hall by Ardent Desire, who was wearing a gown of crimson satin sewn with burning flames of gold. There was no mistaking that this was William Cornish, the genius who devised most of the court revels.

The lords gleefully rushed the fortress to an explosion of gunfire, yet the ladies defended it vigorously, throwing comfits at the besiegers, or sprinkling them with rose water. The men retaliated by assaulting the castle with dates and oranges, and predictably, in the end, the defenders were forced to surrender. The lords took their prisoners by the hand and led them down to the floor, where they danced most elegantly. Katherine could not take her eyes off Henry as he wove in and out among the dancers, bowing, turning and leaping; he was the tallest and most powerfully built among them, and easily recognisable. There was much applause when they all unmasked, then Henry, flushed with pleasure, led Katherine to the chamber appointed for her by Wolsey, where she was to host a lavish banquet for the ambassadors.

Helping himself from the hundreds of tempting treats on offer, and chatting animatedly to the Cardinal and his guests, Henry still betrayed no sign of interest in any other lady present, and when he heartily kissed Katherine good night and thanked her for her hospitality, she felt able to reassure herself that her suspicions were groundless and that the heart and mottos that had struck her as ominous had been mere courtly conceits, a prelude to the pageant.

Katherine, holding six-year-old Mary's hand, was standing in the doorway to the great hall, waiting to greet her nephew Charles. Her spirits had lightened considerably when she had learned that he had at last arrived in England for his betrothal to Mary, and that Henry – who was finally bestirring himself to take command of more state affairs – had overruled Wolsey for once and joined Charles in declaring war on France, determined to halt Francis's ambitions in Italy.

Henry had gone to greet Charles and bring him in the royal barge to Greenwich, and as the young Emperor knelt before her, her heart was full.

'Madam my aunt, I humbly crave your blessing,' he said, and she gave it most gladly, and raised and kissed him.

'I cannot express my great joy at seeing your Majesty.'

Charles's face broke into one of his rare smiles. 'And this is my future bride!' He took Mary's hand and kissed it, and she curtseyed prettily, holding wide her damask skirts. 'You promise to become a handsome lady,' he told her, 'the very mirror of the Queen your mother.'

Mary dimpled and blushed, then showed Charles the new brooch pinned to her bodice. It bore the words 'The Emperor'. Henry had had it crafted for her.

'I am a lucky man indeed to have such a devoted wife,' Charles told her, patting her small red head.

Naturally Henry had arranged tournaments in the Emperor's honour. On the first day Charles sat beside Katherine, watching from the gallery over the tiltyard, and on the next day he jousted with Henry, who took care to ensure that the match was a draw. The delicious supper afterwards was followed by dancing and a masque.

In June the court travelled to Windsor for the formal betrothal ceremony. Katherine watched, greatly moved, as Mary put her tiny hand in Charles's large masculine paw and lisped her vows. She looked so small beside him, in the chapel and at the high table at the feast that was held to celebrate the occasion. It was all quite overwhelming for Katherine, since her delight in her daughter's betrothal was tempered by the knowledge that Mary would be leaving her to go to Spain when she was twelve, and that – God forbid – she might never see her again.

Again, she thought of how small Mary was. She seemed so young for her age, so fragile and vulnerable. All sorts of doubts came rushing into Katherine's mind. How would she fare without her mother's love and guidance? How would she cope with the rigid etiquette of the Spanish court after the greater freedom of the English one? Would she be ready at twelve to bed with Charles – and would he, please God, be gentle with her? She understood now how her own mother, Isabella, had felt when she had had to let her daughter go. Six years, six short years – that was all the time she had left with Mary. It was too short, much too short a time!

Henry was not quite his usual expansive self during dinner, and Katherine wondered if he was feeling the same pangs and misgivings as she was, or if he had another of his headaches. Charles did not seem to notice anything amiss. He was talking about the splendid celebrations he would be ordering for Mary's reception in Spain, and the great household he would provide for her.

'She will have much to learn and accustom herself to,' he said, echoing Katherine's own concerns. 'I wonder – do you not agree that it might be better if she came to Spain earlier, to be educated as befits a future empress and Queen of Spain?'

The food suddenly turned tasteless in Katherine's mouth. She could not, would not, part with Mary a day before she had to.

But thank God for Henry!

'No, brother,' he said. 'If you searched all Christendom for someone to bring Mary up after the manner of Spain, you could not find one more qualified than the Queen her mother. For the affection she bears to you, Katherine will bring her up to your satisfaction. I doubt anyway that Mary will be ready to bear the voyage before she is twelve, or strong enough to be transported to the air of another country.'

Charles nodded politely, as Katherine offered up a silent prayer of thanks.

'The Princess's welfare must come before all other considerations,' he said, but it was clear that he was disappointed.

It was late when Henry arrived in Katherine's bedchamber that night. She was in bed, but he was still fully dressed and seemed restless, pacing the floor before throwing off his gown and settling himself in the chair beside the fireplace.

Katherine got up, drew on her nightgown and took the chair opposite.

'Some wine?' she offered.

'No, Kate, I've had enough.'

'What is troubling you?' she asked. 'I know there is something. Is it the thought of Mary leaving us?'

'It will be a wrench,' Henry said, 'but I have far more on my mind than that. It is the prospect of England becoming just another dominion of the Empire or Spain, which is what will happen if Mary marries Charles and we have no son. As of today it is a very real prospect. I don't want to go down in history as the last King of England.'

Katherine felt the increasingly familiar fear come upon her. What if she never bore another child? It had now been four years since her last pregnancy. She had no words of comfort to offer Henry. He still did not know about the missed courses, and he had not noticed the night sweats that were afflicting her with increasing regularity. Was she ill? Surely, at thirty-six, she was not too old to bear a child? Why, why did God not answer her prayers?

'Kate, I have a son,' Henry said, his voice gentle, his eyes regarding her warily.

'I know,' she answered, trying not to sound reproachful. 'Clearly the fault lies with me.' The words came with difficulty, halting, painful.

'I did not wish to imply that, Kate. God knows, I did not want you to know.'

'You cannot keep secrets in courts, Henry.' She thought she saw him blench at that.

'I was wondering – if God sees fit not to bless us with a son – if there was some way that the boy might be legitimated.'

'No!' she cried out. 'Mary is your heir. She has it in her to be as great a queen as my mother ever was. She has those same qualities, evident already. Married to Charles, she could rule in England.'

'And he would rule through her because she is a woman and subject to him as his wife. No, that is not what I want, Kate, and my people would never tolerate it. You have seen how they dislike and distrust foreigners.'

'They have always shown great affection to me, and taken me to their hearts; they love me almost as much as they love you. And Mary is my daughter and yours. They would love her for our sakes. Henry, you cannot set aside Mary's rights!' And you cannot humiliate her or me by displacing her with your bastard. It was on the tip of her tongue to say it.

'Then what am I to do, Kate?'

'We must keep praying, Henry, and trying for a son.'

'Which is why I am here,' he said, sounding almost weary.

She helped him to undress, unlacing his sleeves and laying the rich clothes over a chest. He clambered naked into bed and clasped her to him. They were as close – almost – as a man and woman could be, and yet nothing was happening.

'I'm sorry, Kate,' Henry muttered at last. 'This is one lance that won't be raised for the attack tonight. I must have drunk more than I realised.' It sounded like an excuse. He had not really been in the mood, that was plain; and she had a horrible feeling that he was here more out of duty than because he wanted to be.

Katherine stretched out her hand to the handsome, swarthy man with the hooked nose that proclaimed his Jewish ancestry, although there could be no question about his Christian orthodoxy. He kissed it and rose at her bidding.

'Welcome to Greenwich, Professor Vives,' she said, smiling. 'It is good to receive one of my countrymen, especially one so eminent. My lord the King has told me much of your learning. We both enjoyed reading your commentary on St Augustine.'

'Your Majesty is most kind to say so.'

'Please be seated. I am interested in your views on education, especially the education of women. You will know of Sir Thomas More, who has had his daughters tutored as well as his son. Having heard of your reputation, he recommended you to the King and me.'

The man in his dark, furred scholar's robes sat down opposite Katherine.

'I am a great admirer of Sir Thomas More, and grateful to him for putting my name forward to your Majesty. He has shown the world that an educated woman can also be a virtuous woman, rather than one who wastes her learning on writing love letters!'

Katherine smiled again. 'My mother, Queen Isabella, held similar views, for which I am grateful. But while I have been able to teach my daughter, the Princess, her letters and her catechism, I am not qualified to be her tutor. Which brings me to the reason why His Majesty and I asked you to come here. I know that you will be staying in England for a time, lecturing at Oxford, but I wanted to ask if you would devise a curriculum for my daughter the Princess.'

Vives's solemn face lit up. 'Madam, I should be honoured. There is no queen in Christendom who is more renowned for her learning than your Grace.'

Over the next week, with Katherine's assistance, he drew up a programme of study that involved much learning of the Scriptures and the ancient classics and histories. Romances were forbidden.

'They encourage light behaviour,' Vives explained, 'but the Princess will benefit from reading moral tales such as "Patient Griselda".' Katherine had read the story in Boccaccio's *Decameron*, and thought that this morality tale of a woman who endured much sorrow and humiliation at the hands of her husband, yet loved him in spite of it, would offer a good example to Mary.

Vives was all fired up with his curriculum. 'Dr Fetherston can have overall responsibility for the Princess's lessons, but I will teach her Latin.' Richard Fetherston, a gentle, devout man, was Mary's chaplain and a fine scholar.

'I myself can help Mary with her translations,' Katherine said, warming to the Spanish professor's dedication and enthusiasm.

'An excellent idea, madam,' Vives concurred. 'She will benefit from your Majesty's erudition.'

He dedicated his treatise to Katherine. 'Govern your daughter by these principles, and she will be formed by them,' he wrote. 'She will resemble your example of probity and wisdom.'

Katherine showed the treatise to Henry.

'Do you think it is a little severe for a child of seven?' she asked him.

He read it, praising it heartily. 'No, I do not,' he said. 'Mary is a clever girl. By God, she will be the best-educated woman in Christendom!'

Maud Parr applauded Katherine. 'I am teaching my daughters to read and write, and I want them to learn French and Latin. In my opinion, girls are every bit as capable of being educated as boys.'

'Many would disagree with you!' Katherine pointed out.

'Let them scorn. One day we will be proved right!'

Mary took to her lessons as a bird to the sky. She was obedient, diligent and hard-working, and always eager to show her parents what she was doing.

'She is a rare person,' Vives said, 'and most singularly accomplished.' He was very pleased with her.

*

That summer Katherine noticed Anne Boleyn going about with a lighter step and a tune forever on her lips, and it was not long before she discovered the reason why. Young Harry Percy was the good-looking heir of the Earl of Northumberland, who had placed him in the household of Cardinal Wolsey, hoping no doubt to secure for him thereby preferment at court.

Katherine liked to welcome young men into her chamber; she enjoyed their company, and they could converse and make merry with her maids-of-honour under her watchful but benevolent eye. Whenever the Cardinal came to court, Harry Percy was always at her door, and it was obvious that he and Anne were deeply smitten with each other.

Then she noticed that another of her maids, Lucy Talbot, seemed put out with Anne. Indeed, it was obvious that she was barely speaking to her.

'I don't know what's got into that girl,' Maud said. 'She's walking around with a face like thunder.'

'Have a word with her, will you, Maud?' Katherine asked. 'Find out what is troubling her.'

Maud returned minutes later, looking exasperated. 'She says it's nothing, madam. She won't be drawn.'

'Best to let her be,' Katherine advised. 'They've probably had a quarrel. She'll get over it. Ah, look, here comes Harry Percy – again!'

Katherine heartily approved of his courtship of Anne Boleyn. It would be a splendid match for Anne, for not only was he ardently in love with her, but he was also the heir to one of the greatest and most ancient earldoms in England. So she encouraged the two young people and looked to hear shortly of their betrothal.

But then came a September day when her maids came running and told Katherine that Anne Boleyn was lying on her bed, weeping inconsolably, and would not be comforted. Katherine saw her alone, and was shocked to see this normally self-assured and exemplary maid-of-honour looking so ravaged with misery.

'Tell me what has happened,' she said, sitting down by the bed and taking Anne's hand.

'I am ordered home to Hever, your Grace,' Anne whispered.

'But why?' Katherine feared the worst, yet she could hardly believe that this girl had it in her to disgrace herself and her family.

'Your Grace will be angry with me if I tell you,' Anne sniffed, choking back tears.

'Your welfare is my concern. You are my maid and I am responsible for you. If aught goes amiss with you, it reflects on me too.'

Anne sniffed again and sat up, her plaited hair askew on her head. 'Well, then, madam, I see I have been very foolish. I entered into a pre-contract with Harry Percy.'

Katherine was startled. What a bold thing to do!

'Did your parents know?'

'No, madam. We are in love. We did not think.'

'That is indeed foolish, Mistress Anne. You should know that a pre-contract is as binding as a marriage, and that you should both have had your parents' permission. Harry Percy is the heir to an earldom, and your father is an important man at court. Men like them do not marry off their children lightly, and in Harry's case the King's permission is needed, for he is of the nobility.'

'I know, I know all that,' sobbed Anne. 'Madam, we did not think they would be displeased, and we did not mean to offend the King, and maybe they would all have been happy with the match, but the Cardinal said no. He had heard gossip about us, and he taxed Harry with it. He called me a foolish girl in front of all his household! He marvelled that Harry had entangled himself with me, and said that if he persisted, his father would disinherit him. And then it turns out that Harry has been betrothed for years to the Earl of Shrewsbury's daughter Mary Talbot.'

All suddenly became clear. Mary was Lucy's sister. No wonder Lucy had been angry with Anne.

'Harry protested, madam,' Anne was saying. 'He did his best, but the Cardinal commanded him not to see me again, and I am commanded to leave court!' Anne was beside herself, and on the verge of crying again. 'Your Grace, I cannot lose Harry – I love him more than life itself – and I do not want to leave your service. Oh, what am I to do?' She buried her dark head in her hands, her shoulders heaving.

'I will speak to the King,' Katherine said. 'But I cannot promise that it will do any good.'

She raised the matter at supper that evening, relating what Anne had told her.

'Boleyn's daughter has aspirations beyond her station,' Henry said, wiping his mouth with a napkin. 'Wolsey told me of his concerns about their affair, and I ordered him to intervene. Percy is betrothed, and it is a fitting match which I heartily approved. Why should he marry beneath him?'

'She is very distressed,' Katherine ventured.

'She said hard words to Wolsey, the pert minx!' Henry frowned. 'It will do her good to rusticate in the country for a bit and reflect on her conduct. We can't have the heirs to earldoms running about and betrothing themselves to any wench who takes their fancy!'

'But what of their pre-contract?'

Henry shrugged. 'Wolsey has taken care of that. On my orders.'

'Nevertheless I am sorry for Mistress Anne. She serves me well, Henry. Will you not reconsider and let her stay? Losing the man she wanted to marry is punishment enough, surely?'

'Wolsey is much offended by her rudeness. I'm sorry, Kate, she must go home.'

And she did. Katherine bade her a concerned farewell.

'When the time is ripe, Mistress Anne, you may be assured of being welcomed back into my household.' She was aware of Lucy Talbot, standing there among the maids-of-honour and glowering at Anne.

'I thank your Grace. You have been most kind. But, madam, I have been treated most unjustly and I have been insulted.' And now the anger beneath the doleful countenance became manifest. 'If ever it lies in my power, I will work the Cardinal as much displeasure as he has done me!' Her eyes flashed.

Katherine was startled by the vehemence in her tone. Even Lucy looked alarmed. The thought came unbidden to Katherine: I would not like to cross her. Aloud, she said, 'I hope that in time you will find it in your heart to forgive him. Now God speed you.'

A graceful curtsey, a wan goodbye, and Anne Boleyn was gone.

Chapter 20

1525

Katherine was on her knees on the prie-dieu in her closet at Windsor, her head in her hands. She was no longer praying, but wondering how to tell Henry that it had been a year and more since her last courses, and that she was fairly certain now that she would never see another. She had asked Margaret Pole what the cessation of her monthly bleeding meant, swearing her to secrecy, and learned the worst. She thought of all the times she had been duped into thinking that she was pregnant, when instead she had been undergoing the change of life. Time was running out for her. Since then, with increasing urgency and fervour, she had repeatedly beseeched God to grant her one last chance to give Henry a son.

She had been ill and feverish from November last year to February – three precious months lost. At one point she had thought she might die, and wondered if that was God's mysterious way of answering her prayers, for if she died Henry would be free to marry again. Weakened by her illness, which Dr de la Saa and Dr Guersye had vaguely diagnosed as an imbalance of the humours, she had descended into misery, and it was only when news came in March of the Emperor's great victory over the French at Pavia in Italy, and the capture of King Francis, that she had begun to rally in spirits.

Henry had been ecstatic to learn that his rival was Charles's prisoner. He'd actually embraced the messenger and told him, 'My friend, you are like the Angel Gabriel announcing the birth of Jesus Christ!' England had erupted in celebration.

When all the euphoria had died down, Katherine began to face the likelihood that she would never bear another child. She had hated deceiving Henry, letting him think there was still some hope of an heir when there was not. And it was not just that. She feared that, if she told him the truth, he would cease coming to her bed altogether. What man could desire an ageing, barren and overweight wife? And yet . . . how could she expect him to respect her when she was not honest with him?

She felt dragged down by a terrible sense of failure. What was worse, she was now afflicted with a horrible, foul-smelling discharge from her woman's parts. She shrank with embarrassment at the thought of mentioning it to anyone, and suffered in silence, assuming it was part of the change she was undergoing.

Henry came to her that night, for the first time since her illness. She was to shudder whenever, in the future, she thought of what had passed between them. In the past his virility had failed him but once, but now it happened again. She was shamefully conscious of the slight stench from her womb, and prayed he had not noticed it, but he was an unusually fastidious man with a sensitive nose, and she sensed him drawing away from her in distaste.

'I think I am too tired, Kate,' he said, sitting up and reaching for his nightgown.

'I am still not well,' she told him, burning with humiliation.

'Let me know when you are better,' Henry said, standing up and sliding his feet into his slippers.

She sat up, hoping for his kiss of farewell. She could not bear to have him think of her as unclean and abhorrent. But Henry merely bowed courteously, which confirmed her suspicion that he was revolted by her. It was all too much. As he picked up his candle and turned to go, she burst into tears.

'Kate, what is it?' Henry asked, hovering by the door.

'There is something I must tell you,' she sobbed. 'There will be no more children. I am past the ways of women.'

There was a silence. It was worse than any storms of reproach.

She raised her wet face to see Henry still standing there. Tears were streaming down his cheeks.

'I am so sorry, so sorry,' she cried, wanting to fly across the room and comfort him.

'All those years, all those prayers,' he said in a broken voice. 'All for nothing. All! Other men have sons! Poor men have more than they can feed. But not me, the King, who needs a son more than anyone else. Why? Why, O Lord!'

It was the bitterest pill for him to swallow. This robust, virile man of thirty-three must face the fact that he would have no more legitimate children. It was a slur on his manhood.

'How can we have offended?' Katherine asked for the hundredth time.

'I do not know!' Henry cried. 'I need time to think about it. I have to decide what I am going to do about the succession. Oh, God!'

He stumbled to the fireside, slumped into a chair and sat there staring helplessly at the flames. 'I must acknowledge Mary as my heiress,' he said at length. 'You know what that means. On my death, as matters stand, England will become a state of the Empire. Charles must be informed. I will have to tell him that you are past the age of childbearing. I imagine he will be pleased to hear it. Another territory to add to the many he already possesses.' His voice was bitter.

Katherine wept again at that, and to hear him so defeated.

'I am sorry, so sorry . . .' she kept saying.

'I'm sorry too, Kate: I'm sorry for you, and for me, and I'm sorry for my kingdom. It galls me to think that the Tudor dynasty will end with me. But I have to secure the succession. Do you think I want Charles to have England? Tell me, what is the alternative?'

'Mary's son could inherit.'

'It amounts to the same thing. A Habsburg on the English throne.'

'Yes, but one with Tudor blood.'

'I *have* a son with Tudor blood,' Henry flung back, suddenly angry, 'only he's not yours, more's the pity. By God, I could have Parliament declare him legitimate and name him my heir; I could even get a dispensation from the Pope and marry him to Mary.'

Katherine was shocked.

'The people would never accept a bastard for their king!' she cried. 'I am surprised you could even contemplate it.'

'I am contemplating it because I have to!' Henry retorted. 'The situation is desperate.'

333

'It could end in civil war,' she felt bound to say. 'There are those who might feel they have a better claim than your bastard.'

'The alternative might be worse. The English people would never take kindly to a foreigner ruling over them. Oh, Kate, I cannot think straight.'

'I am so sorry,' she said again.

'You have no need.' He made a visible effort. 'It's not your fault.'

Afterwards, nevertheless, it felt as if it was, and that he was punishing her. He still came to her bed occasionally, but never made any attempt to touch her. Yet by day he was still his normal affectionate self, the Henry of old. She could not have said there was any breach between them, except in the physical sense, yet she realised, with painful clarity, that his desire for her was dead, and that he visited her bed only because he was concerned to spare her the shame of people knowing that. Servants, after all, could be trusted to gossip.

Yet she still had the feeling that his reluctance to touch her was a form of revenge for her terrible failure. Initiating lovemaking was something she had never done, and had not the courage to start doing now, for she was terrified of being rejected; and anyway, she was still experiencing her embarrassing complaint, and knew she would be offensive to him. So she suffered in silence, turning to prayer to heal the pain of rejection.

Then came an even worse humiliation.

At midsummer Henry appointed a day on which he would ennoble various deserving persons, and there was a great ceremony in the presence chamber at Bridewell Palace in London. Katherine was there, seated beside Henry with her maids and ladies behind her, making herself smile and be gracious, as if all were well. The room was thronged with courtiers, and there was an excited, expectant hum of murmuring. Sir Thomas More was busy with a pile of patents, checking that they were in order before handing the first one to the King. Then he gave the nod.

Trumpets sounded, and the herald at the door cleared his throat.

'The Lord Roos!' he cried.

Henry's cousin Thomas Manners, a bearded man in his thirties who looked so like him, approached the dais and knelt, as More, standing beside Henry, read out the patent of creation that made his lordship Earl of Rutland. Henry stood, belted the ceremonial sword around Roos's waist, and invested him with the mantle and coronet of his earldom.

Then came Henry Courtenay, another of the King's cousins, to be made Marquess of Exeter. They had been brought up from boyhood together, their mothers having been sisters, and Courtenay's wife, Gertrude Blount, was one of Katherine's close friends, so she was delighted for them both.

'Lord Henry Brandon!'

Katherine smiled at the French Queen as a tall knight walked in carrying two-year-old Henry Brandon. How she wished she had a fine boy like that. Henry bent to pat the head of his nephew as the knight, still holding the child, knelt for the ennoblement ceremony, for which the belt, the sword, the mantle and the coronet had all been made in miniature. Katherine caught sight of Henry's face as he created his young namesake Earl of Lincoln: just for an instant he let his guard fall and looked wistful, even emotional. She thought of the little boy's brother and namesake, who had died three years ago, aged six. The French Queen had also known tragedy, but at least she still had a surviving son. Katherine prayed that he would live.

'Sir Thomas Boleyn!'

Boleyn strode up to the dais and knelt in his turn. This blunt-featured, blunt-spoken man had become a great friend of the King and had served him well for many years now. Katherine had never warmed to him, but she recognised that he deserved this honour. Evidently others thought so too, as there was a ripple of hushed comment when he appeared. As he was made Viscount Rochford, a voice behind Katherine murmured, 'The wages of sin!' It was Anne Boleyn, now forgiven and back at court. Astounded both by the remark and the fact that Anne had ventured to make it to the detriment of her own father, Katherine was about to turn and reprove her, but the announcement of another name made her freeze.

'Henry Fitzroy!'

Katherine was dumbstruck. How could Henry humiliate her in public like this? It was outrageous and cruel – like flinging her failure in her face. And everyone was looking, staring, craning their necks to see how she was reacting.

She steeled herself. She would not give them the satisfaction! The smile stayed fixed on her face, yet she could not drag her eyes away from the comely, sturdy six-year-old who came, nobly attended by three earls, and knelt gracefully before the father he so greatly resembled. And now More was reading out a host of honours – Knight of the Most Noble Order of the Garter, Earl of Nottingham, Duke of Richmond, Duke of Somerset . . .

Katherine was appalled. Those were royal titles! Henry's father had been Earl of Richmond before his accession; and the name Somerset would forever be associated with his illustrious Beaufort ancestors. To be bestowed on a bastard . . . it was insupportable! The smile on her face felt as if it were set in stone; she was aware that people were watching her even more closely, and that Wolsey was looking at her, a smug expression on his face. Of course, he was Fitzroy's godfather. No doubt he was behind all this. She stared straight ahead, aware that her cheeks were flushed with anger. How could Henry be doing this to her? It seemed that she was deliberately being slighted. Or was it her punishment for not bearing a son of her own?

She kept her composure through the rest of the ceremony, watched him kiss his son and congratulate him on his advancement, and saw the adulation with which the boy regarded his father. Envy gripped her like a vice. Why was the endearing little fellow not hers?

She would not look at Henry or speak to him as they sat together at the feast held to mark the ennoblements and the disguisings that followed. She was desperately relieved to return to her chamber afterwards, and remained in her apartments for the next few days, keeping her daughter with her lest she hear gossip and ask awkward questions. It was Margaret Pole who told Katherine that young Fitzroy had now been given several high offices, including that of Lord High Admiral.

'It is clear that the King means to have him well brought up like a prince's child in great state,' Katherine observed bitterly.

'Forgive me, madam, but you should know that people are saying he may easily, by the King's means, be exalted to higher things,' Margaret said. It was all too believable.

Katherine was devastated. Henry had delivered a blatant and demeaning insult to her – and to their daughter, which was even harder to forgive. Yet she knew that all she could do was maintain a dignified silence and have patience. And when Henry next visited her, and made no reference to young Fitzroy, she held her peace.

It was a sweltering August day, too hot even for Henry to go hunting. That put him in a bad mood, for the grease season had begun and it was the time of year when he always took a rest from state affairs to indulge his passion for the chase. He could tire eight or ten horses in a day, and his gentlemen sometimes complained that he turned the sport of hunting into a martyrdom. Katherine had known him to sit boasting about his successes for three or four hours over supper. But today he was restless, and in no good mood.

She felt the need to placate him.

'Charles has written to say that he wears the emerald ring you sent him from Mary every day,' she said, her fingers working deftly on the delicate blackwork embroidery that Henry liked to have on the necklines and cuffs of his shirts, and which was copied everywhere now. 'He speaks so warmly of her.'

'Yes, but he continues to press for her to be sent to Spain.' Henry tossed off his doublet and rolled up his shirtsleeves.

'You will not let her go?'

'No, I have said she will not go until the appointed time. But now he is demanding payment of her dowry as an act of good faith. I've written to remind him that it isn't due for another three years.'

Three years, three short, precious years . . . Then it would be farewell to Mary. Katherine could not imagine the enormity of such a parting. Her child, her small, delicate child – surely she would not be ready, there would be a reprieve . . .

'I had best go,' Henry said, rising. 'Wolsey wants to see me.'

He was back within the quarter hour, red with fury, flinging a parchment on the table.

'Is there no faith in the world?' he shouted. 'Sometimes I think I'm the only prince with any honour left! The Emperor,' he fumed, glowering at Katherine as if it were all her fault, 'has declared that, as he has received neither bride nor dowry, he considers his betrothal null and void.'

'No!' Katherine cried, half rising, but sinking back unsteadily into her chair. No, it could not be! Nothing must be allowed to break this most advantageous of alliances.

'Henry, you must do something to make things right. Charles's friendship is so important, to us and to England. Think what his rejection will do to Mary! She has grown up knowing that she will be his empress. She loves him, in her childish way. There must be something you can do, or Wolsey – Wolsey is clever at diplomacy.'

'Kate, if you had let me finish, you would know that there is nothing to be done! Charles has found a richer bride – your own niece, Isabella of Portugal. She has a dowry of a million crowns, far more than I can offer with Mary. What's more, she is of an age to bear children, and very beautiful.'

He was pacing up and down, furious in his impotence.

'I have always dreamed,' Katherine said brokenly, 'of England and Spain being united. It has been my dearest wish that Mary would marry into Spain. This is dreadful. I cannot believe it!'

'*I* cannot credit that Charles could be so perfidious!' Henry barked. 'Wolsey warned me, but I would not heed him, as I know him for a Frenchman at heart. But by God, I can almost feel sorry for Francis, shut up in prison in Madrid.' He sat down, seething, then looked at her challengingly. 'Wolsey wants me to make a new treaty with France, and I tell you I have a mind to do it!'

Katherine was alarmed. 'Henry, please don't make a hasty decision. Wolsey *wants* you to abandon the Emperor; he has not forgiven or forgotten being overlooked in his bid to become pope.'

'What can the Emperor offer me now, madam?' Henry asked, his temper rising again. 'This isn't about Wolsey. It's about maintaining a balance of power in Europe. If Charles wants his freedom, he can have it, but it will come at the price of my signing a new treaty with France, and then he had best look out!'

'Please, Henry, listen to me!'

'Hold your peace, Kate! You are in no position to make demands.'

It was the cruellest thing he had said to her, and it stopped her short. It brought home to her in an instant the stark fact that, thanks to her nephew's betrayal and her own barrenness, her voice now counted for nothing – and for that she chiefly blamed Wolsey. She could easily imagine him dripping poison into Henry's ear, doing his best to undermine her, turning her husband against her.

She would not go down without a fight.

'Your interests are my interests, Henry,' she said, rising steadily now to face him. 'I would never say or do anything to your detriment. I am heartily sorry that Charles has done this terrible thing. But it was no fault in me, and I pray you not to judge me guilty, even though he is my nephew. Were I to see him now, I would give him a piece of my mind!'

'Would that *I* could see him now!' Henry growled.

He left her then, and it was soon clear that Wolsey had once more got to him, for two days later he was back, looking fidgety, a sure sign that he was the bringer of unpalatable news.

'Now that Mary is not going to Spain, she must be prepared for queenship,' Henry said. 'It is what you have always wanted, Kate. You say she has what it takes, that she is Queen Isabella to the life. Well, I hope you are proved right.'

Katherine was astonished. After all he had said, it seemed incredible for him suddenly to have accepted that it was possible for a woman to rule. Her heart rejoiced for her daughter.

'Mary *will* make a great queen!' she assured him. 'I have no doubt of that.'

'We shall see.' He would not concede more. 'I do not intend to make her Princess of Wales, but that role she shall have. You will recall the precedent set by my father and grandfather, who sent their heirs to live at Ludlow—'

'No, Henry,' Katherine interrupted, seeing immediately where this was going. She had just been led to believe that Henry had made the best, the happiest, decision in the circumstances, but she had been wrong, wrong! 'Please, no!'

'But, Kate, it is the best apprenticeship for princes. I wish I had been afforded the opportunity, but I was only the younger son, so Arthur was sent. This is how Mary will best learn to rule. She is nine, an apt age to begin, and I intend for her to stay there until she marries.'

'Henry,' Katherine cried in panic, 'you must know what this means for me. I had counted on keeping her with me, my only child, until she was twelve. She is so young to be parted from us. She needs me, her mother.'

'Kate, it is for her good. I am her father. Do you not think I have her interests at heart?'

'I know you do, of course you do, but what of me? I have no other child to console me in her absence. I cannot bear to part with her. Send her to Ludlow if you must, but let me go with her! I know Ludlow, I was there with Arthur, and I could be a help to her.'

Henry was immovable. 'Kate, your place is with me, as my Queen. You have a role to perform here at court. My mother did not go with Arthur; she knew her duty.'

That stung. But Katherine was frantic. 'Henry, I am begging you!' She fell to her knees and clutched his hands. 'Let her stay with me until she is twelve.'

'No, Kate,' he said, disentangling his fingers, not looking her in the eye. 'Lady Salisbury shall go with her as her governess. Let that be a comfort to you.'

Small comfort, however much I love and trust Margaret, Katherine thought, rising wearily to her feet as Henry left her. I am to be deprived not only of my daughter but also of the best friend I have in England. Again she had the distinct feeling that Henry was punishing her. She gave way then, crying as if her heart would break, and that was how Margaret Pole found her.

'Oh, your Grace, dear me, what is wrong?' Strong, capable arms encircled Katherine, who blurted out between sobs all her griefs – the collapse of the Imperial alliance, the humiliating advancement of Henry Fitzroy, her barrenness, Henry's withdrawal, and now the imminent parting from Mary. 'And I am to lose you too!' she ended.

'Madam, I am so sorry. I know what it is to be parted from a child. But hearken. I am sensible of the honour the King and you have done me, and I promise you, on the safety of my soul, that I will take the greatest care in looking after the Princess. I will be as a mother to her, and make sure that she writes regularly to you. And I will bring her to court whenever His Majesty permits. I will do all the things a good mother would do, as you would have me. Dear madam, do not weep. God sends these misfortunes to try your faith. Remember, we never come to the kingdom of Heaven but by troubles.'

'You are a true friend to me, Margaret,' Katherine said, hugging her. 'It is indeed a consolation to me that you will be with Mary. But you know I think much of this is the Cardinal's doing. He is doing all he can to turn the King against me because he fears my influence. I see the hand of Wolsey in all.'

She got up and began pacing the room, unable to sit still. 'We could stay friends with the Emperor even if he is to marry Isabella of Portugal, and it would be wise to do so, for England does much valuable trade with his dominions; but Wolsey must needs break the alliance because he loves the French and can never forgive the Emperor for not making him pope. He is telling the King that he can make Fitzroy his heir; he has even put it into his head that he can marry the boy to Mary, and she his half-sister! He knows now that Mary will rule after Henry, and fears my influence on her, so he wants us kept apart.'

Margaret frowned. 'Madam, I cannot comment on these matters. I would only advise you not to antagonise Wolsey. He would prove a formidable enemy if provoked. Remember what happened to Buckingham.'

'I can never forget it. Rest assured, I will be careful,' Katherine promised. But she knew how cunning the Cardinal could be. Since that day nine years ago when Henry had cast an envious eye on the glories of Hampton Court, he had never shown any jealousy of Wolsey's vast possessions. But recently she had gained the impression that he was at last growing resentful and jealous of the Cardinal's wealth and power. He was no longer the untried young King whom Wolsey had mentored, but a mature man in his mid-thirties, experienced in statecraft and aware of his own exalted status. On a visit to Hampton Court, Henry had for the first time made pointed remarks about the riches on display in that fabulous palace.

'Thomas, you are more magnificent than your sovereign!' he had exclaimed, clapping Wolsey on the back.

Wolsey, looking uneasy, had hastened to respond, 'It is only fitting that your Majesty's servant should reflect the greater magnificence of his King!'

'Is that so?' Henry's eyes had narrowed. 'Tell me which of my palaces is more magnificent than this?' He waved his arm to indicate the fine tapestries, the carved and gilded plaster frieze of gambolling cherubs, the glowing glass in the oriel window and the abundance of gold plate on the buffet.

Wolsey had hurriedly begun praising the glories of Greenwich and Richmond, and no more had been said. But a week later, Henry had come to Katherine's apartments beaming broadly, with the deeds to Hampton Court in his hand. The Cardinal, no doubt feeling that some sacrifice was expedient, had made the grand gesture of giving his master the palace.

Katherine had seen that as the beginning of the end for Wolsey, but she had been mistaken. If anything, the gift of Hampton Court had shown Henry how devoted Wolsey was to him, and made him love his old friend more than ever.

'Was ever a king so blessed in a servant?' he kept saying. Now Wolsey could do no wrong.

Wolsey came to see her, all rustling red robes and obsequiousness.

'Madam, the King has asked me to consult you in drawing up guidelines for Lady Salisbury as to the régime to be followed by the Princess at Ludlow.' He sat down at the table, without being invited, and produced paper, pen and ink from the bulging leather scrip he always carried.

Katherine bridled. She was Mary's mother, and *she* would decide what was best for her. 'As to that, my Lord Cardinal, I wish Lady Salisbury to have the most tender regard for the Princess's honourable education and her training in virtuous behaviour. Lady Salisbury and I are of one mind about these aspects, and I will tell you about the regimen that *we* have drawn up, which is what you will implement.'

Wolsey frowned. 'If I may advise—'

'There is no need,' Katherine interrupted. 'It is all decided. The Princess is to enjoy plenty of fresh air, and take walks in the gardens for her health and comfort. She is to practise her music, but not too much, for fear of tiring her; and she must continue learning Latin and French, but her studies are not to be wearisome. She enjoys dancing, so she must have time for that.'

Wolsey had begun taking notes in his untidy hand. She waited until his nib had ceased its scratching, trying to remember the myriad things she had ordered for Mary these past years when she had taken it for granted that she would continue to supervise her upbringing. How she would miss being the central focus of her daughter's life. It was essential that the child should not suffer any deprivation while they were apart.

'As to her diet, let it be pure, well prepared, dressed and served with merry conversation, in an honourable manner. Her lodgings, her clothes and everything about her must be kept clean and wholesome, as is proper for so great a princess. There must be no dirt or evil smells, and her servants are to behave wisely, virtuously and discreetly, and treat the Princess with humility and reverence.'

She thought she had covered everything. No doubt she would think of more, but if she did she could write to Margaret and know that her wishes would be respected. She did not ask Wolsey for his opinion of her orders; this was her business, and as far as she was concerned he was here to relay her instructions, no more.

'That will be all, my Lord Cardinal,' she said.

It was late August when all was in readiness for Mary to leave Richmond for Ludlow. Henry and Katherine rode with her as far as the royal hunting lodge at King's Langley in Hertfordshire, and there they bade her farewell. Katherine had been dreading the moment, and feared she might make a spectacle of herself by crying in public, but when the time came for her to gather Mary into her embrace for the last time before parting, she took heart from her daughter's cheerfulness at the prospect of this new, grown-up adventure, made herself smile and gave her a hearty blessing. Then she stood with Henry, watching as the great train set out on its way westwards, until the litter bearing its precious burden disappeared out of sight down the leafy thoroughfare.

Afterwards she tried to be stoical. It would not be for long. It wanted less than four months to Christmas, when surely Henry would summon Mary to court. That would make fifteen weeks at most. She could bear that.

At supper at King's Langley that evening she broached the subject.

'Mary will be coming to court for Christmas, won't she?'

'No, Kate, it's too soon,' Henry said firmly. 'It would only unsettle her.'

'Henry, she has been gone three hours and already I am finding this parting difficult. She is a child, and she needs her mother. Let her come for Christmas, please!' She could hear the note of desperation in her voice.

'Kate, she is a princess and heir to this realm. She cannot cling to her mother's skirts for ever, and you of all people should know that most princesses leave their mothers at a young age. Many never see them again. You must steel yourself to this, as I am having to. She is my daughter too. But I will order that she keep Christmas in as much state as if she were at court. I want her to enjoy it. And we must be happy for her, and learn to let her go.'

Katherine subsided, knowing that further argument was useless. I am Patient Griselda, she thought. I love my husband whatever he does to me, and this is the worst of the blows he has dealt me. He has taken my daughter from me, not understanding the wrench or the pain. Again, I feel he is punishing me. I have not given him a son, and so I have been deprived of the things that make life meaningful: my only child, his body, the alliance that meant so much to me, and my pride. And yet I go on loving him.

She decided not to accompany Henry on his hunting progress. With his permission – a trifle too readily given – she retreated to Woburn Abbey to seek solace for her troubled soul. Abbot Robert and his white monks received her cordially and assigned her a simple room, clean and light, in their guesthouse. Attached to it was a little oratory where she spent many hours praying for strength and resignation.

Then came the thing she had dreaded: a letter from Margaret Pole informing her that Mary was ill.

Katherine caught her breath. No! No! It could not be, not when she was apart from her beloved child. The longing to canter across England to be with Mary was almost unbearable, and only abated when a messenger brought the news that the Princess was on the mend. Katherine wrote letter after letter to Mary, pouring out her love and concern, and telling her how much her absence troubled her.

Mary's own letters, painstakingly composed and regular as clockwork, were a great joy, as were the written exercises that were enclosed with them, even if there were a few forgivable errors. It was clear that Mary still craved her mother's approval in all things and thought of her constantly, and that was balm to Katherine's wounded soul.

Chapter 21

1526–1527

Henry's coffers were running low, but he was still lavishing money on court entertainments. There were not so many tournaments these days, but he insisted on holding one at Greenwich on Shrove Tuesday, even though the weather was likely to be cold. Such minor inconveniences did not bother him. In fact it was freezing, and Katherine did not relish the prospect of spending hours in the royal stand watching him and the other knights breaking lances and engaging in hand-to-hand combat. But there was no help for it. He liked her to be there, cheering him on. And, as on so many previous occasions, he would wear her favour and compete in her honour. It was something she held precious and, given that their marriage was not what it was, these days, not to be missed.

She had her ladies dress her in her warmest gown and kirtle, with furred sleeves and a voluminous woollen cloak lined with sable. On her head she wore a gable hood made entirely of white fur, beneath the hood of her cloak, and as she left for the tiltyard she drew on her thick, padded embroidered gloves. Blanche de Vargas had thoughtfully gone ahead to place a hot brick wrapped in flannel by the footstool where her feet would rest, and when she arrived in the stand she found a brazier burning merrily by her chair. Her women clustered around her, wrapped up warmly, their breath misting the sharp air.

They did not have long to wait before the cheering began and Henry appeared, magnificent in a jousting outfit of cloth of gold and silver embroidered in gold. And Katherine saw the words picked out in silks, 'Declare I dare not', surmounted by a man's heart engulfed in flames – and then it was not only the bitter February cold that chilled her heart.

She tried to tell herself that it meant nothing, that it was a pretty conceit such as the motto Henry had worn – four years ago, was it? – at another joust. And nothing had come of that. She had no reason to suspect anything, none at all. *Be sensible!* she admonished herself. *It means nothing!*

Lord Willoughby was dead of a fever.

Katherine let the letter from Grimsthorpe fall into her lap. Maria's uneven script had betrayed the depth of her grief. 'I can take no food, and only a little wine,' she had written. 'I hardly sleep. If God would summon me to join Him, I would go, gladly.' Katherine tried to imagine how she would feel if Henry died. The world would simply end, she knew, and she would not care what became of her. But others would, as she herself now cared about Maria.

All she wanted was to comfort her friend. In the past years they had corresponded faithfully, sending each other warm, witty letters with accounts of their daily lives and their children, and Maria had visited court three more times, but she had lost another son, Francis, and been immersed in her life in Lincolnshire, so for two years Katherine had not seen her.

'I would like to go to her,' she said to Henry, who had hastened to commiserate with her over the sad news. 'There is no risk of contagion. Lord Willoughby died far from home, on a visit to Suffolk. Maria, to her grief, was not with him.'

It was October and they were at Henry's new palace of Grafton, Northamptonshire, on the last stage of a progress that had begun in Sussex. All was fair between them, and Katherine had almost forgotten her disquiet over the motto she had fretted about in February. Again, it had been meaningless. What had befallen poor Maria was far worse, she thought, recalling her dismay. It was important to keep a sense of proportion.

'It's not so far, Kate,' Henry said. 'But Maria may not want all the ado of a royal visit.'

'I would go as a private person. Please give me leave.'

'Of course,' he said. 'I would not stay you. While you are there I would like you to give Maria a message from me. She will be aware that the Willoughby inheritance now descends to her daughter, who is a minor – and a great heiress. She will not lack for suitors! In the meantime, she is my ward, her father being dead. I want you to tell Maria that for now her daughter may remain with her.'

'That is kind – and very generous.' Katherine was aware that many would be clamouring to buy the wardship of Katherine Willoughby. She hoped that Henry's magnanimity would extend until the girl was of an age to wed.

As Katherine entered her bedchamber in search of her maids and chamberers, whose job it was to pack for her journey, she came upon Margery and Elizabeth Otwell sobbing over the clean linen they were laying away in a chest.

'What is wrong?' she asked.

Margery sprang to her feet and wiped her eyes. 'Your Grace! I am sorry. I will get on with my work.'

Elizabeth's white face registered pure misery. Katherine was touched that they were so moved by Maria's loss.

'It is terrible news,' she said. 'We are all much affected by it.'

The sisters exchanged glances.

'It is, madam,' said Margery. She was clearly making a huge effort to control her tears. 'We feel for Lady Willoughby. How can we help your Grace?'

'I am going to visit her, and need you to make all things ready for me. I will not be gone for more than three or four days.'

Maud came in. 'I've brought your Grace's book,' she said, then noticed the wan expressions of the Otwell sisters. 'Come now, ladies, let us get packing!' she said briskly.

It was a pleasant, mild autumn, with leaves of red, gold and russet adorning the trees, and the roads were dry and free of mud. Katherine's small party covered the fifty miles between Grafton and Grimsthorpe in two days, receiving hospitality overnight from the Abbot of Peterborough.

After supper that evening she walked into the great abbey church, which was lit by a hundred candles. It was empty, and Katherine relished this brief time of solitude. She walked up the nave to the crossing, made her obeisance to the altar, then turned right into the transept and knelt to pray in the chapel of St Oswald, whose arm was one of the abbey's most precious relics. She gazed at it in reverence, then rose and continued around the apse to the beautiful Lady Chapel, and then returned down the north aisle. As she was passing the altar on her left, she paused, halted by she knew not what. It was like a great sense of peace descending on her, a sense of coming home and being lifted up to unimaginable happiness.

She did not know what to think. She would be committing the sin of pride if she allowed herself to think that St Oswald or another of Peterborough's ancient saints had vouchsafed her a spiritual revelation. Maybe she had imagined it – it had only lasted for seconds, and it would be easy in such a holy place to conjure up that feeling of peaceful well-being in Christ. Maybe it *was* a sign, sent to help her comfort Maria. Whatever it was, it was what she had prayed for.

Grimsthorpe was an old castle with a tall tower that had been converted into a comfortable residence sometime in the past. Everywhere there was evidence of Maria's more recent hand, in wall hangings, painted beamed ceilings, tiled floors and carved furniture.

Katherine had come expecting to find Maria in a state of emotional collapse, and to offer support and sympathy, but she found her friend bearing up bravely, and coping admirably with all the sad tasks that widowhood brings. It was only now that she realised how much inner strength Maria possessed. From the moment when they clung to each other in Grimsthorpe's hall, to the time, three days later, when Katherine bade farewell, she never once saw Maria cry.

She had hoped to be in time to attend the funeral, but Lord Willoughby was already buried.

'It was such a short illness,' Maria said, over supper, which was served in a black-hung parlour. 'Such a shock. He rode away in excellent health, looking as handsome and fit as ever, and then I heard he was dead. He was just forty-four.' She paused and breathed deeply. 'I must be grateful that we had ten happy years.'

Katherine reached across to Maria and laid her hand on hers. 'In that you were blessed. And you have your daughter to console you.' She was much taken with her goddaughter, seven-year-old Katherine Willoughby, a sweet, lively child with dark locks and a winning tilt to her nose. 'She favours you in looks.'

'Yes, her nurse calls her the little Spaniard!' Maria smiled. 'How does the Princess?'

'She is ten now, and forward for her age,' Katherine told her proudly. 'I wish you could see her.' *And I wish I could too.*

'I wish it also,' Maria said. 'She is a charming child. It would make me so happy if our daughters could be friends, as we are.'

'God willing, they will be,' Katherine replied, thinking that Maria was still attractive, even in her heavy black mourning gown, although her hair was now silvered lightly with grey. *We are both older*, Katherine thought, but with Maria there was something more. There was a new brittleness to her, as if she were holding herself tightly in check – as well she might, given her situation.

'Roast of kings!' Katherine exclaimed in pleasure, as the lamb dish was placed on the table on its great silver platter. 'I haven't had this for years. I used to love it as a child.'

'Your arrival was well timed,' Maria said, helping Katherine to slices of the meat.

'It's as if you knew I was coming. Mmm, just as I remember it. Peppered to perfection!'

As they ate, they caught up with each other's news. Maria wanted to hear all about what was happening at court, and then she wanted to talk about William.

'It helps to talk about him,' she said. 'It keeps his memory vivid. Thank you for listening.'

Katherine told her about the latest scandal at court. 'The Duke and Duchess of Norfolk have separated, and she has moved into her own house.'

'Was it because of Bess Holland?'

'It was. That has been going on for years, as we all know, and then Elizabeth refused to have the woman in the house, so the Duke cut off her allowance and Bess had her revenge by tying her up and jumping on her chest until she spat blood.'

Maria's dark eyes widened. 'That's appalling!'

'What was worse, Elizabeth had just given birth, and she says the Duke dragged her by the hair from her bed when she complained, and cut her cheek with his dagger. Of course, he denies it, but no one believes him, least of all me! He's a nasty man. Elizabeth says he regards neither God nor his own honour.'

Maria toyed with her food, gave up and poured more wine.

'I don't know what he sees in Bess Holland! She's his laundress, isn't she?'

Katherine shook her head. 'So the gossips say, but in fact she's related to Lord Hussey. Be that as it may, she's a wicked woman.'

As the candles guttered out and the shadows deepened they spoke of other old friends and of various people at court.

'I take it the Cardinal is still riding high?' Maria said, almost innocently. She hated Wolsey as much as Katherine did.

'Indeed he is.'

'It galls me that the King allows him such precedence.'

Katherine hesitated. She felt she should not criticise Henry to her friends. But this was not the court, and it was only Maria who was listening – Maria, whom she could trust. 'Henry remains in thrall to him. Sometimes I think he sees him as a father figure.'

'Your Highness, of all people, should be able to understand what moves the King in regard to the Cardinal.'

'I? Why would I understand?'

'Remember Fray Diego. You behaved as if he were a saint. We all wondered about him, and some raised concerns, but you wouldn't listen. To you, he was perfect, the epitome of sanctity. Maybe that is how the Cardinal appears to the King.'

'As the epitome of sanctity? I doubt it!' Katherine grinned. 'But you may have a point. I was very naive back then, and lonely. I needed a spiritual direction. Fray Diego gave me that – but I also think he took advantage of me.'

'I know he did!' Maria smiled. Katherine was taken aback for a moment, but then she understood that Maria had been referring to the friar's undue influence. No, she would never speak of that night. Older and wiser now, she had come to believe that Fray Diego's interest in her had been more than spiritual, and that he had been deliberately trying to lead her into sin – as, it seemed, he had several others.

It was late evening when Maria called for hippocras to be served. 'Well, it's a special occasion,' she said. 'It's not every day that the Queen of England calls on me!'

'What will you do now?' Katherine asked, as her goblet was filled.

'I am considering my options,' Maria told her.

'The King is content to leave your daughter with you. He asked me to tell you so.'

Maria did not react as she had expected. 'Actually, I have been wondering about that. You see, Highness, I am lonely. William was my life, but that is over, and I would have once more the company of my dear mistress and countrywoman. I would willingly leave my daughter with her nurses and tutors, if I could return to my old position at court.'

'But of course!' Katherine cried, elated at the prospect. She loved Maud Parr and sorely missed Margaret Pole, but Maria was her oldest friend and she was glad to welcome her back into her service, even if Maria had been restored to her for the saddest of reasons. 'You must come as soon as you are ready. And it will not be your old position, for you are no longer a maid. You will be one of the great ladies of my household – and more welcome than I can say!'

When Christmas approached Katherine hardly dared ask Henry if Mary might come to court. It had been sixteen months since she had seen her daughter, and still she felt the parting cruelly. As the days went by and it was November, then December, she thought she would go mad with frustration. If Henry did not bring up the matter soon, she would be forced to speak.

But on St Nicholas's Day he visited her chamber and told her that he had sent for Mary to join them for the festive season. Beside herself with happiness, she threw her arms around him and kissed him, regardless of the stares of her startled ladies.

'I see I shall have to invite Mary more often!' he jested, a little pink in the face.

Mary arrived at court looking and behaving strikingly older than Katherine remembered her. How she clung to her daughter, wishing never to let go . . . Mary wept a little and said how much she had missed her dearest mother. Their days were filled with joyous pastimes, making holly wreaths and singing the old carols and catching up on the myriad things that had happened in the time they had been apart. Katherine was avid to know every detail of her daughter's life, and Mary was eager to tell her. And then there was a Christmas never to be forgotten, with abundant feasting, revelry, masques, disguisings, banquets and jousts. As Henry led Mary out before the court in a pavane, Katherine watched, her heart full, as they danced together and everyone clapped.

It was a magical, golden time. But then, after Twelfth Night, Mary, at Henry's insistence, had to go back to Ludlow, and Katherine was left with only her memories and her longing.

Maria was back in attendance on Katherine by the spring of 1527, when the new Imperial ambassador came to be formally welcomed by the Queen at Greenwich.

It soon became apparent that a decade of married life with an indulgent husband, and the running of a noble household, had changed Maria. She was brisker and more forthright than she had ever been. Understanding immediately that Katherine was deeply unhappy, she was determined to be her champion.

Unlike the circumspect Margaret Pole, Maria did not hesitate to criticise the King. 'He asks too much of you,' she declared. 'He should have a care to your feelings. William always took account of my wishes.' She was fond of reciting William's virtues, and beside him Henry was usually found wanting. 'Your Highness is too meek, too accepting, if I may say so.'

'I am his wife and sworn to obedience,' Katherine insisted.

'You are too kind and courteous for your own good! Men are easily handled. There are ways of persuasion. A little tactical withdrawal? It worked wonders with William. He would do anything for me.'

Katherine, for all her sympathy for Maria, was already growing weary of hearing about how wonderful William had been. 'I doubt Henry would notice,' she said. 'I am not in a position to make tactical withdrawals.'

Maria was about to make some tart retort, and no doubt praise William again, when Anne Boleyn came sweeping in, in the elegant manner that came effortlessly to her, and announced that Don Diego Hurtado de Mendoza, Luis Caroz's replacement following the latter's recall, was waiting in the antechamber with Cardinal Wolsey.

The Cardinal presented the new Imperial ambassador to the Queen, and looked on eagle-eyed as Mendoza bowed and kissed her hand. The Spaniard was a swarthy, attractive man with a shock of dark hair and a very correct manner. Considering that he had just come from an audience with the King, who was still furious with the Emperor, he was remarkably composed.

'Highness, His Imperial Majesty wishes me to convey his most sincere love for you, and enquires after your health.'

Katherine was restrained in her welcome, and conscious of Wolsey's presence. 'I am gratified to hear it, for I have been hurt by His Majesty's neglect. For more than two years I have had no letters from Spain, and yet such are my affection and readiness for his service that I deserve better treatment.'

Mendoza looked uncomfortable. 'Highness, there has been a coolness, shall we say, between His Majesty and the King your husband. His Majesty has not felt able to be in contact with you, and he wishes you to know that he is very sorry about that. But now I hope that matters will improve.'

Katherine guessed that Mendoza was here to mitigate any consequences of Henry's new alliance with France, and that Henry, for all his blustering, was anxious to preserve England's trade with the Empire, even though he and Charles remained, albeit cordially, at odds. Thanks to Henry's efforts, and Wolsey's, naturally, King Francis had been released from his Spanish prison, having bound himself to a draconian treaty of friendship with the Emperor, which was to be sealed by his marriage to Charles's sister Eleanor. Hearing that, Katherine had thought sadly of poor Queen Claude, dead these three years, worn out with childbearing.

But as soon as he'd got safely back home, Francis had broken the terms of that treaty and ratified the alliance with England. Having heard Henry's ambassador in Paris describe the Princess Mary as the pearl of the world, and the jewel her father esteemed more than anything else on earth, he had wasted no time in proposing himself, or one of his sons, as a husband for her. Katherine had been horrified.

'A French marriage for Mary would be bad enough, but giving her to that great Turk would be sheer wickedness!' she had cried. 'Besides, he is sworn to marry my niece Eleanor.'

'I agree,' said Henry. 'It must be one of the sons, the Dauphin Francis or the Duc d'Orléans.'

That was small consolation for giving her only child to a Frenchman, not to mention the prospect of Mary leaving England, perhaps for ever. Katherine had never quite come to terms with the fact that it would happen, the inevitable parting, and she was having a dreadful foretaste of it, with Mary being at Ludlow. She still did not know how she would face it.

Katherine's audience with Mendoza was a short one. Wolsey saw to that.

'There are many important matters that the King wishes me to discuss with you,' he said to the ambassador, after a mere five minutes of courtesies. 'Her Highness will surely excuse us if we take our leave and depart. You shall have an audience at another time.'

It was to prove almost impossible to arrange one; always there was a reason why Mendoza was unable to see her. Usually, as she found out later, he had been diverted or detained by Wolsey. She had the uneasy feeling that she was being watched. Surely it was no coincidence that the Cardinal's servants were always in and out of her apartments on various pretexts? Their presence was beginning to disconcert her. They seemed to contrive to be in her presence chamber whenever she gave audiences, and some were taking an uncommon interest in her maids.

Indeed, there was that minx Lucy Talbot, encouraging one of them with her sideways smile and slanting eyes. Katherine was certain that she was not imagining it all. She wondered if her letters were intercepted; it would not have surprised her. Naturally Wolsey did not want her influencing anyone in favour of Spain, to the detriment of this new alliance.

But there came a day when the Cardinal was away on business and, mercifully, his servants were conspicuous by their absence. She seized her opportunity, letting Mendoza know, by Blanche de Vargas, that she would be taking the air in the gardens at a certain time. They could meet as if by chance. And he was there, the good, faithful man.

As Katherine talked to him, she made a point of looking over her shoulder repeatedly to check that no one was shadowing them.

'It has not been easy to gain access to your Highness,' Mendoza said.

'I am watched,' she told him. 'We are not supposed to be friends with Spain, and my dislike of this French alliance counts against me. But I would never plot against my husband.'

'My master would never expect it,' Mendoza said quickly. 'None-theless, he has been grieved to hear that your Highness is so isolated. Madam, one of the chief reasons I have come into England is to be your friend, and to facilitate your communications with His Imperial Majesty.'

There was no doubting the sincerity in his face and his tone.

'You cannot imagine how much that means to me, Don Diego,' she said, knowing that her eyes were bright with unshed tears.

'It means a lot to me also, Highness,' Mendoza said warmly.

After she had contrived two such meetings, she was in no doubt that the new ambassador was loyal and gallant, a man of astute judgement and deep integrity. He was candid too, but kind, and very wise.

On the second occasion they met she asked if he had any news of her sister Juana. It was twenty years since she had heard from her, and Juana had spent eighteen of them shut up in the convent of Santa Clara at Tordesillas. Mendoza's face darkened.

'There is little news,' he said, clearly choosing his words carefully.

'I understand that she is of quite a different temperament from your Majesty.'

That was true, Katherine knew, for she herself had never been given to tantrums or bouts of melancholy, and she was sure that her love for Henry, deep though it was, was not obsessive, as Juana's had been for Philip. But poor Juana. She thought of her often, wondering what her life was like, immured in that convent.

'You are not telling me everything,' she said.

'I do not want to cause you any grief, madam, but the Emperor has confided to me that she fears the nuns are plotting to murder her. There is nothing in it of course, but since they attend to her daily care and she will not have them near her, it is difficult to get her to eat, wash or change her clothes. It is a great burden on His Majesty. No appeal to reason can move her.'

'I will double my prayers for her,' Katherine vowed. 'I cannot bear to think of her like that. I remember her when she was young and very beautiful.'

'Your Majesty is unhappy,' Mendoza said suddenly, during their third meeting. She had invited him – almost at the last minute, to evade Wolsey's spies – to join her in her barge for a visit to Syon Abbey, where she loved to immerse herself in the holiness of that devout community or browse through the impressive library.

It was a statement, not a question. Katherine was not sure how to answer, lest she appear to be criticising Henry, for whatever she said would be reported back to the Emperor.

'There are sorrows in my life,' she said at length, looking at the water rippling alongside the boat. 'I miss my daughter the Princess more than I can say, but that is the lot of queens.'

'In my opinion, Highness, the principal cause of your troubles is that you identify yourself entirely with the Emperor's interests.'

She was taken aback at that. 'And you, his ambassador, think I am wrong to do so? How can I be a Spaniard and a lover of the French?'

'Highness, I too am a Spaniard. You do not have to explain to me.

But it is no secret that you hate this new alliance with France. My advice would be to pretend otherwise.'

'I am no dissembler,' Katherine declared, wondering as she said it if that was entirely true. Her whole life seemed to be spent dissembling with Henry, so as not to upset the fragile accord between them, and to preserve the vestiges of the happiness they had once shared. 'I find it hard to conceal my feelings on this matter,' she admitted. 'This alliance can bring no good to any of us.'

'It would be so much better if you could make a show of going along with it,' Mendoza urged. 'Wolsey sees your antipathy and fears that you still have influence with the King. He keeps you isolated because of it. That is why he tries to prevent my seeing you. He has no intention of allowing us to discuss state affairs in private, for he thinks we will intrigue against the French alliance. But if your Highness could appear to have been won round to it – then things might go easier with you.'

His argument made sense, distasteful as it was. 'I will try my best,' Katherine promised. And thus it was that, when Henry welcomed a French embassy headed by Gabriel de Grammont, Bishop of Tarbes, who had come to discuss Mary's betrothal, Katherine stood beside him, smiling and gracious, and remained smiling and gracious through the feasting and tournaments that had been laid on to impress the envoys. But she hated herself for it.

The King, the Cardinal and the envoys then sat down to talk terms. Three days later Mendoza came upon Katherine as she and her ladies were in the tiltyard admiring the new banqueting house that had been built there for the visit of the French embassy. It had been designed by Master Holbein, a talented painter from Germany who had been recommended to Henry by Thomas More. The artist had created an astounding interior, with a breathtakingly beautiful ceiling portraying the heavens in all their astrological splendour, and tapestries depicting the history of King David. And everywhere there were Tudor roses and Katherine's own pomegranate, that lying symbol of fertility, which seemed to mock her at every turn.

She steered Mendoza into the tiltyard gallery, saying as she hastened him along that she wanted to show him the new disguising house at the other end. For a short time they were out of earshot of her ladies, but she still had the uneasy feeling that they were being watched.

'I cannot stay long,' she warned him, looking over her shoulder. 'What is it? I can tell by your face, my good friend, that something is amiss.'

'Highness, it seems that the negotiations have reached a stalemate. The Cardinal seems much preoccupied, and the King is in an angry mood, but no one will tell me anything. Whatever it is, they are keeping it very close. Do *you* know what is going on?'

'I know nothing,' Katherine told him, hope springing that the talks had broken down entirely. 'They do not tell me anything. I can only pray that the Emperor will instruct you how to prevent the King from entering into this unfavourable alliance. I would do anything in my power to preserve the old friendship between Spain and England. Alas, though my desire to do so is strong, my means for carrying it into effect are small.'

'The Emperor has as yet sent no instructions, Highness,' Mendoza said. Her heart sank.

'Ah, your Excellency!' said a voice. A dark shadow was cast on the floor. Wolsey stood in the doorway of the disguising house.

Katherine went cold with fear. What had he overheard? Was it enough to convince him that she was actively working against the French alliance? And if so, what would he do?

But he betrayed no hint that he had heard anything untoward; he was his usual urbane self. He bowed to her, then turned to Mendoza.

'Has your Excellency seen Master Holbein's wonderful ceiling?' he asked.

Mary arrived at court after being summoned from Ludlow, to Katherine's great joy.

Then Henry told her that Mary was to remain in her care until the time came for her to go to France.

'You yourself can supervise her studies,' he said. Katherine, speechless with gratitude, had kissed him, hugging him tightly, and been touched when he hugged her back. 'I thought you would be pleased,' he said. It was almost as if he were trying to make amends for the French marriage.

It was wonderful to be once again in charge of Mary's daily life, to sit with her and watch her at her lessons and see the childish mind developing, and to read their favourite books together. But it soon became clear that her daughter needed stretching.

She consulted Thomas More again.

'Mary is older now and her horizons need to be broadened,' she told him. 'May I ask for your help if I need it?'

'Of course, madam, although in my humble opinion she could have no finer tutor than yourself.'

'You flatter me, Sir Thomas! May I ask what that book is you have with you?'

'It's Erasmus's new book, *The Institution of Christian Marriage* – I brought your Grace a copy. I can warmly recommend it.'

'How very kind,' Katherine said, taking the book and glancing through its pages. 'Anything by Erasmus appeals to me.' One passage caught her eye. 'I like the fact that he writes of the holiness of married life. I was brought up to believe that celibacy was the most desirable state, but we are not all cut out to embrace it.' She thought of the passion she had shared with Henry – now shared no longer, but glorious in its day, and sorely missed.

'Your Grace speaks truth,' More said, with feeling. 'It is a dilemma I faced myself. When I was young I felt drawn to the priesthood, but I also craved the love that can be found in marriage. It was a hard decision, but I was forced to agree with St Paul that it is better to marry than to burn, so I left my cloister and took me a wife. I have never regretted it, so I applaud what Erasmus says.'

'This book is of supreme importance,' Katherine said. 'I hope it will be widely read.'

'It's by Erasmus, madam – so you may be assured it will be!'

The French envoys craved an audience with Katherine. They wanted to see the Princess. Katherine was unhappy about the request, having hoped they would have departed for home by now. But it was clear from what the Bishop of Tarbes said that the negotiations were proceeding as planned.

Katherine watched as Mary received the French envoys, curtseying gracefully. She looked so delicate and small that it seemed impossible that she would be ready for marriage in three years, when she was fourteen, as Henry was insisting; and by the looks on the envoys' faces, they were thinking the same thing.

'She is a delightful child,' the Bishop said to Katherine. 'We rejoice to think of the peace this marriage will cement so firmly between King Henry and our master.'

How could any Frenchman think that she, a Spaniard, would rejoice?

'You talk to me of this peace,' she said, unable to help herself. 'It is no doubt desirable. But you say nothing of the general peace that ought to prevail all over Europe.'

There was the briefest of pauses before the Bishop smiled. 'Madam, it is King Francis's sincere hope that this alliance will pave the way for that.'

Empty words, she thought. Francis hated Charles for holding him prisoner; he would never forgive him. Would that he were back in his prison now!

She looked on, feeling physically sick, as Henry solemnly signed the new treaty – to be called the Treaty of Eternal Peace – then stood up and grinned. It was all concluded: Mary was to be married to King Francis or his second son, the Duc d'Orléans. He had set his seal to it. He had even agreed to the choice of bridegrooms.

Katherine put on a brave face as she watched Mary and her ladies dancing in the pageant that followed. There had been few in recent years, for Henry now preferred masques, although Katherine feared that the real reason was that the funds in his treasury were depleted after years of lavish spending. She missed the pageants, equating them with the early, happy years of her marriage, yet could obtain no pleasure from this one, taking place as it did in circumstances that were hateful to her.

In Holbein's exquisite banqueting house she sat enthroned beside Henry, a bejewelled icon of a queen, a puppet playing the role expected of her. Only when the great pageant car bearing its artificial mountain was borne in, and she saw Mary, did her face light up, for tonight her precious child was enchanting in a Roman-style gown of cloth-of-gold taffeta and crimson tinsel, her long, flame-red hair held in place by a caul of gold and a crimson velvet bonnet. So many precious stones sparkled at her neck and on her fingers that the splendour and radiance of them dazzled the sight.

Mary behaved with impressive gravity when, having changed her headdress for a jewelled garland, she played hostess with her parents at a banquet given for the envoys in the Queen's chamber.

'She looks like an angel!' Henry observed to the Frenchmen. 'She is so fair, would you not agree, my Lord Bishop?' So saying, he pulled off the garland and the caul and let fall her tresses.

'Very beautiful, sire,' the Bishop of Tarbes declared.

'As beautiful as ever seen on human head,' agreed his colleague.

Katherine agreed wholeheartedly. But oh, she wished, how she wished, that such beauty would not be wasted on a Frenchman – especially that lecher Francis!

'With this new alliance the power of the Emperor will be curbed,' the Cardinal observed.

'My master can never forgive him for reneging on the terms of his release,' the Bishop said, 'and he realises the necessity for safeguarding the Pope from the Emperor's territorial ambitions in Italy.'

Henry leaned forward. '*I* can never forgive Charles for jilting my daughter! But now she has a more glorious future.'

Katherine suppressed the shudder that his words evoked. Just then she caught Wolsey watching her, a calculating gleam in his eye. Was it triumph that she read there? He must be pleased that he had sidelined her yet again. But then she saw Henry looking almost pensively at Mary, and remembered that every marriage alliance he had made for the child in the past had come to grief. At heart, he could no more relish the thought of Mary marrying into France than she herself did, still less the prospect of England coming under French rule. What was Wolsey thinking of, to inveigle his master into this travesty of a peace? The man was a traitor!

Part Three

The True Queen

Chapter 22

1527

It was her usher Bastien Hennyocke who brought Katherine a sealed letter from the ambassador Mendoza.

'Highness, he slipped it into my hand as I was passing in a gallery, and whispered that I must keep it secret.'

She slid the letter into her sleeve and retired to her bedchamber to read it. Outside the open window the sun was brilliant in an azure sky, the gardens at Greenwich drowsed in the sunshine and birds were singing joyously, but the beauty of the day seemed to mock her as she read, unable to believe what Mendoza had written. 'The Cardinal, to crown his iniquities, is working to separate your Grace and the King.'

Wolsey, he went on, had convened a secret court. Archbishop Warham was presiding, assisted by the Cardinal and a host of bishops and canon lawyers. The King had been summoned, and asked to account for having knowingly taken to wife his brother's widow. He had admitted the charge, confessed that he had had doubts of conscience, and asked for a decision to be given on his case.

Elaborate precautions had been taken to keep these proceedings a secret, especially from the Queen, but Mendoza's informants, and his tenacity, had bested Wolsey. The ambassador requested an urgent audience. He feared, he wrote, that false testimony would be given to the secret court and in time even to the Pope, and desired her to be on her guard.

She sat on her bed, shaking, shattered beyond belief and quivering in apprehension. She had known Wolsey for her enemy, but she had never dreamed that he would go this far. She had no doubt whatsoever that all this was his doing, for Henry had long ago accepted that reservations about the validity of their marriage were groundless. At some point, of course, Henry must have colluded in these proceedings, but he had ever been in thrall to Wolsey, and the Cardinal was clever and manipulative. Yet it hurt her viscerally to know that he had not shared his concerns with her, the other person most closely involved. Of course, Wolsey would have advised against it. Probably he had said that there was no point in worrying her, since it might turn out that there was no case to answer. She could hear him saying it in his unctuous viper's voice.

She sent Bastien to find Mendoza and tell him that she was so afraid that she dared not speak with him, for Wolsey's spies were watching her.

But she needed to do something. She had every right to be represented at this court. Someone must speak for her!

She sent for the tutor, Vives. He was a doctor of law and he had been a friend to her. She saw his face register shock as she told him what was going on.

'I need an advocate,' she told him. 'Will you represent me at this court?'

Shock turned visibly to dismay.

'Madam, I fear I cannot. I dare not offend the King. I am sorry.'

It felt like a bitter betrayal, and it was all the more upsetting because she saw that it was an indication of what others might say if she asked for their help. After all, who would dare to offend the King, his pleasure once being known? It would take a brave man – or woman.

She felt so alone, so isolated. Hurt, she withdrew the pension she had been paying Vives, then worried that she had been vindictive. Yet his refusal had been crushing. Thank God for Mendoza. He was a true friend.

She contrived another meeting in the garden, one evening at dusk, instructing Gertrude Blount to keep watch. She walked a little way and found the ambassador waiting for her in a small banqueting house at the end of a lime walk. As she told him about Vives, it was all she could do to keep her composure.

Mendoza regarded her with compassion. 'Do not distress yourself, madam. I have informed the Emperor of this court. I cannot think that he will permit such iniquitous proceedings to continue.'

'After God, all my hope rests in His Imperial Majesty,' Katherine said, trying not to cry. But it was comforting to know that she had the might of Spain and the Empire behind her.

'It ought also to rest in the people of England, for your Highness is much beloved in this kingdom. There is no doubt that, if the King has your marriage annulled, some great popular protest must ensue. Be assured that there will be many more voices raised in your favour than against you.'

'I would not wish to be the cause of any disturbance in this realm. I came here to bring peace and prosperity, not dissension.'

'It may never come to that, Highness. I will urge my master to put pressure on the Pope to tie Wolsey's hands and, if necessary, have the case referred to Rome for a decision.'

Katherine shook her head. 'There is no need for a decision. The Pope granted us a dispensation to wed, and I cannot understand why that is not seen as sufficient. I assure you, my good friend, that this is all Wolsey's doing, to drive a wedge between England and Spain.'

'Wolsey is universally hated. Rest assured, madam, he will not get away with this.'

As June blazed on in all its golden splendour, Bastien brought another note from Mendoza. The secret court at Westminster had decided that it was not competent to judge the King's case. Henry had gone to the Privy Council for guidance, and his councillors had agreed that there was good cause for scruple about his marriage, and advised him to approach the Pope for a ruling.

'But they are wrong!' Katherine cried. She had told Margaret, Maria and Maud everything, and they were all doing their best to comfort her. 'There is no good cause for scruple, and no *need* for a ruling. Pope Julius gave us a dispensation. Is Wolsey now challenging the infallibility of the Pope, the Vicar of Christ on earth?'

The three women shook their heads sadly as Katherine paced up and down in great agitation.

She had not seen Henry since Mendoza had broken the news about the secret court. He had not visited her chamber, or been in chapel for Mass. She was certain that he was avoiding her – and so he should be, for he had much to explain!

'If the case goes to Rome it will be months before we hear anything,' she said, biting her lip. 'I do not think I can bear it, especially when it is all so unnecessary!'

She broke off as a page announced the arrival of Lord Mountjoy. He entered the room looking unusually distracted, and his air of agitation caught everyone's attention.

'Your Grace, there is terrible news! Rome has been sacked by mercenary troops of the Emperor.'

Katherine's mind reeled, as she and her ladies instinctively crossed themselves.

'The reports are shocking,' Lord Mountjoy went on, 'and I forbear to give you some of the details, but over four days there was such violence and such murder as has never been seen.'

'God have mercy!' Katherine whispered. 'Tell me what happened. I must know.'

Mountjoy swallowed. He was a man of great courtesy and sensibility, and was clearly shocked by what he had heard. And it was against every precept of his well-known chivalry to be discussing such dreadful things with ladies, so Katherine knew they would all receive a heavily censored account. 'Those mercenaries were worse than wild beasts,' Mountjoy said. 'The atrocities they committed were dreadful, and they rampaged unchecked, for neither the Emperor nor any other commander was there to stop it. The soldiers slew at pleasure, murdering women and children. They pillaged houses and churches, even St Peter's itself. There were altars desecrated, prisoners taken, monks and nuns forced to – I will not say it, for shame. To think that such things could happen in one of the world's most civilised cities!'

It did not bear thinking about.

'This is terrible,' Katherine murmured, crossing herself again. 'I have never heard of such evil. All Christendom must deplore and condemn such an outrage. What of his Holiness?'

'The last we heard, he had taken refuge in the Castel Sant'Angelo, north-west of Rome, but he is virtually the prisoner of the Emperor.'

This was appalling. 'But the Emperor was not there! Surely none of this was done by his will or with his consent?'

'No, madam, it was not, and by all reports he is as outraged as anyone else by it, but he has seized his advantage. It suits him well to have the Pope in his power.'

And it will suit me well too, Katherine realised, for with the Pope a prisoner of the Emperor, her nephew, a favourable decision on Henry's case was unlikely to be forthcoming. Immediately she reproached herself for thinking of her own interests when so many had suffered horribly.

'I will order Masses for the souls of the dead,' she said. 'I will pray for them.'

'People are talking openly about the King's case.' Maud was indignant. 'They are calling it the King's Secret Matter, but it's no secret any more!'

'It's true, Highness,' Maria said, her eyes flashing with outrage. 'It's as notorious as if it had been proclaimed by the town crier.'

Katherine's ladies had returned from the gardens in a furious mood. They had cut short their walk after a pair of the court's renowned gossips had stopped them, unable to resist passing on the latest rumours from the City.

'They say that the King has commanded the Lord Mayor to ensure that the people cease gossiping, on pain of his high displeasure,' added Margaret.

'They are even speculating that His Grace might marry the French King's sister,' Maud said. 'God forbid!'

Katherine was horrified. The whole court, and the whole of London, it seemed, knew of Henry's Secret Matter, and yet she, the person most vitally concerned, had not been informed of it. Nor had she seen Henry. That hurt went deep. He could at least have had the courtesy to talk to her about it. There was so much that she was burning to say to him. Maria, furious with him on her behalf, had urged her to find him and give him a piece of her mind; Maud and Margaret, always sensible and cautious, had advised her to ask him if there was anything he needed to discuss with her. Yet she did not want to seek him out, because she feared that what he might say would confirm her worst fears.

But as if thinking about Henry could conjure up his presence, here was Lord Mountjoy announcing the arrival of the King.

'Leave us!' Katherine commanded her ladies, and rose to greet Henry with a graceful curtsey.

She had never seen him looking as nervous as he did that afternoon. He stood before her, a magnificent personage with great presence, but seeming diminished by an unaccustomed diffidence. She gazed at this man who was her husband – whatever anyone said. Never, now that she was afraid she might lose him, had he been so attractive to her: at thirty-six, he was in the vigour of his age. And he was hers – and no man would put them asunder, she vowed it to herself in that moment.

'Be seated, Kate,' Henry said, and took the chair on the other side of the empty fireplace, the hearth of which was now filled with flowers.

He smiled uncertainly at her. 'I trust you are well?' he said.

'I am in health, thank you, and all the better for seeing you.' She tried not to sound reproachful.

'And Mary?'

'She is well too, and Lady Salisbury tells me she is making good progress with her studies.' It occurred to her that Mary, living at court as she did, might have heard the gossip about her parents' marriage. Please God she had not.

'Kate,' Henry said, fiddling with a loose thread on his doublet, 'I need to talk to you. Of late I have been troubled – *much* troubled – in my conscience about the validity of our marriage, and . . . and I am sorry, but I have reluctantly come to the resolution that we must separate.'

It was as if he had dealt her a mortal blow. This could not be Henry, her Henry, saying these things to her.

'Who has put these words in your mouth?' she asked, her voice cracking.

Henry looked disconcerted. 'During the negotiations the Bishop of Tarbes expressed reservations about Mary's legitimacy, and it kept preying on my mind. What he said made me wonder if God had denied you and me sons because our marriage is unlawful. My conscience is troubled, Kate. I am in great fear of God's indignation.'

'Are you sure it is not the Cardinal who has encouraged you to have these doubts?' Katherine asked. 'He wants to get rid of me. Now that you have agreed this French alliance, it is no longer an advantage for you to have a Spanish queen.'

'No, Kate, that is not so.' Henry looked nonplussed, which almost confirmed her suspicions. 'It was Wolsey who assured the Bishop that Mary was legitimate,' he said. 'He does know of my doubts, of course, but from the first he has been against my acting upon them, although he is as anxious as I am to have them allayed. It was he who advised me to ask the Pope to resolve them.'

'There is no need!' Katherine insisted. 'We have a dispensation.'

'But the Bible warns that God will inflict a severe penalty on a man who marries his brother's widow. You know what Leviticus says, Kate! "They shall be childless." Believe me, I have studied the matter, and I am convinced that we have broken a divine law. Surely a marriage that gives me such fear and torment of conscience cannot be lawful!'

'Henry, it *is* lawful! The Pope said so. How can he be wrong?'

Henry got up and began pacing the floor. 'The evidence of God's displeasure is there for all to see. All our sons died soon after they were born. That is our punishment.'

He turned to her and spread his hands open in supplication. 'For a long time now I have felt that I am living under the awful displeasure of the Almighty. Now I know why – and I dread His heavy wrath if I persist in this marriage. That is why, out of regard for the quiet of my soul, and the need to ensure the succession, I have to have these doubts resolved.' Tears glinted in his eyes.

Katherine closed her eyes for a moment, gathering her thoughts. She could not deny Henry's sincerity, yet she needed desperately to convince him that his fears were misplaced. If she could do that, this whole sorry business could be forgotten.

'Have you talked to your confessor?' she asked.

'Yes. He was the first person I spoke to. He was unsure as to how to counsel me, and urged me to seek Archbishop Warham's advice.

Warham held an inquiry. Kate, I'm sorry if this brings you grief, but it has to be resolved.'

'Henry, on what grounds are you doubting our marriage? I came to you a virgin. Arthur and I never consummated our marriage.'

'But you bedded together at sundry times, you lived at liberty in one house . . .'

She was stunned. 'Are you saying I lied to you, that I am lying still?'

'No, I mean, Kate – I do not know! And maybe you don't either. You were an innocent, maybe it happened and you didn't realise it.'

'Oh, Henry! You think I wouldn't know? It was painful the first time with you.'

Henry shook his head impatiently. 'That's all beside the point. Leviticus applies whether your marriage to Arthur had been consummated or not.'

'I don't see how!' Katherine was becoming exasperated now. She was still certain that Wolsey was behind this. 'The barrier to the second marriage only exists if the first has been consummated, and in my case it wasn't. I can't be clearer than that. What else do I have to say to reassure you? The Pope looked at all the evidence over twenty years ago. He would not have issued a dispensation if there had been any doubt. I'll say it again, Henry, there is *no cause* for these scruples of conscience. You have not offended God – and we have not lived in sin these eighteen years!'

Henry glared at her. 'The Pope had no right to issue that dispensation.'

'No right?' She was aghast. 'He is invested with the authority of Christ. Are you challenging that? Are you saying he had no power to dispense at all in our case?'

'That is what I am saying.' Henry sounded defiant, mulish. His piercing blue eyes glittered.

'It is heresy, no less. Do you not see that? Oh, Henry! Do not do this thing, I beg of you.' Spontaneously she fell to her knees before him, raising her hands as if in prayer.

'Kate!' He grasped her wrists. 'Do not do this to me. I am moved only by a scrupulous conscience, and because I despair of having any sons.'

She felt the tears spill over. Henry stared at her, grief in his eyes, and she thought for a moment that he might take her in his arms, but he let her hands drop and she knelt there for a moment, unable to move, then got up and returned to her chair, feeling utterly defeated. Was there nothing she could say that could touch him?

'And if the Pope rules that our marriage is unlawful?' she asked. 'Which he will not, I assure you.'

'Kate, you will want for nothing, not for riches, honour or love. You can have any houses you want.'

'And our daughter? Have you thought of what this will do to her? She is your heir.'

'And as our marriage was made in good faith, she will remain so, until I have sons.'

So he had already thought of taking another wife! And she, his faithful but barren spouse of eighteen years, would be discarded, just like that.

'You want to remarry. Why don't you just say so?'

Anger coloured Henry's face. 'It's not like that. I've told you, I need to set my conscience at rest. But if the only way of doing that is by a divorce, then yes, I must take another wife to ensure the succession and the quiet estate of my realm. It is my duty, no less.' He stood up and walked to the door, then turned to face her. 'All will be done for the best, I assure you, Kate,' he said. 'I ask you not to speak of this matter to anyone, for I fear that the Spaniards in your household might make some demonstration, and I don't want to provoke the Emperor.'

Katherine could not answer him. She could not believe that this was Henry, talking about separating from her and replacing her as queen. As he opened the door to leave, she found she could no longer control her emotions and broke down completely, emitting great, tearing sobs that sounded like an animal in pain. All those years together, all the love that had been between them, the children they had conceived and lost, the joys, the sorrows, the things they had shared . . . They had been one flesh, and now Henry wanted to break them asunder and end it all. It was more than she could bear.

'Oh, God! Oh, Holy Mother!' she keened. 'Oh, please help me!' She sank down on knees that had turned to water, and buried her face in her hands. 'What did I do to deserve this?'

'Kate, don't,' Henry pleaded. 'Please, stop crying. Stop it!'

But the dam had been breached and Katherine could not cease. She knelt there, rocking in misery. There was a long silence, then she heard the latch click. Henry had gone, and the world came to an end.

Her ladies crowded around her, soothing her, bringing dry kerchiefs and wine to calm her. Maud was firm with her.

'Your Grace, whatever the matter is, you must have a care to yourself. All this weeping is not good for you.'

'Here, madam, drink this,' said Maria, handing her a goblet of malmsey.

Katherine gulped and tried to catch her breath. She dabbed at her eyes. The worst of the storm had passed.

'His conscience is troubling him,' she whispered. 'He himself wants to end our marriage. He fears that it is an offence to God.'

Surely not, the ladies said. She must have misunderstood, or the King had been misled by those who should know better. All would be well. If it came to it, the Pope would make all well.

'No,' she murmured. 'He knows what he is doing. He spoke of taking another wife.'

'It is unforgivable of him to do this to you!' Maria said.

'Best not to criticise His Grace,' Maud murmured.

Looking on, her face suffused with sympathy and rage, was Gertrude Blount, Lady Exeter. 'I'll wager I know who is behind this,' she said, shaking her head with its glossy black curls.

Elizabeth Stafford, Duchess of Norfolk, nodded savagely. 'That jumped-up butcher's son!'

Katherine rested her head back on the chair. 'He hates me. I represent Spain, and he hates Spain too. But I dare not openly oppose him. I am alone and without counsel, far from my friends in Spain, and his spies watch my every move. But I have to think of Mary!'

She drew herself up in her chair, more composed now. She remembered that she was the daughter of Isabella the Catholic. She must be firm in her convictions, and have the courage to stand by what she believed to be right.

'My marriage to the King is good and valid,' she declared, her voice strong again, so that it sounded like a battle cry. 'Pope Julius permitted it, and that is sufficient for me. I am the King's true wife, and Mary is his rightful heir. It is Wolsey who has led my lord astray and planted these doubts in his mind. It is my duty to persuade my husband that he is in error, and I will do it, so help me God!'

Her ladies applauded her resolve. She would win through, they assured her. They brought her more wine and the sweet cakes she loved, and books for her diversion. They offered to do anything that might bring her comfort. She looked up into their kind, concerned faces and thanked them, touched by their loyalty and their love for her. And then she saw Anne Boleyn standing to one side, watching her, her face slightly flushed, no doubt from embarrassment at seeing the Queen's loss of control.

'I am all right now, Mistress Anne,' she said, taking the young woman's hand and squeezing it.

Life went on as before, except that nothing would ever again be as it was. No more was said about a separation or Katherine moving to another house, and she remained at court. She spent time each day with Mary, reading, helping with her studies, and sometimes playing and singing with her. She had made a decision never to reproach Henry. She resolved instead to be cheerful and supportive in his company, for no man wanted a wife who was miserable and complaining. That was not the way to win him back!

It seemed that Henry was also trying to make things right between them. He visited her chamber regularly, chatted and played for her, and sometimes summoned Mary so that he could test and praise her progress in her lessons. Things between him and Katherine had been awkward at first, but he was clearly making an effort to return to normal. He was affectionate and respectful, and when they appeared together in public he showed her every courtesy. She began to hope that he had changed his mind about pursuing an annulment.

But then there came an evening when he told her that he hoped before long to hear from the Pope.

'I know what you will hear,' she said, the illusion of security shattering about her.

'Why do you persist in ignoring my scruples?' he snapped.

'I am your lawful wife and your Queen! I stand to lose everything that is dear to me, and what for? A needless doubt planted in your head by my enemies.'

'I've told you, Kate – no one planted it. And you are allowing earthly pride in your queenly rank to stand in the way of my conscience.'

'It is not just pride that prevents me from acknowledging myself to have been your harlot these past eighteen years!' Katherine cried, fearing that she would break down and lose control again. 'It is the love I bear you.'

Henry would not meet her eye. He looked beyond her, staring at the wall.

'You know the right of it is on my side,' she said quietly, 'and on that I will stand firm to my dying day.'

'You would defy me?' he growled, his voice menacing.

'I am, as always, ready to obey you in all things save that which touches my conscience. In all this talk of your conscience, Henry, you have forgotten mine, but it is entirely at peace in regard to our marriage.'

Henry got up. 'That may be so, madam,' he blustered, 'but I must be satisfied nevertheless.' And he stumped out of her chamber.

Katherine wondered if she should ask the Emperor to intercede with the Pope on her behalf. After hours on her knees begging for guidance, she decided that she would seek Charles's help. If anyone could aid her, he could, and the Pope would be looking to please him.

It would not be easy, she knew. Wolsey's spies were hovering, more obtrusive than ever now. How would she outwit the all-powerful Cardinal?

Suddenly a plan occurred to her. She summoned one of her most loyal servants, Francisco Felipez – and she explained, in a low voice, what she needed him to do.

Then she went to the King.

'Sir, my servant Francisco wishes to visit his widowed mother in Spain,' she told him, meek as milk. 'I do not want him to go at this time, for it is inconvenient, but he says his mother is ill, so I cannot say him nay, and so I would be grateful if you would grant him a safe conduct.'

Henry looked at her with narrowed eyes. 'Very well,' he said at length.

He signed the safe conduct that very afternoon. Katherine gave it to Francisco, and then slipped him the letter she had written to the Emperor, which he concealed in his bosom.

'God speed you!' she said fervently.

'Don't try to deceive me again!' Henry roared, as Katherine's ladies scattered. 'This was found on your servant in Calais, where my officers caught up with him and arrested him.' He waved her letter at her. 'He is now back in England, and will not be going to Spain again in the foreseeable future.'

Katherine stood mute. There was nothing she could say in her defence. At least Henry now knew that she was ready to fight to save their marriage. And surely Charles would have heard of her plight from Mendoza?

'Why did you send men after him?' she asked.

'To find out what he was really about. I'm not the fool you take me for, Kate.'

'I have a right to be heard in Rome!' she protested.

'You have no right to incite the Emperor to war, which is how this letter may be construed.'

'That was never my intention!' she cried. 'How could you believe it of me?'

Henry glared at her. 'By the evidence of my own eyes!'

'You believe only what you want to believe,' she said, stung, 'but I assure you, I am your true, loyal wife, and I would never do anything to your hurt.'

'You are no such thing!' Henry retorted, and walked out.

She became aware that she was being watched even more closely. It was the King's own servants who were now infiltrating her household, as well as Wolsey's. She realised that she would have to tread very carefully, especially if Henry believed her capable of inciting war. She must take care not to give him the slightest ground for suspicion.

She was desperate to see Mendoza, but of course he dared not visit her. When they came face to face at a reception for some Italian envoys and he bowed to her, his eyes were flitting about warily. The room was full of people, milling about and chattering. Henry was some way off, surrounded by avid courtiers. His laugh boomed out several times.

'Madam, a word,' Mendoza murmured. 'My master has expressed his indignation at the King's proceedings, which he finds strange. He does not believe it possible that His Grace would go thus far. He has instructed me, for the honour of God, to put an end to this scandalous affair. And I am to give you this. Please move away now.' As Katherine passed, he pressed a folded paper into her hand. No one seemed to notice.

Later, alone in her privy chamber, she read what her nephew Charles had written: 'You may well imagine the pain this intelligence caused me, and how much I felt for you. I have immediately set about taking the necessary steps for a remedy, and you may be certain that nothing shall be omitted on my part to help you.'

At last, she thought, at last – there is someone who is ready and able to help me. I have found my champion.

Chapter 23

It was no longer the King's Secret Matter but the King's Great Matter. That was what people – appalled, approving or simply inquisitive – were calling it. And it did seem that most were appalled. Whenever Katherine appeared in public, crowds gathered, crying, 'Victory over your enemies!' The common people could not believe that their King would be so wicked as to put away their beloved Queen, his true wife. The women, in particular, spoke out loudly for Katherine, making clear their conviction that Henry sought to be rid of her purely for his own pleasure.

'Why,' one ruddy-cheeked fish-seller cried out, 'if the King can put away his old wife, then every lusty fellow'll want to do the same, and then where would we women be?'

Katherine had to smile at that. She felt cheered by the warmth and love of the people. If the matter were to be decided by women, there was no doubt that Henry would lose the battle. But alas, the voices of women, even queens, counted for very little.

At court it was a different story. It was understandable that most people were for the King.

The French Queen came looking for Katherine, and found her in the royal library, trying to make sense of a thick volume of canon law. Without a word she folded her in her arms, plainly emotional.

'I had to come,' she said. 'There is talk everywhere of what is going on here. People speak of little else. I am horrified at what my brother is doing, and I have told him so.' She looked as fearsome as Henry did when his anger was aroused, and Katherine could imagine how the scene between brother and sister had played out.

'Don't provoke him too far,' Katherine pleaded, closing the book. 'He may banish you from court, and I could not stand to lose you, my dear friend.'

'I've said my piece,' the French Queen told her. 'I told him he'd make himself look the biggest fool in Christendom, creating all this rumpus, when the Pope will surely find for you. He didn't like that, though he hasn't sent me away yet!'

'Say no more,' Katherine warned, looking around nervously at the stacks of shelves as if she expected Wolsey's spies to be somehow concealed there. 'Henry has grown very suspicious of late. He accused me of inciting war with Spain, when I had only asked the Emperor to plead my case at Rome.'

'He told me that,' the French Queen said. 'He thinks you are capable of it too. It won't do any harm to let him fret about it. Serve him right!'

'I dare not. He could accuse me of treason.'

'My dear Kate, if – as he maintains – you are not his wife, then you are not his subject, and cannot be guilty of treason. He can't have it both ways!'

Wolsey was on the way to France. Henry said he had gone there to make arrangements for the marriage of the Princess Mary with the Duc d'Orléans, but Katherine suspected that there was more to it than that. The Cardinal might well be trying to enlist King Francis's support for the King's cause.

Just as she was pondering on this, John Fisher, the venerable Bishop of Rochester, came to see her. She knew and liked him for his wisdom and holiness, but today his craggy face was stern. She was dismayed to see him looking so severe.

'Madam, a word of advice from an old man.'

'Pray be seated, my lord,' she said, indicating the chair at the opposite side of the fireplace. 'Some wine please, Maria.'

Maria sped away.

'I saw the Cardinal in Rochester,' Fisher told her, creaking painfully into his seat. 'We discussed the Great Matter at length, and he complained that you were being unduly suspicious of the King's intentions and casting more doubts than the case merited. He told me that you have advertised the matter by your manner and behaviour, and by sending secret messages. Madam, if this is true, then you yourself are to blame for all the notoriety that this case has generated, and for the King's righteous displeasure. I assured the Cardinal that I would expostulate with you for your wilfulness and disobedience.'

Katherine frowned, smarting with the unjustness of these accusations. Now she knew for certain that it was Wolsey who was behind all this trouble. His malice was plain.

'My Lord Bishop, none of this is true,' she said, trying to mask her anger. 'I have done nothing to advertise this Great Matter – rather, I shrink from its being aired in public, and having the whole world gossip over my private affairs. The King prevented me from sending a message asking the Emperor to aid me in Rome, for I have no counsel there. His Majesty accused me of inciting war, which was so far from my intentions as to be ridiculous. It is that which is at the root of these complaints. I would do nothing to harm my husband. I love and honour him.'

'I rejoice to hear you say it, madam,' Fisher said, as if he still felt that she had done something wrong. 'I—' He broke off as Maria returned with two goblets, then took three sips from his and set it down. His expression softened. 'Be wary. Put not a foot out of step. And I will be watchful too.' He waited until Maria had left, then continued in a low voice. 'In the meantime I see no reason to censure you. You know you have my support.'

Late in July Henry gave the order for the court to ride to Beaulieu, his palace in Essex. On the morning they were to leave, Katherine was delayed because she had torn the hem of her kirtle. As she stood waiting by the window, while the Otwell sisters stitched it, she saw Henry mounting his horse by the mews below, where his retinue had gathered.

'Hurry now!' she urged, knowing he would be impatient to be on his way. Then Anne Boleyn entered the room, her sallow face flushed, and asked Katherine if she might leave court to visit her family in Kent.

'This is rather sudden – and short notice,' Katherine reproved her.

'I know, madam, and I am sorry, but it is important that I go.'

'Is anything wrong?' Katherine asked, for Anne seemed agitated.

'No, madam.'

Obviously she was not to be drawn, and Katherine gave her permission to go. Then she hurried downstairs to join the King and thought no more of it.

Beaulieu, the 'beautiful place' that Henry had bought from Thomas Boleyn a few years back and renamed, was now a sumptuous palace, ranged around a main courtyard, where a sculpted fountain spouted water from the mouths of cherubs. Henry and Katherine spent a month there, keeping great state and open house, while Henry hunted and played tennis and Katherine lovingly made two gowns to send to Mary, who was with her household at Hunsdon, and growing fast, Margaret reported. With no more being said about his Great Matter, Katherine began to hope she and Henry would be fully reconciled.

At the beginning of August Anne Boleyn returned to her duties, more expensively dressed than ever.

'That girl gets above herself!' Maria muttered over her embroidery, jabbing in the needle as if she were jabbing it into Mistress Anne's flat chest.

'I have never taken to her,' Gertrude Blount said, 'although I have to admit that that French gown really becomes her.'

'She seems more French than English in many ways,' Katherine observed. 'Of course, she spent many years at the French court.'

'And learned more than French manners there, I'll be bound!' Maria retorted.

'You are lacking in charity, my friend,' Katherine admonished, remembering how Anne had been disappointed in love. 'She has always served me well and been an ornament to my court. I can find no fault in her.'

'But she's not one of us,' Maria complained. 'She always holds herself aloof, as if she thinks she's better than the rest of us. Little Lady High-and-Mighty, I call her!'

'The men flock around her,' said Gertrude Blount.

'That is all they do,' Katherine declared. 'Mistress Boleyn guards her virtue jealously. Remember how she kept Thomas Wyatt at arm's length.'

'He's married. There's no advantage to her in that.'

'Gertrude, don't be unkind. Just because a young woman is spirited and stylish, it doesn't mean she is light in behaviour. She will make a good marriage, you'll see.'

There was revelry planned for the evening, and after supper Henry and Katherine seated themselves in their chairs of estate as the court musicians began playing in the gallery. At once Henry rose and bowed to Katherine, offering her his hand. She smiled and joined him for the opening dance, their courtiers following them on to the floor of the hall.

At forty-one, Katherine felt rather old and stout to be twirling about beside slender young beauties, so after two dances she returned to her seat to watch, while Henry partnered his sister, the French Queen. But when the musicians struck up a fourth tune, to that lady's evident disgust, he walked over to where Anne Boleyn was standing and bowed, then held out his hand. She placed hers in his, and Katherine caught the flash of an emerald ring in the candlelight.

She watched Henry dancing with Anne, aware of a slight ripple of murmuring around the room. She caught people glancing her way. She saw Henry look hungrily into Anne's face as they met in the dance. And in that moment she knew.

When Henry went hunting the next morning, Anne was absent. She had not even asked leave. When he returned late in the afternoon, Katherine looked out and saw Anne, dismounting in her crimson riding habit.

'Look at that,' she said to Maud, bitter bile in her throat.

Maud's full lips set in a hard line. 'There has been talk in the court this past week or so. I did not like to tell you.'

'I wonder how long it has been going on,' Katherine said faintly, fretting about how she could compete with such youth, charm and elegance.

'Not long, I would imagine,' Maud said. 'We would have heard about it sooner otherwise.'

Katherine suddenly remembered the jousts at Greenwich, a year past last February, and the motto Henry had worn. Surely it had not been going on that long? Then she thought of Anne Boleyn's mysterious comings and goings and the increasing richness of her attire. Yet Katherine refused to believe it. It must, as Maud thought, have been a recent development.

'That there is talk now is bad enough!' Katherine exclaimed. 'What if the Princess got to hear it?' She could not bear to contemplate the effect on Mary. 'This is dreadful. Not just because he is being unfaithful, but because he has never, ever made a public display of adultery. It is as if he feels that he is free to do so, and never mind that I am humiliated and slighted by it. I am his Queen! How can he shame me so?'

But Henry could, and he did, and soon, it seemed, the world was full of rumours, fuelled by the King's open – some said blatant – courtship of Anne Boleyn.

Speculation was rampant. She was his mistress, some said; no, said others, he meant to wed her when his Great Matter was resolved. Not so, he was merely trying to get her into his bed!

Anne still attended upon the Queen daily. Never once did she scant her respect to Katherine or conduct herself as her rival. But the other ladies made it quite clear what they thought of her. Their methods were subtle: a slight withdrawing, a hushing of conversation, a disapproving glance; but nothing overt, lest she report them to the King.

Katherine heard from those women what people were saying. She wanted, nay needed, to know, however badly it hurt. She saw too, with her own eyes, how it was between her husband and her maid-of-honour. She watched from her window as they walked in the gardens, arms entwined; she saw Anne at the centre of the privileged crowd who clustered about the King, laughing and jesting and flirting. Her eyes never left Henry and Anne when they danced together, their bodies moving in harmony, their eyes and hands locked.

Henry rarely came to Katherine's apartments now. Every hour of every day, it seemed, he needed to be with Anne. Katherine knew intuitively – who better? – that he was hopelessly infatuated. Everything about him proclaimed it. He had eyes for no one but Anne, and appeared not to care who knew it. But Anne did not seem to have the same need to be with Henry. It dawned on Katherine that her rival was adept at holding herself tantalisingly aloof.

'I fear that she is at the root of His Grace's doubts about your marriage,' Maud told Katherine.

'I had wondered about that,' Katherine said, hoping that Henry was not putting them both through this whole lying affair for the sake of a pair of dark eyes.

The French Queen waxed indignant about Anne. 'I hate that woman,' she declared one evening, as Henry was dancing with his new lady-love. 'She served me in France and I took against her then. She's two-faced and too clever for her own good. Forgive me, Kate, but I'm going home to Westhorpe. I'm not staying here to watch her queening it over the court – because that's what she's doing, mark my words. She means to have your crown, and before you know it, it'll be on her head. Well, she'll never see me bowing the knee to her, the jumped-up little madam.'

Katherine felt cheered by this robust support.

'What of the Duke your husband? Where does he stand in this?'

'Charles? What do you expect, Kate? He is for the King. He has no choice. All that he is, Henry made him.'

'That cannot make for marital harmony.'

The French Queen's expression was grim. 'No, Kate, it does not, which is another reason why I am leaving court.'

'I will miss you, dear sister,' Katherine said, watching Henry pressing Anne's hand to his lips as the dance ended.

As yet Katherine had been afforded no opportunity to ask Henry what was going on between him and Anne, but there came a morning when, arriving in good time to hear Mass, she found him in the royal pew in the chapel, looking over some state papers. She sank to her knees beside him, said a prayer, then raised herself to her seat and summoned her courage.

'Henry, I must ask – I have heard much talk, and I have seen you keeping company with Anne Boleyn. Is there something I should know?'

Henry would not look at her. His eyes were fixed on the stained glass behind the altar. At length he spoke.

'I am in love with her, Kate, and I mean to marry her.'

Katherine drew in her breath. It was what she had feared most.

'So this is why your conscience is troubling you!'

'No, Kate. This is no trivial matter. I know what it looks like, that I am pursuing this divorce out of love for some lady, and not from any scruple of conscience; but that is not true, for I am moved to it *only* to discharge my conscience.'

He turned to face her then. 'Be realistic, Kate. I need a son. You cannot give me one, more's the pity.'

'But if our sons had lived, would you still be saying that our marriage was invalid?'

'If they had lived I would have had proof that God had smiled upon our union. But they did not, God rest them, and I fear greatly for the succession and the future of my kingdom. Dammit, Kate, can't you see reason? The Pope will find for me. He will understand that I need to take another wife who can bear me children. The fact that I have found her is immaterial, really.'

'And what of me?' she asked, trembling with grief and anger.

'I've told you, Kate: you can have anything you want! My case is grounded upon justice, and not from any grudge or displeasure towards you. I mind to treat you as my sister, with the greatest honour and love and kindness. Mary will still have her place in the succession, after Anne's sons.'

His sister! Arthur's widow. But Katherine was spared the necessity of answering because at that moment the chaplain arrived with the children of the Chapel Royal, and the Mass began. She wept most of the way through it. Henry must have seen, but he made no move to comfort her.

'That woman should be suppressed!' Maria hissed. She was in a bad mood these days because, against her will, the Duke of Suffolk had bought her daughter's wardship from the King and been made the child's legal guardian – and he was supporting his master.

'She's no better than a – well, I won't say it!' Maud fumed. 'How can you tolerate her here, madam? Send her home!'

'I cannot do that,' Katherine said. 'That would appear vindictive. And the King would probably recall her and command me to receive her back into my household.'

'Your Grace is a saint,' observed Gertrude Blount, exasperated. 'You show no grudge or displeasure, you just accept things in good part.'

'I try to have wisdom and patience, and I do my best to hold Mistress Anne in estimation for the King's sake. I am still playing Patient Griselda.' Katherine attempted a smile.

'Why do you do it? Other wives would be tearing her hair out.'

'Because when he discards her, as he will, I want him to think kindly of me. And I am the Queen and should show some dignity. Mark me, this lady will have her day, and then she will be gone.'

'She wants the crown of England!' Maria cried, exasperated.

'I know my husband. Once his desire is satisfied, he will soon tire of her. And I am his lawful wife, as will be proved.'

'So your Grace believes that she is his mistress?'

'I am sure of it.' It pained her to admit it, and she knew she should not be talking so disloyally of Henry to her ladies like this, but she had to talk to someone or she would go mad.

'Like mother, like daughter,' Elizabeth Stafford muttered. 'Lady Boleyn had quite a reputation in her youth.'

'And I hear the sister is a trollop,' Gertrude Blount sniffed.

Maud muttered, 'This talk is not seemly for the Queen's ears.'

With an effort Katherine changed the subject, although she would dearly have loved to have pursued it.

Henry was behaving like a man possessed. On the few occasions when they came to have words on the matter, Katherine had to contend with his absolute conviction that he was right. Talk of his passion for Anne Boleyn – and this of a man who had once been the soul of discretion – was rife. He was so amorous and affectionate towards her that it seemed his will was master of all and that discretion was banished. Katherine realised that he was so much in love that only God could abate his madness.

Anne was far more circumspect. She was playing a clever game, no doubt of it, for when Henry was fawning over her – as he did even in full view of Katherine – she appeared cool and detached. Anne was with Henry so often now that Katherine felt that she was living in a *ménage à trois* – as, effectively, she was. Sitting down to play cards with Anne and Henry, she wondered at herself for being so accepting, and at Henry, who apparently saw nothing unusual in including both his wife and his sweetheart in his pastimes.

That day Anne, elegant in black velvet studded with pearls, won the highest stake by drawing a king.

Katherine could not stop herself. She smiled. 'Mistress Anne, you have the good chance to stop at a king, but you are like the others: you will have all or none.'

Henry flushed, and Anne had the grace to bow her head. But the battle lines had now been drawn, and that marked the end of Anne's dutifulness towards her mistress. From now on her hostility was clear. She came and went as she pleased, and behaved towards Katherine with marked disrespect. She missed no opportunity of demonstrating her ascendancy with the King and over the court. She was relentless, and Katherine came to understand that the young woman she had admired and pitied and defended was as dangerous as the serpent who had brought Adam and Eve to grief in Paradise.

With Wolsey still in France, the incessant surveillance of Katherine's movements had abated to a degree, and this time Francisco Felipez succeeded in slipping unnoticed out of England. For many days Katherine remained in suspense, wondering if he had escaped the authorities' vigilance, but as time went by and she heard nothing she began to hope that he had reached Spain and told the Emperor of her plight.

Confirmation came in a letter from Charles.

You can well imagine the pain this news caused me. Were my own mother concerned, I should not experience greater sorrow. I have immediately set about taking the necessary steps for a remedy, and you may be certain that nothing shall be omitted on my part to help you in your present trials. Inform me as soon as possible of the course of this ugly affair, that I may do all that is necessary for your protection and your health.

Thank God, Katherine thought, thank God!

Gossip and speculation that Henry meant to make Anne queen provoked widespread outrage. When Katherine had occasion to go abroad in London, as she did several times over the next few months, the people applauded and cheered her loudly, and shouted their disapproval of Anne.

'We'll have no Nan Bullen!' they cried. 'Burn the whore!'

'God save Queen Katherine!' they shouted. 'Long live the good Queen!'

She prayed that there were no such demonstrations when Mary showed herself in public, and resolved to instruct Margaret Pole to keep the child indoors as much as possible. But Mary could not be confined to her apartments for ever. It made Katherine so angry that this dreadful business was overshadowing their lives to the extent that Mary could not come and go freely. It infuriated her that Henry did not feel these concerns about his daughter. No doubt he was too distracted by the charms of Mistress Anne Boleyn!

Katherine learned that Wolsey had returned when she was sitting in her chair of estate next to Henry in the great hall one evening, about to watch a masque. Anne was there, of course, dressed tonight in white damask with jewels threaded through her loose dark hair. The colour did not become her sallow complexion, but Henry could not take his eyes off her.

Katherine anticipated that the Cardinal would be joyfully received by Henry, especially if he brought news that King Francis was ready to support the divorce. When Wolsey's messenger arrived and asked where his master was to be received, she expected Henry to excuse himself and make his way to Wolsey's private closet to hear his news, as he usually did. But there was Anne, butting in before Henry could answer, and demanding of the messenger, 'Where else should the Cardinal come? Tell him he may come here, where the King is!'

'Yes, tell him to come here,' Henry concurred.

Thus Anne made plain to the whole court her power over the King and her hatred for the Cardinal.

Oh, she is clever, Katherine thought. She remembered a distressed girl vowing vengeance on Wolsey. It came to her that Anne had borne this deadly grudge for, what was it, four years? The thought chilled her, but then it occurred to her that she and Anne had one thing in common: their loathing of Wolsey. For had not she herself borne him a similar grudge, and over a longer period? But, with Henry in thrall to her, Anne could prove a more formidable adversary than Katherine would ever be. She could almost find it in herself to feel sorry for Wolsey, who was visibly squirming to be received like any place-seeking courtier, with his enemies looking on triumphantly.

But then suddenly Anne was gone from the court. No by-your-leave – nothing! Just like she had done in July.

'She left for Hever last night, madam,' said Jane Seymour, Katherine's newest maid-of-honour, looking worried. Katherine liked and approved of Jane – she was no beauty, but then Katherine had thought better, now that she had grown older, of taking on attractive young women to serve her and make a good showing in the court. Jane was of good lineage – a descendant of King Edward III – and the Seymours were a solid English knightly family. Fair, pale-skinned Jane was devout, quiet and helpful, not clever, but shrewd. Her needlework was beyond compare, and one day she would make an excellent housewife. But for whom? Katherine was aware that there had been talk of a betrothal, but that the mother of the young man in question had put a stop to it. Jane had confessed to having been upset about it.

'She felt I was not good enough for her son, madam,' she'd explained, looking mournful.

'Well, Jane, if you are good enough to serve me, you are too good for William Dormer. I am most grateful to Sir Francis Bryan for recommending you to me.'

'He is a good friend to my family, and it is a great honour to serve your Grace.'

Jane's devotion was touching, and it was a relief not to have to suffer Anne's unwelcome and combative presence marring the harmonious atmosphere of the Queen's household. Katherine wondered what had caused Anne's precipitous departure. Was it some new tactic to further ensnare Henry? Absence, people said, made the heart grow fonder. Ah, but there was another old saw too that out of sight meant out of mind. Katherine hoped that might prove true – but her hopes were not high.

In September Sir Thomas More, lately returned from an embassy to Calais, came to see Katherine at Hampton Court.

'I have just come from the King,' he told her. 'We walked in the gallery.' He paused, looking uncharacteristically troubled. 'He asked for my opinion on this Great Matter. He even had his Bible ready to show me, the marker in Leviticus.'

'What did you say, my dear friend?' For Katherine, More's opinion was crucial. She could think of few men who had such integrity.

'I told him plainly that your marriage is good and valid.'

'Thank you for that,' Katherine said, relieved. 'He values your opinion more than anyone else's, as do I. What did he say?'

'He was clearly disappointed, but he accepted it benignly. Then he said I should speak to his chaplain, Dr Fox, who is writing a book setting out His Grace's case. I assured him I would do so, and I will, but that I was unlikely to change my views as they are founded on Scripture. His Grace said he respected that and would not press me.'

'Then all is not quite lost,' Katherine observed. 'Most people seem to be supporting my husband.'

'He is the King, madam. It is only to be expected. Did you know that he has sent an embassy to Rome?'

'No, Sir Thomas, I did not. No one tells me anything.'

More smiled kindly at her. 'Do not fret, madam. You have many friends who wish you well.'

'Yes, my good friend, but I also have powerful enemies.'

'Have courage! His Holiness will set all to rights!'

Anne Boleyn had rejoined the court in time for the Yuletide festivities at Greenwich, and Katherine, again having to suffer the sight of her dancing with Henry, was relieved to find Mendoza standing next to her.

'A very merry Christmas, Highness!'

'And the same to your Excellency.'

The ambassador lowered his voice. 'I must be brief, but there is news I must tell you. The Pope has escaped from captivity, but he is still subject to the Emperor. My master has ordered Pope Clement not to take any steps towards annulling your Grace's marriage, and not to allow the case to be tried in England. The word from Rome is that Cardinal Wolsey has asked his Holiness to grant him the power to hear the case and pronounce judgement. He has also requested the appointment of a fellow Papal legate. He has even sent draft dispensations to Rome, one annulling your marriage, the other authorising a second, to which the Pope need only affix his signature and seal.'

Katherine could hardly take it all in, and there was no time to ask questions . . .

'Thank you,' she murmured, and as Henry, laughing and heated from the dance, returned to his throne beside her, Mendoza melted into the shadows.

'May I speak with you?' Katherine asked Henry.

'Later,' he said, his good mood evaporating. He glared as Francis Bryan led Anne Boleyn out in a round dance.

There was no 'later'. Nor did Henry give Katherine any opportunity of speaking with him alone over the next few days. It was so important, what she needed to discuss. She thought she might go mad with frustration.

During the Christmas season, Bishop Fisher sought out Katherine in her apartments and begged an audience with her.

'Madam,' he said, his gaunt face stern, 'I have been powerfully moved to declare myself in favour of the validity of your marriage, and I will say to you what I have said to Cardinal Wolsey, which is that no divine law prohibits a brother marrying the wife of his deceased brother. You may rely on the Pope's dispensation, otherwise to no purpose would Christ would have said to St Peter, "Whatsoever thou shalt loose on earth shall be loosed in Heaven, and whatsoever thou shalt bind on earth shall be bound in Heaven."'

'Good Bishop, I am heartened to hear you say that,' Katherine told him, deeply moved, and aware that these days it took much courage to oppose the King.

'It must be said, madam. And let no one persuade you otherwise.'

Margaret Pole, who was in attendance at the audience, smiled. 'Your Grace should hear my son Reginald on the Great Matter.' Reginald, Henry's protégé, had not long returned from Italy, where he had been studying for the Church at the King's expense. 'He is of the same opinion as the Bishop here.'

'I am glad to hear it, Lady Salisbury,' said Fisher. 'I suspect also that Archbishop Warham is none too pleased about this business.'

'But he was one of those who advised the late King against my marriage,' Katherine pointed out.

'Well, madam, take it from me, he is not happy. Warham is sufficiently the King's man to support him in his quest to have the validity of the marriage established. Warham told Wolsey that, however badly your Grace might take it, the truth must be sought out and followed. But he is a conservative in every respect and would never countenance any attack on the authority of the Pope. Remember, there are those who see this case as a means of exposing corruption in the Church.'

'Let us hope that it never comes to that,' Katherine said.

She faced Henry at last across the table in Wolsey's closet. She would have preferred to see him alone, but he had insisted that Wolsey be present. It was late and the candlelight was dancing on the painted panels that lined the walls. The Cardinal stood to one side, warming his hands at the fire.

'I hear that you have sent an embassy to Rome,' Katherine began, refusing to be intimidated by the steely expression on Henry's face.

'It is no secret,' he replied. 'I have sent to enquire as to whether the dispensation issued by Pope Julius is sufficient, for I believe it was founded on certain false suggestions.'

'What false suggestions?' Was there to be no end to these fantasies?

Wolsey hastened to intervene. 'Madam, the King is absolutely resolved to satisfy his conscience. He never wished for this marriage.'

'*That* is an outright lie!' she cried, remembering the distant day when Henry burst into her poor lodging and claimed her for his own. She could not bear to have such a precious, treasured memory tainted by this falsehood. She turned to the King. 'My lord, surely you will refute it!'

Henry looked uncomfortable. 'All I hope for, madam, is that the Pope will ease my conscience.'

'It is the vehement desire of the whole nation and nobility that the King should have an heir,' Wolsey said.

'The Pope will never consent to our marriage being annulled,' Katherine insisted. Thank God that Charles was keeping Clement on a tight rein.

'If your Grace is thinking that the Emperor's will holds sway in Rome, you are mistaken. I have assured his Holiness that, if he grants what the King asks, His Grace is ready to declare war against the Emperor to procure the freedom of the Holy Father.'

Katherine was dumbstruck. Was Henry really offering to take on the might of Spain and the Empire? Heaven help her, it seemed he was ready to move Heaven and earth to be rid of her.

How had it come to this? Where was the golden young man who had come to her at Greenwich, here, in this very palace, and offered her his heart? She looked at him now, sitting glaring at her across the table, and thought she would die of grief.

Wolsey had brought Henry to this – Wolsey and Anne Boleyn, two devils, seated at either shoulder of their victim, dripping venom in his ears. This was not the Henry she knew and loved. He had been led astray, corrupted by these evildoers.

'You are the cause of all this, my Lord Cardinal!' she flung at Wolsey. And with that she rose, made a curtsey to the King, and left the two of them gaping at her.

Wolsey caught up with her in the gallery. His face was drawn in the moonlight spilling through the latticed windowpanes.

'Madam, I beg of you to hear me,' he asked, breathless and grim-faced. 'I did not seek this divorce. It is the King's will. I have no choice but to do as he bids me. If the Pope is not compliant, my life will be shortened, and I dread to anticipate the consequences.'

Katherine heard the desperation in his voice. It surprised her. He had sounded so confident back in the closet.

'I am not your enemy, madam,' Wolsey went on. 'You and your daughter have my sympathy. If it were up to me, I would not be putting his Holiness in this impossible position. Disregard for the papacy is growing daily, and it worries me that this Great Matter will only make things worse. And when the King declares war on the Emperor, and believe me it will happen in the next few weeks, your position will be even more precarious. I would not add wood to the fire. But Mistress Anne and her friends have undermined my influence with the King. He does not listen to me these days, yet he needs me, for he knows that, if anyone can get him what he wants, I can. So my hands are tied.'

'We all do as we must,' Katherine said, relenting only a little, 'and I suppose you have much to lose if you forfeit his favour.'

'As do we all, madam. I am aware of that. And now I must go, for I cannot risk being seen talking privily with you. I wish you a good night.'

She watched him go, noticing for the first time the stoop in his shoulders, the defeat in his demeanour. Could it really be that a slender girl had the ability to bring down the great Cardinal?

Chapter 24

1528

Henry was beside himself with terror. The hot summer had brought with it a new outbreak of the dreaded sweating sickness. Thousands had perished in London, and the epidemic seemed to be spreading at a frightening rate.

Katherine was alarmed when the King burst into her chamber one morning. 'Three of my servants died during the night,' he told her, his face a white mask of fear. 'It's under our own roof!'

Before the implications of what he had said sank in, Katherine knew a moment's pleasure that he had come to her in his time of need, when he had mostly been avoiding her of late and could have sent a messenger. Then she thought of Mary, and her heart froze like ice.

'We're leaving at once,' Henry told her. 'I'm taking a reduced household to Waltham Abbey. Tell your women and Lady Salisbury to make ready with all speed. Hurry!' He was in a frenzy to be gone. Katherine remembered how frightened he had been when the terrible disease had struck eleven years ago – in another life, it seemed now. At least he was taking her with him. Maybe this new threat had made him see things in proportion.

When she arrived in the courtyard, holding Mary by the hand, Katherine saw Anne Boleyn standing with Henry in the midst of a small throng of courtiers and household officers, all impatient to leave. For once, Anne was wearing a gable hood instead of the French one she usually affected, and it had the new-fashioned short lappets. Someone had said something that amused her, for her shoulders were shaking with mirth. It brought to Katherine's mind the memory of that woman sobbing in the Tower, nearly twenty years ago.

The image of that weeping woman was still vivid, even now.

But there were more pressing things to think about. Of course, at such a time, and especially if he had come to his senses, Henry would want to say goodbye to Anne – and good riddance, as far as Katherine was concerned. As she made her way to where her litter stood, trying to put on a cheerful countenance for Mary, people around them were speculating fearfully as to where the sweat might spread next. But Katherine was not listening. She had watched Anne mount her horse, had heard her say, 'When we get to Waltham . . .'

How could Henry do this to her, and to Mary? It was as if Anne had robbed him of his humanity. It was bad enough suffering Anne's presence in a crowded court, but in a much-reduced household it would be unbearable. Yet there was nothing she could do, so she climbed into her litter, leaving him to ride on ahead with his sweetheart at his side.

The great abbey of Waltham was an ancient and popular place of pilgrimage. Katherine had been here several times, and prayed before the great black marble cross that was said to work miracles, although it had never done so for her. A mile off stood Dallance, Henry's own property. It was not a large house, but one he liked to visit when he had some leisure time, for the hunting was good thereabouts. He would not be going hunting now, though. He had made it clear that he was staying indoors, to avoid any evil humours in the air.

There was a King's Side in the house and a Queen's Side – and nothing, apart from the Princess's rooms, a hall and offices, in between. Anne would have to lodge with the Queen's ladies, of whom there were now few. And Mary would be in Katherine's company daily. Katherine saw with a sinking heart that it would be impossible for her and the Princess to avoid Anne here.

Anne was nowhere to be seen when Katherine's women were laying away her clothes and other belongings. Grateful for the respite, she sent Mary off to have her lesson with Master Fetherston, and opened the window to look out on the pretty pleasance below, then wished she hadn't, for Anne and Henry were there. A sick feeling came over her, until she heard raised voices and realised that they were arguing.

'It's an order!' Henry shouted.

'Have it your own way!' Anne flounced away, fury in her every movement. A few moments later there were footsteps on the stairs, and she entered the Queen's chamber and made her curtsey.

'Ah, Mistress Anne, at last,' Katherine said. 'I have a task for you. Please unpack my books.'

'Yes, madam.' Anne's look would have felled armies. She was in a foul mood. The other ladies exchanged amused glances.

Anne took her time arranging the books on the shelf. Katherine saw her open one, peruse it and frown. Then she put it away.

Two days later, when Katherine was seated at the centre of a sewing circle, Henry appeared, looking around the room warily.

'Good evening, Kate,' he said. 'Ladies, you may leave us.'

As the women rose from their curtseys and hastened through the door to the inner chamber, Anne glared at Henry, but he avoided her gaze and said nothing, so she had to follow the others.

'Would you like some wine, sir?' Katherine asked.

'Yes, Kate, that would be pleasant on this warm evening. Can you close the window? Just in case the contagion is in the air. I trust you are comfortably settled in?'

'Yes, thank you.' Katherine handed him the goblet, thinking that this was the Henry of old. Maybe he *had* tired of Anne. She dared to hope that the scene she had witnessed in the garden signalled an end to all this madness. Then he would forget the nonsense about a divorce and come back to her. Her heart overflowed with forgiveness. Just let all be as it was before . . .

'Kate,' Henry said, loosening his shirt collar, 'I have been wondering. In fact, I am afraid, and not just of the sweat. Tell me, do you think this plague is a visitation from God?'

'There is no doubt of it,' she said, hope springing stronger in her breast.

'That is what I believe. He is displeased with me, and He is visiting His wrath on my kingdom. But why, Kate? Why?'

She could have answered that, but she just shook her head sadly.

'Is God displeased with me because I have remained in an incestuous marriage? Or because I have sought to put you away?'

'Why are you asking me this?' she said. 'You know what must be my answer. I thought you were convinced of the rightness of your case.'

'But that was before this visitation, Kate. I know that I have offended God in some way. I just wish I knew how.'

'Have you asked your confessor for his opinion?'

'Yes. He advised me that I should return to you until my case is resolved – and so, Kate, here I am.' Henry spread his hands and gave her a wry smile.

It was not what she had hoped for, but it was something.

'I am so glad of it,' she said, finding that her eyes were filling with tears. She even had it in her to feel sorry for Anne, who had clearly been dismissed.

'I hope to have a ruling soon – by autumn, if all goes well,' Henry was saying. 'The Pope is sending a cardinal to try the case with Wolsey. You'll remember him – Cardinal Campeggio.'

Katherine forced herself not to cry. He still wanted to be rid of her. He was still talking to her as if she were a disinterested party, not the wife he wished to discard. In an instant, joy had turned to misery.

'Yes,' she said, picking up her sewing and bending her head over it. 'He came here a few years ago. You made him Bishop of Salisbury.'

'He's good, Kate. Erasmus thinks he's one of the most learned men living. And he'll be impartial.'

Katherine sighed. 'I pray God grants him wisdom,' she said, wishing that Henry would see sense. Surely God had made His displeasure clear enough? 'I long for the day when we can put all this behind us. And your people long for it too.'

Henry frowned, but said nothing. She was sure he knew what she meant. How could he be deaf to the complaints of his subjects, whose prosperity had suffered since he had declared war on the Emperor? He must know how badly England's trade was suffering!

Draining his goblet, Henry leaned back in his chair. 'I think we did the right thing in sending Mary back to Hunsdon. I'm sure it's safer for her, being deep in the country. I trust that Fetherston is pleased with her?'

'He is indeed,' Katherine replied, angry with him for avoiding the subject. 'I've already heard that she is settled there and doing well.' Pray God this Great Matter would be resolved before it touched her adversely. She was twelve now, old enough to be wed to the Duc d'Orléans, although all talk of her marriage had ceased now that Henry's nullity suit had cast doubts on her legitimacy. She was certainly old enough to understand what was going on. Katherine and Margaret Pole had done their best to shield her from it all, yet the country was lively with gossip and it would be a miracle if Mary had not heard some talk.

'Let's hope this sickness passes soon and we can see her again,' Katherine said. She hated being apart from Mary, especially at such a time. Her longing to be with her daughter was a constant ache.

'Amen to that.' Henry swallowed. 'Kate, let us set our differences aside for now and wait to see what God wills in this matter.'

'I am content to do that,' she agreed. 'What of Mistress Anne?'

'She is . . . not content,' Henry admitted. 'Kate, you have it all wrong about Anne.'

'How can you say that?' Katherine asked. 'Have I ever complained about her, or criticised her? I treat her with honour, for your sake.'

Henry shrugged. 'She might see it somewhat differently. But never mind. What I want you to know is that she does have the qualities that make a good queen. She *is* virtuous, believe me, whatever people say about her.'

Katherine pursed her lips. 'The world says she is your mistress.'

'No, Kate. That's what I'm trying to tell you. I can assure you, none better, of her constant virginity. And she is descended of right noble and royal blood; she's well educated – and apparently apt to bear children.'

'Given her constant virginity, how can you know that?' Katherine had not meant to argue with Henry, but she could not help herself, and she knew she sounded tart.

'She is young,' Henry said.

That was cruel, and it spurred Katherine to further tartness. 'She is older than I was when we wed. And she spent years at the French court, a byword for licentiousness. They say never a gentlewoman leaves it a maid. Truly Mistress Anne must be remarkable.'

'I don't like what you're insinuating, Kate.'

The pink flush in Henry's cheeks should have warned Katherine, but her proud Spanish blood was up. 'I insinuate nothing! But a woman who encourages the attentions of a married man – and steals another woman's husband – cannot be virtuous!'

'Kate, I am not your husband!' Henry said angrily.

'I say you are! And until the Pope has confirmed it, Mistress Anne should not be getting ideas above her station. And *you* are wrong to encourage her, for she is going to be bitterly disappointed!'

'I've had enough of this!' Henry barked, and stood up.

'Henry, why are you doing this to us?' Katherine cried. 'We have a good marriage, and you are destroying it – *and* you are breaking my heart!' Great, tearing sobs burst out of her; she could not help herself. 'My grief is the greater because I love you so much!'

'You know very well why I am doing this,' Henry said coldly. 'You just don't listen, do you? You don't want to listen.'

'I could say the same about you!' Katherine retorted, dabbing at her eyes. As she looked up, the door slammed. Henry had gone.

She spent a miserable afternoon, trying to be cheerful for her ladies' sake but fearing that she had wrecked this special opportunity of a reconciliation with Henry. After all, he had come to her, ready to share bed and board until the Pope had spoken, just in case he was wrong. She prayed that Clement would not delay too long.

In the evening she was looking for her psalter when she saw the book that had made Anne Boleyn frown. Of course. It was Queen Elizabeth's old missal, the one in which Henry had written, in that golden summer when the world was young and glorious, 'I am yours for ever.' He will never love Anne like that, she told herself.

To her astonishment, he came to her bed that night. At the sight of him walking through the door, candle in hand and a damask robe over his nightgown, her heart leapt with joy. It had been so long, so very long . . .

'Kate,' he said, 'I'm a plain man. Maybe I was a little unkind earlier. I was thinking, people are dying out there – hundreds of them – and we should not be at odds with each other.'

'No, we should not,' Katherine agreed, wanting to open her arms to him as she used to do, and yet unsure as to whether she should. What did he expect from her? Was this just for form's sake? Or had he remembered the many loves they had shared, and realised that he wanted her after all?

He came to the bed, set down the candle, took off his robe and climbed in beside her. Then he lay down on his back, staring up at the canopy, and reached for her hand.

'Kate,' he said, 'there is a woman in Kent, a nun, who is reputed to have the gift of prophecy; she claims to have had holy visions.'

'Elizabeth Barton,' Katherine said, hoping that this conversation was not the only purpose of Henry's visit.

'You know of her?'

'I do. She asked if I would see her, and of course I said no.' The woman had prophesied that, if Henry put away his lawful wife, he would no longer be king and would die a villain's death. Katherine had known she could not risk any taint of association with such dangerous ideas.

'Very wise, Kate, very wise. She's a lunatic, and what she preaches is treason; yet people are credulous, and if she persists, we will have to deal with her.'

'I pray she sees the error of her ways,' Katherine said. 'She sounds a simple, misguided soul.'

Silence descended. They lay there for a while not moving, then Henry bade her good night and turned away from her. As he began to snore gently, tears dripped on to Katherine's pillow. It *had* been for form's sake, after all. Nothing had really changed. She wished he had not given her cause to hope that it had.

'There are forty thousand cases of the sweat in London,' Henry said, his face ashen.

Katherine crossed herself. 'Those poor souls,' she murmured. 'I pray

God that Mary will be all right!'

'Fear not, there are no cases of the sweat at Hunsdon or within several miles, thanks be to God,' Henry said fervently. They were at dinner, just the two of them, for he did not like too many people coming near him, but suddenly the door opened and there was Mistress Anne. There was none of her usual hauteur in evidence; her face appeared unusually white and drawn.

'Forgive my intrusion, your Graces, but I must tell you that my maid has died of the sweat.'

'By God, it's reached us here!' Henry cried, jumping up and nearly upsetting the table. 'We must leave at once. Where is safe? Let me think. Hunsdon – I have it! Yes, we'll go to Hunsdon and be with Mary. Kate, have your women make ready to leave within the hour.'

'I will help,' Anne said.

'No,' Henry told her, quite adamant. '*You* are going home to Hever, right now, and you will stay there until it is clear that you are not infected with this plague. I pray to God you are not!'

Katherine heard the agony in his voice, but she also noticed that he made no move towards Anne; rather he seemed to be shrinking from her. It seemed that his fear of the sweat was greater than his love for his mistress.

'God keep you!' he said, as Anne departed, glowering.

'May He watch over your Grace too,' she answered, ignoring Katherine.

'I had to send her away,' he said brokenly, when she had gone, as if he were apologising to Katherine for depriving her of her maid. 'I have no son to succeed me, and I dare not risk catching the sweat. Come, Kate, we must make haste to Hertfordshire!'

At Hunsdon, for much of the time, Henry shut himself up in a tower with his physicians, no doubt fretting about Mistress Anne. Each day, his household diminished, as more and more of his attendants were sent away. The fewer people he had about him, the less chance there was of his being infected with the sweat.

He was playing skittles in the hall with Katherine and Mary on the day that a letter arrived from Wolsey. His eyes narrowed as he read it, the dangerous flush infusing his fair skin. Mary was regarding him with apprehension, and Katherine, having seen the Cardinal's seal, hurriedly sent her away to fetch her needlework. She watched with relief as the door closed behind her – and just in time.

'The Cardinal's gone mad!' Henry bellowed. 'By God, how dare he preach to me? He fears that this sickness is a manifestation of God's wrath, so in all conscience he begs me to abandon all thoughts of a divorce. Has he forgotten that *I* have a conscience too? Where has he been this past year and more? Have I been wasting my breath?' Henry began pacing up and down the floor, incandescent with rage. 'I'll have him in the Tower for this! They can string him up and cut him down and make collops of him. This, mark you all, is the man who sang Mistress Anne's praises to the Pope, the man who vowed to make her my Queen. No, Kate, do not look at me like that. It's only a matter of time now, and you may as well get used to it. I will have her, by God! And I swear I would give a thousand Wolseys for just one Anne Boleyn. None other than God shall take her from me!'

Katherine rose, made the briefest of curtseys and left the hall. She would hear no more. It was intolerable, having to sit there and listen to Henry voicing his determination to replace her. It was not only Wolsey who had gone mad! Again, she felt that unwilling pity for the Cardinal, quickly quelled because, cornered by Henry in a rage, he was likely to prove even more dangerous, to save his own skin.

She fetched her writing chest – given to her by Henry, and therefore, like so many things, a reminder of much happier times. It bore his coat of arms and was adorned with the painted figures of Christ, St George and others from myth and legend, among them Venus, who represented love and fertility. Katherine did not, could not, stop to think on that now. Haste was imperative, for Cardinal Campeggio was probably well on his way from Rome, and time was short. She must file an official protest against the case being heard in England, for she knew she would never be accorded an impartial hearing.

*

Anne had the sweat.

Henry was in tears. In such feverish agitation that Katherine thought he had it too, he had come to her room during the night and woken her. He thought she should know. Anne's father was also infected.

Katherine knew a guilty moment of huge relief when she heard the news. God Himself was settling the Great Matter! Then, at once, she reproached herself for entertaining the hope that her rival might die. That was grossly uncharitable. *Forgive me!* she prayed silently. She could guess what Maria might say.

'Where is Dr Chambers?' Henry kept asking. No one could find him. Then a groom in the stables said he had taken his horse and ridden to an afflicted household, to tend the sick.

'Send for Butts!' Henry commanded, frantic now. 'Make haste!' Everyone scattered.

Dr Butts, Chambers's subordinate, came quickly. He was a cultivated, learned man with an urbane manner and a kindly face, and his soothing presence calmed the King.

'Remember, sire, that many have this sickness and recover,' Dr Butts assured him. 'I will go immediately to Hever.'

'Wait!' Henry called for writing materials and scribbled a note. 'Take this to Mistress Anne.' Dr Butts bowed and was gone.

Katherine, feeling that she had become invisible, was about to return to her bedchamber, but Henry came after her.

'Kate, I do not want to be alone tonight,' he said plaintively.

She did not want him, not when his thoughts were with Anne, but he was her husband, so she could not refuse him. And it *was* good to be needed; despite herself, she was touched that it was to her that he had turned when he wanted comfort. Tonight she could see in this big, powerful man – who in so many ways now seemed alien to her – the young boy, untouched by life, he had once been.

When they lay in bed together she did not hesitate to wind her arms around him and draw him to her. And he came to her, not as a lover, but as a lost soul. He was so near to her, yet so far, and she ached for him – and for them both.

*

405

They waited a week for news. Every day Henry was on his knees in chapel, bargaining with God, offering all manner of things if He would only spare Anne.

Katherine, kneeling beside him, could not but be aware of his anguish. It was compounded by tidings that one of his favoured gentlemen, Anne's brother-in-law, William Carey, had succumbed to the sweat; and when they came to tell Henry that his good friend Sir William Compton had also died of it, he was plunged into an abyss of grief – and a fresh martyrdom of anxiety for Anne.

Katherine made herself pray for Anne to be restored to health, even though some inner demon was telling her that she ought to be praying for her death. Without Anne, Henry's doubts of conscience would miraculously disappear, she was certain. But she could not find it in herself to ask God for such a favour; it would be wrong, evil – and so she did what she knew to be the right thing.

At last – Katherine could hear Henry holding his breath and feel his apprehension – there was a letter from Dr Butts. Henry gave a shout, almost leaping for joy.

'Anne is past the danger!' he exulted. 'She is making a perfect recovery.'

'I am glad for her,' Katherine said, trying not to wonder why God had seen fit to spare a woman who was becoming the scandal of Christendom.

Henry was in no doubt about that. 'It is a sign that God approves of my future Queen,' he declared.

Katherine was grateful for the respite afforded her by Anne's long convalescence, and it was a relief to hear, when the sweat had died down and her rival returned to court, that she was no longer to be required to suffer her constant presence, for Henry was having an apartment off the tiltyard made ready for Anne. He could not have his future Queen waiting on his present one.

When Anne arrived at Greenwich, she was prouder and more insufferable than ever because she believed that God was smiling upon her. And there was Wolsey, hastening to greet the favourite, obsequiously bowing and presenting a costly gift, with Henry looking on, beaming.

But it seemed that an apartment at court was not sufficient for Mistress Anne's vanity. Soon afterwards Katherine learned that her rival was to have an establishment of her own, at Durham House, where she herself had lived during those dreary years after Arthur's death. Henry had charged Thomas Boleyn with refurbishing the property to a standard fit for a royal bride-to-be, and an army of servants and ladies-in-waiting was to be installed there, so that Mistress Anne could keep as much state as if she were queen already.

'I'll warrant that this is because she hates having to bow the knee to you,' Margaret Pole said, tart. 'She cannot bear the fact that you rank high above her, so she must needs queen it over her own court.'

'At least I do not have to watch her doing it,' Katherine observed.

Henry was now dividing his time between Greenwich and Durham House. Although he would plainly have preferred to be with Anne, he could not be seen to be living with her, and was taking care to keep Katherine at his side for appearances' sake. Outwardly all was cordial between them, and when Mary was with her parents no one would have guessed there was anything amiss. Henry was his old genial self, in high good spirits in anticipation of the arrival of Cardinal Campeggio.

'You rejoice prematurely,' Katherine could not resist telling him. 'Do not think that this Pope will overturn the decision of his predecessor.'

'My case is righteous!' Henry retorted. 'God and my conscience are perfectly agreed on that point.'

'And what of my conscience?' she countered. These days they often squabbled like this in private.

'You are a good woman, Kate, but you are misguided. And you don't listen!'

He was working on another book, in which he was setting forth his arguments against their marriage. He was up late most nights scribbling away, despite the headaches that had begun again to plague him.

'I will give it to you to read when it is finished,' he told Katherine. 'It may help you to understand better, although I suspect you are being obstinate rather than stupid.'

'I have heard your arguments many times, so I have no need to read them again. It is you who are being obstinate!' And so it carried on. Katherine prayed that the legate would come soon. This state of affairs could not continue.

Cardinal Campeggio was here!

At last, *at last*, Katherine thought. There would be an end to this intolerable waiting.

Henry had been all for offering Campeggio a state welcome to London, but the Italian Cardinal refused it, and arrived discreetly by barge. Then, Katherine heard, he took straight to his bed. It was understood that he had gout, and that the long journey had been a martyrdom for him. Certainly he had taken an unconscionable age to get to England.

'Maybe he was told to delay!' Maria opined. 'Or maybe he was chosen because he would be like a little snail, shuffling across those foreign lands.'

'I cannot believe that,' Katherine said. 'His Holiness would not think of doing such a thing.'

Maria stabbed her needle into her tapestry frame. They were working on a set of hangings depicting the heroic deeds of Antiochus the Saviour, King of Syria, which helped to fill the long, dragging hours. 'Highness, you are too trusting for your own good! Think about it. There is the Pope, still frightened of the Emperor, but also frightened to offend the King. Who could blame him if he played for time, hoping the King will tire of Mistress Anne?'

It dawned on Katherine that Maria might be right.

For some days she heard nothing. Almost cloistered in her apartments at Bridewell Palace on the banks of the Thames, she was isolated from what was happening beyond her doors. Then one morning, Maria came in, fuming.

'That woman is back!' she said, clenching her fists. 'She has been installed in a fine lodging here.'

'What woman?' piped up little Anne Parr, Maud's daughter, who had recently joined Katherine's household as a maid-of-honour.

'Mistress Anne Boleyn!' Maria barked, as Maud shook her head furiously, signalling to Maria to shut up.

Anne's return could only mean one thing, Katherine realised – that Henry was anticipating a speedy and successful outcome to his case.

Even if Clement failed her, Katherine knew she had one powerful champion. When Margaret Pole brought her a package from Mendoza – 'And don't ask me how I managed to evade the Cardinal's spies!' the Countess said, smiling – Katherine knew it was something of great importance, for the ambassador rarely attempted to communicate with her these days. And it was.

At first Katherine thought it was a copy of Pope Julius's dispensation, but then she read the Emperor's letter, which explained that it was actually a copy of a second dispensation issued at the request of Queen Isabella. The original had permitted Katherine to marry Henry even though her first marriage had perhaps been consummated, but in this version the word 'perhaps' was missing.

Katherine looked up at Margaret. 'I have much for which to thank my mother. She was concerned to avoid all doubt. Now it is clear that, even if Arthur and I had lived as man and wife, my marriage to the King would be good and valid.'

Immediately she took the document to Henry, whom she found walking in a gallery, deep in discussion with Wolsey.

'I thought you should see this, my lord,' she said. Henry read the document and frowned, then passed it to Wolsey without comment.

The Cardinal studied it. 'Madam, it seems strange that no one in England has ever heard of the existence of this dispensation,' he said, 'and I'm afraid that leads me to conclude that it must be a forgery.'

'Are you accusing the Emperor of being a liar?' Katherine demanded of him.

'Of course not, but there may be those in his service who are not so scrupulous.'

Her blood was up. 'I hope you are not suggesting that Mendoza is one!'

'I did not say that, madam.'

'You should have informed me of the existence of this dispensation before,' Henry reproved her.

'I did not have it, or know of it. It arrived only today, and I brought it straight to you. The Emperor writes that the dispensation was found when a search was made among the papers of Dr de Puebla, and that this is a true copy.'

'It may be so,' Henry grunted, 'but it is only a copy, and cannot be submitted in evidence. We need to see the original.'

'His Grace is right,' interjected Wolsey, 'and as your Grace looks for the continuance of his love, you will send to Spain for it, as the lack of it might ruin your case, and endanger your child's inheritance.'

Katherine's cheeks burned with indignation. How dare this upstart butcher's son speak to her so insolently! She would have liked to give him a piece of her mind, but Henry was glowering at her, and she feared to provoke his anger.

'Very well,' she said, 'I will send my chaplain.'

She chose one of her English chaplains, a young cleric called Thomas Abell, whom she had recently taken into her service as master of languages and music. He had helped her to perfect her English, which she now spoke as well as her native tongue but still pronounced awkwardly, and he was in charge of her musicians. Already he had become indispensable to her, and she knew she could rely on his loyalty.

Father Abell left for Madrid that very day, with a letter requesting the Emperor to send the dispensation to England. Katherine dared not entrust him with any message of warning; instead, as she bade him an anxious farewell, she was praying inwardly that Charles would have the wisdom to read between the lines and refuse her request, for she was sure that, once that dispensation was in England, genuine or not, it would conveniently disappear.

Katherine stood in her privy chamber, clutching the table for support, as she stared at the paper in her hand in horror. It was signed by the whole Privy Council. She could not quite believe what she was reading. Mute and distressed, she passed it to Margaret Pole.

'This is ridiculous!' the Countess declared briskly, after a cursory perusal of the opening sentences. 'The King resents you for refusing to heed his doubts about your marriage? He is irritated by the way in which you seem able to rise above your misery and appear cheerful? He is persuaded by your behaviour that you do not love him?' She shook her head. 'Madam, words fail me! Let's make no bones about it, it is His Grace who has put you in this misery, and if anyone has cause to doubt that they are loved, it is you!'

'That is bad enough,' Katherine said dully, 'but read on. They are threatening me.'

Margaret read. 'This is nonsense! What plot to kill the King and the Cardinal? And they think you had some part in it! If it could be proved the Queen had any hand, she must not expect to be spared. They have taken leave of their senses.'

'I love him, God help me,' Katherine said. 'I would do nothing to harm him.'

'Well, they know that. I know it. Everyone knows it.'

Katherine took back the letter and read it again, much as it pained her to do so. 'It seems I have not shown as much love for the King as I ought; and now that he is very pensive, whatever that means, I am accused of manifesting great signs of joy, setting people to dancing and other pleasures, out of spite to the King. Heavens, if I were to go about wailing and weeping, and not put a brave face on things, that would be wrong too! I can do nothing right. They censure me for showing myself too much to the people, and working on their affection by being civil and graciously bowing my head. What, am I to appear rude to them? I cannot win, whatever I do. And now the King has concluded that I hate him.' The tears began to fall. 'It is this last bit that hurts. They write that, as they in their consciences think his life is in danger, they have advised him to separate himself from me, both at bed and board, and to take the Princess from me. And they warn that I would be a fool to resist the King's will.'

Margaret rose, knelt down by the chair and hugged Katherine. 'Dear madam, I cannot see you looking so devastated. Listen to me. It is all a pretext to discredit you in Cardinal Campeggio's eyes, so that he will look with favour on the King. It is cruel and it is all lies, but your fame goes before you, and most people know you for the sweet, kind lady you are. They love you for it, whereas the Boleyn strumpet is hated and reviled – hence the need to show you in an unfavourable light.'

Katherine leaned her head on Margaret's shoulder. 'What would I do without you, my dear friend? You make that horrible letter sound like a silly rant.'

'Which is all it is!' Margaret cried. 'Madam, you should hear what the people are saying in the streets – when the legate goes abroad in London, they yell that the King only wants another wife for his own pleasure, and if there are lone voices that speak out against them, they are hot to defend you. Truly, you are loved.'

'Nevertheless, I must be careful,' Katherine said. 'This is a warning.' And it comes direct from him. Who is doing the hating here?

She took care not to leave the palace unless she had to. She adopted a grave demeanour and dressed in sober colours, so as not to draw attention to herself. The time she had spent in making merry with her ladies she now spent on her knees, so that they were stiff from kneeling. And still that was not enough. The Council made her sign an oath not to write anything but what the King commanded her. And in case she broke it, there were the Cardinal's spies, always watching her. She suspected that even some of her women were in Wolsey's pay, or had been bribed to report everything she did and said. Lucy Talbot had come to her in tears and said she must leave court, now, with no reason given. When pressed, she would only say that she could no longer injure a kind mistress.

They were trying to get rid of her, by fair means or foul. If they could find any slight pretext for proceeding against her as a bad wife, she knew they would not hesitate to seize it.

It was in the third week of October that the two cardinal-legates, Wolsey and Campeggio, came to the Queen's apartments. Katherine had donned her regal robes, her velvets and furs and jewels, and one of her costliest gable hoods, but when she came to look at her reflection in the mirror, she lamented her haggard appearance. She was nearly forty-three, and could not expect to look like a fresh young maiden, but she looked ten years older. It was what all this grief and strain had done to her.

Campeggio came leaning heavily on a stick, his florid face strained and severe; Wolsey was his usual unctuous self, but his brow was furrowed and his manner tense – as well it might be! But he was Henry's man, Katherine reminded herself; he had got himself into this position and did not deserve her sympathy. Campeggio too was looking as if he would rather be anywhere else. Well, they would find that she was not to be intimidated. She kept them standing, to remind them that she was the Queen.

They began civilly enough.

'Madam, we have been appointed as indifferent judges in the King's case,' Campeggio told her. Seeing her expression, he went on, 'his Holiness cannot refuse justice to anyone who demands it, but this Great Matter is full of difficulties, and he counsels you that, rather than face a trial, you should take some other course, one that would be satisfactory to God and your conscience, and would be to the glory and fame of your name.'

'And what is that?' Katherine asked, intrigued, hoping that the Pope, in his wisdom, had thought of a solution that had occurred to no one else.

'It would greatly please his Holiness if you would enter a convent,' Campeggio said.

There was a moment's silence.

'No,' she replied, quietly but hard as iron.

'But, madam, there is an honourable precedent. You will have heard of Queen Jeanne de Valois, the first wife of King Louis of France. She could not bear him children, so she agreed to a divorce and became a nun. She founded a holy order, and is now popularly reputed a saint. Could any woman ask for more?'

'I have no vocation,' Katherine said, 'and I have my daughter to consider.'

'Your Grace should think of your position,' Wolsey intervened. He was visibly perspiring, despite the autumnal chill.

'His Majesty has studied this Great Matter with such diligence that

I believe he knows more about it than the greatest theologian,' Campeggio said. 'He told me in the plainest terms that he wants nothing but a declaration of whether your marriage is valid or not. But, madam, I truly believe that even if an angel were to descend from Heaven and tell him that it is lawful, he would not be able to persuade the King of it.'

'My husband has been unduly influenced,' Katherine said, barely suppressing her anger.

Campeggio gave her a smile of rare sweetness. 'There are the strongest arguments in favour of your Grace entering a nunnery. Your piety is renowned. Your daughter's rights would be preserved, and you could see her regularly. If you took this course, the Pope would issue a dispensation allowing the King to remarry, and the Emperor could not possibly object. His Majesty could then take another wife and have sons. You would still keep your honours and your worldly possessions. Most important of all, the peace of Europe and the spiritual authority of the Holy See would no longer be under threat.' He paused, looking distressed.

'How can it be under threat?' Katherine asked. 'Is not the Pope Christ's representative on earth?'

'Madam, the King warned me only today that, if this divorce is not granted, the authority of the Holy See in this kingdom will be annihilated. Yes, I see you are shocked by that, as am I.'

Yes, but it is bluster, Katherine thought. I know what Henry is like when he doesn't get his way. She said nothing.

'So you see,' Campeggio continued, 'it is in your best interests to make a graceful exit. This solution will be extremely pleasing to the King, who is prepared to be very generous. You stand to lose only the use of his person by entering religion; and some comfortable house can be found where you can still enjoy any worldly comforts you desire.'

'No,' said Katherine again.

Campeggio and Wolsey exchanged exasperated glances.

'Madam,' Campeggio went on, 'it pains me to say this, but His Grace will not return to you, however things fall out. But if you show yourself compliant, he will allow you whatever you demand – and he will settle the succession on your daughter, if he has no heirs by another marriage. You will lose nothing by it, as you have already lost the King as a husband.'

Katherine stood up. 'My lords, you speak of practical solutions, but you are forgetting the most important issue at stake, which is whether or not my marriage is valid, and whether Pope Julius's dispensation is good or not. If the Pope finds it good – as surely he must – then my husband must return to me.'

Campeggio looked pained. 'Madam, it is not easy to reason with the King. Evidently he is so blindly in love with a certain lady that he cannot see his way clearly, and he is determined upon this divorce.'

'He has to have grounds for it first!' she snapped. 'My lords, I can affirm to you, on my conscience, that I did not sleep with Prince Arthur more than six or seven nights, and that I remained as virginal as when I came from my mother's womb. So how can my marriage to the King be invalid?'

'His Majesty insists otherwise,' Wolsey said.

'Does he call me a liar? He knows the truth, in his heart. And I intend to live and die in the estate of matrimony to which God called me. I assure you, I will always remain of that opinion and will never change it.'

Campeggio spoke. 'It would be better to yield to the King's displeasure rather than risk the danger of a sentence given in court. Consider how great your grief and trouble would be if it went against you. Think of the scandal and enmities that would be bound to ensue.'

Katherine's anger flared. 'I will not yield when I know I am in the right!' She turned to Wolsey. 'And for this trouble, I have only you to thank, my Lord Cardinal of York! Because I have always marvelled at your pride and vainglory, and hated your voluptuous life, *and* cared little for your presumption, you have maliciously kindled this fire – and mainly on account of the great grudge you bear to my nephew the Emperor, because he would not gratify your ambition by making you pope by force!'

'Madam,' Wolsey protested, visibly trembling, 'I am not the beginner or the mover of the King's doubts, and it is sore against my will that your marriage ever came into question. I give you my solemn promise that, as legate, I will be impartial. Believe me, I would obtain a happy solution with my own blood, if I could!'

'I do not believe you,' Katherine said, and noticed Campeggio watching her with sympathy and – she suspected – admiration. God knew she had need of both!

'Believe it or not, I wish you nothing but good,' Wolsey said, looking at her almost pleadingly.

'I think we must leave Her Grace to think this over,' Campeggio told him.

'There is nothing for me to think about,' Katherine declared.

'Then we must leave you for now.'

'Will you hear my confession?' she asked.

Wolsey looked stricken. Of course, he knew what she would say, and that Campeggio would believe it.

She knelt behind the grille. She could see Campeggio's face in thoughtful profile beyond it.

'Bless me, Father, for I have sinned,' she began, then enumerated all her little transgressions, and the greater ones of envy and wrath and pride. Then she said, 'I have not lied. I swear to you, upon the salvation of my soul, that I was never carnally known by Prince Arthur. And you may tell that to the world if you wish.'

Campeggio made no comment. He absolved her, blessed her and gave her a light penance of ten Ave Marias and a Pater Noster.

The next day he and Wolsey returned.

'We are here at the King's request,' he informed her. 'He asks again if you will enter a nunnery, and we urge you – nay, we beg you – to comply, lest some dire punishment befall you.'

'I will do nothing to my soul's damnation or against God's law,' Katherine declared. 'I will abide by no sentence save that of the Pope himself. I do not recognise the authority of the legatine commission to try the case in England, since I believe it to be biased in my husband's favour.'

'Madam, the King's wrath can be terrible,' Wolsey warned her, naked apprehension in his eyes.

Katherine feared he might be right. The Henry she knew had always been a reasonable and just man, but this Great Matter was changing him. Yet there was a principle at stake. If she acquiesced, and the Pope was forced to undo what his predecessor had done, it could bring grave discredit on the Holy See. Many might be led astray into thinking that right and justice were not with him. So for the sake of herself, her daughter, the Holy See and all Christendom, she was ready to stand firm. This was her time of trial, and she must be equal to it.

'Neither the whole kingdom, nor any great punishment, even though I be torn limb from limb, can make me alter my opinion,' she insisted, her voice becoming impassioned. 'And if, after death, I should return to life, I would prefer to die all over again rather than change my opinion.'

For weeks Henry had been conspicuous by his absence from Katherine's apartments, but now, suddenly, here he was, and in no very good mood.

'I will be brief, madam,' he said. 'I came to say that it would be better for you if you went of your own volition to a convent, otherwise you will be compelled to do so.'

Katherine forced herself to reply with the calm dignity of a queen. 'It is against my soul, my conscience and my honour. I am your wife, and I have done you no wrong. No judge will be found unjust enough to condemn me! Force me into a nunnery if you will, but you cannot make me say the vows that will free you from our marriage.'

Henry threw her a furious look, then stamped out without another word.

Hard on his heels came Campeggio.

'Believe me, it is in your Grace's interests to enter a nunnery as soon as possible, so that you can avoid the embarrassments that might arise if the case goes to trial. You do realise that the – ahem – intimate details of your married life will be exposed to public scrutiny?'

'I am prepared for that,' she said, keeping her voice as calm as possible. Inside she was shrinking from the prospect, but it was another thing that had to be faced. She knew that they were trying to make things as difficult as possible for her.

Then Mendoza smuggled a message to her. There was a rumour in Rome that certain persons in England were plotting to poison the Queen if she persisted in her obstinacy. That chilled her to the very marrow, but still she stood firm.

She got Maria to take her answer. 'The Queen is ready to incur that danger rather than be a bad wife and prejudice her daughter.' No one was going to rob Mary of her birthright.

Katherine knew that the citizens of London were growing increasingly hostile to the divorce and not afraid to voice angry objections. The Great Matter was now notorious, and it was impossible to go abroad in the City, even on the rare occasions when she now ventured forth, and not sense the public mood.

Henry was clearly aware of it too. Her ladies were abuzz with speculation because he had invited all his lords, councillors, judges, the Lord Mayor, aldermen, sheriffs, masters of the city guilds, and many others to Bridewell Palace. One lowering November afternoon all these dignitaries assembled in the presence chamber to hear their King address them.

Katherine watched with Maud Parr from behind a lattice in the gallery facing the royal dais. She saw the august gathering kneel as one as Henry entered and mounted his throne. He had put on his richest clothes and his most appealing manner, and that air of majesty he wore so easily.

'My trusty and well-beloved subjects,' he said, his voice ringing out, 'you know well that I have reigned for nearly twenty years, during which time I have so ordered, thanks be to God, that no enemy has oppressed you. But in the midst of my glory, the thought of my last hour often occurs to me, and I fear that if I should die without an heir, England should again be plunged into the horrors of civil war. These thoughts are continually pricking my conscience. This is my only motive, as God is my witness, which has made me lay this Great Matter before the Pope.' He placed his hand on his heart, raking the room with his piercing gaze. 'And touching the Queen, if it be adjudged that she is my lawful wife, nothing will be more pleasant or acceptable to me, for I assure you that she is a lady without comparison. If I were to marry again, I would choose her above all women.'

Katherine felt Maud stiffen beside her. Henry was a fool if he thought that people would be taken in by that.

'But,' he was saying, 'if it is determined that our marriage is against God's law, then I shall be sorrowful parting from so good a lady and so loving a companion, and lament that I have so long lived in adultery, and have no heirs of my body to inherit this realm. For although she and I have a daughter, to our great comfort and joy, I have been told by many learned men that she is not legitimate because the Queen and I have lived together in open adultery. And when I remember that I must die, then I think that all my deeds are as nothing if I leave you in trouble. For if I leave no true heir, just think what shall befall you and your children. Mischiefs and manslaughters will be the least of it! Think you, my lords, that these words touch not my body and soul? These are the sores that vex my mind; these are the pangs that trouble my conscience. And if any oppose my just cause, there is never a head so dignified but that I will make it fly off!'

When the King had gone, and a hubbub of chatter broke out, Katherine and Maud left.

'He should never have raised the matter in public!' Katherine said, as they hurried back to her lodgings.

'I fear it will win sympathy for His Grace though,' Maud said.

'That is my concern too, and that it will win over some who were lukewarm or even hostile.' Katherine sighed. 'Now it has come to the point where people are being threatened – I am being threatened. I have never felt so anxious and perplexed in my life.'

But there was heartening news waiting for her in a note from Mendoza, smuggled in by Isabel de Vargas, telling her that the Emperor had refused Father Abell's request to send the original of the second dispensation to England. Immediately she sent her chamberlain to inform the cardinals of that. She could not face seeing them herself. She wondered what they would do.

There was also a letter from Erasmus, praising her piety and gently urging her to enter religion. Even he had deserted her, she felt. At least Vives had written begging for her forgiveness after the way he had seemed to abandon her; and now, with her leave, he came to see her.

At the sight of his kind, familiar face, which brought back memories of happier days, Katherine opened her heart. 'I am in great distress that the man I love more than my own self should be so alienated from me, and that he should think of marrying another.'

She wept then, and the wise, gentle scholar put aside all protocol and took her hands in his.

'Do not blame me for attempting to console your Grace,' he said. 'Everyone praises your moderation. When others would have moved Heaven and earth, or sought revenge, you ask merely not to be condemned without a hearing.'

'I just want my husband back,' Katherine sobbed.

Chapter 25

1528–1529

When the court moved to Greenwich in December, Henry still kept up the pretence that all was well between them. He was plainly on his best behaviour, for surely Campeggio would be sending regular reports back to Rome. He visited Katherine almost every afternoon, as he had used to do; he dined and supped with her; and he sometimes spent the night with her.

'You do realise, Kate, that my confessor has forbidden me to touch you while my case is undecided,' he said, as they lay two feet apart in the wide bed. It was a convenient excuse, she thought, trying to suppress her longing to be lovers once more. She had thought, when she was young, that those fires might be dampened with the advancing years, yet they were as lively as ever, her passion refusing to be stilled. Having Henry so near, and yet forbidden to her, was cruel and frustrating, especially since the symptoms that had offended him had now disappeared.

One night it got too much to bear, and she could not stop the tears flooding her pillow. Instinctively she moved towards Henry for comfort, but he put out his hand and stayed her. Then he got out of bed and drew on his nightgown. The fire was dead and it was cold. She could hear him fumbling for the candle.

'Kate,' his voice came out of the darkness, 'are you not aware of the danger that may ensue to me by using you as my wife?'

'I have told you a hundred times, your conscience may rest easy,' she replied, hurt beyond measure by his rejection.

'It has nothing to do with my conscience, but with my person,' he told her. 'I have refrained from mentioning it, for fear of embarrassing you, but you have a woman's disorder, and I fear it may infect me, so I am sorry, but I am utterly determined never to sleep with you again after tonight.'

Katherine was so mortified she could not find the words to protest that she had recovered from her affliction. This was humiliating beyond words, and heartbreaking. She wished now that she had plucked up the courage to consult one of her physicians long ago. She supposed it was natural for Henry to have been put off by her secret ailment, although she was almost sure that it was not catching, just unpleasant. In fact, she even wondered fleetingly if it was at the root of his crisis of conscience. But did he have to be so brutal about it?

She was relieved when the door closed softly behind him, glad that he had not made a light and seen her flaming cheeks. Yet still she wept, for her lost love and her shame. Would there ever be any loving and gentleness between her and Henry again?

After that night Henry came less frequently to her chamber and her table, and soon she learned the reason why. Mistress Anne was installed at Greenwich, in a very fine lodging near the King's own.

Maria was outraged. 'Greater court is now being paid to that slut than has been paid to your Grace for a long time!'

'I see they mean to accustom the people by degrees to endure her, so that when the great event comes off it may not be thought strange,' Maud observed.

'I think the people have her true measure,' Katherine said.

'They hate her, and they would do more if they had more power,' Maria declared. 'When that woman rides abroad in London, they still shout, "Nan Bullen shall not be our Queen! We'll have no Nan Bullen!" It does my heart good to hear it!'

'The only thing that can do *my* heart good now is a just judgement on the King's case,' Katherine said. 'But I do not look for it in this English court. I just cannot understand why there are all these delays, and why the Pope cannot confirm that the dispensation is good. This waiting is killing me.'

'They say Mistress Anne is tired of waiting too,' Gertrude Blount offered.

'As well she might!' chimed in Elizabeth Stafford, who, for all she was Anne's aunt, hated her. 'She's nigh on twenty-eight, and long past her first youth.'

'I hear that she is forever complaining to the King, and it's obvious that there is no love lost between her and Wolsey,' Margaret said. 'For some reason she hates him.'

Katherine remembered an angry young girl who had been deprived of her lover. But the breaking of her pre-contract with Percy had not been solely Wolsey's doing; he had been acting on the King's orders. Katherine wondered if Anne knew that. More likely it was the Howards, Anne's aristocratic kinsmen, who had poisoned her mind against the Cardinal.

It was a miserable Christmas. Katherine found it hard to feel her usual joy in this holy season, her mind was so troubled. Wolsey and Campeggio were the King's guests of honour, but Wolsey was clearly feeling the strain. Henry's welcome had been less gracious than before, and once, at table, he spoke angrily in a low tone to his former friend, the man who at one time could have done no wrong in his eyes. A tense atmosphere pervaded the jousts, the banquets, the masques and the disguisings, which had all been laid on ostensibly for the cardinals' pleasure.

Katherine's only enjoyment was in the company of her daughter, who had come up from Hunsdon to court for the festive season. Henry, as proud and loving a father as ever, made much of Mary. But more than once Katherine caught Mary's small, serious face regarding him warily. Of course, the child – although she was nearly thirteen now – must by now have heard something of the Great Matter.

Katherine asked Margaret Pole if Mary ever said anything about it.

'No, madam, and it has not been my place to raise the matter. I have done my best to protect Her Grace from idle gossip, and her household have strict instructions, but people will talk. Would you like me to speak to her, madam?'

'No, Margaret. I will talk to her.'

One morning Katherine took Mary aside and sat her down.

'I think you have heard something about what people call the King's Great Matter?' she said gently.

Mary swallowed. 'Yes, madam.'

'You must not worry about it,' Katherine said. 'Your father has certain doubts about the dispensation given to us by Pope Julius, but Pope Clement is looking into the matter and has sent Cardinal Campeggio here to try the case with Cardinal Wolsey. I have no doubt that the matter will soon be sorted out, and that His Grace's mind will be set at rest.'

She thought she had managed rather well, and that if Mary had heard wilder tales, this reassurance would make a nonsense of them. But then Mary spoke.

'But my father wants to marry Mistress Anne Boleyn.' It was not a question, just a statement. Of course the child could not have been blind to what was going on at court. Henry had spared no thought for her, had made no effort to be discreet.

'If the Pope finds our marriage invalid, then of course he must marry again, and he wishes to see if Mistress Anne has it in her to be a good queen.' It was only what Henry had said himself, and it still sounded unconvincing.

'But she is not royal and she is not very nice,' Mary said.

'Not very nice?'

'She scants her respect to me! And to you! I hate her!'

Katherine was taken back by the venom in her daughter's voice. She had never heard her speak thus before, and it broke her heart to see how Mary had been suffering on account of this sorry business. How, she asked herself, yet again, could Henry inflict this suffering on his child?

'We must be charitable towards her, for the King's sake.'

The child's eyes, childish no longer, flashed with anger. 'My lady mother, I cannot, even to please you. She is a wicked woman, stealing my father away from you.'

'Mary!' Katherine placed her hands firmly on her daughter's shoulders. 'Never let the King, or anyone else, hear you say things like that. You owe him respect and you must not arouse his anger at such a time. Soon all will be well, and Mistress Anne will be forgotten.'

Mary stood up. 'I pray for it. May I go and play with my puppy now?'

Katherine watched her go, her heart breaking.

Anne was determined to play her part in the festivities, even though she could have no official role. While Henry and Katherine kept open house at court, she did the same in her luxurious apartments, and there was a scramble of courtiers, eager to stay in favour, falling over themselves to visit her there. It was clear that Henry was unwilling to flaunt her in front of the cardinals, but Katherine also suspected that Anne did not want to come face to face with her.

'She is too proud to bow the knee to your Grace,' Maria sneered.

'Presumably she agrees with the King that your Grace is not his lawful wife,' Maud said drily.

'Well, she *would*!' Gertrude Blount put in.

'There is more to it than that,' Maud said. 'It seems she is now setting herself up as the champion of reform within the Church.'

'Some say she is a heretic, and that her brother is more Lutheran than Luther himself!' That was Maria, who tended to exaggerate, bless her.

'If that is true, then she is more of a threat to the unity of Christendom than I feared,' Katherine observed. 'In his besotted state, the King might well heed her!'

Her situation was becoming even more intolerable. It hurt to see Anne going about decked in the jewels Henry had showered on her, and she found it almost unbearable to see him caressing the woman openly in public, as if she were already his wife.

With the case looming, Mary had been sent away from court. Katherine could not forget the child's wan little face as they said farewell. Wolsey too was looking wan and haggard, and the suave Campeggio gave little away. Fearing more than ever that she would get no impartial justice from either of them, Katherine lodged a formal appeal in Rome against the authority of the legatine court.

Sometimes she wondered if it would ever sit. She was now convinced that the Pope had ordered Campeggio to drag out matters as long as he could. First Campeggio had been ill; then there had been the drawn-out business of the second dispensation. It was not until Easter that Wolsey smugly informed Katherine that he had sent envoys to Rome to make a search for the Vatican's copy, but they had found no trace of it.

'That does not surprise me, my lord!' she retorted.

'Probably they did not look hard enough!' Maria commented afterwards, and Katherine feared she was right.

Then more envoys had been dispatched to Spain to see the Emperor's copy. This time Wolsey took evident pleasure in informing her that it was clearly a forgery, and that there was no point in producing her copy as evidence in court.

'He would say it was a forgery, even if the Angel Gabriel told him it wasn't!' Maria averred.

Throughout these terrible months of waiting, people talked of nothing but the Great Matter and the coming trial of the King's case. The very machinery of government all but ground to a halt as preparations went ahead for the hearing.

In April, when the court was at Richmond, Henry visited Katherine. 'I want you to choose the best clerks of my realm to act as your counsel and do the best for you,' he said.

She did not tell him that she had no intention of recognising the court. As an obedient wife, she chose Archbishop Warham and John Fisher, Bishop of Rochester. Fisher was staunch in her cause, Warham cautious and ill at ease.

'Remember, madam, *ira principis mors est!*' he kept saying. 'The wrath of the prince is death!'

There was no help to be had from Warham, that was clear. She reminded herself that her counsellors were still her husband's subjects, and if the verdict should go in her favour, the King's anger, and Anne Boleyn's too, might well be visited upon them. She did not expect them to give her disinterested advice. Instead, she continued to pray that the Pope would realise that she could hope for no justice in this English court, and revoke the case to Rome.

The court had moved to Bridewell Palace in readiness for the hearing at the adjacent Black Friars' monastery when Katherine contrived another 'chance' meeting with Mendoza in the gardens. Under cover of admiring the early blooming roses, he murmured that the Emperor had insisted that the Pope revoke the commission granted to Campeggio and Wolsey; but it was thought that Clement was too well disposed towards Henry to agree.

She was just digesting this unpalatable information when Mendoza, that good, loyal man, turned to face her. He seemed to be struggling with himself. At length, he said, 'I must tell you that the Emperor wishes to demonstrate his disapproval of the King's case by not being officially represented in England while it is being heard. So, Highness, it is with the profoundest regret that I must take my leave of you, for I have been recalled to Spain.'

Katherine could have cried. To be deprived of this true and indefatigable friend in her hour of need was a bitter blow. But she remembered her dignity and the courtesy due to Spain's ambassador.

'I am heartily sorry to hear that,' she said. 'I cannot thank you enough for all your kindness to me, and your support. I hope that you will return to England when this sorry business is over, and that we shall meet again in happier times.'

'It is my fervent wish also, Highness,' said Mendoza, with feeling. 'May God preserve you and send you a happy outcome to your troubles. I will pray for you.'

'God go with you,' Katherine said, and extended her hand to be kissed.

It was June, and the day when the King and Queen would be summoned before the legatine court had dawned at long last. Katherine commanded her ladies to attire her in a gorgeous gown of crimson velvet edged with sable, its skirts open at the front to display a kirtle of yellow brocade. From her girdle they hung her gold pomander with its watch dial. On her head they placed a hood lavishly adorned with goldsmiths' work. If she could not look beautiful, she would at least look queenly.

Crowds had massed outside the hall of the Black Friars where the court was to sit, and when Katherine passed along the open gallery that connected Bridewell Palace with the monastery, they shouted their support. 'Good Queen Katherine! How she holds the field! She's afraid of nothing! Victory over your enemies!'

She paused, nodding and smiling, and waved, then went into the monastery.

It was obvious that great thought had been given to preparing the hall, for of course it had never been heard of for an English king to be summoned to appear in a court of law, still less to await the judgement of a subject, and the arrangements made must reflect the importance of the occasion. On the dais at the far end, behind some railings, the legates sat on two chairs upholstered in cloth of gold. Before them was placed a table covered with a Turkey carpet for their papers, of which there were several piles. To the right, below the dais for once, was the King's throne beneath a cloth of estate, and to the left a rich chair awaited the Queen.

As Katherine entered a hush descended on the packed hall, and there was a scuffling and a scraping of chairs as nobles, lawyers, theologians and prelates all leapt to their feet and bowed. Katherine was aware of a hundred eyes watching her speculatively as she walked to her place, four of her ladies following. She was grateful to have the support of a simmering Maria and stout-hearted Maud on this fateful day.

Then Henry arrived. How handsome he still was! She could not help thinking it, even now, when he was attempting to divorce her. Tall, majestic and gorgeously dressed, he dwarfed and eclipsed every man in the room.

As soon as the King was seated, the crier demanded silence and called, 'King Harry of England, come into the court!'

'Here, my lords!' Henry answered in a loud, firm voice, in which could be heard confident anticipation.

The crier than called, 'Katherine, Queen of England, come into the court!'

Katherine sat there, her heart pounding. She would make no answer. Henry gave her a questioning look, to which she remained impassive, and there was a bewildered pause before he turned to the legates.

'My lord cardinals, I am come here because I wish to have my doubts resolved for the discharge of my conscience,' he said. 'All I ask is that you determine whether or not my marriage is lawful. I have, from the beginning, felt a perpetual scruple about it.'

Katherine's resolution to keep quiet flew out of the window. She could not let that pass. 'This is not the time to say so after so long a silence!'

Henry looked at her sorrowfully. 'If I kept silence, it was on account of the great love I had, and still have, for you. Madam, I desire more than anything else that our marriage should be declared valid.'

'And do you think it will be in this court?' she asked him. 'It is no impartial court for me.' She turned to the legates, who were regarding her with some severity. 'I beg you, my lords, to have the case referred to Rome.'

'You are being unreasonable, madam,' Henry objected. 'The Emperor has the Pope in his power. You are loved in this country, and you have your choice of prelates and lawyers. You cannot say that this is no impartial court. Now, let us begin!' He tapped his foot impatiently.

'Katherine, Queen of England, come again into the court!' called the crier.

Gathering her wits and her courage, Katherine decided that the only course left to her was to appeal to Henry's chivalry and his better instincts – and whatever vestiges of his love remained. She would tell the world how it had stood between them. She would stand up for her rights and make sure that that wan look was banished from Mary's face for ever.

She made no reply to the crier, but rose and walked across the crowded courtroom to where Henry sat on his throne. As she fell to her knees at his feet, raising her hands in supplication, indrawn breaths and gasps could be heard in the court.

'Sir,' Katherine said, loud and clear, 'I beseech you, for all the loves that have been between us, and for the love of God, let me have justice and right. Take pity and compassion on me, for I am but a woman and a stranger born out of your dominions. I have here no true friend, and no indifferent counsel. I flee to you as the head of justice within this realm.'

She paused, disconcerted by the fact that Henry was staring straight ahead, clearly uncomfortable, his lips pursed, that threatening flush mounting in his cheeks.

'Alas, sir, how have I offended you?' she asked. 'Or what occasion have you for displeasure, that you intend to put me from you? I take God and all the world to witness that I have been to you a true, humble and obedient wife, ever conformable to your will and pleasure. I have been pleased and contented with all things in which you took delight. I have never grudged you anything, or shown a spark of discontent. I loved all those whom you loved for your sake, whether I had cause or not, and whether they were my friends or enemies.'

Not a flicker of recognition. This was truly terrible. But, having started, she must go on. 'These twenty years and more I have been your true wife, and by me you have had many children, though it has pleased God to call them out of this world, which was not my fault.' She faltered, but whatever it cost her, this had to be said. 'And when you had me at the first, I take God to be my judge, I was a true maid, untouched by any man; and whether it is true or not, I put it to your conscience.'

She looked directly at Henry's face as she spoke, willing him to remember that first night of sweet loving, but apart from a small twitch of his mouth, he seemed immovable. It was plain to her that he was not going to make any answer. All the same, she must finish what she had to say.

'If there is any just cause under the law that you can allege against me, to put me from you, I am content to depart, to my shame and dishonour. But if there is none, I must beseech you, let me remain in my royal estate and receive justice at your princely hands. Many learned men have said that the marriage between you and me is good and lawful. But it is a wonder to hear what accusations are invented against me, who never intended aught but honesty! And now I must submit to the judgement of this new court, in which you may do me much wrong. But you must understand that your subjects cannot be indifferent counsellors, for they dare not, for your displeasure, disobey your will. Therefore, most humbly do I beg of you, for the love of God, to spare me the extremity of this court. And if you will not, I commit my cause to God.'

Still Henry would not look at her. He said not a word. She rose to her feet, curtseyed low to him, then found that she was trembling so much that her legs would not carry her. Hurriedly she beckoned to Griffin Richards, her receiver-general, and leaned gratefully on his arm.

'Take me out of this place,' she whispered, and he escorted her through the silent, watching hall to the great doors. She heard Henry command the crier to call her back.

'Pay no heed,' she said to Griffin Richards. 'It is no indifferent court to me, therefore I will not stay.'

When she emerged outside the Black Friars' monastery she was greeted by crowds of Londoners, most of them women, who shouted their encouragement. She nodded weakly and smiled. 'Remember me in your prayers, good people,' she cried, her voice barely steady. Then she mounted the stairs to the gallery and returned to a well-nigh deserted Bridewell Palace.

That evening, as she was trying to calm her tumultuous thoughts, Bishop Fisher came to see her, his face grave.

'Madam, you think you have no impartial counsel, but I assure you that is not the case. I would not have advised making that appeal to the King, and it might have gone better for you if you had acknowledged the court and then given evidence, though I understand your concerns.'

Katherine nodded, grateful for his honesty. 'What happened after I left?' she asked. 'Pray sit down and tell me.'

'The King spoke,' Fisher related, easing his ageing bones into the proffered chair. 'He said you had always been as true, as obedient and as conformable a wife as he could desire. He said he had been fortunate to be blessed with such a queen, and took God to witness that no fault in your Grace had moved him. He spoke of how your sons had died soon after they were born, and called it a punishment of God. He is adamant that his concern is chiefly for the succession. He insisted he had not brought these proceedings for any carnal desire or dislike of your person.'

That was a lie, Katherine thought. It is all lies. He is mad to marry

Anne Boleyn. That is why he is turning the world upside down and I am suffering and Mary's future is hanging in the balance.

'He ended,' the Bishop concluded, 'by saying that he would be well content if your marriage was found to stand within God's laws.'

'There is little chance of that in this court.'

Fisher sighed, his angular, ascetic face creased with sadness. 'I regret to say that I agree with your Grace. This afternoon the King produced a parchment on which was set forth the case he had to answer, and he said that every bishop in England had set his hand and seal to it. Well, I denied it!' He could not hide his outrage. 'I told him I had never signed or sealed such a document. But there it was, my seal, and my signature, forged, and Archbishop Warham had the temerity to affirm that both were mine. The King said it did not matter, as I was but one man. Believe me, madam, they will stop at nothing to have their way.'

'I know it,' Katherine said, sinking into despondency.

Fisher rose. 'They have me to contend with!' he snorted, his eyes alive with zeal. And he blessed her and signed her forehead with the cross – and then, to her surprise, he patted her shoulder.

The court sat again on many successive days. Katherine maintained her resolve not to attend, and Bishop Fisher kept her up to date with developments. It seemed that most of the time was taken up with counsel for either side arguing about whether her first marriage had been consummated.

One evening Fisher stayed for supper in her chamber. 'The King's lawyers are saying that your marriage was invalid from the beginning because you had carnal knowledge of Prince Arthur,' he told her, as soon as the servitors had withdrawn.

'That is not true!' Katherine protested, then remembered her manners and passed the dish of salad. 'How many times do I have to say it?'

'Madam, I told them it was very doubtful,' Fisher said, helping himself to just two leaves of lettuce. 'Warham is little help – he might as well be representing the King – and he is very argumentative! That young priest Ridley who's assisting me thinks it disgusting that your private life is coming under scrutiny in open court.'

'Amen to that,' Katherine said fervently, 'although, given the nature of the case, I have no choice but to endure it. At least I do not have to listen to it.'

'What irritates me most,' Fisher said, 'is the King's righteous conviction that, if he takes another wife, Heaven will vouchsafe him a son. I felt bound to ask him, "*Who* has promised you a prince?"'

'No doubt Mistress Anne has.'

'Then it remains to be seen whether Heaven complies!' And the Bishop's ascetic face creased into what, with him, passed for a grin.

One morning in late June Katherine was surprised to receive a visit from Henry, who appeared agitated and peevish. But he was courteous enough, and commented approvingly on her black damask gown with its cloth-of-silver sleeves.

'I am glad to see you so royally attired, Kate, as I want you to accompany me to the Black Friars'. The legates are no nearer a conclusion than when they first sat, and we both want this case resolved.' He held out his hand. 'Will you come?'

'If I must,' she said, allowing him to lead her away.

Again they sat in their chairs of estate, while Henry addressed the cardinals. 'The Queen and I are weary of waiting for a verdict,' he told them. 'We beseech you to reach a final end. For my part, I am so troubled in spirits that I cannot attend to anything for the profit of my realm and my people.'

Katherine said nothing, but at a nod from her Fisher stood up and declared that she would abide by her appeal to Rome. Henry glared at her, but held his peace until they had reached the privacy of her apartments.

'Appealing to Rome will just prolong the whole damned business,' he snarled. 'What are you thinking of, Kate? Why do you have to be so difficult?'

'Why do *you* have to question a perfectly good marriage?' she flung back.

'Not that again!' Henry almost shouted, and stormed out in a temper.

'The King has clearly gone to great lengths to seek out witnesses to your wedding night with Prince Arthur,' Fisher told Katherine when next he came to see her. 'Nineteen of them gave evidence today. I will not repeat their testimony, as it would be deeply embarrassing to your Grace and all right-thinking people; and anyway, none of it was conclusive, and much was hearsay. The sight of elderly lords queuing up to attest that they were potent at Prince Arthur's age was most distasteful, and I think the legates were of that opinion too. Of course, several of these witnesses were of the Boleyn faction. One was Mistress Anne's brother, who wasn't even born at the time of your first marriage, and I fear that others were bribed. You will be glad to hear that young Ridley made it clear that your Grace had often said that your first marriage had not been consummated. I, of course, upheld that.'

'You have ever been a staunch friend to me, my good Bishop,' Katherine said. 'Tell me truly, do you think we stand a chance of winning this case?'

'I think our insistence that the marriage was lawful carries a lot of weight with many. Even Cardinal Campeggio seems to approve.'

'Then why does he not pronounce sentence? It is all taking so long.'

'He must hear all the evidence – such as it is. I think the delays are trying the King's patience to the limit too. I was told that he summoned Wolsey to Bridewell Palace and castigated him for over four hours. Many heard the shouting, and I was waiting at Blackfriars Stairs for my barge when the Cardinal emerged, making for his. He looked sick, and the Bishop of Carlisle, who was also at the jetty, tried to make pleasantries, and observed that it was a hot day. The Cardinal agreed, and said that, if the Bishop had been as well chafed as he had been, he would say it was very hot. I never thought to feel sorry for him, but I believe he is doing his utmost best for the King against impossible odds.'

'He is in a difficult position,' Katherine conceded.

Fisher stood up. 'Well, madam, I must take my leave and prepare my papers for tomorrow. I pray you, try not to worry. We are doing better than I had hoped.'

Katherine summoned her ladies and they all got out their embroidery frames and settled down to work, chatting as they did so. She was relieved to have a quiet evening with simple diversions, and to be afforded some space in which to think of more pleasant things than the weighty proceedings that were blighting her life.

It was less than an hour later when an usher came to say that Wolsey and Campeggio were waiting upon the Queen in the antechamber. Katherine rose, bidding her ladies to attend her, and went out to greet her visitors.

'Welcome, my lords. You see my employment.' She pulled off a skein of white silk that was hanging around her neck. 'In this way I pass the time with my maids.'

'Madam, may we speak to you in private?' Wolsey asked. He looked old and ill, and unaccustomedly flustered.

'My lord, if you have anything to say, speak it openly before these ladies, for I fear nothing that you can say or allege against me, and would prefer that all the world should both see and hear it.'

'Madam,' Wolsey said, with evident reluctance, 'we have come on the King's command to know what you are disposed to do in this matter between the King and yourself, and to offer our opinions and our counsel.'

Katherine turned to Campeggio. 'Will any Englishman counsel or befriend me against the King's pleasure?' she asked, wishing that Fisher was here to speak for her. 'Alas, my lords, I am a poor woman, lacking sufficient wit and understanding to answer such wise men as you in so weighty a matter.' She paused, seeing Wolsey visibly sag, as if he were on the verge of collapse, and took pity on him. 'Come, we will go into my privy chamber,' she said, and took him by the hand, leading the way, Campeggio and her women following.

'I thank you for your kindness, madam,' he said, sinking heavily into the chair she indicated. 'It has been a somewhat trying day.' He mopped his brow. 'It is the King's wish that you surrender this whole matter into his hands. He fears that, if the case goes against you, some judicial condemnation might follow, and then shame and slander might accrue to you. His Grace wishes to avoid all occasion for that. He asks you, as his wife, to remit your cause to him.'

435

'But he is trying to prove that I am not his wife,' Katherine protested. 'He cannot have it both ways. As for this judicial condemnation with which you threaten me, there is no crime with which anyone can charge me.'

'Perhaps I should have said censure, rather than condemnation. If the case goes against you, and you persist in maintaining an adulterous marriage, we, the legates, and perhaps even his Holiness, may feel that some admonishment is in order . . .'

Katherine snapped. 'God knows, and you know, that my marriage is not adulterous! I am the King's true wife, and I will remain so until my dying day!'

There was a pause as the cardinals looked at each other in despair.

'Madam, we will report your answer to the King,' Wolsey said, rising creakily to his feet, and with that they took their leave.

It was now the third week of a hot, sultry July. Katherine longed to leave London and go into the country, where the air was fresher and there was no stink from the river or the overcrowded streets – and no threat of plague. It seemed that the court hearings would never end. But now, hours before she expected him, here was the faithful Bishop Fisher, his gaunt features transformed.

'A victory, madam, a victory!'

'The court has declared for me?' Katherine cried, hardly able to believe it.

'No, madam – but your plea has been answered: the case has been revoked to Rome. His Holiness himself will pass judgement.'

It was not quite what she had hoped for – but it augured well for her, and for Mary, and her heart filled with thankfulness.

'Tell me what happened,' she said.

'There were strong signs that Cardinal Campeggio was about to pass sentence, and the King came into the court with the Duke of Suffolk, hoping to hear it. But Campeggio stood up and said he would give no hasty judgement until he had discussed the proceedings with the Pope, for the truth was hard to determine. And then he adjourned the court, saying he was referring the case back to Rome. Well, madam, I wish you had been there. The King got up and walked out with a face like thunder, and then uproar broke out in the court. The Duke of Suffolk swore by the Mass that the old saying was true, that it was never merry in England while we had cardinals among us. And Wolsey reminded Suffolk that if he, a simple cardinal, had not been there to rescue him when he married the King's sister, he would have had no head on his shoulders and no tongue to spite him.'

'Wolsey must be in a bad way,' Katherine said. 'This is a grave defeat for him, and he stands to forfeit the King's pleasure because of it.' Again, she felt a twinge of pity for her old enemy.

'He looked like a man stunned,' Fisher told her. 'While all this rumpus was going on, the legates just sat there looking at one other, utterly astonished.'

'Campeggio has nothing to fear, for he can go back to Rome,' Katherine said, 'but Wolsey must stay and bear the brunt of the King's anger.'

'There is no doubt that the King has taken this disappointment very displeasantly, and no wonder. The Papal court will not sit until October, and its proceedings progress slowly, so it might now be a matter of months, if not years, before the Pope reaches a decision. Do not look alarmed, madam, for his Holiness is now friends with the Emperor, and judgement will probably be given in your favour.'

There was a sudden commotion outside, raised voices, and then the door was flung open and there stood Henry.

'Out, Bishop!' he barked at Fisher, who frowned, made his bow and left. Henry slammed the door behind him.

'This is your doing,' he said to Katherine. 'You made those appeals to Rome, and now judgement is further delayed! Do you think my royal dignity will admit of my being summoned to appear at the Papal court? By God, my nobles and subjects would never allow it! I tell you, madam, that if I go to Rome, it will be at the head of a great army, and not as a supplicant for justice!'

'At least it would be impartial justice!' Katherine retorted.

'What, with the Pope hand in glove with the Emperor, and Charles and Francis about to sign a peace treaty? Do you realise that will leave me isolated? What impartial justice will there be for me?'

'The Pope will do what is right, Henry.'

'The Pope is a man like any other, and fallible, as was his predecessor in granting that dispensation.'

She was shocked. 'That is heresy! You are questioning the authority of the Holy See, an authority that was entrusted to it by Our Lord Himself!'

'Kate, the Holy See is corrupt. Everyone knows that. Money talks in the Vatican, and might too. And I see plainly that money must have changed hands when Pope Julius granted that dispensation back in 1503. He had not the authority to do so. Scripture is clear on that.'

'Why must you constantly misinterpret Scripture?' she cried.

'Hold your peace, woman!' Henry was red with fury. 'I will argue with you no more, as you refuse to see reason. We're leaving tomorrow for Greenwich, and then I'm taking Anne on progress. We'll be staying away for the hunting season. You, madam, will take yourself elsewhere!'

Chapter 26

1529–1530

For all his anger, Henry eventually relented and summoned Katherine to join the progress at Woodstock. She suspected that this was less on account of any consideration for her than the angry reaction of his subjects when they saw him parading his mistress in his wife's place.

She did not want to go to Woodstock, the scene of happier days; it was hateful to her to see Henry with Anne, and she knew they would both be hostile towards her. She would far have preferred to have visited Mary, whom she longed to see. But she owed Henry obedience as his wife, so she gave orders to pack and depart. As her small procession made its way along late-summer lanes drowsy with sunshine, she reflected that she was luckier than Wolsey, for she had heard that the Cardinal was out of favour and had retired to his Manor of the More in Hertfordshire. It was widely held that the legatine court's failure to declare for the King was Wolsey's fault.

Henry's welcome at Woodstock was cool. There was about him that air of suppressed anger that Katherine had noticed increasingly in recent months. Anne Boleyn mostly avoided her, but when they did come face to face, Anne's dark eyes flashed with unmistakable fury. Katherine was only grateful that Mary was not at court and spared the spectacle of the woman's malice.

The atmosphere became even more charged when the Pope's summons citing Henry to appear at the Papal court was served on him, prompting another outburst of fury. Katherine trembled to witness it, fearing that the calling of the case to Rome would alienate Henry still further from the Holy See. She was also brooding over the news that the King had summoned Parliament to meet in November. What did he intend now? Maria, candid as ever, was of the opinion that he would bring about the divorce on his own authority. Katherine had replied that he would never dare. But Henry was in a strange, defiant mood these days; who knew what he might do next?

It was under this lowering cloud of discontent that, in September, on the feast of the Nativity of the Virgin Mary, they arrived at the old royal hunting lodge at Grafton Regis. Hard on the heels of the court rode Cardinal Campeggio, come to take formal leave of the King before returning to Rome. Katherine saw him arrive from her window, which overlooked the courtyard. Wolsey was with him – she had not expected that – but of course, his fellow legate must be there for courtesy's sake.

The two men, both of them grey-haired and portly, alighted from their horses at the gates, and household officers hastened to conduct Campeggio to the rooms that had been made ready for him. But no one came for Wolsey, and he was left standing at a loss in the middle of the courtyard. He had aged so much in these past months and become an old man, shrunken and uncertain, all his hauteur gone. He looked so pathetic that Katherine was moved by his plight, and found herself wishing that someone would come to his rescue. Then she saw Sir Henry Norris, the King's Groom of the Stool and great friend, approaching, his handsome face full of apology. The two men spoke, and Norris led Wolsey away in the direction of his own lodging.

Later that afternoon Katherine took her place beside Henry in the refurbished medieval hall where he was to receive the cardinals. The room was packed, and although Mistress Anne was not present, her faction was there in force. The Dukes of Norfolk and Suffolk, her brother, George, and a horde of Boleyn connections were all prowling like predators waiting for the kill, watching the King closely and enjoying Wolsey's discomfiture as the two cardinals approached and fell to their knees.

But Henry confounded them.

'My Lord Cardinal!' he cried. 'You are most welcome!' And he actually stepped down from the dais and helped Wolsey up, then led him by the hand to a window embrasure where he spoke with him privately. Katherine, making polite conversation with Campeggio, was aware of the irate faces of the Boleyn faction, and tried not to smile. Then she heard Henry say to Wolsey, quite genially, 'Go to your dinner, and after dinner I will talk with you again.' Whereupon Norfolk and George Boleyn immediately left the room, no doubt to report back to Mistress Anne.

Katherine dined alone, with just the Otwell sisters in attendance, acting as servers, and looking grand and pleased with themselves in the new gowns of tawny damask lined with velvet that she had ordered for all her chamberers. Henry, she guessed, was with Anne. But when she walked in the gardens late that evening, savouring the sweet-scented night air and the solitude, she looked up and saw Henry and Wolsey silhouetted in a window, deep in conversation. She wondered, with some trepidation, what this portended. Was the Cardinal back in favour? If so, he would no doubt be so grateful that he would redouble his efforts to get Henry what he wanted. And Wolsey was a clever man . . .

The next morning Wolsey sat in council with the King, which gave rise to much angry muttering among Anne's supporters. The atmosphere was icy. But there was Anne Boleyn, apparently blithely unconcerned, giving strident orders for a picnic to be prepared, to be taken in the open air before the afternoon's hunt. Henry duly left with her, having bidden a warm farewell to Wolsey in front of everyone.

'I will be back before you depart for London,' he said.

But he wasn't. The hour when he had said he would return came and went. The cardinals waited as long as they dared to leave Grafton before night fell and the roads became dangerous. Katherine did her best to entertain them, aware that Wolsey was growing increasingly anxious. She watched him droop with disappointment, and at length rise reluctantly, an old, defeated man once more, to take his leave of her.

'I had hoped to see the King before I left,' he said.

'I am sure your Eminence will see him soon,' Katherine replied, with more assurance than she felt.

'No, madam,' he said. 'The night crow has got at him. She seeks my ruin. He will not send for me again.'

Katherine could find no words to answer that. She knew that Wolsey was right.

It was several hours before the hunting party returned. Mistress Anne was in an especially gay mood, flashing her dark eyes at Henry, who was gazing at her with hungry adoration. There was about the woman an air of triumph.

Katherine suppressed her distaste.

'The cardinals left hours ago,' she said. 'They had hoped to see your Grace, and were sorry that they could delay no longer.'

'I am glad to see the back of them both,' Henry said.

Katherine had not been informed that the Emperor was sending a new ambassador to England, so she was delighted when Eustache Chapuys, a black-gowned man in his late thirties, was presented to her at Grafton. For months she had felt the lack of a stout supporter such as Mendoza had been, and when she met the dark-haired, sober-faced Savoyard lawyer and cleric with the large kind eyes and prominent nose, whom Charles had sent to represent her interests and his own, she knew within a few minutes of their conversation that she had found another champion.

'His Imperial Majesty would like to do so much more for your Highness,' Chapuys told her, 'but the Turks are at the gates of Vienna, and he must needs deploy all his forces to push them back. However, we are confident that the Pope will give a ruling very soon, and in the meantime, if your Highness has any concerns, you may rely on me to address them.' He spoke with vigour and assurance.

'I could never consent to the use of armed force against the King my husband,' Katherine said, touched by the zeal of the new ambassador, but alarmed at the implications of what he had said.

'Highness, rest assured, my master hopes it will never come to that, and has asked me to use gentleness and friendship to bring about a reconciliation between your Grace and the King.'

'Alas, I fear the King will not listen. Cardinal Campeggio tried to do that, and failed.'

'There is no harm in trying again, Highness.' Chapuys smiled. 'I hear that my predecessor found it difficult to speak privately with you.'

'The Cardinal set his spies to watch on me, but they are gone now.'

Chapuys lowered his voice. 'The word is, Highness, that the Cardinal is finished. The Lady – you know to whom I refer – would have it that way, and it is clear that she rules all.'

Katherine was impressed at his speedy and astute summing-up of the situation. 'She is all-powerful here, and I can have no peace until my case is decided at Rome.'

'I am confident that the Emperor will ensure a favourable outcome, and soon.'

'God let it be soon,' Katherine said. 'I have been wondering if his Holiness has determined to delay judgement indefinitely in the hope that the problem will resolve itself.'

'Judging by what I have seen of the King's affection for the Lady, I regret to say that I do not think it will. But rest easy, Highness – an end to your troubles is in sight.'

Katherine was not surprised to hear that Wolsey had been stripped of his office of Lord Chancellor, or that, for accepting the office of Papal legate back in 1518, he had been deemed guilty of introducing an illegal foreign authority into England. For this, his lands and goods were declared forfeit, and he was ordered to retire to his house at Esher. *How are the mighty fallen*, she thought, but there was no sense of triumph in her. Instead she could feel only sympathy for the ageing man who had done his best to serve his King and failed.

Henry gleefully appropriated York Place, Wolsey's London house.

'He is having it done up for *her*,' Maria sniffed. 'It is to be renamed Whitehall.'

'I imagine she is elated about that, for it lacks a queen's lodging, and for a long time she has resented having to give me precedence,' Katherine said. 'Well, I shall be glad not to be there to watch her holding court as if she had usurped my place already.'

When the court was at Greenwich that autumn, Chapuys came to see Katherine, looking worried. She dismissed her ladies, anxious about what he might say, and gestured for him to sit with her by the fire.

'Highness, when Parliament sits next month, I fear that something may be brewed there against you.'

'I fear it too,' Katherine said. You never knew with Henry these days. One day he was like his old self, the next hostile and cruel. He was a man possessed – and a thwarted man possessed at that. She believed he would stop at nothing to have Anne, and she supposed she should not be surprised that bending Parliament to his will would be his next move.

Elizabeth Stafford, Duchess of Norfolk, had friends in high places, and had warned Katherine that Henry had been using his persuasions on several lords known to be waverers.

'My husband has played his cards so well that he is likely to get a majority of votes in his favour,' Katherine told Chapuys. 'He may be tempted to obtain by this means what he has not been able to get in any other way.'

'His Majesty has banished the one man who could help him.'

'Poor Wolsey, I pity him,' she replied. 'I pray the King now leaves him in peace.'

'That is unlikely, Highness, if the Lady's party has anything to do with it. But I have better news to impart. I've just heard that the King has chosen Sir Thomas More to replace Wolsey as chancellor. He is an upright and learned man, and a good servant of your Highness.'

Katherine's heart leapt. There could be no better man to replace Wolsey. Surely More would exert a restraining influence on Henry, who utterly revered him.

'Now that *is* good news!' she declared.

After Chapuys had gone she sent for More at once. As he was ushered into her apartments, she rose from her chair to welcome him.

'I hear that you are to be congratulated, Sir Thomas,' she said, smiling. 'I cannot tell you how delighted I am to learn of your advancement.'

'It is a great honour, of which I am unworthy,' he said, his sensitive face troubled. 'And it is a bait to catch a quarry, I fear, for the King wants my support in his Great Matter. Having little skill in spiritual law, I have never meddled in the divorce, yet His Grace has for some time been earnestly persuading me to agree with him on the matter. Alas, I cannot do so, even now, and that saddens us both. I fear he is disappointed in me.'

Of course Henry was disappointed. More had a great reputation throughout Christendom, none better, and his scholarship and his wisdom were universally respected; thus his support would be of inestimable value.

'Did he press you?' she asked.

'No, madam. He told me he does not wish me to do or say anything against my conscience; he said I must first look to God, and after God to him. But his mood may change, as it often does these days. So you can see why I am reluctant to accept the chancellorship. It will be no easy office. And my lord of Norfolk, who is a friend of mine, is now made Lord President of the Council, but he is uncle to Mistress Anne, and she is above all. Her brother boasts that the lords have no influence except what it pleases her to allow them.'

'This is nothing new,' Katherine said. 'Her pride will be her undoing in the end. The King will come to resent her interference.'

More shook his head.

'Alas, I fear that day is a long way off. You will have heard that the Boleyns have a new chaplain?'

'Why should I have heard that?'

'Because it may be significant. The man is called Thomas Cranmer. The King's secretary, Dr Gardiner, met him when he lodged at Waltham Abbey after returning from Rome last month.'

'What was he doing in Rome?' Katherine asked sharply.

'He was there on the King's business, but I gather that his Holiness would make no concessions. What worries me more is the influence of this Dr Cranmer, who is a dangerous radical. He gave it as his opinion that the King's case should be judged by learned doctors in the universities of Europe, and not by the Pope. When the King heard of this from Gardiner, he summoned Dr Cranmer to see him, and the man is now writing a treatise on his views. Mistress Anne's faction, needless to say, is fawning over him, and her father has made him his chaplain.'

Katherine frowned. 'I do not like this,' she said. 'It smacks of heresy. Even if all the universities pronounce in my husband's favour, only the Pope can dissolve our marriage. But what if the King acts without the Pope's sanction? Where would I stand in the eyes of the Church, and Mary?'

More shook his head. 'In faith, your Grace, I cannot say. I fear that the whole of Christendom will be turned upside down. You will recall what I said to you many years ago – that if the lion knew his strength, it would be hard to rule him. With the Cardinal gone, the King is now intent on becoming absolute ruler in his realm.'

Katherine could not but be aware that Henry and Anne had moved into Whitehall Palace. Her ladies were scandalised by it.

'She is attended like a queen, she goes about decked like a queen, and she dispenses patronage like a queen!' Elizabeth Stafford fumed, turning up her aristocratic nose. 'It is your Grace who should be there beside him, not abandoned here at Greenwich!'

Katherine sighed. What could she do about it?

'Mistress Anne pretends to be devout!' Maria sneered. 'They say she makes a big show of reading St Paul's letters, but she makes no secret of the fact that she hates all priests, and she has no love for the Pope.'

'She is a heretic, and may lead the King into sin if he is not careful,' Katherine said, her heart bleeding for the man who had once defended the Holy See against such attacks.

'I heard that she complains about the long delay in settling her future, with no end to it in sight,' Elizabeth Stafford related.

'I might say the same myself,' Katherine observed wryly, 'although it seems strange to be in agreement with Mistress Anne.'

'But, madam,' Elizabeth answered, 'you bear it in patience. She is become vindictive. You should be wary of her.'

'She is insecure,' the Marchioness of Dorset observed, 'and she knows that all she has is the King's love. Unlike you, madam, she lacks powerful friends abroad. And she is developing a great talent for making enemies!'

If only Henry were not so blind, Katherine thought.

*

Katherine sat close to the fire, embellishing the neck of one of Henry's shirts with the blackwork embroidery for which she had become famous. It pleased her to do the ordinary domestics tasks for him, just as she had always done: it gave an illusion of normality.

After opening Parliament he had returned with Anne to Greenwich, and seemed to be at pains to convince everyone that he and Katherine were still on good terms. She was summoned to accompany him whenever he appeared in public, and both of them took care to observe not only the courtesies but to put on a display of togetherness. It was exhausting to maintain a mask of calm dignity while her emotions were in turmoil. To be so close to Henry, knowing that he wished her elsewhere, was torture.

'Your forbearance is more than human!' Maria told her, scowling at the shirt. 'This pretence of the King's is all a means to an end, to convince the Pope – and the world – that he is sincere in his love for you.'

Katherine winced. Sometimes Maria could be too outspoken. But she spoke truth, for in private Henry never came near her. She was surprised therefore when, on a stormy November night, he joined her for dinner in her chamber.

She welcomed him with a hopeful smile, and hastened to give him the shirt she had just finished, but although he thanked her it was clear from his face that this was not just a courtesy visit. Almost as soon as the venison had been served and the attendants had withdrawn, he was telling her how disillusioned he was with the Holy See.

'I've been abandoned by the Church of Rome,' he said plaintively. 'It's all political, of course. The Vatican is a mire of corruption. And you don't help, Kate. You show no understanding of my frustrations.'

Suddenly Katherine could not eat. 'I have tried all along to understand why you are doing this but I still cannot agree with you,' she said, laying down her knife.

Henry glared at her. 'You don't try hard enough!' he snarled. 'I need an heir, and no one takes account of that. Clement's in Charles's pocket, and you won't set me free.'

'Even if our marriage were invalid, I would not see you demean yourself by marrying a woman who is the scandal of Christendom!' Katherine said quietly. 'You never think, do you, of what that would do to Mary? But I do! God knows, I have suffered the pangs of purgatory on earth because of this Great Matter, and I feel very badly treated, especially when I am deprived of my child's company because I dare not bring her to court for fear of what she might witness – and I am lonely when you don't visit me in private.'

Henry banged down his goblet on the table. 'You have no cause to complain of bad treatment, Kate, for you are still queen and mistress in your own household, and can do what you please. Don't accuse me of not thinking of Mary – I too think her best away from court at this time. And I have not visited you because I've been much engaged with business. The Cardinal left affairs in great confusion. And I am not your legitimate husband. I have been assured of this by many learned doctors.'

'Doctors!' Katherine cried, her temper rising. 'You know yourself, without the help of any doctors, that you are my husband and that your case has no foundation. I care not a straw for your doctors!'

Henry flushed. His eyes glittered malevolently. 'I warn you, madam, that I intend to canvas the universities for their opinion on my case, and if they decide for me, I will not fail to have their opinions forwarded to Rome. Then, should the Pope not declare our marriage null and void, I will denounce him as a heretic and marry whom I please!'

She was horrified to hear him talk like that, and prayed inwardly that it was all bluster.

'You know what the opinions of the universities are worth against the authority of Rome,' she told him, 'and you know too that the best lawyers in England have spoken on my side. Let me collect opinions as you are doing, and for every doctor or lawyer of yours, I will find a thousand to hold our marriage good.'

Henry stood up, puce in the face. 'I will not stay to listen to your malice,' he growled. 'I am going to seek more congenial company.' And he stamped out, slamming the door behind him. The shirt, which she had spent hours lovingly embroidering, lay forgotten on the floor.

Katherine was in great grief. The foundations of her world seemed to be crumbling. Henry's threat had struck a chill into her very soul, and she feared not only for his spiritual well-being, but for the future of Christendom itself, for what might ensue when kings like Henry began questioning the authority of the Pope?

She was brooding miserably on this when Chapuys sought an audience.

'Is there word from Rome?' she asked, but the look on his face told her there wasn't.

'The King has created the Lady's father Earl of Wiltshire,' he said, 'and now all must defer to her as the Lady Anne Boleyn, while her brother is to be known as Lord Rochford.'

Henry is preparing her for queenship, Katherine thought. It is less demeaning to marry the daughter of an earl than the daughter of a knight. May God help us.

She invited Chapuys to be seated.

'The King held a banquet at Whitehall to celebrate, and the Lady sat by his side, in the Queen's throne,' he related. 'I am sorry to be the bearer of such news, but, madam, it was like a wedding banquet. There was dancing and carousing, and it seemed as if nothing were wanting but the priest to give away the nuptial ring and pronounce the blessing.'

'I do not want to hear it,' Katherine said, sickened.

Chapuys spread his hands helplessly. 'It cannot be ignored, madam. Such is the blind passion of the King that I fear that, one of these days, some disorderly act will take place.'

'That is my fear too,' Katherine admitted. 'I think it is no longer a case of what the King might do, but what he will do.'

It was Christmas Eve. Katherine was watching with Mary and Henry as, accompanied by much mirth and good cheer, the Yule log was hauled into the great hall and placed on the hearth, where it would burn throughout the festive season. But Henry seemed to take no pleasure in it. He had been in a prickly mood all evening, no doubt because his sweetheart was absent at Hever, and still there had been no word from Rome. Katherine saw Mary watching her father, saw the incomprehension in the troubled little face. Her constant prayer was that Clement would speak soon, not only for her own sake, and Mary's, but because it might be the one thing that would deflect Henry from doing anything rash.

Towards the end of the evening, after Mary had gone to bed, hippocras and marchpane comfits were served to the King and Queen, and Katherine accepted them with a smile.

'I don't know what you've got to look happy about,' Henry muttered. 'You should be considering your future.' His voice was blurred; he was slightly drunk.

'I consider it constantly,' she told him.

'Then mind this,' he said. 'If the Pope pronounces sentence against me, I will not heed it.'

'Sir!' Katherine hissed. 'I cannot believe I am hearing this. I beg you to think on what you are saying, and consider the safety of your soul.'

'Oh, I know what I am saying, madam,' Henry answered, his tone menacing. 'I would have you know that I prize and value the Church of England as much as people across the Channel prize the Holy See, and if I have to, I will sever it from Rome.'

Katherine summoned her courage. 'Sir, that would be a thing repugnant to all the faithful, and I cannot believe that it is what you really intend.' It was the drink talking, it must be.

'And do you not believe that this long silence from the Pope is proof that my case is being deliberately shelved? That being so, why should I not take matters into my own hands?'

'I beg of you to wait!' she urged, trying to keep her voice low, for people were staring at them.

'I cannot and will not wait any longer,' Henry insisted.

'Does that mean that you have consummated your relationship with the Lady Anne?' She was surprised at her own boldness, but the question had to be asked.

Henry rounded on her. 'No! Would that I had!'

450

'The King says she is not his mistress,' Katherine told Chapuys two days later when he sought an urgent audience with her. 'I do not know if I believe it.'

'Many say that she is,' he answered, 'although it makes no difference, save to confirm everyone's low opinion of her. But I came to tell your Grace that I have discovered something that may help your case. My spies tell me that the King once meddled with her sister.'

'Mary Carey? Never!' She could not credit it.

'Apparently it is true. Gossip has it that one of her children is the King's.'

'My good friend, I would not heed the gossips. They will tell you anything, and they enjoy making mischief.'

'I had this from at least two reliable sources, madam. Concerned people have spoken quite openly of it. Think on its significance, for had the King listened to his conscience, as he asserts, there would be a greater affinity in his intended marriage than in yours. Your Grace could expose him as a hypocrite.'

Katherine sighed. 'I would have known, I'm sure. I was aware that Mary Carey had a reputation, but I cannot believe there was anything between them. And if your informants are wrong, I would make a great fool of myself in Rome by alleging this impediment.'

'Let me find you proofs, Highness.'

She smiled sadly. 'The fact that you are offering to do so confirms my suspicion that your information is flawed. No, Messire Chapuys, do not take this further. I command it. I still live in hope that my husband will eventually come back to his senses.'

There was compassion in Chapuys's eyes as he regarded her. She knew he did not believe it. But he did not know Henry as she did. Remove Anne Boleyn's influence, and the King would be a different man.

It was spring again. As Katherine rode with Henry to Windsor, the trees were glorious with blossom and lambs gambolled in the fields – but her heart was heavy, for Henry had ordered Mary to remain at

Beaulieu, and still the Pope had not spoken. She thought she would go mad with frustration. She had sent letter after letter to Rome, beseeching Pope Clement to pass sentence soon, but there was never a reply. She had, though, been cheered by the demonstrations of love that the common people hereabouts had made when she passed among them. Henry had been plainly furious to hear them calling out their support for her, and had reined in his horse beside her litter and abruptly ordered her to stop nodding and waving at them.

Now here he was again, angrily invading the peace of her chamber where she was composing a new letter to Dr Ortiz, whom the Emperor had recently appointed to represent her interests in Rome.

'Do you know what the common people are saying? They are spreading rumours that I have separated you from Mary, out of spite. This is your fault, madam – you have long encouraged them to think ill of me. Well, I will put paid to this nonsense. We'll have Mary brought here to give the lie to it.'

That at least was good news, but Katherine knew that Henry was summoning Mary from Beaulieu, where she had been living since Christmas, only because he was concerned about his popularity. Yet she was overjoyed to see her daughter – it had been too long since they had been together.

'My dear child!' Katherine cried, embracing Mary as she arrived with her ladies and servants in a flurry of activity the next day. 'Let me look at you!'

Mary was growing up fast. Every time Katherine saw her there had been a change. The Princess was fourteen now, still small and slight, but showing the first curves of womanhood. She retained her childish prettiness, and her manner was as sweet and charming as ever. Yet there was that wariness, that nervous reserve about her that troubled Katherine.

Waiting behind Mary was Margaret Pole. Katherine raised her from her curtsey and kissed her warmly, delighted to be reunited with her old friend. 'We must talk later,' she said. 'I shall look forward to it.'

She spent the rest of that day with Mary, asking her about her lessons, her daily life and her devotions. She could not have been more pleased with the child's answers, but then Mary said, 'My lady mother, I have been worried about you.'

Katherine was taken back.

'There is no need to worry about me,' she said, 'I am very well.'

'But my father's Grace is still trying to put you away.' There was such a pitiful look of distress on the child's face that Katherine's heart turned over.

'We are both waiting for the Pope to pronounce sentence on our marriage,' she said carefully. 'I am sure he will do so soon. There is nothing to worry about. Your father and I are as perfect friends as ever.' If only it were all true!

'But he is always with the Lady Anne.' Mary seemed to be on the verge of tears.

Katherine made a supreme effort. 'He will only marry her if he is not allowed to return to me, which is what he wants, of course. And that is unlikely to happen, so please do not fret about it. Now, let me hear how you play on the virginals!'

Mary stared at her with eyes that looked old before their time, eyes that said she was a fool if she really believed what she was saying. But the girl was dutiful; she said nothing.

As Mary was playing – and playing beautifully – Henry came in. Immediately she curtseyed gracefully, then knelt for his blessing. He swept her up into his arms.

'How does my dear child?' he asked, kissing the wary look away.

'I am well, sir. I trust that your Grace is too.'

'That was an excellent performance,' he complimented her. 'I could hear it as I approached.' Henry sat down next to Katherine, who could see Mary eyeing them both speculatively. 'Now, how are you progressing in your studies?' he asked.

It was a pleasant interlude – almost like old times. He stayed for two hours, and was even merry with them. His love for Mary was a pure thread in his life – there was nothing feigned about it, and in that he shared a common bond with Katherine. When he left, Katherine was in little doubt that Mary's fears had been allayed.

*

'The Princess is certainly troubled about the situation,' Margaret Pole confided later, when Mary had gone to bed and she and Katherine were catching up over a late-night posset of aleberry, which Blanche de Vargas had fetched from the servery of the great kitchen. 'She does not say anything, but she clearly knows more than she lets on.'

'It is not surprising, considering that the matter is notorious,' Katherine observed. 'Fortunately His Grace spent time with us both this afternoon, and I do believe that Mary was reassured by it. But, Margaret, it does worry me how this may affect her. This long delay in obtaining sentence does not help. She is getting older and wiser, and we cannot protect her for ever.'

'Rest assured, dear madam, I will continue to do all I can to shield her,' Margaret promised.

'I cannot thank you sufficiently. You are a true friend. And it is clear that Mary has blossomed in your care.'

Katherine went to bed feeling somewhat relieved. It was wonderful to have Mary with her, and to know that she was in good hands when she herself could not be with her.

But the next morning, as she sat going over a French translation with Mary, a messenger came to inform the Queen that the King was leaving Windsor for Whitehall, and that she and the Princess were to remain until the time came for Mary to return to her household at Hunsdon.

He was leaving them, without even saying goodbye, to go off with his mistress. Katherine struggled to hide her dismay from Mary. Then she saw that nervous look in Mary's eyes once more. Her heart burned with fury at Henry, who had done this to their precious, precious child.

Wolsey had been sent north to York, there to carry out his duties as archbishop.

'The Lady would have had him arrested for treason, but the King refused to proceed against him,' Chapuys told Katherine as they stood in the garden at Beaulieu, watching the courtiers playing bowls in the summer sunshine. He lowered his voice. 'The Lady is a dangerous enemy to have. She has not ceased to work against the Cardinal.'

'I thank God that so far the King has resisted her demands,' Katherine murmured. 'I never liked Wolsey very much, and he was no friend to me, but it saddens me to see him treated so ungratefully. At least he has retained his archbishopric of York.'

'And by all reports carries out his duties diligently and reverently,' Chapuys informed her. 'Bravo!' he cried out loud, as everyone clapped.

'I used to deplore his worldliness,' Katherine said when everyone's attention was back on the game. 'All those benefices and high offices – and no sense of piety. Yet now, in adversity, he seems to have found his true calling.'

'There is something interesting I have to tell you, Highness,' Chapuys went on, bending to her ear. 'It seems that the Cardinal has not quite bowed himself off the political stage. I had a letter from him, enquiring how your case is progressing and urging strong and immediate action in it. He plainly thinks that, once this business is settled, he has a good chance of returning to power.'

'The Cardinal is working for me?' Katherine asked, stunned.

'I think he was for you all along, madam. I am informed from Madrid that he supports the Emperor in asking the Pope to order the King to separate from the Lady until judgement is given.'

'Well, I am surprised, to put it mildly. And I am grateful to the Emperor for his efforts on my behalf.'

'My master has not ceased to press his Holiness to pronounce in your Highness's favour. Yet he fears that the King will marry the Lady with or without the Pope's consent, and because of that he is granting me special powers to act on your behalf.'

'My dear friend,' Katherine said, touched to the core, and liking Chapuys more every time she saw him, 'you cannot know what it means to me to have you and your master so zealous in my cause.'

Chapuys flushed with pleasure. He bent over her hand and kissed it. 'I am proud to serve so virtuous and high-hearted a lady,' he said.

As the summer faded into a cool and wind-whipped autumn, Katherine embraced her beloved child, helped her into her litter and watched her disappear into the distance. Then she returned to Richmond with the court, deeply uneasy about her future.

'I think the Pope has abandoned me,' she confided to Chapuys, as they strolled through the cloisters surrounding the gardens, Katherine's ladies following at a discreet distance. 'It's a year now since we expected judgement to be given, and already this dreadful business has dragged on for over three years.'

'Your Highness might be forgiven for thinking that,' Chapuys replied. 'It is not for the want of pressure, Highness. The Emperor, Dr Ortiz and I myself have all urged his Holiness to proceed to sentence. And the King has too, many times, I have no doubt.'

Katherine had no doubt either. Where others would ask, Henry would bully. He was like a baited bear these days. Anger at the interminable delays, and frustration at not having his way, were changing him. He was less kind, less considerate, more sharp-tongued, more suspicious, and apt to flare into frightening tempers.

She looked at Chapuys anxiously. 'It is more imperative than ever. The Princess is older now, and all too aware of what is happening. I do not want her anxieties prolonged, or her faith in the Holy See to be undermined.'

'Madam, the King approaches,' Chapuys said suddenly. 'It would be better if I took my leave.' He bowed and disappeared into a doorway, just as Henry hove into view, coming towards Katherine with a purposeful stride. It was at once clear to her that he was in no good mood.

'Well, Kate, what do you think of this latest iniquity from Rome? By this his Holiness loses all credibility, and does his office no service.'

'Why, sir? Tell me, what does he say?'

'His Holiness has suggested that I might be allowed two wives, and says he could permit that with less scandal than by granting an annulment.' Henry snorted in disgust.

Katherine was outraged. 'But that is against all the laws of Scripture!' She was shaken, not only at the very idea, but also by the fact that the Pope – the Vicar of Christ! – had felt driven to suggest it. 'I cannot understand why finding our marriage good could cause scandal.'

'Well, *I* could,' Henry said, glowering at her. 'It is scandalous that we have lived in sin all these years.'

'I find it more scandalous that you should even think it!' she retorted, stung. She could not bear anyone to think that she was the kind of woman who would live in sin with a man.

'My conscience tells me I am right,' Henry countered, 'and I regard my conscience as the highest and most supreme court of judgement and justice. I know that God is guiding my actions.'

'How can you know that? I must say it is presumptuous, and it takes no account of the fact that my conscience tells me differently.'

'You have always taken a subjective, ill-informed view, Kate.' Henry's blue eyes narrowed. 'But I'm warning you, my patience is wearing out. I will no longer tolerate any defiance. There is this matter of your chaplain, Father Abell.'

Katherine felt the hairs on her neck rise in fear. That good, brave man. He was not only true and loyal, he was writing a treatise in her defence . . .

'I hear he intends to publish a book, in which he argues that by no manner of law is it lawful for me to be divorced,' Henry said. 'Well, I will not have it! If he dares, I will have it banned and every copy destroyed. He will learn that he defies me at his peril.'

'You will not harm him?' Katherine asked, fearful for her faithful chaplain.

'Not if he abandons his cursed project,' Henry said. 'But if he persists in his mischief-making, it will be another matter.'

'So are you saying that men cannot now speak out in my defence? That you will punish them if they do?'

'I will punish those who defend the indefensible!' Henry snapped. 'Go carefully, Kate, and watch that you do not incite your friends to disobedience.'

Katherine was too horrified to argue. How far would Henry go? Were these latest threats just his temper speaking, or was he really resolved to break all opposition to his will?

Chapter 27

1530–1531

Wolsey was dead.

Elizabeth Stafford had come to tell Katherine the details of his end. Despite the sad circumstances, Katherine was pleased to see her, for the Duchess rarely waited on her these days. The Duke, her estranged husband, was firmly allied to Anne Boleyn and disapproved of his wife's friendship with the Queen. But Elizabeth loathed her husband, for his misplaced loyalty and his flagrant infidelities; she was seizing every opportunity to support Katherine.

'Of course, my lord did not tell me the details himself, as he refuses to speak to me,' the Duchess said, rolling her eyes. 'I had them from my son Surrey. My lord was sent to Leicester to escort the Cardinal to London, to be tried for treason, but Wolsey collapsed at Leicester, and the monks took him into their infirmary. Soon afterwards he died and they buried him there in the abbey. When he lay on his deathbed, he said that if he had served God as diligently as he had done the King, He would not have given him over in his grey hairs.'

Katherine crossed herself. 'I will pray for his soul,' she said, her voice croaking, which was a legacy of the feverish cough that had racked her these past weeks. She was surprised at how emotional she felt at hearing of Wolsey's passing, but it was understandable, she supposed, for she was only just recovering and still weak. Henry had not bothered to visit her; he had been disporting himself over at Hampton Court with Anne Boleyn. He had written to excuse himself from coming in person, saying he had heard that there was plague in Richmond, and then – ignoring the fact that Katherine was confined to her bed, shivering and burning up with the ague – he had hectored her again to take the veil.

'They have no pity, none of them!' Elizabeth spat. 'My lord cared not a fig for Wolsey's sufferings, or the Duke of Suffolk. They offered him no comfort.'

Katherine could imagine that. King's men, both of them. They would have been merciless.

'This comes of Mistress Anne's malice,' the Duchess said, as Maria and Gertrude entered the room. 'I have no doubt that it was she who prevailed on the King to have the Cardinal arrested.'

'It must have been, for it was Henry Percy who was sent to make the arrest!' Maria exclaimed, as she set a hot posset down on the table, within reach of Katherine's chair, and spread the warm blanket over her mistress's skirts; it was a fierce winter and the Queen must be kept warm. 'It's all over the court!'

'There's some justice in his being chosen,' said Gertrude, tart, bending to rake up the fire.

'I never thought to say it, but I feel grieved for Wolsey,' Katherine admitted. 'It was an ignominious way to die.'

'Better to die ignominiously than by the headsman's axe,' Maria observed. 'Some might say it was less than he deserved.'

'We must be charitable, my dear,' Katherine reproved her, sipping the posset. 'I cannot believe that His Grace would have gone so far as to execute a cardinal in holy orders. How would that serve his case in Rome?'

Henry seemed fairly nonchalant about Wolsey's death.

'He failed me, but I wish he had lived,' he said, when finally he came to see Katherine. She took it as proof that he would never have had the Cardinal executed.

But Anne Boleyn's vindictiveness towards Wolsey was as lively after his death as it had been before. Informed that there was to be a masque staged at court, Katherine joined Henry on the dais to watch the evening's entertainment, but was shocked when it turned out to be a cruel farce about Wolsey going to Hell, which had been devised by George Boleyn. Everyone seemed to find it hilarious, and roared with laughter at the sight of the King's fool, in red robes padded out to make

459

him look corpulent, being dragged down by demons into a fiery pit. Glancing at Henry's stony face, and, a little further away, the jubilant triumph of Anne and her relations, Katherine felt sickened, and retired as soon as she decently could.

Chapuys had been stalwart. He had never ceased pressing the Emperor to ensure that her case was brought to a final conclusion. He understood the urgency, even if no one else seemed to.

'The King stops at nothing to gratify his blind, detestable and wretched passion for the Lady!' he announced one day, as he and Katherine were coming from the chapel after Mass. 'They are still canvassing the universities now, and she is preparing for queenship.'

'What worries me is that there is a growing number of men holding radical or even heretical views in the universities these days,' Katherine told him, leading him up the secret stair to her lodgings. 'Luther's heresies proliferate. It seems that the word of God is now debated by all and sundry, and that the Church is held increasingly in disrepute. If only his Holiness would speak – and confound them all!'

'Take heart, madam. For every radical doctor there are probably ten who hold to the old faith,' Chapuys reassured her.

They had reached her apartments, where she had ordered her ladies to set out places for two for dinner in the privy chamber.

'How very kind of your Grace to invite me!' Chapuys exclaimed.

They sat as the waiting ladies arranged their napkins over their shoulders and poured wine, then they broke the manchet bread on the side plates and helped themselves to the rich venison stew.

'This will make your Grace smile,' Chapuys said. 'The Duchess of Norfolk told me yesterday that the Lady had commissioned the College of Arms to draw up a family tree tracing her descent from a Norman lord who settled in England four hundred years ago.'

'I thought her forebears were merchants,' Katherine interjected.

'And so, I believe, they were, so this genealogy was patently an invention, and the King was most displeased with it. But he was even more displeased to learn that the Lady had provided her servants with new liveries embroidered with the device *Ainsi sera, groigne qui groigne.'* So it will be, grumble who may.

Katherine laughed. As she and Chapuys well knew, the true and proper form was *Groigne qui groigne, vive Bourgogne!* Grumble who may, long live Burgundy! It was a device of the Emperor and his forebears, the dukes of Burgundy.

'Yes, madam, and the King told her whose motto it was, and he said she must not suffer her servants to wear those liveries.' Chapuys was gleeful. 'She was mortified!'

'It is a pity he does not curb her in other ways,' Katherine said, dipping her bread in the spicy sauce. 'That masque, for example. It was scandalous. And the King let her do it.'

'One day, we must pray, he will tire of her behaviour.'

'That day cannot come soon enough!' Katherine said, with some vehemence.

At Christmas Katherine joined Henry for the traditional festivities at Greenwich. She was overjoyed that Mary was there, too, although concerned to see that haunted look on her daughter's face, and the stiffening of her expression whenever Anne Boleyn was mentioned, or made her presence felt – which she did often, paying the barest of reverences to the Queen and the Princess.

'I detest her!' Mary burst out in private. 'She is a wicked woman. How can my father do this to you, madam?'

'Hush, child! You must not speak of your father so, and you must be charitable towards the Lady Anne for his sake.'

'My lady mother, you have the patience of a saint!' Mary cried. 'I cannot be like you, however hard I try.' Katherine started. Was this her meek and dutiful daughter? But there were tears in the girl's eyes. Seeing them, Katherine was seized inwardly with fury. Why should her cherished child's young life be blighted in this way? Henry must stop flaunting his mistress in front of her!

On Christmas Eve, when he came to her chamber, she was ready for him.

'You are setting a scandalous example by associating with the Lady Anne!' she said. 'Mary is very upset at having to witness it.'

'There is nothing wrong in my relations with the Lady Anne, madam, as I have told you!' Henry barked, clearly riled. 'I intend to marry her, and marry her I will, whatever the Pope might say, so Mary had better get used to the idea.'

He was immovable. Katherine had chosen the wrong moment, for over the holiday it became clear that he was feeling very sorry for himself. Even at Twelfth Night, when they sat enthroned together and there were masques, games and a great banquet, he was full of self-pity, and did little but grumble about the interminable delays in Rome and how badly the Pope had used him. In the end Katherine gave up trying to get him to show some mirth for Mary's sake. She almost felt sorry for him. This madness was all of his own making, yet she still believed he had been led astray. Once she had blamed Wolsey, but now she knew who the real culprit was. And Henry was too greatly in thrall to see it!

She was sure that, for all his bluster and unkindness, his natural virtues and goodness would win through in the end. If only she could have him with her for a reasonable time – for just two or three months – as he used to be, she would be able to make him forget all about a divorce. But, of course, Anne was clever. She knew that Henry's heart really lay with his wife, so she was constantly trying to prevent his being with Katherine. And while Henry was with Anne, he remained under her influence.

New Year's Day had not long dawned when Chapuys came to Katherine's chamber, in some alarm.

'Highness, I have been told by a well-informed gentleman that the King's marriage to the Lady will be accomplished in this coming session of Parliament.'

'That is what we feared last year, and the year before,' Katherine reminded him, sounding more positive than she felt, 'and still it has not happened. Anyway, the King cannot marry her without first obtaining a divorce.'

'The Lady feels assured of it, I hear.'

Maria, who was present, snorted in disgust. 'She is braver than a lion! Do you know what she said to me the other evening? She said that she wished all Spaniards were in the sea. I told her such language was disrespectful to her mistress the Queen, but she said she cared nothing for the Queen, and would rather see her hang than acknowledge her as her mistress.'

'You see her malice plain, Highness,' Chapuys chimed in, openly angry.

'I care not what the Lady Anne thinks,' Katherine said. 'Her enmity is born of insecurity.'

'Pah! I'm sorry, madam, but she is becoming more arrogant every day, even to the King!' Maria persisted. 'The Duchess of Norfolk says he has complained several times to the Duke that she is not like your Grace, and that you had never in your life used ill words to him. And when he said this he had tears in his eyes.'

Katherine felt like crying too. It was hard to imagine Henry comparing her favourably to Anne, but maybe he was seeing sense at last.

'He will tire of her soon, mark my words,' said Chapuys.

'Pray God let it be so!' she breathed.

These days Henry was in an even angrier mood. The Pope had finally cited him to appear in Rome to defend his case.

'I intend to ignore his summons,' he growled across the dinner table one dark January night. His face was flushed in the candlelight.

'But, Henry,' Katherine protested, 'this is the way to get our case decided.'

'Do you think I'm going all the way to Rome as a plaintiff?' Henry roared. 'What of my kingdom? I'd be away for months – years, knowing how Clement dithers. No, Kate, I am finished with the Pope.'

His words struck chill into her heart. He had threatened this before, but somehow this time it seemed more than bluster.

'My lord, I beg of you to consider well what you are saying,' she pleaded.

'I have thought of little else!' he shouted. 'I am convinced that the English Church would be better off with myself, the King, as its head, rather than owing allegiance to this weak, dithering pope.'

Katherine dropped her knife in shock and sat, frozen, aghast at the heresy of his words. He was threatening everything she held sacred. If Henry abandoned the Holy See it would mean schism and the overthrow of religion. It might mean war. She must stop him at all costs.

She rose and walked around the table, then fell heavily to her knees. 'Sir, you are known as a good son and champion of the Church,' she remonstrated. 'I beg of you, do not break with Rome! It would be the work of the Devil!' Of course she knew perfectly well that Anne was behind this – Anne and her faction, who were hot for Luther's heresies and enemies of the true Church. Devils all of them!

'Kate, get up,' Henry said. 'If anyone is in league with the Devil, it's Clement. He serves Mammon rather than God. He is meant to be defending and promoting God's laws, yet he shrinks from his duty for political considerations. How can Christ's vicar stoop so low? You must agree – it is a scandal.'

The awful thing was, she did agree. Yet respect for the Holy See was so ingrained in her that she could not bring herself to criticise it.

'But he has summoned you, Henry. He will give judgement soon.'

Henry frowned. 'I care not a fig for his judgements!'

That the King was in earnest very soon became clear. Over supper one evening, Chapuys informed Katherine that the clergy had assembled at Westminster.

'I think this meeting will be significant, Highness, and that the King desires the bishops' consent to some matter of great moment.'

Katherine swallowed. Was Henry about to carry out his threat to divorce her without recourse to the Pope? And if he did, where would that leave her? Completely isolated, she suspected – which was probably what he wanted.

'I hope it is nothing too extreme,' she said at last, pushing her plate away, her appetite gone.

There was a pause – just a heartbeat.

'Does your Grace know Thomas Cromwell?' Chapuys asked.

'Slightly,' Katherine said, signalling to Maria to pour more wine. 'He was in the Cardinal's service, and I believe he has now transferred to the King's. I see him sometimes about the court.' He was a thick-set, portly man in his forties with black hair and small, porcine eyes, and rather clever, by all reports.

'He has just been appointed to the Privy Council.'

'Why are you telling me this?' Katherine asked.

'Because this is a man with few scruples, and he is high in the King's good graces. Like the Cardinal, he comes from lowly stock; the Duke of Norfolk in particular looks down on him because he is the son of a blacksmith, and because he is hot in the cause of church reform. The Duke, as you know, is a great conservative, and a snob.' Chapuys permitted himself a grim smile, but his face instantly became serious again. 'Thomas Cromwell is all for having a sovereign state supported by Parliament, the law and an efficient civil service. There is no room in his vision for the Church of Rome. I'll wager that he is behind this summoning of the clergy.'

Katherine shivered. 'It sounds as if I have another enemy to contend with.'

'I fear so,' Chapuys said. 'I have been watching Cromwell's moves for some time. He is a radical in his opinions. He wants the Bible to be made available in English, that all might read it.'

'But it is for the clergy to interpret the Scriptures! It is heresy to read them in any language other than Latin. And the King would never agree to it. He has banned William Tyndale's translation.'

'Do not underestimate Cromwell,' Chapuys warned. 'He is no Thomas More. With him it is more expediency than principle, and he grows more powerful by the day in the King's service.'

'I had not realised,' Katherine said, toying with her napkin. 'My husband has not mentioned him to me.'

'That does not surprise me, Highness. His Grace does not like to show his hand. He prefers to keep you in ignorance of what is going on. And Cromwell is a discreet presence at court. People discount him as just another councillor. But I know him. We are neighbours in the City of London, and cordial as such. Cromwell confides in me – to a degree. He accounts me a friend, I do believe. That may be useful.'

'You like this man?' Katherine was surprised.

'Well enough, Highness, although there is plenty that divides us.

There is an amiability about him that conceals much. He appears guarded, but when you talk to him, that reserve gives way to joviality and banter, and he becomes very animated. He is a congenial host, full of graciousness and good cheer, and keeps a generous table. He was loyal to the Cardinal, even after his fall, and now he draws those of Wolsey's former affinity to him like a magnet. Yet he has a mind that can be cold and calculating, and when it comes to politics he becomes detached from human feelings. People are beginning to sense that he has influence, and seek his favour. I have no doubt that he is making himself indispensable to the King, and I wanted you to be on your guard. Your Highness is not eating.' Chapuys offered Katherine some more pheasant, but she shook her head.

'Norfolk and Suffolk hate Cromwell,' he went on. 'They call him a foul churl, but only because he is eclipsing them in the King's counsels. Of course the Boleyns have taken him up, the Lady calls him her man, and I do not doubt that he is working hand in glove with Dr Cranmer on her behalf.'

'This is most disturbing,' Katherine said, thinking of just how many forces were combining to defeat her and deprive Mary of her rights. And this unscrupulous radical, Thomas Cromwell, was revealing himself as the most formidable, and sinister, of those forces.

'It is, Highness. Frightening, even. Only this week Cromwell told me himself that there was no need for the King to wait for the Pope to consent to a divorce. He said that every Englishman is master in his own house, and why should His Grace not be so in England? Ought a foreign prelate to share his power with him? He said that His Grace was but half a king, and his people were but half his subjects.'

'I fear he will have said as much to my husband,' Katherine said, laying down the crushed napkin and trembling for the future of her daughter and her adoptive land.

'I rather fear that too,' Chapuys replied, his dark eyes troubled.

Parliament was sitting. Every day Katherine waited in trepidation for news. When, on a crisp bright day early in February, Chapuys asked for permission to walk with her as she was taking the air in her privy garden, she saw by his expression that he brought bad tidings.

'Highness, is there somewhere private where we can talk?' he asked, his tone urgent.

'It is too cold to sit here,' she said. 'Let us go to my privy chamber.' As she led the way along the path towards her lodgings, she heard a slight rustling behind the nearby hedge, and glimpsed an almost imperceptible movement through the dense wall of box. She stopped and put a finger to her lips.

'Who goes there?' she called.

No one answered. She had the impression that someone was standing behind the hedge, holding their breath.

'I know you are there!' she cried. 'Show yourself at once.'

Chapuys inclined his head towards the hedge, mouthing that he would go and investigate. Katherine nodded, and he set off for the next garden. In seconds he was back.

'No one was there, Highness.'

'I do not think I was mistaken.'

'I heard it too,' Chapuys said.

'No one should be behind there,' she told him. 'These are my private gardens.'

She walked on, deeply troubled. 'I remember how the Cardinal's spies used to watch me,' she said, 'but they did so openly, on various pretexts. I think I have been shadowed today – or am I being fanciful?'

'Not at all, Highness.' Chapuys frowned. 'It is said that Cromwell's spies are everywhere, and it would not surprise me if he was having you watched. The King fears your communicating with the Emperor. I too feel that I am being kept under observation.'

They had reached Katherine's apartments. She dismissed her women and sat down by the fire. 'Do come and warm yourself,' she bade Chapuys, indicating the other chair. 'Now, tell me the news. Spare me nothing. I need to know what is happening.'

Chapuys took a deep breath. 'This morning, Highness, the King stood up in Parliament and demanded that the Church of England recognise and acknowledge him as its supreme head.'

'Heaven protect us!' Katherine cried. 'Surely Parliament resisted.'

'It did not, madam. Even the clergy raised no protest. None dares defy the King. And I am told that every day leave of absence is granted to those Members of Parliament who support you. I find that ominous.'

'You think that Parliament will comply and enact a law making the King head of the Church in England?'

'I think it will.'

'Then God help us all.'

A few days later Henry came to see Katherine. His gaze was steely, his manner imperious; she saw that he was in no mood to brook any opposition. Dismissing her ladies, he sat down and leaned forward, his beringed hands placed squarely on his knees.

'No doubt the Imperial ambassador has informed you of the proceedings of Parliament, madam?' he said.

'Indeed he has, sir,' Katherine answered, bracing herself for a fight. 'And I have to say—'

But Henry did not wait to hear what she had to say. 'You should know,' he went on, 'that Archbishop Warham has said that the clergy are ready to acknowledge me as Supreme Head of the Church of England, as far as the law of Christ allows.'

'It does not allow!' Katherine flared, determined to make him see sense. 'Who are you to usurp the authority of Christ's vicar on earth? You may cow your English clergy, but you will never persuade the world at large of it. You will be called a heretic and a schismatic, and no prince will want to be your friend.'

'Enough, madam!' Henry shouted. 'I have not come to ask for your opinion! I came to tell you – so that there should be no misunderstanding – that the English Church no longer recognises the authority of the Holy See, and that the Pope is from now on to be referred to as the Bishop of Rome.'

'Henry, you cannot do this!' Katherine insisted.

'You will find that I can,' he said. 'I will be king and pope in my own realm, and I will look to my subjects' spiritual welfare. There will be no corruption in my Church, as there is in Rome! And I will deal severely with any person who dares to defy me!' He glared at her, almost provoking her to do so.

'Henry, my dear lord, what has happened to you?' Katherine asked. 'Who has got at you, that you are driven to do something as evil and wicked as this?'

'Credit me with some sense, Kate!' Henry snapped. 'I am no one's puppet. Don't you realise that I am only returning the English Church to its sacred roots? The popes in former times usurped authority here from my predecessors, and I and my people will no longer suffer it. I have a right to be emperor in my own kingdom, like King Arthur was, and henceforth I will recognise no superior but God. Do you understand me?'

'I understand you all too well!' she retorted. 'It appals me that you are prepared to divide Christendom just as a means to marry the Lady Anne.'

Henry stood up and came over to her in one bound. He bent down, so that his face was almost touching hers, his expression glacial. 'Do not thwart me, madam, and do not impute to me dishonourable motives. I will not have you question my judgement!'

He straightened up. 'I will leave you now, so that you can think on this and consider your position.'

That I should live to see this day, she thought, as the door closed behind Henry. The enormity of what he was doing was beyond comprehension. What would happen to them all, to every soul in England, to devout young Mary? And how could she bear to be cut off from the true Church? Deprived of its ministry and consolations, she would be damned – and the whole kingdom with her! It was a shattering prospect.

Chapuys arrived half an hour later.

'I see by your Highness's face that you have heard the news,' he said, his expression grave.

'The King told me,' Katherine said, desperate to speak of her fears. 'I cannot quite take it in. Surely people will speak out?'

'So far there has been little resistance.'

Katherine caught her breath. It was incomprehensible that Henry could carry this through unopposed.

Chapuys was shaking his head. 'It seems that most of the nobility support the King, and the clergy have no choice. The Lady is making such demonstrations of joy as if she had actually gained Paradise, and her father said to Bishop Fisher that he could prove by the authority of Scripture that, when God left this world, He left no successor or vicar. I have no doubt, Highness, that he and his daughter are the principal cause of the King breaking with Rome.'

'They have much to answer for. And, it must be said, so does his Holiness. If he had given judgement promptly, instead of allowing this matter to drag on and on, he would have saved us from this iniquity.'

Chapuys was firm. 'I have to agree with your Highness. His timidity and dissimulation have prejudiced your interests and the authority of his office.'

'What I fear is that the King will now proceed to have our marriage dissolved unlawfully,' Katherine said.

'I am sure that Cromwell is working on it, but I have taken steps to protect you, as much as I can,' Chapuys assured her. 'I spoke to the Earl of Shrewsbury, who has your crown in safekeeping, and he has promised that he will not allow it to be placed on any other head than yours.'

'I am grateful to you, and to him, but I do not see how he could defy the King's command to relinquish it. It would be a brave man who did that.'

'He seems quite resolved. We shall live in hope. And you have another ally in Bishop Fisher, who has openly said that it is against God's law for the King to be head of the Church of England.'

'Thank God for men like Fisher!' Katherine said. 'He was ever a good friend to me.'

She was so agitated that she could not bear to sit still. Wrapping herself in her cloak and pulling on her gloves, she made her way out of the palace and walked along the broad pavement fronting the river, trying to calm down. To her left the iron-grey waters of the Thames flowed unheedingly past, carrying with them the odd ferry or barge, and to her right the red-brick buttresses of the palace soared skywards. There were few people about, for it was very cold, although the guards were on watch at the palace doorway, and they had lowered their pikes in salute as their Queen passed.

It all looked comfortingly familiar, the Greenwich Katherine had always known, but the world had changed, and it was as if the ground were crumbling beneath her feet. The old certainties were gone, and the beliefs she held sacrosanct were being wickedly undermined. She could not come to terms with it. That Henry, her beloved Henry, the man she had married, could have created this schism was unbelievable, and she trembled for his immortal soul. What if he were eternally damned and they could never meet in Heaven?

Having walked as far as she could and got chilled through, she retraced her steps back to the palace. Coming in her direction was a well-built man, soberly dressed, but in good cloth, with his bonnet pulled down over his ears. With him was a clerk, and she heard the man say, 'Take this letter to Master Sadler; and this is for the relief of the poor people of London. See that it reaches the Lord Mayor by nightfall.'

'Yes, Master Cromwell,' the clerk said, taking the purse. 'I'm sure the poor will bless you for your bounty.'

He hastened to a waiting boat and Cromwell walked towards Katherine. He bowed, but she would not give him her hand to kiss. They faced each other, two antagonists who – at least on her part – had much to say but did not know where to begin. And it was up to Katherine to initiate a conversation.

'I have been hearing a lot about you, Master Cromwell. I was told that you were loyal to the Cardinal, even after his fall,' she said.

The shrewd little eyes looked wistful. 'He was a kind master, madam, and good to me.'

'He had his faults, but he would never have sanctioned what is going on now,' she said, her anger flaring. 'It is a pity you did not esteem him enough to follow his example.'

'I am the King's servant now,' Cromwell said, his expression bland. 'The world has moved on since Wolsey died. It is advisable to move with it.'

Katherine could not stop herself. 'Advisable for whom? For self-seekers, who look for preferment by giving the King what he thinks he wants? I tell you, Master Cromwell, some of us do not do what is merely advisable – we do what is right!'

Cromwell regarded her wearily. 'They warned me that your Grace was intractable, and I see that they spoke truth. My advice to you would be to move with the times and accept that change is necessary.'

'These changes are but a means to an end, to get rid of me and make the Lady Anne queen,' Katherine retorted. 'They do not take account of principles, or my daughter's rights!'

Cromwell remained unruffled. 'There are wider issues at stake, madam. The King's Great Matter has served to bring them into focus. It has exposed all that is wrong and corrupt in England – and in the Church itself. Are you not aware that there is bitter resentment in this kingdom against the papacy, that ordinary people are angry at having to pay tithes to a church that is obscenely wealthy, that they see the corruption in it and are sickened, and that they want to read the word of God for themselves?' As he spoke he had become passionate, and Katherine could now see the animation to which Chapuys had referred. 'Madam, I assure you, I too do what is right, and not merely because it is advisable!'

'I fear for you, and I fear for England,' Katherine said, shocked and shivering, and not just from the cold, 'because you cannot see that you are in grave error and are casting yourself into the abyss. I will pray for you!'

Unable to bear Cromwell's company for another moment, and very near to tears, she walked away, into the palace, past the guards whose faces remained impassive. She did not look back.

Gertrude Blount was out of breath. 'I have run all the way here,' she said to Katherine, sinking into her curtsey. 'I had to tell you immediately. People are saying that there has been an attempt on Bishop Fisher's life!'

'No!' Katherine and Maria exclaimed, crossing themselves in unison.

'What happened?' Katherine asked.

'His cook is said to have poisoned the soup. There were at his table, his family and household, and the poor whom he fed out of charity. Seventeen people are said to be gravely ill, and two have died.'

'What of the good Bishop?'

'He escaped, praised be God. He ate only a little soup and suffered only stomach pains, although I hear they were grievous. The cook has been arrested.'

'Why would he want to murder his master?' Katherine wondered.

'Maybe he was bribed to do so,' Maria suggested.

'That is what people are saying.' Gertrude nodded. 'They whisper that he was acting on the instructions of my lord of Wiltshire, who is said to have given him the poison and bribed him to put it in the food.'

'That's believable!' Maria snorted. 'I'll wager that woman was privy to it all.'

'We do not know that,' Katherine said quickly. 'This is all pure speculation.'

But Chapuys, arriving soon afterwards to inform Katherine of what she already knew, was of the opinion that the rumours were well founded.

'The Bishop is outspoken in your Highness's cause, and the King is becoming increasingly irritated by it, while the Lady and her faction are furious. It is entirely credible that they plotted to silence the Bishop.'

'And where does the King stand in this?' Katherine faltered. She could not in her wildest dreams imagine Henry resorting to murder. He had surely not sunk *that* low.

'The King refuses to credit the rumours, but expresses outrage at the crime. I do not think he is involved. But, Highness, be on your guard. Those who perpetrated this deed will not hesitate to strike again by such underhand means. I beg of you, be watchful. If a bishop's cook can be bribed, so can a queen's – and your Highness stands more solidly in their way than Bishop Fisher.'

'I will be vigilant, I promise you,' Katherine vowed, her heart lurching at the thought of the danger she might be in.

'I myself will taste your food,' Maria declared stoutly. 'We can't be sure that your official assayer isn't open to bribes.'

'You are a dear, brave friend,' Katherine said, deeply touched, reaching over and squeezing Maria's hand. Then a terrible thought struck her. 'But what of Mary? How safe is she?'

Maria and Gertrude looked shocked. 'They would never dare!' Maria declared.

'Harm the King's own daughter?' Gertrude cried. 'No, your Grace need not fear. No one would even contemplate it.'

But the world was turning on its head already. Was anything certain? Katherine asked herself, even as she agreed with her ladies. And there were those to whom Mary represented a threat: heiress to the throne, of unquestionable legitimacy, and the enemy of the Lady Anne.

Henry came. This time he was in a better mood, although he appeared deeply troubled.

'You have no doubt heard the gossip about Fisher's cook,' he said. 'I came to tell you that there is nothing in these wild accusations.'

Katherine said nothing. She wished she could believe it. She hoped fervently that Henry had not been duped, because if the Boleyns had not tried to poison Fisher, then she herself and Mary were in no danger.

'To prove it, I intend to make an example of that wretched cook,' Henry went on. 'Poisoning is the most abominable form of murder. I abhor it, and I'm having Parliament pass a new law providing that poisoners are to be deemed guilty of treason and boiled to death.'

Katherine shuddered. The thought of such torture sickened her. 'Why not hang them like other felons?' she whispered.

Henry's voice was steely. 'Because poisoning is an especially foul and secret way of murdering someone, and it requires a meet punishment, to deter others.'

Such a terrible fate did not bear thinking about – and it would be the worst cruelty to inflict it on a man who had been the tool of others, while the real culprits got away with their wicked deeds.

But Chapuys, with whom she spoke later, was of a different opinion.

'The King is wise to deal so severely in this case,' he said, 'and the cook was culpable, because presumably of his own free will he put the poison in the food. I do not imagine that the Lady Anne or her father were standing over the cooking pots. Nevertheless, the King's vengeance cannot wholly absolve them from suspicion.'

'I hope in Christ that they are innocent, and I pray that this poor cook is given strength to bear the ordeal in front of him,' Katherine said fervently, crossing herself. All the same, she could see that Chapuys was right, and that such a cruel punishment would act as a deterrent to any who might think of poisoning Mary.

Chapter 28

1531

'It is not good news, Highness,' said Chapuys, as he came upon Katherine in her privy garden one afternoon in March. 'It has been announced in Parliament that the universities of Europe have pronounced on the King's case. Only four out of sixteen have declared for you.'

'They have been bribed!' she said, bitter.

'I have no doubt of it. The majority have declared your marriage incestuous and against the law of God; they say it is therefore null and void, and that Pope Julius had no business in the first place to give a dispensation.'

'I will never accept that,' Katherine declared.

It seemed that the women of London agreed.

'They are demonstrating in the streets,' Gertrude Blount reported the next day. 'They cry out that the King has corrupted the learned doctors.'

'The women of England have ever taken your Grace's part,' Maud observed.

'It's a pity the men don't heed them!' Maria sniffed. 'But of course we are idiots without powers of reasoning!'

Bishop Fisher sent a note to Katherine. He had heard, he said, that even the heretic Luther had declared that on no account could the King separate himself from his Queen. Not, Katherine thought, that Henry would take any notice of a man he had called a sick and dilapidated sheep.

There was a cool response again from his subjects when Henry's own book about the Great Matter, *A Glass of the Truth*, was finally published that spring. 'The people deride it,' Chapuys told Katherine. 'Your Highness should hear what is being said in the taverns and – quite openly – in public. You should take heart from it. The people love you. They will tolerate no one else for queen.'

'I wonder the King does not punish them,' she said.

'Did you not know? He is unwell and has taken to his bed. They say it is in consequence of his grief and anger at what his subjects are saying.'

She was hurt that no one had told her. She must go to him. She must see for herself that he was not seriously ill. The habit of caring for him, of loving him, of fearing for him, was too deep-seated in her.

'It's just a fit of pique, I suspect,' Chapuys opined. 'For effect!'

'Nevertheless, I will send to ask after His Grace's health, and if I may visit him,' Katherine said. 'I will write a note.'

As soon as it was finished she sealed it and gave it to Maria. But when Maria opened the door, it was to find one of the Queen's ushers crouching at the keyhole. The man leapt up, shamefaced, and made for the stairs, but too late. They had all seen him. Chapuys raced after him and hauled him back into the Queen's presence.

'What were you doing listening at my door?' Katherine asked him.

The man stared at her sullenly.

'Answer Her Highness!' Chapuys barked.

'I wasn't listening, your Grace,' the man said. 'I had dropped a button and was looking for it.'

'Did you find it?' Katherine asked.

'No, your Grace.'

'Go and look, Maria.' Maria went, and came back.

'There is no button to be seen, madam,' she reported.

'I must have lost it elsewhere,' the usher said.

'Show us where it is missing,' Chapuys demanded. 'Is it from your doublet or your sleeve?'

The usher held out his arm. A button was missing from his shirt cuff. Katherine wondered if he had pulled it off while they were waiting for Maria. She did not believe his excuse, and neither, plainly, did Chapuys. But there was nothing to be done about it.

'You may go,' she said, 'and make sure you are not found loitering by my doors again.'

The man went. They listened to his footsteps fading into the distance.

'Check that he has gone,' Maria said. Chapuys went to the door. There was no one there.

'One of Master Cromwell's spies, I'll wager,' he said. 'I have reason to think that the court is full of them. I could even point out one or two known to me personally.'

'I said nothing I would not say to the King's face,' Katherine asserted.

'All the same, Highness, please be careful. It's an old saying, but in this place the walls really do have ears. And there are those who would twist your words to make them sound seditious.'

'This cannot go on for much longer,' Katherine said. 'I do believe that, in the face of these public protests, the King will not dare to make this other marriage.'

It was unsettling to find that the others were looking at her doubtfully. But before they could say anything, the King was announced.

'I must go,' said Chapuys. 'He must not find me here.'

'Go out through the postern,' Katherine directed, and Maria led the ambassador through to the bedchamber, where a spiral interconnecting stair led down to the King's lodgings and then to the privy garden below.

Henry missed Chapuys by seconds. When he arrived Katherine and Gertrude Blount were sitting there sewing smocks for the poor, as if they had been at it all afternoon.

Henry did look ill. He had clearly just struggled out of his sickbed.

'Kate, I have to tell you that Mary is seriously ill,' he said, his voice a mere croak.

'No!' Katherine cried in alarm. 'What is it?'

'The physicians cannot say for certain, but she has kept no food down for eight days.'

Immediately she thought of poison. 'All this time, and they didn't tell us?' She was furious.

'They will answer for it, I promise you,' Henry vowed.

'Let me go to her,' Katherine begged. 'I must see her. I can nurse her back to health better than any doctor!' And I can protect her.

Henry regarded her for a long moment. 'You may go to Hunsdon and see her if you wish – and stop there.' For all Katherine's distress, the emphasis in his tone alerted her. The implication of his words was ominous. Surely he wasn't stooping so low as to take advantage of their daughter's illness to his own purpose? But there was still that calculating gleam in his eye. She knew then. He was trying to provoke her into giving him grounds for a divorce by deserting him.

Her maternal instincts demanded that she be with Mary, to look after her, keep her safe from her enemies and bring her through this sickness; her place was at her daughter's side, and she was desperate to be on her way. But now she saw that she must stay, to protect her child in another way. All along, she had comforted herself with the knowledge that, even if the Pope declared her marriage invalid, it had been made in good faith, and its issue would be deemed legitimate. Mary was Henry's heir; no one could ever deny that or deprive her of her rights. But if Henry divorced her mother for deserting him, and married Anne Boleyn, their children would displace Mary in the line of succession.

It was an agonising decision.

She met Henry's gaze. 'But my place is here with you, my lord. You are unwell too, and I would not leave you at such a time.'

His eyes narrowed. He knew she had bested him.

'I will send my physicians to Mary,' he muttered.

'And I will write to Lady Salisbury and ask her to take the greatest care of her and get news to us regularly,' Katherine said. 'I will also send some delicacies to tempt Mary, and pray for her speedy recovery.'

The letter she wrote to Margaret Pole was a masterpiece of ambiguity. She urged, she counselled, she pleaded, that Mary be kept safe, begging that Margaret would read between the lines. For two days she worried and fretted and prayed, desperately beseeching and badgering God, the Virgin Mary and the whole company of saints to restore her daughter to health.

One morning Henry, looking much better, joined her in the chapel and knelt beside her, adding his prayers to hers.

Eventually she rose from her knees, ready to go to dinner.

'I am still concerned about Mary's health,' Henry said, rising too, his manner quite different from what it had been two days before, which led her to hope that his mind had been temporarily disordered by his illness. Today there was a gentleness about him that she had not seen in years. 'She *should* be with you, her mother,' he conceded. 'I am recovered now, and her need is greater. I have arranged for her to be brought by litter to Richmond Palace, and for you to join her there.' It was the nearest he would come to admitting he had been wrong – and unkind.

'Oh, thank God! And thank *you*, Henry!' Katherine breathed, relief flooding her. 'I have been so scared that something terrible might befall her, and I not with her.'

Katherine was ever afterwards convinced that her arrival had been a turning point in Mary's illness, and that the Princess had begun to mend from the moment they embraced. She was shocked at the change in her pretty girl, who had always been slight and slender but was now thin and pale. *Had they tried to poison her?*

'We have done everything we could,' Margaret Pole assured her, her long face drawn and tired, for she had had little sleep these past days and nights.

'Why didn't you inform me how poorly she was?' Katherine asked, trying not to sound too aggrieved, and scarcely crediting that her friend had been so remiss.

'Oh, but I did, madam. I wrote on the second day.'

'I never received the letter,' Katherine said, suspecting that it had been kept from her, and not daring to wonder why. 'No matter, I am here now.'

She sat with Mary, feeding her heartening broth and poached fish and almond milk with her own hands. She read to her, fables and stories and the romances that young girls loved and Vives had deplored; she watched over her while she slept; she bathed her face and hands and combed her hair. Gradually she saw her improve, until there came the joyous day when Mary was well enough to get out of bed and take a few wobbly steps.

While Mary slept in the evenings, Katherine took much pleasure in chatting with Margaret by the fireside. She had greatly missed seeing Margaret daily, and it was good to be together again, just the two of them. But she was perturbed by what Margaret had to tell her.

'At fifteen the Princess should not be suffering from so many ailments, madam. I know it's a difficult age for girls, having brought up my Ursula, but Her Grace seems over-prone to painful and irregular courses and dreadful headaches.'

'She has had a lot to cope with,' Katherine said, suppressing her mounting anger that Mary had had to suffer like this. 'The troubles between the King and me must cause her great anxiety. I have seen it with my own eyes.'

'I agree, madam. She loves His Grace and yourself equally, but it is clear to me that her sympathies lie with you, although she never criticises the King. She often says she longs to see and comfort you in your trouble. I know that she also worries about her future. She is grown very devout, and I believe she finds much solace in religion.'

'She has always been a pious child,' Katherine observed. 'I am glad she finds comfort in it at this time.'

'So am I, madam. It is as if it represents the security she knew when she was little, before all this happened – a fixed mark in a changing world. It hasn't surprised me when she has got into a passion and said she loathes heresy in any form. I cannot tell you how greatly these latest reforms are grieving her, for she will not discuss them.'

Katherine could have wept. Poor Mary.

'My dear friend,' she said, 'when the subject comes up, please assure her that I am as cheerful as may be, and that I have good friends to support me. Tell her to continue as she is, and trust in God that all will be well, as I do. And, as ever, see that she gets plenty of good food and fresh air, and keeps busy, so that she does not have time to dwell on her worries. I, for my part, will write to her regularly, and visit her whenever I can.'

When Katherine returned to Greenwich in April, leaving a much-restored Mary in the safe hands of Margaret Pole, it was to hear welcome news. Parliament had risen without making any pronouncements on her marriage – for now. Immediately she wrote to the Emperor, urging him to insist on the Pope giving sentence before Parliament reconvened in October.

Henry was still, even now, keeping up the charade that he and Katherine were happily married, notwithstanding the fact that the Lady Anne was very much in evidence. Early in May the King and Queen dined together in public, with courtiers standing around them in the presence chamber. Chapuys was there too, watching the proceedings, and within earshot. Henry conversed amiably with Katherine, keeping to the pleasantries; she responded in kind, although it took some effort because she was worried about Mary, having that morning received word from Margaret Pole that the Princess was again a little poorly. The news had resurrected her fears that Mary was being poisoned, and it seemed all wrong to be donning cloth of silver and eating rich food off gold plate when she should be winging her way to her daughter.

She was in no mood therefore to look lightly on Anne Boleyn arriving late, making her curtsey and seating herself – when everyone else was standing – on a chair that had been set at the side of the chamber. The woman thought she could do as she pleased – and Henry allowed it. He was even smiling and nodding in Anne's direction – and Anne did not scruple to dart a smirk of triumph at the Queen.

Katherine gathered her courage and turned to Henry. Her voice was low, but audible to all, as she intended.

'Sir, will you not dismiss that shameless creature?'

Henry flushed. 'No, madam, I will not.' There was a silence, as if the court were collectively holding its breath. Only the Lady Anne smiled in obvious and triumphant amusement. Henry looked furious, then visibly made an effort to master his rage. 'May I help you to some syllabub?' he muttered, as if nothing had happened.

The next day Katherine felt the force of his wrath. She had spent a sleepless night worrying about Mary, and knew she must go to her, for her own peace of mind.

Henry received her coldly when she sought him out. His lips were pursed tight, his gaze icy.

'Sir, might I have leave to visit Mary?' Katherine asked. 'She is still unwell.'

'Go if you wish and stop there!' he snapped. This time there was no mistaking his meaning.

'Sir, I would not leave you for my daughter or for anyone else in the world,' Katherine declared, desperate, crushingly disappointed, and almost in tears. 'Perchance Mary could be brought to court?'

'No,' said Henry. 'She is better where she is. She is in good hands. Now, if there's nothing else, I have state affairs to attend to.' Katherine knew herself dismissed.

The very next day she was perturbed to be waited upon by a deputation of lords and bishops from the Privy Council.

'The King has sent us, madam,' Edward Lee, who was Archbishop of York in place of Wolsey, explained, as they knelt before her. 'The Bishop of Rome has sent a nuncio to tell His Grace that his case can only be tried in Rome and nowhere else. Naturally, the King will never consent to such a thing, even if the Pope were to excommunicate him. He therefore wishes you to be sensible and withdraw your appeal to Rome, and bow to the judgement of the universities.'

Katherine stood up. 'I am his lawful wife, and will so remain till the court of Rome has given judgement.' She fixed her steady gaze on the men before her. Did they not fear for their souls?

The Archbishop swallowed audibly. 'Might I remind your Grace that the King is now head of the Church of England and does not recognise the authority of Rome?'

'The Pope is the only true Vicar of Christ, and he alone has power to judge spiritual matters, of which marriage is one!' Katherine insisted. 'I love, and have loved, my lord the King as much as any woman can love a man, but I would not have borne his company as his wife for one moment against the voice of my conscience. I came to him as a virgin, I am his true wife, and whatever proofs others may allege to the contrary, I, who know better than anyone else, tell you they are lies and forgeries. Go to Rome and argue with others than a lone woman!'

'But, madam—' the Duke of Suffolk began.

Katherine cut him short. 'God grant my husband a quiet conscience, but I mean to abide by no decision save that of Rome. And tell the King that I am ready to obey him in everything save for the obedience I owe to two higher powers – God and my conscience.'

Once more Henry relented, and allowed Mary to spend a few days with Katherine at Windsor after the court moved there in June. She had been hugely relieved to find her daughter so much better, yet there was now a sad, tormented look in Mary's eyes, as if she bore the cares of the universe on her shoulders. It was as well that Henry had taken Anne Boleyn off to Hampton Court for the hunting.

With the King away the ancient royal lodgings at Windsor felt empty, but the weather was good, so when Mary's lessons were over, Katherine took her for long walks in the park, enjoying the peacefulness of it all. When Henry returned with Anne, Katherine kept to her apartments, not wanting Mary to see the woman flaunting herself.

On the few occasions she herself came face to face with Henry, he was still irate with her. It did not help that he had recently turned forty, middle-aged by anyone's standards, which made his lack of a male heir even more of a tragedy. Yet he was still a fine and regal figure of manly beauty. Looking on him, even as he berated her for her obstinacy with that hard-done-by, accusing expression on his face, Katherine missed more than ever the closeness of their lovemaking.

She was weary of their endless wrangling, and she suspected he was too. They seemed to go round in circles, never getting anywhere. He often accused her of never listening to him, but she did – she did! It was just that what he said made no sense to her.

The court was due to leave Windsor on 14 July. Everything was in readiness. That morning Katherine rose and heard Mass as usual. It was only when she was served breakfast afterwards that she became aware of a stillness about the castle. Normally before the King removed to another house there was much commotion and bustle, but not today. Katherine stood up and looked out of her window. The upper and middle wards were empty. No carts, no pack horses, no officers shouting orders, no servants racing hither and thither.

She sent Lord Mountjoy to find out if the court was leaving after all.

'Madam,' he told her, 'the King left for Woodstock early this morning.'

That was strange. Henry would surely have told her that he was going on ahead? But no doubt he had wanted to ride with the Lady Anne, and his wife's presence was inconvenient.

'Am I to follow?' she asked.

'Madam, I cannot say. I have no instructions.' Mountjoy was absent-mindedly fingering his golden beard, a sure sign that he was perturbed.

Perplexed, Katherine went to her daughter's lodging. All Mary's belongings were packed and waiting.

'Are we going to Woodstock today?' Mary asked.

'I do not know,' Katherine admitted. 'We must await the King's pleasure. He has left no orders.'

Dinner was served at eleven o'clock, and Katherine and Mary ate it with due ceremony in the Queen's privy chamber. The cloth had only just been lifted when a messenger wearing the Tudor livery arrived.

'Ah, now we shall be on our way,' Katherine said.

But the messenger, a pleasant-faced young man, seemed a little diffident about delivering his message. He looked, in fact, as if he would rather be anywhere else. At length he blurted out, 'Your Grace, I am to inform you that it is the King's pleasure that you vacate Windsor Castle within a month.'

It took a moment for the implication of his words to sink in, and when it did she began to tremble.

The enormity of it overwhelmed her. Henry had left her.

Chapter 29

'Go where I may, I remain his wife, and for him I will pray,' she told the messenger, striving to keep her voice steady, for Mary was watching with a bewildered look on her face. 'Pray say farewell to the King for me,' Katherine continued, 'and tell him how sad I am that he did not say goodbye to me. And please tell him that I asked after his health, as a good wife should. It would be a consolation to me to hear that he is well.'

The messenger looked stricken at that, and she suspected that Henry might be given a somewhat censored version of what she had said, so she repeated it.

All she wanted to do was cry. She badly needed to throw herself on her bed and weep her heart out. But there was Mary to think of, Mary, who was looking at her questioningly, wondering what was going on.

'We are not to leave after all,' Katherine said, keeping her voice light and smiling. 'The King your father wishes us to remain here for now.' There was no need to say any more. Henry had gone from here for a brief visit to Hampton Court recently, so Mary must be led to believe that he would return again, once he had exhausted the hunting at Woodstock. He could well have a change of heart in the next few days, so there was no need to upset Mary in her present fragile state. Yet deep within her Katherine knew that this parting was final.

Would the next thing she heard be that Henry had divorced her by unlawful means? What could she do then? She was alone, cut off from the court, and – which was worse – from Chapuys, her confidant and the vital link to her nephew Charles, the one person, beside this vacillating pope, who could help her. Did she dare write to him? Or would Cromwell's spies intercept her letter and show it to the King? A means must be found for sending messages privately to Chapuys. But how?

She was still pondering on this that evening, after Mary had gone to bed, and thinking about seeking the advice of Maria and Margaret Pole, when another messenger was announced. The man was English and wore no livery, and she wondered whether it was wise to receive him. But it was too late to send him away: he was already kneeling before her.

'Your Highness, I am come from Messire Chapuys,' the man said. 'He thought it best that I did not wear his livery. I am to tell you that he knows about your situation and will do everything in his power for you.' He handed her a letter.

She opened it and read. Chapuys wrote that he had been present when her message had been delivered to Henry.

His Grace became very angry. He asked me to tell you that he does not want any of your goodbyes, and has no wish to afford you consolation; and that he does not care whether your Grace asks after his health or not. He says you have caused him no end of trouble and have obstinately refused the reasonable request of his noble Council. He knows that your Grace depends on the Emperor, but states that you will find that God Almighty is more powerful still. He commands that you stop it and mind your own business, and he wants no more of your Grace's messages.

Her heart broke all over again as she read Henry's brutal words. And there was worse, further down the page . . .

Now that the Queen was banished, Chapuys had written, the Lady was trumpeting that it would be only three or four months until her wedding. 'She is preparing her royal state by degrees, and has just taken on new officers. Foreign envoys have been warned to appease her with presents. You may be assured that she will not receive one from your good servant.'

It did sound as if Henry meant to take matters into his own hands, which was a chilling prospect. Yet for all Anne's optimism, it seemed that he was in no hurry. He had had the declarations of the universities since March – four months now – but had not so far acted on them. If it had been his intention to push the matter through Parliament, he could have done it by now. Katherine suspected – and fervently hoped – that he believed the Pope would speak soon and spare him the necessity for rending Christendom asunder. Then he could be received back into the fold, like a lost sheep, and be a good son of the Church once more.

The fragile edifice of her hopes came crashing down with the arrival of a letter from Henry, warning her that it would be a good deal better if she spent her time in seeking witnesses to prove her pretended virginity at the time of her marriage, than in talking about it to whoever would listen to her. 'You should cease complaining to all the world about your imagined wrongs!' he ended.

She was taken aback at the unjustness of it. Most of the people of her acquaintance were for the King; she had few friends in England. Presumably, by 'all the world' Henry meant the Emperor, the Pope and Chapuys? But what did he expect her to do? Let him ride rough-shod over her principles without complaint? Abandon the fight for her daughter's rights? Make a mockery of the Holy See? As for her 'pretended' virginity, he knew, none better, that that was a lie.

She did not answer. There was no point in stoking up Henry's rage any further. It would burn itself out eventually, as it always did, and one day surely he would see the light and return to her, as loving as before.

Katherine arrived at Easthampstead Park in August. It was a spacious royal hunting lodge in the middle of the royal forest of Windsor, and although it had been standing for two hundred years, and had a history that stretched back to Saxon times, it was as comfortable and well appointed a residence as any queen could wish for. It had three wings ranged around a large courtyard, and was surrounded by a moat, which was spanned by two drawbridges leading to twin gatehouses.

Katherine had feared that Henry would send her to some mean house for the purpose of breaking her resistance, but at Easthampstead there was room for her entire household, including her two hundred and fifty maids-of-honour, and she was sufficiently provided for to live in great state, as she was accustomed. Yet for all her people around her, she still felt isolated, and deeply saddened at being parted from Henry, and from Mary, whom he had sent to Richmond. Katherine had written asking if Mary might remain with her, but he had refused. She suspected that it was another way of punishing her for opposing him. But was it fair to punish Mary too? His unkindness preyed on Katherine's mind.

She missed the fiery company of Elizabeth Stafford, and the devoted loyalty and proud Spanish spirit of Gertrude Blount; both had been forbidden to visit her, although Elizabeth had twice sent her gifts of oranges in which she had hidden messages telling Katherine that she had taken great pleasure in impugning Mistress Anne's ancestry and in warning her to stop interfering in the marriages of Elizabeth's children. 'She wants to marry them off to her supporters, but I told her I was having none of it!' Katherine had to smile at the thought of the feisty Elizabeth Stafford taking her hated niece to task.

Gertrude Blount had determinedly written several times and sent her maidservant, Elizabeth Darrell, to wait on the Queen in her place and act as go-between for them. Years ago, Elizabeth's father had been Katherine's vice-chamberlain, so she was pleased to receive the girl. Mistress Darrell, who soon became known to all as Eliza, was not yet twenty and was golden-haired, green-eyed and very beautiful, and she soon became devoted to her new mistress. Of her many maids-of-honour, Katherine quickly came to love her best, although she also cherished the quiet mouse Jane Seymour, and Blanche de Vargas. Isabel de Vargas was loyal, but she was lazy; whenever Katherine wanted something done, she was nowhere to be seen, but would reappear as soon as she was no longer needed. Of the twins, Katherine far preferred Blanche.

As for the great ladies of her household, only Maria and Maud were with her now, while Margaret was looking after Mary, thank the Lord. The rest – or their husbands – had deemed it politic to make their excuses and leave her service. That had hurt – but at least it had left her with those who were congenial to her, and whom she could trust.

Katherine had been greatly cheered by the reception she had received from the people when she had ridden to Easthampstead from Windsor. They had come running across the fields and lined the dappled summer lanes to see her, crying out their support, and their anger against Anne and Henry.

'Truly you are beloved by these islanders,' Maria had observed. 'The King should listen to his subjects!'

Katherine knew she allowed Maria too much licence in speaking critically of Henry, but the fact was that Maria was usually right. She might be abrasive at times, but she was a staunch friend, so much could be forgiven her. And often Maria voiced what Katherine herself was too reticent to say. Katherine dared not admit that she was missing Henry dreadfully and longed for his presence. At court, she had known that he was nearby and might visit her, or that they might meet by chance; here she was cut off from him and condemned to a purgatory of loneliness and wanting, and had to hold her peace about it, for she knew exactly what Maria would say.

She had been at Easthampstead for two months when, as the golden, rust-brown leaves of October were falling, another deputation of lords of the Council arrived. She received them with Maria and Jane Seymour in attendance.

Archbishop Lee was again their spokesman. 'We are come to advise your Grace to be conformable to the will of God, and to inform you that all the universities have clearly determined that the Pope can in no wise dispense with your marriage to the King, therefore the dispensation in which you trust is clearly void and of no effect.'

Katherine made herself stay calm. She had to show them that she was not to be moved or swayed by lies. She knelt with quiet dignity before these hard-faced, intractable men, and raised her hands as if in prayer.

'I am the King's true wife!' she declared. 'He has yielded to mere passion, and I cannot think that the court of Rome and the whole

Church of England will consent to anything that is unlawful and detestable. But still I say I am his wife, and for him I will pray.'

The lords regarded her sternly.

'It is our duty to warn your Grace of what the King might do to you if you persist in your defiance,' the Archbishop told her.

'I will go even to the fire if the King commands me!' Katherine declared, meaning it, but inwardly shrinking in terror.

'It may yet come to that,' she was told, brutally. When they were gone, bowing themselves out, her courage deserted her, leaving her in misery and fear. She was shuddering, rooted to the spot, and Maria and Maud came hastening to help her up.

'He would never hurt you!' Maria cried. 'You have committed no crime.'

'It seems that in England it is a crime to oppose the King,' Katherine gasped through chattering teeth, a great pall of fear engulfing her. 'Yet I cannot believe that His Grace means to proceed so harshly against me.' She was praying that, when her words, said so impulsively, were reported to him, they might not take root in his mind. She should not have courted martyrdom while she had Mary to think of!

A few days later she received the King's command to leave Easthampstead and go to the More, Wolsey's old house. As Katherine's small cavalcade passed on its way, crowds gathered to see her. 'We will always hold you for our Queen!' they cried out.

There was no diminishing of her state at the More. It was a house of great splendour, built of red brick and surrounded by excellent hunting parks. There were wonderful sets of tapestries, several of them embroidered with Wolsey's coat of arms, and there were other reminders of the Cardinal too. His portrait hung on one wall, and his stall was there in the chapel. What magnificence he had lived in once, Katherine mused – and what had it availed him? Because, in the end, all turned to dust, and he had been brought lower than he'd deserved, another victim of the Lady Anne's malice. She shivered at the thought of the night crow's power.

To her surprise, a few local worthies and gentlemen visited her. The

Venetian ambassador and his suite of thirty finely dressed Italians came too. She enjoyed playing hostess and impressing them with the magnificence of her estate, and when they came to watch her dine, she took care to see that thirty maids-of-honour stood around her, while a further fifty waited at table. Let none doubt that she was the true Queen of England! And all the while she was asking herself why the Venetians had felt it politic to visit her. Did they know something she did not? Had they gained the impression that she was about to be recalled to court? But they gave nothing away in their conversation, and she concluded that they could not be aware of the true situation, and were merely there to pay their respects, as was customary. After all, Henry's courtiers had stayed away.

Soon afterwards there arrived a letter from Chapuys, who had diligently maintained contact ever since Katherine had left court. Bishop Fisher had told him something disturbing: the Lady had sent a message warning Fisher not to attend the next session of Parliament in case he should suffer a repetition of the sickness that had struck him down in February.

'How could one not now conclude that she was behind that attempt to poison him?' Chapuys asked. Here seemed to be proof indeed, and the worst of it was that Anne clearly thought she was invincible and could get away with murder. At the very least it was a threat made in the worst taste. Either way, it made Katherine feel especially vulnerable, and even more fearful for Mary.

But when a summons came from the King, bidding her attend the annual feast for newly appointed sergeants of the City of London at Ely Place in Holborn, her spirits rose and she felt more optimistic than she had for a long time. For she and Henry had attended this feast on several occasions in the past, and the fact he had commanded her to be present could only be construed as an olive branch. He would be there; she would see him again, see his beloved face, hear his voice. In the months of their separation, she had found that it was possible to forget his unkindnesses – which were all due to Anne Boleyn's pernicious and bewitching influence, of course – and remember increasingly the loving husband he had once been.

'Surely your Grace is not going?' Maud asked, when Katherine ordered her to brush and lay out her crimson velvet gown.

She stared at Maud. 'Not going? The King has summoned me. I must obey.'

'Forgive me, madam, but your attendance may purely be a formality, and I fear you may regret it.'

Maria looked up from her sewing. 'Maud is probably right, madam. His Grace seems set on this course he has taken; otherwise, surely you would have been summoned back to court.'

She frowned at them. She *knew* Henry, knew the way his mind worked. He hated to admit he was wrong. He would not make the first overt move. He would want to test the water in a neutral setting. She was sure of it.

'I appreciate your concerns, but I assure you both that you are probably worrying needlessly.'

She left the More in a state of hopeful anticipation. She could even see this event marking a public reconciliation. Perhaps – she tried not to let her hopes run away with her – Henry had already sent Anne away, in readiness for Katherine to resume her rightful place at court.

She was cheered when she saw the avenue of flares lighting her arrival at Ely Place, that great palace that was the London house of the bishops of Ely and had been home to many royal personages over the centuries. And there was the beautiful chapel, dedicated to St Etheldreda, soaring gracefully above the other buildings in the rambling palace complex. At the entrance to the state apartments she was received with a fanfare of trumpets and courteously welcomed, then conducted by the new sergeants-at-law to a fine chamber where tables had been set out, with a chair of estate at the centre of the high table – a single chair, to which she was shown. But where would Henry sit? Was he not here after all?

Her heart sinking fast, she asked where the King was.

'His Grace will be dining in the great hall,' she was told, 'and the ambassadors in the little hall.' At that moment another fanfare could be heard, and much cheering, which could only signal Henry's arrival. Katherine, walking to her place past ranks of bowing guests, no longer had a view of the entrance. He was here, so close, and yet she could not see him – and she was being deliberately kept apart from him, whereas in previous years she and Henry had dined together in the great hall. It was cruel – cruel! And although she should have been glad to be gracing a state occasion again, she was sick to her stomach and could barely eat a thing.

How she made conversation she did not know. All she could think was that Henry was here and yet had made no attempt to see her. She was only present, no doubt, because the sergeants-at-law had invited her, according to custom, and it would have looked odd if she'd stayed away. She could fool herself no longer: this arrangement of separate feasts was almost certainly at the King's command.

Her only hope was to see him as she left, although what she might say to him on so public an occasion she did not know. Dare she throw herself on her knees and make an abject plea to him? If there was any chance that it would move him, she was ready to abase herself. But because she had to get back to Hertfordshire, she was obliged to leave early, so even that opportunity was denied her. As she thanked her hosts at the outer door, she could hear music and the loud hum of conversation coming from the great hall. It took all her resolve to walk away and climb into her litter, leaving Henry behind.

The next day she wrote to the Emperor.

What I suffer is enough to kill ten men, much more a shattered woman who has done no harm. I can do nothing but appeal to God and your Majesty. For the love of God, procure a final sentence from his Holiness as soon as possible. I am the King's lawful wife, and while I live I will say no other.

She read it over, and signed it:

At the More, separated from my husband without having offended him in any way, Katherine, the unhappy Queen.

She gave the letter to Maria to pass on to Chapuys's messenger when next he came.

'It is yet another appeal to His Imperial Majesty,' she said, shaking her head, because after four years all the pressure that Charles had so far brought to bear on Pope Clement had been to no avail.

Maria's temper flared. 'I cannot bear to see your Highness so sad. It is a very strange and abominable thing, that the lust of a foolish man and a foolish woman should hold up a lawsuit and inflict an outrageous burden upon such a good and blameless queen!'

'Enough, Maria! You must not say such things of the King. Whatever faults may be imputed to him, he is still my husband and sovereign of this realm.'

Maria fell to her knees. 'Forgive me, Highness! It is just that I cannot bear to see you suffer!'

Katherine smiled at her sadly. 'I understand that. Get up, my friend; never feel you have to kneel to me. I know God sends these trials to test me. Sometimes I think He must love me to confer on me the privilege of so much sorrow!'

'Dear madam, let us pray that the Pope soon puts an end to your suffering.'

Late in November Maud Parr caught a chill that rapidly settled on her lungs. Deeply anxious about her friend, Katherine summoned Dr de la Saa, who prescribed a posset infused with chamomile and poppy juice, but it made no difference. Maud lay there pale and wan, her skin clammy, her curly hair damp with sweat. Fearing for her, Katherine summoned Dr Guersye, but he was of the opinion that Dr de la Saa's treatment had been the most appropriate and that they should try it once more. Again, Katherine was distressed to find that it proved ineffective.

She sat with Maud, chafing her hands and willing her to get better. Maud was not yet forty – far too young to die – and her children still needed her. Katherine herself needed her! She knew how Maud fretted about her clever daughter, Kate, now nineteen and married to an ailing husband. The younger daughter, Anne, was sitting at the other side of the bed, weeping, frightened that her mother might die. Anne had often hinted that she missed the court and all its excitements and longed to be back there, but for now the only place she wanted to be was with her mother.

On the first day of December Katherine went into Maud's chamber to see how she was, and found little Anne Parr weeping over a corpse.

'Oh, madam, she's gone! Oh, Mother, Mother!' Anne laid her head on the dead woman's breast, sobbing woefully.

Katherine crossed herself. 'Oh, my dear child.' She raised Anne and clasped her in her arms. How tragic for the poor girl, to lose her mother at such a vulnerable age. Anne was not much older than Mary.

'She did not know me,' the girl wept. 'I tried to rouse her, and speak to her, but then I saw that her eyes were open and that she had stopped breathing.' She broke into more heart-rending sobs.

Katherine stroked her hair and made her kneel with her by the bed. She grasped Maud's limp hand. 'Blessed Mother of God, pray for her. Holy Mary, Mother of God, pray for us sinners now, and at the hour of our death . . .'

Anne joined in, as the other ladies clustered into the room, each silently kneeling in turn and joining in the prayers.

When at last Katherine rose, and laid Maud's hands in the form of a cross on her breast, Anne wept again. 'Oh, Mother, my mother! What shall I do?'

'You will come with me and have some wine to calm you.' Katherine felt her own voice break. Maud had been her friend for so long, and she could not imagine a world without her. As she led the sobbing Anne from the room, she looked back at the still figure on the bed. We are all going to miss her dreadfully, she thought.

The Emperor, Chapuys reported, was now pressing the Pope to excommunicate Henry, in the hope that it would bring him to his senses. Katherine was shocked to the core. Charles had gone too far this time! Never would she have sought such a thing, however well meant, or wished it on her husband. For once, she was glad that Clement was reluctant to provoke Henry; and she resolved to oppose his acting on the Emperor's suggestion.

'The Lady governs all,' Chapuys had written. He had heard from a

Venetian envoy that there had been an ugly incident in London recently, when Anne was dining in a house by the Thames. Word had apparently spread quickly through the City that she was there, and before long a mob of seven or eight thousand women, and men disguised as women, attempted to seize her. 'Had she not escaped by taking to her barge and crossing the river, she would have fallen a victim to their anger.'

'It would have solved a lot of problems!' said Maria, tartly. 'And good riddance too!'

'I could not wish that on anyone,' Katherine said, 'but I do wish that the Lady Anne would go away, or that the King would tire of her. Were His Grace once free from the snare in which he has been caught, he would confess that God had restored his reason – I know he would. But she and her friends goad him on like a bull in the arena.'

She did not think she could take much more. Some days she thought she would give in and go into a nunnery after all; to be truthful she would welcome the peace and tranquillity, and be glad to escape this miserable world. But there was Mary to consider; she had to stand up for Mary's rights. And what if she took holy vows, and the Pope then found her marriage good? Whatever Henry had done – the schism he had caused, his blind passion for Anne, the statutes he had passed – she remained convinced that, beneath the bluster and the threats, he was still at heart the man who had been a good son of the Church, and that a favourable judgement from Rome would bring him to his senses. And so she must hold herself in readiness for when that day came.

'Oh, if only his Holiness would put us all out of our misery!' she said, sighing. 'I do not see the difficulty, and I must confess that I am amazed at him. How can he allow a suit so scandalous to remain so long undecided? His conduct cuts me to the soul.'

Christmas was wretched, celebrated with great solemnity, yet lacking in merriment and jollity, and Chapuys reported that it had been the same at Greenwich. 'Everyone said that there was no mirth because your Grace and your ladies were absent.'

Katherine spent the season missing Henry and wishing that Mary could have shared it with her, but Henry had commanded that Mary keep Christmas at Beaulieu, her own residence. It was clear to Katherine that Henry was keeping her and Mary apart, careless of his own daughter's happiness. *He fears that I might try to influence her against him!* But that was unfair, for Mary had eyes, and she had ears, and she was of an age to make up her own mind, and had done so without her mother's help.

Katherine had always given Henry a special gift at New Year, and she was determined that this year should be no different. As his wife, she would be failing in her duty if she did not send him something. So she ordered a gold cup, and dispatched it to Greenwich with a loving and humble message, to which he could not possibly take exception. But back came the cup, with a curt message enclosed. 'I command you not to send me such gifts in future, for I am not your husband, as you should know.'

That almost broke her. But still she would not be cowed.

In January, to Katherine's astonishment and joy, Mary was permitted to visit her at the More. It had been six months since they had seen each other, and Katherine was moved to see that her child, at nearly sixteen, was now become a woman.

But growing up had brought a new gravity to Mary. She was too serious, too opinionated for someone so young, and over-preoccupied with rights and wrongs and the sheer awfulness of what her father was doing. Katherine's heart bled for her. Mary should not be burdened with such things; at her age she should be thinking of her studies, of pretty clothes to wear, and perhaps of handsome young men.

They talked. How they talked. Even at night Mary would appear at Katherine's door, needing comfort and reassurance, and they would cuddle together in the big bed. Katherine knew that Mary was struggling to reconcile Henry as he had been with Henry as he was now, and knew that it was important for the girl to be reminded of the good that was in him, and how much he really loved her.

But then the conversation would stray into dangerous waters, with Mary voicing her vehement hatred of Anne Boleyn, and hotly defending the Pope and the Church, and bursting into tears at the thought of the evil that Cromwell and Cranmer and other heretics were wreaking.

'Hush!' Katherine would soothe. 'Forget them. Let us enjoy this quiet time together.'

And for hours on end they did. They read together, as they had always done, played music, took walks in the wintry gardens and played endless games of cards by the fire.

Katherine wondered what had prompted Henry to send Mary to her at this time. Was it just an unexpected kindness on his part, intended mainly for Mary? Or was he worried about public opinion? For surely there would be murmuring at his wife and daughter being kept apart.

Katherine knew he was worried about her influencing Mary against him, so she voiced no opinion on the divorce. She did not need to: Mary did it for her, and quite vociferously too. She had to warn her to watch what she said in the presence of others. Even to sympathetic friends it did not do to criticise the King so passionately.

All too soon the day came when Mary had to leave. Katherine held her close, kissing her sweet face, and urging her to have patience and pray for strength, for all would soon be well. Then she let her go, and watched the too slender figure of her precious child clamber into the waiting litter. A last smile and a wave, and Mary was gone.

Katherine walked slowly to her favourite part of the garden, seeking solace in the warm May air and the scent of spring flowers, holding Chapuys's latest letter. The news that Sir Thomas More had resigned as Lord Chancellor had saddened her deeply. He had surrendered the Great Seal of England to the King, pleading ill health, but Katherine knew that his conscience could never be reconciled to Henry's demands.

The clergy of England had not been so scrupulous. They had renounced their allegiance to Rome, and been pardoned by the King for their misplaced loyalty, on payment of a heavy fine. Henceforth they would answer to their sovereign only.

To Katherine, isolated and hearing only the news that Chapuys could smuggle to her from court, it felt as if the world had shifted further out of kilter. Her faith and obedience to the Holy See remained as strong as the day she made her first confession, yet the man she loved most had made a mockery of all she held dear.

She hoped that Henry's admiration and respect for his old friend was staunch enough to override any anger and disappointment he felt over More's resignation. She knew how much he would have given to have More support his cause. But, by the very act of resigning at such a time, More had made it plain that he could not give it, or endorse the King's reforms. Surely, for all his silence on the subject, that meant that he was against the divorce? It was a comfort to learn that he had been allowed to return to his house at Chelsea to enjoy a quiet retirement with his family and his books.

Katherine sat down on a stone bench to read on. She waved her ladies away, wanting to be alone to absorb the news. She was fearfully aware that More's resignation had left Cromwell free to push through his reforms unhindered. Chapuys had recently warned her that Cromwell had risen above everyone save the Lady Anne, and currently had more credit with the King than even Wolsey had enjoyed. 'Now there is not a person who does anything except Cromwell,' he had written. Who knew what Cromwell would do now? He had made his malice towards her and the Church all too evident.

When Katherine read that Cromwell's friend Thomas Audley was to be made chancellor in More's place, it became more than clear to her which way the wind was blowing. But now here was a surprise. Chapuys wrote that Archbishop Warham, whom Katherine had thought a staunch King's man, for he had never put much heart into her defence, had spoken out against Henry. Warham was ageing now, and ill, and she could only conclude that he was less in dread of an earthly king than a celestial one, for he had stood up in Parliament and protested against all laws that impugned the Pope's authority. Effectively, he had denied the King's supremacy over the English Church.

Reading that, Katherine held her breath, wondering what had befallen Warham for his defiance. But it seemed that Henry had let him be, by which she supposed that he believed that the old man was not long for this world. At least he had not vented his anger on him, which was a good sign. She wondered if Warham had supported her all along but been afraid to say so. She was glad that she could think of him more kindly now, for without the Archbishop's cooperation there could be no formal declaration that her marriage was invalid. In the end, he had served her magnificently.

It seemed, from Chapuys's letters, that the world was full of protests. 'The Abbot of Whitby has slandered the Lady Anne,' Katherine told Maria as they lingered at table after supper one evening. 'I will not, for delicacy, repeat what he said, but he has been censured for it.' And the Nun of Kent had waxed vocal again. 'She has accused the King of wishing to marry the Lady Anne only on account of his voluptuous and carnal appetite. I rather wish she would stop. She only angers him the more by her sayings and prophecies, and she embarrasses me.'

'You did well to refuse to see her, madam,' Maria said, sipping her wine.

'I will not give them any grounds for complaint,' Katherine said drily, returning to the letter and reading on. 'Listen to this! You remember Friar Peto, who was the Princess's confessor? Well, on Easter Sunday he preached before the King and the Lady Anne at Greenwich, and warned His Grace that their marriage would be unlawful, and that if the King went ahead he would be punished as Ahab was, and his blood would be licked up by dogs.'

'By God! What did the King do?'

'He was so angry that he walked out of the chapel, with the Lady Anne following, and then he had one of his chaplains preach a sermon denouncing Peto as a dog, a slanderer, a base and beggarly rebel and a traitor. Now he has put Friar Peto in prison.'

Even the King's own sister, the French Queen, had stood up for Katherine. 'For some years now she has refused to come to court when the Lady Anne is there, but now she has criticised her openly, deploring her morals and her lack of decorum.'

'That will ruffle the Duke's feathers,' Maria observed gleefully. She hated Suffolk, hated his being her daughter's ward. 'I would not like to be at their breakfast table right now. I imagine the atmosphere will be frosty, to say the least!'

'A Member of Parliament has moved that the Commons ask the King to take me back,' Katherine went on, scanning Chapuys's long letter. 'The King told the Speaker he marvelled at it, and said the matter was not to be determined in Parliament, for he said it touched his soul, and he wished for our marriage to be found good.'

'Hah!' interjected Maria. 'We've heard that before.'

Katherine frowned at her in reproof. 'But he also said that the doctors of the universities had determined it to be void and detestable before God, and it was his conscience that caused him to abstain from my company, and no foolish or wanton appetite.'

Maria muttered something that could have been, 'Arrant nonsense!'

'The King reminded Parliament that he is forty-one years old, at which age the lust of man is not so quick as in lusty youth.'

'Really? He *is* feeling sorry for himself!'

'Maria!' Katherine reproved again. 'I have commanded you to show no disrespect to the King.'

'I apologise, Highness.' Maria bit her lip, her eyes fiery.

'It does not matter, my dear friend. I know you mean well.' Katherine smiled at her and went back to Chapuys's letter. 'The Commons fear that a divorce could have an impact on England's trade with the Emperor's territories. Messire Chapuys thinks that Parliament ought to petition the King to take me back and treat me kindly.'

'As he should! Is there any news from Rome?'

Katherine read on. 'Only that the Pope has postponed the hearing yet again, until November.' She sighed in exasperation. 'It seems it will never end!'

'I grieve for your Grace,' Maria said, reaching over and taking Katherine's hand. 'But take heart. The King did allow the Princess to visit you in January.'

'I think he felt he needed to placate the people,' Katherine murmured. 'But that was four months ago. I have asked several times since if I might see Mary again, and every time I have been told no. I fear that it suits His Grace to keep us apart. The Princess is growing older and he fears us intriguing with the Emperor against him. As if we would do such a thing! And keeping me from my daughter is a way of punishing me for what he sees as my obstinacy.'

She bent her head, perusing through a blur of tears the last few lines of Chapuys's letter. 'I do not like this,' she said. 'England and France have signed a treaty of alliance against the Emperor. You know what this means. The King now feels that he can count on King Francis's support. The King of France is a good son of the Church and has influence in Rome. The King is going to meet him at Calais in the autumn.'

'But your Grace has the support of the Emperor, and he will never allow the French King to browbeat the Pope,' Maria said.

'I doubt this Pope will be browbeaten by anyone,' Katherine commented resignedly. She had almost given up hope of any good tidings from Rome.

When the King's order to move to the palace at Hatfield came a few days later, Katherine was relieved, for life at the More, for all its splendour, had been tedious and monotonous. It would prove to be the same at Hatfield, no doubt, but at least it was a pleasant change of scene.

She liked the house, which was built of red brick, with four wings around a courtyard. Like Ely Place, it had once been owned by the bishops of Ely but had often been used by royalty. She could remember Henry telling her that he had stayed there as a child, and that his baby brother Edmund had died there. That was probably why he rarely used it. But it was in good order, if not as grand as the More or Easthampstead, and it was spacious, and the grounds and gardens were lovely.

She was not left in peace to enjoy them for long. One afternoon she was in her spacious presence chamber, playing cards with her women, when Lord Mountjoy was announced. She knew, as soon as she saw the distress in his face, that he brought bad news.

'Madam,' he said, 'I have received an order from the King. He commands that Lady Willoughby leave your household and that you are not to communicate further with her.'

Katherine felt as if someone had punched and winded her. Maria was her oldest and dearest friend, and one of her staunchest supporters. Save for those ten years of her marriage to Lord Willoughby, whose perfections she still trumpeted, she had been with Katherine through tempest and calm, and was a vital link to their lost youth and the land of their birth.

'Why?' she gasped.

Mountjoy swallowed. 'I was told that she has been spreading sedition.'

'That is ridiculous!' Even as she said it, Katherine knew that, in Henry's eyes, Maria's constant criticism of his behaviour could amount to sedition. But how would he have known? Did the walls have ears? Had Thomas Cromwell planted a spy in her household?

'I cannot let her go, I cannot!' Katherine burst out, as Eliza Darrell tried in vain to comfort her. Maria was not there; she had gone to the steward, to hector him over the dusty state of the great hall, which Katherine wanted made ready for the receiving of guests – should there be any.

'Madam, the King has commanded it,' Lord Mountjoy said miserably.

When Maria returned, to find her mistress weeping inconsolably on Eliza Darrell's shoulder, Lord Mountjoy looking helpless in the face of such distress, and the other women shaking their heads, she was horrified to learn the cause.

'I will not go,' she declared, her eyes glittering with fury. 'I will stay. Let them try to move me!'

Katherine roused herself and lifted a ravaged face. 'You *must* go, my dear friend,' she said. 'You must not disobey the King's order. Think how that would look. It would reflect on me.'

'Madam, I cannot leave you,' Maria protested.

'Maria, I command it!' Katherine ordered.

The King's order was to take effect immediately. It was a highly emotional farewell. Not only was Katherine losing her oldest friend, she was also losing the last of her ladies-in-waiting. There were all gone now – Margaret to Mary, Maud to death, and now Maria to banishment. Now she would have only her maids for company. Not that she did not love them – but it would be a sorry household for a queen who had been served by the highest ladies in the land, and without the one who was especially dear to her.

'I will return as soon as I may,' Maria promised. 'Oh, madam . . .' She broke down – Maria, who never cried.

'God keep you, dear friend,' Katherine said, her voice hoarse. 'Take this.' She pressed into Maria's hand a little miniature painting of herself holding her pet monkey. (Poor, sweet Carlo, he had not lived long.)

'I will treasure it, madam!'

A last hug, and Maria too was gone from her.

Just hours later, as Katherine was trying to resign herself to being deprived of Maria's company, there was a great banging on the outer door of the palace.

'Open in the name of the King!' a man shouted.

'What in the world . . .' Katherine gasped, emerging from her apartments as a company of armed soldiers entered the hall. 'Why are you here?'

The captain bowed hastily. 'We are come to arrest your Grace's chaplain, Father Abell.'

'My chaplain? On what charge?'

'For publishing a seditious tract against the King, madam.'

She had feared that this would happen, feared it from the moment Father Abell had told her that he had gone ahead and published his book.

'I assure you, Captain, there is not a seditious bone in Father Abell's body,' Katherine declared.

'Then, madam, I must show you this.' The captain drew from his pouch a rather crumpled bundle of pages, smoothed them out perfunctorily and handed them to her. She read the title: *Invicta veritas. An answer that by no manner of law, it may be lawful for the most noble King of England, King Henry the Eighth, to be divorced from the Queen's Grace, his lawful wife.*

'But this is not sedition. It is an honest opinion, the same opinion that I myself maintain. What crime has Father Abell committed?'

'It's not for me to question the King's orders, your Grace. Father Abell is to come with us.'

Katherine sent Eliza to find the chaplain. 'Tell him to hurry and pack some warm clothes and books,' she whispered.

Father Abell remained composed when told that he was under arrest. His homely, amiable countenance seemed untroubled as he blessed Katherine and bade her farewell.

'Do not fret about me, my daughter,' he said. 'God will protect the righteous.'

But he left her distraught. Was it now a crime to speak out against the divorce? If so, what punishment might she herself merit?

Chapter 30

1532–1533

Archbishop Warham had died. Katherine received the news in August, not from Chapuys, whose letters came ever more infrequently these days – which was worrying in itself – but from her chaplain, Father Forrest, who had heard it when assisting at Mass in the parish church at Hatfield.

She dismissed Father Forrest and sat alone in her chamber, cold with sorrow and worry despite the hot summer's day. What would happen now? Who would replace the Archbishop?

Katherine did not have long to speculate. Chapuys managed to get a letter to her.

'Thomas Cranmer is nominated to the See of Canterbury,' she read. That was bad news indeed, with Cranmer being the creature of the Boleyns; Katherine had not forgotten that it had been his idea to canvas the universities. Such a man would not scruple to give Henry what he wanted.

She was even more disturbed to read that Anne Boleyn's enmity towards Mary was now as great as it was towards herself. 'The King dares not praise the Princess in the Lady's presence for fear of provoking her temper, and he keeps his visits to the Princess as short as possible because the Lady is so jealous,' Chapuys had written. 'She has boasted that she will have the Princess in her own train and might one day give her too much dinner, or marry her to some varlet.'

'Oh, dear God!' Katherine cried aloud, every instinct urging her to fly to Mary and protect her. And it was clear that Chapuys was alarmed too, for he had again mentioned the attempt on Bishop Fisher's life, and stated that he did not doubt that the Lady was capable of putting her threats into effect. He would be doubly vigilant, he promised, and knowing his zeal towards Mary she had no doubt that he would – but he was not living at Beaulieu or Hunsdon, where Mary's household lodged. Who would protect her there?

Misery swamped Katherine. How could she bear to live in such fear for her daughter? Dare she write to Henry, begging to visit Mary, or have the girl come to her? But she must, she must!

Chapuys's next letter brought a brief glimmer of hope. The King, he wrote, had made the Lady a peer of the realm in her own right, something that had never before been granted to a woman in England. She had been created the Lady Marquess of Pembroke, with much pomp and ceremony. 'It is important, however, to note that the wording of the patent of nobility leaves some room for speculation,' Chapuys had observed, 'since the phrase "lawfully begotten" has been omitted in reference to any male issue to whom the title might one day descend. Some think this an indication that the King has tired of her and is pensioning her off and providing for any bastard she might bear him.'

But there could be another interpretation, Katherine thought. Maybe Henry was ensuring that any child he conceived with Anne would have a title in the event of his dying before he could marry her.

Either way, it could only mean one thing: that Henry and Anne really were lovers. And although Katherine had assumed that all along, for all Henry's protests that she was wrong, having it confirmed at last hurt deeply. It was as if she had lost him all over again.

She picked up the letter once more, tears misting her vision. It was clear from what Chapuys had written that there was no question of Henry tiring of Anne. 'The King cannot leave her for an hour. He accompanies her to Mass – and everywhere. He is even taking her to Calais to meet the King of France. He told me that he meant to marry her as soon as possible. I fear they will do so while they are in France.'

The same thought had occurred to Katherine. *I pray we are both wrong*, she said to herself, and wept again.

The royal messenger's expression was impassive as he stood before her. 'The King requires your Grace to deliver up to him the Queen's jewels.'

'For what reason? I am the Queen, and they were entrusted to me.'
They were very precious to her, and she had always felt privileged to
have been consigned such special pieces.

'The King orders that you surrender them now, so that the Lady
Anne can wear them in France.'

The fierce blood of Isabella the Catholic welled up hotly in Katherine.
'The Lady Anne, not being queen, has no right to these jewels! Besides,
this request is offensive and insulting to me. It would weigh upon my
conscience if I were to give up my jewels for the base purpose of
adorning a person who is a reproach to Christendom, and is bringing
infamy on the King through his taking her to France!'

The messenger had gone red in the face. 'Your Grace, I have my
orders.'

'But I do not have mine!' Katherine retorted. 'You may tell the King
that I refuse to surrender my jewels without his express command in
writing, since he has commanded me not to send him anything.'

The man withdrew, looking harassed. Of course she knew that she
was only delaying the surrender of her jewels, yet she was glad she had
made the protest. Someone had to.

Everything she held sacred was being challenged. Worse still, she
knew, from what her maids and servants told her, that the true faith
was being steadily undermined in England. And much of this was down
to Anne Boleyn and her pernicious influence. As to what might come
of this meeting between Henry and Francis, she dared not think.

She wrote to the Emperor.

I must warn your Majesty of the consequences of the Pope's
endless delays. There are many signs of the wickedness being
meditated here. New books are being printed daily, full of lies,
obscenities and blasphemies against our holy faith. These people
will stop at nothing now to determine this suit in England. The
coming interview between the kings, the companion the King
takes everywhere with him, and the authority and place he allows
her, have caused the greatest scandal and widespread fear of
impending calamity. My conscience compels me to resist, trusting

in God and your Majesty, and begging you to urge the Pope to pronounce sentence at once. What goes on here is so ugly and against God, and touches so nearly the honour of my lord the King, that I cannot bear to write it.

As inevitable as death came the King's written order to surrender her jewels, and with a heavy heart she gave them up.

But it seemed that Anne was angered at her obduracy, and that the jewels were not enough to satisfy her. Katherine was horrified to hear from Chapuys that she had made Henry give her the Queen's barge, then had Katherine's coat of arms shamefully mutilated before it was burned off. 'The King was very much grieved,' Chapuys wrote. 'God grant that the Lady may content herself with your Grace's barge, your jewels and your husband.'

Katherine was at least gratified to learn that none of the French royal ladies were prepared to receive Anne. Yet the Lady was still going to Calais. Chapuys had written: 'Many people speculate that the King will secretly marry her in France, although I can hardly believe that he will be so blind as to do so, or that the King of France will lend himself to it.' (The King of France, Katherine thought, would lend himself to anything, if it were to his advantage.) 'But the Lady,' Chapuys continued, 'has made it very clear that she will not consent to it. She will have it take place here in England, where other queens have usually been married and crowned.'

Pray God his Holiness speaks soon! Katherine thought, in desperation.

At Henry's order, Katherine spent Christmas at the royal manor of Enfield, a three-sided courtyard house with large bay windows, much older than Hatfield, and not so luxurious, but in good repair and comfortable; if the move was a subtle way of telling her that she would suffer materially if she persisted in her obstinacy, then Henry would soon realise that a less splendid residence was not going to make a difference.

Katherine could take no joy in the season, though, for Henry had again refused her request to have Mary spend it with her. She had not seen her daughter for ten months now, and she was missing her dreadfully. She could only hope that Margaret Pole was taking care to ensure that Mary's Christmas was as full of good cheer as possible.

She felt more isolated than ever, for Henry had now specifically forbidden her to communicate with Chapuys. She had always prided herself on being an obedient wife, but in this she was prepared to defy him, and she was aided by Chapuys himself, who stationed one of his men at an inn near the palace, and arranged a rendezvous with Eliza Darrell at a postern gate in the grounds, where letters could be passed through a lattice.

By this means Katherine continued to press for the Pope to give sentence. 'I take full responsibility for the consequences,' she wrote. 'I still believe that, if the Pope decides in my favour, the King would even now obey him, but if he does not, I will die comparatively happy, knowing that the justice of my cause has been declared and that the Princess will not lose her right to the succession.'

She wrote too of her fears for the Church.

The Pope must be warned that the King has already seized for his own use much of the wealth of the Church, and he will be encouraged to go further because of the kind of people who surround him, like the Lady and her father, staunch Lutherans both of them. If sentence should be pronounced now, the majority of people here are such good Catholics that they would compel the King to obey. But unless the Pope acts at once, he will be deprived little by little of his authority here, and finally his censures will go unheeded.

In the letters smuggled in by Eliza, Chapuys showed himself confident that, if provoked, the people of England would rise on her behalf. 'If a tumult arose in your favour, I know not if the Lady, who is hated by all the world, would escape with life and jewels.'

Katherine hoped it would never come to that; she could not bring herself to wish it on even her rival. In fact, she hoped to forestall such an evil. Wrapped in furs against the cold winter night, she had candles lit and sat down by the fire to write again to the Emperor, once more impressing on him the urgent need for the Pope to act. 'There can be no danger in what I ask,' she told him. 'As you know, the thunders of this land hold no lightning for any head but mine.'

Katherine sat alone at her writing desk. Through the closed door she could hear the bustle of life elsewhere, servants moving about the house and her maids giggling as they stepped lightly through the corridors, intent on their little interests and intrigues. They were young girls still, she thought, and for a moment her mind wandered to the children who should have been gathered around her. Tall, red-headed sons; sisters for Mary to gossip with. Her tiny Isabella would have been fourteen now. She blinked back tears and looked again at the pile of letters she had received since her husband had sent her away.

Little information reached Katherine nowadays. Chapuys clearly had to pick his moments to write to her, for his movements were probably being watched, but she knew that Father Abell had been released from the Tower and was on his way to her. This gladdened her immeasurably. God must have touched Henry's heart. For a while she had hoped it was true that he was tiring of Anne – Heaven knew, by the sound of it, that he had cause – and was about to acknowledge the error of his ways.

But then Eliza brought another missive from Chapuys, who confessed that he had concerns about Thomas Cranmer, who was waiting for the Pope to confirm his appointment as archbishop. Katherine had not thought it strange that Henry had sent to Rome for that, for it was proof that he had no intention of creating a permanent breach with the Holy See. But Chapuys was worried: 'If the Pope knew of the reputation Cranmer has here of being devoted heart and soul to the Lutheran heresy, he would not be hasty in approving the appointment. Dr Cranmer is a servant of the Lady's, and should be required to take a special oath not to meddle in the divorce. But I fear that he may authorise the marriage in this Parliament.'

She prayed that Chapuys was wrong. Surely his Holiness would never sanction the preferment of such a man?

She was surprised and alarmed to receive a letter from the Council. It informed her that the King's chief councillors had assembled several doctors and proposed to them that the unanimous opinion of the universities was that, if her first marriage had been consummated, her second was null.

'But it was *never* consummated,' she said aloud, for all that she was alone in her bedchamber. Yet there was worse to come. The King, she was told, had found a document, which he had shown to the Council, in which his father and King Ferdinand had stated that her marriage to Arthur *had* been consummated.

'*What document?*' Katherine cried out. There was no such thing. It was a forgery!

Nevertheless, the Council had accepted it as proof and agreed that it only remained for the King to proceed to his purpose by the authority of the Archbishop of Canterbury. There was no doubt in Katherine's mind what that purpose was.

He was going to take matters into his own hands, as she had feared. He really was going to set her aside and marry Anne Boleyn, regardless of the consequences.

She waited in a fever of agitation to see what would happen next, bracing herself to stand up for her rights, and the authority of the Holy See, in the face of any pretended divorce that Henry might push through. She waited in vain for a letter from Chapuys, who must have been aware of the situation. But what came, in February, was an order from the King to move to Ampthill Castle in Bedfordshire.

Katherine had stayed at Ampthill several times; it had been one of Henry's favourite places to stay when the court was on progress, for the air was healthy and the castle was surrounded by a well-stocked deer park. But it was nearly fifty miles from London, and it felt as if she were being banished there. That impression deepened as her cavalcade approached and the dark, ribbed walls and high battlements took on a sinister aspect, silhouetted against the early dusk.

They are trying to break my resistance, she thought. Yet her apartments were luxurious enough, and there was a pretty garden for her use.

'May I go abroad from the castle?' she asked Lord Mountjoy, who had escorted her to this place and was to remain in charge of her household.

'My orders are that your Grace is to stay within its precincts,' he told her, looking uncomfortable. That was not surprising. He was an honourable man, and he had given her impeccable service for twenty-four years, yet she knew it was more than his office was worth for him to speak out on her behalf or defy orders.

'My lord, am I a prisoner?'

'Not strictly speaking, no, madam. You are to enjoy every comfort and go where you will in the castle and gardens.'

So it was to be a gilded cage. Now she knew how her sister Juana must have felt all those years ago – and, for all she knew, felt now. She wondered if it would be better if she were insane like Juana, and in happy ignorance of what was going on around her. Yet poor Juana had endured her incarceration for over a quarter of a century now. It was a living death, and one that no human being should suffer. Living under house arrest, in luxury, could not compare with it.

But when one had known freedom, one chafed at even small restrictions – the inability to go hunting, or to send letters to friends. The order came – delivered by an evidently shocked Lord Mountjoy – that she was not to correspond with Mary, and that was the hardest thing to bear. Evidently Henry feared that she would incite Mary to defiance. It was intolerable, being cut off from her child, and from news of the outside world. Strict watch was kept on the comings and goings of Katherine's household, and she worried that any attempt on Chapuys's part to communicate with her would be discovered. Then she would be in an even worse state. He, brave man, was now the only channel through which she might get news of her daughter.

She was painfully aware that her servants were being punished for their loyalty with what was effectively imprisonment. Most of them bore it cheerfully, for love of her, which touched her deeply; but when she saw little Anne Parr leaning out of a window, tapping an impatient foot and gazing wistfully at the world outside, she felt dreadful. What life was this for a young girl? What life was it for any of them? It was then that, for the first time, she knew a moment of doubt. She had only to say the words, the words Henry wanted to hear, and they would all be free. But those same words would brand her child a bastard.

She could not give in. Too much was at stake.

It was early April, and the trees were festive with blossom, when the deputation from the Council, headed by the Dukes of Norfolk and Suffolk, came to Ampthill. Lord Mountjoy conducted them to Katherine's presence, and she received them seated in her high-backed chair by the hearth, filled with trepidation but determined not to let them see it. For when she saw the two dukes she knew that they must have brought her news of some import.

Norfolk acted as spokesman, his manner as blunt and abrupt as ever. 'We have come to inform your Grace that you must not trouble yourself any more in the Great Matter, nor attempt to return to the King, seeing that he is married.'

Married? She started at that, and her temper rose. Yes, he *was* married – to her!

'Henceforth you are to abstain from the title of Queen and be called the Princess Dowager of Wales,' Norfolk continued in his rasping voice, 'though you will be left in possession of your property.'

Lord Mountjoy stepped forward. 'That means, madam,' he said in a quiet voice, 'that the King will not allow you to call yourself Queen, and at the close of one month after Easter, he will not defray your expenses or the wages of your servants.'

Katherine stood up. She was incandescent. 'As long as I live I will call myself Queen!' she vowed. 'As to supporting my household, I do not care to begin that duty so late in life. Failing for food for myself and my servants, I will go out and beg for the love of God!'

'Do as you please. You have been warned,' Norfolk barked. And with that the lords left her.

She slumped back into her chair, trembling in disbelief and shock. The words *he is married, he is married* kept repeating themselves in her brain. How can his conscience allow it? she asked herself. Cranmer has not even proceeded to a judgement on our marriage – it has not been dissolved! This is bigamy, no less. What do the opinions of the universities count against the authority of the Church?

She summoned her household and told them what the deputation had come for. 'Henceforth,' she said, 'if you wish to remain in my service, you will not address me by any title other than Queen. Those who wish to leave may do so now, for you should consider that it may go the harder for you if you disobey the King's command.'

No one moved. She could see the outrage in their faces, and felt comforted. But after they had all dispersed, Anne Parr hung back.

'Your Grace, might I go to court?'

Katherine was startled.

'Not without the King's permission. You are his ward.'

'Will you ask him for me, madam?'

Katherine would have given much to say yes. She had seen for herself how bored and unhappy the girl was here, and she knew that Maud had fretted about her daughter's future. If Anne stayed, no man of any standing would ask for her.

'I am afraid that you must ask him yourself, child. I am forbidden to contact him.'

'Yes, madam.' Anne scuttled away eagerly.

To her surprise, Henry said yes, and soon Anne was excitedly waving them all goodbye and setting off for London with a small escort, bound for the court. And – there was no doubt about it – the service of Anne Boleyn. It was a small betrayal beside the many others Katherine had suffered, but it hurt. Maud would have been horrified had she known, and Katherine gave thanks that she was not here to see it.

Henry himself was not ill-natured, she told herself, as the clock struck four and still she was awake. It is Anne who has put him in this perverse and wicked temper. When the Emperor heard of this latest outrage, there was no telling what he would do. It might mean war – not that she would sanction that. There must be a better way to root out the Lady and her adherents. She did not doubt that, once this accursed Anne had her foot in the stirrup, she would do Katherine and Mary all the ill that she could. And, which was the most chilling prospect of all, if she had her way, the kingdom would be given over to heresy.

These fears, and the enormity of what had happened, plagued Katherine's mind as she went about her quiet daily affairs. There was no means of discovering what was going on in London. For all she knew, Anne might be crowned by now. She crossed herself at the thought. God was a little hesitant with vengeful thunderbolts these days, but she must have trust in Him, for everything happened for His greater purpose. Doubtless He was testing her – but, sweet Jesu, when was it going to stop?

A week after the deputation had left Ampthill, Lord Mountjoy came before Katherine. Looking shamefaced, as well he might, he made the mistake of calling her the Princess Dowager.

'That is not my title!' she blazed. She had never had occasion to speak so sharply to him.

'But, madam, the Council has issued an order commanding that from henceforth you be styled Princess Dowager.'

'I shall not talk to you if you address me thus,' she insisted. 'I reject it utterly.'

'Then, madam, I cannot give the courtesy that is your due. I came to tell you also that I have received a message from the King, bidding me warn you that you must soon retire to some private house of your own, and there live on a smaller allowance.'

He named a figure that would scarcely be sufficient to cover her expenses for three months.

'I shall beg my bread,' Katherine declared. 'How will that look to the King's subjects, and to the world at large? I cannot believe that a prince of His Grace's great wisdom and virtue will consent to putting me away thus. If he has no regard for men, he should have some respect for God! I have been married to him for nearly twenty-five years. We have a daughter endowed with all imaginable goodness and virtue, and of an age to bear children. Nature alone must oblige the King to consider her rights.'

'Madam, I may not comment on such matters,' Mountjoy said, clearly distressed.

'Be assured that the Emperor will never recognise the Lady Anne as queen, and that any annulment the King has procured can have no validity in law!' Katherine asserted.

When the chamberlain, looking mournful, had gone, and her anger had burned itself out, she sat back and took stock. The future looked black indeed, unless by a miracle the Pope came to her aid. It dawned on her that now, more than ever, her very existence posed a threat to Anne's security. Anne, she knew, could be vindictive, and her influence over the King was considerable. Remembering what had happened to Bishop Fisher, Katherine would be on her guard from now on.

At the end of April she received a summons to appear before a special ecclesiastical court that Archbishop Cranmer was convening in the priory at Dunstable, just four miles away. Now she knew why she had been sent to Ampthill. They had planned this all along.

She would not go. She would not collude in this travesty. It showed only how low her husband had sunk. Where was his care for the succession, that he had thought fit to enter a bigamous union that any fool might dispute?

'I utterly refuse to accept Archbishop Cranmer as my judge,' she declared. 'I look to none other than the Pope for a decision on my marriage.'

The young clergyman who had brought the summons regarded her with piteous contempt. 'May I remind your Grace that the recent Act Restraint of Appeals prevents any person from appealing to Rome for any cause whatsoever.'

'If I am not the King's wife, then I am not his subject and therefore not bound by his laws,' Katherine said.

'The Archbishop may declare you contumacious,' the objectionable young man warned.

'Let him!' she replied.

*

518

'Look at this, madam!' Blanche de Vargas cried, thrusting into Katherine's hands a pamphlet. 'It was pushed under the door.'

Katherine looked. The pamphlet was entitled *Articles devised by the whole consent of the King's most honourable Council, to exhort and inform his loving subjects of the truth.*

She did not need to be told what it contained.

'Burn it!' she ordered. 'I will not read these blasphemies.'

Later that day she summoned Eliza. 'My dear friend, can you do me a great favour? Do you have any kinsfolk who live near London?'

'My brother and his wife are lodging in London, for he is sitting in Parliament.'

'Good! Can you pretend that his wife is ill and asking for you?'

'Of course, madam,' Eliza agreed. 'I would do anything for you. My sister-in-law will not mind. Edmund is for the King, but secretly she supports your Grace.'

'Then ask Lord Mountjoy for permission to visit her. I want you to get a letter from me to Messire Chapuys. I will give you gold. Go to your brother's lodging, so that none suspects you, then when he is out hasten to the convent of the Austin Friars in Broad Street, and ask for Messire Chapuys's house. I know it lies near their church. Make sure this reaches him.' She gave Eliza a note folded into a tiny square. 'I have not signed it. He will know who it is from.'

In fact it bore just the one line: 'Tell the Emperor and the Pope that I now consider my cause to be desperate.'

She prayed that her message would reach Chapuys. Its very brevity would make clear to him the seriousness of her situation. She did not know how he could do more than he had done before, but she was hoping that, once the Pope heard of Henry's illicit marriage to Anne, he would be provoked into giving judgement. And that could not be a moment too soon, for if Anne were to become pregnant and bear a son, the King was sure immediately to have Parliament swear fealty to him as his heir. There was no time to lose!

It was Lord Mountjoy who acted as spokesman for this latest deputation from the Council, who waited on Katherine at Ampthill early in July, and his demeanour was grave. Katherine forced herself to stay calm and dignified. Whatever they said, she would not be cowed.

Mountjoy cleared his throat, obviously not relishing his task.

'Madam,' he began, and he did not call her by any title. 'I am commanded to inform you that the King is lawfully divorced and married to the Lady Anne, who has been crowned queen.'

'How can that be?' Katherine asked, stunned. 'The Pope has yet to give judgement.'

'The Bishop of Rome has no jurisdiction in this realm,' Norfolk interjected.

Katherine outfaced him. 'I will abide by no sentence save that of Rome.'

'It is too late for that, madam,' Mountjoy said. 'The sentence has been given by the judgement of His Grace of Canterbury. The King cannot have two wives, and therefore he cannot permit you to persist in calling yourself Queen. As his marriage to the Lady Anne is irrevocable, and has gained the consent of Parliament, nothing that you can do will annul it, and if you persist you will only incur the displeasure of Almighty God and of the King.'

He handed her a parchment, not looking her in the eye. 'Here are the King's terms for your submission, and your acknowledgement of his marriage.'

Katherine turned to Blanche de Vargas. 'Bring pen and ink,' she said, and when it was given her she sat down at the table, took the parchment and struck through the title Princess Dowager wherever it appeared, so vehemently that the nib tore the parchment.

'I am not the Princess Dowager but the King's true wife!' she declared. 'And since I have been crowned and anointed queen, and had lawful issue by the King, I will call myself Queen during my lifetime!'

'Madam, the rightful Queen is now Queen Anne,' Lord Mountjoy said, looking warily at the scowling, wrathful lords.

'All the world knows by what authority it was done!' Katherine cried. 'It was much more by power than by justice. There has been no true divorce, and the whole matter depends not on the universities but on the Pope.' She paused, calmer now. 'It is not that I desire the name of

Queen, but only for the discharge of my conscience that I declare I have not been the King's harlot for the past twenty-four years. I do it not for vainglory, but because I know myself to be his true wife.'

Mountjoy addressed a point past her shoulder. 'As the King's subject, you are bound to obey him.'

'You call me the King's subject?' Katherine cried. 'I was his subject while he took me for his wife. But if he says I am not his wife, I am not his subject! I did not come into this realm as merchandise, but as his lawful wife – not as a subject to live under his dominion. I have done England little good, and I should be loath to bring it any harm. But if I should buckle to your persuasions, I should slander myself and confess to having been the King's mistress – and that I will never do!' Her steady gaze took in every man in the room. 'This cause has been determined here in the King's realm before a man of his own making, not an indifferent person, I think; being the King's subject, his judgement is partial and suspect. I think there would have been a more indifferent outcome had the case been judged in Hell, for I think the devils themselves do tremble to see the truth so oppressed.' She spread her hands in earnest. 'If it can be proved that I have given occasion to disturb or offend my lord the King or his realm in any way, then I desire that I be punished according to the law.'

Mountjoy looked stricken. Norfolk growled at her. 'Your obstinacy might cause the King to withdraw his fatherly love from your daughter. That ought to move you, if nothing else does.'

It was a bluff – surely? Henry would never take out his anger against Katherine on Mary. But he had already, hadn't he, by keeping them apart.

'The Princess my daughter is the King's true child,' she replied, 'and as God has given her to us, so I will render her up to the King, to do with her as his pleasure dictates, trusting to God that she will prove an honest woman. Neither for my daughter, nor for any worldly adversity or the King's displeasure, will I yield in this cause, or put my soul in danger!'

The Duke of Suffolk stepped forward. 'By your obstinacy, you are indeed putting yourself in danger of the King's anger and its consequences!'

Katherine stared at him evenly. 'Not for a thousand deaths will I consent to damn my soul or that of my husband the King.'

The lords looked at each other, shaking their heads.

'There's no more to be said,' Norfolk muttered. 'We are wasting our time.'

They turned to go.

'Wait!' Katherine said. They looked at her, plainly hoping she had come to her senses, as they would see it. Well, they would wait for ever.

'I have to ask you,' she said. 'Was any judgement given concerning the status of the Princess? For even if my marriage *were* null, she is legitimate, owing to the lawful ignorance of the King and I when we entered into it. Surely the Archbishop has not dared to be so shameless as to declare her a bastard?'

'He has not, madam,' Dr Stephen Gardiner said, his manner terse. He was Henry's man through and through, and had been active on his behalf in Rome itself.

'That is one blessing,' Katherine sighed. 'Has the Princess been informed of his judgements?'

'We informed her ourselves,' Norfolk told her. 'And we have commanded her, in the King's name, not to communicate in any way with your Grace.'

Katherine felt as if she were dying inside, but she smiled grimly. 'By that, I take it that she told you that she would accept no one for queen except me.'

They would not tell her, but she saw in their faces that she was right.

She was punished for her defiance. Before that month of July was out, the King's command came: she was substantially to reduce her household and remove to the Bishop of Lincoln's palace at Buckden in the county of Huntingdon.

Go where I may, I am still his wife! she said to herself, as she fell to pondering on who should be let go. It was a difficult choice, but Lord Mountjoy had informed her that there would not be room to accommodate everyone, and on her reduced income she knew it would have been a struggle to support all her servants.

With a heavy heart she summoned her people and dismissed those she could not take with her, thanking them with all her heart for their service. It was hard to let them go, to see the tears in their eyes as they took the blow and the money she pressed into their hands. She realised that it would not be easy for them to find new places, for who would take on any who had loyally served a discarded queen? Yet she had no choice – they understood that.

When they had dispersed to gather up their belongings, she gave the order to pack, trying not to cry at the prospect of the difficult farewells that lay ahead, and thinking that it was not only in the big things that wrong had been done to her, but in seemingly small, insignificant matters like these.

Chapter 31

1533

As her cortège wound its way to Buckden, late in July, the country people ran after it in hordes, wishing her joy, comfort, prosperity and all manner of good things, and they were vehement in invoking misfortune on her enemies. Men and women, some with tears in their eyes, came begging her to let them serve her, and several declared that they cared not a fig for the King or his harlot, and that they were all ready to die for her sake. She thanked them all for their kindness and goodwill, and continued on her way, her litter crammed with humble gifts of posies, butter, eggs, cherries, honey and home-made wine.

As they drew nearer to their destination, Katherine noticed a gradual change in the countryside. Soon they were crossing tracks along dykes built across a vast, flat landscape of water and sedge. Here and there were a few humble dwellings of wattle, daub and thatch. Occasionally they saw the odd, barely human person making his way across the wetlands on a flat boat or even stilts. The inhabitants looked bent but hardy, their skin leathery from long exposure to the weather. The wind blew unhindered here, and the place felt remote and inhospitable.

'This is the Great Fen, madam,' Lord Mountjoy told her, riding alongside the litter.

In this strange world of endless water, reed beds and wet woodlands, Katherine espied beavers, otters and numerous birds.

'It looks to be a very unhealthy place,' Blanche said, peering out through the curtains with dismay. She and Eliza were sharing the litter with Katherine. 'Mark me, we'll all catch fevers.'

'I trust not,' Katherine said, hoping that wasn't what Henry had intended. Certainly he had meant for her to be even more isolated from the court and the world at large. It was his revenge on her for her defiance. In this desolate wilderness it would be even more difficult to maintain contact with Chapuys and her other friends.

Her spirits sank lower still when Buckden loomed up ahead. It was a forbidding place with a high old tower, and it was surrounded by a secure moat and a wall, and set apart from the nearby church and tiny village. The only good thing one could say for it was that it was near the Great North Road, which, she realised, might make communication with Chapuys possible.

All the houses in which Katherine had lived since leaving court had been suitably grand and well maintained, but it was clear from the first that at Buckden she would be living in greatly reduced circumstances. She was dismayed to be shown to apartments located in a corner turret of the Great Tower, which was fifty years old and looked it. Immediately she became aware of the damp that rose from the Fens. It was apparent in the stale air and in ominous green patches on the walls. Even though it was July and warm outside, she ordered that a fire be lit, but the rooms remained chilly and uncomfortable.

An attempt had been made by the custodian to brighten up Katherine's lodging with woollen hangings and embroidered cushions, and when her own furniture and belongings had been set out, the rooms did look more welcoming. But the dampness prevailed. Despite the hot bricks placed in her bed by her chamberers, the sheets felt clammy at night; mould formed in unworn shoes, and her lodgings never got properly warm. It was not long before she found herself with a permanent sore throat and wheezy cough, and her attendants frequently complained of sore eyes and skin rashes. It was all down to the damp, she was sure.

She lay in bed at night wondering if Henry had known about the state of Buckden. Certainly he had chosen it for its remoteness, but her whole being shied away from the possibility that he had also had a sinister motive in sending her here. Probably he had hoped thereby to secure her speedy submission, and had intended all along to move her on quickly to a more salubrious house. She could not believe he had purposed anything worse. She knew Henry. He could be cruel when thwarted, he could be vengeful, but he liked everything to be lawful. He was not a man to do things in an underhand way, and he would never stoop to murder. It was not his way. He would readily threaten those who opposed him, but with the full might of his laws.

Anne Boleyn was another matter. Katherine was sure that she would have no compunction in doing away with her enemies by secret means. One only had to remember the attempt on Bishop Fisher, and Anne's threats to him and to Mary. Katherine could imagine Anne secretly seeking out the most unhealthy houses in England, and then making an innocent suggestion to Henry, twisting the truth to suit her purpose.

Katherine would not be intimidated. She would stand fast, whatever they made her suffer.

'Visitors are forbidden, by the King's express command,' Lord Mountjoy had said when Katherine arrived, 'and no one is permitted to leave the house without permission.' But pretty Eliza had no trouble flirting with the guards at the gatehouse, and before long she had prevailed on them to let her out to buy food in the village.

'If they tell Lord Mountjoy,' she said, 'I will show him what I have bought.' She produced for Katherine a loaf of new bread, some cheese and a pot of quince marmalade.

It was but a step from there to smuggling out a letter to be given to a carter bound for London – and then it was a matter of hoping and praying that it reached Chapuys. In the meantime Katherine fretted about how little money she had to support herself and her servants. They would have to live carefully, and what there was to spare she would give in alms to the poor folk hereabouts.

Fortunately the Fens provided a great abundance of fish. Her table was graced with perch, roach, turbots and lampreys. Of meat there was little, but that did not worry her, for she had taken to fasting for the health of her soul, not just on Fridays but at other times. Through self-denial and penance, she might the better reach God and move Him to look kindly on her.

It was in prayer that she found the greatest solace. There was a little chamber with a squint that afforded a view of the altar in the castle chapel. Here Katherine would kneel, all by herself, for much of her days and nights, praying at the window, leaning on the sill. Often she left it wet with tears shed in loneliness, in sorrow, and in yearning for Henry and Mary. The rest of the time she spent with her women, making altar cloths and vestments that were to be given to churches near Buckden. That way she could continue to do good to her adoptive land.

They had not been at Buckden long when Lord Mountjoy brought a letter for Jane Seymour.

'Is it bad news?' Katherine asked gently, observing the young woman's face as she read it.

'Yes, madam. My father commands me home without delay. He says that he has found me a place at court, and has bought it dearly for me.'

'With the Lady Anne?' Who else would Jane serve at court? Sir John Seymour was evidently a man who seized his advantage.

'I fear so, madam.' Jane was weeping. 'Let me stay, your Grace! Oh, do let me stay! You could write to my father and command it . . .'

'Hush, child, do you think my word would carry any weight? Besides, it is more to your benefit to be serving one who is in favour than one who is not. Your father is wise; he sees this.'

'But I cannot serve her. I hate her and all she stands for!'

Katherine was startled to see the normally meek Jane so vehement.

'I am very sorry,' she said, 'yet there is no remedy. You must obey your father and go, but you go with my blessing.'

At that, Jane wept afresh. 'I will never have such a kind mistress,' she sobbed, her pale eyes pink with distress. 'I wish – I so wish – your Grace and the Princess a happy ending to your troubles.'

In streams of tears Jane went away and packed her things, while Lord Mountjoy arranged horses and an escort to take her south. She clung tightly when Katherine embraced her and bade her farewell.

'Your Grace knows that I am not going willingly!' she cried.

'I know that,' Katherine soothed. 'May God be with you always.'

527

One final curtsey and Jane was gone.

She watched from her window as the little cavalcade set off down the drive and the great doors of the gatehouse swung open to let it through. How she envied Jane, going to freedom, going to court, going where Henry was . . .

The royal messenger bowed and presented the letter. Katherine took it warily, broke the seal and read it. It was from the Privy Council. The King had requested the Princess Dowager to send the rich triumphal robe and bearing cloth that she had brought from Spain to wrap up her children for baptism, for the use of the child that his most entirely beloved wife, Queen Anne, was soon to bear him.

Katherine had suffered many blows in the past few years, and endured many cruelties, but this felt like the ultimate betrayal. It was tangible evidence that her husband now belonged to another, even if he was not lawfully married to her, and it brought home to Katherine a new and painful awareness of the intimacy between those two.

And that was not the whole of it! Was Anne not sufficiently satisfied with what she had taken from her already, that she should demand that her own child go to the font in the robe that Katherine's daughter and her precious firstborn son had worn? The idea was not to be borne! Besides, the robe was Katherine's personal property, given to her by her mother; it lay, yellowing slightly but cherished and lovingly folded away, in the bottom of her travelling chest. She wondered how Henry could have been so insensitive to agree to such a request. No doubt he feared to anger or upset Anne when she was near to her time.

She sent the messenger to the kitchens for something to eat – poor fellow, it was not his fault that he had brought such shocking news – and sat down to compose a reply. It was brief but succinct. 'You may tell His Grace that it has not pleased God that I should ever be so badly advised as to give assistance in a case as horrible as this.'

There was no response. It was a little victory.

Eliza's plan had worked. Katherine's message had found its way to Chapuys, who now had one of his men lodged in the Lion Inn at

Buckden. She thanked God fervently. At last she was in touch once more with her dear friend, who was still working tirelessly in her cause.

Mary was well. That, above all else, was what she wanted, and needed, to hear. But one other piece of news stood out from Chapuys's letter, and it made Katherine go cold. Henry's sister, the French Queen, was dead. She had been ailing for some time, apparently, of a disease in her side, and had passed away at Westhorpe in June. *And I did not know!* Katherine thought. Her sister-in-law had been, what, thirty-seven? Far too young to die and leave behind her children. All that golden brightness and beauty brought low, never to shine again. The French Queen had been a good and outspoken friend, fearless of offending her brother the King, who must, for all their disagreements, be feeling her loss. Katherine grieved for her, and for Henry.

Wiping away a tear, she turned to the rest of Chapuys's news. His Holiness, angered that the King had gone ahead and married the Lady without Papal sanction, had immediately declared their union null and void. Furthermore, he had threatened the King with excommunication if he did not send the Lady away by September.

'Heaven forbid!' Katherine cried out loud, bringing her maids running to see what ailed her. 'I would never wish that on anyone, least of all my lord.' She could not bear the thought of Henry being cut off from the Church and all its consolations, and cast out of the Christian community. Immediately, she wrote to the Pope. 'I beg your Holiness not to put the sentence of excommunication into effect, lest it should drive the King further into schism and wreck my hopes for a reconciliation.' For, of course, Henry would blame her, since it was she who had made the appeal to Rome. Then Eliza took the letter, flirted her way past the guards and tripped off jauntily into the village. Soon it was an established routine.

It was some days before a note came from Chapuys. Katherine was both heartened and alarmed to read that the Emperor was outraged at the way in which she had been treated, and had declared that, if she expressly wished it, he would declare war on England on her behalf.

'No,' she said to herself. 'Never!'

Her maids looked up in puzzlement and she sensed that she had again spoken aloud. Not for the first time she regretted the fact that, since Maria's departure, her household had been bereft of great ladies in whom she could confide. How she missed Maria and Margaret and Maud. She could not speak freely to Lord Mountjoy, who was in a difficult enough situation as it was. Nor dared she speak of her fears to her maids-of-honour. Willing, loving, loyal as they were, they were still young and loved to gossip, and they were not her equals. They had not yet learned the discretion that comes with age and high rank. And war was a serious matter indeed.

Trembling a little, she read on. It was clear that Henry feared what Charles might do. Cromwell had sounded out Chapuys on the likelihood of an invasion. 'But I would not be drawn,' the ambassador wrote, for of course he did not yet know what course she herself would take. She sensed that he was hoping that she would tell the Emperor to do his worst. It was what Chapuys, given his head, would have done; he would have said that Henry deserved to have the might of Spain and the Empire vengefully descending upon him.

Cromwell knew her courage, and evidently he feared her. He had observed to Chapuys, 'It is as well that the Princess Dowager is a woman. Nature wronged her in not making her a man. But for her sex, she would have surpassed all the heroes of history.'

She was gratified to hear it, but she did not want war. It was the last thing a good wife would wish on her husband, and she resolved again never to sanction it. She would not call down more ills upon a people who had so warmly taken her to their hearts. Besides, if Henry got any inkling that she had in any way endorsed, or appeared to endorse, the Emperor's threats, he could righteously proceed against her for incitement to war, which was treason in anyone's book, never mind the niceties about whose subject she was.

The next news from Chapuys was incredible. It seemed that Henry had begun to tire of Anne. He had been unfaithful. Chapuys did not say who the lady was; he was more concerned to report that, infuriated by the Lady's tirades when she found out, the King had told her she must shut her eyes and endure as well as more worthy persons had done; and she ought to know that it was in his power to humble her again in a moment, more than he had exalted her before. He had not spoken to her for two or three days, and after that relations between them had been frosty. Katherine was beginning to hope that this was the beginning of the end, when she saw that Chapuys had dismissed it all as a love quarrel and warned her to take no great notice of it.

But there had to be more to it than that, Katherine thought. Not a year before, Anne had been the mistress and Henry the adoring servant. Probably he was discovering that Anne was not fitted to be queen. What had been alluring in a mistress did not always become a wife. It was satisfying to know that he had compared her with his true Queen and found her wanting. He might well have gone to other women for what he could not enjoy with Anne while she was pregnant, but the fact that he could even contemplate doing so led Katherine to hope that his feelings for the Lady were no longer as intense as they had been.

When the church bells started pealing one morning in early September, Katherine stopped what she was doing, catching her breath at the realisation that they might be ringing out in rejoicing for the birth of a son to Henry and Anne. If so, she did not think she could bear it. So when Lord Mountjoy came and announced in clipped tones that a princess had been born, she did not know whether to exult or weep.

Chapuys wrote that Henry and Anne had shown great disappointment at the child's sex. 'They hold it a great reproach to all the doctors and astrologers who had predicted that it would be a boy. I can only conclude that God has entirely abandoned this King.'

Katherine was horrified to learn that Gertrude Blount had been appointed one of the godmothers – and she suspected that Gertrude's father, Lord Mountjoy, was too, although he would never have let it show. 'Lady Exeter wanted nothing to do with it,' Chapuys related. 'She had refused to attend the Lady's coronation, but was commanded in this case, and she and her husband were warned by the King that they must not trip for fear of losing their heads.' Henry had Gertrude in a corner, for her very public role at the ceremony would lead people to think that she had abandoned Katherine. But Katherine could not believe it. It is an honour born of malice, she thought.

'The little bastard's christening was cold and disagreeable,' Chapuys continued. 'There were no fireworks, or any bonfires lit in the City of London.'

Little bastard or not, the child, who had been given the name Elizabeth after Henry's mother, was still being vaunted as his true-begotten heir, while the rights of Mary were apparently being ignored. And yet Mary had the prior claim to the succession. Katherine felt desperate. What could she do? She was helpless, immured here at Buckden. She could only cling on to her much-tested faith in Henry's innate goodness and his love for Mary, and pray that his sinful passion for Anne would die.

Chapuys mentioned, almost in passing, that the Duke of Suffolk had remarried. Katherine found that shocking, given that the poor French Queen had been in her grave for less than three months, but as she read on her eyes widened. His new wife was Maria's daughter, her own godchild, Katherine Willoughby. Katherine did a rapid calculation: the girl was just fourteen, whereas Suffolk must be all of fifty! And he had not waited to observe a decent period of mourning. Of course, he had coveted Katherine Willoughby's estates and riches, she being a great heiress. But – wait a minute – had not the girl been betrothed to his son some years ago? She was sure she remembered Maria telling her that. In which case, he had wronged not only his late wife's memory but also his own flesh and blood. And – she almost smiled to herself – he had got with his stolen bride a mother-in-law who loathed him! She could imagine how relations stood between those two: Maria, the great friend of the Queen, and Suffolk, the willing tool of the King. It seemed there was some natural justice in this world after all.

Eliza had told Katherine that the guards were now not averse to sharing a bit of gossip, but one day she came back from her errands crying her eyes out, and it took some persuading before Katherine could get her to repeat what they had told her.

'They said that the next Parliament would decide if your Grace and the Princess were to suffer martyrdom,' she sobbed.

Trembling uncontrollably, Katherine sent for Lord Mountjoy and asked him if it was true.

His heavy-lidded, watchful eyes filled with the compassion he dared not admit to. 'The soldiers have pre-empted me, madam. I was about to inform you that I have received instructions from the Council to warn you of the danger.'

She felt sick to her stomach at hearing that, but outraged too.

'It is nothing but a malicious ploy to frighten me into submission!' she declared, sounding a lot braver than she felt. Lord Mountjoy said nothing, but his eyes were eloquent. She thought he was trying to tell her that it was just that.

But what if it was true?

'I am ready to face martyrdom,' she informed Chapuys, 'and I know the Princess is just as staunch in her convictions.' The thought of Mary, her innocent, sweet-natured child, facing martyrdom was nevertheless unbearable, but she held to her resolve. 'I hope that God will accept it as an act of merit, as we shall suffer for the sake of the truth. Rest assured, I do not fear it.'

For all her brave words, she became horribly afraid when Chapuys wrote that he thought it ominous that her guardians had been instructed to break her resistance by relaying such threats. 'The King has no legal grounds for proceeding against you, but the Princess is without doubt his subject, which is why I fear for her.' Reeling at that, Katherine could only conclude with Chapuys that the English government had gone mad. It was a relief to know that he had written to the Emperor, imploring him yet again to press the Pope to delay no further in pronouncing sentence. The matter was now urgent, he had stressed, for the recent arrest for treason of the Nun of Kent showed that Henry meant to deal harshly with those who opposed him. Katherine prayed that, when it came to her and Mary, his fear of reprisals from Charles would stay his hand.

She prayed too for the Nun of Kent, that poor, misguided creature. She thanked God that she had consistently refused to grant the woman an audience, for had she done so, it would be easy for them to implicate her in the Nun's treason. No doubt Cromwell was now doing his efficient best to discover if she had ever written or sent a message to her. But she was perfectly at ease on that score.

Lord Mountjoy stood before Katherine. He had aged in her service during these past, difficult years, and was a shadow of the handsome, assured young scholar he had once been.

She realised that the latest threats against her and Mary had strained this good man's loyalty too far.

'Your Grace,' he said, his voice breaking, 'I have come to tell you that I have asked to be relieved of my duties as chamberlain.' He hesitated as he saw her eyes fill with tears. 'I can no longer be a party to the ill-treatment to which you are being subjected. I do not see it as my part to vex and disturb you, for the King's Grace had me sworn to serve you to the best of my power. I would rather serve him in any cause, even a dangerous one, than meddle further in this.'

'Oh, this is a very sad day, my lord,' Katherine said, touched beyond measure at such candid and loyal support. She had long suspected that Lord Mountjoy was deeply unhappy about carrying out the orders that came from the Council, but she had never expected him to speak out openly against the King.

'You have served me faithfully for so many years,' she said, just holding herself together. 'I will be deeply sorry to see you go.'

But as she prepared herself to lose yet another true friend, the King's answer was returned. Henry would not permit Lord Mountjoy to resign.

'I am so glad,' she told him, overwhelmed with relief, and grateful that Henry had unwittingly left her an ally.

He looked at her a little shamefacedly. 'From now on, I will do all in my power to make life easier for you,' he assured her.

'That will be a great comfort to me, my lord,' she told him. 'And if you have to be severe to me in the presence of others, I will understand.'

News from Chapuys came fairly regularly now. No one seemed to suspect that Eliza's forays into Buckden were for any purpose other than buying provisions. Katherine heard that the Nun of Kent had been made to do public penance, walking through the streets of London to Paul's Cross, where a sermon was preached against her. 'The King wants Parliament to pass an Act of Attainder condemning her,' Chapuys told her. 'He does not want her tried in open court, for he fears demonstrations against himself. Even King Richard the Third was never so much hated by his people as this King, and there is little love for the Lady.'

In December Katherine learned that Anne's daughter had been given her own household at Hatfield. Mary had refused to recognise Elizabeth as their father's heir, and had bravely insisted that she alone was the King's true daughter, born in lawful matrimony. She had spoken up and declared that she would be slandering and dishonouring her mother, her father, the Holy Church and the Pope if she falsely confessed herself a bastard.

No one could make her a bastard, Katherine was certain. Her parents had married in good faith. Yet evidently that was what they were trying to do. And if Mary continued to defy the King, they would surely redouble their efforts. While she applauded Mary's courageous stand, she feared it had been unwise.

'The King himself is not ill-natured,' Chapuys observed. 'It is this Anne who has made him like this, and alienates him from his former humanity.'

Anne was patently jealous – and she was aware that Mary was popular, and that her own child was seen by many as a bastard. No doubt she feared – and rightly – that Mary would become a focus for those who opposed her marriage. And so she was taking her revenge. Katherine was appalled to hear that Mary had been deprived of the title of Princess; her palace of Beaulieu had been given to George Boleyn; her jewels had been taken from her and given to Anne herself, who had said that the King's bastard daughter could not be permitted to wear what was meant for his lawful heir. Then came the shocking news that Mary's household had been disbanded and she herself sent to Hatfield to serve as a maid-of-honour to Elizabeth. Worse still, her beloved Lady Salisbury had been dismissed for refusing to surrender Mary's jewels to

Anne Boleyn, and in her place was Lady Shelton, Anne Boleyn's aunt, who by all accounts was treating Mary harshly. Katherine knew that Mary was afraid of being forced into a compromising situation that would besmirch her honour, and was therefore constantly on her guard.

Katherine suffered agonies at the thought of what her poor child was enduring. It frightened her to hear that Mary's health was deteriorating. Chapuys had written that Mary lived in fear of being poisoned, and Katherine's fevered imagination took flight at that, for her daughter was surrounded by hostile Boleyn kinsfolk and adherents who were unkind and often insolent, and might not scruple to stoop to evil.

That winter was bitter. Much of the Great Fen was flooded, and when the water froze the inhabitants could be seen crossing it on skates made of animal bones. The winds that blew unhindered across the flat land whistled and roared through every crevice in doors and windows, and down chimneys, and the old tower seemed damper and colder than ever.

Katherine knew that her health had suffered from living in such severe conditions. She had a vague, ill-defined feeling of creeping malaise, nothing she could describe specifically, but debilitating all the same. Dr de la Saa and Dr Guersye prescribed endless cordials and herbal infusions, but none helped. Even her younger maids were complaining of chilblains and perpetually runny noses.

They could not go on like this. The place was gradually killing them.

Katherine sent a message to the Council, asking if the King would permit her to move to a healthier house. But before they could respond a letter came post-haste from Chapuys.

The Lady has urged that your Grace be moved to Somersham Castle, another residence surrounded by deep water and marshes. The King, who dares not contradict her, has agreed to shut up your Grace in this island and to accuse you of being as insane as Queen Juana is reputed to be. I protested in the strongest terms that Somersham is the most unhealthy and pestilential house in

England, and thanks to my intervention the King has changed his mind, although he was not best pleased that I had interfered. Still, he is in fear of the Emperor.

Sure enough, Lord Mountjoy was soon telling Katherine that the King had offered to move her to Fotheringhay Castle, which she herself had once owned in the days when she had been the unchallenged Queen. But Chapuys had been deceived. In those distant, early years she had lavished money on it, yet hardly visited enough to justify the outlay, which had been wasted anyway, for long afterwards both she and Henry had been informed that the refurbishments had not saved the ancient fabric of the buildings from advancing decay. Heaven only knew what condition Fotheringhay was in now – it was probably in a more pitiful state than Somersham.

The worst thing was that Henry knew it.

Katherine turned to Lord Mountjoy. 'I have no mind to go to Fotheringhay, although I very much wish to leave this place.'

'I will write to the King,' the chamberlain said.

Katherine hoped she would hear no more of the matter. Christmas was almost upon them, and while Katherine was steeling herself to endure another Yuletide without Mary, the household at Buckden was doing its best to put on a brave face in honour of the season and make meagre preparations for some good cheer, although inevitably it looked as if fish would be on the menu as usual. Then suddenly the Duke of Suffolk arrived, at the head of a detachment of the King's guards.

Suffolk was no longer the handsome and debonair gallant who had clandestinely married the King's sister. The man who bowed before Katherine was running to fat, and his spade-shaped beard was streaked with grey. Even so, the likeness to Henry still struck her, though God forbid that her husband would ever look as decrepit as the Duke. How must Maria feel, seeing her daughter tied to this miserable specimen of manhood?

Huddled in his furs, Suffolk edged closer to the fire beside which Katherine was sitting. She was glad that he was experiencing for himself the biting cold and the unhealthy miasma of this place; hopefully he would report back to his friend the King.

He stood before her, the big fellow, looking unaccustomedly awkward. Katherine wondered why he had come.

'How is my goddaughter?' she asked, since he seemed to be in no hurry to inform her of the purpose of his visit.

Suffolk frowned. 'I did not come to exchange pleasantries, madam,' he blustered. 'It's about other matters.' He paused, shifting his weight from foot to foot. She guessed that he did not relish what he had come to say, and was wishing himself back with his young bride, in the warmth and splendour of a court preparing for Christmas.

'Madam,' he said, his voice gruff, 'I had hoped on the way here to meet with an accident that would have prevented me from carrying out my orders, for I am commanded to dismiss all but the most necessary of your servants. Those who remain are to undertake not to address you as Queen, but as Princess Dowager.'

'You must do as you are commanded, but you know, for I have told you myself, that I will never acknowledge that title,' Katherine said sternly.

'You had best beware how far you provoke the King, madam. You see these letters . . .' Suffolk produced from inside his doublet a sheaf of papers and handed them to her. They were copies of her letters to the Pope.

'May I remind your Grace of how you have sought means to bring grief to the King and his realm? Well, I am here to ensure that henceforth you shall not be suffered to do that.'

Katherine retorted heatedly, 'And may I remind *you*, my lord, that it was my plea to his Holiness that saved the King from excommunication! My husband knows that I wish him no harm, and that I render obedience to him in all ways save those that touch my conscience. He knows too that, when it comes to the legality of our marriage, I would rather be torn in pieces than admit I am not his wife!'

'I see you are as obdurate as ever,' Suffolk sighed, 'and that being so, I am commanded to escort you to Somersham without delay.'

'No,' Katherine said. 'I am not going. I would be putting myself and my servants at peril if I did. This house is unhealthy enough, but Somersham is worse. The King knows that, and that I do not want to remove there.'

'The King is adamant.'

'I have told you, it is out of the question.' She could feel her temper rising again.

'Madam, if you don't go of your own accord, I will have to make you. Those are His Grace's orders.'

'I have said no! Did you not hear me, my lord?'

'I have my orders, madam!'

This was not to be borne! She would not go. She would stay here, and let them dare try to force her. She was so furious she was shaking. Without a word she stood up and in a few quick steps had made the safety of her privy chamber, slamming the door behind her and dropping the thick oak bar into its metal cradle.

'If you wish to take me with you, you will have to break the door down!' she cried, her heart pounding.

The Duke banged on the door. 'Madam, come out!' he called. 'It is useless to defy the King's orders. Do not make things worse for yourself.'

'It will be the worse for me if I go to Somersham. It will kill me!'

'The King may construe your disobedience as treason.'

'And I may construe his orders as inhumane! Does he want my death on his conscience?'

They argued for at least ten minutes, until the Duke fell silent. After a space Katherine heard men's muted voices in the outer chamber. She bent her ear to the keyhole.

'I dare not break down the door or seize her by force,' Suffolk was saying. 'She is the Emperor's aunt, and there might be repercussions. Let us proceed to the dismissal of her servants. My Lord Mountjoy, will you summon them here?'

Katherine stood tense, listening, on the other side of the door. She heard the Duke reading out a list of the members of her household who were to leave. Such trusted, familiar names . . . And after years of good service, to be cast off as if they had done something wrong. She could hear a woman sobbing, and felt like crying herself.

'You are commanded in the King's name to refer to your mistress in future as the Princess Dowager,' Suffolk was telling them.

'My lord, hear us out.' It was her chaplain, Father Abell, who spoke. 'We have all sworn our oaths of service to Queen Katherine, and cannot perjure ourselves by calling her anything else.'

'I was told that you were a troublemaker,' Suffolk growled. 'Take him and this other priest – aye, and anyone else who causes mischief – and keep them in custody in the porter's lodge.'

There was a scuffle, then the outer door banged shut.

'I'll write to the King tonight and ask what I should do with them,' Katherine heard Suffolk say. Then, in a louder voice, 'Now, those of you remaining must swear a new oath of loyalty to the Princess Dowager.'

There was a chorus of protests, as the Duke blustered and threatened, and in the end yelled that he would report their disobedience to the King that very night. In the end, some capitulated and took the oath. Katherine heard them with a heavy heart, although she was grateful not to be deprived of all her servants. They had made their objections known, and given in out of consideration for her.

But then the most dearly loved voices spoke out: Eliza's, and the Otwell sisters', and those of her other female attendants. No, they would not swear such an oath!

'Then you are dismissed,' Suffolk said, and Katherine sank to the floor, her hand pressed to her mouth to stifle her outburst of protest and her sobs.

There was a muted shuffling of footsteps, and then silence. Katherine stayed on the floor, her back pressed against the door, sunk in misery. All whom she had left were the Vargas twins, who, as Spaniards, could not be made to swear the oath. Blanche was dutiful enough, although she was fifty now and creaking in the joints, but Isabel, although a witty companion, had always been indolent and next to useless. How she would miss Eliza – Eliza, with her resourceful links to Chapuys! But it would not only be on account of that. She would miss Eliza's merry soul, her kindness and her strength. And Margery Otwell, who had been so supportive these past months. And the rest, dear, good companions whom she had cherished . . .

She was aware of a footfall behind the door and then Suffolk spoke.

'Madam, please come out!'

She would not answer. Instead, she remained on the floor, leaning against the heavy oak door, clutching her rosary.

'Madam, it will go the worse for you if you persist in this folly! Listen to reason, I pray you.'

'Your Grace, the Duke speaks sense!' That was Lord Mountjoy.

'What you are doing is against all reason,' Suffolk chimed in.

'I will not come out, and I will not go to Somersham unless you bind me with ropes and violently force me to it!' Katherine said at length. 'And I will not be served by any sworn to me as the Princess Dowager.'

'Madam, your necessary women will be replaced with those who are more obedient to the King's Grace.'

'I will not accept any others!' she cried. 'Failing proper attendants, I will sleep in my clothes and keep this door locked!'

Again there was muttering outside the door. 'By her wilfulness she may feign herself sick and keep her bed, or refuse to put on her clothes, or otherwise conduct herself in some other foolish way,' she heard Suffolk say. 'By God, she is the most obstinate woman!'

'But she must be adequately served,' Mountjoy murmured.

'Very well,' Suffolk called. 'Two of your English women may remain. Who are they to be?'

Katherine breathed deeply in relief. 'Thank you, my lord! I will have Elizabeth Darrell and Margery Otwell.'

'Very well,' the Duke said. 'But they are not to address you as Queen. And you must come out.'

'No,' Katherine said.

She heard Suffolk sigh.

'Is the only remedy to convey her by force to Somersham?' Mountjoy asked. 'I must admit I find the prospect distasteful.'

'I too,' Suffolk grunted. 'My mother-in-law will never speak to me again, although that would be a blessing, I promise you! But I can't just manhandle her out of the house. I must ask what the King's express pleasure is in regard to it. I hope to God I hear back by the twenty-first, otherwise there won't be time before Christmas to remove her.' He lowered his voice, but Katherine could make out his words. 'My lord,' he murmured, 'I have found things here far from the King's expectations.'

'How does your lordship mean?'

'His Grace imagines that the Princess Dowager is in high health and fighting spirits, and ready to make war on him. But I was shocked to see how she has deteriorated in health. She has lost weight and looks ill. Believe me, I do not relish harrying a sick woman to move to a ruinous house. If the King knew, I am sure he would choose some other lodging.'

If the Lady Anne would let him! Katherine thought grimly, struggling to her feet and moving into her bedchamber. She did not want to hear more. She was disturbed by Suffolk's concerns about her health, for she had not realised that she looked so ill. It was true, she had lost weight, but that was the consequence of so much fasting, and the monotonous diet she was served. She had felt that vague sense of malaise increasingly lately, but had put it down to the cumulative effects of the damp, cold conditions at Buckden.

She peered at herself in her glass. A pale, haggard face stared back. Faded, sunken . . . old. Her looks had gone, but that was to be expected at forty-eight. She did look drawn, but who would not, in her circumstances?

The voices had ceased now. She was all alone at the top of the tower, with no one to attend her. She had not eaten, but that did not matter, for she was not hungry. She tried to pray, but was too disturbed in her mind, and fearful of what the morrow might bring. There were no rushlights to light the candles, so her rooms were in darkness, and they were freezing. Lacking her maids, she could not unlace her gown and undress for bed, but no matter, it was too cold to disrobe. Removing her hood, her shoes and the pendant she always wore – the cross with the three pearls that Henry had given her long ago – she climbed fully dressed into bed and huddled down under the covers.

She was woken the next morning by Suffolk banging on the door. She ignored him and sat at her mirror, trying to tidy her hair and arrange her hood. It was so cold that she hunted out a thick shawl and wrapped it around herself.

Lord Mountjoy was at the door now, calling out that he had brought her some food with which to break her fast. She was light-headed with hunger, but dared not open the door, lest she be seized and taken by force to Somersham.

'Take it away!' she cried. He pleaded with her, but she stuck to her resolve.

Shivering, she went to her window to look down on the frost-covered world beyond, and then she saw a strange thing. There were men – local farm-workers and labourers, by the look of the homespun clothing in which they were bundled – and they were gathering silently beyond the wall that encircled the palace, ranging themselves at intervals along the perimeter. They had in their gloved hands scythes, pitchforks and other farm implements, and they were holding them at the ready, as if they were weapons. They did nothing, but stood there, watching and waiting.

Katherine stared at them for a long time. What did they want? Why had they come? Then she saw one of her dismissed servants among the watchers, and enlightenment dawned. Those of her people who had been sent away must have told the local folk what was going on in the tower. And so they had come, these good, true men, to make their silent protest and protect their beloved Queen. The sight cheered her immensely.

Later that day she was overjoyed to hear Eliza's voice at her door.

'Madam, I have brought you food. The carpenter is with me. He will knock out one of the lower panels of the door, so that I can pass it in.'

Thanks be to God, Katherine breathed. She was near to fainting through lack of sustenance.

'Is Margery still here?' she called.

'Yes, she is to stay too, madam.'

'I am so pleased. I asked for you both. The Duke would only let me keep two of you. I hope that Margery is not upset about Elizabeth having to leave.'

'She understands, madam. Do not worry.'

A few bangs with a hammer and the panel was on the floor. Above the din, Eliza called, 'Look out of your window, your Grace! The commons hereabouts are come to support you. The Duke is most uneasy about it. He will do nothing more until he receives instructions from the King.'

Katherine went back to the window. There were more men gathered below now, all of them just standing and watching. But there was an air of menace about them. She was not surprised that Suffolk was afraid.

On the last day of December, when she had been shut in her privy chamber for nigh on two weeks, Lord Mountjoy came to tell her that Suffolk had left for the court, and that the King had ordered that she was to remain at Buckden for the present. She sighed with relief, then looked again out of her window. The labourers, who had stayed on watch, changing shifts, all this time, had gone, and by that she knew that it was safe to open her door.

She emerged into a presence chamber stripped of its chair and canopy of estate, and called for her household to attend her. But pitifully few came. Two years ago she had had two hundred and fifty maids-of-honour, but now she had just three, Eliza Darrell, Blanche and Isabel de Vargas, and her sole remaining chamberer, Margery Otwell. Even though Margery protested that she was rather old, in her late thirties, to be a maid-of-honour, Katherine resolved immediately to promote her to the same rank as the other three, as compensation for the dismissal of her sister. Besides these ladies there was her tailor, Mr Wheeler; his wife, Dorothy; her two physicians; her apothecary, Master Juan; and her grooms and ushers, Philip, Anthony and Bastien. She had also been left her laundress, her cook, the little maids who cleaned for her, her goldsmith, the faithful Francisco Felipez, and her Spanish confessor, the Bishop of Llandaff. They were most of them growing long in the tooth now, and her doctors certainly should have been enjoying a tranquil retirement. This was not the life they had been destined for, yet they had all chosen to stay and share her privations. It humbled her.

'They let me remain, madam, because they thought I would do less harm than anyone else,' the Bishop told her. 'But your English chaplains, Father Abell and Father Forrest, were made to leave.'

She embraced them all, deeply grateful to have their friendly faces about her. And then she called for a good dinner – or what passed for one here – at which everyone, even the astonished laundress, was to be seated at her table.

Chapter 32

1534

Katherine had feared that her defiance of Suffolk would lead to greater restrictions being placed on her household, but Eliza was able to come and go as before, and that was how Katherine learned from Chapuys that – at last, at last – Pope Clement had convened the consistory court that would decide the King's case.

'Eliza, there is no time to be lost. Is there any way we can get a letter to the Emperor?' she asked.

'I will do my best, madam,' the girl promised. Later that day she returned from the Lion Inn and reported that there had been a ship's master there, home between voyages to visit his family. He was soon to return to his vessel at Boston, and would be visiting Bruges, where he said a ship could be found to convey a letter to Spain.

'Oh, that is wonderful!' Katherine cried. 'Thank you, dear girl!'

She called for writing materials and wrote to her nephew. If anyone could influence this new Papal court, he could. 'Beg his Holiness to act as he ought for God's service and the tranquillity of Christendom,' she urged. 'All other considerations, even the lives of myself and my daughter, ought to be put aside. There is no need to tell you of our sufferings. I could not endure so much, did I not think these things suffered for God's sake. As long as I live, I shall not fail to defend our rights.'

The weeks went by as January gave place to February, and when Katherine thought she might begin to look for a response, a letter came from Chapuys. She was disturbed to learn that he had again urged the Emperor to declare war on Henry; but Charles had informed him that, though he was bound to his aunt, this was a private matter, and public considerations had to be taken into account. In future, she was to communicate with him through Chapuys, rather than directly, to avoid any accusations of her inciting war. It was well meant, but it confirmed what Katherine had recently begun to suspect, that her nephew did not regard her sufferings as politically critical. And that came like a slap in the face.

That February, whether it was from the stress of worrying about what the Pope would say, or the effects of the bitter winter, Katherine fell ill and had to take to her bed. She lay there feverish and shuddering, coughing incessantly, while her maids soothed her raging brow with damp cloths and Dr de la Saa tested her urine and prescribed feverfew, although when he had gone Margery Otwell was adamant that a slice of toast soaked in vinegar and applied to the throat would be more effective, while Blanche said that her grandmother in Toledo swore by eating spiders coated in butter. Katherine was too poorly to care. Her feet and legs had swelled, and in the mornings her eyes were puffy. Dr de la Saa said it was dropsy, and shook his head, looking worried.

But gradually Katherine began to recover. Early in March she was well enough to leave her bed and sit in her chair, but she was thinner than ever and her once-golden hair had turned completely grey. *What would Henry think of me now?* she wondered. *And Mary?* Perhaps it was as well the dear child could not see her looking so old and ill.

A letter came from Chapuys. Eliza, that resourceful girl, had kept him informed of her mistress's progress, and he had been most concerned. 'I rejoice to hear that your Highness is better,' he had written. 'I was worried that means were being employed to hasten your death. I feared that they were trying to give you artificial dropsy. It is a relief to me to know that you are recovering.'

Had there been an attempt on her life? Much perturbed, she consulted both Dr de la Saa and Dr Guersye, but neither of them took the possibility seriously.

'I have seen these evil humours many times,' Dr Guersye said. 'Had your Grace been living in a better place, you would have recovered sooner.'

Katherine's convalescence received a setback when news came that the Lady was expecting another child. 'She wishes to bring the Princess Mary over to her side,' Chapuys wrote.

When the Lady visited the little bastard, she urged the Princess to visit her and honour her as queen, saying it would be a means of reconciliation with the King, and that she herself would intercede with him for her. The Princess replied that she knew no queen in England except her mother, but if Madam Boleyn would do her that favour with her father, she would be much obliged. The Lady repeated her offer, but to no effect, and in the end she made all manner of threats to the Princess Mary, but could not move her. She was very indignant.

Katherine was glad to hear that Mary was standing up for what was right, but fearful lest there should be consequences. Worrying about her daughter kept her awake at night, and hindered her recovery. Then, to her dismay, she heard from Chapuys that Mary had refused to accompany Elizabeth's household when it moved to the More, and had been manhandled into a litter. 'This is my fault,' the ambassador confessed.

In order to prevent her father and his lady from thinking she was worn down and conquered by ill-treatment, I had advised her to speak out boldly, but not to do anything so extreme that it led to her being taken by force, for fear of irritating her father. Now the King is very angry with her, and the Princess is in great distress. Three times she has written to me from the More, to know what to do. I have warned her not to behave as she did, and enjoined her to obey her father in all matters save that issue that touches her conscience.

It was sound advice, Katherine knew. Yet for all her fears for her daughter, something inside her thrilled at Mary's defiant stand.

*

Soon afterwards Lord Mountjoy sought out Katherine.

'I bring important news that will affect you, madam,' he informed her. 'Parliament has deprived you of the lands settled on you as queen, and returned to you those that you once held as Prince Arthur's widow. The Queen's lands have been assigned to Queen Anne.'

'Not all the estates in the kingdom can make her queen in truth,' Katherine said.

'Your Grace must not say so,' Mountjoy reproved her, with a smile that belied his words. 'I am also commanded to tell you that Parliament has passed an Act confirming the judgements of His Grace of Canterbury that your marriage is invalid and that the matrimony between the King and Queen Anne is good and lawful.' He swallowed. 'And that your daughter, the Lady Mary, is declared illegitimate in law. Madam, pray allow me to finish! This Act also settles the succession on the issue of the King and Queen Anne, and it requires all the King's subjects, if so commanded, to swear an oath acknowledging Queen Anne as the King's lawful wife, and the Princess Elizabeth as his legitimate heir – and recognising His Grace as Supreme Head of the Church in England under Christ.'

'I will never swear to any of it!' Katherine vowed.

'Anyone refusing to swear will be accounted guilty of misprision of treason and sent to prison,' Lord Mountjoy warned her.

'I might remind you, my lord, that I am already a prisoner, but if the King wishes to send me to the Tower, I am ready to go!' she countered. 'I will never say that my marriage is not lawful and that my daughter is a bastard. And she is the *Princess* Mary, not the Lady Mary!'

The Pope had finally spoken: her marriage was lawful and valid.

She felt her knees buckle beneath her as she read Chapuys's letter, and sank down on a stool. Evidently the news had spread by other means as well, for they were ringing the church bells in Buckden.

Unable quite to believe it, she summoned her household and told them the good tidings, then she left them rejoicing and hugging each other, and went to the chapel to render profound and hearty thanks to God, who had vindicated her at last. Seven long years she had waited for this moment, and she could hardly believe it had come. She *was* the King's true wife. No one could now deny it. Nor could they deny that Mary was his legitimate daughter and rightful heir. Her daughter's anxieties could be laid to rest now. There would be no more wrangling, no more waiting, no more unpleasantness.

For the King, Chapuys had written, had been ordered by the Pope to resume cohabitation at once with his lawful wife and Queen. 'He has been instructed to hold your Highness and maintain you with love and honour, as a loving husband, as his kingly honour requires him to do, and if he refuses, he will be excommunicated. He is also to pay the costs of the case. Already the people are celebrating in the streets . . .'

Indeed they were! Looking down from the tower she could see a crowd gathering at the gates, cheering and calling for her. She waved, smiling, bowing her head in thanks. Soon, surely, she would be riding down the Great North Road to London and the court, and more people would come running to see her, and she would express her deepest gratitude for their steadfastness and loyalty.

There would be no bitterness, no reproaches. She would return to Henry brimming with love, and with forgiveness in her heart, happy to be restored to her rightful place. She would not be vindictive to Anne, but would show herself generous. Anne would have to leave court, of course, taking her infant with her, and Mary would be reinstated as Henry's true heir. No doubt Henry would find Elizabeth a husband in time. He had provided handsomely for his other bastard.

Katherine sent for Lord Mountjoy and knew by his jubilant expression that he had heard the news.

'You have learned of the Pope's sentence, my lord?'

'Yes, your Grace, I have. May I be the first to congratulate you?' He beamed at her. He too was pleased that this dreadful business was at an end.

'Have you heard from the King?'

'I have heard nothing as yet, madam.'

'I am sure we will hear soon. I should be making ready to return to court.'

Lord Mountjoy frowned. 'I regret that I cannot allow your Grace to leave without the King's sanction.'

'Of course.' She smiled at him. 'It will not be long to wait!'

As Lord Mountjoy left her chamber, Katherine paused to wonder how Henry was feeling. She remembered him saying vehemently that he would not heed the Pope, whatever judgement he gave, but she knew that, underneath the anger and the bravado, there lurked a true son of the Church who had been led astray, and she could not believe that he would ignore this ruling. It would jolt him into the comprehension of what he was doing, and how he had put his immortal soul in peril. No man liked to be proved wrong, especially kings, and Henry had been infatuated with Anne. Yet maybe the signs had been accurate, and he *was* tiring of her. Her new pregnancy complicated matters, of course, but no one could argue with the Pope's declaration. Katherine would go gently with Henry. She would give him time and win back his love by kindness.

She had her maids pull her gowns out of the chest. They were all showing signs of wear.

'I think the crimson velvet will pass,' she said. 'Have it brushed and hung up to air. And there's a biliment on my gold hood that needs stitching back on. I want to look my best for His Grace.'

Her maids washed her hair in water and wood ash, and laundered her finest body linen. The summons would come soon, she was sure, and she wanted to be ready to leave immediately. Happily, she immersed herself in plans for reinstating her dismissed servants, for inviting Maria back to court and for recalling Margaret Pole to be Mary's governess. Maybe Henry would look kindly on reestablishing Thomas More as chancellor. Now that there was no Great Matter forcing people to take sides and causing bad feeling, the world could set itself to rights.

There remained the question of the succession, but Mary was now of marriageable age. She could be wed to Reginald Pole, as Katherine had long desired; their union would surely find favour with the people, and the royal houses of York and Tudor would again be united. Their marriage would also lay to rest the spectre of civil war that had haunted Henry for as long as Katherine could remember, for if Mary bore a son that would solve the problem of the succession. Katherine could see the years stretching ahead, herself and Henry growing mellow with age together, surrounded by grandchildren, at peace with Christendom.

But a fortnight passed, and no summons came. Gradually the bitter truth dawned: nothing had changed as far as Henry was concerned. He was entirely Anne's creature, and Cromwell's, so much so that he remained determined to defy the Holy See.

This was the most crushing disappointment that Katherine had had to bear. It was cruel, *cruel*, to have won her case, only to have it made plain to her that it made no difference. All along she had never doubted that Henry would abide by the Pope's judgement, but now she saw how far he had separated himself from Rome.

She wept – how she wept! Abandoning the proper distance imposed by rank, she sobbed in Eliza's arms, crying out against the unjustness of it all. And when she thought of Mary, and how this would affect her, she cried and raged all the more.

She dragged herself out of her misery and wrote to Chapuys. 'I imagined that, when the Papal sentence was delivered, the King would return to the right path. But I now realise that it is absolutely necessary to apply stronger remedies to this evil. What they are to be, I cannot say, but a means must be found to bring the King to his senses.' After the letter had been sent, she realised that anyone reading it might be forgiven for thinking that she was sanctioning war, but what she really hoped was that the Emperor and the Pope would content themselves with threats that Henry could not ignore. What he did not know was that she had no real expectation of Charles doing anything more for her.

But Chapuys replied that the Emperor would not fail to do what was necessary for the execution of the Pope's sentence. That heartened her, until she read on: 'What is necessary, your Highness, is armed force, but His Imperial Majesty will not take that course unless you yourself specifically ask it. He means to compel the Pope to ex-communicate the King, in the hope that it will bring him to his senses.'

That sounded a sensible, if drastic, course, and Katherine hoped against hope that Henry would take heed and soon be restored to the fold.

She hoped too that Charles would act soon, because it seemed that Henry was now determined to punish any who opposed him.

'No one dares speak out against him,' Chapuys informed her. 'Cromwell is rigorously enforcing the oath, and most are taking it without demur.' But Bishop Fisher had refused to do so. 'I am told that he received terrible letters from the King about it. Now he has been deprived of his office, attainted for treason and imprisoned in the Tower, in great danger of his life, even though he has written to His Majesty protesting his loyalty.'

Katherine's heart pounded in fits and starts as she read this, and she had to sit down. That good, upright man, who had been such a friend to her and was respected by all. How could Henry treat him so badly? And how, being advanced in years, would he fare in the Tower? Who would dare send him food and warm clothing?

But even more terrible news followed. She could not believe that Henry had also sent his good friend, Sir Thomas More, to the Tower. He loved More! He had always admired and revered him, and hung on his every word. But More had refused the oath. It had not counted that he had declared himself the King's loyal subject and denied he had ever been against Henry marrying Anne Boleyn. Even the royal commissioners had wanted to discharge him, Chapuys reported. 'But the Lady, by her importunate clamour, sorely exasperated the King against him. Many are shocked by his arrest. I am convinced that the harassment to which he and Bishop Fisher have been subjected is entirely due to their having espoused your Highness's cause.'

No doubt Cromwell had done much of the harassing, Katherine thought. She had been crushed to learn that, after being appointed to a succession of ever higher offices, he had now been made principal secretary to the King, which meant that he could wield even greater influence over Henry. And Henry, as Katherine knew, was suggestible. With such a man at the helm of affairs, there was no knowing what might happen. Between them, Anne and Cromwell had gained the King's heart and mind, and under the pretence of serving his will were using him for their own evil, heretical ends. And Henry was too besotted to see it!

Katherine was horrified to read in Chapuys's next letter that the Nun of Kent and five of her supporters, among them two priests, had been executed before a great crowd at Tyburn. 'They were drawn on hurdles to the gallows, and there the Nun was hanged until dead, then beheaded. The men suffered hanging, drawing and quartering.' It was the first blood spilt as a result of the Great Matter, and Katherine, fighting down terror, feared that it would not be the last. It was a measure of Henry's anger with the Pope that he was prepared to go this far in order to deter opposition. But that he could put priests to death like common felons was not only horrible – it was sacrilege!

The world had definitely gone mad. Katherine trembled to think how much further Henry would go. Would she be next?

Mary was ill. After four months of misery and ill-treatment in Elizabeth's household, her health had broken down. Katherine read Chapuys's letter aloud to Eliza, needing to share her anxiety.

"'I have pleaded with the Council and with Master Cromwell to let the Princess come to your Highness," the ambassador writes, "and I have promised that I myself will stand surety for the good conduct of you both, but the King does not trust me. He fears that, if you and your daughter are allowed to be together, you will plot against him and summon the forces of the Emperor to your aid. I sought Cromwell's help, but he will only promise to ask the King to send his physician to the Princess, but I do not think he will keep his word, or that the King would make much account of it. Cromwell's words are fair, but I fear he really desires the Princess's death. He told me that her present predicament was her own fault, and that if it pleased God . . . He left the sentence unfinished. This worries me, and I feel I must alert your Highness to the danger, for I have heard the Lady say she will not be satisfied until you and your daughter have been done to death by poison or otherwise. Therefore I beg you to exercise constant vigilance to ensure that your food is prepared only by those servants you trust.'"

Coming on top of the news of what had befallen Fisher, More and the Nun of Kent, this warning struck terror, physically, into Katherine's heart. As Eliza knelt before her, taking her hands in hers and trying to offer some comfort, Katherine had to pause until the palpitations had stilled and she had got her breath back. Then she took stock, steeling herself to face the truth.

Henry had not scrupled to send her to Buckden, which he knew to be unhealthy, and he had tried to make her go to Somersham, a house in even worse condition. She might be forgiven for concluding that he wanted her dead, save for the fact that he was in thrall to Anne Boleyn, and it was clear that *she* would stop at nothing, and that she was in a strong position to have her way. The child she was carrying might be a boy, but until she had a son she was insecure on her throne. If Henry's love for her had diminished, there was always a chance that he would heed the Pope's sentence and return to Katherine. Katherine knew she was still popular, and that the rift between the King and the Emperor over the Great Matter had had a bad impact on England's trade with the Low Countries. No wonder the people wanted her back! And no wonder they hated Anne.

There could be little doubt that Anne saw Katherine and Mary as deadly threats to her security. 'Neither you yourself, nor the Princess, will be safe for a moment while the Lady still has power; she is desperate to get rid of you,' Chapuys warned in his next letter.

Katherine would not criticise Henry to her maids, but she was desperate to unburden herself over Anne. Gone were the days when she had preserved the proper distance between mistress and servants, and Eliza had already heard something about the threat hanging over her. Eliza, Blanche, Isabel and Margery were Katherine's friends; they were near at hand, and they were willing to listen and help her if they could.

'The Lady Anne ruthlessly hounded Wolsey to his ruin,' she reminded them, as she sat by the fire one evening, her maids kneeling by the hearth. 'Messire Chapuys believes her to be capable of using poison to get rid of me and my daughter. He tells me she plots day and night against the Princess. The King is planning to visit France, and she has said openly that while he is there she will do away with Mary, either by hunger or otherwise.'

Eliza's hand flew to her mouth, as the other three gasped.

'It is true,' Katherine said, feeling the fluttering in her chest she had come to dread. 'And when her brother warned her that it would anger the King, she said she did not care, even if she were burned alive for it. You see how ruthless she is.'

The ladies did their best to comfort her. From now on, they said, they would oversee the preparation of her food themselves. But they could not give such an assurance about what Mary ate, and it was that which continued to give Katherine nightmares. When Eliza, Blanche and Margery – Isabel had managed to absent herself as usual – descended on the kitchen and insisted on supervising the cooking of their mistress's meals, there were protests and complaints from the cook and his staff. In the end, Eliza had the steward rig up a hook for a cooking pot over the fire in Katherine's room, and a spit on the hearth.

'Henceforth we are going to cook your meals ourselves, madam!' she announced.

It was a kind and noble gesture, but none of them could cook, although they had been brought up to supervise kitchens, as gentle-women should. The food was invariably either raw or burned, and some of it was inedible. Moreover, a permanent smell of cooking pervaded the bedchamber. Katherine bore it all patiently, and gratefully. It was better by far to suffer these inconveniences than to risk being poisoned. She clung to the faint hope that Mary had such vigilant attendants.

When the Archbishop of York arrived to administer the oath to Katherine and her household, she braced herself to remain resolute. Although she and Mary were in a dangerous situation, she could not put her immortal soul at risk by forswearing herself.

She faced the Archbishop, holding herself as a queen should.

'I refuse the oath,' she said, her voice steady. 'If I am not the King's wife, as he maintains, I am not his subject and cannot be required to take it.'

She held her breath, expecting the Archbishop to say that she must go to the Tower, like Fisher and More. But he did not.

'Very well. Summon your servants,' he ordered.

They came, hostile and mutinous, prepared to defy him.

'No,' they said, one after the other. 'I will not swear!' Most of the Spaniards, who had been in England for over thirty years, suddenly appeared not to understand English.

'I have taken an oath of allegiance to my mistress, Queen Katherine,' Francisco Felipez said boldly. 'She still lives, and during her life I know of no other queen in this kingdom.'

'Let the King banish us,' said Bastien Hennyocke, 'but let him not order us to be perjurers.'

'I cannot make foreigners take the oath,' the Archbishop admitted, exasperated, 'but those of you who are English and will not swear are dismissed.'

Katherine's maids and servants looked at each other, then they nodded and, one by one, took the oath.

'We had agreed beforehand that, if we had no choice, we would do it with inward reservations,' Eliza explained. 'An oath made under duress is no oath at all. Besides, madam, we could not leave you all alone to fend for yourself.'

'Bless you all, my true friends,' Katherine said, thanking God for their staunchness.

Chapter 33

1534–1535

Katherine thought she was again being punished for her obstinacy when, at the end of April, an order came from the King, commanding her to remove to Kimbolton Castle, in the shire of Huntingdon, which was further from London than any of the houses in which she had been immured since leaving court. It was not a place she knew, but she had heard nothing bad about it, and Lord Mountjoy had said it enjoyed a much better climate, being away from the Fens, and that he was very pleased about that, as his health, which was not good, had suffered as hers had. The poor man, he was a martyr to rheumatism. So all she could feel was relief.

'At last we shall sleep in dry beds!' she said. 'In truth, I cannot wait to leave this place.'

Lord Mountjoy, who was getting rather stout and breathless these days, informed her that two officers of the Crown, Sir Edmund Bedingfield and Sir Edward Chamberlayne, had been appointed her custodians at Kimbolton. She sensed that he had concerns about that, since his increasing infirmity of body was making it difficult for him to serve and protect her as well as he wished, and yet she knew he did not want her to be exposed to unkind treatment, for he had told her firmly that he would be staying on as her chamberlain to look after her.

Katherine had heard of Sir Edmund Bedingfield's bravery in Henry's French wars, but could not remember meeting him. Sir Edward Chamberlayne she knew slightly, for he had been at court in the early years of Henry's reign, before becoming a Member of Parliament.

'I trust that my household will be allowed to accompany me,' she said. 'There are not many, just twenty persons.'

'They may go with you to Kimbolton, but they will only be permitted to remain with Sir Edmund Bedingfield's approval. From what I've heard he's a fair man.'

Bedingfield replied promptly to Katherine's request. The Princess Dowager might bring her servants with her. However, he could not commit himself to exempting all her servants from the oath required by the new Act.

One May morning, he came himself, with a party of soldiers, to escort Katherine and her household to Kimbolton. He was courteous but formal, bowing and doffing his hat, a lugubrious-looking man with a grey beard and black brows. But he would not address her as Queen, and therefore she was not prepared to talk to him. They walked in silence to the waiting litter.

Their party travelled westwards into Huntingdonshire, and after about twenty miles they came in the evening, weary and hungry, to the castle. It looked like a large manor house, but it was strongly fortified and surrounded by a double moat. Katherine's litter jolted on the cobbles as the horses clattered through the archway under the gatehouse, which proved to be the only means of access. She realised that she had exchanged one prison for another, and as the great doors clanged shut behind her she had the sensation of being swallowed up, which brought on another attack of palpitations.

Grooms brought torches to light up the courtyard, and as Katherine made to descend from her litter, Sir Edmund dismounted from his horse and came over to assist her. She accepted his hand and stood up shakily, suddenly overcome with breathlessness. Another man stepped forward and bowed.

'Welcome to Kimbolton, madam.' This must be Sir Edward Chamberlayne, an owl-faced man with a hooked nose and kindly eyes. 'I trust you are not too wearied after your journey. Come, let us show you to your lodging.'

Holding a lantern aloft, he and Sir Edmund escorted her through the courtyard and into the castle, with Lord Mountjoy labouring behind and her household following.

It was soon clear that this was not another Buckden, and that Henry had provided well for her, showing consideration for once, which was perhaps another sign that Anne's influence was waning. Gradually her beating heart slowed down to normal.

'The castle is owned by Sir Charles Wingfield, who has placed it at the King's disposal,' Sir Edward said, as they entered a great hall with a high timber roof. 'His father was a wealthy man and high in favour with the King, who granted him the castle some dozen years ago. As you can see, he spent lavishly on it, building fair new lodgings and a new gallery.'

Katherine could see. Costly tapestries hung in the hall, the floor was tiled and the solid oak trestles were of good craftsmanship.

Sir Edward lifted one of the hangings and led Katherine through an arched doorway in the centre of the wall behind the dais.

'This is the south wing,' he told her.

They passed into a withdrawing room, also adorned with fine hangings, and then into the gallery of which Sir Edward had spoken. It was an impressive room with three large windows, a battened and painted ceiling, rush matting on the floor, and portraits on the walls. One was of Henry as a young king, and it gave Katherine's heart a jolt to see it. This was the way she remembered him, before Anne Boleyn had got him in her talons – handsome, vigorous, ardent and full of hope for the future. She could have wept for the loss of the young man he had been, even as she rejoiced in the fact that she would see his beloved image whenever she passed this way.

At the end of the gallery Sir Edward opened a door.

'This will be your bedchamber, madam. There is a closet beyond, and a door from it leads to the chapel gallery. Sir Edmund and I hope that you and Lord Mountjoy and your ladies will join us for meals in the dining room beyond the great hall.'

Katherine entered the room. It was not large but that did not matter, for it was warm and dry, and a good fire was burning merrily on the hearth. Linenfold oak panels lined the walls, and the mullioned windows had greenish-glazed diamond panes and were hung with bright curtains on rings. A large tester bed with green hangings occupied most of the space and had been made up with clean bleached sheets and a fur counterpane. There was a carved chest at its foot, pegs on the wall for hanging clothes, as well as two high-backed chairs on either side of the fireplace, a prayer desk, a turned stool and a small table. New rush matting covered the floor, and a small piece of Turkey carpet lay beside the bed. Beyond, through the door to the closet, Katherine could see a close stool and another chest on which were set a copper basin and ewer.

It was more than she could ever have expected, and she was so relieved that she could have cried.

'It is charming,' she said. 'I thank you both, Sir Edward and Sir Edmund, for making me so welcome. Tell me, where are my servants to sleep?'

'Lodgings have been prepared for them on the north side of the Castle Court, where Sir Edmund and I have our apartments, madam. I will have some supper sent up to you, and your servants will be given food in the kitchens.' Sir Edward turned to Sir Edmund. 'We must summon the grooms to have the Princess Dowager's baggage brought up here.'

Katherine bridled. 'Sir Edward, I am grateful to you for your kindness, but there is one thing that you and Sir Edmund must understand, which is that I will not be addressed, or referred to, by any title other than Queen.'

The two men stared at her.

'We are forbidden to use that title, madam,' Sir Edmund said. 'If we do we will incur the anger of the King.'

'Parliament has deprived your Grace of that title,' Sir Edward said. 'It is illegal to use it.'

'I care not a fig for what Parliament has done. The Pope declared my marriage lawful, and I am the true Queen. I will not speak to anyone who calls me Princess Dowager. And if you persist, I will stay in my rooms.'

The knights looked at each other.

'Then so be it,' said Sir Edward. 'We will be very sorry to be deprived of your company and conversation, but you will understand that we have our orders.'

*

At first, she was glad just to luxuriate in a warm, dry bed and be free of the smell of damp and mould. Her rooms felt like a haven, and through her open window she could watch the flowering of the spring and smell the scented air. The food delivered to her door was good, and it was varied and fresh. She did not lack for company, for her days were spent with her maids, sewing, reading and taking turns on Eliza's lute; and for spiritual comfort she had the regular visits of her confessor. Her doctors were pleased to see an improvement in her health. Here, she thought, she could get better.

But after a time she began to feel too confined, and to wish that she could leave her rooms and enjoy the spaciousness of this lovely house and its gardens. She hardly ever saw her custodians, and her servants had told her that Sir Edward and Sir Edmund kept mostly to their apartments across the courtyard, but she did not wish to risk meeting them in the gallery, the great hall or the chapel. The less unpleasantness there was, the better, for she feared that her unpredictable heart could not take much more of it.

Katherine had been at Kimbolton for three weeks when Bishop Tunstall of Durham came to require her, once more, to take the new oath.

'No, Bishop, I will not,' she declared. 'I do not acknowledge the Lady Anne as queen or the King as head of the Church in England. I am the true Queen, and the Pope is the true successor of Christ!'

'Madam, you must not call yourself the King's wife, because he has remarried and had a fair child, with more likely to follow, by God's grace.'

Katherine was adamant. 'I will never quit the title of Queen, but retain it till death. I am the King's wife, not his subject, and therefore not liable to his Acts of Parliament.'

'You will go to prison if you persist in your obstinacy,' Tunstall warned. 'These are dangerous times, and for some of us these changes are hard to accept. For myself, I would not advocate civil disobedience.'

Katherine's anger flared. 'Hold your peace, Bishop!' she cried. 'These are the wiles of the Devil! I am queen, and queen I will die! By right, the King can have no other wife. Let this be your answer.'

Tunstall frowned. 'Madam, you might be sent to the scaffold if you do not take the oath.'

'And who will be the hangman?' Katherine countered. 'If you have permission to execute this penalty on me, I am ready. I ask only that I be allowed to die in sight of the people.'

'Forgive me, madam,' Tunstall begged, wringing his hands. 'I did not mean to frighten you. I have no such instructions. The penalty for refusing to swear the oath is imprisonment, not death, and you could be said to be suffering that already. But I do fear for you, and I thought to frighten you into submission for your own sake. The King is in an angry mood, and Queen Anne is jealous. Who knows what they might do.'

'I fear God more than I fear them. I cannot do other that what my conscience dictates.'

'I wish that it was otherwise for you, madam. But ask yourself, is it all worth it? If you swore the oath, the King would be ready to grant you your heart's desire. You could live in palaces, have the company of your daughter and your friends, enjoy freedom once more – and you will have His Grace's brotherly love.'

His words had twisted the knife. She felt her heart lurch. Get thee behind me, Satan! 'And when I come before God's judgement seat and am accused of putting worldly considerations before the health of my soul and the weal of the Church, what shall I answer then? God knows, my lord, do you think I would stay here and suffer as I do, with my daughter exposed to all manner of evils, if there was any other way open to me?'

Tunstall shook his head sadly. 'No, I do not, madam. In the end, we all must do as our consciences dictate, and face the consequences. For some, I fear, they will be serious.' Katherine knew that he was thinking of More, his fellow humanist, with whom he had once been great friends. 'This afternoon I will administer the oath to your Spanish servants,' he added.

'They are not the King's subjects,' she reminded him. 'A few do not understand English properly.'

'Nevertheless, if they are to continue to serve you, they must take it,' Tunstall said.

That alarmed her, and while he was having his dinner with her custodians, she summoned her Spaniards.

'Listen very carefully,' she said. 'The Bishop is going to ask you to take the oath. Do not refuse. You must ask to take it in Spanish, and say, "*El Rey se ha heco cabeza de la Iglesia.*"'

They smiled at her, comprehending, and Bishop Tunstall, having expected a lot of opposition, was surprised to find them so cooperative, and went away satisfied.

Katherine found herself laughing as she had not laughed these many years.

Eliza and the other English maids stared at her, puzzled. *They think I have gone mad*, she thought. 'I must tell you,' she said, smiling, 'that, instead of recognising the King as head of the Church, my Spaniards have acknowledged only that he has made himself head of the Church!'

Katherine had been worried about maintaining contact with Chapuys after moving to Kimbolton, but her fears were again unfounded. The town had a weekly market, and Sir Edward and Sir Edmund had made no quibble about her servants going there for provisions. Thus word was got through to Chapuys that Katherine could send and receive letters, and soon his man had taken a room at the Sun Inn, with Eliza acting as go-between, as before. Katherine suspected that there was some dalliance going on between her maid and the Spaniard, as Eliza was always so keen to go on her errands and would not hear of anyone else doing them.

It was a comfort to Katherine to be back in touch with Chapuys, but things were as bad as ever. Now the Lady had said she would not cease till she had got rid of her rival. 'As the old prophecies say that a queen of England is to be burned, she hopes it will be your Highness, to avoid the lot falling upon herself.'

Chapuys was still putting pressure on Katherine to sanction an Imperial invasion; even though the Emperor had his hands full with pushing back the Turks from his borders, the ambassador seemed convinced that his master was ready to fight on another front as well. But she was adamant that she would never do so. 'Your loyalty to the King is heroic,' he told her.

'If I am too scrupulous, it is because I have great respect for the King my husband,' she wrote back. 'I would consider myself damned if I took any course that led to war.'

In his next letter Chapuys warned Katherine that Mary would soon be required to take the oath. The news plunged her into an agony of anxiety. This was to be Mary's testing time. The Emperor had advised them both to take the oath rather than lose their lives, protesting that they took it out of fear. But Katherine was resolved to stick to her principles, and hoped that her daughter was too. Mary must be encouraged to stand up for what she believed to be right, and to face the consequences.

Katherine wrestled with herself and came to a decision. She must defy Henry's ban on communicating with Mary and trust Chapuys to get a letter to her. She wrote:

Daughter,

I heard tidings today that the time has come for Almighty God to prove you. Be sure that He will not suffer you to perish if you take care not to offend Him. Obey the King your father in everything, save only that which imperils your soul. For I am sure that all will end well, and better than you can desire. I would to God, good daughter, that you knew with how loving a heart I write this letter to you. And now you shall begin, and by likelihood I shall follow. I set not a rush by this oath; for when they have done the uttermost they can, then I am sure all will be amended. I pray you, remember me to my good lady of Salisbury, and pray her to have a good heart, for we never come to the kingdom of Heaven but by troubles. Daughter, take no pains to send to me. If I can, I will send to you.

Your loving mother, Katherine the Queen

God send that Mary would know how much feeling was encapsulated in those words.

When Eliza had departed with the letter, Katherine sank to the floor, keening, her fist in her mouth. Had ever mother been placed in such an impossible position? For what she had effectively done, in counselling Mary to do the right thing according to her conscience, was encourage her child to court martyrdom.

Mary had refused the oath. She had said that she was not prepared to renounce her title of Princess. Katherine was so sick with worry about what Henry – or rather Anne – might do to her daughter that she became ill. Suffering from those wretched palpitations, dizzy spells and an irritating cough, she took to her bed.

Her doctors seemed worried. When they conferred with each other it was outside her room, not at her bedside, where they did their best to reassure her that she would be better soon. The way she felt, that did not seem likely. She was so weak, so racked by anxiety.

'Madam, you must calm yourself,' her confessor admonished her. 'The Princess is in God's hands, and you must get well.'

Eliza encouraged her to eat, though she had little appetite. It was a good thing that her people were allowed out to the market, she reflected, because of late there had been a marked deterioration in the standard of the food that came from the kitchens. Whether it was due to negligence or spite she could not say. Sir Edward and Sir Edmund came to her lodging rarely, and only then stiffly to impart necessary information. She did not answer, of course, because they would not address her as Queen, but Sir Edward had popped his head around the door as she lay ill, and wished her well. Even he had looked concerned at the sight of her.

She called for her glass and was shocked at what she beheld. She was a spectre of her former self, white-faced, white-haired, the skin of her cheeks sagging.

'Take it away,' she said.

She forced herself to eat, for she must get better. She had to live, for Mary's sake.

Gathering her strength, she wrote to Chapuys, 'Please come . . .'

'Madam! Madam! Look!' Eliza and Blanche were at the window; Eliza was nearly jumping up and down with excitement. 'There are men in the Spanish ambassador's livery outside the walls, waving to us.' They waved back.

Katherine struggled to sit up in bed. Was he here? Was Chapuys really here?

'Help me up,' she said, but when they assisted her to her feet she felt so faint that they had to lay her down again. When they had made her comfortable they hastened back to the window.

He was coming, as she had known he would, defying the King and that great black spider Cromwell, who sat at the centre of affairs, luring the unwary into his web. This very day Chapuys would be here, and she could unburden herself of all her troubles and confide in him about the things she dared not commit to paper, and he would take steps to ensure Mary's safety. Meanwhile, her maids were still waving and calling down to his men, and local people were hurrying out to embrace them with as much astonishment and joy as if the Messiah had descended to earth.

But Chapuys did not come, and by and by the crowd dispersed and his men went away. That night Katherine felt so low and ill that she feared she might die.

In his next letter Chapuys explained what had gone wrong. He *had* tried to see her. Alarmed by her urgent message and reports of her poor health, he had asked several times for permission to visit, but the King and Cromwell had always refused. 'His Majesty said he feared that I would strengthen you in what he calls your obstinacy, or that we might intrigue to spirit your Highness and the Princess out of the realm. But I kept asking, saying that I wished only to offer you what comfort I could, and in the end His Grace said I might go, on condition that I undertook not to discuss politics.'

He had set off at once, but when he was but five miles from Kimbolton a royal messenger had caught up with him and ordered him to return to court immediately. 'You may imagine how angry that made me,' he wrote. 'I told Master Cromwell I should have judged it more honourable if the King had informed me of his intention before I left London. All he said was that I would not be permitted to visit your Highness in the future.'

Katherine laid down the letter, trying not to weep. He had been coming to see her, that dear, good man; he had been almost here. If only the messenger had missed him! What a comfort the sight of him would have been to her.

In late July the weather was glorious, warm and sunny with a light breeze that gently billowed out the curtains. It did the soul good, she thought, and recognised that she was feeling a little better. Soon she was able to get out of bed and sit in her chair, and after a week her doctors suggested that it be moved into a sheltered place in the garden below her window, so that she could enjoy the healthy air that would hasten her recovery.

'I will ask permission, madam,' de la Saa said. He knew that she would never do it herself.

Back came the answer: no. 'They said that, when your Grace is ready to be addressed by your proper title, then you may go where you please.' The good doctor looked outraged.

It was petty and it was cruel. Lord Mountjoy thought so too.

'I would readily tender my resignation again in protest, for I have come to detest my office,' he said. 'But it would not be accepted, and I am loath to leave you at the mercy of those indifferent gaolers.' He inclined his head in the direction of the north wing. 'I will not see you treated badly.'

'My dear friend, I thank you for your kind service to me,' Katherine said, extending her hand – the hand of a queen. Mountjoy knelt, his bulky frame creaking, his breathing heavy, and kissed it fervently.

'I will serve you till death, your Grace,' he vowed.

It was all very strange, Katherine thought. According to Chapuys, the Lady was not to have a child after all. But she *had* been pregnant, hadn't she? It would be no easy thing to fake over so long a period. When had the news been announced? In the spring? And apparently the baby had been due in August. Her condition must have been unmistakable.

Then the likely truth dawned. The child had been born dead, and there had been a veil of secrecy drawn over it.

It was easy to understand why. Henry needed the world to know that God smiled upon his union with Anne. The birth of a son would have been proof of that. But it was as clear as day to Katherine, as it must be to everyone else, that a daughter and a dead baby – probably a son, or why the secrecy? – betokened God's displeasure. The question was, when would Henry come to his senses?

Katherine would not have wished a stillborn child on anyone, however wicked – she knew all too well how devastating a loss it was. But she could not help seeing it as a blessing, for it seemed to have turned Henry against Anne. Chapuys had also reported that Henry was in love with a beautiful lady of the court. 'The Lady wished to drive her away, but the King has been very angry and said she had good reason to be content with what he had done for her, which he would not do now if he were to begin again.' Chapuys warned that it was best not to attach too much importance to this quarrel, considering Henry's changeable character and the craftiness of the Lady, who well knew how to manage him. *Ah*, Katherine thought, *but it sounds as if he is growing tired of being managed.*

November brought her great sadness, for Lord Mountjoy had a sudden seizure, fell down and died. She feared he had been overburdened with worry and cruelly torn loyalties on her account. He had been a true friend to her, to the best of his ability, and Katherine mourned him deeply.

She wondered whom Henry might appoint in his stead, but presently a message came from the other side of the house to say that the Princess Dowager's chamberlain would not be replaced. In her circumstances, she did not need one. That irked, but it was true. She could manage well enough without. Two rooms did not a palace make.

Pope Clement had also died that autumn. She prayed for his soul, that it might be spared purgatory; he had been the cause of most of her troubles, but it would be uncharitable to remember that now. How different things would have been if he had given judgement back in 1527! Henry had been a good son of the Church then; he would have accepted Clement's ruling, and all the terrible things that had happened since would have been avoided.

The new Pope, Paul III, was a resolute man, Chapuys reported, and consumed with a crusading fervour. He was resolved not to countenance King Henry's disobedience, and one of his first acts was to threaten to put into effect the sentence of excommunication drawn up by Clement. Henry had paid no heed, but Katherine knew that he really could not afford to ignore the threat. Let Pope Paul publish the bull of excommunication, and the Emperor might be provoked to make war on Henry of his own accord; and as an excommunicate ruler standing alone, Henry could not expect to receive aid from the other Christian princes of Europe. Remote from these great events in her room at Kimbolton, Katherine prayed that matters would never reach such a pass.

In February God sent her another heavy cross to bear. Mary was lying ill at Greenwich, where Elizabeth's household was staying. Chapuys did not mince words: it was feared that the Princess would die.

'The King is alarmed,' he wrote, 'but he refuses to heed the advice of his physicians, and my pleas, that she should go to your Highness, for whom she is pining. He told me he wishes to do the best for his daughter's health, but he must be careful of his own honour and interests, which would be jeopardised if she were conveyed abroad, or if she escaped, as she might easily do if she were with your Highness, for he has some suspicion that the Emperor has designs to get her away.'

As if I would risk my child's health by sending her on a sea voyage at such a time! Katherine fumed, remembering how ill she had been when she sailed to England from Spain.

In a frenzy of agitation, trying to ignore the pains and the pounding in her chest, she wrote desperately to Cromwell himself, begging him to urge the King to let her nurse Mary at Kimbolton. 'A little comfort and mirth with me would be a half health to her. I will care for her with my own hands. For the love of God, let this be done!'

But Cromwell did not deign to reply.

Katherine did not wait to see if his letter had been delayed. She called for Dr de la Saa. When he arrived in her chamber, he asked immediately what was wrong. She asked if he would go to Greenwich to treat Mary. There was an awkward pause, in which she realised that this was something he was reluctant to do.

'Why not?' she asked, seeing his frown.

'Madam, I fear what I might discover, and that I might be powerless to stop it, or even be implicated.'

Her jaw fell. Was this what Chapuys really dreaded? But even as she thought it, her mind rejected that notion. It was impossible! Henry loved Mary; he might bluster and threaten, but he would never harm her, Katherine would stake her soul on it. But there was that other, whom Wolsey had once called the night crow, who would not scruple . . .

'All the more reason for you to go!' she said sharply to Dr de la Saa.

He went unwillingly, and was away a week. The time seemed endless, and for most of it Katherine was on her knees imploring God to preserve Mary's life. It was an utter relief when the doctor returned with good news.

'The Princess's health is improving, but I am concerned because her illness is so prolonged.'

The room was suddenly swallowed up in blackness and when Katherine came round she was lying on the floor, her doctors and maids peering at her in concern.

'You fainted, madam,' Dr Guersye told her. 'Just lie still and when you are a little recovered we will lift you on the bed.'

'I am all right,' she said, struggling as they all helped her to sit up, and remembering the news about Mary. 'I am more worried about my daughter. Dr de la Saa, you said you were concerned about her illness being prolonged.'

'Madam, calm yourself!' the doctor said.

'You must return to her! Make her better!'

Dr de la Saa hesitated. 'My place is with you here, madam, until you are yourself again. The Princess is in the care of her own physicians.'

'I have Dr Guersye to look after me. I am commanding you to go back to Greenwich!'

'Madam, I am not welcome there!'

That aroused her suspicions all over again.

'Is my daughter's life in danger?' she asked, her voice sharp.

Dr de la Saa's face sagged. 'I wish I could reassure you about that, madam.'

He and Dr Guersye bade her rest, but how could she rest in the circumstances? She lay down on her bed to please them, but when they had all left her to sleep she got up and, though she still felt dizzy, wrote a letter to Chapuys.

I beg you to speak to the King, and desire him from me to be so charitable as to send his daughter and mine here to me, because if I care for her with my own hands, and by the advice of my own physicians, and God still pleases to take her from this world, my heart will be at peace. Say to His Highness that there is no need for anyone to nurse her but myself, and that I will put her in my own bed in my own chamber, and watch with her when needful. I have recourse to you, knowing that there is no one else in this kingdom who will dare to say to the King my lord what I am asking you to say.

She did not care that Henry would know that she had defied his ban on communicating with Chapuys. The only thing that mattered now was that Mary should be safe.

When Eliza came to check on her mistress the letter was signed and sealed.

'Invent an errand!' Katherine told the young woman.

'There is no need, madam,' Eliza said, smiling. 'The innkeeper has promised us a chicken!'

She was desperate for an answer, counting the days until she could expect to receive one. She was praying that Henry would show compassion to Mary, and to her, yet full of fears of how he would react when he realised that she had been communicating with Chapuys against his express orders. Depending on his mood, he might use her disobedience as a justification for punishing her further. She could only count on his being as anxious about Mary as she was.

She waited and suffered for a whole week, and was frantic by the time Chapuys finally wrote that, as soon as he'd received her letter, he had gone straight to the King and made no bones about the appeal coming direct from Katherine. She drew in her breath at that. But Henry had made no comment, which gave her to believe that his concern for Mary overrode all other considerations, as she had hoped. All the same, he had been adamant that she and Mary be kept apart, but he had consented to Mary being moved to a house near Kimbolton, and to allow Katherine's physicians to attend her, but on condition that Katherine did not attempt to see her.

It was not what she wanted, but at least Henry had been willing to compromise, and Katherine was profoundly grateful.

She was in chapel giving thanks for having found some common ground with Henry, and hoping that it would lead to a new rapport between them, when news came from Chapuys that Mary had had a relapse and was thought to be in danger of dying. In anguish, Katherine again wrote to the ambassador, urging him to beg Henry to let her see their daughter, but the King was as immovable as a rock. Chapuys reported that he still entertained the ridiculous notion that Katherine might yet take Mary's part. 'He said that you are a proud stubborn woman of very high courage, and thinks that if you took it into your head to take your daughter's part, you could easily take the field, muster a great array, and wage against him a war as fierce as any your mother, Queen Isabella, ever waged in Spain.'

How could Henry put such considerations before their daughter's well-being? Katherine asked herself bitterly. How little he knows me, she thought. I would never, never sanction anything that would harm him; I love him too much. He was so suspicious these days, and it was Anne, working her evil wiles, who had made him overly so – and Anne, no doubt abetted by Cromwell, who had made him see malice where no malice was intended.

Still there came no word that Mary had been brought from Greenwich to Huntingdonshire, and Katherine, with a faltering, juddering heart, supposed that it must be because her daughter was too ill to be moved. Her joy was therefore boundless when she learned that Mary was recovering, even if she would not be coming within a few miles of Kimbolton.

Chapter 34

1535–1536

Katherine's realm had shrunk to just two rooms, and with only her servants for company she sometimes felt entirely isolated from the world outside. With Mary's health so improved, she could rest at last, sitting in her chair by the open window, with her maids beside her and the warm air easing her chest. But soon the summer was tainted with stories of such horror that she was filled again with fear.

Three priors of the Carthusian Order and a monk of Syon Abbey had been executed as traitors for denying the royal supremacy and protesting their allegiance to the Pope.

'They were as joyful as bridegrooms going to their marriages,' Chapuys reported. 'They were forced to wear their habits, and dragged by horses through the streets of London, then strung up on the gallows and left to hang until they had half-choked. Then they were cut down and revived with vinegar, so that they might suffer the full horrors of their punishment.' He did not need to spell out what those horrors were, for Katherine was well aware that the dread penalty for treason was castration, disembowelling and decapitation. Afterwards the bodies of traitors were cut into quarters, which were publicly exhibited on the gatehouse of London Bridge or elsewhere, as a warning to others.

The Carthusians had died bravely. 'The people were horrified to see such unprecedented and brutal atrocities,' Chapuys recounted. 'They muttered in whispers and blamed the Lady.'

In June ten more Carthusian brothers accused of treason were chained, standing upright, to posts and left to die of starvation. Truly, these were evil times, when a king might with impunity put to death holy men dedicated to God. If Henry could do that, what, goaded by

Anne, might he not do to those he had loved? The answer came all too soon.

'The Lady is triumphant,' Chapuys wrote.

She hosted a great banquet for the King at her mansion at Hanworth, where she laid on several brave mummeries. Her chief purpose was to allure him with her dalliance and pastime to put Bishop Fisher and Sir Thomas More to death. Two days later the Bishop was tried at Westminster Hall and condemned to death. When the King learned that the Pope had made the Bishop a cardinal, and was sending his red hat to England, he raged, 'Afore Heaven, he shall wear it on his shoulders then, for by the time it arrives he shall not have a head to place it on!'

Katherine wept for that virtuous and loyal man, who was full of goodness and had been a staunch friend to her, and prayed with all her might that he would be given the strength to face his ordeal. She wept too for Henry, for what he had become. He never used to be so cruel and ruthless.

The next letter Eliza brought back from the Sun Inn contained terrible tidings. Bishop Fisher was dead. Henry had commuted his sentence to beheading after public outrage at the prospect of such a holy man facing a traitor's death, and the Bishop had died bravely on Tower Hill. His head, that learned and wise head, had been set up on a pole on London Bridge. Strangely, it was showing no signs of decay, which people were saying was a sure sign of sanctity.

That was not all. Three more Carthusian monks had died traitors' deaths at Tyburn.

Katherine felt as if she could not take any more. The knowledge of these dreadful events had made her ill again, and convinced her that she and Mary were in more danger than ever. For they had refused to take the oath, just like the Carthusians and Fisher.

Then one morning she heard distant hooves on the road to Kimbolton, followed by stamping footsteps and clinking spurs on the stairs to her rooms. Her maids gathered around her, and Katherine could sense them shaking, as she was, with terror. It was a deputation of the Council, headed by the Duke of Norfolk.

She was sure they had come to arrest her and take her to the Tower and certain death. They did not hang, draw and quarter women for treason; they burned them at the stake, and Katherine's flesh shrank from what now seemed to be the very real prospect of the flames licking at her feet and then flaring up to consume her. She could not imagine such agony. How long would it last? She had heard of heretics taking three-quarters of an hour to die.

The councillors told her that they had come to search her rooms. They implied that they expected to find something compromising or incriminating, so that they would have cause to arrest her. She prayed that they would not discover Chapuys's letters, cleverly hidden by Eliza behind a loose piece of panelling. She held her breath and prayed as she had never prayed before, while the search was taking place.

The councillors found nothing, much to their anger. His face suffused with rage, Norfolk shouted at her, 'We know you are in communication with the Emperor and his ambassador! Rest assured, your intrigues will not go undiscovered, and then there will be a reckoning!'

Katherine stood there trembling, her chest tight with shooting pains, her heart racing.

Norfolk thrust his face into hers. 'If God took you and your daughter to Himself, this whole dispute would be ended, and no one would doubt or oppose the King's marriage or dispute the succession!'

She quailed before the malice in his eyes.

'Have you come to harry a sick woman, my lords?' she challenged them. 'Shame on you! I have committed no treason. I wish only good to the King.'

'You should know that your former confessor, Father Forrest, is in prison in hard durance and has been sentenced to be burned.'

Katherine's hand flew to her mouth. 'What has he done?' she cried in anguish.

'He has openly opposed the King's supremacy, and spoken out against it. We thought we would warn you, madam, of what happens to those who incur the King's displeasure.'

Katherine saw the malicious gleam in Norfolk's eyes as he left her almost collapsing in grief at this appalling news. That night she could not sleep. She called for the Bishop of Llandaff, in desperate need of spiritual guidance.

'I can feel no ease or comfort till I have written to Father Forrest,' she told him.

'Then write, my daughter; it will bring comfort to you both. And remember that it is a great privilege to be called to combat for the love of Christ and the truth of the Catholic faith.'

It was the most difficult letter she had ever written. How did you console someone who was about to meet the most horrific death? Exhorting Father Forrest to bear up under the few short pains of the torments prepared for him hardly addressed the dreadful reality; and it sounded so glib to assure him that he would receive an eternal reward. But then, suddenly, God gave her the words, and her pen flew across the page.

O happy you, my Father, to whom it has been graciously granted that by a most cruel death, for Christ's sake, you will happily fulfil the course of your most holy life and fruitful labours. But woe to me, your poor and wretched daughter, who, in the time of this my solitude and the extreme anguish of my soul, shall be deprived of such a father, so loved by me in Christ. I confess that I am consumed by a great desire to be able to die, either with you or before you, which I would purchase by any amount of the most terrible torments.

She told him she could never allow herself any joy in this miserable and unhappy world. 'But when you have fought the battle and obtained the crown, I know I shall receive abundant grace from Heaven by your means. Farewell, my revered Father, and on earth and in Heaven always have me in remembrance before God.' She signed it, 'Your very sad and afflicted daughter, Katherine.'

She did not expect to receive a reply, but Father Forrest responded quickly, saying that her words had infinitely comforted him. He ended:

'Pray for me, that I may fight the battle to which I am called. In justification of your cause, I am content to suffer all things.' Enclosed was his rosary. That broke her, and she laid her head in her arms and howled. Her women came running, but she would not be comforted, and it was a long time before the tears ceased flowing.

In the days that followed she dragged herself around in a stupor of grief. That a good man should have to suffer such torments on her account was unendurable. Her relief was overwhelming, therefore, when another letter arrived from Father Forrest. The King had been graciously pleased to commute his sentence to life imprisonment.

On her knees Katherine thanked God fervently and asked for His blessing on Henry, who had perhaps realised that enough blood had been shed to prove his point. And she rendered thanks again when she heard that the good Father was in touch with Father Abell, who was again in the Tower for speaking out on her behalf. She prayed that these brave, devout men might be strengthened by their faith and soon freed.

But then came perhaps the worst news of that terrible summer. Sir Thomas More had been tried for treason and beheaded. He had mounted the scaffold on Tower Hill and died bravely, declaring that he was the King's good servant, but God's first. 'The whole world is horrified,' Chapuys wrote. 'Everyone is saying that the King has gone too far this time.'

The shock and grief were more than Katherine's wasted frame could withstand. She lay on her bed, her chest tight and painful, her heart thudding alarmingly, trying to get her breath. She wept, and wept again, feeling as if she had shed enough tears to fill a lake these past weeks. She mourned More profoundly. He had been one of the best men she had ever known, brilliant, principled and full of integrity. The world would never see his like again. She cried for his family, that close-knit circle that had revolved around him. If she herself was devastated by his death, how must they be feeling?

When Anne Boleyn faced God's judgement, she would have much to answer for.

*

Thomas Cromwell, Chapuys wrote that autumn, was bragging that he had promised to make the King rich. Katherine knew that much of the fortune Henry had been left by his father had been spent on palaces and pleasures and the pursuit of glory in war, and guessed that by now he must be in need of money to replenish his treasury. Chapuys had learned that Cromwell had compiled a report detailing the financial state of the Church in England. 'It seems that, not content with forcing the clergy to withdraw their allegiance to Rome, and fining them for it, the King is planning to divest the monasteries of their wealth and treasures. Already his commissioners have commenced their visitations of some of the smaller religious houses. I do not like this at all.'

Neither do I, thought Katherine. It was as if the whole fabric of civilisation in England was being dismantled, and she trembled for the future of religion in this kingdom. Pray God the King did not lay sacrilegious hands on the property of the monasteries, much of which had been given as pious bequests and donations by people laying up treasure in Heaven. It was not Henry's to take – it was God's!

October came in with winds and lowering skies, as if the heavens were showing their displeasure at what was happening in this fair but troubled land. The leaves lay in russet heaps strewn over the grass, and Katherine, looking out of her window and stifling the cough that had grown more persistent, felt the autumn chill in her bones and wondered if she would live to see another spring.

Her health was declining, she knew it. She was becoming increasingly breathless and troubled by the palpitations and giddy spells. Some days she felt so weak she could only lie in bed, barely able to hold a book. She had little appetite, and was skeletally thin – she, who had once fretted about being overweight and unattractive to Henry. What would he think of her now?

What concerned her more was her own future – or rather, the likely lack of it. For she could see the very image of Death in her face and her wasted body, and she was in torment worrying about how Mary would fare when she herself had gone from this world. Who would protect her child then, and look out for her as she, her mother, had?

She was plunged into further emotional turmoil when she learned from Chapuys that the Emperor had at last crushed the Turks. 'The King and the Lady were so astounded at the news, they looked like dogs falling out of a window.' And no wonder, because Charles was now free to invade England on his aunt's behalf, were he so inclined. It was what Henry feared most, Chapuys wrote. And the time was ripe for it!

At Kimbolton, as elsewhere, the bad weather had ruined the harvest, and the people, who faced a lean and hungry winter, were blaming the King, for they saw it as a sign from God that He was displeased with Henry for marrying Anne. Chapuys reported that there was mounting unrest, and that many were still muttering their disapproval of the executions of More, Fisher and the Carthusians.

Their terrible ends were preying on Katherine's mind too, along with her fears for what Henry might do to the Church in England. She felt driven to write to Pope Paul, begging him to find a remedy. 'Most holy and blessed Father,' she began:

> I entreat you to bear this realm especially in mind, to remember the King, my lord and husband, and my daughter. Your Holiness knows, and all Christendom knows, what things are done here, what great offence is given to God, what scandal to the world, what reproach is thrown upon your Holiness. If a remedy is not applied shortly, there will be no end to ruined souls and martyred saints. The good will be firm and suffer. The lukewarm will fail, and the greater part will stray away like sheep without a shepherd. I write frankly to your Holiness, as one who can feel with me and my daughter for the martyrdom of these good men, John Fisher, Thomas More and the unfortunate brethren of the Charterhouse. I have a mournful pleasure in expecting that we shall follow them in their torments. We await a remedy from God and from your Holiness. It must come speedily or the time will be past.

She knew that, in writing such a letter, she was putting herself in grave danger, for if it were intercepted, it could be used as evidence that she had tried to incite the Pope to excommunicate the King, or call for a crusade against him – and that, in anyone's book, was treason.

Chapuys's next letter, which arrived in November, sent new shivers of alarm through Katherine.

> The Lady is again *enceinte*, and has bewailed in the King's presence how much afraid she is at the thought that their child might one day be excluded from the throne by supporters of the Princess; and she has extracted a promise from him to have the Princess put to death, rather than that should happen. She has let it be known that, if the King does not make an end of his daughter, she herself will. She said that, if she had a son, as she hopes shortly to do, she knew what would become of her.

Katherine read on with mounting horror. The King had told his Privy Council that he would no longer tolerate the trouble and fear and suspicion that she and Mary had caused him. He had demanded that the next Parliament pass an Act of Attainder against them, or he would not wait any longer to seek a remedy himself! 'When he saw the dismay on the faces of his councillors, he told them it was nothing to cry or make wry faces about. If he was to lose his crown for it, he would do what he had set out to do.' But it was the Lady whom Chapuys feared more, for she was the person who managed and ordered and governed everything, and whom the King dared not oppose, especially in her present condition.

Katherine had to sit down. She was shaking, and only slightly comforted to read that the Emperor thought that these threats had been made merely to frighten her and Mary; but if they really were in danger, then he urged them to yield and do what the King wanted. Yield? After all this time? Katherine knew she could never imperil her immortal soul by doing so, and she was sure that Mary would not either.

Mary was in low spirits, Chapuys had continued, but when he suggested to the King that she be permitted the company of friends who could cheer her, Henry had exploded, shouting that he would ensure that soon she would not want any company, and that she would be an example to show that no one ought to disobey his laws, and that he meant to fulfil what had been foretold of him, that at the beginning of his reign he would be gentle as a lamb, and at the end worse than a lion.

Katherine felt faint on reading that. She cried out aloud, and there came the running of hasty feet and willing arms helping her to her bed.

'I must go to her!' she cried. 'I must protect her! He cannot do this to his own child!'

Her maids tried to soothe her, but she would not be soothed. 'I cannot rest until I know that she is safe. I must pray for her.' She struggled up.

'Rest, madam! Please!'

'Your Grace should lie here awhile.'

'No! If ever there was a time to pray, it is now!' She slid off the bed and swayed a little, but staggered dizzily towards the prie-dieu, sinking down gratefully to her knees. 'Oh, sweet Jesus, save my child!' she begged, clenching her hands together. 'Watch over her and protect her!'

Suddenly she felt a sharp, stabbing pain in her chest. As she clutched herself, gasping for breath, her maids came running, lifting her up and laying her on the bed. The doctors were sent for, and by the time they had arrived the pain had mercifully lessened, but it was still there, still gnawing, and her heart was leaping erratically.

Dr de la Saa ordered her maids to disrobe her and put on her night-rail. Then he examined her, probing her on the chest and back, and asking her to cough. For a moment his face looked grave, but then he saw her staring questioningly at him and put on his usual urbane smile. She was not deceived. The way she was feeling, she would never rise from her bed. Time, she feared, was running out for her. And then what would become of Mary?

But within a few days Katherine was miraculously better, and her household rallied around her to celebrate her fiftieth birthday. The maids wanted to make her something special to eat, but still she could not face food.

'What I could fancy is a little broth,' she said, to please them.

'I'll make it for your Grace,' said Margery, and busied herself at the hearth while Eliza strummed the lute and they all sang songs to cheer

Katherine. The broth, when it came, was not very appetising – Margery had overdone the herbs, Katherine thought – but she ate a few spoonfuls to please her. That afternoon she had a bad attack of breathlessness and stomach cramps, but they passed, and in the evening she was able to sit by the fire and do some embroidery. But she continued to fret about Mary, terrified lest Anne Boleyn persuaded Henry to carry out his threats.

Katherine was still holding her own a week later, when Christmas came. Sir Edward and Sir Edmund sent a servant with a flagon of wine, but she refused to drink it, fearing it might be poisoned, so they had ale from the kitchen. Eliza's parents had sent a goose in honour of the season, and they roasted that on the spit and trilled the old carols and wished each other a merry Yuletide. Katherine lay back in her chair, smiling at them, but her thoughts were far away with Mary, praying that God would keep her in His gracious protection, and wondering how she was passing this holy season. She thought too of Henry. If only she could see them both, her adored husband and her beloved child, just once more, in this life. It was all she asked for now.

The next day, the feast of St Stephen, Katherine was up and sitting in her chair, swathed in shawls, when suddenly she found that she could not breathe. Panicking, she tried desperately to draw in air, as her maids came running and began thumping her on the back. Her chest felt as if it would burst, her vision was blurring over. She was going to die, here, now, and with no chance of making her peace with God. Then, miraculously, she felt her lungs expand, but still it felt as if there were a vice-like band suffocating her. Coughing and in pain, she was forced to take to her bed again. Dr de la Saa and Dr Guersye were called, but they could do little to relieve her. The ravening wolf in her chest gave her no peace, and she could take little rest. If this went on, she knew, she would die. Surprisingly, she felt no fear, only bitter regret that soon she might no longer be here to love and protect Mary.

As the days dragged by, the pain grew worse. Eliza sponged her brow and tried to divert her by reading aloud; Margery made her herbal cordials, bitter but warming, to soothe a throat raw from coughing; and Blanche wrapped hot bricks in flannel for her feet and kept the fire stoked up to keep her warm. Isabel – well, Isabel contrived to look busy, but she did attempt to cheer Katherine with some jests.

'Let me summon the King's physicians,' Dr de la Saa urged. Katherine realised, from the edge in his voice, that he was anxious lest he be accused of negligence or worse. But why would anyone bother? Anne wanted her dead. Then it dawned on her. He thought she had been poisoned. Bringing in the King's doctors would relieve him of all responsibility.

'No,' she said. 'I have wholly committed myself to the pleasure of God.'

She thought his fears unfounded. This illness was but a progression of the symptoms she had been suffering for some time. She tried patiently to bear the pain, but it would not leave her. It was as if she was being devoured from within. She could not rest, and she could not stop trembling. She was breathless all the time.

On the last day of the old year she received a brief note from Chapuys, warning her to have her chamber well locked from night till early morning, and carefully examined that none was hidden there, for he believed there was a danger that someone would play some macabre trick on her, either an injury to her person or an accusation of adultery or to find proof that she was plotting an insurrection.

'Adultery! As if I could even think of it, in my state,' she said weakly to Eliza, who was regarding the note with horror. She wondered what had prompted Chapuys to send it. He must have heard something that alarmed him, or maybe he was just being overcautious. She hoped it was the latter.

On the afternoon of New Year's Day, the first day of the year of Our Lord 1536, Katherine lay half dozing, thinking that at court they would now have exchanged gifts and be preparing for the traditional feast. She had had no wherewithal to buy gifts this year, or even the strength to think about it.

The door opened. Blanche stood there, her face alive with excitement.

'Your Grace, you have a visitor!'

Katherine turned her head as a man swathed in a black cloak entered the bedchamber. It was Chapuys!

'Oh, dear God! How wonderful!' she gasped, and was overtaken by a fit of coughing.

Chapuys waited until it had subsided then he knelt by the bed and kissed her hand. 'Your Highness, I had to come.' He was looking up at her with eyes full of pity, and no wonder, for she must be a sorry sight, lying wasted in her bed and unable even to sit up. She could not express how overjoyed she was to see him.

'Now I can die in your arms, not abandoned like one of the beasts,' she said, as her maids came forward to take Chapuys's cloak and bring him some ale, warmed with a hot poker. Katherine would have liked to talk to him there and then, but he had ridden a long way, and because she was a queen and knew that certain courtesies should be observed, she said, 'You will be weary from your journey. We will speak later. I myself shall be glad of sleep. I have not slept two hours these past six days; perhaps I shall sleep now.'

Chapuys bowed. 'I will return later,' he said, his face filled with compassion.

After supper, he sat with her, taking a chair by the fire and putting on fresh logs himself. Eliza and Blanche, observing the proprieties, asked if they should stay, but Katherine sent them away.

'If I need you, Messire Chapuys will call for you.'

When the door had shut, she turned to him. 'I cannot believe that the King let you come.'

'I told him I had heard that your Highness was very ill, and asked if I might visit you. He said I might go to you when I liked.'

Katherine suspected that rather more than that had been said, but she held her peace. She wondered if Chapuys thought she was dying, and had persuaded Henry of it.

'I also asked for permission for the Princess to visit you,' he said, 'but this the King refused.' That was a blow.

'Look at me,' she said. 'Do I look as if I am in any state to plot treason and invasions?'

'No, Highness,' Chapuys replied, regarding her sadly. 'But with God's grace you will be better soon.'

'You have been a true and trusty friend to me,' she told him. 'You have been tireless in my cause, and have gone a long way beyond the call of duty. I cannot express how grateful I am. Without you, I think I should have felt entirely abandoned.'

'I have been honoured to serve your Highness, and to uphold the rightness of your cause. What is happening in this kingdom is wicked. The Lady has her foot in the stirrup and none dare gainsay her, even the King. If she bears a son, I dare not think what might ensue.'

'My husband seems to be a changed man,' she said sadly. 'Yet I am sure that it is the Lady who has done this to him.'

'He is a frustrated man. He cannot have what he wants, so he lashes out at anyone who opposes him.'

Katherine sighed. 'I can understand his frustrations. I, of all people, know how much he desires a son. And I was as frustrated as he was at the long, long delay in obtaining a Papal sentence. Tell me, my dear friend, do you think he will ever come back into the fold?'

'Not while the Lady holds sway.' Chapuys grimaced.

'There is one more thing, one vital thing, that I must ask of you,' Katherine said, trying to rise in her bed.

'Say it, Highness, and it will be done.'

'Look after Mary for me, dear friend. You have always had her interests at heart and been a true champion of her rights.'

Chapuys's face softened. 'And will continue to do so, Highness, I vow it. I hold the Princess in the highest esteem, and I will endeavour to my utmost power to keep her safe, for your sake and her own. You may rest assured on that.'

Relief flooded her, and profound gratitude. This kind, good, true man had taken up her burden of love and care, had lifted it from her weary shoulders and made it possible for her to depart this life at peace with herself. She knew that she would never see her daughter's cherished face again, but she had done the very best she could for her, and could take comfort in that.

'I thank you from the bottom of my heart,' she said to Chapuys.

He smiled at her. 'You did not need to ask.'

They had been chatting for two hours when there was a knock on the door, and Eliza came in to say that Katherine had a visitor. Behind Eliza, Katherine could hear raised voices along the gallery, one of them a woman's, strident and insistent. No – it could not be!

But it was. Seconds later, Maria Willoughby whirled into the room.

'Thank God!' she exclaimed. 'I never expected to see your Highness alive.'

Katherine could not believe her eyes. God had been bountiful enough in sending Chapuys to her, but to have two of the people she loved best in the world visit her here in this lonely place, and on the same day, was the most manifold blessing.

Maria embraced her, leaning back and shaking her head. She looked not a day older than when Katherine had seen her last, three years ago, but Katherine knew that she herself was a shadow of the woman she had been then, and she could see in Maria's face that she was shocked at the change.

'Oh, my dear friend!' Katherine breathed. 'Did the King allow you to come too, as he has Messire Chapuys?'

'No, Highness. Reports that you were ill reached me at Grimsthorpe, and I knew I must come. I made all the haste I could, but it's fifty miles, and in this weather it's a hard ride. The inns along the way are atrocious. It's been four days and I'm freezing.' She strode over to the fire and held out her hands. 'When they opened the doors in the gatehouse, I insisted on coming in, but those two wretches who call themselves custodians tried to shut them in my face. So I thrust my foot in the way, and told them I had with me plenty of letters that were sufficient to exonerate them from any blame, which I would show them in the morning.'

'And do you have such letters?' Katherine asked.

Maria smiled. 'Of course not. I think they're looking for me. Lock the door!'

Miraculously Sir Edward and Sir Edmund did not come banging on the door, demanding to see Lady Willoughby. Even they must have realised that the time for plotting was long past.

Maria was not interested in what Sir Edward and Sir Edmund thought. She was tutting at the state of the hearth.

'Don't tell me someone's been cooking in here,' she said, sniffing at the ever-present smell of stale meat fat.

'My maids cook for me,' Katherine explained. 'I dare not eat anything else, for fear of poison.'

'I will make you something,' said Maria.

'You can cook?' It seemed incredible that the proud daughter of a Castilian grandee should stoop so low.

'No!' Maria grimaced. 'But I can learn!'

The stew she prepared, having sent Katherine's maids racing down to the kitchens for the necessary ingredients, was surprisingly good. Maria gave Chapuys some, and spooned it into Katherine's mouth herself.

'I am not hungry,' Katherine told her. 'I have no appetite these days. But I will eat a little because you have been so kind as to make it for me.'

'That's what I want to hear!' Maria said brightly. 'Good food will make you better.'

Katherine doubted it, but she went along with the pretence.

'Where will you sleep?' she asked Maria. 'You can share my bed, if you wish?'

'If Messire Chapuys will take the chair,' Maria agreed.

'Of course,' Chapuys said, 'but now that Lady Willoughby is here, my presence is no longer necessary and I should leave, for I can be of more service to your Highness elsewhere.'

'Do not go just yet,' Katherine pleaded. 'It is so pleasant to have your company, and it will be a health to me.'

'I will stay a little longer then,' he smiled.

Chapuys was ready to leave. He had come to take his farewell.

Katherine put on a brave smile.

'It is good to see your Highness looking more cheerful,' he said.

'That is thanks to you and Maria,' she said.

'I am leaving two of my people to entertain you, and to keep me informed of your health,' Chapuys told her. One of them, Katherine guessed, was the young man who had been passing on the letters she had entrusted to Eliza, for she had just seen Eliza's face light up.

'So now it is goodbye,' Katherine said, extending her hand to be kissed. She wanted to weep and beg Chapuys to stay, but she was resolved not to embarrass him or make him feel guilty about leaving.

He knelt and grasped her hand in both of his, kissing it fervently. When he looked up there were tears in his eyes. 'You are the most virtuous woman I have ever known, and the highest hearted. But Highness, you are too quick to trust that others are like yourself, and too slow to do a little ill that much good might come of it.'

She managed another smile. 'Are you still nagging me to incite war? My faithful, trusty friend, will you never give up? I will not waver from what I have said.'

Chapuys regarded her ruefully.

'Was I right?' she asked him. 'Was I right to make a stand against what I believed to be wrong? Even though many ills have come from it? I have been asking myself this a lot lately. I must be quiet in my conscience.'

'Never doubt it, Highness,' Chapuys said. 'The world would be a better place if there were more like you. And now, farewell. May God keep you and restore you to health. Rest assured that I will never forget my promise to look after the Princess.'

'Farewell, dear friend! Thank you!' She watched him leave, knowing she would never see him again, and then the slow tears trickled down her cheeks.

At least she now had Maria, who had made it her business to take charge of the four maids and assign them different tasks. Katherine suspected that Eliza was a little put out, having managed quite capably for so long, but the girl said nothing. Instead she willingly agreed to be responsible for looking after Katherine's personal needs. Margery and Blanche were to do the cooking, and Margery was to continue making the herbal cordial, for Maria considered it beneficial to their mistress. Isabel, made to bestir herself, was to see that all things needful were obtained from the kitchens and elsewhere, and was to bully those lazy wretches in the north wing to rouse themselves if what she wanted was not forthcoming.

Katherine could only lie there and watch and listen, for she barely had the strength to raise her arms now. The palpitations and breathlessness were worse than ever, and sometimes her heart raced so fast that she feared it would burst. She was always cold and trembling, no matter how warm the room. Her feet and hands were freezing.

She was dying, she knew it. No one could be this ill and recover. But she was calm and resigned. In some ways it would be a relief to be out of this world with all its sorrows. It was only the thought of Mary, motherless and friendless, that brought her grief – and of Henry, for whom her love had never died. Of all the things she had loved on this earth, Mary would be the hardest to let go of.

She must make her will now, before it was too late. She asked that pen and paper be brought, and summoned the Bishop of Llandaff to set it all down, and Maria and Eliza to be witnesses. Then she dictated her last wishes.

'Write that I desire King Henry the Eighth, my good lord, to pay my debts and recompense my servants for the good services they have done for me. I ask to be buried in a convent of the Observant Friars, and that five hundred Masses be said for my soul, and that someone make a pilgrimage on my behalf to the shrine of Our Lady of Walsingham.' She paused, thinking about what bequests to make. 'To my daughter, the Princess Mary, I leave a collar of gold that I brought out of Spain and my furs.' What money she had left, and the rest of her belongings, she left to the faithful Francisco Felipez, her four maids and her other servants.

When the will was drawn up and she had used her remaining strength to sign it, Katherine had to rest. She felt utterly drained, and knew that Death was stealthily approaching. Maria ordered Margery to bring Katherine some cordial, and they raised her up so that she could sip it. She could take very little and signed to them to lay her down to sleep.

She woke when it was dusk, to hear Maria grumbling.

'Where is that woman?'

'She went into the garden to gather some herbs.' That was Blanche.

There was a swish of skirts as Maria went to the window. 'I can't see her. She's been gone since dinner time.'

'Maybe she's with Bastien?' Eliza suggested. 'She likes him.'

'Bastien was with Philip in the kitchen when I went there a few minutes ago.'

'Shall I go and look for her?' Blanche asked.

'Yes, and take Isabel. Search the gardens. Check the kitchens.'

'She has gone, my lady.' It was Isabel speaking.

'Gone?'

'I think she has left the castle. Her things have gone – her clothes and her travelling chest.'

'What?' Maria, for once, seemed at a loss for words. 'Show me!'

There was the sound of footsteps receding, then returning, and urgent voices murmuring in the closet.

'Madam,' Maria said. 'Are you awake?'

'Yes,' said Katherine. 'Has Margery left the castle?'

'It seems that she has. Of all the ungrateful . . . and after you so generously provided for her in your will.'

'Do not be angry with her,' Katherine said. 'She has had her fair share of suffering. Do not ask me to elaborate, but I can assure you of it. This is no life for her, nursing a dying woman. It is no life for any of you.'

'I never did like her,' Maria sniffed. 'But to steal away without telling us, or bidding you farewell! You have been a good mistress to her. You deserve better!'

'Leave it, Maria. There is no room in my heart for anger. I am sure she had a good reason.'

Eliza spoke up. 'She was meeting a man,' she said. 'He came more than once, and they met at the Sun Inn. I saw them there.'

'And you never told the Queen?' Maria was outraged. 'Do you not realise that the conduct of her maids reflects on her? She is responsible for your moral welfare.'

'Enough, Maria,' Katherine murmured. 'I am too weary to listen to this. I would like to think that Margery has seized her chance of happiness. Please write to her sister for me and explain what has happened, and that I am ill. I can do no more.'

Maria snorted her disapproval, but she left Katherine in peace, and Eliza to sit with her.

The pain and the palpitations were bad. Katherine felt light-headed and disorientated. She wished she could sleep again and escape this torment. She lay there, trying to think of something pleasant. In her mind she wandered through the gardens at Greenwich, where once, long ago, Henry had given her a rose as they planned their wedding. How he had loved her then! She had given him her whole heart – and it was still his. She wanted him to know that, while there was still time.

He had forbidden her to communicate with him, but she could not die without expressing her love – and her forgiveness.

'Eliza,' she said, 'will you write a letter for me?'

'Of course, madam. Who is it to?'

'It is to the King. Write it down as I say it.' She took a laboured breath and strove to order her thoughts. 'My lord and dear husband, I commend me to you. The hour of my death draws on fast, and my case is such that the tender love I owe you forces me to remind you of the health and safety of your soul, which you ought to prefer before any consideration of the world or the flesh, and for which you have cast me into many miseries and yourself into many cares. For my part, I do pardon you all; yes, I do wish and dearly pray God that He will also pardon you. For the rest, I commend to you Mary, our daughter, beseeching you to be a good father to her. I entreat you also, on behalf of my maids, to give them their marriage portions, which do not amount to much, there being but three of them. For my other servants I solicit a year's pay more than they are due.'

She paused, struggling again for breath. The effort she had made to dictate the letter had been too much for her. She forced herself to finish. 'End it thus, Eliza: "Lastly, I vow that my eyes desire you above all things."'

Eliza looked up. Her eyes were brimming with tears. 'Shall I help you to sign it, madam?'

'Yes.' Eliza fetched another pillow, which raised Katherine up slightly, and helped her to grasp the pen. Katherine traced the words across the page, slowly, painfully. 'Katherine the Queen,' she wrote, the letters straggly and awry. Those three words symbolised all that she had stood and fought for during the last bitter years. They were her final defiance.

On the seventh morning of January, Katherine awoke in the depths of the night. She had slept fitfully. The pain had worsened; she could hardly breathe. She knew that the time had come for her to make her peace with God.

Maria was sitting beside her.

'What time is it?' Katherine asked.

'An hour after midnight, Highness,' Maria whispered.

'Is that all? I had hoped that day was approaching, so that I could hear Mass and receive the sacred sacrament. But it is too early for Mass. I must wait until an hour before dawn.'

'No matter, I will fetch your confessor,' Maria said. She sped off on slippered feet through the silent house and returned with the Bishop of Llandaff, who was in his night robe.

'Madam, I will say Mass if you wish it,' he said.

'No, Father, I cannot ask you to go against the Church's ruling. I will lie here and say my prayers, and I will look for you at dawn.' She trusted she would still be alive then. She willed herself to be.

When the sky lightened, the Bishop returned and celebrated Mass. Katherine was now very weak, but she received the sacrament with great fervour and devotion, feeling uplifted beyond earthly concerns, and confident that the joy it gave her was a foretaste of the glories to come. In Paradise there would be no giving or taking in marriage, no divorce and no shedding of blood. Her mother and father were waiting there for her, and Juan, and those good men who had suffered for her sake, and all those cherished tiny babes she had lost. Soon she would be with them. It would not be long now.

But in the little time she had left her thoughts were with Mary – and Henry.

'I pray that God will pardon the King my husband the wrong he has done me, and that divine wisdom will lead him to the true road,' she said aloud. 'I pray that He comforts my child when I am gone.'

They were gathering around her bed now, and she saw that even Sir Edward and Sir Edmund had come to witness her receiving extreme unction. Everyone was on their knees. She felt the Bishop anointing her with holy oil on her eyes, ears, nose, lips and hands.

'Through this holy unction and His own most tender mercy, may the Lord pardon thee whatever sins or faults thou hast committed by sight, by hearing, by smell, by taste or by touch,' she heard him say. 'By the sacred mysteries of man's redemption may Almighty God remit to you all penalties of the present life and of the life to come; may He open to you the gates of Paradise and lead you to joys everlasting.'

It was done, the last rite. She was free to go. Miraculously the pain had gone, and she was able to sleep.

When she awoke, her household were still gathered around her. It was yet day. She felt as if she were far away, lifted to another plane. If this was death, it would be easy to drift away.

Gradually she felt a change come over her, a gentle fading away, not frightening, but serenely comforting. But even now she was mindful of setting a good example. She had been taught from her childhood that it was important for a Christian to make a good death.

'Lord, into Thy hands I commend my spirit,' she whispered, and then she had the sensation of falling down into a dark tunnel that seemed to go on and on, and at the far end she saw little children holding out their arms to her, and there were winged angels beckoning her to a glorious light, and it was more beautiful than anything she had ever seen; and she knew that the light was love, and that it was peace.

Author's Note

In telling the story of Katherine of Aragon, I have kept closely to the
historical record. I have taken some dramatic licence in fleshing out
minor characters, and I apologise to the shade of the Imperial
ambassador, Eustache Chapuys, for inventing a few letters and putting
others' words into his mouth. But in recounting the tale from
Katherine's point of view, I have had to take into account what she
knew about events and how, especially in the years of her exile, she
would have found out what was going on in the world – and in those
years Chapuys was her chief link. However, many of the letters quoted
in the text are genuine, even if I have slightly modernised the language.
The same is true of a substantial amount of the dialogue.

Thanks to recent research by Giles Tremlett and Patrick Williams,
we can now be fairly certain that Katherine's marriage to Prince Arthur
was not consummated and that Arthur died of tuberculosis. Dr Alcaraz's
testimony, given in 1531 at Zaragoza, is the basis for my account of
Arthur's illness.

Writing the story from Katherine's point of view has enabled me to
give a different and intimate psychological perspective on this indom-
itable, courageous and principled woman. Some modern observers
suggest that Katherine should have taken a more pragmatic approach to
the divorce and thereby saved herself a lot of trouble and grief. But such
a view does not take into account the priorities of the early sixteenth
century, a world that was vastly different from our own. In transporting
the reader to that world, I have tried to show that the past was indeed
another country, and that modern preoccupations with women's rights,
feminism and political correctness had no place in it. Katherine's
situation, as a woman, and her willing subjection to Henry in all things

except those that touched her conscience, may seem shocking to us, but for her they were normal, right, and not to be questioned.

I have tried in these pages to evoke the sights, textures, sounds and smells of an age, a lost world of splendour and brutality, and a court in which love, or the game of it, held sway, but where dynastic pressures overrode any romantic considerations. It was a world dominated by faith and by momentous religious change – and a world in which there were few saints. This was Katherine's world, and we can only understand her properly within its context.

Huge thanks go to Mari Evans at Headline and Susanna Porter at Ballantine for commissioning this book and giving me the opportunity to revisit a subject by which I am endlessly fascinated. I am enormously grateful to them both, and to their enthusiastic and dedicated teams for the care and thought they have taken in developing this project and for their staunch support. I wish also warmly to thank my editor, the wonderful Flora Rees, whose accomplished revisions have transformed the text; Jo Liddiard of Headline and Philip Norman of Author Profile, for invaluable help with marketing and social media; Frances Edwards, for editorial support and advice; Caroline Pretty, for copy-editing; Sarah Coward and Elisabeth Merriman for proof-reading; Caitlin Raynor for great publicity; Siobhan Hooper and Patrick Insole, who designed the beautiful jacket; the Balbusso Twins, for the delightful artwork; and Barbara Ronan and Frances Doyle, Sales and Digital Strategy directors.

Profound gratitude goes to my agent, Julian Alexander, for bringing me and Headline together, and for his ever-valuable advice and tremendous support. And to my husband, Rankin, my rock and anchor, without whose endless thoughtfulness and support I could not write.

Dramatis Personae

In order of appearance or first mention. Names in italics indicate where the actual name is unknown.

Catalina/Katherine of Aragon, daughter of the Spanish sovereigns King Ferdinand of Aragon and Queen Isabella of Castile.

Maria de Salinas, maid-of-honour and friend to Katherine.

Arthur Tudor, Prince of Wales, eldest son of Henry VII, King of England; betrothed to Katherine.

Henry VII, King of England, first monarch of the House of Tudor.

Elizabeth of York, Queen of England, wife of Henry VII.

The Lady Margaret Beaufort, mother of Henry VII.

Dr Roderigo de Puebla, resident Spanish ambassador in England.

Doña Elvira Manuel, Katherine's duenna.

Isabella, Queen of Castile and Spain, Katherine's mother.

Isabel and Blanche de Vargas, twins, maids-of-honour to Katherine.

The Count de Cabra, the head of Katherine's Spanish escort.

Don Pedro Manrique, first chamberlain to Katherine; married to Doña Elvira Manuel.

Juan de Diero, second chamberlain to Katherine.

Alessandro Geraldini, Katherine's chaplain.

Ferdinand, King of Aragon and Spain, Katherine's father.

Juan, Prince of Asturias, Katherine's brother; heir to the Spanish kingdom.

Isabella of Aragon, Queen of Portugal, Katherine's eldest sister.

Alfonso of Portugal, first husband of Isabella of Aragon.

Juana of Castile, Katherine's second sister; later Queen of Castile.

Maria of Aragon, Katherine's third sister; later Queen of Portugal.

Cristóbal Colón (Christopher Columbus), an Italian explorer who discovered America.

Philip the Handsome, Archduke of Austria, husband of Juana of Castile; later King of Castile.

Manuel, King of Portugal, husband in turn to Katherine's sisters Isabella and Maria of Aragon.

Margaret, Archduchess of Austria, wife of Juan, Prince of Asturias; later Duchess of Savoy and Regent of the Netherlands.

Francesca de Cáceres, maid-of-honour to Katherine.

Isabella of Portugal, Dowager Queen of Castile, Katherine's maternal grandmother.

Richard III, King of England, last Plantagenet monarch, of the House of York.

John of Gaunt, Duke of Lancaster, fourth son of King Edward III, ancestor of the Tudors and the monarchs of Castile.

Catalina of Lancaster, Queen of Castile; Katherine's great-grandmother.

Edward Stafford, Duke of Buckingham, English nobleman descended from King Edward III.

Prince Henry, Duke of York, second son of King Henry VII; later King Henry VIII.

Margaret Tudor, eldest daughter of King Henry VII; later Queen of Scots.

Mary Tudor, third daughter of King Henry VII; later Queen of France and Duchess of Suffolk; known as 'the French Queen'.

Edmund Tudor, youngest son of King Henry VII.

Henry Deane, Archbishop of Canterbury.

Don Pedro de Ayala, Spanish ambassador to Scotland and envoy to England.

James IV, King of Scots, husband of Margaret Tudor.

Anthony Willoughby, gentleman to Prince Arthur.

Dr Alcaraz, Katherine's physician.

Sir Richard Pole, chamberlain to Prince Arthur.

Margaret Plantagenet, Lady Pole, wife of Sir Richard Pole; later lady-in-waiting to Katherine, and Countess of Salisbury.

Edward IV, King of England, first monarch of the House of York; father of Elizabeth of York.

Edward V, King of England, son of King Edward IV; second monarch of the House of York and the elder of the Princes in the Tower.

Richard, Duke of York, brother of Edward V and the younger of the Princes in the Tower.

Perkin Warbeck, pretender to the throne.

Edward Plantagenet, Earl of Warwick, nephew of King Edward IV and King Richard III, and brother of Margaret Plantagenet/Pole, Countess of Salisbury.

George Plantagenet, Duke of Clarence, brother of King Edward IV and King Richard III, and father of Edward Plantagenet, Earl of Warwick, and Margaret Plantagenet/Pole, Countess of Salisbury.

Henry Pole, son of Sir Richard Pole and Margaret Plantagenet/Pole, Countess of Salisbury.

Ursula Pole, daughter of Sir Richard Pole and Margaret Plantagenet/Pole, Countess of Salisbury.

Reginald Pole, son of Sir Richard Pole and Margaret Plantagenet/Pole, Countess of Salisbury.

Gruffydd ap Rhys, gentleman to Prince Arthur.

Maurice St John, groom to Prince Arthur.

Dr Miguel de la Saa, Katherine's physician.

Dr Balthasar Guersye, Katherine's physician.

Don Hernán Duque de Estrada, Spanish ambassador to England.

Pope Julius II.

Father Duarte, Doña Elvira's chaplain.

William Warham, Bishop of London; later Archbishop of Canterbury.

Master Giles Dewes, tutor to Prince Henry.

John Skelton, poet, tutor to Prince Henry.

Juan Manuel, brother of Doña Elvira and Spanish ambassador to the court of Philip the Handsome.

Herman Rimbre, envoy of Philip the Handsome.

Don Guitier Gómez de Fuensalida, Spanish ambassador to the court of Philip the Handsome, and later Spanish ambassador to England.

Eleanor, Archduchess of Austria, daughter of Philip the Handsome and Juana of Castile.

Charles, Archduke of Austria, eldest son of Philip the Handsome and Juana of Castile; later King of Spain and Holy Roman Emperor; Katherine's nephew.

Fray Diego Hernandez, an Observant Friar, chaplain to Katherine.

Signor Francesco de Grimaldi, banker of Genoa.

Maximilian I, Holy Roman Emperor, father of Philip the Handsome and Margaret of Austria, grandfather of the Archduke Charles.

Luis Caroz, Spanish ambassador to England.

William Blount, Lord Mountjoy, chamberlain to Katherine.

Desiderius Erasmus, renowned scholar, humanist and man of letters.

Agnes de Vanagas, maid-of-honour to Katherine, wife of William Blount, Lord Mountjoy.

Jorge de Atheca, an Observant Friar and Katherine's chaplain; later Bishop of Llandaff.

Elizabeth Stafford, Lady FitzWalter, sister of the Duke of Buckingham and lady-in-waiting to Katherine.

Anne Stafford, Lady Hastings, sister of the Duke of Buckingham and lady-in-waiting to Katherine.

Elizabeth Stafford, Countess of Surrey, daughter of the Duke of Buckingham and lady-in-waiting to Katherine; later Duchess of Norfolk.

Sir Thomas Parr, comptroller to Henry VIII; father of Queen Katherine Parr.

Maud Green, Lady Parr, wife of Sir Thomas Parr and lady-in-waiting to Katherine; mother of Queen Katherine Parr.

Jane Popincourt, a Frenchwoman, maid-of-honour to Katherine.

Mary Roos, maid-of-honour to Katherine.

Sir William Compton, Groom of the Stool and friend to King Henry VIII.

Charles Brandon, a knight, friend to King Henry VIII; later Duke of Suffolk.

Louis XII, King of France.

Sir Francis Bryan, a knight, gentleman and friend to King Henry VIII.

Thomas Wolsey, almoner, friend and chief adviser to King Henry VIII; later Archbishop of York and cardinal.

Richard Foxe, Bishop of Winchester, Lord Privy Seal.

Thomas Howard, Earl of Surrey; later 2nd Duke of Norfolk.

Katherine of York, Countess of Devon, daughter of King Edward IV and sister of Queen Elizabeth of York.

Henry, Prince of Wales, eldest son of King Henry VIII and Katherine of Aragon.

Sir Thomas Knyvet, Chancellor of the Exchequer.

Sir Thomas Boleyn, a diplomat and courtier; later Viscount Rochford and Earl of Wiltshire.

William Parr, son of Sir Thomas Parr and Maud Green.

Kate Parr (later Queen Katherine Parr), daughter of Sir Thomas Parr and Maud Green.

Louis d'Orléans, Duc de Longueville, a French nobleman held captive by King Henry VIII.

Nicholas Carew, gentleman to King Henry VIII.

Mary Boleyn, daughter of Sir Thomas Boleyn; later the wife of William Carey, gentleman to King Henry VIII.

Elizabeth Howard, daughter of Thomas Howard, Earl of Surrey, and wife of Sir Thomas Boleyn.

Bessie Blount, kinswoman of William Blount, Lord Mountjoy, and maid-of-honour to Katherine.

Elizabeth Carew, wife of Nicholas Carew.

William, Lord Willoughby, husband of Maria de Salinas.

Francis I, King of France (Francis of Angoulême).

Louise of Savoy, mother of King Francis I.

William Cornish, musician and Master of the Revels to King Henry VIII.

The Princess Mary, daughter of King Henry VIII and Katherine of Aragon; later Queen Mary I.

Lady Margaret Douglas, daughter of Margaret Tudor by her second husband, the Earl of Angus.

Margaret, Lady Bryan, governess to the Princess Mary.

Edmund de la Pole, Duke of Suffolk, nephew of King Edward IV and King Richard III.

Richard de la Pole, 'the White Rose', brother of Edmund de la Pole.

Henry Willoughby, son of Lord Willoughby and Maria de Salinas.

James V, King of Scots.

Sir Thomas More, Privy councillor, renowned scholar, humanist and man of letters; later Lord Chancellor of England.

Lady Alice More, wife of Sir Thomas More.

Francis, Dauphin of France, son and heir of King Francis I.

Isabella, daughter of King Henry VIII and Katherine of Aragon.

Henry Fitzroy, bastard son of King Henry VIII and Bessie Blount; later Duke of Richmond and Somerset.

Gilbert, Lord Tailboys, husband of Bessie Blount.

Martin Luther, a monk of Wittenberg, Germany, religious reformer and founder of the Protestant religion.

Margery and Elizabeth Otwell, sisters, chamberers to Katherine.

Sir John Peche, a knight of Kent.

Claude of Valois, Queen of France, wife of King Francis I.

Madame de Châteaubriant, mistress of King Francis I.

Anne Boleyn, daughter of Sir Thomas Boleyn and sister of Mary Boleyn.

Pope Leo X.

Gertrude Blount, daughter of William Blount, Lord Mountjoy, and Agnes de Vanagas, and wife of Henry Courtenay, Marquess of Exeter, a cousin of King Henry VIII; lady-in-waiting to Katherine.

Henry Courtenay, Marquess of Exeter, son of Katherine of York and cousin of King Henry VIII.

Jane Parker, daughter of Lord Morley, wife of George Boleyn, son of Sir Thomas Boleyn.

Juan Luis Vives, Spanish professor and educationist, tutor to the Princess Mary.

Dr Richard Fetherston, chaplain and tutor to the Princess Mary.

Harry Percy, son and heir of the Earl of Northumberland.

Lucy Talbot, daughter of the Earl of Shrewsbury and maid-of-honour to Katherine.

Mary Talbot, daughter of the Earl of Shrewsbury and sister of Lucy; betrothed to Harry Percy.

Thomas Manners, Lord Roos, Earl of Rutland, cousin of King Henry VIII.

Henry Brandon, Earl of Lincoln, son of Charles Brandon, Duke of Suffolk, by Mary Tudor 'the French Queen'.

Isabella of Portugal, daughter of Manuel, King of Portugal, by Maria of Aragon, and wife of the Emperor Charles V.

Katherine Willoughby, daughter of Lord Willoughby and Maria de Salinas; later Duchess of Suffolk; Katherine's godchild.

Thomas Howard, 3rd Duke of Norfolk, son of the 2nd Duke and husband of Elizabeth Stafford.

Bess Holland, mistress of Thomas Howard, 3rd Duke of Norfolk.

Don Diego Hurtado de Mendoza, Spanish/Imperial ambassador to England.

Henry, Duc d'Orléans, second son of King Francis I.

Gabriel de Grammont, Bishop of Tarbes, French envoy to England.

Hans Holbein, court painter to King Henry VIII.

Bastien Hennyocke, Katherine's usher.

Pope Clement VII.

Francisco Felipez, Katherine's servant.

John Fisher, Bishop of Rochester.

Thomas Wyatt, courtier, poet and diplomat.

Jane Seymour, maid-of-honour to Katherine.

William Dormer, suitor to Jane Seymour.

Cardinal Lorenzo Campeggio, Papal legate.

Elizabeth Barton, the Nun or Holy Maid of Kent.

Dr John Chambers, physician to King Henry VIII.

Dr William Butts, physician to King Henry VIII.

Anne Parr, daughter of Sir Thomas Parr and Maud Green.

Thomas Abell, chaplain and master of languages and music to Katherine.

Jeanne de Valois, Queen of France, first wife of King Louis XII.

Griffin Richards, receiver-general to Katherine.

Nicholas Ridley, a young cleric.

Sir Henry Norris, Groom of the Stool and friend to King Henry VIII.

Eustache Chapuys, Spanish/Imperial ambassador to England.

Dr Thomas Cranmer, a reformist cleric; later Archbishop of Canterbury.

Dr Stephen Gardiner, secretary to King Henry VIII.

Dr Ortiz, Spanish/Imperial envoy in Rome.

Thomas Cromwell, Privy councillor, chief adviser and later Principal Secretary to King Henry VIII.

Edward Lee, Archbishop of York.

Elizabeth (Eliza) Darrell, maid-of-honour to Katherine.

Friar William Peto, confessor to the Princess Mary.

Father John Forrest, Katherine's chaplain.

The Princess Elizabeth, daughter of King Henry VIII and Anne Boleyn.

Anne, Lady Shelton, aunt of Anne Boleyn and governess of the Princess Mary.

Philip and Anthony, Katherine's grooms.

Sir Edmund Bedingfield, Katherine's custodian at Kimbolton.

Sir Edward Chamberlayne, Katherine's custodian at Kimbolton.

Cuthbert Tunstall, Bishop of Durham.

Pope Paul III.

Timeline

1469

- Marriage of Ferdinand of Aragon and Isabella of Castile

1479

- Spain united under the joint rule of the Spanish sovereigns, Ferdinand and Isabella

1485

- (August) Battle of Bosworth. Henry Tudor defeats Richard III, the last Plantagenet king, and becomes Henry VII, first sovereign of the royal House of Tudor
- (December) Birth of Katherine of Aragon, youngest daughter of Ferdinand and Isabella

1486

- Birth of Arthur Tudor, Prince of Wales, eldest son of Henry VII

1489

- Treaty of Medina del Campo between England and Spain provides for the marriage of Katherine of Aragon and Arthur Tudor, Prince of Wales

1491

- Birth of Henry, Duke of York, second son of Henry VII

1492

- The fall of Granada, the last Moorish stronghold in Spain, completing the Christian reconquest

1501

- Marriage of Katherine of Aragon and Arthur Tudor, Prince of Wales

1502

- Death of Arthur Tudor, Prince of Wales

1503

- Betrothal of Katherine of Aragon to Prince Henry, now Prince of Wales

1504

- Death of Queen Isabella; accession of Katherine's older sister Juana as Queen of Castile

1507

- Ferdinand of Aragon becomes regent for Queen Juana, who is deemed incapable of ruling

1509

- (April) Death of Henry VII; accession of Prince Henry as Henry VIII
- (June) Marriage and coronation of Katherine of Aragon and Henry VIII

1510

- Birth of a stillborn daughter to Katherine of Aragon and Henry VIII

1511

- (January) Birth of Henry, Prince of Wales, to Katherine of Aragon and Henry VIII
- (February) Death of Henry, Prince of Wales

1513

- (June) Katherine appointed Regent of England for Henry VIII, while he is away campaigning in France
- (August) Battle of the Spurs; Thérouanne falls to Henry VIII
- (September) James IV of Scots killed at the Battle of Flodden, a decisive victory for the English
- (September) Tournai falls to Henry VIII
- (October) Birth of a short-lived son to Katherine of Aragon and Henry VIII

1514

- Henry VIII breaks the alliance with Spain, makes peace with France and marries his sister Mary to Louis XII of France
- Birth of a short-lived son to Katherine of Aragon and Henry VIII

1515

- Death of Louis XII; accession of Francis I as King of France
- Thomas Wolsey, Henry VIII's chief minister, made a cardinal

1516

- (January) Death of Ferdinand of Aragon
- (February) Birth of the Princess Mary, daughter of Henry VIII and Katherine of Aragon

1517

- Juana's son Charles I becomes her nominal co-ruler and effective King of Spain
- Martin Luther publishes his ninety-five theses in Germany and inspires the Protestant Reformation

1518

- Birth of a short-lived daughter to Katherine of Aragon and Henry VIII

1519

- Election of Charles I as the Holy Roman Emperor Charles V
- Birth of Henry Fitzroy, bastard son of Henry VIII by Elizabeth Blount

1525

- Henry Fitzroy created Duke of Richmond and Somerset
- The Princess Mary sent to Ludlow; stays for two years

1526

- Henry VIII in pursuit of Anne Boleyn

1527

- Henry VIII questions the validity of his marriage to Katherine of Aragon and asks the Pope for an annulment

1528

- Cardinal Campeggio, the Pope's legate, comes to England to try the King's case

1529

- The legatine court sits at the monastery of the Black Friars in London, where Katherine of Aragon appeals to Henry VIII for justice; the case is referred back to Rome
- Cardinal Wolsey falls from favour; Sir Thomas More appointed Lord Chancellor
- Eustache Chapuys appointed Charles V's ambassador to England

1530

- Henry VIII begins canvassing the universities for their views on his case
- Death of Cardinal Wolsey

1531

– Thomas Cromwell emerges as Henry VIII's chief minister

1532

– Sir Thomas More resigns the office of lord chancellor
– (August) Death of William Warham, Archbishop of Canterbury, paving the way for the appointment of the radical Thomas Cranmer

1533

– (January) Henry VIII secretly marries Anne Boleyn
– (April) Parliament passes the Act in Restraint of Appeals (to the Pope), the legal cornerstone of the English Reformation
– (April) Anne Boleyn appears at court as Queen of England
– (May) Cranmer pronounces the marriage of Henry VIII and Katherine of Aragon incestuous and unlawful, and confirms the validity of Henry's marriage to Anne Boleyn
– (June) Coronation of Anne Boleyn
– (September) Birth of the Princess Elizabeth, daughter of Henry VIII and Anne Boleyn

1534

– (March) The Pope pronounces the marriage of Henry VIII and Katherine of Aragon valid
– Parliament passes the Act of Supremacy, making Henry VIII Supreme Head of the Church of England, and the Act of Succession, making the children of Queen Anne the King's lawful heirs
– Imprisonment of Sir Thomas More and John Fisher, Bishop of Rochester, for refusing to swear the oath of Supremacy

1535

– Executions of John Fisher, Bishop of Rochester; Sir Thomas More; and several Carthusian monks

1536

– (January) Death of Katherine of Aragon

Reading Group Questions

- Throughout *The True Queen*, Alison Weir shows how Katherine was raised to conform to contemporary cultural and religious norms, and how this influenced her thinking and her actions. What impression did this make on you, and did it aid your understanding of her dilemmas and conflicts? Did this take on her story allow you to empathise more closely with Katherine's choices?

- There is a huge cast of supporting characters in *The True Queen*. Who in particular stood out for you and why? How does Alison Weir contrast the more demure Katherine with her outspoken friends Maria de Salinas and the French Queen, and what do these characters gain from each other?

- Alison Weir tells the story entirely through Katherine's eyes. What does this technique add to the richness of Katherine's character and the power of the narrative overall? What advantages are there to using a single character's point of view in this way? Are there any disadvantages?

- Arthur's brief marriage to Katherine is one of uncomfortable silences and confused emotions, and historians have long argued over whether their marriage was in fact consummated. Do you agree with Alison Weir's version of events? How do you feel Arthur and young Henry compare as princes and future kings?

- *'His was to be a new golden age, an age of open-handedness, magnificence and glory.'* How does Alison Weir depict this golden age of Henry and Katherine's early marriage, bringing to life the boldness and glory of the bustling court? How does the tone and colour of the narrative here contrast with that of Katherine's uncomfortable marriage and widowhood in Part One and, later, her exile from court?

- Katherine sees Queen Isabella as an ideal role model, whereas Henry seems determined to make his reign the opposite of his father's. How do Katherine and Henry, both children of monarchs with great power and high expectations, react to their parents' influence? Which other parent-child relationships did you find interesting, and why?

- We see Henry VIII only through Katherine's perspective, which is coloured by her all-encompassing love for him, but nonetheless allows us a deep insight into this complicated and dominating king. What is your impression of his character in *The True Queen*? How does it compare to your own assumptions about Henry VIII?

- As a princess of Spain, Katherine is accustomed to having power rather than seeking it. Does she ever become ambitious? How does she learn how to use her power over Henry? How does it affect her when she finds this waning? When she asserts herself as the True Queen, is she seeking to save her husband, her throne or her soul?

- Loss is a major theme in *The True Queen*. Katherine grieves for the deaths of her brother, her mother and her children among many others. How does this underlying sorrow affect the development of her character, and how does it test her faith? How does her response to loss contrast with other characters' reactions?

- Katherine finds herself influenced by diverse powerful and intriguing people – including Cardinal Wolsey, Thomas More and Thomas Cromwell. These historical figures have been written about many times, but how does Alison Weir choose to portray them? How does Katherine's relationship with each man move the story forward, and who do you think has the most impact on her life?

- *'What she wanted did not matter. When her parents commanded, she must obey.'* Katherine is sent to England as a bargaining chip, left powerless at Arthur's death, and increasingly loses control over her own life as Henry fights for a divorce. Yet she retains great strength of character and is praised for her learning and intelligence. Do you see her as a passive or active character? In what ways does she manage to live on her own terms? How does she choose which battles to fight, and do you feel she ever wins?

- Henry's councillors push Katherine to accede gracefully to his demand for a divorce, offering her a comfortable life with her daughter and friends in return. How does the strength of her principles and her devout faith make this impossible for her to accept? Do you think she made the right decision, and was it worth the price?

- *The True Queen* is the first in Alison Weir's new series about the six queens of Henry VIII, and many of their storylines will overlap. What did you think of the introduction and characterisation of Anne Boleyn and Jane Seymour here, through Katherine's eyes? Which queen's story are you most interested in reading, and why?